PROJECT:

Dragonslayers

K. Rowe

Black Rose Writing

www.blackrosewriting.com

The final approval for this literary material is granted by the author.

First printing

ISBN: 978-1-935605-07-2

PUBLISHED BY BLACK ROSE WRITING

www.blackrosewriting.com

Printed in the United States of America

Project: Dragonslayers is printed in 11.5-point Cambria

Dedication:

To the men and women of the US armed forces: Courage is knowing when to keep your head down and using it to get you home alive. You will never be the same after you have tasted battle.

Acknowledgements

My husband Scott-for all you do and have done
My best friend Jessica Betancourt-
who I blame for getting me into this writing stuff
Mary Mearns-UK
Suna Akiah-UK
Members of the 305th/87th Medical Group:
Dr. M. Louis Weinstein
TSgt Timothy Vickerie
SSG William Johnson (US Army)
SSgt Alison Legarda
SrA Brian Weigandt
SrA Richard Salazar
Carol Korn
Dave Bryk
Evelyn Soto
Cathy Coyle
Connie Rothman
Barbara Walker-McBean
TSgt Lance Srp, 96th MDG- for a 7 week "mental vacation"
Tony Capone (Ft. Dix VA Clinic- PTSD group)

Valenzano Winery- for your wonderful "creative juices" that have
occasionally helped me in my creating.

Cover

Totally T-Shirts, Signs and More- Pemberton, NJ (patch)
Albey's Dry Cleaners and Alterations- Wrightstown, NJ (uniform alterations)
SSgt Jesus Amador- 87 MDG- uniform model

CHAPTER ONE

She was late. This was her first meeting as a full-fledged member of a Joint Services Sub Committee, and the meeting was going to start without her. The whole morning had started out as a disaster: the alarm clock failed to go off, the Metro got stuck under the Potomac River because of unseasonably bad May flooding, and now she was lost. Her heels clicked loudly across the old tile floor of the Pentagon Metro station. Flashing her ID at the guard, she asked him for directions, (although it was his first day on post and he was no help) then she hurried inside to the maze of hallways that made up the Pentagon. "Now what was that room number?" She growled, her voice tinted with a Nordic accent. She had been in the building many times before, but this time they were doing renovations on the area she was familiar with and she now had to go into unfamiliar territory. Digging through her attaché, she hurried along, "Damn, where is it?!"

In her haste, she collided with a gentleman dressed in civilian clothes, who was evidently trying to locate some place himself. As she bounced off him, the heel of her shoe twisted and broke, sending her tumbling backward to the floor. Her attaché spilled sending papers everywhere.

"Oh, terribly sorry ma'am," the man replied as he immediately started to pick up her papers. He looked at her out of the corner of his eye. She was beautiful. Perhaps five foot six, skin of pale porcelain, hair of the lightest blonde, with white bangs and eyes that shimmered a deep icy blue. She looked to be in her mid thirties and was dressed in Air Force Service Dress with a skirt that stopped just above her knee caps. He noticed the silver maple leaves on her shoulders.

"Now what else can go wrong? I'm going to be late for my meeting," she snapped, picking up her broken heel and examining it, "Don't suppose you have some Super Glue?"

"Afraid not ma'am," he said handing the papers back to her. Their eyes met for a brief moment and the woman realized that the man was nearly the epitome of tall dark and handsome. But there was no time to gawk; she had to get to the meeting.

"Thank you," she sighed and stuffed the papers back into her attaché. The man gently helped her to her feet and she hurried away.

"Good luck ma'am," he called in a soft voice.

After obtaining more directions, the woman found the meeting room. As she opened the door, all eyes turned her way. "Glad to see you could join us colonel," a gray haired admiral called from the head of the table, a hint of disdain in his voice. He was probably in his mid sixties and it appeared to take a great amount of effort to get his massive girth into his Navy Service Dress uniform. He had a mustache that made him look somewhat like a walrus.

"Sorry I'm late, they don't make shoes like they used to."

"Take your seat," the admiral motioned to an empty chair, "Gentleman, this is Lieutenant Colonel Eagle Tryggvesson. She represents the Air Force."

Eagle sat quietly organizing her papers. She removed the weighty proposal from her attaché and ran her hand over the powder blue cover. There was a shield with a dragon's head and up-thrust sword. The word "Dragonslayers" was printed at the top of the shield. The Department of the Defense saw fit to stamp across it in red letters "PROJECT" designating it as something that had not been approved yet. Eagle hoped that she would soon change that into a reality.

The admiral spoke up, "For those of you who do not all ready know me, I am Admiral Richard Westland, Chairman of the Joint Sub-committee on Defense Spending," he paused, "We are here today to discuss Congress' proposal to put ninety billion dollars back into the Defense Department budget. We need to spend this money wisely, Congress has said this is a onetime deal," he sipped on his coffee, "Are there any opening ideas?"

The room broke into a mass of chatter with several voices being louder than the others, calling out ideas. Eagle said nothing; there was no way she could compete. There would be the right moment. After a few minutes, Westland called the room to order. "Now that your creative juices are flowing, I think we should take a look at what we can do with Base S-2301." He removed his own proposal and opened it, "Concerning S-2301, I believe you all know which base I am referring to. There are plans to send up six HA 901 keyhole satellites into orbit to provide worldwide data coverage for the base. We currently have funding for four units. The additional units are thirty billion each. I believe this is necessary to complete the data gathering systems of the base."

"Sir?" An Army colonel spoke up, "Who is designated to get control of the base?"

"Currently it's up in the air. My thoughts were for a joint services pact where each service would send specialists to provide manning."

Eagle perked up immediately. Joint services, those were the magic words, my foot in the door, she thought as she raised her hand. Westland tried to ignore her until he could no longer.

"Yes colonel, what is it?" He huffed in an annoyed voice.

"Sir, I think I have just the thing." She stood up and picked up her proposal, "I have detailed plans in here about a Joint Service Special Forces Team that might do well with being located at that base."

"Colonel," Westland spoke up, "I think your proposal is out of context. This base will not be able to support a team like that. It's designed to be used as an information gathering platform, there has been no allocation to have personnel come and go with any expediency. The only way to and from the base besides the service road is by helicopter."

"Yes sir, I know that, but included in my proposal are detailed designs for the construction of a short take off fighter aircraft. And according to the layout of the base, there is a nice flat area to the northwest that would suit a runway quite well, even a C-130 or maybe a C-17 could land there."

Westland decided to put her on the spot, "And how much is this elite team going to cost the Government?" He snapped.

"Well sir, I have allotted for seven people total, plus the cost of five SF 87 Wolverine aircraft and five AH 88 Badger attack helicopters, and one Warhawk transport helicopter, plus all our armament. Any other support personnel will fall under the base manning roster."

"And how much is all of this going to cost?" He replied impatiently.

Eagle cleared her throat, this was the big moment, "Sir, I can get all that for under 80 billion."

The room broke into laughter. One of the Navy captains called out, "Where are you going to buy your aircraft K-Mart?!"

"No sir," she answered calmly, "I have a good number of contacts within the Black Projects community, they said that they could do it relatively inexpensive."

"Sure and what about cost overruns and delays on parts? We all know contractors like to take their time so they make more money," the captain fired back.

"Like I said, I have many contacts, they won't let me down."

The room continued in laughter until Westland called them back to order. Eagle got the impression they didn't think she had a single bit of knowledge as to the workings of the government. What they didn't know was that she had more than just an understanding of what goes on; she knew how to cut through the red tape that surrounded many of the new development programs and get to the bottom of things. She all ready knew whom she would need to talk to and what they would do for her. Her only stumbling block seemed to be this meeting, which clearly was not going well for her.

The group adjourned for lunch. Eagle picked up her things and quietly left the conference room. She hunted around a few offices and finally found some Super Glue. After repairs to her shoe were complete, she headed to the cafeteria for lunch. Mindlessly, she filed through the line, getting only a small amount to eat. She sat down and picked at her food, the proceedings of the day had ruined her appetite. Westland had made it apparent that he didn't think she should be part of the committee. Eagle wasn't part of the "Good Old Boys" club, she wasn't anywhere close to being a Flag grade officer, and she was female. As far as he was concerned, she was a fly on the wall.

Thoughts wandered through her head and she wondered if getting on this committee was such a good idea. She was out of her element. Her career so far had been medical school, getting commissioned, doing a surgical residency and then on to flight school. She became a flight surgeon and did over a year of flying generals around. She enjoyed her job, but there was more out there that interested her. Occasionally she would meet up with someone from a sister service and take leave so she could train with them. Special Operations was where she really wanted to be. It wasn't considered "woman's work"; she hoped to maybe change that.

Out of the corner of her eye, she saw the man she had run into in the hall. Being in such a hurry, she only got a quick look at him. He was tall, perhaps six one or two, well built with broad shoulders. She could not see much of his front because he was turned away from her and heading to the far side of the dining room. He was dressed in a comfortable pair of dark grey linen trousers and an off white heavy cable knit pull over sweater. His hair was almost black and styled in the typical military fashion. She watched as he walked around looking for a table, he carried himself like an officer. How old was he? Late twenties? Early thirties? It was hard to tell. The man finally found a small table and sat down. Darn, Eagle thought, his back was to her. Perhaps if she wasn't so much of a chicken, she would get up and talk to him. No, she reminded herself, she was not here to start some relationship, she was here to play hardball with the big boys, and needed to keep her focus on the meeting.

A few minutes passed and a woman sat down with the man. She was dressed in a light brown business suit with skirt, her hair pulled tightly back into a bun. She wore the most unattractive glasses. Eagle thought she looked like a Librarian. The woman took a large brown envelope from her briefcase and laid it on the table. The man picked it up and peered inside without removing any of the contents. They exchanged a few words and the man nodded. The woman got up to leave but he put his hand up to stop her. He said something to her; she shook her head and pushed on by him. He tucked the envelope under his tray and continued to eat.

What had just transpired? Eagle wondered. Dining facilities were not the usual place one conducted business in, especially sensitive business like that appeared. Perhaps it was nothing, just delivering a Birthday card around so that the whole shop could sign it without the boss knowing, or something else trivial. She finished her lunch and left, never looking back at the man.

Over the next six weeks, Eagle immersed herself in committee work. She fought long and hard, sometimes even resorting to dining with the "enemy" in order to win them over to her idea. Truly this was not the part of politics she liked, she felt rather cheap in having to result to something just shy of bribery, or extortion to get her point across. But she held to her morals. Several times after dinner, she was invited to some hotel room, but she always managed to graciously decline. *That* she was not stooping to in order to gain favor.

Eventually her efforts began to pay off. More and more of the committee members began to see the merit of her project. Westland resisted, claiming that Base S-2301 provided an extremely safe location where the higher ups could keep an eye on the world without being constantly bothered. The very area that Eagle suggested would make a fine runway, Westland all ready had ideas for a nine hole golf course. The tenth floor of the building was designed with luxury apartments, meeting room, private dining room with kitchen staff and other amenities. The rest of the building was appointed with all the finery expected by the high ranking officers who were to frequent the base.

Accessibility to the base was difficult. The service road was temporarily paved and had been used to move only the very heavy items that could not be airlifted. It was a long and dangerously twisting road that when the base was completed would be destroyed. That left only the air. Set high in the Sierra Nevada mountain range, the nearest military installation was the staging base nearly thirty miles to the northwest. Lake Tahoe and Reno were within short flying distance to the northeast, just far enough away that civilian aircraft wouldn't bother flying over the jagged peaks that neighbored the base.

Westland knew what Eagle's proposal was all about. He had heard enough scuttle-butt going through the committee to know that if her idea was approved, his cozy little vacation spot would be ruined. And now in the final days of the committee, she was even more determined to present her ideas. The old committee rule held true: If it wasn't presented, then it wouldn't be voted on.

Lunch had just ended and the last of the committee members were filing in and taking their seats. This was the time to make her move. Eagle felt confident that she had at least six of the fifteen committee members in her back pocket. Six was by no means a majority; some of the others were tempted to change their opinions in her favor. She had to strike quickly and catch Westland off balance. In the "war of the words" he (or she) with the sharpest tongue would win.

Eagle rehearsed her attack strategy. It wasn't anything glorious, just down and dirty hard ball. She was going to take command of the floor and not give him a chance to push forward any other ideas. The consequences of her action might be severe, he could have her removed from the room and make sure she never stepped foot on a committee ever again. Her career would most likely be ruined if she did not play her cards right. Now was the time. Eagle took in several deep breaths and prepared to do battle.

Two days later, the committee voted ten to five in favor of Eagle's plan. She had won. As the members of the committee filed out she sat in the room quietly contemplating her victory. Looking at the calendar in her day planner, she noticed it was the seventeenth of June. Maybe this was a good day, maybe it wasn't. She was happy that she had finally realized her dream, but the next year would be a busy one. Once funds were allocated in October, she would meet with the design team at the Lockheed Skunk Works to start building the aircraft. Then it was off to find a suitable training place for the team. The base where they were to be permanently stationed was far from finished. Lastly, she would begin the process of selecting her team. Pulling everything together was going to be a major undertaking, but she was confident her organizational skills would serve her well.

She stood and gathered her papers together. Westland came back into the room to pick up his coffee cup. Eagle did her best to ignore him; she knew he was angry with her for pulling off a victory that should have been his. As she put several papers back in her attaché, she could feel Westland behind her. Not choosing to engage him, she continued packing her things. She had an uneasy feeling that something was not right. A moment later, Westland grabbed her from behind and shoved her forcefully against the table, leaning his weight into her, "This is far from over colonel," he whispered into her ear. Eagle froze. She was somewhere between panic and the instinct to fight back. Just what was Westland going to do? He was a high ranking officer, how much would he choose to abuse that rank? Letting out a low growl, Eagle was preparing to make a stand when Westland let go and stomped out of the room. She was fairly confident he wouldn't have pulled anything. The room was empty, but a busy hallway was just outside and voices would have been heard. Closing her attaché, she got the distinct feeling that Westland was just trying to show his dominance over her. Well, soon enough she would be leaving the Pentagon and heading out west to get things started. Hopefully her further dealings with Westland would be over the phone from now on. Any time she had direct dealings with him, she always felt creepy. There was just something about him that didn't set right with her. She would be more than happy to put several thousand miles between them.

Admiral Westland secretly swore the battle was not over. He would put an end to her precious Dragonslayers. It was just a matter of time. The big players in the Pentagon could be persuaded to see things his way and Eagle would be shut out. He also feared that having a team directly under him would compromise his other job, stealing secrets. For the last ten years he'd managed to quietly smuggle numerous plans and schematics for classified weapons systems. Most of his sales were to Amir Kemal, an Iranian arms dealer who had a direct line to his government. The pay was far more than he made as a Rear

Admiral, his personal comfort after retirement was assured. He had several other buyers for information, but they were small compared to the Iranian.

Sitting in his office, Westland looked at a copy of her proposal. He needed to find some way to discreetly sabotage her team. If she was to fail in the first few weeks of the project, the money would go up for grabs and he could make a play for it. Perhaps an untimely end to her group? Or better yet, an untimely beginning. Yes, he smiled, that was it. He made a few notes on a pad of paper and closed her proposal with a hint of finality, "Good luck colonel, you're going to need it!" He laughed. Eagle had requested the privilege of choosing their training location and the men who would make up the team. Westland decided that he would take care of that for her, making her job all the more difficult.

Picking up the phone, he dialed the number for the Pentagon Judge Advocate General, "Yes, this is Admiral Westland; I need to speak to General Smith..." He waited until his call was transferred, "Hello Brad, Richard here. I wonder if you can help me? I have a little project that could use some help...Yes, I'm aware of that. Can you find me six court martial cases that may want to take some orders in lieu of hard time? No, branch of service does not matter, just some bodies to fill slots. No particular skills needed. Yes, take your time; they'll probably be needed in six to nine months...All right, I'll draw something up and send it over to you for review... Okay, thanks, goodbye."

Eagle stood in the doorway of Brigadier General Spears' office. He was a small man in his early sixties with a wiry build and far too much energy for a man his age. His short gray hair ringed his head, leaving a shiny bald patch on top. She had known him since her surgical residency when she helped take care of his wife, Rose, who was dying of breast cancer. The general found her compassion unmatched. He got to know her enough that he had more or less adopted her as a third daughter. He provided mentorship in her career and sometimes just a fatherly shoulder to cry on when things weren't going well. He enjoyed seeing her succeed and occasionally helped her career along with a gentle push.

"Well, how'd it go?" The general asked.

"I did it; I got them to vote for the team!" Eagle grinned.

"Congratulations! We should go celebrate."

"You didn't perhaps talk to anyone on the committee did you?" She said suspiciously.

"No, I most certainly did not. Yes, I pulled a string or two to get you on the committee, but I in no way influenced anyone to vote in your favor. My dear, you did that all on your own... And I'm very proud of you." He stood and motioned for her to come around the desk. Eagle closed the door. The general held his arms out, "Now come give your 'Dad' a hug."

Eagle wrapped her arms around him and he gave her a firm hug. The general wasn't a big man, but his hugs could squeeze the wind out of someone who wasn't ready for it. "Thanks sir. I'm going to work very hard to make this a success."

"I know you will. You have a lot of passion for what you believe in. I'm sure you'll be a fine leader for your team."

"This is by far the biggest challenge of my career."

"I'm confident that you'll do just fine. When are you leaving DC?"

"Probably in the next couple of weeks…Have to move out of my apartment and get things situated."

"Well, I'm very happy for you, but sad that you'll be leaving me…I shall miss our Sunday morning breakfasts."

Eagle smiled, "Yeah, me too…But I gotta grow up sometime."

For some particular reason, nature decided to make it the hottest September ever recorded at Holloman Air Force Base in New Mexico. The sun scorched the earth and sand storms howled through on regular intervals. Everyone did their best to stay out of the heat. To most, conditions were beyond unbearable. First Lieutenant Douglas MacArthur Elliott (or as he preferred to be called, D.M.) stood at the window of his apartment just off base. Another fine Holloman day, he thought with contentment as he watched several F-117s take off. He was both Desert Rat and Air

Force Brat. That pretty much summed his life up. Having spent the first part of his life growing up in the north of Spain, he didn't have a problem with hot and dry.

D.M. was stationed there with the 49th Fighter Wing. He'd transitioned from flying F-15 Eagles to flying F-117 Nighthawks. Not particularly his favorite airframe, D.M. thought it looked like a fat gopher. It was far slower and less lethal than his beloved Eagle. It was useless to being stealthy since radars had been improved to the point that it could now be seen. The Eagle was fast, agile and much more capable to handle a rough mission, but the Air Force was slowly fazing them out. This fat gopher had to live in a special hanger and could hardly carry any payload. D.M. wished he could go back to Nellis and his Eagles. The lieutenant had been forced to make a decision about his career, fly the Nighthawk or become a "banked" pilot riding a desk until an airframe came available. He had opted to stay in the air, moving from Nellis to Holloman. That part didn't bother him; he was just swapping one desert for another. What did bother him was his father was a colonel stationed across base as the commander of the 4th SPCS- Space Control Squadron. Unfortunately for D.M. there were not enough miles between them to make him happy.

Things were due to get even more uncomfortable for a while. The base was undergoing a SAV, a Staff Assisted Visit for the next two weeks. D.M.'s father had been tasked to review his squadron. His father wasn't a pilot, so he would probably be doing some of the ground inspections. Humm, perhaps I can hide out in the cockpit and he won't notice me, D.M. thought as he turned and looked in the mirror. No, won't work, it was hard enough to cram all six feet six inches, two hundred and fifty pounds of him into the cockpit of a fighter jet. Having required a height waver, D.M. was restricted from flying the smaller aircraft like T-38's and F-16's. He wasn't interested in flying heavy lift, he wanted to go fast. At thirty four years old, most considered him a grandfather when it came to fighters. Having decided to complete his Master's Degree, he entered Officer Training School later than most. He found flight school fascinating and quickly rose to the top of his class.

The door opened and D.M.'s roommate Lt. Austin Ramirez

strolled in, “Hey, we gonna go to the O’Club?” He was dressed in his flight suit and carried his gear bag. Austin stood nearly a foot shorter than D.M. and kept his head shaved.

“I really don’t feel like it. And I bet it’s crowded with all the SAV inspectors,” D.M. replied, rubbing his dark brown eyes and wiping his hand over his face. He had flown so much in the last few days he was truly tired. He contemplated getting out of his flight suit, taking a long hot shower and calling it a day.

Austin chuckled, “We oughta call them ‘Staff Appointed Vipers!’ After what they've done to us... Come on man; don't make me go there by myself.”

D.M. smiled and grabbed his flight cap, pulling it on over his spiky raven black hair, “Okay, I’ll go, but I’m not drinking.”

“Oh, come on one beer won’t do you any harm,” Austin teased.

“Well, maybe just one.”

The Officer’s Club was booming with noise. Pilots were crammed elbow to elbow at the bar toasting everything under the sun. A jukebox belted out the latest tunes, and several men and women were dancing in between the tables. They made their way through the throng, finding a table tucked away in the corner. Austin purchased the first round and returned to the table, “Here you go. A toast... to breaking some more records for the SAV.” Austin hefted his mug and gulped down the foaming amber liquid. D.M. held the mug to his lips and took a small sip. He frowned, American beer really tasted foul to him. The beer in Spain was much more agreeable.

Austin slammed his mug on the table and wiped his mouth with the back of his hand, “Come on man, kill it. You need to get a couple in ya before these inspectors drink the tap dry.” D.M. looked at his watch. The first sortie for his squadron wasn’t until fourteen hundred the next day. That left plenty of time for the ‘bottle to throttle’ rule to be safe. The little voice in his head was telling him not to. You can’t hold your liquor, no, don’t do it, the little voice just kept repeating.

He looked at the mug full of beer, “Shut up,” he said softly and tipped the mug to his lips.

***

D.M. awoke wet and shivering. His head pounded and stomach teetered on the verge of vomiting. He looked at the ceiling. Where was he? Why was he so cold? His eyes tried to focus. Bars. Shit. He propped himself up on one elbow and slowly analyzed the situation. Dim light, cold hard floor and bars. Yes, he was in jail. But how? What had he done? Trying to think back, D.M. remembered finishing off a second beer and that was it. Everything after that was a blank. Stupid! You should have known better! No, no, just ignore your conscience; think that you can be just like the others.

He rubbed his eyes and sat up all the way. His stomach threatened more forcefully. Oh God, where was the can? He looked around. In the corner, good, he thought, no, not so good, he needed to get there right now. He could feel his stomach tighten. Got to hurry. D.M. tried to stand, but his legs would not oblige him. Hell, crawl, and hurry. He could feel it in the back of his throat. Crawl quicker. He reached the toilet just in time and spent the next few minutes praying to the porcelain goddess as he emptied the contents of his stomach.

A while later a Security Policeman came in, "Well sir, I take it you've sobered up a bit."

D.M. groaned. His head pounded with one of the worst headaches he'd ever had.

"I don't suppose you remember what you did?"

The lieutenant shook his head slowly.

"I was told you picked a fight with some colonel, punched him out and went after two others who tried to pull you off. To say the least, they're in the hospital with numerous broken bones."

D.M. thought hard for a moment, his head still heavily clouded from the alcohol. Was his father there? Oh, this was really not turning out to be a good day. "What was the name of the Bird I busted?"

"Colonel Theodore Elliott."

D.M. slumped to the floor, "Oh God," he said softly.

"That's not all lieutenant; you also resisted arrest and took a swing at one of my men. You're in deep shit sir."

He looked up, "I don't remember any of that."

"How much did you have to drink?"

"I only remember having two beers. For some reason I don't hold my alcohol too well."

The SP shook his head, "You probably only *remember* having two. Chances are you probably had a good half dozen."

The lieutenant slowly rose to his knees and then got to his feet. He approached the SP, "Well I guess I really fucked my career up. My old man's gonna make sure I twist in the wind for this one. Shit, for that, I wish I would have killed the bastard."

"Colonel Elliott is your father?"

"Yeah. Ain't that something? He's caused me nothing but pain all my life. Just wish he was gone so my suffering would end."

The SP leaned against the bars, "If I may ask, what'd he do to you?"

D.M. turned away into the darkness, "I'd rather not talk about it," he walked over and sat down on the cot.

Hallelujah! Pay day! Jake thought as he slipped the gate guard twenty dollars and pulled onto the base. The tarp in the back of the Humvee moved conspicuously, "Come on dar'lin, settle down, I don't wanna get caught," he called over his shoulder while trying to maneuver between companies of men marching on the road. The weather was warm for late September, and the humidity was miserable. Dothan Alabama was in the middle of a heat wave.

For Army Corporal Jake Collins this was a weekly ritual. Besides being one of the head grease monkeys for Fort Rucker's award winning helicopter maintenance company, he was also the proprietor of a highly successful business run out of an old armory on the back side of the base. The troops called it 'Collins's Cat House', and for fifty to one hundred dollars a sex starved service member could indulge his hormones.

General Peterson watched from his office as Jake drove by, "There he goes, I want him followed. No man is going to get away with running a whorehouse on *my* base!" He said with a southern drawl as he slammed his fist on the desk.

"I'll get right on it sir," the aide replied as he opened the door,

"I think I know where he's hiding out."

"Where?"

"In one of the old condemned armory buildings."

"Are you sure?" The general pressed.

"Pretty sure. I overheard a couple of men talking about it."

"If you're sure, get the MPs and meet me there in two hours. We'll give Corporal Collins quite a surprise party. Better yet, my gift to him will be matching bracelets," the general grinned.

Jake looked at his watch. It was 1730. His first clients would be arriving shortly. Ducking inside the heavy steel doors, he made one final check of his girls. Yes, they were ready. The heat had lessened somewhat but the air remained sticky. He paused at a shelf on the wall and grabbed a bottle of tequila. He took a few swigs, tapped a cigarette out of a pack and lit it. After taking a couple drags, he inhaled deeply, holding the smoke in his lungs and closed his eyes. A moment later he exhaled, blowing the smoke out in a series of rings. Jake stood maybe five feet seven, had dark brown hair which usually needed a hair cut to be in regulation. He was on the small size of average and had dark hazel green eyes. At twenty three, he was in the prime of his life.

Outside, the men were beginning to show up. He could hear them talking excitedly. Time to make some money, he thought and went out. Four men stood with money in hand. Jake quickly took their money and let them in. Another six came down the worn path, and soon a line formed. When one would come out, he would let another in. Business was looking good for the evening.

"How ya do'in this fine evening?" He asked one of the men.

The man smiled, "Oh, fine, just fine," he replied, "How much?"

"For how long?" the corporal answered.

"The maximum time."

"That'll be a hundred bucks," Jake smiled.

The man reached in his pocket and moved his hand toward Jake. The corporal reached to take his money. Instead of getting cold hard cash, he got the cold hard grasp of a handcuff as it snaked its way around his wrist. Jake groaned, there was no getting out of this one. Several of the men in line saw what happened and started to run, but the MPs that were waiting further out quickly captured them. General Peterson made his way over to Jake, "You're gonna pay real good for this corporal."

As Jake was being led off to the awaiting patrol car, he looked back at his little empire. Well, at least I made some damn good money off this place, too bad it had to end now, he thought.

CHAPTER TWO

Naval Air Weapons Station, China Lake was considered anything but the perfect California vacation spot. Of those who lived and worked there, the general consensus was that it wasn't too far from hell. Summer temperatures reached unbearable triple digits and frequent sandstorms blew up from the dry lake bed. It was a bleak, unforgiving place that worked hard to swallow up all that tried to live there.

This was perfect, Eagle thought as she stepped off the plane. It was one year to the day since she'd won her battle against Westland and the Committee. The seventeenth of June now seemed like a good day to remember. She took in a deep breath of air. It was so hot she could feel her lungs burn. Just another obstacle for them to overcome, of course me too, she thought. Questions raced through her head. Who were they? Did she know any of them? Would she be able to form the team and have them mission effective? Westland had denied her the privilege of choosing her own team. He had simply stated that men would be provided. Eagle had protested his decision, but he vehemently refused to let her choose her team. The suspense was driving her mad. But she would have to wait. All the personnel records were packed somewhere in the pile of boxes that came with her. Tonight she would know.

One of the ground crew approached and informed her that there was going to be a delay in transporting her to the camp. I should have known, she thought and headed inside to the air-conditioned comfort of the small terminal. She found a drink machine and got a can of soda. As she sat looking out into the bleak landscape she wondered if she had enough training to pull this off. The men were supposed to be trained in the basics, but she would have to take their training to a whole new level. The hardest part was she had roughly six months to turn them into a functioning team. From her experience working with other services, she knew that it took years sometimes to make a cohesive team that was ready to handle tough missions. This was going to be the biggest obstacle.

Marine Sergeant Frank Elliott watched as the endless miles of sand passed by. Sure, the biggest beach in the world, but somebody forgot the water, he thought as he wiped the sweat from his brow and ran his hands through his short wavy brown hair. His cobalt blue eyes searched for some sign of life. The class B service uniform he wore made him feel like he was cooking in an oven. How could D.M. love this shit? He wondered about his elder brother of five years. The man must definitely have a screw loose somewhere to love the desert like he did. Yes, that was it, he was crazy.

The Humvee turned east and bumped along a poorly graded dirt road. It seemed to take an eternity. China Lake was a huge facility with miles of endless dirt roads. There were jagged, dark volcanic mountains to the north and east that seemed to be the only real color change for miles. Patches of salty alkaline sand dotted the landscape from when the area used to be a lake millions of years ago. The only greenery was small bushes of sage and tumble weed that seemingly grew against the will of nature. Finally, Frank saw three low tan Quonset huts in the distance that appeared to push themselves up from the barren sand, "We still on the lake?"

"This is the northern part, not much out here. Guess you're not here on vacation," the driver replied.

"No, I don't think I'd ever vacation in a place like this, I like water with my sand," Frank replied.

They stopped in front of the middle hut. The letters BOQ were painted crudely over the door in red. "Bachelor Officer's Quarters?" Frank looked at the other huts, but nothing was painted on them, the hut to his left had a padlock on it. He went to the hut on the right and tried the door, locked. "I guess the BOQ is where I'm supposed to be," he said in dismay. He turned the knob on the door and pushed. It creaked loudly and scraped as it opened. The driver quickly removed Frank's bags and tossed them on the ground. He had other things to do besides cook in the desert heat.

"Ciao!" He hollered and drove off.

Frank stood in the doorway looking inside. Thin rays of light filtered through the dirty windows. The air was a bit cooler and smelled like stagnant water. Four sets of bunk beds were arranged two on each side divided by sets of miss-matched wall lockers. A large picnic table with benches sat near the back of the room. A doorway led to the back. "Hello?" Frank called tentatively. The wind whistling through a crack in the window was his only reply.

Closing the door, he walked further into the hut. Next to the doorway was a kitchen service window with pots and pans hanging within view. He walked through the door into the back. A row of sinks with mirrors were on the left, three latrine stalls on the right and three shower stalls were against the back wall of the kitchen. A door on the back wall led outside. Frank opened it and stood in the glaring sun. There was a gentle breeze but it provided no comfort from the stifling heat. Loud rumbling sounded above him as the air conditioning came on. He turned around, unsure of the noise. Realizing what it was he sighed, "Air, thank God for that," and closed the door.

Retrieving his bags from out front, Frank found a bottom bunk, took off his coat and lay down. Even with the air conditioner running, the hut remained stale and musty smelling. He tried to take a nap, but the strangeness of the situation would not permit. If this is for officers, I feel privileged to have lived in the splendor of Boot Camp. This place is shit. Who would get assigned here? And why would they need me? And for what? I'm just a washed up light armor vehicle repairman turned lowly kitchen labor. His thoughts wandered on.

Several hours later, Frank heard the crackle of car tires on the gravel outside. He went to the window and tried to see through the filth. Someone in pale gray-green camouflage Army Combat Uniform was heading toward the hut. He turned toward the door. The knob turned and a foot kicked the door with great force. It flew open, smashing Frank and knocking all six feet three and two hundred and forty pounds of him to the floor. The man walked to the middle of the room and dropped his bags. He turned and saw Frank sitting on the floor rubbing his face.

"Great, Fuck'in Jar Head. Just my luck," the man growled.

Frank got to his feet, dusted himself off and approached the man. He offered his hand, "Frank Elliott."

The man looked at him for a moment then walked away. Frank had noticed the man's last name and rank on his uniform, "Okay Corporal Collins, you can be an asshole if you want, but at least tell me your first name."

"Jake," he said lowly as he sat down on the table.

"Thank you," Frank replied sarcastically and lay back down on the bunk.

There was an uneasy silence between the two men. Frank was content to lie on his bunk and stare at the ceiling. He knew that it was useless to try and talk to the Grunt; he would talk when he was ready.

Jake sat picking at his fingernails. Perhaps he shouldn't have been so nasty. Who knows? This might be the only other person here. He felt a bit stupid for acting that way, but it was going to be hard to admit truce. His ego just didn't do well with that. "This place is a real shithole eh?" He finally broke the silence.

Frank ignored him, choosing to give Jake a taste of his own medicine. The corporal hopped off the table and started rummaging through his bags. The sergeant watched out of the corner of his eye. Jake retrieved a plastic bag that contained a small amount of a dark greenish substance. He then found a pack of cigarette papers. Returning to the table, he proceeded to sprinkle some of the contents onto one of the papers.

It was then that Frank realized what the corporal was doing; rolling a joint. He couldn't believe it. Here was a man dressed in a United States Armed Forces uniform about to smoke weed. "You're not gonna smoke that are you?" Frank asked.

"Naw, I made it so I can shove it up my ass and fart smoke rings," Jake snapped as he finished rolling the joint and stuck it between his lips, "You got a light man?"

Frank shook his head. Jake got up and went through his things until he found a book of matches. Grabbing his paraphernalia off the table, he disappeared into the back.

An hour passed and Frank heard another car pull up. This time he went to the window on the other side of the door and peered out. Through the dirt he could see a very large man dressed in blue carrying luggage toward the door. Frank opened the door and stood looking out. The two men's eyes met in immediate recognition.

"D.M.!" Frank shouted.

"Frankie? What the hell are you doing here?" He replied dropping his bags in shock. Frank bounded out and gave his brother a hug.

"Hey man, been a long time," Frank smiled as he picked up the lieutenant's bags and carried them inside.

D.M. removed his cap and threw it on the first top bunk on the right, "Mine," he said protectively.

"Be my guest, only one other person is here. And *why* he's here is beyond me, he's a real loser," Frank chattered as he hovered around his brother, "By the way, do you have any idea why we're here?"

"Special Forces I was told," D.M. said lowly as he removed his coat,

"What?! No way! I'm not cut out for that kind of work!"

D.M. sat down on the bottom bunk facing his brother, "Evidently someone thought we were. I don't think they were right in the head, but someone signed our paperwork to be sent here."

Frank stood up, "Shit, I wanna talk to my assignments officer, I think they messed up. I didn't think those orders I took in lieu of time was gonna be like this."

"Why? What did you do?"

"I got busted for screwing up on the job. I blew an engine in an LAV, so for punishment they made me do KP duty. I was out behind the kitchen peeling potatoes and a car went by. I didn't realize it was a general's car. I threw a couple of taters and one broke the back side window and hit the general. To say the least, he was really pissed. He pressed charges, and here I am."

The lieutenant rubbed his eyes; it had been a long day, "Well, I'm pretty sure this is where I'm supposed to be, versus the chopping block too."

Jake came from the back, a half-smoked joint dangled from his lips sending wisps of smoke into the air. "Oh, this is even better, got the Air Fags in this too," he grumbled.

D.M. stood and approached Jake. The corporal showed no fear of the giant. "I don't have to tell you that's very illegal corporal," D.M. warned.

Jake took a long drag and blew the smoke in the lieutenant's face, "So, what cha gonna do about it *sir*?" He replied in a derogatory tone.

The lieutenant stood motionless for a moment, then seized the corporal around the throat in a vice-like left handed clinch. Jake gasped for air. D.M. flicked the smoldering joint from his lips and smashed it out with his foot. "Now you little piss ant, shit for brains, low on the food chain corporal, if you ever fuck with me or my brother, I will personally see you are sent out of here in a body bag."

Jake gasped harder and tried to pull D.M.'s hand off. The lieutenant only tightened his grip, "And I never wanna catch you smoking any of this shit again. Is that understood?"

The corporal's face was growing pale. He nodded the best he could. D.M. loosened his grip and shoved Jake backward to the floor. He landed hard, gulping in deep breaths of air. D.M. returned to his seat on the bunk.

"You're certainly not the brother I remember. I think that's the most I've heard you say in quite a few years. And you've gotten a lot meaner," Frank said softly.

"I learned that nice guys finish last. I'm not a loser, I'm a survivor," he replied bluntly. Three months of pretrial confinement to the base and losing his promotion to captain had taught him that. He figured it must have been his father that kept him from doing hard time in Leavenworth. The old man could have pushed for prison, but he settled with this punishment. Technically, his career should have been over.

"The last email I got from you, you were flying '15's at Nellis. You're lousy about keeping in contact."

"Yeah. Well, I'm a pilot, and I'm busy."

"What happened?" Frank pried gently, knowing his brother was not one to talk much.

"I got transferred to 117's at Holloman. One night I went to the O'Club and got in a fight, they said I punched out father and put a couple other guys in the hospital. All I remember is waking up in jail feeling like I got hit by a train."

Frank shook his head in disbelief, "Whoa, wait a minute, you punched out our father?!"

D.M. lay back on the bed and collected his thoughts. It was several moments before he spoke, "We never got along, you knew that."

"Yeah, but still..."

"Okay, I admit I screwed up, but life goes on," he said in a soft voice.

Frank looked around the room. This was just too strange. They were out here in the middle of nowhere, now his brother saying something about Special Forces. Things were just not adding up. Jake shuffled over and crawled up on the top bunk farthest away from D.M.

"We're probably some kind of kamikaze squad. You know, 'send in the crazies,' let *them* get killed," Jake growled.

Frank regarded his brother for a moment, "Do you think so? Would they really do something like that?"

The lieutenant rubbed his forehead in concentration. The little punk had a point. This could be his old man's revenge. Send him somewhere he'll never come back from. Yes, this was very possible. And the more he analyzed it, the more sense it made. Probably everyone in the room had done something to get them in a lot of trouble. He looked at Frank, who seemed to be waiting for an answer, "Yes, Frankie, I think they would do it."

Frank put his hand on his head, "Oh God."

Jake sat up, "I'd rather die with a rifle in my hands than

rotting in jail..." he paused for a moment, "It's a more honorable way to go."

D.M. gave Jake a hard stare, "What the hell do you know about honor?"

"Hey, I happened to be the leader of one the toughest gangs in south Jersey. We knew about honor."

"Honor among thieves maybe," D.M. mocked, "*True* honor comes with bravery, compassion, humility, sacrifice, and loyalty."

"Yeah, Jake, how much of that do you really have?" Frank scoffed.

Jake said nothing in reply. The man was right. Better to face defeat quietly.

Frank walked around the room, "Gee, I wonder if this place is gonna be home for good? If it is, we sure need to do some serious decorating."

"I dunno Frankie...I dunno," D.M. said softly.

Eagle loaded the last of her things into the truck just as the sun was setting. They had made her wait almost six hours because of the damn truck. She tried to calm herself by thinking of the task at hand. Tonight she would finally meet her team.

Her stomach flipped with butterflies as they bumped down the dirt road. In the distance she saw a dim light in the blackness of the desert. That must be it. The butterflies were now pulling five-g turns and her whole body tingled with excitement.

As the truck stopped in front of the hut to the farthest right, she looked over at the BOQ. Lights were on and she could see movement inside. She fished the key from her pocket and hopped out of the truck. Unlocking the door, she pushed it open and peered into the darkness. After fumbling for the light switch, she flicked it on.

She was standing in a small office area with a desk, chairs, and a file cabinet that all looked like they were left over from the Korean War. A doorway led into the living area. There was no TV, just an old couch with an end table and desk lamp that reeked of government issue. Behind the couch was a small area that she could set up as her mini infirmary. On the back wall were a kitchen service window and a doorway that led to where her sleeping quarters and bathroom were.

Jake opened the door part way and peered out. Two men were busy unloading boxes into the hut next door. D.M. sauntered over and stood looking over his shoulder, "Think the C.O. is here?"

"Dunno, didn't get to the door in time," Jake replied, sensing that D.M.'s hostilities toward him had ceased for the moment.

The lieutenant collected his towel and soap. His watched beeped and he noticed it was 2100. After countless hours in his dress blues, he knew he needed a shower. On his way past the kitchen, he leaned in the kitchen door. Frank was straightening up from dinner. "That was a great dinner Frankie, where'd you learn to cook like that?"

"Eight months of KP."

D.M. raised an eyebrow and shook his head, "I'm gonna get a shower." He disappeared into the back. Frank heard him turn the water on. Several moments later, he heard a cry from D.M. He hurried around the corner to see his brother staring wide-eyed over the top of the shower stall.

"Oh, sorry, I forgot to tell you, we have no hot water," Frank smiled; he rather enjoyed seeing his brother in an awkward moment. D.M. was always the one who was cool and in control of the situation, no matter how bad it was.

"Right, thanks, a little late though," the lieutenant gasped.

Frank chuckled and walked out.

Eagle stood in front of the mirror carefully taking down her hair. She hated wearing it up, it felt like it was trying to strangle her head. And after such a long journey, it was in need of some attention. Gently working out the tangles, she slowly returned her shoulder length hair to its natural silkiness. "There," she said brushing her paper white bangs off to the sides and pulling her hair back into a pony tail, "Let's go meet the troops." She would deal with the pile of boxes tomorrow; there was plenty of time for that.

***

D.M. sat wrapped in a towel trying to figure out which bag he had packed his underwear in. Frank and Jake had settled their differences and were playing cards at the table. The door opened and Eagle walked in. D.M. looked up, surprised at seeing a woman, not to mention a beautiful one, standing in front of them. His eyes focused on her Airman's Battle Uniform. She was wearing an Air Force tape above one pocket and her name above the other, but it was long and too small to read. Her rank stated she was a Lieutenant Colonel and D.M. knew what that meant, "Room ten hut!" He called as he sprang up. The other two scrambled to their feet.

Eagle took a few steps further. D.M. realized that his towel had started coming loose. This was not good, you don't flash the boss when you first meet *her*, he thought as he stood stone still. She made her way over and inspected Jake. His uniform was tattered and full of wrinkles, "You know corporal, a uniform like that could almost get you some jail time...How about having some pride?"

"All right," he answered dully.

"Try 'Yes ma'am.' Now drop and give me twenty," she growled. Insubordination was not tolerated.

Jake got down on his hands and knees. He had plenty of practice with this. She moved on to Frank. His uniform was much neater. This troop seemed to have his act together. Looking up at his eyes, she sensed this was a Marine who lacked the killer instinct. He seemed too peaceful. "Tell me something Marine. Could you kill someone?"

Frank's brow furrowed, "Ma'am, I believe I could if I had to."

Eagle shook her head, they weren't making Marines like they used to. Where did these guys come from? Neither of them really looked like they were Special Forces. And they were not officers as she had requested. Something certainly wasn't right. Looking at D.M., she made her way over to him. He squirmed as the towel slipped again. Oh, shit, he thought, please don't fall down. He bit his lip in frustration.

The woman stood and looked him over. Now *this* was what

she had in mind for her team. He was big, strong, and broad shouldered with a deep chest. His jaw was solid and rippling muscles covered with smooth olive skin; his mind was intently trained on something serious. It wasn't until he squirmed again that she realized what he was concentrating so hard on. This could prove amusing, Eagle thought. "Well soldier, since this is certainly not the uniform of the day, how about a name and rank?"

"First Lieutenant D.M. Elliott, U.S. Air Force, ma'am," he stated crisply.

"Good, an officer," she paused and then looked at Frank, "You are not related are you?

"Yes ma'am, Sergeant Elliott is my brother."

Eagle scratched her head, any more surprises? If this was Westland's work, he'd sure gone to great lengths to make her job difficult. D.M. grunted as the last fold of towel was inching loose.

"Is there a problem lieutenant?" She smiled.

"Yes ma'am, my towel is slipping," he said hurriedly.

"Well then, I *suppose* you should fix it."

D.M. sighed and fixed his towel, making sure it was firmly tucked in,

"At ease everyone," Eagle said as she casually circled the room, "I am Lieutenant Colonel Eagle Tryggvesson," she announced, "It appears that we have all had a cruel trick played on us." She sat on the table with her feet on the bench, "Originally I had requested six men, officers, with Special Forces training to take these positions. Evidently that is not going to happen, and I have a firm belief that we were sabotaged from the very beginning."

D.M. spoke up, "Ma'am? What's gonna happen to us?"

She eyed him with curiosity, "What do you mean?"

"Well, we're obviously not what you wanted, so I assumed..."

"You assumed wrong lieutenant. Just because you don't currently fit into my mission requirements doesn't mean I'm going to give up and reassign you. If I did, by God I'd never get the people I need and Westland would have won the war," she snapped fiercely.

"Ma'am, who's Westland?" Frank spoke up.

"Rear Admiral Richard Westland, Head of the Joint Forces

subcommittee, and also our boss."

"Hang on a second," Jake interjected pointing his finger in the air, "Lemme get this straight. This guy is our boss, but he doesn't want us to succeed?"

Eagle nodded.

"With all due respect ma'am, that's fucked!"

"Yes it is. But if we can show him up..."

Frank chided in, "What makes you so sure we can?"

"We can and we will. It may take a little longer than I expected, but you should all be perfectly capable of the task ahead." She stood and went to the door, "I will brief everyone more thoroughly in the morning after the others have arrived... Until then, goodnight gentlemen." The door closed behind her with a hint of finality.

They stood in silence for several moments before D.M. returned to his luggage, "Shit, where the hell is my underwear?"

"Is that all you have to say?" Frank blurted, "Don't you realize what's going to happen to us?"

D.M. studied Frank. His deep brown eyes twinkled black in the dim light. "Yes, I know. And I'm responsible for my actions. I certainly consider this better than hard time in Leavenworth."

"Dear brother..." he said in an adoring voice, "You are missing the big picture..." he spread his arms out wide, "We are cannon fodder, target practice, lambs to the slaughter. It's just a matter of time before we're butchered and sent home in garbage bags-*big black ones!*" He crawled up on his bunk. "I once heard about this Airborne unit that went to Lebanon, some kind of freedom fight, they didn't come home alive, none of 'em."

D.M. knew the grim facts. Yes, they would probably die miserable deaths for a country that didn't really care. This was the perfect way his father was going to get even.

"Well, we're here, there's no changing that. Guess we might as well make the best of it with the time we have," Frank said softly.

"Fuck that! I'm not going to stick around and get killed. The first available moment I get, I'm outta here. This place isn't that far in the middle of nowhere. You can get out if you really want," Jake replied.

"And if she catches you, she'll make sure you're sent to a

prison cell so far down that you'll never see the light of day again. And what happened to your honor?" D.M. retorted.

"At least I'll be alive."

"I wouldn't wish that terrible existence on anyone. I would think you'd wanna live life to the fullest, no matter how long it is. Besides, here we have one thing that prison doesn't," the lieutenant spoke softly, "Freedom."

CHAPTER THREE

Morning arrived. During the night two more men had been added to the team. Navy Petty Officer Second Class Sam Waters lay curled up on the bunk under Jake still dressed in his dark blue digital Navy Working Uniform (NWU). The other bottom bunk held Army Sergeant Max Hauer, face down dead asleep. His class B service uniform wrinkled beyond repair. It was 0600 and all was quiet, at least for a short while.

Eagle stretched and yawned. Reaching over she smacked the alarm clock with enough force it bounced to the floor. Time to wake the troops. Sliding out of bed, she went to the window. The horizon looked fuzzy, rather dusty. Not a sandstorm all ready, she thought as she slowly dressed. First she would wake the troops and then come back over for a shower and breakfast. She pulled on a light pair of sweat pants and fixed her t-shirt. It was too warm to sleep in much. Now, what would wake up those dead heads? She pondered as she looked around the hut. Finally deciding on a large pan and spoon, she went to the door. The wind had picked up and sand swirled in the air.

Quickly crossing the distance between huts, she opened the door carefully and crept into the middle of the hut. As her eyes adjusted to the dim light, she saw two more additions. Time to rise and shine. Holding the pan at arm's length, Eagle smacked it several times. Immediately bodies began to springing up, faces looking around wildly. "Good morning gentlemen, it's 0615, time to get up. You will be showered and fed by 0730. I want everyone out in front not one minute later than that. The duty uniform is whatever service utilities you have. Is that understood?"

Several low growls were the reply.

"Excuse me? Did I hear all of you say 'Yes ma'am'?"

"Yes ma'am," they replied weakly.

"What? Did I hear something?" She cupped her ear with her hand for emphasis.

"Yes Ma'am!" They called louder.

"Can't hear you."

"**Yes Ma'am !**" The five shouted at the top of their lungs.

"Good, now that you have wasted five minutes learning how to speak up, I suggest you get off your back sides and get ready." She turned on her heel and left.

D.M. collapsed back on his bunk, "Did she get up on the wrong side of the bed this morning?"

"Shit, I'm just glad you didn't call the room to attention," Frank replied as he hopped from his bunk and strode to the bathroom completely naked.

"Don't worry, I wasn't," he called as he jumped down to follow dressed only in his underwear.

Jake leaned over the side of his bunk and looked at Sam, "So who gave you permission to sleep here?"

"I didn't think it mattered at two in the morning. Why you got a problem with it?" He gave Jake a hard glare with blood shot blue eyes.

"You're a Squid. I don't like Squids."

Sam crawled from the bunk, "Hey, how about we try this again? I'm Petty Officer Sam Waters," he said, offering his hand. He stood roughly five feet nine and had light brown hair with lighter blond hairs mixed in from being in the sun. His build was average and he weighed roughly one hundred and seventy pounds.

Jake wrinkled his nose and sat up, "I don't make friends with Squids."

D.M. came from the back, "Shut up Jake, you don't like anyone in here. I think you're the one with the problem." He noticed the other new arrival had gone back to sleep. "Hey why don't you wake up your fellow Grunt and get him going?"

"Not my job man. I gotta get ready too."

D.M. gritted his teeth. He wasn't used to being treated like some enlisted person. But this wasn't the time to pull rank, and it probably would have had little effect anyway. He crossed the room and approached the sleeping sergeant. "Hey, time to get up," he said giving Max a firm slap on the shoulder.

"Fuck you let me sleep."

"Sorry, can't do that."

"Who the hell do you think you are?"

"I'm *Lieutenant* D.M. Elliott, that's who the hell I am."

Max bolted upright, "Uh, sorry sir." He regarded the lieutenant with tired green eyes. Rubbing his face, he ran his fingers through his dark sandy brown hair. Climbing from his bunk he stood. He was about six feet tall and weighed probably one hundred and eighty pounds.

D.M. noticed the nametag on the sergeant's uniform, "Well Sergeant Hauer, what time you finally get in?"

"Four I think," Max replied as he rubbed his eyes, "My name's Max, sir." He offered his hand. The lieutenant shook it.

"Better get your act together. A nice cold shower should bring you 'round quickly."

"I hate cold showers."

"Sorry, it's all we have."

0730 arrived and the team tumbled out into the bright sun. The sand storm had changed course and the desert was deathly quiet. Eagle was waiting for them. They quickly lined up and D.M. called them to attention.

She made a quick but thorough inspection and then resumed her place in front facing them. "At ease. Not a half bad inspection considering some of those uniforms look like they've been packed away for a while."

D.M. knew the comment was directed at him, it had been God knows how long since he had worn his ABUs, a flight suit was his normal wear. He watched as Eagle removed a small knife from the side of her boot, flipped it quickly so she caught it by the blade and then offered it to Sam, who stood at the beginning of the line.

"Now, I want you to take off your rank."

The men regarded each other with concern. Sam gently took the knife and carefully cut away some of the stitches on his collar. When he had enough to hold onto, he made one quick rip. He repeated the operation for the other side. The stripes he had worked so hard for lay tattered in his hand. He passed the knife to Jake, who had simply to pull the Velcro tab off the front of his uniform and passed it down the line. Eagle followed behind collecting their rank.

D.M. stood holding the knife in his hand. How could she do this to him? Here were several years of his life about to be stripped away. As he reached up to cut the threads on the first patch, Eagle approached him and held out her hand. She looked up at him, her lips forming a soft smile. He stared back with hatred in his eyes. Her smile broadened and she winked reassuringly at him. She motioned at him to give her the knife. He handed it back and sighed. Walking back in front of the group, she stood looking at them. Overall, they didn't seem like much. Their uniforms were a colorful contrast to the bleak desert sand; splashes of green, blue and gray in an otherwise tan landscape. Besides the lieutenant and his brother, the other three were fairly average in height; the Army corporal was the smallest of the group.

"How would you like to trade these in for bars?" She said, holding their rank up for all to see.

"Exactly how are we going to do that?" Jake replied sarcastically.

"I spent a great deal of time on the phone over the last year speaking to a friend of mine at the Defense Education Office. I've been developing a curriculum that can be considered beneficial for advancement. It was geared toward officers, but I may be able to see if it can be approved as a commissioning program."

"You mean go to school? Here? How?" Frank spoke up.

"By dividing up what you learn into course hours and giving tests."

"Tests?" Max groaned.

"Oh yes, I was planning on tests anyway. Most were to be skill demonstrations, but I can make up written tests so a grade can be submitted to them."

Several more groans and complaints rose from the group.

D.M. stepped out and faced them, "Hey, if I were you guys, I'd be glad this chance was coming my way...Do you realize how much more an officer gets paid? Or how much more respect you get? It's the ultimate show of dedication and responsibility. You do not follow blindly, you are there to lead and be a decision maker for your troops."

Jake pointed his finger at D.M. "So what, you threw away your career."

"Yeah, I screwed up, but I still have my integrity, that's what counts." He stepped back into line. Eagle studied him for a long moment. Yes, he was the one to lead. Here was a man who was most certainly angry over being transferred here, but he had enough integrity to swallow his pride and stick up for her cause. Very interesting, she pondered. Taking her foot, she dug a shallow hole in the sand.

"All right, those who wish to put forth the effort and are willing to work, take your stripes and bury them," she offered her hand out. Max was the first to step forward. He took his stripes from her, placed them at the bottom of the hole and sprinkled some sand over them. After, he stepped behind Eagle to show that he was on her side. One by one the others came forward until Jake and D.M. remained.

Eagle walked up to the lieutenant, "Remember you are equal with the rest," she said softly with a slight smile.

D.M. smiled back, "Yes ma'am." He took his place with the others. Jake stood alone, arms folded in resistance.

"Well corporal, you seem to be the only one left," she announced, "What's your decision?"

Jake stood silent for quite some time. He was not going to give in that easy. "So what happens if your plan doesn't work?"

"Even if the DEO doesn't approve us, you're still going to receive the same training."

"What about the written tests?" The corporal growled.

"I might keep to that idea just to see how book smart you are."

"What's a matter Jake? Can't read? That why you're so afraid?" Frank teased.

"I can read!" he snarled, "Just not good at taking tests and stuff like that."

Eagle held her hands out, palms up to show her doubt. "If that's all you're worried about, don't. You shouldn't be afraid to ask for help. We're all on the same side and must work together as a team. Where one is not so strong, the others help to share the load."

Jake smiled devilishly, "That mean somebody's gonna do my homework and take my tests?"

"Not hardly. But someone will help you."

"Jake, for the love of God would you get your head out of your ass? You have nothing to lose," D.M. added.

"I don't wanna go to Leavenworth."

"I don't think that would happen. And wouldn't you be proud to stand up and receive your bars? That alone makes this little scene look like bullshit," the lieutenant replied. He was quickly becoming irritated with the corporal.

The others readily agreed. Jake stepped forward, took his stripes, and tossed them in the shallow 'grave,' kicking sand over them. The group cheered. This might turn out okay after all, Eagle thought.

"Come on gentlemen, let's go in, it's getting a little hot out here," she ushered the group to the far hut and quickly unlocked the door. Inside they found the floor covered with exercise mats and various pieces of martial arts equipment lined the walls. In the back was a simple weight room set up. "Please everyone boots off and have a seat on the center mat." Eagle instructed as she pulled her boots off.

Once everyone was seated she proceeded to explain roughly how the team would function and some possible applications that they might be used for.

"...Counter terrorist, reconnaissance, air to ground combat, air to air, hostage situations. The list of our applications is endless."

Max held up his hand, “Ma'am, may I ask a question?”

“Certainly,” She replied.

"Why is this unit called the Dragonslayers? Sounds a bit archaic."

Eagle wiggled a bit to try and get more comfortable on the floor, "Well, according to the Department of Defense, our nomenclature is: Joint Special Operations Command, Detachment Five...But that doesn't sound very exciting... In my culture, which is Viking, for many thousands of years there were dragons. Yes, you all may be thinking this is just fantasy, but there really were great beasts."

"How come scientists have never found one?" Jake interrupted.

"Because when a dragon dies, its body decomposes, all of it, flesh, bone, scale, horn. Nothing remains that touches the earth... That's why there has never been one found... There were also good and bad dragons. Some were friendly and others were just out to make a meal of whatever they chose... So in order to fight the bad dragons, clans put together groups of their most elite warriors. These were the strongest, bravest, most intelligent men that could be found. Usually they were organized in teams of six to twelve. Their mission was to find and slay these evil dragons."

"And are all the dragons gone?" Sam asked.

"There is one left. He is a good dragon. He goes by the name Sjø Drage, or the Sea Dragon. He is important in ceremony and rituals for my people."

"And does he just come up for a visit or is he called?"

"No. You have to be in the...oh, what would you call it?...Uh, the in between land. Almost like a dream I guess,"

"What? Something like purgatory?" D.M. said.

"I can't quite explain it. But you have to be very special to get an audience with him."

"Have you ever seen him?" Max inquired.

"No, unfortunately I haven't."

"So the 'dragons' we're to fight will be whatever evil rears its ugly head?" Frank said, scratching his chin.

"Pretty much. I just thought it was a good name for us. The Dragonslayers of old were revered by the people. They were highly prized for their skill not only in slaying dragons, but for their prowess on the battlefield as well." Just as she was finishing up, the door opened and the last member made his entrance. All eyes turned to him.

"He ain't one of us," Frank said softly to D.M.

The Lieutenant shook his head, "No, he's not."

Eagle stood and approached the man. He stiffened to attention and saluted, "Ma'am, Sergeant Tigge St. Ivor, Australian Special Air Service Regiment...But everyone just calls me Tige." His accent was so strong she stared blankly at him for a moment trying to figure out what he had just said. He stood probably five feet ten and had short medium brown hair. His eyes were a deep bluish green and she could see he had the "thousand yard stare," something only men who have had serious combat experience displayed. The sergeant was of average build, but he carried himself proudly. He was dressed in Australian Army Service Dress, his sand colored beret sitting smartly atop his head. She guessed his age to be late thirties or early forties.

She returned the salute, "Report-no-later-than date was yesterday sergeant."

Tige looked at his watch, "Umm, what day is it ma'am?"

"Thursday."

"Oh, terribly sorry. There was a problem with my paperwork."

"Well, since you have found this place, I assume you're supposed to be here. You'll find a bunk over at the BOQ." She turned to the group, "All right everyone that's all I have for now. The rest of the day is for you to unpack and get the barracks organized. The place looks like a pigsty. I expect it to be military clean by tonight. There are cleaning supplies in the cupboard behind the hut. Sometime later this evening I will be calling you over individually to review your records and sign in on the manning roster, until then, dismissed."

D.M. lay on his bunk watching the others unpack. Looking around the room he made a curious observation. The bunks were arranged four on each side. But the only inhabitants of the bunks on the right side were himself and Tige. He wondered why that was. The others had gravitated to the left side and occupied all the top and bottom bunks, yet there were two bunks available on his side. He listened as Jake argued with Sam about finding another bunk. The Petty Officer flatly refused and told Jake he better learn to live with it. Max took the bunk above Frank. The two laughed and joked apparently having hit it off. The team was now complete. On the whole, D.M. thought, they didn't look like much. Everyone was of average size and build, with the exception of himself and Frank. They didn't look much like a Special Forces team. He had envisioned a team of big strong men with Rambo-like temperaments. Most of these guys looked like they had a hard time dealing with everyday life.

Jake was a burned out druggie gang-banger. Sam felt the Navy screwed him over, which was not entirely unfounded. Max was suspected of stealing sensitive documents; of course he plead innocent. Frank was all ready doing K.P. for screwing up and his tossing a few potatoes at a passing general's car just added to his troubles. D.M. hadn't heard the new guy's story. He figured he must have screwed up really bad to get sent out of his own country. This Admiral Westland guy must certainly have it in for Eagle.

Tige started to unpack his duffel. A large silver case leaned against his bunk.

"What's in the case?" D.M. asked.

"Huh?"

"What's in the case?" He pointed to it.

"Oh, my rifle…I'm a sniper."

"Ah, I see. Interesting. How'd you end up here?" D.M. said as he leaned over and watched the sergeant.

"Got in a bar fight."

"Oh, do I know how that goes."

"Did you kill a man?" The Australian said flatly.

"No. I wish I would have though," the lieutenant replied lowly.

"Yeah, well. The bloke started in on me and I kept telling him he didn't wanna mess with me. He kept pushing my buttons. I refused to engage him. Then he pulled a knife on me and that was all it took. With the blink of an eye, I had the knife out of his hand and buried in his carotid artery."

"Yikes."

"The American courts ruled that it was done in self defense, but my government wasn't going to take the heat because I was a loose cannon and basically disowned me. I was in a military jail for about six months before they decided what to do with me."

"Guess we've all had a rough go of it," D.M. said as he lay back down on his bunk and picked up a magazine he had bought in the small terminal on the main part of the base.

Jake stood in front of his bunk. He took off his ACU blouse and hung it on the corner of the bed. Pulling off his t-shirt he tossed it in his duffel bag which was now his dirty clothes bag. Frank looked over at him and noticed all the tattoos on his chest, back and shoulders. "Got enough artwork?"

Jake looked at him, "Oh, these? Just part of being in a gang."

"How many do you have?"

"Ummm, eight or nine." He looked about his body, "Nine I'm pretty sure."

"Why do you do that to yourself?"

"It's a sign of solidarity, fraternity, and shit you do when you get too drunk and fucked up!"

Frank laughed lightly, "Well, you can keep 'em, none for me thanks."

The sun had just set when Eagle knocked on the BOQ door.

"What!?" Jake hollered.

The door opened partway and Eagle poked her head in, "Lieutenant, may I see you please?"

"Yes ma'am, I'll be right over," he replied hopping down from his bunk. Eagle had closed the door and headed back to her hut.

"My dear brother, got a date all ready?" Frank teased.

"Paperwork remember?" D.M. snapped defensively.

"Oh yeah, that's what *she* said!"

D.M. frowned at his brother as he left the hut and wandered across the thirty foot gap between huts. He knocked lightly on the door. "Come in lieutenant," Eagle called from behind her desk as she busily shuffled papers. The stifling heat had forced her to change out of her uniform and adopt some cooler clothing. She was dressed in a loose Air Force PT shirt and a pair of running shorts. D.M. opened the door cautiously, not exactly sure how he should approach. Military greeting or not?

"You wanted to see me ma'am?"

"Yes, please, have a seat," she motioned to a chair in the corner. D.M. moved it in front of the desk and sat down gingerly. He still felt uneasy about the woman. She was so remarkably beautiful it made him nervous. Her hair was, as best he could describe it, light golden blond. Her bangs though, were paper white and very unusual. D.M. wondered if she dyed it that way or she was born like that. He remembered something from biology class; they called people like that piebalds. Her pale skin resembled fine porcelain and her icy blue eyes made it even more pale looking. She was beautiful in a mysterious way.

"Relax lieutenant, this isn't going to be the Spanish Inquisition," she said softly, noticing he was sitting rather stiffly.

"Sorry ma'am," he replied trying to settle into the small chair.

"Oh, please, you don't have to call me ma'am, at least while no one else is around. It makes me feel like some kind of old maid," she cracked a smile; "I'm not wrinkled and gray quite yet!"

Humm, she's such a looker I wonder who she slept with to get her silver leaves so quickly, D.M. thought.

"Don't be thinking I slept with every general in the Air Force to get these," she tugged at her collar where her rank would have been. D.M.'s cheeks flushed, he rubbed his face in embarrassment. The woman must be psychic.

"Yes lieutenant, a lot of people think that unfortunately. I'm not exactly as young as I look. I've done a good many years in the Air Force."

D.M. lowered his eyes, "Sorry."

"It's all right, I'm used to it," she shrugged her shoulders as if to shake the comment off. This was not good, D.M. thought, why did he have to screw this up? At least when he was flying, he was on top of the world, soaring high in *his* Eagle. This was a totally different Eagle, a very *female* one. He could feel he was heading for a crash-and-burn. His track record with women was far from sterling.

She continued flipping through his record. Nearly everything was perfect. The lieutenant seemed to be a model officer.

"I see you spent much of your younger life in Spain."

“My father was stationed at Zaragoza Air Base as a Space and Missile Operations officer when he met my mother. She was Spanish. And rather than try to move her and children, he took quite a few short tour assignments and left us there. He would come back every year or so… My mother pretty much raised me Spanish. I speak the language fluently, went to bull fights and lived like a Spaniard. It was good growing up there… I was almost sixteen when our mother died. She had complications giving birth to Ben, my youngest brother. My father decided it was time to come to the States, so he ended up with orders to Vandenberg. To say the least, I didn’t even feel like an American for quite a while.”

As she flipped up another page she stopped. There it was. The reason he was here. Deciding not to push things too far she simply stated, “According to this you lost your line number for captain. Ouch.”

“I should have lost a lot more than that. What I get for a lapse of reason,” he said lowly, “So much for my military career.”

“Don't write yourself off just yet,” she flipped up another page, "I see here you graduated all your schools with honors," she broke the uneasy silence, “And you attended MIT? A Masters in Chemical Engineering, impressive.”

"Uh, yes…I like to learn," he felt like he had just stuck his foot in his mouth.

"Good. How do you feel about teaching?"

D.M. raised an eyebrow, "Teaching?"

"Yes. I need someone who can help teach these guys to fly. I can, but you have far more flight hours than I. You'd be the best man for the job."

"What are we flying?"

"Whatever I can get my hands on. Westland is being such a hard ass it might as well be paper airplanes."

D.M. laughed lightly, he was trying to push the fact that Eagle was a woman to the back of his mind and think of her as one of the guys. It wasn't easy, but that was going to be the only way he could handle the situation. She was just so beautiful he was fighting every screaming hormone to keep his composure. "Sure I'll help any way I can," he replied dryly, trying not to let his emotions win the battle, "Seems like you have your hands full."

Eagle nodded, "It does seem a bit inundating at the moment. Once things get rolling I expect the team to shape up nicely." She handed him some papers and pointed to where he needed to sign.

"I bet you hate him," D.M. said lowly.

"Who? Westland? I hate him only because he's such a chauvinist. He doesn't believe women should be in the military, let alone Special Forces. As far as he's concerned, we're all supposed to be barefoot and pregnant... No, his opposition represents a challenge for me to overcome."

D.M. looked up as he finished signing the papers. Their eyes met and he felt an unusual sensation course through his body. It was something he'd never felt before. Every nerve in his body tingled, yet in his mind there was an extraordinary, if not terribly unnatural calm. He averted his gaze, trying to make the feeling go away; but it persisted. What's going on? He thought as he glanced down attempting to fight the unusual sensation. What's happening? Thoughts began to fly through his head. He swallowed hard. It wasn't an unpleasant feeling, just a very new one. D.M. handed the papers back to her.

"There, you're all mine," she said with smile and a sigh that made her chest rise.

D.M. bit his lip, "Was that all?"

"Yes, I think so."

The lieutenant stood to leave. He paused, "Where are you from?" He asked in a soft voice, all the while fighting to keep his composure.

Eagle studied him, "Northern Norway...My father came to the states and got citizenship so he could work. I guess he thought he would change things for the better for my people. Unfortunately the only work he could find was a coal miner even though he had far greater skills. I lost my mother when I was ten. I came here when I was twelve."

"And you still have such a strong accent?"

"I've spent as much time in my home country as I could. Before I came to the desert, I went home for almost a month. My accent will eventually get watered back down."

"I like it," he smiled, feeling a bit more cooled off, "And your name, that's quite unusual too."

“What? Eagle?”

“Yeah.”

She laughed lightly, “My mother was very pregnant with me. One day she went out to pick multebær, umm, uh, I think you would call them cloudberries, and she saw a mated pair of sea eagles out hunting. She wanted a beautiful but strong name for me, so she decided to call me Ørn, which is Norwegian for eagle. My last name traces way back to Olaf Tryggvesson from about one thousand A.D.”

“Interesting,” he opened the door, "Should I send someone else over?"

Eagle looked at her watch, they had been talking for a while and she'd started later than planned. Leaning back in the chair, she stretched. Mercy! She wasn't wearing a bra! D.M. knew he had to get out of there.

"No, I feel like procrastinating," she smiled.

D.M. attempted to meet her expression, but knew any more temptations like that and he would be groveling at her feet. He turned to the door, "Okay, I'll see you in the morning." He closed the door carefully.

Eagle sighed deeply, closing his file, "My God, he's a handsome one!”

CHAPTER FOUR

The next morning everyone was waiting outside. Eagle made a quick inspection and directed them to the training hut. "Nice to see everyone falling into a routine. As of tomorrow that will all change." She waited until everyone was seated, "Tomorrow you will fall out at 0400 for calisthenics and a run. After that, showers and breakfast. 0700, report directly here where class will continue until noon. At 1400 training will resume until 1900," she paused for a moment, "I know this makes for a very long day, but we have much to learn in a short time. Westland gave me an ultimatum of activating the unit sometime near Christmas."

Tige quickly did some finger addition, "That's only six months from now!"

"I realize that. Some of the *required* courses such as English, Math and History will have to wait until after the team is commissioned, so most of you will be wearing your bars on 'credit'. If anyone fails to pass all the required courses, you will most likely be transferred out to Leavenworth to finish your time."

"Me too?" D.M. asked.

"Don't count yourself exempt just because you have a commission. There are ways you can screw up."

D.M. nodded slowly. He knew she meant business.

"All right, enough from you gentlemen. Now it's my turn for twenty questions." She picked up a clipboard and pen, standing in front of them. "I want all of you to think of any special talents you posses that might benefit the team."

"Yeah, like what?" Jake interjected.

"For instance, D.M. is a pilot. He's agreed to help teach all you land lovers how to sprout wings and fly."

"Fly?" Frank raised an eyebrow.

"Flying, fixed and rotary wing, self defense, marksmanship, assault tactics, explosives, first aid, and much more," she answered, "There is much to learn in the time we have."

Frank shrugged his shoulders, "What can a light armored vehicle repairman turned lowly kitchen help contribute?"

"A lot, you will be surprised. I'm sure you'll prove invaluable when we train with vehicles. Until then, your expertise in the kitchen should be appreciated by all," she jotted down his skills. Several men chuckled. Eagle pointed to Jake. "Okay, how about you? How did you serve the Army?"

"Usually doggie style," he replied without the slightest hesitation. The hut boomed with laughter.

Eagle frowned, "That's not what I meant!"

Jake regained his composure, "I was a 'screw' chief in the rotary wing company. I fixed Apaches."

"Good, someone else with mechanical background," she made notations on the paper.

"So, are we really gonna fly choppers?" Jake asked with great interest.

"As well as jet aircraft."

"Yeah? I can fly an Apache," he boasted.

"No way!" Frank butted in.

"I can, really," he gestured with his palms in the air like it was no big deal.

"And where did you receive your flight training?" Eagle pried, nibbling the end of the pen. There had to be a good story to go with this claim.

"Used to trade favors with some of the pilots. You know, drop a new engine in some guy's Corvette and he'll give you a month of flying lessons on the QT. I reckon I have about three hundred hours flying."

"But you have no formal training?"

"Naw, but I can fly those babies like a bat out of hell," he replied with a stiff grin.

Eagle made a notation, "I can't make any promises about that." She turned to Tige, "And what about you?"

"I'm ranked fourth in the world in sniping, with fifty six kills. I hold a black belt in Judo, and served an extended tour on a Commando team as a rifleman trainer."

"Excellent!" She scribbled furiously, "You're going to be a valuable asset to the team."

Tige scratched his head, "Actually I thought I was on my way to Ft. Benning to train with Lieutenant Westmoreland, the number one sniper in the world. Guess fate wasn't gonna have it. I ended up in a bar fight and Her Majesty decided she didn't wanna bail me out. So I kind of got disowned by my own country. I'm still wondering how I ended up here."

Eagle looked at Tige and then D.M. "What is it with you guys and bar fights? I'm beginning to see a trend here...Well, unfortunately sergeant we can't have everything. Be assured your expertise will be well exploited here." She paused, "Sam what about you?"

The sailor shook his head in disgust, "Uncle Sugar played a mean trick on me," he traced an imaginary figure on the mat in front of him, "I *almost* have an Associate's degree in Applied Science, surgical technician. I was a surface fleet Independent

Duty Corpsman. The Navy promised me I could finish my school... So much for job security. They decided they had enough IDC's and sent me to school for Explosive Ordinance Disposal. But mainly I built bombs... I got pretty pissed at my commander and blew up his staff car. To say the least, that's why I'm here."

"Talents from both your careers will be used to the fullest," she added.

"Guess that leaves me," Max spoke up. Eagle had her pen ready. "I'm a ninety-seven Lima, translator/ interpreter. I speak seven different languages: Spanish, German, Russian, Arabic, Chinese, Korean and Farsi," the sergeant stated flatly. "I was also used as a courier in diplomatic missions and gathering intel."

"Good, if we ever get lost in some foreign country, you can stop and ask for directions!" The colonel cracked. The others chuckled in amusement. "No, seriously, you will be valuable when it comes to foreign intelligence." She studied all the notes she had scribbled, "I think with the skills you all have, we should be able to pull this off. Each one of you must be a good teacher and an even better student. I'm counting on all of you. The sooner we start working as a team, the better off we'll be."

D.M. raised his hand.

"Yes D.M.?" She had taken to calling them all by their first names when they were in a group, that way she avoided the rank conflict.

"And what do you have to offer the team?" He said.

Eagle handed the clipboard to him, "Okay, for starters I hold a Doctorate in medicine, my specialty is trauma surgery. I have a minor in genetics. I'm an Air Force flight surgeon. I have been certified to fly the F-16, but mostly I flew the C-20, C-21 and a few other aircraft to include rotary wing. I'm a black belt in Aikido. I hold a Marksmanship ribbon with both the M-16 and 9mm. I speak Norwegian and my native Sami languages, which will probably be no help. I've done some training with the SEALS and also the 82nd Airborne- off the record of course." She looked over at D.M. who was trying his best to take frantic left-handed notes. He looked up when he had finished.

"So, do you think I have enough to offer the team?"

"Definitely," he replied handing the clipboard back to her.

***

The next morning the team stood dressed in PT gear. The sun was just starting to come up and the eastern sky was bright pink. Eagle came from her hut dressed in Air Force PT clothes. D.M. called the team to attention. She stopped in front of the group, "At ease...This may be group PT, but I think we can leave the formalities out of it. Just be out here and ready to go to work. And I don't care what you wear for PT, just as long as it's decent." She walked in a couple small circles, "I normally start my day off with a five mile run. I'll be nice to you and we'll just do two miles today. I need to see how fit you all are." She started walking and waved the others to follow. They walked three laps around the compound to get warmed up. Then she led them in some gentle stretches. "All right, let's go," she said, starting off at a light jog. The others fell in behind her; D.M. quickly caught up and kept pace with her. "I'm not going to run you into the ground am I?" She said, picking up the pace.

"After spending the last three months confined to the base, I didn't have much to do, so I spent lots of time in the gym and on the track. I was running at least three miles a day, six days a week."

"Good, sounds like fitness won't be a problem for you," she looked over her shoulder and saw the rest of the group starting to lag, "Come on, get the lead out!" They sped up, fighting the heat and sand. It was obvious to Eagle that some of them were not in very good shape. She continued to run, checking her watch every so often. When she had hit her time for the mile, she made a smooth turn and headed back. D.M. kept right with her. Tige followed along, although he was feeling the effects of sitting in jail for six months. Normally a couple mile run was nothing for him, but not having run in a while, he knew it was going to take a few weeks to get fit.

D.M. looked over his shoulder; he could see Jake lagging far behind. He dropped away from Eagle's side and ran back to the corporal, "Come on, motivate!" He barked and gave Jake a shove in the back.

"Screw you!"

"The team has to stick together. Get your ass in gear."

"I'm trying all right?" Jake said with labored breathing.

"Don't try, do." He kept running behind him, nudging him on. Soon Frank had dropped back and was nudging Jake from the other side. They ran with him all the way back to the camp.

Eagle stood watching them. Tige, Sam and Max were walking around trying to cool off. They had finished shortly after her. It took Jake nearly two minutes before he stopped in front of her; leaning down and putting his hands on his knees. Frank and D.M. left his side and cooled down, they said nothing; they knew what needed to be done.

"When was the last time you did any running?" Eagle said as she grabbed Jake and stood him up. "Come on, you need to walk."

"I don't remember the last time I ran. I'm not much for running either."

"Well I suggest you change that mindset. You're going to be doing a lot of it."

After breakfast the men reported to the training hut. Eagle stood in the middle, her ABU blouse and boots off. They removed their boots and joined her. "I figure we should start with the basics of hand to hand combat…Besides Tige, do any of you have fighting skills?"

"Street fighting is about all I can do," Jake said.

"That might help you out a little, but learning to incapacitate an enemy will be your greatest advantage," she motioned to D.M., "And size doesn't matter."

The lieutenant stepped forward, "Why do I get the feeling this is going to hurt?"

"I promise it won't hurt too bad."

D.M. groaned, "Okay, what do you want me to do?"

"Just make a grab for me," she said, standing with her arms at her sides. The lieutenant stood motionless for a few moments. He then made a quick left handed grab at Eagle. She reached up, grabbed his thumb and made a subtle move that immediately sent him to the floor. A searing pain went up his arm.

"AH! Uncle!" He cried.

Eagle let go. D.M. grabbed his thumb and held it until the pain subsided. She reached down and offered her hand to help him up, "Sorry, I didn't mean to pick on you because of your size, I was just making a point."

D.M. got to his feet, "Remind me to never to tangle with you in a dark alley."

Jake knocked on Eagle's door. He was holding a towel to his nose to stop the bleeding. She opened the door and saw him, "All right, who the hell did this?"

"D.M.," he replied.

"Get in here."

Jake walked in and climbed up on her treatment table. Eagle retrieved several packs of gauze and tore them open. The men had only been there a couple of days and she was already having to doctor wounds from fights. She figured the lieutenant would have exercised better self control, but she guessed that might have been an error in judgment on her part. She handed the gauze to Jake to hold against his nose. "And who started this fight?"

"It wasn't exactly a fight...I said some things I probably shouldn't have and he punched me."

"Great, just great...Just keep holding pressure on the area. I'll be back." She stomped over to the BOQ and shoved the door open with force, "Lieutenant, in my office now!" She barked.

D.M. grimaced, he knew what was coming, "Yes ma'am." He followed behind her and stood at attention in front of the desk. Eagle attended to Jake and then excused him. The corporal walked out, saying nothing. The colonel sat down at her desk.

"Lieutenant, would you please care to explain yourself?"

"Jake's been picking on me all day. I mean Frank and I did our best to help him during the run, and he just can't leave well enough alone. For some reason he feels the need to tease me. I finally got tired of it and confronted him. I told him to cut the shit out, that I'd had enough. He hit me in the chest, not hard, but he hit me. I didn't intend to hit him very hard, I just wanted to get the point across that I was tired of being harassed. I popped him in the nose with my right hand. Didn't think he'd bleed like that.

I'm really sorry."

"So he started it and you finished it?"

"It wasn't the desired result, but I was tired of being picked on."

"I'm a bit disappointed with you," she said, resting her arms on the desk.

"Pretty sure you are. Sorry, I'm not trying to cause trouble for you."

"Try a little harder."

"Yes ma'am."

"You will go over and apologize to the corporal. He will need to apologize to you for his actions as well. If he does not, tell me... Dismissed."

D.M. saluted and left. Eagle grabbed each of their personnel records, put a blank sheet of paper in and documented the incident. She hated paper trails, but in some situations they were necessary. This was surely a team with their share of problems, and if she had to process any of them for further discipline actions, she had to make sure it was on paper.

As the days turned into the first month, Eagle learned more and more about her team. She found out what tactics inspired them to work harder, and how each man fit into the team. She also knew that they would begin to feel the stresses of all the training and that's when she expected trouble. The team had developed a natural chain of command. Eagle was of course the top, D.M. second, only because she had more or less dumped a lot of the responsibility on him to keep him out of trouble. Tige fell into third. Occasionally he stepped on D.M.'s toes and would start trouble for the lieutenant. Jake was fourth because he was always outspoken. Frank fifth because D.M. refused to stick up for him, telling him he had to learn to fight his own battles. Max was sixth; he just tried to avoid conflict. Sam was last because he stayed rather removed from the rest of the group. And it was quite obvious that D.M. and Jake were not getting along. They argued and had numerous shouting matches. As hard as it was, Eagle learned to trust them. Now more than ever that trust would be put to the test. Tomorrow the weapons were to arrive.

"Are you sure you don't want some help with that?" D.M. asked as Eagle was preparing to jump on a crow bar that was shoved under the lid of a crate.

"No thanks, I have a bit of frustration to vent. This is a good way."

"Better it than us," the lieutenant smiled.

After the crates were opened, and a quick inventory of all the rifles, handguns, ammunition, targets and cleaning equipment was completed, Eagle started handing out rifles.

"Oh, not the M-4 again, I'm not very fond of it," Tige grumbled, "I got my rifle in the barracks. Can't I use it?"

"No. You practice with what everyone else is using. Any use of that unauthorized weapon will be on your own time and cleared through me first. Understand?" She stood her ground.

"Yes ma'am," he replied curtly, taking the weapon and handling it with disgust.

D.M. was the last in line. Rifles were something new. He'd never handled or fired one, not even as a kid. His service 9mm spent probably 364 days a year in the holster. He wasn't overly gun crazy and the rifle Eagle held across her chest looked particularly menacing.

"Well D.M., I bet you're eager to get your hands on one of these," she patted the rifle.

Actually I'd like to get my hands on what's on either side of it, he thought, noticing the way she held the rifle made her breasts more prominent. "I'm not really the gun type," he replied sheepishly.

Eagle cocked her head to one side in a most seductive way. "Oh come now D.M.," she said as she daintily ran her hand over the rifle, "I thought you'd be dying to get your hands on some fire power," licking her lips as she caressed the barrel gently. D.M. swallowed hard. The woman could make a cruel instrument of human destruction erotically interesting. Eagle seemed to understand his certain moods and could play off his emotions better than she could the rest. Perhaps she had him figured out?

Not a chance, he thought.

"Come on D.M. It's only a cold hard piece of steel, it won't bite," she said with a smile, "This will become your best friend." She played her index finger over the flash suppressor at the end of the barrel.

D.M. bit his lip. Enough of this torture. "O-kay," he grunted and reached to take the weapon. Eagle carefully presented it to him. He took the rifle tentatively, feeling the moist warmth on the steel where Eagle had held it against her chest. It didn't seem so bad, perhaps a bit awkward and out of balance, but he'd have to overcome that.

Admiral Westland slid into the back seat of an unmarked blue sedan. The door gently closed behind him. His adjutant, Lieutenant John Farlow took his place in the driver's seat. "Same area Boss?" He asked as the car edged out of the Pentagon parking lot.

"Yes, and put the air on," Westland replied as he stripped off his service coat and loosened his tie. "Damn humidity. Why the hell can't it just rain?"

"The weather report said good chance of thunderstorms this afternoon."

The car cruised along the surface streets crossing the bridge into the District. Farlow took as many different routes as possible to prevent detection. This was the monthly "milk run." They would make a trip to some café or deli, usually in Rockville or Georgetown to make a long distance phone call to Amir Kemal. Westland's security clearance allowed his fingers to do the walking through some heavily classified military projects.

"How's this place sir?" Farlow broke the silence, "It's not too busy and has a phone outside."

"Yes, that's fine. Did you get me a new number?"

"In my pocket."

Westland used random calling card numbers to further prevent detection. So far, all these years he had managed to elude the top anti-espionage agencies.

Picking up the phone, Westland punched in the number

Farlow had given him followed by the country code and then Kemal's private phone number.

"Yes?" The heavily accented voice answered.

"Blue Mole," Westland gave his code name.

"Go ahead."

"I feel the Little Bird might be in the position to cause us trouble. I've done my best to make sure things are difficult for her. It appears she's more adaptable than thought."

"And her charges?"

"Her last report states they are progressing well, unfortunately. I think once they are activated I may have to go dark to prevent detection."

Kemal grew agitated, "There are things I need from you, specifically the item I mentioned in our last conversation. You cannot go dark. Find things away from you for them to do. Send them to Russia for Allah's sake!"

"Good possibility, better go."

"Remember, without me, you wouldn't have that offshore bank account."

With that, the line went dead. Westland stood looking at the handset for a moment before replacing it on the cradle.

Farlow came from the deli, a half- eaten sandwich in his hand, "Hey, this is good food, we'll have to come here again sometime."

"We have other problems, let's go," Westland snapped.

"Can I finish this first?"

"I *said* let's go."

Farlow regrettably threw the sandwich away and got the door for the admiral. They returned to the Pentagon and wrote the outing off as lunch.

D.M. jumped as the rifle recoiled in his arms. He clearly did not like this. Resuming his stance and raising the rifle, he prepared to take another shot. Just as his finger wrapped around the trigger, Tige came up from behind and hit him in the back of the knee with his rifle. D.M. fell backwards onto the searing sand. A wild shot went into the air.

"Don't lock your front knee, makes the rest of you stiff and not as accurate."

D.M. scrambled to his feet. The whole day the Aussie had been picking on him. It started with Tige standing on his ankles while he tried to shoot in the prone position. After that the day seemed to go downhill with him finding fault in everything D.M. did. He had had enough. Swinging the rifle up, he leveled it at Tige's head. His temper flared.

"If you're gonna aim that thing at me you better be prepared to us it," Tige growled, "You wanna shoot me? Go ahead. I'm not afraid to die." Sweat dribbled into D.M.'s eyes but he did nothing to stop it. His eyes were fixed on the target that filled his sights. "Come on lieutenant, you chicken shit?" The Australian teased.

The rest of the group had gathered at a safe distance. D.M.'s eyes narrowed, trying to convince himself that he could do this. Eagle stood quietly. She knew there was nothing she could do. D.M. was a strong individual, but he would not shoot, not now at least.

"Come on D.M., shoot," Tige insisted. D.M.'s hands were shaking and sweat poured down his face. His heart was pounding so hard it was difficult to breathe. Slowly he lowered the rifle. He stood looking at the weapon before throwing it to the ground and walking off. Eagle took several steps toward him.

Frank stopped her, “Don’t. He needs to work this out for himself.”

Eagle figured Tige was the type to take revenge. She didn't expect it so soon. The team was just starting their second month. It had only been a couple days after D.M. had threatened Tige with the rifle. It was late afternoon and she sat in her office doing paperwork. The men were in the hall working on martial arts. Suddenly she heard Frank and Max hollering frantically for her. Jumping up, she ran to the door and opened it. She saw the two men dragging a barely conscious and bloody D.M. toward her.

"Oh shit," she growled, "Come on get him in here." They laid D.M. on her exam table. Eagle quickly inspected his wounds.

"Tige beat the liv'in shit out of him. Poor D.M. kept trying to get up and Tige would just keep going after him," Frank rattled.

"We yelled and tried to get him to stop, but he wouldn't," Max shook his head, "He just kept beating him. None of us were crazy enough to try and break it up; Tige would have probably killed us. We had to stand there and watch until he was satisfied with the beating."

Eagle pulled on a pair of gloves and ripped open a pack of gauze, "I'll deal with Tige later. I need you two to get everyone back in the barracks. Send Sam over here, I need his help.

The men left and a couple minutes later Sam came in, "You need help?"

"Yes, scrub up and get in here. Time to take advantage of your talents."

"Yes ma'am," he replied and quickly washed his hands.

Eagle checked D.M.'s pupils, "He's got one hell of a concussion. I pity him for the headache he's going to have later."

Sam looked over her shoulder as he dried his hands, "Do you want me to sew, or just assist?"

"No, I'll do the sewing. Most of the supplies are in that cabinet."

Sam gathered everything they would need, "You have a nice little set up here."

"I can treat most things, but broken bones and big stuff needs to go to the hospital." She continued to check him over.

D.M. began to moan and writhe around. "Shhhhh D.M. hold still, we're trying to help you," Eagle said softly. The lieutenant continued to struggle, his fighting getting worse. Sam found a vial of Valium.

"Hey, think we might just wanna give him a dose of Prince Valium?"

"Good idea. Give him ten milligrams IV to start with," she replied, trying to hold down an arm for Sam to stick. "D.M. hold still!! Damn it hold still!" She yelled.

"Okay, here comes," Sam said as he found a good vein and pumped the Valium. The effect didn't take long. D.M. relaxed and went quietly to sleep. Eagle retrieved more gauze and saline and began to clean him up. Sam prepared the suture tray. "What size silk do you want?"

"Six-oh nylon please."

"That's awful tiny."

Eagle inspected the damage to D.M.'s lip. "Yuck," she said carefully opening his mouth and running her fingers over his teeth. Several teeth on the left side of his lower jaw gave as she touched them. "Damn, I'll have to take him to the hospital. He's got three loose teeth, and I bet a broken jaw as well." She sighed deeply. This was going to be a *long* night. "Okay, let's get sewing," peeling off one pair of gloves and putting on a sterile pair, she took the needle and forceps from the tray. Starting on the gash above his eye, she carefully made tiny sutures until the wound was closed.

"That's some mighty nice work ma'am," Sam commented as he opened another package of suture nylon and dropped it in her sterile field.

"There's no place for scars on a handsome face," she said unemotionally. In truth, she was furious. Tige was going to pay for this, she hadn't figured out what she was going to do, but it wasn't going to be pleasant. D.M. didn't deserve to be cut and beaten for what he had done to Tige.

Eagle studied the ragged gash under his left eye. The skin had begun to purple with bruising and she could tell that he was going to have a nasty black eye. Carefully, she manipulated the flap of skin until it closely matched where it had been torn from. This was going to be a real challenge. All her practice with cosmetic suturing would be put to the test. "Okay, here goes nothing..."

An hour and a half later and nearly fifty stitches, Eagle bandaged D.M.'s wounds. The lieutenant was awake; his eyes closed trying to keep the light from making his headache worse. "Eagle," he said without moving his mouth. "It hurts to breathe."

"Your ribs?"

"Uh huh," he motioned clumsily to his left side. Eagle pulled his shirt up and carefully palpated his ribs. D.M. let out a stifled cry when she touched the ribs just under his armpit.

She shook her head in frustration, "We'll have to get those x-rayed too."

Eagle went around the back of her hut. A Humvee had been

brought out so the team could get back and forth to the main part of the base. She climbed in and tried to start it. The engine rumbled but refused to start. She tried again with the same result. Smashing her fist into the steering wheel, she growled. Her patience was wearing thin. Climbing out, she went over to the BOQ and knocked loudly. Frank opened the door, "Yes ma'am?"

"Can you see if you can get the Hummer started?"

"Sure. Give me a couple minutes to get what tools I have and I'll be over."

"Thanks. I need to take D.M. off base to the hospital."

Frank met Eagle and quickly went to work on the vehicle. He opened the hood and started checking areas that were likely problems. After several minutes he pulled out a filter and pounded it on the chassis. Dark goo fell out and dribbled down the fender.

"That's pretty gross," Eagle said as she watched him.

"Gimme just a minute to get it back together and then try it ma'am."

Eagle climbed back in the driver's seat and awaited Frank's signal. He installed the part, reached around the hood and gave her a thumbs up. She tried the ignition again and the Hummer started with effort. Frank hopped down and closed the hood, "Just leave it running while you get D.M. loaded."

The colonel hopped out, "Thanks Frank. Do you think I'll have any more trouble with it on the way home?"

"No ma'am, you should be fine. But if you like, I'll take a better look at it later."

"Yes, I think that would be wise."

He wiped his hands on a rag, "You'd better get him to the hospital."

CHAPTER FIVE

Eagle and D.M. returned from the hospital just as the others were waking up. Their trip had shown that the lieutenant had two broken ribs, a fractured jaw that wasn't deemed bad enough to wire, and three teeth needed to be bonded. A CAT scan of his head showed a minor blow out fracture of his left orbit, no doubt a result of one of Tige's kicks. D.M. was going to spend quite a bit of time on the side lines. Eagle wasn't particularly worried, he was a bright individual; what he couldn't learn from watching, he would pick it up later.

The colonel sat in her office. This was the part of her job she hated the most, discipline and punishment. A single knock sounded on the door. "Enter," she called. The door opened and Tige marched in. He stopped in front of her desk, snapped to attention and saluted in customary Australian fashion with an open facing hand. She stood, returned the salute and then sat back down.

"Tell me sergeant, how long have you been in the Army?"

"Fifteen years ma'am," he stated crisply.

"And how long have you been with the SAS?"

"Ten years ma'am."

"Then you of all people should know how important unit cohesiveness is. Each member of the team has to be able to trust and rely on the other members...You disappoint me. I thought you would bring many skills to the team, not to mention your understanding of how a team operates... Can you explain your actions yesterday?"

The sergeant stood silent for a few moments, "I'm sorry ma'am... I let my anger control me. And that's unacceptable...I have no excuse for my actions."

Eagle flipped through his personnel record. There wasn't much in it; the Australian government didn't send the entire record since most of it was classified. "From what I see in your record, you seem to have a problem with anger and discipline. Unless you wanna go to Leavenworth, I suggest you pull your head out of your ass and straighten up. Is that clear sergeant?"

"Yes ma'am!"

"Now, an offense like this must carry a punishment. For the

next two weeks you will be the lieutenant's personal assistant. You will do what he says and help him out. If you complain or backtalk to him, you will get a day of punishment added for each time you open your mouth...Now, you will go over and apologize to the lieutenant in front of the rest of the men. Any more trouble out of you and you'll be on thin ice. Dismissed."

Tige saluted and quickly turned to leave.

"Oh, and sergeant?"

He slowly turned, "Yes ma'am?"

"If you're going to be a part of this team, you'd better bloody well learn to salute like us damn Yanks."

Tige stiffened to attention and carefully brought his hand up and made a conscious effort to salute with his palm facing down.

"Better, keep working on it."

"Yes ma'am." He turned and left.

He returned to their hut and stood at attention in front of D.M., who was sitting on the bottom bunk of his bed, "Sir, I apologize for my actions yesterday. They were uncalled for, and I am sorry," he announced.

The lieutenant stood with great effort, his ribs hurt with even the smallest movement, "I accept your apology and I apologize in return for my actions on the firing line."

"My punishment is to be your personal assistant for the next two weeks. I will do as you say," Tige said with remorse.

A five ton truck ground to a halt in front of the small base. The team was just coming out of the training hut for lunch. Two men dressed in civilian clothes got out and went to the back of the truck. One climbed up in the bed of the truck and the other stood on the ground below. Boxes of supplies were soon handed down and placed on the sand. Eagle motioned the men to help and get the boxes inside their hut. They quickly formed a line and passed the boxes inside to Frank who was hurriedly stacking them on the kitchen floor. After several minutes of furious stacking, he could hear the truck starting up. He looked at the dozen boxes and tried to make sense out of the contents. Two immediately caught his attention as being perishable so he grabbed a knife and opened them. Max came in and peered into the kitchen, "Need some help putting the groceries away?"

"Yeah, can you put these two boxes in the fridge?"

"Sure," he took one and set to unloading it. "Think some of this needs to go over to the boss?"

"She told me the first time we got supplied to just unload it all over here and she'll come 'shopping' later."

"I don't see why she doesn't just come over here every night for dinner."

"Dunno, we can make the offer. I'm sure she's tired at the end of the day, and having to cook all by herself is probably a real pain in the ass."

"At least we gang up and get it done with several people," Max said as he grabbed the second box and unloaded it.

Sam wandered into the kitchen and started making sandwiches for everyone, "We get anything good this time?"

"Naw, more of the same. At least it's not field rations."

"I'm happy they're remembering to bring us food. We're not exactly down the street a couple blocks from the super market."

"At least we have a way to get back if we get forgotten."

D.M. tapped on Eagle's door. "Come in," she hollered from the kitchen. He opened the door. "Oh, hello lieutenant," she called.

"Am I interrupting something?"

"No, just putting my dinner in the oven."

"I can come back later if you wish," he replied and turned for the door.

"That's all right. What'd you want?"

"It's been a two weeks. You said my stitches might be able to come out?"

"Has it? My, the time is flying. Yes, I did say that didn't I?" She washed her hands, "It'd probably be better if you lie down on the table, you won't move as much."

"It's not gonna hurt is it?" He replied as he carefully lay down.

Eagle rummaged through her supply cabinet and found a

suture removal tray. Opening it, she placed it on his chest. "Humm, need some more light." She rolled a portable lamp over and plugged it in. The light flicked on and D.M. groaned. "Sorry, I should have warned you." Inspecting the sutures, she picked up a pair of tweezers. D.M. eyed her suspiciously. "No, it shouldn't hurt, as long as you hold still." Eagle carefully clipped the sutures and pulled them out. The lieutenant lay quietly with his eyes closed. "Did Tige apologize to you?"

"Yes he did, and he told me what his punishment was."

"Good and you've held him to it?"

"Most definitely."

After she had finished, Eagle stepped back to inspect her work, "One of my best jobs I think."

"I'm not some piece of artwork to hang on a wall," he said lowly.

"Sure you are. The human body is a beautiful and functional piece of art. We're so complex that we haven't even got ourselves figured out."

D.M. sat up with great effort, his left arm trying to protect his broken ribs.

"How are your ribs?" She replied as she motioned for him to lift up his shirt.

"They still hurt a lot. I really haven't been sleeping well, that's the side I prefer to lay on."

Eagle gently ran her fingers across his ribs. D.M. winced slightly. "Unfortunately for you lieutenant, ribs take a very long time to heal because they're always moving."

"I wish there was something that could be done. I don't like the thought of missing so much training. I need to learn this stuff." He shook his head slowly. Eagle hopped up and sat next to him. She studied him for a long while before coming up with a possible remedy.

"Well, there is something we can try..."

D.M. looked up, a glimmer of hope in his eyes. "What?"

"There is a drug, still very experimental. The research group I work with has given me some to conduct further field trials. The stuff is pretty neat. It helps the human body heal itself up to seventy-five percent faster."

He rubbed his jaw, "Sounds good, load me up."

"Not that fast. This might be a wonder drug, but it has some problems."

"What? Am I gonna grow another arm or two?" He joked.

"No, but there is a risk of an allergic reaction."

"So, I'm willing to be a guinea pig for science," he pleaded.

Eagle slid off the counter and went to a locked cabinet. Quickly undoing the padlock, she removed a small bottle. "I'm going to try the good stuff on you."

"Gee, thanks. Glad to know I'm worth it," he managed a smile.

"There are two varieties. H.C.15 is the strongest, but it has the highest rate for reactions. H.C.13 is not nearly as effective, but it does work."

"I just wanna get better," he replied softly.

Eagle drew up a small syringe full of the drug, "I think a couple c.c.'s should be enough to test you."

The lieutenant pulled his arm out of the sleeve of his ABUs, "So what kind of reaction can I expect?"

"Perhaps nothing. If you do have one, you might experience severe pain at the injection site, have problems breathing, or die." She swabbed his arm with alcohol and drew her hand back.

"Great, I hope I don't get the *dead* kind of reaction." He grunted as the needle bit deeply into his biceps, and there was a burning pressure as she pushed the plunger.

"There, all done," she said upon removing the needle, "Now we wait."

"How long?"

Eagle discarded the syringe into a sharps box and took D.M.'s medical record from the shelf, "About fifteen to twenty minutes should be long enough." She placed a blank sheet of paper in the front of his record and annotated her test information. After, she flipped through his record. What better way to find out about someone? There wasn't much of anything that piqued her interest. Lots of flight physical notes, a couple of drug allergies, several x-ray reports and labs that all read normal. The only thing that did get her attention was his commissioning physical notes. On the form there was a drawing of his back showing numerous scars. They all seemed to be going the same direction and appeared to have been made by the same weapon- something straight and blunt.

D.M. sat on the table in silence, his head down. For some reason the whole experience was awkward. All he could do was sit and wait for something (or nothing) to happen. Eagle too was feeling uneasy. She felt the need to inquire about the scars, "What are all those scars on your back from?" She had read the doctor's notes, but felt she needed to hear it from him.

The lieutenant turned and looked at her, his eyes had changed from peaceful to that of a scared rabbit. "Uh...umm...I got beat up in a fight in high school. Six guys jumped me and beat me up with a piece of pipe," his voice trembled slightly. Eagle studied him, she knew he was lying. Eventually she would get the truth out of him. A wonderful aroma drifted from the kitchen. D.M. took several sniffs, "Mmm, that smells good. What is it?" He quickly tried to change the subject.

"What you might call meatballs Norwegian style," she replied as she darted into the kitchen to check on it.

"By the smell of it you must be a good cook."

"I really don't like to cook, I just follow recipes."

"Frank said if you don't feel like cooking every night you can join us for dinner. He's actually pretty good in the kitchen."

"I may take you up on the offer. Hard just cooking for one, and I'm not a fan of leftovers," she checked her watch one last time. "Okay, time's up. I think you should be all right with more." Washing her hands, she returned to D.M. and gathered together all the supplies for starting an I.V. "I'm going to put in what's called a Hep-Lock. It will stay in for the next couple days and save me from having to stick you every time we do the treatment."

"How much of that stuff do I get?"

"Two hundred c.c.'s diluted in one liter of saline a night for three nights. That should give your body enough help to get healed quickly."

D.M. watched as she prepared everything, "That thing stays in me?"

"Just until after the last treatment. It shouldn't bother you much...Now let me see your hands."

He offered both hands to her. She poked around until she

found a suitable vein, "You are left handed?"

The lieutenant nodded. Eagle pulled on a pair of gloves, "Good, the best vein is in your right hand anyway." Tying the tourniquet around his wrist, she thwacked the back of his hand to make the veins rise. Taking an alcohol pad, she wiped the area and prepared to make the stick. "Hold real still, I only wanna do this once." D.M. closed his eyes and tried not to flinch as she slid the catheter under his skin.

"Man, he's been over there for almost an hour. Dinner's just about done," Frank commented as he chopped onions and sniffed back the tears from their pungent aroma.

"Maybe he and the boss woman got a little more going than we think," Jake teased as he stood in the kitchen doorway watching.

"No, I don't think so. He really hasn't been feeling well. He says his ribs hurt so bad they keep him awake at night."

Jake hopped up and sat on the counter, "Oh come on, you don't really believe he'd be over there getting doctored?"

"Actually I do," Frank scraped the onions into the sauce and stirred it. "And to prove it, I'm gonna bet you five bucks that's what he's doing."

"You're on."

Frank washed his hands and the twosome headed for the door. "Where are you guys going?" Sam called.

"To see if D.M.'s gonna join us for dinner," Frank answered as they left the hut. They reached Eagle's hut and Frank rapped on the door.

"Just a minute!" Eagle hollered from the kitchen. She quickly finished rescuing some green beans from a pot of water and went to answer the door. D.M. was crashed out on her sofa sound asleep. An I.V. line ran to a bag that hung on a pole next to him.

"Hi. What do you two want?"

"Uh, I was just checking to see if D.M. is gonna join us for dinner," Frank said nervously.

Eagle smiled slightly, "I don't think he's going to do much of anything..." she opened the door all the way so they could see where he was. "A little Demerol does wonders."

"I guess so. At least he's not in pain," Frank replied, "Thanks."

"No problem, see you in the morning."

As they walked back to their hut, Jake produced a pack of cigarettes and lit up. "Shall I forget that you owe me five bucks?" Frank teased.

"Naw, I'll pay up. No big deal, I got plenty of dough."

Frank disappeared into the hut and Tige came out, "Hey mate, can I bum a fag?"

Jake stared at him blankly. Did this guy just ask him for a *fag?* No, this couldn't be. Tige wasn't that familiar with his background.

"Hey, can I have a cigarette?" Tige asked again, motioning to the pack.

"Oh yeah sure," Jake stammered, still thinking about what Tige had just said. He offered him the pack and lighter.

"Where I come from we call's 'em fags," Tige added.

"Ah, I see."

The Australian lit up and took several long drags. "This is crazy..." he took another drag, "Trying to make a special team out of us. It takes a lot longer than six months. I don't know how she'll do it- if she even can."

"I don't either. All I know is the twelve hour days are not my idea of fun."

"That's nothing compared to spending a week in the bush with no sleep and very little tucker...But there's only so much she can teach here in the desert...If she thinks were ready after just this training, she's got another thing coming."

"So we're looking at the possibility of being butchered our first time out?"

"Probably," Tige said flatly as he finished his smoke. Smashing the butt out on the door frame, he went inside.

Jake stood looking at the sunset. The sky was painted a beautiful salmon pink with a few wispy clouds that gave it a silvery touch. He wasn't one to appreciate what nature had to offer, but tonight for some reason he felt compelled to stay until the sun had dipped below the horizon and the mountains to the east faded to a blue gray. Maybe it was good to appreciate what he might not see too many more of.

***

Eagle had taken the team into the main base so they could do laundry and stock up on supplies. It was Sunday, their only day off from training. The team was now two months into training. They had just returned back to their little base when Tige approached Eagle, "Ma'am, can I ask a favor?"

"What?"

"I'd like to practice some with my rifle. You know, so I can keep my edge."

"All right. Keep it pointed down range. Understood?"

"Yes, ma'am. Thank you." He jogged off to the BOQ and retrieved his rifle case and a target. Scrounging around in the pile of crates that were between huts, he found part of a crate lid to hold the target. He walked out to where their designated firing line was and set his rifle case down. Taking his target and the lid, he began to walk. Soon, the others came out to see what was going on.

"Where's he going?" Frank said as he watched Tige walk past where their targets were usually posted.

"He's a sniper. A thousand yards is like a golf putt for him," Jake replied. Max, Sam and D.M. wandered out after they had put their clothes away.

"Eagle's gonna let him practice huh?" the lieutenant said, putting on his hat and sunglasses. The desert was blindingly bright.

"I guess so," Sam added as he pulled up a crate, flipped it over and sat down on it. Tige continued to walk for another few minutes. Finally he set up his target and started the long walk back. Several minutes later he returned to the group.

"What? Expecting a show?" He said as he opened his rifle case and pulled out a thin shooting mat. Laying it on the ground he then pulled out his spotting scope and set it up on the mat, "Any volunteers for a spotter?"

Max stepped forward, "I know a little bit."

"Good, on your belly mate," Tige said as he took out his rifle and flipped down the bipod legs on the front. He flopped down on his stomach and opened the covers on the scope. Reaching over into his case, he retrieved a set of small hearing protectors and a box with twenty five rounds of ammo. Max fished around in his pocket and found a pair of foam ear protectors. Rolling them between his fingers, he shoved one in each ear. It would help reduce the noise some. He looked at Tige's rifle. Something seemed odd about it.

"That doesn't look like any standard issue sniper rifle I've ever seen," Max commented, noticing the stainless barrel and bolt assembly.

"It's not. This rifle was given to me by my grandfather. I started hunting with it when I was just ten. When I joined the SASR, they had me shooting with their standard issue, a .338, I couldn't hit a bloody thing with it. So one day I brought this one in and started shooting at targets nearly eleven hundred meters out. I hit every bull's eye. The commander quickly decided that I should stay with what I knew. So this has been my trusty partner for the last ten years of service."

"What is it?"

"A very old .375 Holland and Holland magnum... I've had to replace the barrel only once on it and I swapped out the beautifully carved wooden stock for a composite stock. Those changes took me over a month to get used to."

"So you really are married to that thing huh?" Jake said from behind.

Tige looked over his shoulder, "Yes, you are. Once you find the right rifle, you'll do anything to keep it in excellent working order. It's your life. Rarely is there ever a divorce!"

The men chuckled.

"How many kills do you have?" Frank asked.

"Fifty six," he pulled a round from the box and dropped it into the chamber. Closing it, he reached down and picked up a small amount of sand. Tipping his hand slowly, the sand fell out and blew the direction of the wind. Tige leaned down and found his target. "Right, five knot wind from the west, afternoon heat, and very low humidity," he adjusted his scope and turned his hat around backwards. Settling down, he let his finger slowly wrap around the trigger. His breathing slowed and his body did not move. With the most gentle of pressure, he squeezed the trigger. A loud report sounded as the round went down range.

Max adjusted the spotting scope so he could find the bullet strike on the target, "A bit high and to the right."

"Correction?" He looked over at Max.

"Huh?"

"What would my correction be?" Tige knew what the correction was; he just wanted to make sure Max knew what he was talking about.

Max looked though the scope again, "My guess would be one down and one left."

"Very good," Tige made the adjustment and ejected the spent case. Pulling another round out, he dropped it in and locked the bolt. Eagle came out from her hut to watch. Sam motioned her to join him on the crate. He slid over and made room for her. She sat down and held her fingers up to her ears. Just as Tige prepared to fire, she shoved her fingers in her ears. Another loud report went through the camp.

"Dead on!" Max cheered.

Tige rolled over partway and looked back at the group, "Now see, there's no reason to be blowing a hundred rounds of ammo for just one kill. Even in the heat of battle you can exercise some control. Your ammo will last a helluva lot longer."

"So why don't you use the .50 cal?" Frank asked.

"Granted it's the King of sniper rifles, but when you get a bit older, you just don't feel like lugging that thing all over the place. It's bloody heavy! Yes, you can get a kill from nearly two miles out, but I find I'm more comfortable with my old friend here. If I have to close the distance a bit to make my shot, I'm fine with that."

"Don't you guys shoot with silencers?" D.M. added.

Tige reached over and grabbed a cylindrical leather case. Popping the top, he slid an eighteen inch long silencer out. Lying on his side, he pulled the rifle back until the barrel was level with his shoulders. Carefully he screwed the silencer on then pushed the rifle back into position. "Yes, we shoot with them, but as you will see, the term 'silencer' is rather inaccurate. It does greatly reduce the muzzle noise, but it doesn't get rid of it completely. As the calibers get larger, it's harder to keep the rifle dead quiet," he took aim and fired. The noise was almost half what the other shots were.

"Dead on again," Max called.

"Good," Tige ejected the spent case, closed the bolt but left the handle up. He flipped the scope covers down and got to his feet. He began his long trek down range to collect his target.

"Are you done?" Frank hollered.

Tige turned, "Sorry, snipers are lousy showmen. We like to use as few rounds as possible to get the job done," he walked off.

Eagle and the rest of the team returned from their morning run. They were now up to running three miles and were keeping together as a group. She was pleased to see their progress. After cooling down and more stretches, she dismissed them to get showers and breakfast. The colonel went back to her hut and into the bathroom. Turning on the shower, she stood waiting. There was a knocking noise in the pipes and a dribble of water came out.

"Oh, just great," she groaned. Opening her back door, she walked out to the small well house and opened the door. She stood staring at the pump works clueless as to what was wrong. Returning to her hut, she tried again. No luck. She wandered to the front of the hut and opened the door. Frank stood with his fist up, just about to knock.

"I know. No water," she announced with dismay.

"We're dry over there too."

"Any of you guys know about wells?"

"Mmmmm, maybe, if it's mechanical. I'll get my tools and grab Jake. Maybe we can figure it out."

"I just hope the damn thing's not dry. I was told it's over six hundred feet deep."

"Crap, that's the last thing we need to go wrong out here." He hurried back to the hut. A few minutes later he and Jake went out back and started to work on the pump.

"Let's check the electrical first," Jake said as he opened the electrical panel and began pulling fuses and looking them over. He put them all back in and threw the main power. The well pump motor made grinding noises. Quickly he turned off the power. "Well, that doesn't sound very healthy."

"Think it's in the gears or something?"

"Dunno. I'm used to working on fuel pumps on helicopters." He poked around the well components. Flipping the screwdriver out of his Leatherman, he opened the top of the motor. "Humm, wonder if it's got some sediment built up in it?" Reaching up, he turned the power back on. The motor made some grinding noises and a blast of muddy water shot out, covering both the men. Jake frantically turned off the power. They stood looking at each other laughing. The rest of the men were looking out the back door of their hut, laughing at the spectacle.

"Yeah, that was just brilliant," Frank teased.

"Well, uh, I don't have any experience with these things!" He put the cover back on and screwed it down, "Let's see if we broke loose what was stuck." Turning the main power on the motor growled and rumbled. He turned to the group, "Hey, someone go see if we got water."

Max tried the tap and came back out, "We got a dribble of muddy water, that's it."

Jake shut off the power and stood thinking. He held his finger up, turned and went back into their hut. A few minutes later he returned, wearing a set of steel toe combat boots. "Okay, outta the way," he stepped in and gave the well motor several hard kicks. Reaching up, he turned the power back on. The motor hummed. "Hey, see if you got water now," he hollered.

Max checked again, "Yeah, it's a bit muddy, but we got pressure again." The others cheered.

"Let run for a few minutes to see if the mud goes away," He looked over at Frank, "Damn, finally found a use for these steel toes after all." He closed the door to the well house and trudged over to Eagle's hut. Knocking on the door he stood for a few moments before she answered. She looked at him standing there splattered with mud.

"Okay, we have water again," he smiled through the grime.

"Excellent! What'd you do?"

"I kicked the shit out of it, literally...I'd open all your taps and let them run for a few minutes, the water's a bit muddy right now."

"Good job corporal, you saved the day."

"You're welcome. I'm going to get a shower; I more than need one now."

Frank walked back to their hut. He was going to head in the back door when something caught his eye. The back of their hut and Eagle's hut had a small clapboard storage area attached to them. The men had discovered that was where the brooms, mops and cleaning equipment were. Frank stopped at the shed and looked at it. He opened the door that faced the back and saw all the cleaning supplies. Closing the door, he walked around to the left and found a door that faced between the huts. He flipped open the latch and peered inside. "Well shit!" He laughed.

D.M. came around the back and stood looking at him, "What?"

"Come here my dear brother, have a look."

The lieutenant peered into the darkness and then started to laugh, "Son of a bitch, guess we should have looked all over this place before we settled for cold showers."

Frank reached in, flipped the switch and turned it on, "At least I won't have to hear you bitching about another cold shower."

D.M. grabbed Frank and gave him a hug, "I knew I kept you around for something."

"Yeah, Mr. MIT can't figure out where the water heater is!" He walked over to Eagle's storage unit and checked hers, "Ah, she must have been smart enough to figure it out."

"All right, all right, rub it in will you? I don't see you working on long and short chain polymers any time soon though."

"I'm just happy to be a mechanic. My skills are in demand too," he playfully punched him in the shoulder.

At the three month mark, Eagle decided it was time to start their flight training. So far they had demonstrated that they could function as a team and work together reasonably well. Fights and squabbles were few and far between and she could see some friendships forming. She had set aside time each afternoon for D.M. to conduct 'ground school' for the rest. They had taken to the thought of flying with great enthusiasm and had kept the poor lieutenant on his toes with an endless barrage of questions and comments.

It was shortly before dawn when the team rolled out for their morning run. Eagle was waiting for them. "Good morning gentlemen. Today I have a little surprise for you. Instead of going to the training hut after breakfast, I want everyone out here dressed in some form of duty uniform. D.M. time to dust off your flight suit."

"We flying?" Jake spoke up.

Eagle nodded and cheers went up from the group. This was the day they had been waiting for. "Listen up!" She brought the group back to order, "The only way I could get this past the Brass here was to tell them you are all officers...Yes, I could get my ass in a sling for this, but when your training is complete, you *will* be officers. So for now, you have your bars on credit. Remember you are officers now, you must act like them. Don't forget that the enlisted will salute *you*. I suggest that you all brush up on your customs and courtesies so you don't make any mistakes. I expect all of you to look and act sharp. You are a part of a Special Forces unit; enjoy the prestige that goes with it," she paused for a moment to collect her thoughts, "And if you all succeed in behaving yourselves, I *MIGHT* take you to the Officer's Club tonight."

The group broke in to wild cheers. D.M. approached Eagle, "And who's buying the first round?" He smiled.

Eagle wrinkled her nose, "Humm, I guess if they *earn* it, I will."

D.M. turned to the group, "Hey, she says that if we do well, she'll buy the first round." More cheers came from the group. He looked over his shoulder at her, "Amazing what a little beer will do for morale."

"Yes, now go get them ready."

"Yes ma'am!" he replied smartly. "Team tinge HUT!" The men snapped to attention. "Everybody needs to get ready real quick. Fall out!"

The team made a quick stop by clothing issue to get flight gear. Eagle watched as they all strutted around proudly in their flight suits. "Ma'am?" The clerk approached Eagle, he carried a manila envelope, "This arrived for you a couple weeks ago."

Eagle opened the envelope, "Ah yes, I've been waiting for these. Thank you." She walked over to D.M. and pulled off the old squadron patch on his left shoulder. The two sides of Velcro separated with a loud rip. The lieutenant regarded her with suspicion. Reaching into the envelope, she removed a new patch. With careful precision, she applied the Dragonslayer's patch to his arm.

"Cool, thanks," he smiled broadly, "Do you want me to pass them out to the others?"

"No, have them come over to me. I wanna do it."

"Do I detect a hint of personal satisfaction?"

Eagle grinned, "Yessss!"

After Eagle's brief decoration ceremony, in which she presented squadron patches and also bestowed Second Lieutenant bars on the enlisted men, they headed for the hanger. D.M. was the first through the door. He stopped and let out a disgusted groan, "Are you sure this is the right hanger?"

"Yes, I'm sure."

"You've got to be kidding me. We can't fly these pieces of shit."

"Didn't they retire them over thirty years ago?" Jake inquired.

"Oh, at *least*," Frank chided.

Max scratched his head, "They still make parts for them?"

"Cannibals," D.M. replied flatly, "They take parts from retired planes and use them to keep these running."

"Well that doesn't sound so good," Max added.

"What's wrong with F-4's? They performed very well in Vietnam," Eagle stated.

"Yeah, that's just it. How long ago was Vietnam? These planes are long past their service life," D.M. added.

Eagle walked around one of the planes and noticed that it had seen a lot of action. The grey fuselage was at least four different colors of primer and there was even some rust on a couple spots. The plane indeed looked tired, ready for the bone yard. This was the best they had to offer? No, must be Westland again. She returned to the group, who had made themselves comfortable on a pile of drop tanks and were reading flight manuals. Walking up, she reached the pile of their flight gear. Helmets and bags were stacked haphazardly. She picked out D.M.'s helmet, the only one with any decoration, and tossed it at him, "Come on. Shake down time." He put down his flight manual and followed her. Eagle reached into her bag and took out a small notebook and handed it to him. "Preflight," she said with little expression.

D.M. walked around the plane. He couldn't believe he was going up in this junk heap. Nothing looked safe. As he climbed up to check the cockpits, he stopped. There were three holes drilled on either side of the inside cockpit rail at the level where the stick was. Humm, curious, he thought. He reached down and stuck his little finger into one of the holes. Metal shards stuck to his skin. He stood on the ladder thinking. Then it dawned on him. China Lake was a weapons testing facility. They needed old planes to test ordinance. If he was right, this plane was on its way to being a target drone. The holes were to mount the equipment that would allow the plane to be flown like a giant radio controlled airplane. He was really not feeling good about this now.

After the plane was preflighted and taken out onto the tarmac, Eagle climbed into the rear seat. D.M. looked up at her from his place on the ground, "How long are we gonna go for?"

"About half an hour."

D.M. climbed up the ladder and squeezed into the cockpit, "Hey, anybody got a shoe horn?" He joked as he wiggled into his seat. Once buckled in, he contacted the tower and got clearance. The rest of the team came out to see them off. They waved as the plane taxied down to the runway.

Once in the air, D.M. brought the plane up to two thousand feet and leveled off. "Okay lieutenant, I want you to change course to zero-eight-five and show me what you got."

"Roger that," he replied flatly. For some reason Eagle seemed to be giving him the cold shoulder. She usually had more to say; or at least in a more civil tone of voice. He brought the plane around and performed a few smooth textbook loops and rolls.

Eagle yawned loudly. She wanted to make sure D.M. heard it, "I thought I recall saying that I wanted to see what you got. I know you can fly like a textbook. I wanna see what you can do with this bird. Now *fly!*"

"Yes ma'am!" He replied and cranked the stick hard to the right and pushed the throttle to the stops. The plane lurched forward in an immense burst of speed. He gained altitude and then leveled off.

"Ah, much better," she sighed, "You have a MiG on your six, shake him."

"Yeah? What kind?"

"MiG twenty nine."

"Right," he yanked up and brought the plane into a steep climb. The G's pushed them deeply into their seats. D.M. then pushed the stick to the left and nosed the plane into a roll followed by a dive. "Is he still on me?"

"Like white on rice."

D.M. growled. Eagle was not playing nice. He understood the point of her exercise, but he wasn't really in the mood to fly so hard. She continued on for the next half an hour calling directions and telling him the whereabouts of the "bogie." Finally she allowed him the pleasure of getting behind the pretend fighter and taking it out with a "missile." When they were back on the ground, Eagle hopped out of the plane and walked off like nothing had happened. D.M. sat in the cockpit for a few minutes, exhausted, his flight suit drenched with sweat. It had been a long time since he'd had to fly like that. In the back of his mind he felt satisfaction that he'd been able to keep up with her. He wondered what it would be like to fly against her. Was she that good?

The team finished their first day of flying. Eagle and D.M. had taken turns giving rides to the others. They had done well. The colonel held up to her promise and took them to the Officer's Club. The men bellied up to the bar and ordered their first round. They devoured their drinks as if they had never tasted anything so good. Eagle sat at the end of the bar and watched as she sipped on a brandy. They all looked so proud. Heads held high, they looked as if nothing could stop them. This was the attitude that would keep them alive. In time that attitude would manifest into quiet courage. Without it, they would die their first mission out.

D.M. saw Eagle sitting alone and approached her, "May I join you?" He could see she was tired; the sparkle in her eyes had dimmed considerably. She nodded slowly. D.M. pulled up a stool and sat down, "Something wrong?"

"It's not easy keeping up with all of you," she rubbed the edge of her glass with her finger.

"We're not exactly angels," he took several swallows of soda. They sat in silence for some time. Silence between them usually felt awkward for D.M., but for some reason this time it didn't bother him, "How much longer do we have here? Or is this permanently home?"

Eagle sipped on her brandy, savoring it at length before she replied, "Training is half over. I see everyone becoming a team. This is good. There are still more things to learn before we move on."

"So we have three months more of this holiday paradise? Then what happens? Do we live here forever?"

"Heaven's no!" She perked up, "We're only at the 'China Lake Fitness Club' in order to toughen all of you up. No, I hate this place too, but it's a harsh environment with few distractions."

D.M.'s eyes followed a lovely blonde waitress as she walked by.

"Like I said *few* distractions!"

D.M. turned his attention back to her and smiled, "Just kidding."

Eagle reached over and playfully smacked him on the shoulder, "I'm so glad we're out in the middle of nowhere, otherwise I'd never get an honest day of training out of any of you."

"Hey, we're men, we can only concentrate on one thing at a time," he laughed.

CHAPTER SIX

Weeks flew by and it was now beginning the last month of

their stay at the camp. Eagle was amazed at how fast they had learned to fly. It seemed to her that they were all large sponges soaking up every drop of information that was given; turning it into immediate and sometimes terribly proficient skill. She was now faced with the fact that she must let them spread their wings. D.M. had proven to be a wonderful teacher. He made sure safety took precedence over everything else, but allowed them to have fun as well. It was now time to test them on what they knew. It was time to let them fully take control of the planes and fly.

Eagle gave D.M. the honor of being the back seat examiner. He would test them on what they were capable of doing, but try not to help them. He would be the ultimate judge of their abilities. If he said they passed, Eagle would let them have their wings. She knew D.M. would not let her down. He understood the importance of what they had been taught and knew if he failed Eagle would probably never forgive him.

D.M. stood in front of the last two men. Max, Tige and Frank had earned their wings. He felt good about his teaching; everyone had done well so far. He now had to choose who was to go next. It was late afternoon and Eagle had told him there was time for one more flight. Taking the pre-flight book from his bag, he presented it to Jake, "Let's do it," he said calmly and started off toward the plane. He still had misgivings about the corporal, and their personalities always seemed to clash. They had nothing in common except they were here because they had been in trouble.

"Yes sir!" Jake snapped and quickly collected his gear. This was the moment he had been waiting for. He loved to fly, and now he was nearing the point where he could do it without breaking regulations. Helicopters were still his favorite, but jets gave him something new- Mach speed.

"All right Jake, let's get this junk heap in the air," D.M. hollered from the back cockpit. Every time he went up as a back-seater, he felt an uneasy sensation in the pit of his stomach. He was not completely in control anymore. He was at the mercy of someone else.

"Okay, all done. Can we go now?" Jake called from the ground several minutes later.

"If you think we're ready."

Jake took one quick look at the preflight manual and tossed it in his bag. He climbed the ladder and crawled into the front seat. He had been in the seat many times before, but today he felt just like he had the first day he had taken the plane up as a pilot. Butterflies zoomed in his stomach and he felt almost lightheaded. He strapped himself in and made contact with the tower. It was all up to him now.

The plane taxied to the end of the runway and stopped. Jake made one final check of all the instruments and fixed his eyes down the runway. "Okay, here's for all the marbles." He shoved the throttle forward and guided the plane down the runway. It jostled unsteadily on the uneven pavement until the front gear lifted free. Jake eased the stick back further and the plane broke free of its earthly bonds. "God I love this!" He bellowed over the mike.

"Ascend to angel's seven and take a heading of zero-two-nine, speed four hundred knots," the lieutenant called.

"Roger that. Ascending to seven thousand feet, bearing zero-two-nine at four hundred knots," he replied crisply as he made the course correction. The plane cruised along smoothly. D.M. started his test by having Jake perform several loops and rolls. He then had him make rapid changes of direction and altitude. Jake carried out each task with effortless precision. Now came the last part of the test, the part all the others had nicknamed "the pipe." It was a narrow canyon that snaked between tall mesas. The object of the exercise was nape of the earth flying. The pipe had to be negotiated carefully; sharp rises and falls in the contour of the canyon floor made navigation difficult. A slight oversight in speed or navigation would send the plane slamming into one of the walls or the canyon floor.

"All right, this is where it gets hard," D.M. broke the silence.

"Bring it on baby."

"Reduce speed to two hundred knots and come around to three-two-zero."

"Altitude?"

"Whatever you feel comfortable with. Mind the fact I would like it to be somewhere below the canyon rim, and above the level of the dirt and cactus," D.M. joked. He was trying not to be nervous, but this part of the test really played havoc with his nerves.

Jake brought the plane around and began his descent into the canyon. D.M. watched as the walls closed in around them. The plane slalomed smoothly around the bends. The canyon floor rose and fell beneath them. "How am I doing?" Jake asked.

"Very good."

An instant later a loud crash rocked the plane. Warning lights and buzzers went off. "Shit!" D.M. hollered.

"What happened?!" Jake fought the stick to keep the plane level, "I got bells and whistles like crazy. Left engine is out and I'm getting a fire warning light."

"Get us up and out of here, quick!"

Jake battled to get the plane above the rim, "D.M. I don't think I can hold it much longer."

"Give it some right rudder and gain some altitude. If we have to eject, we need to be higher," he keyed the mike, "Mayday, mayday. China Lake control this is Delta Sierra three-one-five, we're having problems. Left engine out, we now have a fire warning light and are losing hydraulic pressure."

"Roger Delta Sierra three-one-five you have dropped off radar. What is your position?"

Jake fought with the plane but soon lost control and they started to spiral uncontrollably. "D.M. I lost it, I can't get control."

D.M. tried to read the control panel to check their location but his eyes would not focus in the blur of motion.

"Delta Sierra what is your location?" The tower radioed again.

"Shit I don't know, but we're going to have to eject," D.M. snarled. "Jake, hold on, I'm gonna punch us out."

"D.M. I got a fire light on the right engine."

"Time to get out of here. Decrease your speed and I need you to get us upright and level for just a moment."

"I'll try," he throttled back and jostled the stick. The plane flipped upright and Jake managed to hold it for a few seconds.

"Eject! Eject! Eject!" D.M. closed his eyes and pulled the

handles. The canopies blew off and D.M. was rocketed clear of the plane. He tumbled, the force of the ejection knocked him unconscious.

Eagle paced nervously in the control tower, "Did he say what his coordinates were?"

"No ma'am," the controller replied.

"Where was their last radar contact?"

"Last contact was at sixteen twenty five. They were bearing zero-three-three at about three hundred feet."

"You lost them at three hundred feet? What the hell kind of radar do you have?!"

"An old one," another controller answered.

Eagle turned to the map on the table, "Zero-three-three at how many miles out?"

"About eighty."

She plotted out their course and studied it, "Humm, if they kept on their last known course, they would have ended up somewhere near Death Valley...But if they went out of control..."

White. White all around. Was this heaven? No, way too hot for that. D.M. sat up and pulled the parachute off. He scanned the area. Where was the plane? Slowly, he got to his feet and took off his helmet. He was standing near the mouth of a large canyon. The walls rose steeply and were colored with shades of brick red, sandstone, and black volcanic rock. Wind worn peaks protruded like jagged knives. D.M. squinted his eyes from the sun. There, about midway into the canyon, something glittered. Plane wreckage, he guessed, gathering his parachute and helmet he set out for it. He walked several hundred feet before he stopped to survey the wreckage. Bits and pieces of plane were scattered for at least five hundred yards in every direction. There wasn't much left. A flutter above him on the ridge caught his attention. A parachute! Jake must have made it out after all. He walked further into the site to try and get a better look. There he was, about fifty feet up the cliff wall jammed between a couple boulders. "Jake!

Jake!" He hollered trying to see if he was conscious. There was no response. The lieutenant began to pick his way up the steep cliff. This was going to take time.

"Why haven't they contacted us? Surely they were able to eject safely," Sam commented.

"Maybe not. From what the controller said it seemed like they were in a mess of trouble," Frank replied glumly.

Tige approached Eagle, "Should we send out a search party? Maybe we can find the wreck."

"I'll see what I can do, but it's getting dark. It'd be near suicide to try and search through that country. It's full of deep canyons, jagged mesas, and stone towers. Besides we have no idea where they actually are."

"Eagle, we can't just leave them out there, it's going to get below freezing tonight. If they are alive, they could freeze to death by morning," Frank protested.

"D.M. has trained everyone on survival skills. We just have to hope for the best."

The lieutenant wedged himself between a boulder and the cliff face. He was within arm's reach of Jake. "Jake? Jake? Can you hear me?" He reached out and took hold of him and tried to pull him over. "Shit, why did you have to go and get stuck all the way up here?" He growled and tried to inch closer. After several minutes of struggling and cursing, D.M. managed to get Jake's limp body onto one of the boulders and cut free of the parachute. He checked his breathing, pulse, and then started to look him over for injury. Jake's visor had been smashed and little bits of dark plastic poked out from his bloodied face. Blood stained the left elbow of his flight suit. D.M. crawled over to get a better look. He pulled out his knife and carefully cut back the tattered, blood soaked sleeve. A large shard of metal protruded from just above the bend in his elbow. This didn't look good. D.M. grabbed some of the parachute and cut it up. He removed Jake's field bandage from his survival vest and carefully dressed the wound. Taking the shreds of parachute, he bandaged over the dressing to help keep it clean. The rest of Jake's body was riddled with little bits of shrapnel. D.M. guessed that he had been ejected just as the plane exploded.

He looked down at the wreckage; it was too spread out to have hit the ground and broke up. There was no scar in the earth from where the fuselage would have hit and slid. He turned his attentions back to Jake. He lifted one of his eyelids and then the other. One pupil was larger than the other, no doubt a concussion from the blast. Now, to get him down from here. D.M. looked for a better way down, but the best way was how he had come; threading his way between the boulders and crevices.

Hefting the corporal over his shoulder, D.M. began to pick his way back down the cliff. The progress was slow, but he wanted to make sure they both made it down alive. Once at the bottom, he found a soft sandy spot and carefully laid him down. Taking off Jake's helmet, he checked his head over for any bleeding other than his face; which had stopped and had started to dry. "Jake? Hey, anybody in there? Come on man, talk to me," he tapped him on the shoulder, hoping he could get him to wake up. No response.

D.M. went through the pockets of his survival vest. Emergency water packages, sunscreen, compass, trusty Swiss Army knife, preserved food of some sort, flare gun, flashlight, radio...Radio! He hurriedly turned it on and adjusted it to an open frequency, "Mayday, mayday, this is Delta Sierra three-one-five does anybody copy?"

"Roger Delta Sierra, are you okay?" The tower responded.

"No, we seem to be without the fucking plane!" D.M. snarled, "My pilot is hurt, unconscious, he's got a large piece of metal in his arm and is bleeding pretty good."

Eagle tore up the stairs of the tower. The controller immediately gave her the microphone, "D.M., what is your status?"

"Jake's hurt pretty bad. I'm okay. Please come get us."

"Where are you?"

"I haven't got a clue. The plane was completely out of control. Last place I really remember was in the pipe. We're just inside the mouth of some big canyon. The walls are steep and there's a big flat top mesa to my north."

The controller quickly scanned the map, "Here's the pipe. They were going north east. Now the only area that fits that description is over here," he pointed to an area a considerable distance further to the east, "They are almost two hundred miles out. They aren't even in the range anymore."

"Can we get a rescue team out there?" Eagle questioned.

"Too dangerous, they would never approve of it."

"Well I suggest you check in to it right away."

"Yes ma'am."

Eagle returned to the microphone, "D.M. we believe we've located where you are. They say it's too dangerous to send out a rescue team; you'll most likely have to wait until morning. Can you manage taking care of Jake?"

"I guess I have no other choice. You know it's going to freeze tonight."

"Yes, I'm aware of that. Do what you have to. Can you get wood for a fire?"

D.M. looked around, "Negative, nothing here."

"I promise we'll be out there at first light. Do you have a flare gun?"

"Affirmative."

"When you hear us, send it up," Eagle replied. "And maintain radio contact with us every hour. Let me know if anything changes in Jake's condition."

"I will, don't worry. Delta Sierra out." D.M. knew the battery wouldn't last long if he kept chatting. He needed to hurry and get some kind of shelter constructed so they wouldn't be out in the cold. Wandering through the crash site, D.M. poked through the rubble. Engine and fuselage parts lay scattered over a wide expanse. A gentle breeze made something flutter a few yards away. He walked over and picked up part of the intake fan. It was covered with blood and a large, black, mangled feather fell out and floated to the ground. "Bird strike," he said softly and put the piece back where he had found it.

Dragging pieces of the plane over, he constructed a makeshift lean-to around Jake. He scrambled back up the cliff and retrieved the other parachute. They were going to need everything possible to keep warm. The sun was setting quickly and soon the darkness and freezing cold would make matters worse. D.M. kept a close watch on Jake. He covered him up with one of the parachutes and watched for signs of shock. It was only a matter of time.

Jake groaned. D.M. checked his watch. It was 1900, the sun was down and they were left in near blackness. The plane had gone down almost three hours ago. "Jake? Jake? Hey, come on, wake up," D.M. nudged his shoulder. Jake groaned again and tried to open his eyes. "No, don't open your eyes, it'll probably make you feel worse."

"D.M.," Jake gasped.

"Yeah, I'm right here."

"I gotta..." he muttered and vomited. D.M. quickly rolled him over on his side to clear his airway. He had stopped breathing and was beginning to struggle.

"Easy Jake, let me help you," he said as he stood and quickly gave him three hard blows right between the shoulders. Jake wheezed, trying to get air in. D.M. hit him again and heard something, "Hold on Jake, I'm trying." He reached around to his head, "You bite me you little puke and I'll let you die. Now open your mouth." Jake opened his mouth and tried to get air in. "No! You shit; whatever's there'll go back down!" He reached inside Jake's mouth and carefully tried to find the obstruction. He felt something, just out of reach. "Jake, I need you to puke again. I think that'll make it come out." He reached up and pressed his finger against the roof of his mouth. He could hear Jake's abdomen all ready at work. He rolled him over further and held his head. Jake wretched violently and finished emptying the contents of his stomach. When his throat cleared, he took in ragged gulps of air.

D.M. pulled out his flash light, leaned over and looked at the vomit. He almost lost his own stomach when he got a whiff of it. Something black, cylindrical, and about three-quarters of an inch long lay in the pile. What the hell was it? Some type of rubber gasket from the plane? How'd he manage that? "Jake? You okay?" He noticed that he was pale and his breathing did not sound good.

"Water," Jake gasped.

"Okay, hang on a second," he replied and quickly retrieved a packet of water. He cut the top off and held it to Jake's lips. "Here, drink." Jake took a few sips and lapsed back into unconsciousness.

D.M. turned on the radio, "Control, this is Delta Sierra, do you copy?"

"Roger Delta Sierra. How are you guys?" Eagle replied.

"Jake is looking real bad. His breathing is shallow and ragged."

"I need you to check for internal injuries; his chest and ribs especially. Give me your report on next check in."

"Roger that. Delta Sierra out." D.M. set to the task of checking Jake over. He found three broken ribs on his left side. Had one of them punctured a lung? There was no telling. Jake was going to be lucky if he made it through the night.

CHAPTER SEVEN

Something was making noise. What the hell was it? Lick, lick, lick. What was that light? D.M. pushed the parachute off his face. The sun was just starting to come up. Something living was on the other side of Jake. D.M. rose up slightly, enough that he could see over Jake and the lean-to. His eyes met with a large pair of amber eyes. Shit, not now. Not more problems. The large cougar stared back, not moving a muscle. D.M. held the animal's gaze, not moving. Jake began to stir. "Jake, don't move, we got unwelcome company." He inched his hand down to his knife sheath. No knife. Where was it? He carefully searched around with his hand, not taking his eyes off the cougar. The big cat growled and hissed. "Nice kitty, why don't you run along and play with someone your own size?" D.M. said slowly sitting up. His hand found a fair sized rock and he carefully pushed the chute away to free his arm up for throwing. It would be awkward, right handed, but perhaps it would chase the cat off.

D.M. raised his arm. The cat backed up and let out a loud roar.

He had heard that roar so many times on nature shows on TV. To say the least it was far more frightening in person. "Come on cat, I don't have all day to screw around. Now why don't you act peaceable and leave," he said boldly. The cougar did not move. D.M. let fly with the rock and smacked the cat squarely in the shoulder. The cougar snarled and trotted off to a safe distance and watched. D.M. scooped up another rock and hurled it at the animal. It fell short, splattering the cat with bits of rock. Growling, the cougar lumbered off in search of an easier meal.

The Huey helicopter hovered near the crash site looking for a place to land. Sam sat on the door ledge with his feet dangling out. Eagle found a spot and set the helicopter down in an open patch of sand nearby. Sam grabbed the first aid bag and stretcher and hurried over to where Jake lay. "Nice to see you could fit us into your busy schedule," D.M. announced sarcastically.

"Sorry sir, they said it was too dangerous to come out last night. I see why," Sam replied as he quickly took Jake's vitals and assessed his wounds. Jake still had not completely regained consciousness. Eagle ran over to them.

"Sam, how is he?"

"His pulse is weak, BP a bit low, his breath sounds suck. I think he's got a pneumothorax."

Eagle took the stethoscope and listened to Jake's breathing, "I think you're right. We need to get him straight to the hospital. Get him ready to travel."

"Aye aye!" He quickly prepared Jake for transport.

Eagle walked over to D.M. "How are you?"

"Fine," he growled, turning away from her.

"I know you're angry for being left out here, but there was nothing I could do."

"Bullshit."

"Lieutenant..." she said firmly, "I didn't wanna leave you out here. On the same token, I wasn't going to endanger more lives to come find you."

He spun around and faced her, his eyes filled with rage, "He could have died!"

"Ma'am, I could use some help here," Sam called.

"We'll discuss this later. Come on, we need to get Jake taken care of."

After Jake was loaded, Eagle climbed into the pilot's seat and started the engine. D.M. sat next to her, looking out the side window. His anger had not diminished. They made the flight to Ridgecrest Regional Hospital in an uneasy silence. Jake was taken to surgery upon arrival. D.M. declined the doctor's attentions, stating that he was fine. He sat in the waiting room with his head in his hands. Eagle sat down next to him, "Please tell me what happened up there," she said in a soft voice.

D.M. lifted his head and looked at her, "Bird strike. Went down the left intake and FODed out the engine."

"You know this for fact?"

"I saw blood and feathers at the site."

"A team of investigators will still wanna talk to you and see the site."

D.M. nodded. He was tired from being up all night in the cold. His eyelids felt like lead. Eagle got up and went to the desk. She said a few words to one of the nurses and returned. "I know you're tired. I got you a bed if you wanna get some rest, we'll be here for a while."

"Thanks..." he replied, "I'm sorry for being so angry earlier."

"No need to apologize, I probably would've been too. I felt bad that my hands were tied; God knows I wanted to help."

D.M. got up to leave. Eagle caught his hand and stopped him, "Are you okay to go back up?"

"Yeah, I'm fine. Just a bit shook up. I'll finish what I started. There's only one left to go." He slipped her grasp and walked off.

The hours passed and finally the surgeon came out.

"How is he?" Eagle stood up to meet him.

"He's going to be okay. I put a chest tube in to alleviate the pneumothorax, he's got four broken ribs, and his whole body was riddled with shrapnel. My biggest concern was his left arm. The piece of metal had just barely missed his axillary artery, but it did nick his cephalic vein. Fortunately it stopped bleeding, but I had to do some venous repair."

"Thank you for your help doctor," she offered her hand to him. He took it and gently shook it.

"No problem. Glad I could be of service."

Jake was to spend three weeks in the hospital. His lung proved stubborn to heal because of his smoking. The team visited him every couple of days to help keep his spirits up and inform him of what was going on with training. He had no problem with good spirit. Every nice looking nurse in the place was fighting over who would give him a sponge bath.

It was 2100 on a Sunday night. The team had just returned from seeing Jake. Eagle could not sleep. She had read in the paper that there was supposed to be a meteor shower starting soon and went outside to survey the night sky. Her whole life she had been fascinated by the stars. There was nothing more beautiful than a clear dark night where the stars shone brightly. She found the switch and turned off the compound light. Ah, total darkness, she sighed and turned her attentions to the heavens. A dull popping sound reached her ears. She looked around for the source. The lights were on in the training hut and the noise seemed to be coming from there. Quietly, she walked over and slipped in the door. In the dim light she could see D.M., his shirt off, using one of the bamboo practice swords. He batted at a punching bag that hung in the rear of the hut. Eagle took her shoes off and crossed to the center mat. She watched him for a while. D.M. was unaware of her presence and continued to fight his pretend foe.

"You hold that sword like a child..." she spoke up loudly. D.M. spun around in surprise. "Either put it away, or learn how to use it properly."

The lieutenant approached her. His body glistened with sweat. He stopped in front of her and turned the sword point down to the mat and rested his hands on the pommel.

"I take it that means you want to learn."

D.M. nodded slowly, his eyes fixed and determined.

"All right. I will teach you. But you must first answer this: why the sword?"

The lieutenant raised the sword and held it in a firm two handed grip, "I like the feel of it."

"You know that you will face your enemy in battle. He will not be just a missile shot, or a figure in your cross hairs. You will face him and ultimately kill him with your hands. Can you do that?"

"Yes," he replied coldly.

Eagle studied him for a moment. He looked magnificent holding the sword. The weapon seemed to suit him. This was her chance to train someone in the old ways, to make him more than just a soldier. D.M. possessed the intelligence, strength and power to become a warrior.

"Kneel. Place your sword on the ground in front of you." She went to a small locker and opened it. Carefully, she removed a real sword that rested in its sheath and returned to him. She held the sword up like a cross and kissed the hilt in the center. Muttering something in Latin, she drew the sword and held it out, the handle in her right hand, her left supporting the blade.

"Repeat after me," she said, "No me saccas in razon..."

"No me saccas sin razon..."

"No me envainas sin onor," she continued.

D.M. repeated, "No me envainas sin onor."

"Do you know the meaning of that lieutenant?"

"Yes. 'Do not draw me without cause: do not ensheath me without honor'... You forget I grew up in Spain."

"Do you believe in these words? And will you swear by them?"

"I swear," he said solemnly.

Eagle bowed her head and brought the sword forward to him, "Kiss it," she said softly. D.M. cradled the blade in his hands and kissed it. "Han som kjemper med sverd, vil bli dømt etter sverdet," she announced loudly in Norwegian and added the translation for D.M.'s benefit, "He who fights with the sword, shall be judged by the sword." She took the sword and held it like a cross, kissed it, and returned it to its sheath. "Take thy weapon and rise. Your education begins."

The lieutenant stood, taking up his sword. Eagle returned the real sword to the cabinet and found another bamboo practice one. Taking off her ABU blouse, she tossed it on the floor. "How much do you know about this weapon?"

"Not much. Used to watch the matadors use them during bullfights."

"Humm, I wouldn't call that much of a sword fight, rather one sided I'd say."

"Not really, the bulls have two swords- one on either side of their head. And sometimes they managed to put a world of hurt on those guys."

She stepped up to him, her sword in her right hand, "The first position you must learn is en garde. This is the position of ready," she stood with her right foot forward, left foot back, knees bent slightly and her sword pointed at him, "Your weight is mostly on your back leg, this gives you flexibility to move your front leg to start an attack." D.M. mirrored her position since he was left handed. "You need to stay loose and fluid. A sword fight is always changing, evolving. You never know what your opponent will do," she lunged forward and struck her sword against his, the lieutenant made a clumsy block. "And you have to be fast," she stepped in, lunged, blocked his sword and firmly tapped him on the chest.

"Shit," D.M. said as he looked down at the bamboo blade against his skin.

"Okay, in order to block my attack, you must parry. There are many different directions you can try to divert my blade to, but the simplest is off to one side, preferably the outside," she held her sword up and out at him. He made his best attempt to parry. "Not bad, but try this. Hold your sword out." D.M. held it out with the blade level. "If my blade is inside yours, you will have difficulty trying to force me to the outside. So you want to get to the inside, and you do it like this," she positioned her blade outside his, "It's simple, and you don't wanna make the movement too big," she dropped her blade to just below the level of his, quickly moved it inside then parried his blade out of the way, "Now is the riposte," she lunged and tapped him on the chest again.

"Is this harder because I'm a leftie?" He said taking his position.

"Yes, a bit. You're making me have to think a bit more... Okay, your turn," she held her blade out to him. Carefully D.M. practiced the movement she had just shown him. He lunged and stopped just short of her chest.

"What? Afraid to hit a girl?" She teased.

"Well, I don't wanna hurt you."

"This is a Viking you're taking to... Hit me... You must learn to control your blade. I can hit you so soft you barely feel it or I can cut your head off. Control is the key."

"Right," he stood en garde. Eagle advanced and beat his blade a couple of times. D.M. wasn't sure what to do. He stepped back.

"Come on," she said as she lunged. He parried her blade and riposted, landing a hit right between her breasts. Immediately he stopped, worried that he had hurt her. Eagle advanced again, he had hit her fairly hard, but that wasn't going to stop her. She was a Viking and this part of her life.

"Are you okay?" He said as he backed away.

She attacked again. Blocking his blade she closed the distance, spun until her back was against him and with all her might, hit him in the abdomen with the pommel of the sword. D.M. fell backwards to the mat holding his stomach and coughing.

"Oh fuck!" He coughed, "You're one tough broad. Maybe you should have been a Marine instead."

"Ja, that's what the SEALs said!" She laughed and offered him a hand up.

He got to his feet, still rubbing his stomach.

"Oh, and I forgot to tell you, Vikings don't fight fair."

"Thanks, I'll remember that for next time."

She took his sword and put them away, "So you want a next time eh? You like this?"

He picked up her blouse and handed it to her, "Yes, actually I do."

"All right. I'm sure we can find time to practice once or twice a week."

"Thank you. Where did you learn to use the sword?"

"My father taught me some. He protested though, saying that

good Viking women didn't need to practice with swords, they needed to practice with spoons and rolling pins."

"That's a bit chauvinistic."

"That's how my society sees things...I also studied more in depth at Harvard. I was on their fencing team for nearly four years."

"Is there anything you aren't lethal in?

"Well, I haven't managed to kill anyone yet with my cooking. But I suppose there is always a first!" They both laughed.

D.M. lay awake in the middle of the night. Some sort of noise had awoken him. He listened, trying and find the source of the noise. A few moments later he heard it again. The noise was coming from Tige's bunk. It sounded perhaps like he was having a dream, and it didn't sound like it was a good dream either. After a few minutes, there was a loud commotion followed by the resounding thud of a body hitting the concrete floor. "Ahhhhhhhhh!" Tige hollered. D.M. jumped out of his bunk and turned on the lights. The others had been awakened and were looking wildly around.

Tige lay on the floor on his left side. His left arm twisted unnaturally above his head. He writhed in pain. It was obvious that his arm was either broken or dislocated.

"Sam!" D.M. hollered and knelt down next to Tige, "What the hell happened?"

"Fuck'in flashback," Tige replied through clenched teeth.

Sam scrambled from his bunk and hurried over to help, "We need to get him on his back, carefully." D.M. helped roll Tige over. The Petty Officer did a quick assessment of the injuries. "I don't think he broke it, I think he's got a nasty shoulder dislocation."

"I coulda bloody well told you that!" Tige growled.

"Can you get it back in?" D.M. asked.

"Oh, I could, but I think we'd better take him over to the boss, she's got the happy drugs." They carefully helped him to his feet and went Eagle's hut. D.M. banged on her door. After several moments the door opened.

"What the hell happened?" She said, noticing that Sam held

Tige's arm while D.M. helped hold the sergeant up.

"He said he had a flashback. Must have been a good one because he came clean out of bed and hit the floor."

"Flashback huh?"

"Yeah, I get those once in a while. The joys of living a life of combat."

"No doubt you suffer from post traumatic stress disorder."

"I'd say," Tige replied

"His shoulder's dislocated," Sam said as they helped him inside and got him up on her treatment table.

"Well, at least that's an injury we can deal with here." She opened her drug cabinet and got out a vial of valium. "Ever had a dislocation before sergeant?"

"Yeah, the other shoulder about five years ago."

"Wasn't from flashback was it?" D.M. joked. He was trying to be upbeat about the situation, although he knew all too well about flashbacks himself.

"No. I was on a training mission. We were fast roping out of a helicopter and the bloke above me fell and took me out."

Eagle drew up the valium and got her supplies together. She tied the tourniquet around his arm and found a good vein. Tige didn't even flinch when the needle bit into his flesh. He knew this was the easiest way to get his shoulder fixed. He sat quietly waiting while the drugs took effect. After a few minutes he sighed deeply.

"How are you feeling?" She asked.

"A bit dopey. I have a rather strong tolerance for narcotics."

"Ready to give it a try?"

"Sure, what the hell."

"Sam, if you could assist me please," she reached out and took Tige's arm. Sam grabbed hold of Tige and helped to hold him still.

"Need my help?" D.M. said as he watched the spectacle.

"I think we're okay for now," Eagle replied, taking a firm grasp of the sergeant's arm, "Ready?"

"Let's do it," Tige said clenching his teeth.

"Okay, one, two, three!" She yanked on his arm. Tige let out a loud howl as his shoulder popped back into joint.

"Bloody hell!"

Eagle palpated the area to make sure the joint had been reduced back into place. She went to one of her supply cupboards and got a sling and long ace wrap. Sam helped her get the sling around Tige's arm and fastened. Then the ace wrap was placed over the sling, immobilizing his arm.

"You're gonna have to rest that for probably a week or more. I only hope you didn't tear your rotator cuff or anything else," she said as she helped him to stand.

"I healed okay from the last one. But I'll let you know if it's not going well." He headed back over to their hut, D.M. and Sam by his side.

Tige sat down on the bottom bunk, "I think I'll be sleeping here for a while."

"That's probably a wise choice," D.M. replied as he reached up and grabbed Tige's pillow and sheet from the bunk above and placed it next to him. Frank and Max had climbed from their bunks and were standing around Tige.

Sam leaned against Tige's bunk, "You got PTSD huh?"

Tige looked up, "Yeah mate. If you'd killed fifty six people, you'd have some problems too…Have any of you ever taken a life?" He looked around the room at the others, "Sam? Max? Frank? D.M.? I'm sure as a fighter pilot you might have shot someone down."

"No. But there were missions in Afghanistan that we were given to go find a certain set of coordinates and bomb it. I was pretty sure they were supposed Taliban hideouts, but from over ten thousand feet, you just don't see much." He shrugged his shoulders.

"Great, so the lot of you are cherry. That just makes this harder. Not everyone can pull the trigger. No, in fact there are very few of us who can do it and not have a problem with it."

"Yeah, they call you psychopathic killers," Sam added.

"No, I'm not a psychopath. A psychopathic killer lacks the basic reasoning skills to discern right killing from wrong killing. They kill for the joy of it. I, however, do possess those skills. If I did not, you would have all been dead long ago." The others exchanged glances between themselves. Tige was right.

"But you still need to have a screw loose somewhere to be

able to kill without remorse. There's a line drawn between those who can and those who can't," Sam added.

"Partly, yes. But if you all wanna survive, you're gonna have to cross that line too. It's bloody hard the first time. But after that, it gets easier each time after."

"And what happens if you like it too much?" Max asked.

"Then you've crossed the line too far and you get what's called blood lust."

"What do they do with you if that happens?"

"Humm, well, if you're a soldier, they find the nearest war and drop you in the middle of it." They all laughed. Although Tige's words came as a joke, all knew the meaning behind them. If they were going to survive their missions, they were going to have to kill. It was just part of the job. The true test would be the first mission. Who would be able to pull the trigger?

The next day, Eagle procured another plane so D.M. could give Sam his flight test. He knew Sam wasn't an aggressive pilot like Jake, so he expected a soft ride. He delivered a textbook flight and D.M. could feel his nerves finally start to relax. Everyone was done. All had passed. Even Jake was awarded his wings, despite having not completed the test. D.M. congratulated them on a job well done and asked Eagle if he could buy them a round at the club.

"I see no problem with that, but you have one test left," she smiled.

"What?" D.M. furrowed his brow in confusion.

"You need to be tested," her smile broadened.

"Moi? Tested? You've got to be kidding!" He laughed.

"So am I to assume you're going to turn down a good old fashioned dog fight?"

"Against you? Hell no! Come on, let's go." He picked up his gear and walked to the plane. The rest of the team cheered him on. Another plane was brought around and Eagle performed a thorough preflight before she climbed into the cockpit. Over the months, they had formed a comfortable working relationship. The lieutenant had learned that Eagle actually did have a sense of humor, contrary to what the others believed. The time he had spent with her learning the sword had shown him she was more than just stiff and starched; she had plenty of personality, a strong sense of duty, and worked tirelessly to make sure the team succeeded. D.M. taxied up to where she was and keyed the mike, "I'm going to enjoy this. I rarely get to pick on someone *not* my own size!" He announced.

Eagle looked over at him, "I suggest you get your ass in the air. I like to play rough," she teased seductively, letting her Norse accent flow thick. At times, she let her hardcore professional persona go out the window and allowed herself to have some fun.

"Oh, don't turn me on like that! I love it when you talk dirty to me." He checked the flaps on the wings, "But there's just not enough room in this cockpit to hold any more of this cock- unless you wanna help with that problem?"

"When I get done with you, it'll be tucked between your legs!" She barked.

D.M. laughed, "God I love a woman who has good cockpit talk." He pushed the throttle forward and taxied past to the runway.

Once airborne, Eagle joined up with D.M. They flew together long enough for Eagle to lay out the rules of engagement. The hard deck was five thousand feet, and other than that, the rule book was thrown out the window. She knew D.M. could fly, but could he best her? She had proven absolutely lethal in the F-16; they just wouldn't let her fly in combat. "All right lieutenant, the battle has begun," she banked the plane hard and hit the after burners so she could make a quick escape. D.M. held to his present course, he was in no hurry. He knew Eagle would find him soon enough. Tipping the nose of the plane to the sun, he gained altitude. If Eagle was to come at him, his best advantage was to be in the sun. He was going to make her come up to him. Checking the radar, he could find no trace of her. Where had she gone? Certainly she would not have gone below the hard deck, Eagle wasn't one to break the rules, but she would bend them sometimes. An image showed on his radar. There she is. She was heading away from him. What an easy target, he thought. Come at her from above and behind and get an easy kill. Maybe that's what she wants? He pondered as he maneuvered the plane. Surely she has me on radar and knows where I am. He keyed the mike, "White Feather this is Lone Wolf. What the hell are you doing?"

"I want you to come down and play with me," her voice came back over the radio. She was sounding even more seductive.

"Roger White Feather, I'll come play, but I wanna be on top," he nosed the plane over into a steep dive and readied his weapons. "I got a big Sparrow I'd love to put up your tail pipe," he chided as he got into position.

"Oh, how big is it?" She replied. There was the sound of a zipper over the radio.

"Is eight plus inches enough?" He was nearing radar lock.

"Please, don't insult me!" She yanked up on the stick and brought the plane around so they were coming head on. "So how are you going to take me? On the left or the right?"

"Come on, I told you I wanted to be on top."

"Sorry, I don't like to be dominated," she had radar lock on him.

"Oh, you bitch! I guess I'll have to go...Left!" He broke hard and spiraled out of her sight. They continued their friendly dogfight until Eagle decided to call it a draw. She joined him on his right wing.

"Come on now ma'am, we both know there's only one winner in a dog fight." D.M. teased.

"Yes, I know, you're too good looking and I don't have the heart to kill you. So I'll buy you a drink. You did good."

"Good?! Is that all I rate, just 'good?' Come on baby I'm much better than that," he argued playfully.

"I've had better," she laughed.

D.M. pulled off his mask and looked over at her with disbelief, "How do you do it?"

"Do what?" She pulled off her mask and smiled at him.

He had to ask the question that had been burning in him since they first met, "Make things that deal with death so damned erotic?"

"Don't you know that we Norwegians are very erotic people?"

"No, I didn't... But if plane sex is anything like phone sex, I'll have to get a larger aircraft to accommodate me!" He laughed. Eagle joined in his laughter. She knew the lieutenant had been under a lot of pressure and figured this would be a good way to help him relax.

Once back on the ground, Tige approached D.M. He offered him a cigarette. "What's this for?" The lieutenant asked.

"Gotta have a smoke after good sex mate," Tige replied slyly. D.M. took the cigarette and Tige offered him the lighter. The lieutenant occasionally found the taste of a cigarette pleasing and relaxing when he had been under great stress.

"Don't tell me you guys heard the whole thing?" D.M.'s face went pale.

"I'll talk to the Air Boss; maybe he can get you a C-5 Galaxy next time."

"Oh God!" He slapped his hand to his forehead, his cheeks flushed crimson.

Tige put his hand on D.M.'s shoulder and stepped close to him, "Mate, I've never met a man so well endowed that he had to use an F-4 as a condom."

Eagle came around the corner and the rest of the team burst out into wolf whistles, cat calls and raucous laughter. She saw the lieutenant several shades of red, "D.M., what's going on?"

"They heard the whole thing."

Eagle put her hand over her mouth. Her cheeks were turning red far faster than the lieutenant's had. "Oops!" She smiled demurely. The men gathered around them and started to cheer. D.M. turned to Eagle. A broad smile curled to his lips. He shook his head and put his arms around her in a friendly embrace.

"Thanks Eagle that was fun."

That night, Eagle decided to have dinner with the team. The embarrassment of the day had passed and she was just too tired to cook for herself. She watched as they worked together in the kitchen, each man had a task he was responsible for. In the simplest of terms, they were working together as a team for a common goal. Frank was in charge of the meals, his skill in the kitchen more or less meant he commanded the others.

“Ma’am? Would you like carrots or beans?” Frank called through the window.

“Carrots please,” she said, taking a seat on bottom bunk under

D.M.'s. She was so tired she almost didn't feel like eating, but with the rigorous training schedule, she had to keep her body fueled. Keeping up with six men was quite the task.

D.M. brought out the plates and set them on the table, "Chow time!" He said loudly enough that he startled Eagle; she had just closed her eyes for a moment. Yawning, she got up, taking a seat on the bench. The others came out and sat down. They ate dinner discussing the day's activities.

"Ma'am, when are we going to fly choppers?" Max asked, "I don't see any on the base."

"Well, unfortunately Westland didn't approve any for here, but we'll get to them later," she said, taking a mouthful of spaghetti. That seemed to be one of the dishes Frank was quite proficient at making.

"Darn, I was looking forward to flying through the pipe in one. Would be quite the ride."

"I'm sure you'll find equally challenging places to fly," she replied.

After dinner the men sat around the table playing cards. They chatted and told stories back and forth. Eagle had returned to the bottom bunk and was listening to them. It wasn't long before she was fast asleep. Her head and body were on the bunk, her legs hung off touching the floor. Pure exhaustion had taken its toll. Frank looked over and noticed her crashed out, "Hey, bro, I think you might wanna wake the boss and send her home."

D.M. looked over his shoulder, "Yeah, she probably doesn't want to hear some of you guys snore all night." He got up and approached Eagle. Leaning down, he reached out and touched her arm. She opened her eyes and looked at him. "Hi," he said softly, "Tired?"

"Yeah, I guess so."

"I don't think you wanna sleep in here tonight, a couple of these guys snore pretty loud."

"Mmm, thanks," she stretched and sat up. He stepped out of the way so she could get up. Eagle stood, stretched again and headed for the door, "Goodnight all."

“Goodnight,” they replied in near unison. She left the hut and returned to her own.

CHAPTER EIGHT

It was Thanksgiving when Jake returned home from the hospital. The team planned a grand feast. Eagle had purchased a dozen bottles of rather expensive wine. They cooked enough food to feed an army. Frank enjoyed playing master of the kitchen, especially when he got D.M. to do the menial labor of peeling potatoes. The whole team got involved in the celebration. Tige opened wine bottles and kept glasses full. Sam and Max helped out wherever they could. A small stereo blared tunes from someone's CD collection. Jake sat back and enjoyed the spectacle with Eagle.

When the table was set, everyone gathered around. A chair was set at the end of the table for Eagle. The team remained standing as she took her place. She picked up her glass and held it up, "I have two toasts to make before we eat...First, to Jake, welcome home. I'm glad to see you in such good health."

"I had great nurses!" Jake laughed.

"To Jake!" Eagle held her glass high and then took a drink.

"To Jake!" The others toasted and drank.

"Second..." she paused to collect her thoughts, "I drink to all of you...You have done the near impossible, and done it with the deck stacked against you. I see a team before me, not just a rowdy bunch of men. And a team of your merit deserves a place better than this..." The men looked at each other. "...Tomorrow afternoon, we will leave this place, and go somewhere that befits our purpose and status," she raised her glass again, "To leaving here!"

"To leaving here!" They toasted merrily. Eagle took her seat and the feast began. They ate, drank, and even occasionally danced until late in the night. The party grew louder with each bottle of wine that was opened. D.M. stepped outside to get some air, Eagle slipped out behind him. "Hello," she said as he almost closed the door on her.

"Oh, hi. Just a bit loud in there for you too?"

"Yes. I didn't expect them to get so drunk. But I guess here is better than at the club where they can get into trouble," she said.

"I know how that goes," he replied.

She leaned against the door frame, "I need to talk to you. Now is not a good time. Do you fancy a walk early tomorrow?"

"Sure, I don't think I'll have much trouble slipping out. I think they're all gonna be pretty hung over."

"How come you weren't drinking?" She inquired.

"I don't seem to be able to hold my alcohol. It was two beers that got me sent here in the first place."

Eagle remembered reading the incident report of what happened at Holloman. "I'm glad you take responsibility and know what not to do," she put her hand on his shoulder, "I'll see you at dawn," she smiled and headed to her hut.

Admiral Westland looked at the progress report that Eagle had sent him. How could this be? He'd gone to great lengths to put them somewhere so nasty that most would have curled up and died. The aircraft they were given to fly were going to be used as target drones, there was no such thing as safety with them. All the firearms were ones that were supposed to be recalled due to defects. He had made every effort to send her the most incorrigible personnel he could find, and yet the report showed that they were quickly becoming a team. Eagle had to be lying to him. There was no way she could take those delinquents and make them into a Special Forces unit; there was no way in hell. He crumpled up the report and threw it in the trash. They still had a few more weeks before the commissioning ceremony, maybe he would get lucky. If they made it past that then he was running into dangerous territory. He would stand to lose nearly all the funding and worse, his job on the side may be threatened. If they got activated, he needed to find a way to make life as difficult for them as possible. Should all of them be dead in less than a year, he would be quite happy.

Dawn arrived and Eagle stood outside waiting. A cold wind blew across the dry lake bed and she had put on a jacket. She knew that she needed to talk to D.M. alone. This was stuff that wasn't said in the presence of others. The door to the BOQ creaked as he slipped out. He carefully closed the door and met her half way between huts. "Good morning," he whispered. He was dressed in his ABUs, but with the cold chill of the morning he had put on his leather pilot's jacket. Mixing and matching of uniforms was generally frowned upon, but he didn't think there was anyone out here in the middle of nowhere that would care. Eagle was certainly one to bend the rules when it came to comfort and the weather. She was dressed in her ABUs with an old woodland camouflage gortex jacket.

"Good morning," she whispered back. They walked in silence for a while until they were certain no one could hear them.

"So where is this little stroll taking us?" D.M. broke the silence.

"See those rocks?" She pointed ahead.

D.M. squinted, "Way out there? It'll take forever to get there!"

Eagle picked up her pace. D.M. strode along next to her. "So what did you wanna talk to me about?"

"Do you feel you're ready?" She stated.

"Ready? As in 'ready' to go out and kill bad guys?" He put his hands in his pockets, "I honestly can't say... Yes, I've learned a great deal, but you never know if you're ready until you're thrust into the situation...We're all still pretty green, each in our own areas."

"Do you feel the same about the others?"

D.M. pondered the thought before answering, "Yes, I think I can say the others would feel the same way." They walked along in silence until they reached the rocks. Eagle crawled up a narrow crack between two rocks and sat down facing the rising sun. D.M. had to take a running leap in order to make it up. He occasionally envied her for her ability to just go and do something, like climb up the crack between the rocks with great ease. Once seated, he turned slightly to face her. "Now what was it you wanted?" He asked again, knowing that there was more on her mind.

Eagle ignored him. She was having trouble finding the right words. Everything she had rehearsed last night had just gone away with the wind. Her mind was blank. She knew what she had to say, but there were no words that came to her lips. Her eyes looked to the heavens for some sort of help; her face was drawn and worried.

"Eagle? Is there something wrong?" He pried gently. Rarely did he call her by her first name; he respected her rank in the group. But it seemed something personal was on her mind. He tried not only to be a good leader to the rest of the team, but also to be someone she could talk to if she wanted. Once in a while she shared things with him, but mostly she stayed aloof.

She turned and faced him. The words might not have been what she wanted, but she needed to convey her thoughts, "From the moment I saw you, I knew you had something the others didn't. You have what it takes to be a great warrior and leader." She reached into her pocket with one hand and took his hand with the other. Carefully, she pressed a small object into his hand and held hers over it so he could not see. "I need you to lead them." She removed her hand and allowed him to see what she had given him. He looked down and saw a small golden maple leaf Major's insignia.

"Major? You're promoting me to major?!" He cried excitedly.

"You've earned it," she replied softly.

"Oh thank you!" He grabbed her and gave her a huge bear hug. Eagle lost her balance and began to slide off the rock. D.M. tried to stop her but slid off as well. It was nearly six feet down. She landed on her back in the soft sand with a thud, D.M. right on top of her.

"Sorry," he quickly lifted some of his weight off her. Eagle laughed, thoroughly enjoying the situation. Their eyes met. D.M. could resist no longer. He leaned down and gently kissed her on the lips. "I've been crazy about you from the very first day we met." He leaned to kiss her again, but Eagle put her hand against his chest. He rolled off her and sat up, "Have I screwed this up?" He said softly, rubbing his forehead in frustration.

"No," she replied, her voice trembled slightly, "D.M. you don't understand... You and I...We cannot be."

"Why? Because of the chain of command bullshit?"

She shook her head, "That, and I am Eagle the White Feather. I am the last of the ancient and royal Sami line of the Norse. I cannot marry just anyone."

D.M. cocked his head in confusion, "Let me get this straight. You're royalty? And do they arrange your marriages?"

"I'm free to marry who I wish as long as they are of royal blood. My clan is very small and quickly being swallowed up by modern Norwegian ways. My father left them because he felt that there had to be a better life here in America. He thought maybe he could work here for a while and then go home and make things right. He'd lost his faith in the clan and when he got here he soon realized that even though he was of royal blood, he didn't have enough money to live in the upper class where he thought he belonged. Instead, the only work he could find was mining coal. He died in misery, afraid to go home to his people in disgrace."

"But why?"

"My people hope that someday a Sami will take the throne and our line will rule in glory. In truth, I am their last hope. I may never see the throne, but my people want the chance."

D.M. sat with his head bowed. He was at a loss for words. Over the last few months he had realized that his feelings for her were very real. He knew that relationships in the chain of command were forbidden, but he just couldn't get the feelings he had for her out of his head. Yes, it was love, no denying that. And here before him was the woman that he loved more than anything else, refusing him. He fought to keep his emotions at bay, but as hard as he tried, a single tear still rolled down his cheek. "But if you're royalty, then why are you taking such a risk by leading a Special Forces team? There's always a chance you could get killed."

"Yes, I know. You have no idea how hard it is for me. I want so much to be there for my people, but there is a big part of me that lives for this kind of life. All that training I did with the other SF units just fueled my passion for it. I guess that's the Viking part of me, I seem to relish a good fight. I know by regulation I'm not allowed in combat, and I'll try to respect that. That's where I need your strength. You will lead them into combat. I'll be there to bring you home." She paused for a moment, "D.M.," her voice trembled on the verge of crying, "This hurts me too. I care greatly for you, you have no idea." Tears began to roll down her cheeks. She reached over and put her hand on the side of his face. He looked up and saw the anguish on hers. He held his arms out to her. She slid into his embrace and cried.

It was several minutes before she regained her composure. She'd never felt like this before about a man. He was everything she had ever dreamed of and more. Tall, dark, handsome, intelligent, mature, funny sometimes, but mostly she loved being around him because he was the epitome of the warrior class. It didn't matter to her that he was couple of years younger; his level of maturity was years ahead of his age for the most part.

The lieutenant flopped back onto the soft sand, his fingers laced across his chest, "So what are we going to do about this?"

"Not much we can do I'm afraid."

"Sure there is. I like you and you like me, why can't we be fuck buddies until Mr. Right comes along?" He joked.

Eagle reached over and swatted him on the arm, "I can't believe you just said that!"

"Hey, I'm male. We never turn down an opportunity," he laughed lightly.

"Well, sorry, not happening either... Tradition requires I remain chaste until married."

"You're joking."

"No."

He rolled over onto his side facing her, "Now that really sucks!"

She propped herself up on one elbow and turned toward him. She looked into his deep brown eyes and sighed, "Yes it does sometimes."

He felt his spirits fade, "So there's no way is there?"

"No. I'm sorry." She stood up, brushing the sand off her uniform, "And even if you were Mr. Right, you and I both know relationships in the chain are taboo."

D.M. stood up. His heart ached but there was little he could do. She was right. If they did have a relationship and were caught, it would spell the end for one or both of their military careers. It was going to be tough to fight the feelings he had for her, in his eyes she was the most perfect woman in the world for him.

Three transport trucks arrived at the camp. The men worked on getting their things packed and loaded. The training hut was emptied and the contents placed into boxes and crates for shipment to the new base or transfer to logistics support where it would be sent to public auction. It was time to move to a new home and the energy in the air was undeniable. Frank and D.M. had quickly packed their bags and were helping Eagle get all her medical equipment loaded. She was glad she had bothered to bring it out, the number of injuries from fights early on and training and was considerable. She'd lost track of how many sutures she had put in, or how many cuts she had doctored. Now they could move to a new home where medical care was at its best.

"Ma'am, where do you want these to go?" Frank said as he carried two large boxes of medical supplies.

"In truck two, they can come with us."

"Roger that," he headed out the door and nearly collided with his brother who was on the way back in.

"Okay, what do you have left?"

"Humm, just these two boxes and that's it," she replied pointing to the boxes that sat on the floor. D.M. scooped them up and left. In the back of her mind she thought that maybe she might miss this place just a little. It was, after all, the birthplace of the Dragonslayers, as dusty and grimy as it was. She looked around at the bleak surroundings that had been home for the last six months. They had accomplished over eighteen hundred hours of training, learned countless skills, and proved that they could function like a Special Forces team. There was still the matter of the SF community taking them seriously. Being the newest team, they were sure to have their share of criticism and jokes. They had a tradition of warfare, just not one that America was familiar with.

Hopefully that would all change.

Eagle closed the door to her hut and walked slowly to truck. The rest of the team was piled in the back sitting on the bench seats. D.M. sat on the end looking out at her. She looked around at what had been their home. Would she ever see this place again? Would she ever *want* to see this place again?

D.M. hopped out of the truck and stood waiting to help her into the back. Despite her rank and position, she insisted that she ride in the back with the rest of them. A team stuck together no matter how bumpy the road was.

"Ready?" He said, trying to be cheerful despite how he felt.

"Yeah, let's go," she put her foot on the tailgate ladder and started to climb. D.M. put his hand in the middle of her back to steady her. Once she was seated, he scrambled in and sat down. Jake was sitting farthest up front. He reached up and banged on the cab to tell the driver to go. The trucks growled to life and started down the long dusty road toward the main part of the base. They watched out the back as the Quonset huts disappeared into the desert.

The trucks dropped them at the small terminal where they would wait for their ride to the new base. The air was cool and crisp; the only inclination that winter was approaching in the desert. Eagle sat on a bench outside the terminal watching the men play football. She had a book to read, but was more interested in watching them. They were playing surprisingly nice. Most of the time their games were heated and fairly rough in nature. There had been many times that someone would knock on her door to have their knees or hands treated and bandaged from playing. She figured because they were playing on the concrete apron by the terminal, they better not get too rough or someone might get hurt.

They played for nearly an hour. Finally they tired of their game and most went to relax on their pile of gear. D.M. approached Eagle, "May I join you?"

She looked up from her book, "Sure."

He sat down, keeping his distance somewhat. He was still upset by what had been said earlier, but he was trying to be the consummate professional, as hard as it was. "Nice day huh?"

"Yeah." She continued to read her book, fighting to be disinterested in him.

He turned slightly toward her, "Look, I'm sorry about what I said and did earlier. I've never felt this way about someone before. Yeah, I've had a few girlfriends, but this is totally different."

Eagle slipped her bookmark in the page she was reading and snapped the book shut. She knew she had to put an end to this, "Listen lieutenant, you may have feelings for me, but as you now know, there can be nothing between us...We're adults, and we are also officers in the military. We're held to higher standards than others...My best suggestion to you would be to get this out of your mind so you can stay focused on the job. You have five other men to worry about leading."

He leaned forward, resting his forearms on his thighs. There was nothing he could say. Normally he wasn't one to get his feelings hurt, but this time he felt like Eagle had ripped his heart out. It was going to be tough to work with her. Maybe over time his feelings would diminish and he could feel comfortable around her. For now though, it was going to be sheer hell.

Eagle was fighting her own battle. She really had feelings for him, but it was her responsibility as the senior officer to keep the relationship professional. Deep down inside she wanted to bend those rules. Even if D.M. wasn't the one for her, it was hard to deny that he possessed everything she was looking for in a man.

CHAPTER NINE

The C-130 transport plane arrived at the terminal. The team stood ready to be taken to their new home. Once their gear was loaded they clambered on board and the plane lifted off. They flew north until they were deep in the Sierra Nevada Mountains. The plane began to descend through the clouds and circled for a landing. Sam looked anxiously out the window, "Ma'am? Is there really a runway down there?"

"Yes, there's a runway, and a whole lot more."

He pressed his face against the glass, "Are you sure? All I see are trees and mountains."

"It's there, trust me."

The plane circled once more and came in for a landing. It taxied to the end and turned down the narrow taxiway. Turning once more onto the runway, it stopped and the Loadmaster opened the back door. The team peered out into their new environment. A cold wind blew from the west and caught them by surprise. "Burrr! Did someone turn down the air conditioner?" Sam joked.

Eagle took in a deep breath and sighed loudly, "Ahhh, just like home!"

"Where exactly are we?" Jake asked as he surveyed the area from the bottom of the ramp. The sun shone brightly on the autumn landscape.

"We are deep in the El Dorado National Forest in part of the Sierra Nevada mountain range," she replied.

"Ah, then we have found it," Max chimed in.

Eagle looked at him quizzically, "What?"

"Over the mountains of the moon, down the valley of the shadow, ride boldly ride the shade replied- If you seek El Dorado," Max said with a flourish.

"Oh yes. Right. Well gentlemen, it appears that we've found our El Dorado after all."

From their vantage point out the back of the plane, they could see an oval twelve story glass and steel building sitting on the rise of a small man made hill. To the west there was a forest that ran up and over the lip of the valley, to the north and east, a steep cliff face. A rim of mountains surrounded the whole base. In the distance, tall peaks rose up through misty cloud layers. The air was thin and cold. The snow had not yet arrived.

The team loaded their gear into an awaiting truck. The nearly six thousand foot altitude had everyone breathing hard after only minimal work. They followed Eagle as she made the roughly one hundred yard walk up the hill to the main door of the building. D.M. brought up the rear of the group; he was still rather upset and wanted to avoid conversation with her. "Welcome to the Knight's Keep, your new home gentlemen!" She exclaimed, almost out of breath. She opened the door for them. They stepped inside to warmth and an immense lobby resembling a fine hotel. Large plants grew from massive pots; the back of the lobby was lush and inviting with a glass enclosed conservatory and lounge chairs for sunning. Next to it were the doors leading to the Olympic sized swimming pool.

"This is *way* cool!" Jake gasped as he turned around in circles taking it all in.

"Glad to see it meets with your approval. This is just the beginning; we have more to see up stairs." She pushed the elevator button. The doors opened and they shuffled in. She punched several numbers on a keypad, the doors closed and the elevator started up, "Access to our floor is restricted to those who live there, or those who need to work there. Our area is considered classified."

"Have you been here before?" Sam asked.

"I got to make a quick visit here about six months before it was finished. Our floor was still a bit rough, but I could see it was going to be quite nice."

The elevator stopped and the doors opened. They stepped out into a hallway that curved away from them in either direction. The walls were light gray; the carpet was a darker shade. In front of them on the wall was a mirrored sign in the shape of a sword with the word "Dragonslayers" written in futuristic black lettering. Eagle stepped close to the sign, pressed her hand to her lips, reached up and touched the hilt of the sword, "For luck," she said softly. One by one, the others repeated the motion and followed her down the right side of the hallway. Three large wooden doors were spaced evenly along the wall to their right. She stopped at the second door and opened it. "This is the dining room. Breakfast is at 0600, at which time we will have morning muster and meeting." There was a large oval table that roughly matched the shape of the building. Seven chairs sat around it. The outer wall was solid glass, giving an amazing view of the valley below.

Frank wandered back toward the kitchen, "I'm not gonna

have to cook am I?"

Eagle smiled and shook her head, "No, you've earned the right to be cooked for." She headed out of the dining room and continued to show them around. Their floor was equipped with a full gym, whirlpool spa, sauna, briefing room, commander's office, and ready room. She took them down the hall to the room next to the briefing room. It was a good sized recreation room that she had thoughtfully planned out. Knowing men were usually like big kids, she had made sure that the room has its share of toys. A full sized pool table sat off to the left side; a foosball table next to it. There were comfortable recliners that faced a large empty wall where an overhead projector would show movies or play video games. A pinball machine and two old style arcade video games were tucked away in the far corner so as not to disturb those who were trying to watch TV. On the right side of the room were three small tables with chairs where board games such as chess could be played. A dart board hung on the back wall. There was a refrigerator, microwave and small sink near the tables.

"Oh, I've died and gone to heaven!" Frank exclaimed.

"Bloody nice play room," Tige said as he looked around.

"Now this is totally *way* cool!" Jake added.

"Well, I know how you boys are with your toys, so I had this done up special so you'd have a nice place to relax."

"This certainly beats the SAS hands down!"

Frank walked over to the pool table, "What the Marines called a rec room was a disgrace compared to this place; they had chairs and old magazines to read. There was nothing very recreational about that."

Jake chuckled, "Only if the magazines were Playboys."

Frank smiled and shook his head, "No such luck there!"

Eagle walked around the room. It had turned out much nicer than expected. She was pleased they all liked it. Much of the building amenities Westland had designed for his use, now it was home to the Dragonslayers. She knew he was probably spitting nails over her gaining control of the base. "Well, come on gentlemen; let's go check out your new living accommodations."

Jake opened the door to his room, expecting to find just that, a room. He stood in the doorway in awe. He walked down the two steps into the living room. There was a small dining table with four chairs and a kitchenette behind that. A large sofa to his left with a matching recliner, entertainment center with a fairly good sized TV, and a stereo system. The place was nice, very nice. He walked into the back. The bedroom housed a Queen sized bed which the headboard backed up to a wall of glass. There was a chest of drawers and closets along one wall, the bathroom was to his right. Jake turned the light on and wandered into the bathroom. It was large and decorated in a trendy modern motif. He thought it resembled some of the nice hotels back in Atlantic City.

The team met for dinner at 1800. They sat around the table chatting noisily about their new quarters. Eagle came in; D.M. stood up and motioned the others to do so. They stood and waited until she found her chair and sat down. "As you were," she smiled, "I guess I did make gentlemen out of you after all."

A waiter came from the kitchen and announced the choices for dinner: grilled fillet mignon, or chicken, with fresh steamed carrots and green beans, baked or mashed potatoes, salad, and something special for desert. They ordered and chatted amongst themselves. Two bottles of wine were brought out and put on the table. "Ma'am, are we gonna eat this good every night?" Frank inquired.

"No, not quite this good, but for our first night, I told them to do something really nice." She looked at D.M.; he sat quietly reading a book. She knew he was still upset, he hadn't said anything to her since that morning. "So is everyone satisfied with their accommodations?" Everyone except D.M. offered praise for their new quarters. He sat, still reading his book. "D.M., how do you like your quarters?"

D.M. poured himself a glass of water and then went right back to reading his book, "It's fine," he replied with disinterest. What made it worse; he was living right next door to her. How much more torment was she going to subject him to?

***

Eagle pushed the doorbell to D.M.'s room. Several moments later he opened it. His expression changed when he saw who it was.

"May I come in?" She asked softly. He stood to the side so she could enter. Walking down the two steps she stopped in the middle of his living room and turned around to face him, "All right, I'm going to level with you. I know you're upset, but you can't let this affect your work performance. I need you to be sharp and ready to deal with any problems that might come up. Your personal life has to stay out of this. The team doesn't need to know that you have problems other than theirs, especially during a mission."

D.M. sat down on the top step. He really didn't want a confrontation with her, but it was going to come to that. He cleared his throat, "I don't think I can work with you…Every time I see you my heart aches. I love you and you can't love me back. This is pure torture," he said, his voice starting to show anger.

"Oh? And do you not consider that I might have the same feelings? I've spent most of my adult life looking for the right man. It's not easy for me either," she snapped back.

"You're just making my life a living hell. I never thought I'd have feelings like this, I can't get you out of my mind." He stood up and began to pace in a circle.

"If you can't handle the situation, I'll promote someone who can," her voice got louder.

"That's not fair and you know it...You know I'm the only one who can do the job, don't toy with me, I'm not going to tolerate it," his voice was matching her intensity.

She stepped closer to him, "You're not in a position to 'tolerate' anything. I have the final say on everything around here. I can send still you to Leavenworth in a heartbeat!"

"But would you really do that? Huh? I don't think so…You love me enough not to do that."

Eagle turned away from him and strode to the center of the room. She wanted to end this argument peacefully. D.M. was not the person to make angry. His temper raged on the edge of volatile, and she didn't want him to reach the boiling point. He could be a very violent person, she had seen some of his outbursts during training, and had read about some of his others. The odd part of it all was she couldn't pin point why he could be so violent. For the most part everything she had read about him showed him to be a loyal and reasonably peaceful person.

"I really don't wanna fight D.M., I want us to be able to work together and be friends...I hope that you'd want the same. Please, try and forget what's gone on between us, it will make life in the future much better."

"And you expect me to dismiss these feelings like a bad dream?" He replied, still upset, but not wanting to take the issue any further.

"Don't make this so hard on yourself. You're acting like some high school freshman that's just been jilted by his first girlfriend."

D.M. smiled slightly, "You're certainly not the first, but you are by far the most significant."

She sighed deeply, "I can say the same about you...Boy, it's going to suck...I have to find someone who can match up to your standards...That isn't going to be easy!" She laughed lightly, trying to bring the situation back into a more favorable light.

"Well, if you should fail to find someone..."

"You're at the top of my list." She approached him and held out her hand, "Friends?"

He looked down at her hand then gently took it, "Friends."

The roar of a jet engine roused D.M. from a sound sleep. He lay there for a moment trying to figure out what kind of plane it was. Certainly nothing like he had ever heard before, he sat up in bed and pulled the curtain back. As he peered out into the darkness he could see the faint outline of a plane on the runway, its engines blasting out blue flame. With the blink of an eye it hurled down the runway and was away in the dark sky. D.M. watched it disappear over the ridge. He looked at the clock, it was only 0430. Who was up that early? Snuggling back down into bed, he closed his eyes and went back to sleep.

***

The team mustered in the dining room for breakfast. Eagle was nowhere to be found. D.M. sat in his chair sipping a cup of coffee. He had taken the liberty of switching chairs so he would be on Eagle's right hand side. He was after all, her right hand man, albeit, left handed. He had taken some time to rethink his feelings and emotions. Even if he couldn't be the man in her life, he still needed to be her second in command. She needed his strength and character to lead the team, and he didn't want to let her down.

The clock on the wall read quarter past six, still, no sign of Eagle. The men were getting restless and hungry. Well, D.M. thought, now would be a good time to make a command decision. Eagle was not there, so it was going to be up to him to get the situation in hand. "All right everyone, take your seats, I guess we'll start without her," he said.

The men were half way through breakfast when Eagle walked in. She was dressed in a black flight suit and was carrying her gear bag. Quickly, they all stood as she entered, "As you were," she called with authority as she dropped her things and sat down. The team settled back into their seats. She looked over at D.M. and smiled, "Good morning."

"So it was you who woke me up," he said, feeling more comfortable interacting with her.

"What?" She raised an eyebrow.

"That was you out flying this morning."

Eagle gave the waiter her breakfast order and poured herself a cup of tea, "Yes, it was me. I wanted to check flight one of the new toys."

"What was that thing?" He pried, wanting to know all the details of their new aircraft.

"Oh, I'll show you later," she replied with a devilish grin.

After breakfast, Eagle ran down the list of the day's activities. First, a stop by clothing issue to be supplied with uniforms and to be measured for their dress uniforms. The commissioning ceremony was only a week and a half away and Eagle needed to make sure they were properly attired for the occasion. After that, one of the Intelligence officers was to take them on an extended base tour. Eagle needed to catch up on some paperwork and figured it would do them good to meet some of the other personnel on the base. But first, she was going to give D.M. a quick sneak peek of the new planes.

The elevator stopped at the basement, the doors opened. Eagle stepped out into the dim light, D.M. followed, lost as to why they were going to the basement to see a plane. He thought hard for a moment. He didn't recall seeing any hangers when they landed, just lots of grass and trees. "Why are we in the basement?" He asked, feeling a bit stupid.

"You'll see..." she stepped onto a small rail trolley. D.M. joined her. She pushed the throttle forward and headed off down a tunnel. In the distance, D.M. could see a series of red lights spaced evenly apart on either side of the tunnel. Eagle passed the first red light. D.M. noticed that they illuminated what appeared to be a large steel door. Stopping at the second light on the left, she got out and went to a keypad under the light. Punching in the combination, the door opened with the effort of a large bank vault. D.M. watched as the door opened into blackness. Eagle walked inside and loudly called, "Lights!" The lights came on, but not from above, they were set into the floor in a ring around the plane. D.M. stepped inside to get a better look at the plane. It immediately reminded him of some sort of insect. The plane was fairly low to the ground, the landing gear holding it up in a seemingly crouched position. The nose section had a long pitot tube and the general shape resembled an SR-71. The rest of the plane looked like a hybrid of the F-117A Stealth and perhaps an F-14 Tomcat, as it appeared to have variable sweep wings. It was small, maybe the size of an F-16 Fighting Falcon and painted completely black.

"So this is the little noise maker," D.M. said as he walked around the plane. "What do you call it?"

"The SF-87 Wolverine."

"Strategic Fighter? That doesn't sound right."

Eagle walked over to the plane, reached inside the nose gear door and flipped a switch. The canopies opened and a small ladder folded out of the body. She climbed the ladder and slid back to the rear cockpit and sat on the canopy rail. "It got that name because it can do the job of an SR-71, by providing high altitude reconnaissance, and still maintains the capability of shooting down anything that might just get in its way."

D.M. climbed up and sat on the rail of the front cockpit. He looked inside. Despite being a small plane, the cockpit was roomy, not giving the pilot the impression he needed to be shrink-wrapped to get into his seat. Eagle reached in and booted up the system, "Go on, climb in if you want." The plane glowed inside from all the computer screens and colorful buttons. D.M. slid in behind the stick. The seat was reclined more than he was used to, giving him the feeling that he was lying down rather than sitting.

Eagle slid forward until she sat on the rail above him. "Now, see that monitor on the right? That's your weapons panel. You have a toggle on the stick in which to make your selections. Besides a twenty millimeter gun, you have a rotary belly launcher with either AiM-10 Mongoose, or AiM-12 Diamondback missiles. You can carry Sidewinders, but I find them rather inaccurate. I think you'll like these munitions much better."

"Why didn't you just have the weapons mounted externally?"

"No, wouldn't work. Not because of the plane being extremely stealthy or anything, but the fact this little thing can do some serious speed. They tried and it ripped the munitions pylons right off. You can mount things like contoured drop tanks and oxygen outside, especially if you plan to be up for a while."

"Oxygen?"

"Yes, that little thing we all need. When flying at very high altitudes and at very fast speeds, the plane cannot do that without the help of oxygen bled into the combustion chamber. It's also handy for when you need to get out of dodge quick. The effect is somewhat like nitrous oxide. Not to mention the humans need it too."

"And what's the ceiling on this baby?"

"You can happily cruise at eighty thousand feet. Normally, forty five to sixty is a good working ceiling."

"How fast?"

"In excess of Mach three when going full out... The engines

are amazingly tough. They were designed by a friend of mine who just happened to be a Russian defector. He knows how to build 'em right, and inexpensive. This plane is built rather old fashioned; the weapons and avionics are the most high tech part, the rest is tough and built to last."

"Mach three, that sounds like fun. I'm a bit of a speed freak." He jiggled the stick, getting the feel of a different hand grip, "This thing is more like an SR-71 than a fighter. Does it have the same problem with the fuel tanks leaking?"

"No, we solved that by making them with bladders inside. The skin of the aircraft will heat up. If it gets too hot, you run the risk of igniting the fuel in the tanks. There's a gauge for that. I don't recommend you push it either."

"And I thought they had to use special fuel, oil and hydraulic fluid in the Blackbird."

"Not needed here. The service ceiling is just low enough that none of it will freeze. The Wolverine will happily take JP-8 fuel and everything else is just standard aviation grade oil and hydraulic fluids. I was trying to be as cost effective as I could."

"Then why didn't you just use off the shelf technology?"

"Nothing would work for the desired mission roles, and it's not like this is a really long runway. I had several variables to work with."

"What's the cost?"

"About twenty two million each."

"Shit, you really were cost effective!"

"I had a rather tight budget to work with. Westland was not going to give me a penny more than I was allocated." She looked at her watch, "Hey, I need to get back to my paperwork, and you need to get with the rest of the group."

D.M. climbed out and she closed up the plane. They walked out of the hanger. "So is this whole platform some sort of elevator?" D.M. questioned.

"Yes, the doors above open and the plane is lifted up. Neat idea huh? Almost like the elevators on aircraft carriers. It reduces the foot print of the base, and also makes it less interesting to spy on." She closed the door and stepped into the trolley.

"And what's on the other side?" He pointed to the doors that were on the right.

"Those are the Badger helicopter hangers. You'll meet them all later."

D.M. caught up with the group at clothing issue. Most had their measurements taken and were gathering all the items to go with their uniforms. The standard day-to-day uniform was a medium shade of gray. It was based on the old style Battle Dress Uniforms that were worn by most of the military branches for nearly thirty years. A black T-shirt, belt and combat boots accompanied the uniform. All the men were issued black berets with the unit crest affixed to the rise over the left eye. They also had the option of a gray patrol style cap for wear in the field. Tige looked skeptically at the new uniform, "I think I can safely say that the only place this will camouflage into is an office environment." The others chuckled.

The tailor leaned across the counter, "Sir, the uniform is called the IGU, or In Garrison Uniform. It's not supposed to be any sort of camouflage, although you're right, it does seem to blend in well with the walls and carpet...It's a simple but sturdy uniform designed for everyday wear when training."

Tige held the uniform against the wall and laughed, "Right, it does...But what do we do when we have field operations?"

"You come down here and get issued some of these," the tailor opened a large cabinet to reveal several shelves stocked with various patterns of camouflage, "You all have lockers upstairs to keep everything."

Tige looked at the selection of uniforms, "Gee, don't get this many choices of uniforms normally."

"This is a small team, so there is less to outfit making it easier to have the right uniform for the right job."

"Thank God somebody finally figured out there isn't one uniform for all occasions."

"Tell me about it," D.M. replied, tugging on the front of his ABUs.

They would leave their new uniforms to get name tapes sewn on. Their current uniforms would have to suffice for a few more days. The service dress uniforms would have to be tailored to fit and would be ready shortly before their commissioning ceremony. Every man on the team knew this was the real deal. In a few weeks, all they had trained for would come to fruition.

CHAPTER TEN

Admiral Westland picked up the phone. This was another one of the "milk runs" in which he made contact with Kemal. "This is Blue Mole...The Little Bird and her charges will be activated next week."

"And you still think they will represent a threat to your operation?"

"I can't completely rule them out. When the information is acquired, we might have a problem with loose ends," Westland expressed his concern.

"Have them sent out on an assignment before. Send them to me and I will take care of them," Kemal hissed.

"And where should I send them?"

"My house on the California coast, near Los Angeles."

"I know the one... I'll send them out shortly before the other job goes down and hopefully there will be none of them left," Westland replied, "I will call you the week before so you can get your men ready."

"That will be fine," Kemal hung up the phone.

Eagle sat at the desk in her office. For some funny reason she thought she had done all this paperwork just six months ago. Now that they were in a new base, she had to do the whole thing over again. This office was far plusher than the old war leftovers at China Lake. The desk was bought out of her own money; she saw it in an antique store and had to have it. It was solid English oak with ornate carvings and Queen Anne legs that ended in a clawed foot that rested on a ball. It gave the impression that if it were to come to life; it might try to eat you. Eagle liked the imposing nature of the desk, feeling that if she were not intimidating enough, it might help. The rest of the office was furnished with overstuffed leather chairs and a long leather sofa. Behind her was a wall of glass.

There was a knock at the door. "Come in," she hollered, knowing the door was very solid. Frank opened the door and crept inside. He stopped in front of her desk.

"You wanted to see me?"

"Yes. I need you to do some more paperwork. Pull up a chair."

Frank grabbed a chair and sat down. Eagle pulled his file and opened it to the appropriate page. She paused for a moment; the thought of D.M.'s inexplicable temper had been bothering her. Maybe Frank might just know why D.M. had such a violent temper? They were brothers after all, even though they really didn't act like it. Well, it was worth a shot anyway. "Frank?"

"Yes ma'am?"

"You know D.M. pretty well right?"

Frank rubbed his chin, "He's not the brother I grew up with, but yes, I know him reasonably well."

"He seems like a nice enough guy, but where did he get that violent temper?"

He ran his fingers through his hair and sat thinking for a few moments, "You know, I remember him being easy going when our mother was alive. When she died, then he seemed to get a bit nasty and short tempered. I don't know if her death caused him a lot of grief, but I hardly think it would change his attitude that much," he paused, collecting his thoughts, "I hadn't seen him in two years before we came to China Lake. He had his moods, but now he seems to be far more aggressive than I remember."

"How was his relationship with your father?" She pried, feeling like an interrogator.

"They didn't get along very well, especially after mother died."

"Did they fight a lot? Physical fights?"

"Ummm...I remember a lot of arguments. Father hit him once that I can remember because D.M. started swearing at him in

Spanish... Father made the rule that D.M. was not to speak Spanish in the house."

"Do you speak Spanish?"

"No, not really, I know all the cuss words and that kinda stuff," Frank replied.

Eagle mulled the information over in her head. She was beginning to piece things together. Evidently D.M. had not had a very happy home life after his mother died. Some of the things Frank told her helped to make the picture a bit clearer. She picked up her pen and handed the file over for him sign. He signed and returned it to her. "Thank you, that's all I needed," she said softly.

Frank stood to leave, "D.M.'s not an easy person to figure out...When you do, let me know, because he sure won't let me in his life past the front door," he turned and left.

The day had come. Every member of the team had worked tirelessly toward this moment. Now they would become an official unit. The stage was set, the chairs in their place. The ceremony was to take place in the Great Hall on the third floor. The mess kitchen bustled with activity preparing for the reception after the ceremony. Distinguished guests began to arrive in their helicopters or on the C-130 transport. It was 1100, one hour to show time.

Eagle sat at the dressing table brushing her hair. The doorbell rang. She went to see who it was. D.M. stood at the door holding a red sash in his hand with a puzzled look on his face. He looked splendid dressed in his service dress uniform. The uniform was medium gray, somewhat reminiscent of an old West Point dress uniform. The coat was fitted, tailored closely at the waist. The collar was upright; a gold unit pin on the left, an empty space on the right where his new rank would go. The pants were gray; a one inch black stripe ran down the outside of each leg. His black dress shoes shined with many hours worth of polishing. The black beret sat atop his head crisply.

"Let me guess, you need help?"

He nodded and handed the sash to her. She motioned him inside. He stopped next to her dining table. "Take your coat off, it makes it much easier," she said as she folded the sash to make it even. D.M. wiggled out of his coat and set it on the back of a chair. Eagle stepped to his left side and placed the middle of the sash against his waist. "Hold that right there," she instructed as she wrapped her arms around his waist and brought the sash to meet on his right side and grabbed it with one hand. Next, she crossed the sash and repeated the process leaving the loose ends on his left side. Then D.M. watched as she proceeded to tie the sash in somewhat of a backward Windsor knot. "There, all done."

"Thanks, I'm sure you'll have more customers to get all tied up."

"Humm...Bondage...Interesting concept!" She smiled devilishly.

"Oh no! I'm not even gonna touch that one!" He grabbed his coat and darted out the door, leaving Eagle laughing.

The guests were seated and back stage the final touches were being readied for the ceremony. The team had rehearsed every night for the last week; they were as ready as they would ever be. Eagle paced nervously as the hall was called to order and Admiral Westland strolled up to the podium. She stood peeking around the curtain as he made his opening speech. All a bunch of lies coming out of his mouth, she thought as he took all the credit for getting the team started and spearheading their training. Oooohh, I'd like to spear him! Eagle's temper boiled as Westland continued on with his lies. Politics were the worst part of the job, but unfortunately a very necessary part of it. She gave up listening to the speech for its content; rather she just listened for their cue to get lined up. "All right, line up," she whispered as Westland started his conclusion.

The men fell into formation and stood silently until they were called upon. They all looked so handsome in their dress uniforms. At the precise moment, Eagle led them out on stage. They walked boldly, there was nothing going to stop them from achieving their goals. The men held their heads high, pride gleaming in their eyes. All that they had worked for was now becoming reality. Eagle stopped on her mark. The others stopped. As one, they executed a slow, precise left face to the crowd, heels clacking loudly as they snapped to attention. The room was brought to attention as Eagle presented each man with appropriate rank. D.M. received his major's leaf for real; Tige was bestowed with captain's bars, Max with first lieutenant, because he was only one class short of his Bachelor's Degree, and the others with second lieutenant. The team was put at ease and the room allowed to be seated. Eagle stepped to the podium and started her speech.

D.M. stood looking out into the crowd. He was good at seeing a lot without moving his eyes much and looking obvious. A pair of familiar cold blue eyes stared at him. The hair on the back of his neck stood up and his mouth went dry. Who the hell had invited him? This was the proudest moment of his life and someone had to invite the one person who had made it so miserable. He tried to look elsewhere, but the cold eyes of his father seemed to burn right through him. He wished he'd never looked out there, just kept his gaze at the back wall, it didn't look back. Sweat began to bead on his forehead and his stomach tightened. He tried to concentrate on Eagle's speech. Having heard it so many times, he knew it almost by heart. Her words soothed him somewhat; he knew the next part was for him.

"Major? Do you take the Oath of Blood?" She said turning her head in his direction. D.M. stepped forward one pace, did another left face and solemnly approached her. He stopped in front of a small table. This was where the ceremony got a bit painful. A Viking warrior to show his unquestioned loyalty to those he served performed the Oath of Blood. Eagle stepped from the podium and met him at the table. She removed a jeweled dagger from its sheath and held it to him. He reached up and took it by the blade with his left hand, holding it firmly. Lowering the dagger to waist height, he took her hand and placed it on the handle and covered it with his. His left hand loosened slightly so the blade would not bite too deep.

"I take the Oath of Blood as my undying sign of loyalty and allegiance," he said as he pulled the dagger out quickly. Eagle sat the dagger on the table and retrieved a small bowl containing red ocher powder. She held it to D.M. who let some of the blood drip into it. A piece of white gauze was wrapped around his hand and

Eagle mixed the blood with the ocher using the dagger. She dipped her finger into the mixture and carefully painted a line under his right eye that went up his cheekbone and angled down toward his ear. "This is the sign of a warrior whose loyalty is without question," she announced loudly. The rest of the team began to applaud, and soon the rest of the room started in. "I give you the Dragonslayers!" She hollered as the room rose to their feet applauding louder.

Eagle wandered through the reception. General Spears came up to congratulate her, "Ah, you did it! I'm so proud of you," he said as he shook her hand.

"Thank you sir. I must admit, I had my moments of doubt in the beginning."

"But you pulled it off. You showed them all you could do it." He looked at his watch, "I have to run; I have another meeting back in Washington early tomorrow. I wish I could stay a while and chat, but duty calls."

"I'll call you sometime next week and let you know how things are going sir."

"Splendid. You take care my girl," he said softly and headed for the door.

Eagle continued on through the hall, she was looking for D.M., who had mysteriously disappeared. Frank was mingling the best he could; his father had not yet come to congratulate him. Eagle made her way over to him, "Lieutenant? Have you seen the major?" Frank almost didn't realize she was talking to him; he'd never been called lieutenant before. Most of the time in the desert, she used their first names.

"He went to the medical floor, said he was gonna get some stitches."

Eagle slipped away from the reception and went to the fourth floor. She found D.M. in one of the treatment rooms, a technician carefully sewing the wound on his hand. "I guess you grabbed it a bit harder than I told you," she said as she leaned against the door post.

"My concentration got a bit messed up... I saw someone who I wish had not bothered to come... I certainly didn't invite him." His voice was low and bristled with hatred.

"Your father?"

D.M. nodded. The technician finished suturing and carefully bandaged his hand. He picked up his things and left. Eagle sat down in the chair across from him, "Is that why you came down here right after the ceremony? You didn't want to have a confrontation with him."

"You can call it running away with my tail tucked if you want," he replied folding his arms and bowing his head in disgrace.

"No, I would call it pretty damn smart. You knew better than to start something, so you removed yourself from the temptation. There should be no reason to fear your father. I think you could easily best him."

"That's the problem; I'm not afraid, well, kind of. I see myself getting the chance and tearing him limb from limb."

Eagle thought this was a good time to find out why he hated his father so much. She had a pretty good idea of what he might say, given the information she had gathered over the months and also what Frank had said. "D.M.?" She said softly, he looked up at her, "Why do you hate him so much?"

D.M.'s eyes narrowed and his face grew tight as he clenched his jaw. He stood up and walked away, his back turned to her. He stopped at the counter, resting his hands on it. "You wouldn't understand," he said flatly.

"I'd like to understand," Eagle knew she was no psychiatrist, but perhaps he would open up to her, since they were good friends.

He looked over his shoulder at her, how could she understand? She had never been through what he had. He turned away and stared at the cabinet. "Eagle, you can't possibly understand."

She reached over and closed the door quietly. Her intention was not to trap him, but to keep prying ears away. This wasn't going to be easy, and she couldn't think of any better way to handle the situation. "Did he abuse you?" She asked softly. D.M. stood motionless for several moments before nodding his head slowly. All right, he's opened the door, she thought as she gathered her thoughts and prepared to ask him another question. If she said the wrong thing, he might just clam up and ruin her chance of trying to help him. "So those scars on your back are from him?"

Again D.M. nodded. He kept his face turned away from her; there was no one, not even Eagle who could comprehend what was going on inside his head. He wanted to lash out in rage, cry, scream at the top of his lungs, and jump off a building. His emotions were confused. This was not a new feeling. He'd felt like this the first time his father had abused him. He was sixteen, huddled in a closet, his back stinging from his father's belt wondering what he'd done to deserve a beating like that. Now he was faced with the same feeling, but this time he was now much older and needed to take responsibility for his life.

D.M. took a few deep breaths and turned toward her. Eagle immediately noticed his face was very pale, almost death-like. He stood with his head bowed and shoulders rounded as if he was a child being scolded, "He started beating me after our mother died... I think he somehow blames me for her death...I was too scared to tell anyone because he could have had his career ruined."

"You said nothing because of his career?" Eagle replied flabbergasted.

"I thought that if I said something and he went to jail, who would take care of the three of us?"

"How often did he abuse you?" She knew she might be crossing the line, but it was worth knowing.

D.M. sat down. He rubbed his forehead apprehensively as he tried to collect his thoughts. This was not easy. There was no way of putting it except to say it how it was. "He used to beat me once or twice a week...Sometimes he would only hit me a few times, other times he would beat on me for a while...I used to know when he had had a bad day at work because he would take it out on me... He did that for about a year...then..." D.M. swallowed hard, this was the skeleton in his closet that no one knew about. "...He started to molest me." He closed his eyes and buried his head in his hands.

Eagle was at a loss for words. She never imagined that

someone could be so horrible to another human being, let alone someone in their own family. In her eyes D.M. was a wonderful person: intelligent, strong, handsome, a well-rounded being. It amazed her to think that he had gone through all of that and still managed to be somewhat emotionally stable. It certainly explained his violent temper and hatred of his father. She knew that she should refer him to a proper counselor, but she wanted him to go on his own accord. "I appreciate your courage in telling me these things... I think it would be best if you talked to a counselor who might be able to help you work through this... I will leave that to you... But know I'm here if you just wanna talk." She slid around the table and gently wrapped her arms around his shoulders. D.M. kept his face buried in his hands and cried softly. He knew weakness and emotion weren't part of being a warrior, but he felt so much like a train wreck there was nothing he could do about it.

After a few minutes he sat up and looked at her, "You know... I wonder..."

"What?"

"I wonder if that bastard had a little change of heart."

"What do you mean by that?"

"He had me dead to rights. I punched him out. He could have had me sent to Leavenworth so easily... I think that he knew I might still be able to say something to ruin his career. He probably told them to find some other interesting punishment instead."

Eagle scratched her head. It was plausible. Her question was how did Westland find all these troubled men to send her? "And did they say why they chose you to come here?"

"No. I knew it was in lieu of hard time, but I don't really know who came up with the orders to send me here."

"I'm absolutely sure Westland had something to do with it. I haven't figured out the connection yet."

"From everything you've told me about Westland, he seems like he wants us to fail."

"Yes. Well, he did. If we were to fail, nearly all the money that I got appropriated to us would go back into the pot. He could then make a play for it. I knew pretty much from the beginning when I met all of you that he wanted us to fail. That's exactly why I worked so hard in succeeding."

D.M. smiled slightly, "Well, you succeeded."

Eagle got up to leave, "I need to get back to the reception. Stay down here if you want, or go up to your room. You don't have to put yourself in a situation."

"Thanks."

Eagle returned to the Great Hall. The reception was in full swing. Admirals, generals and colonels mingled talking mostly politics. She found Frank talking to his father. The colonel was close in size to Frank, had tired blue eyes and looked about forty pounds overweight. There wasn't much family resemblance to D.M. from what she could see.

"Ma'am, this is my father Colonel Theodore Elliott."

The colonel offered his hand. Eagle shook it, but she could feel her blood begin to boil and the hair on the back of her neck stood up. It was going to be extremely hard to be civil to the man, considering what she had just learned about him, "Nice to meet you sir," she said gritting her teeth.

"I was surprised to hear that two of my sons were in this unit. Not common that something like that happens."

"Fate has a strange way of showing itself."

"I find it interesting that you promoted D.M. to major," the colonel said with a hint of disdain.

"He's been a model officer. D.M. has shown that he has the will and desire to lead the team." The more she spoke to the colonel, the less she liked him. She was having to fight her own internal battle. Every ounce of her just wanted to punch his lights out.

"Just make sure he doesn't lead them down the wrong path."

Eagle balled up both her fists. She had to get out of there or she'd do something regrettable. Her Viking temper flared. "I don't think that would happen. Excuse me sir; I have other guests to attend to." She made a hasty exit and went upstairs to her office. She was just opening the door when D.M. came down the hallway toward the dining room. He could see she was flustered.

"Are you okay?"

She pushed the door open and stomped inside. D.M. followed, closing the door.

"Arrrrrrrrrrrrhhhhhhhhhh!!!!" She roared, taking a few wild swings at the air.

The major kept his distance, "I take it that's a no."

She spun around and faced him, "Argh! You were right! He's a bastard!"

"I take it you met the old man?" He said calmly.

Eagle paced around her office trying to settle down. Her temper was almost out of control.

"He's quite the piece of work huh?" D.M. said as he walked over to the window.

"I wanted to kill him!"

"Welcome to the club," he said over his shoulder.

"I can't believe the remarks he said about you. And he said them in front of Frank."

"He doesn't give a shit about any of us."

"That was rather obvious. It only looked like he was trying to be nice to Frank because he had to."

"Yeah, I've seen it all before."

"Oh, and get this, he was not very happy over you making major."

D.M. turned and walked over to her, "I bet he wasn't. He got me demoted, and you promoted me to a higher rank."

"He said he hoped you wouldn't lead the team down the wrong path."

The major cracked a stiff grin, "I'm surprised you lasted that long talking to him. I figure you would've punched him out."

"Oh, I was so tempted. That's why I had to come up here."

"And I had to live with him all those years."

"You've certainly got more mettle than I major... I would have killed him."

"Lord knows I wanted to."

After the last guests departed, the men gathered in the rec room for some much needed relaxation. Sam had brought in several DVDs and they decided to watch Predator. The room was equipped with a projector TV and the movie was shown on the wall. They were all happily changed out of their uniforms and were wearing civilian clothes.

"Man, feels good to be somewhere clean and neat for once," Frank said as he plopped down in a recliner.

"No more dust storms. No more hundred and twenty degree days. Shit, this place is paradise!" Jake exclaimed.

"I wouldn't call it that," D.M. said, "This area gets a good amount of snow."

"I'll take the snow over the heat any day," Max replied.

"We'll see about that here shortly. The weather report is calling for snow tonight."

The team awoke the next morning to four inches of snow on the ground. It wasn't much considering the annual snow fall for that area was sometimes measured in yards. They couldn't wait to get outside to play in it. The weather was a comfortable thirty eight degrees and the snow wasn't going to last long.

D.M. stood looking out the main doors to the Knight's Keep. He happily decided to stay in the warm building and play spectator. Snow was not his thing. The others were out playing in the snow like a bunch of kids. He smiled as he watched them throw snow balls at each other. Frank saw him standing there and threw a snow ball at the door. It hit just were the major's face was. D.M. leaned aside and held his hand up with middle finger extended. Frank laughed and made another one. Just as he was preparing to throw it, Jake came up from behind and shoved a handful of snow down the back of his jacket. Frank made several wild gyrations trying to shake it loose. He turned and saw Jake making a hasty retreat.

"Jake, you punk!" He hollered and ran after him.

D.M. laughed, watching their antics. He wasn't above horse play; it was just too cold for him at the moment. His Spanish blood ran thin and hot, summer was his favorite time of year.

They played for probably an hour before deciding it was getting colder and they were tired. It was going to take time to get used to living above six thousand feet. Most of the team had been suffering mild headaches and fatigue. The medical floor had done well helping them try and adjust, and keeping them plied with Motrin until the headaches subsided.

"All right everyone, gather 'round," Eagle said as she made her way over to a bench. They were down on the seventh floor which contained the indoor small arms range. "Time to get familiar with your new firearms," she opened a cabinet and took out a pistol, "This is the Sig Sauer P220 in .45 ACP. Threaded for a silencer with adjustable combat night sights. It has either and eight or ten round magazine," she handed it to D.M., "Merry Christmas major."

"Uh, thanks," he took the pistol and looked it over. After all the time at China Lake, he was now more than comfortable with firearms.

Next she took out a submachine gun, "Your next tool of the trade is the Heckler and Koch UMP chambered in .45 as well. You can get about six hundred rounds a minute and have a twenty five round mag... There are many accessories you can each customize your own with," she handed it to Jake.

"Wise choice to have one caliber for the both," Tige observed.

"Good knock down power and only one caliber to carry. Makes it more versatile," Eagle replied. Retrieving the next weapon, she laid it out on the counter, "Meet the H and K 417, your main battle rifle. Chambered in seven-six-two by fifty one millimeter. It has a five to six hundred round per minute firing rate. You can fix an AG-C/EGLM grenade launcher to the lower Picatinny rail. Once again, you can all customize them to your liking," she handed it to Max.

The last weapon she took from the cabinet was a shotgun, "And finally, the Mossberg 590 Special Purpose. Chambered in 12 gauge, it can take nine shells. It has a collapsible stock and a very smooth racking action," she handed it to Sam. "This range can handle everything up to .270 Winchester magnum. Anything bigger than that and you'll have to go down to the basement range."

"And what's the distance of that range?" Tige said as he reached over and took a UMP from the cabinet.

"It's an impressive sixteen hundred feet bored out of solid rock. It runs parallel to the flight line just to the west of the Wolverine hangers."

"Sounds like I'll be spending a lot of quality time down there."

"I'm sure you will. And whomever you're partnered with will also be spending plenty of quality time down here too," Eagle replied.

Jake fiddled with the UMP, "So who are we going to be teamed up with?"

"You'll find that out tomorrow."

"Well who ever I'm teamed up with better be ready to work. I may play bloody hard, but I'm no bludger. They're gonna have to learn how to be my spotter, and that's gonna take time. I'm sure they're gonna make their share of blues, but then after time, their blood'll be worth bottling."

Jake looked at Max, "What the fuck did he just say?"

"I dunno, I'm not his translator. I don't speak Aussie,"

Eagle laughed lightly, "Humm, after all this time, we still have a language barrier."

"Hey, at least I learned to salute like you bloody Yanks...I said I was not a lazy person and that my partner is gonna make his share of mistakes. But when he gets it, he's gonna be mighty helpful to me."

"Very well. I would suggest captain that you try to tone down the slang so we all stand a chance of understanding you."

"Yes ma'am...Oh, that's gonna be trouble."

CHAPTER ELEVEN

The team stood waiting outside the basement door that led to the flight simulators, gear in hand ready to play. Eagle met them there a few minutes later. She wasn't going to let any of them get behind the stick of a new aircraft without plenty of simulator time. "All right gentlemen, I hope you each brought a large pocketful of quarters 'cause these will be the best video games you've ever gonna play."

"Cool!" Jake exclaimed, "I rule at video games!"

Sam shook his head in dismay, "Another wasted life!" The others chuckled at Jake's expense. Eagle opened the door and let them in.

"Okay, before we start, I think I should name off the permanent team assignments. D.M. and Jake, you are team one; Tige and Sam, team two; and Max and Frank, team three." She walked over to the control console and turned it on. "Now that we're starting to gear up for missions, I think we should choose our call signs." She picked up a piece of paper and a pen, "My call sign is 'White Feather', D.M., I know yours is 'Lone Wolf', how about the rest of you?

Jake spoke up, "I was always known as the 'Kingpin' of Atlantic City."

Eagle wrote it down, "Do you have a particular symbol or image associated with that?"

"Humm, we used to think it was cool to go bowling sometimes…I guess maybe a bowling pin."

"Tige?"

"I got the call sign 'Wombat' because I used to skitter around on my belly during sniper training, everyone said I looked like one, so it stuck."

Eagle wrote it down, "Sam, how about you?"

"I had the rotten habit of being in the wrong place at the wrong time when we were working with small explosives, I was lucky I didn't lose any body parts. My classmates christened me 'Ground Zero' because I was always right in the middle of something when the explosion went off."

"And you Frank?"

"Tater…After my crowning achievement of screwing up my career with a couple of potatoes."

Eagle raised an eyebrow, "Are you sure that's what you want? It doesn't sound very positive."

"Yeah, that's what I want. Besides when we were growing up, D.M. used to call me 'Mr. Potato Head' because the majority of my diet consisted of fries and mashed potatoes."

Everyone laughed. Eagle turned to Max, “Right, you’re the last.”

Max stood thinking for a few moments; he had never done anything noteworthy enough to warrant a nickname or call sign, he had simply been happy to blend in with the world around him.

“I don’t know. I’ve never had a call sign before.”

“Come on man, you can think of something,” Jake encouraged.

Max thought harder, “I did have a pet Bull Dog when I was stationed in England. We were the best of friends. He died rather tragically of a kidney disorder. I really miss him.”

“What was his name?” Sam asked.

“Hamlet.”

Jake scratched his head, “Naw, Hamlet is too wishy washy, you need a tough call sign. How about just plain old ‘Bull Dog’?”

Max smiled, “Okay, Bull Dog it is.”

Eagle made the last notation and put the paper down, “Right gentlemen, now that we have that settled, let’s get to the fun stuff...Who wants to go first?" The men exchanged looks and Jake held up his hand.

"We'll go ma’am," he replied enthusiastically. D.M. groaned. He was not pleased with being teamed up with Jake. Although they had more or less settled their differences, they still did not get along very well.

"Get settled in and give me a chance to get the computer up and running."

"Do we need all the flight gear or just helmets?" D.M. asked as he dug through his bag.

"Helmets are fine."

“Okay...Can I talk to you later about something?” The major said as he pulled his helmet on and found his gloves.

“Yes, later.”

They hurried inside the door to the simulator. Tige approached Eagle, “Ma'am, I was wondering, why’d you pair me with Sam? Max has more skill in spotting and I thought he'd be the logical choice.”

“Maybe so. But you have the opportunity to train a spotter up exactly how you want. Sam is quite smart. I'm sure he'll pick up on it quickly.” She poked a few buttons on the control panel, “If you took notice, I paired you up a certain way: one skilled and one not so skilled. This is so we continue a learning environment...The teams are not set hard and fast, you may get paired up with someone else if there is a mission that requires two different specialties."

"I see. I'll do my best to train him."

Once they had buckled in and Eagle had the computer running, the others crowded around the display monitor to watch their first "flight." D.M. was at the controls and Jake was sulking in the back seat because the major would not let him fly first. "I'm ready, how about a seventy-five cent ride?" D.M. teased as he readied for takeoff.

"Remember these are *Short* Take Off and Landing aircraft, so the end of the runway will be closer than you're used to," she reminded.

"No problem," he replied.

Eagle punched a few keys on the keyboard, "You're clear for takeoff."

"Roger. Dragon One is rolling." He pushed the throttle forward and the display started to move. The simulator bumped along as if it were on a real runway. Suddenly he could see the face of a cliff coming at them.

"D.M. I think you need to go faster," Jake warned.

The major looked at his air speed indicator, not going fast enough. He pushed the throttle forward to the stops and pulled back on the stick in a desperate attempt to get the plane airborne. No such luck. The screen flashed red and a buzzer sounded. He had hit the cliff. "Shit!" He growled. This was very embarrassing. You don't normally crash on takeoff, especially as many hours as he'd spent behind the stick.

"Major, when I said short take off, I really did mean it," Eagle announced over the intercom, "The key to starting off right is to keep the brakes on until you're at about sixty percent on the engines, then you let off and hold on for dear life. It's just like being shot off an aircraft carrier."

"You forget I was in the Air Force. Carriers are a bit foreign," he replied with a hint of sarcasm. "Let me try that again."

"As you wish," she restarted the program, "And don't forget I was Air Force too." He followed her instructions and soon they were airborne. "Hey, how come you were able to get it in the air the other day?" D.M. said, remembering her early morning flight.

"I spent a month playing test pilot. I know these planes quite well."

Jake sat in the back rather bored as D.M. put the "plane" through its maneuvers. The simulator was unique in that it was designed to allow any kind of movement that the real plane was capable of, even inverted flight. "Jake? Are you bored back there?" Eagle asked as she noticed he was sitting with his arms folded with a bored expression on his face.

"Yes, I'm bored. Fly boy up there won't let me have any fun."

"How about a couple bogies to liven things up?" With a few strokes of the keys, two MiG aircraft appeared on the screen. One broke formation and immediately headed for their tail.

"Thanks ma'am," Jake responded, "I wanna get my quarter's worth too."

She let each man fly for about ten minutes, enough to whet their appetite for flying the new jets. Then they moved on to the helicopter simulator. Jake proved without a shadow of doubt that he was king of that simulator. Eagle had never seen anyone more lethal than him; he obviously wasn't lying when he said he could fly like a bat out of hell. And all the years of video games hadn't hurt either.

Eagle stepped out the door of her room. She was dressed in a comfortable pair of pants, a burgundy scrub shirt and a lab coat. With all the paperwork finally done and the team settled in to a routine, it meant some time for her. She walked to the elevator and pushed the button. A few moments later the door opened and D.M. stepped out. "Evening," he said politely as he passed her, "Where are you off to?"

"I have a small lab on the fifth floor. I'm on my way to do a bit of research."

D.M. raised an eyebrow, "Lab? They have labs here?"

"Yes, there are five or six...Why? Are you interested in doing research of some sort?"

"Well, my degree from MIT was in Chemical Engineering. I have a lot of equipment in storage that I bought in hopes of someday having my own lab." He stepped back into the elevator and followed her to the research floor. Eagle went to her lab and punched a combination on a keypad opening the door. He stepped inside and looked around. Her lab was indeed small. It resembled a cross between a blood lab and a computer lab. Several monitors were set up amongst microscopes, centrifuges and other related equipment. "So what kind of research are you doing?"

"My minor is in genetics, I really prefer this to studies in trauma surgery." She replied as she sat down to a computer and turned it on. "This may sound a bit weird, but I hope perhaps to find my future husband among all this DNA data."

"You're right, it is weird. So you're choosing your husband solely based on his DNA? So much for looks and personality!" He scoffed.

"It's not quite like that. The DNA helps me map out a family tree. I can then trace it back and see if there's any blue blood in them."

"Aren't there plenty of Royals in Europe? Why don't you pick one of them?"

"I've done lots of research. The hard part is most of the men who are about my age, or within ten years of my age are already married."

"That sucks," D.M. reached over and took an empty blood vial from a rack, "Okay, call me a bit selfish. If I can't have you, I wanna make damn certain of it." He offered the vial to her. She studied him for a moment, noticing the determined expression on his face. What could it hurt? At the worst it would prove once and for all that D.M. wasn't of a royal line.

"All right. But I all ready traced your line based on your father's information and it came up a dead end."

"Humor me," he replied flatly and insisted she take the vial. Eagle got her supplies together and drew his blood.

"This'll take a while to process."

"How long is a while?"

"My computer system is a bit out of date; it might take a few weeks to actually get an accurate mapping of your DNA and your associated family tree."

"Humm, sounds like you need a serious software upgrade."

"So what was it that you wanted to talk to me about earlier?" She said, looking up from the computer.

"Why'd you pair Jake and me up? You know we don't get along very well."

"That's partly why. Everyone in this team has to learn to work together. Perhaps the two of you spending more time together will forge a working relationship. You also have a lot of discipline, which Jake clearly does not. I'm hoping that some of your maturity will also rub off on him."

"Mmm, that's a tall order for a burned out druggie gang-banger."

"People can change if they have the proper motivation."

"Yeah, right, this is Jake we're talking about," he scoffed.

"Well, consider him your pet project. If you're able to turn him around, it'll be quite a testament of your leadership skills."

D.M. sighed, "I hope he learns to behave, otherwise I'm going to be mentoring him with my fist, and doing some wall-to-wall counseling."

"You'll do no such thing major," she warned sternly.

"I can always dream..."

A week later and the team had spent many exhaustive hours in both simulators. They were getting proficient in take-offs and landings. Eagle wasn't quite sure they were ready to tackle the genuine articles, if one crashed, that only left one other spare plane for the time being. Two more were being built, but their delivery date was not for another seven months. So she had to be sure they were ready. The last thing she wanted to lose was any personnel or equipment. In the mean time, the men would have to settle for rides in the back seat so they could get a feel for the aircraft. D.M. argued vehemently that he was ready to fly on his own. Finally Eagle broke down and gave him his chance.

They sat at the end of the runway while D.M. finished his

checks of the instruments. Eagle sat quietly in the back with her fingers crossed. "Right, feet on the brakes, bring throttle up to sixty percent," he calmly recited his actions, "At sixty percent, brakes off." The nose gear sunk towards the ground as the plane rocketed forward down the runway. D.M. held it steady as they headed toward the "line of no return" - a white line painted across the runway to remind the pilot that he better get the plane in the air or else they would end up splattered all over the cliff face.

"D.M., I think you should pull up," Eagle reminded him calmly. The line was getting very close. "Pull up D.M.," her voice got louder. They were almost upon the line and D.M. had made no action to bring the plane up. "Pull UP!" She screamed as the granite cliff rushed up to meet them.

The major yanked back on the stick and the plane shot into the sky. He was breathing hard and his whole body flushed with sweat. Eagle was right when she said "Short take off" he thought as he tried to regain his composure.

"What happened back there major?" She asked softly.

"I'm sorry. I thought I really had a feeling for the plane, but I guess I was wrong. This is much harder than it looks. One second we were at the far end of the runway, the next, we were about to be part of the mountain."

"After your little experience, do you think the others should start flying?"

"Oh, hell no. I think we all need more time in the simulator."

"That's what I thought. At least you're honest enough to admit you were wrong. Not many people, especially those in a position of leadership can do that."

“Nobody’s perfect…” he maneuvered around several of the tall peaks, “What kind of fly by wire does this have?”

“Fly by human mostly.”

“What’s that supposed to mean?”

“It means you have total control of the aircraft. It will do as you tell it, even crazy things. The only time the computer will take control is if it feels you have become unresponsive because your hand is not applying enough pressure to the stick.”

“Like when you G-loc huh?”

“Lose consciousness, or in some way become incapacitated.”

D.M. banked hard a few times pushing the aircraft through more difficult movements. He found it to be very responsive and agile. "This is one strange plane. And why the variable sweep wings?"

"Take us up to angel's fifty and open it up."

"Roger that!" D.M. increased the altitude and pushed the throttle forward. Out of the corner of his eye he could see the geometry of the wings beginning to change. Instead of sweeping back, they angled forward and part of the wing root had transitioned to the rear, bringing the tips of the wings to the front of the fuselage in a forward sweep. The wings took on an elongated diamond shape. As they increased in altitude, his ears popped a few times from the cockpit pressurizing.

"You just effectively reduced your wing area, now you can go even faster with less drag," she said checking the airspeed indicator. They were traveling at Mach two. "Come on, I thought you wanted to go fast?"

"I'm getting there, don't rush me," D.M. remarked.

"Humm, I thought you men were quick to get to the business?" She teased.

"Oh no! You're not gonna start that all over again are you? Come on, we're in the same plane this time."

Eagle laughed lightly, "No, I just thought you'd like to indulge the speed freak side of you."

The major pushed the throttle forward almost to the stops. In the thin air the plane picked up even more speed. Before long, they were cruising at Mach three. "Sweet, I love it!" He increased altitude until he was nearing the service ceiling. The sky around them took on an eerie appearance, dark above and light below. He looked at the altimeter and noticed they were nearing eighty thousand feet. Rolling the plane gently over he looked at the ground far below, "Now this is as good as it gets," he sighed.

"Well, I hate to break up this new love affair, but we need to get back. We didn't start with a whole load of fuel on board."

"Oh, all right," he groaned and turned for home.

It was Christmas morning. A large storm had arrived two

days earlier leaving the whole mountain range covered in a couple feet of snow. The men stood looking out the dining room window in amazement. For some, it was their first white Christmas. Before the storm hit, Frank and Jake had trudged out into the forest and had returned with a scraggly little pine tree. They decorated it with whatever they found that looked seasonal. It was going to be a simple holiday, the only family around was their teammates.

The dining room table was not set for breakfast in the usual manner. Instead, identical boxes sat at each man's spot. D.M. studied the box without moving it. It was perhaps fifteen inches square and professionally wrapped. He could tell because they all looked precise in every way. The wrapping paper and bow were tastefully masculine; the gift tag filled out in perfect calligraphy. No, Eagle wouldn't have had time to do this. She had probably slipped out without their knowledge, or was busy on the internet.

"Good morning gentlemen, and Merry Christmas," Eagle said loudly as she strolled in. They all stood.

"Merry Christmas," they replied in near unison. She sat down and the others joined her.

"I thought you gentlemen deserved to have a nice little Christmas present…Go ahead, open them."

Jake wasted no time. He tore through the wrapping paper and quickly opened the box, "Oh, this is great!" He exclaimed in delight, pulling out a black flight helmet with his call sign "Kingpin" and an expertly painted picture of a bowling pin on it.

The others opened theirs, holding them up for each other to see. They thanked Eagle graciously and tried them on. She laughed as they played about, teasing each other and making jet noises and "talking" over the radio.

"This was very nice," D.M. said as he returned the helmet to the box and set it on the floor next to him, "But we didn't get the chance to get you anything."

"Seeing you all happy was a perfect gift in itself."

Later in the day, Eagle pulled on her flight suit and picked up her gear bag. She left her room and went to Jake's. She knocked on the door and a few moments later he answered, surprised to see her.

"Well ma'am, what do I owe this visit?" He smiled.

"I thought I would see how you do in the real thing. Get your gear and meet me in the hanger bay in fifteen mike." She turned and headed for the elevator.

Jake met Eagle and they made their way to the helicopter hanger. It would be his first time flying the real thing. The hanger doors opened to reveal a sleek black helicopter sitting in a ring of dim lights. The craft appeared much smaller than the Apaches he was used to working on. The canopy configuration was similar, one behind the other and the back one just a bit higher. Small stub wings came from the body and angled backwards about forty degrees.

"Sweeeeet! Looks even better in person," Jake commented as he made his way around the craft touching the smooth contours of the body. Eagle opened up the cockpits and climbed into the front seat. Jake had proven himself in the simulator that he was quite adept at flying helicopters, so she had no reservations in letting him take the controls the first time out.

"Are you gonna stare at this thing all day? Or are you going to preflight it so we can get going?" Eagle called.

Jake dug the flight manual from his gear bag. He made his preflight walk of the aircraft and then settled down in the back cockpit. It was exactly like the simulator and he knew every button and knob on the control panel. Of all the books that were given to him, his Badger flight manual was the most tattered from use.

Once in the air, Jake put the helicopter through some simple maneuvers. With minor exception, it handled just the same as the simulator. He felt very comfortable at the controls, almost as if he were part of the craft. The lieutenant gained altitude and banked to the west. He dropped into a neighboring canyon and explored it, skimming just above the tree tops. Eagle was enjoying the ride. She had been too busy to take time and see the beauty that was beyond the valley of the base. The snow covered peaks towered above the landscape clothed in a heavy white blanket. Fresh deer tracks could be seen in the clearings below.

"Well lieutenant, this has been a very nice ride, but I thought you'd wanna see just what this thing could do."

"Oh, yes ma'am, I do, I was just getting warmed up." With that, the lieutenant pulled up on the stick and brought the aircraft to nearly vertical. He shoved the throttles forward and Eagle could feel the G's pushing her deep into her seat. He banked hard to the left and then proceeded to fly as if he was trying to shake off an attack. Jake continued to climb, dive and bank so hard that Eagle was beginning to feel queasy. She had never before flown with someone who could control a helicopter like the lieutenant could. He seemed like he was made for the job. There was no doubt in her mind that he would be lethal with this airframe.

"Jake."

"Yes ma'am?"

"I think we should head for home," Eagle said as she swallowed hard to fight back the nausea.

Jake leveled the helicopter out and slowed down, "Aw, I was just getting warmed up."

"Sorry. I have a teleconference in an hour and I need to get ready for that."

"Aw, and I was just getting warmed up," he teased and turned for home.

The phone rang and Kemal picked it up, "Hello?"

"Blue Mole." Westland identified himself.

"So is it time?"

"Yes. I will be acquiring the goods in three days. Are your men ready?"

"Of course. Send those Special Forces impersonators out; I will make sure they have a welcome that they will never forget," Kemal hung up the phone. He turned to one of his assistants, "Alert the guards at my home in Isla Vista that we will be having some unwanted guests. I want them dispatched in as many pieces as possible." The assistant bowed lowly and hurried off. Kemal hated to do someone else's cleanup work, but this was going to be worth millions in the end. If Westland delivered what he had promised, Iran would have a cheap, medium range missile in which to strike Israel. With a bit more work, the missile would be able to strike Europe. Iran was growing tired of the sanctions that had been placed upon it because of its nuclear program. There was only so much they would put up with.

The end was in sight. Or was it? Eagle slept with her head down on the desk in her laboratory. She had loaded the last of the forty-three tapes that made up her database of genetic information. It had taken every moment of the last month in order to process D.M.'s DNA. The computer had to search through the tapes to find a match close to his. Her system was so old that it had crashed several times causing her to take far longer to complete the search then planned. Eagle had to change tapes at least three times a day, and her enthusiasm had certainly diminished for the project. In nearly all other cases, a match had been made in less than thirty-five tapes. But nothing had surfaced for the major. She began to wonder if he was part alien or something strange and would not have a match. Nonsense! He was human and there had to be DNA somewhere that would match.

0200, the incessant beeping of the computer roused the colonel from her sleep. She rubbed her eyes and stretched. Looking around, she noticed the monitor flashing red. Pushing the mouse with her finger, the screen blinked to a page filled with data. She rubbed her eyes some more and tried to focus on what it said. As she scanned the data her heart began to beat faster. Hitting the print button, she wanted to see the words on paper before she was convinced. The printer finished printing and she swiped the paper. As she studied the data a smile curled to her lips. She was out the door in a flash and to the elevator.

The doors opened and Eagle sprinted down the hall. She stopped at D.M.'s door and quickly entered in the override code to open the door. The lights were off, but she knew her way around. Darting into his bedroom she jumped onto the bed next to him.

D.M. sat up in surprise and hurriedly turned on the light. "What the hell do you think you're doing?!" He growled as he pulled the covers around his waist. Eagle offered the paper to him, a smile beamed on her face from ear to ear. "What's this?" He rubbed his eyes and tried to look at what the paper said.

"You are *not* your father's son," she announced proudly.

"Huh?"

"You are the son of the King of Spain."

"Don't bullshit me; it's too early for that."

"I'm sorry major, but DNA does not bullshit. Your father is not Theodore Elliott."

D.M.'s eyes cleared enough that he could read the paper. How could this be? His mother had married Theodore Elliott, and nine months later he popped out. Or was it nine months? His mother had told him that they had had a short engagement before getting married. Was there someone else?

"Your mother worked in the palace as a maid. She evidently caught the eye of the King and they must have had a brief affair. In order to keep from bringing dishonor on the royal family, she was sent home to Zaragoza where she quickly found Theodore and married him so the baby would appear to be his."

"Whoa! Hang on a minute! This is just too weird for this hour of the morning," he rubbed his forehead trying to collect his thoughts.

"D.M.? Do you know what this means?"

The major regarded her with a blank expression.

"You are of a royal line," she smiled and wrapped her arms around his waist. D.M.'s mind was still a bit fuzzy, but he wasn't going to pass up an opportunity to hold the woman he loved. He let his arms slide around her, his lips moved down her neck kissing her gently. Eagle made no motion to resist; instead she snuggled against him and stroked his chest with her hand. D.M. decided to test the waters a bit further and rolled over until he was lying almost on top of her. He pressed his body firmly against her; his mouth searching hers out in a kiss that embodied all the passion coursing through his heart.

He drew away and sighed deeply, "I think I'm the luckiest man in the world," he whispered, "But what about the chain of command bull shit?"

She studied him for a few long moments before tightening her arms around his back, "Bull shit," she whispered, "I won't tell if you don't." A broad smile beamed to her face. He met her smile with one of his own. Perhaps he'd finally found happiness.

He leaned down and kissed her again, his hand found its way under her shirt and he caressed her breast. Eagle let her lips wander down his neck until she reached the base. She nibbled playfully at his neck. D.M. gasped as jolt of pure energy raced through his whole body. Cold chills of excitement shot down his spine and goose bumps flushed his skin. No woman's ever done that to me, he thought, God it was amazing! He pressed himself against her harder. Eagle could feel the fullness of his manhood bearing between her legs through the sheets. The temptation was great, but she had to put the thought in the back of her mind.

D.M. was working her shirt up in an attempt to find a breast to kiss. His lips had no more than touched her creamy skin when the phone rang. He growled fiercely and rolled over to answer it. "Yeah?" He grunted, pausing to hear the message, "Okay. Thanks." He hung up the phone.

"What was it?" Eagle asked as she sat up and rearranged her clothes. Perhaps this was a good stopping point, before things got too out of hand.

"We've been put on alert. Looks like we got our first job."

"All ready? I was hoping we'd have a little more time to work with the planes before a real mission. Guess we'll just have to hope for the best," she said as she climbed off the bed.

"Maybe we'll get lucky and not need them. It could just be a helicopter insertion."

CHAPTER TWELVE

By 0400 the team was gathered in the briefing room eagerly awaiting information about the mission. Outside, a cold front had brought snow that was drifting down in huge flakes. Eagle came in with a brown folder tucked under her arm. She joined the others at the table and opened the file. "Good morning gentlemen," she yawned, "It appears that our services have been requested in the matter of an Iranian scumbag by the name of Amir Kemal. Word has it he has an affinity for American things- especially top secret things." She handed out several photographs of Kemal and his house on the California coast.

"I take it he's got something the government would like back?" Jake said as he studied one of the pictures.

"A couple of micro disks that contain plans for a long range ballistic missile that could be easily modified to carry chemical weapons, or maybe even nukes."

Max edged into the conversation, "I thought they had missiles that could do that. What's so special about these?"

"A new propulsion system that makes them one third smaller but provides the same range and payload. It's also very cheap to build," she replied, taking out a rough diagram for them to see.

"So what's the plan?" D.M. spoke up. He sat with his elbows on the table, one hand balled inside the other with his chin resting on them.

"According to intelligence, this should be an easy job. But we all know about intel-reliability is not always their strong point. The house is right on a cliff overlooking the ocean. There's a stairway from the beach to the house... I think if we land on the beach, it might be a good insertion point."

Over the next few hours the team hashed out the details of the mission. Eagle had told them to try all their gear on and become familiar with it. D.M. and Jake were the first ones in the ready room. Each man had a locker in which to store his equipment. D.M. stood in front of his locker dressed only in a pair of boxer briefs. He was just beginning to pull on his pants when he felt a pair of eyes staring at him. He turned to see Jake looking at him.

"Okay, why are you looking at me like that?" The major said lowly.

"Just appreciating your physique," Jake replied sheepishly.

"You're not going gay on me are you?" D.M. snapped back.

Jake stood quiet for a few uneasy moments, "Um...No."

"Why does that answer not sound very truthful?"

Jake sat down on the bench. He tried to gather his thoughts. This was something that he hoped would never get out, but it seemed that now he would have to come clean. "No, I'm not gay. Bisexual I guess... There were things I did in my younger life I'm not very proud of," he paused trying to find the words, "In my early gang-banger days I got so hooked on cocaine that I would sell myself to the highest bidder so I could feed my habit. Male, female, it didn't really matter. I had to feed it. In the beginning I really didn't like having to sleep with guys. Of course I prefer women, but after a while, I came to terms with what I was doing. And when I was so deep into the drugs, something changed and I began to find the experience rather erotic."

D.M. turned away from Jake and finished putting on his uniform. "You don't have feelings for any of us do you?"

"No...Well, with exception of Eagle, no. And I know where you stand on that issue," he said as he turned away. D.M thought for a moment about what the lieutenant had just said. Did he perhaps know about him and Eagle?

Several minutes later the rest of the team straggled in and began to prepare. They dressed in black BDUs and began to get familiar with their new gadgets. Jake pulled out a tangled mess of black nylon webbing, "Wadda ya make of this?"

Frank stepped over and inspected the tangle. "I think it's like the old load bearing gear... See, this part goes over your shoulders and around your waist...But this other part... I haven't got a clue."

Max joined the conversation, "It looks like that part goes on your legs," he turned the webbing over several times until it resembled a skeleton pair of pants.

"Yeah, but what do you do with it?" Jake replied. Frank opened a box that sat in the bottom of Jake's locker and pulled out a black pouch with Velcro tabs on the back. He reached over and attached the pouch to the webbing.

"Hey, that look right?"

Jake and Max nodded and quickly set to helping each other

into their gear and attaching pouches. When they were done, Jake stood looking into his locker, "Hey, aren't we supposed to have some sort of body armor or something?"

Tige turned around, "Mate, if we wore body armor, we would be weighted down and not able to move around well."

"So we go in naked? Shit, we really are a Kamikaze squad after all."

"I'm really not liking this idea...We're gonna be lambs to the slaughter," Max added.

"Well then mate, I suggest you learn to move faster. There's only so much area that body armor will protect anyways. Your lower body, arms and perhaps your head are still exposed."

It was midday when the team gathered for lunch. They talked excitedly about the mission. D.M., however, sat quietly. He was worried. Something about the assignment made him feel uneasy. Was it just too soon after their commissioning? The fact that they were told it was going to be an easy job? How did intel find out who had stolen the disks? The answers did not add up correctly to him. His food arrived and he sat picking at it. Eagle noticed he was not eating, "Got a case of the nerves major?"

He studied her for a moment, "Yeah, I suppose so."

"It's Wednesday, you know what that means?"

"Sure. You think it's a good idea?"

Eagle finished chewing a mouthful of food, "Practice will help you relax some."

"All right. After lunch?" He asked. His appetite seemed to be improving and the large hamburger on his plate was definitely looking delicious. Eagle nodded, trying to slurp down her pasta.

Snow was falling harder. The ground around base was completely white. Eagle stood at the window on the training floor and watched as Jake, Frank, Sam, and Tige played football in the snow. It appeared though; they were more interested in throwing snow balls than really playing football. She smiled at their childish antics.

D.M. came up behind her and put his hands on her shoulders. She looked back at him, "Beautiful isn't it?"

"I'm not much for snow."

"You're not much for mountains or trees either."

D.M. let his hands slide down to her waist, wrapping his arms around her he stepped close, "I like the desert...This probably sounds bizarre, but I feel like the trees keep too many secrets."

"You're right, it does sound bizarre...But I think I see what you mean," she slid from his grasp and retrieved two steel practice swords, handing one to him. They walked to the center of the room and faced en garde. She lunged forward in an aggressive attack sending D.M. into a retreat. "Come on major, I know you can fight, show me something!"

The major battled back and soon had Eagle on the retreat. She was not about to give up that easy. With a quick flick of her wrist, she knocked the sword from his hand and sent it sailing to the floor behind him. Without hesitation, D.M. performed a graceful back handspring, caught his toe under the sword and lifted it back into his hand. He stood ready to face her. Eagle let the point of her sword droop to the ground. Amazing! She never expected something like that from him. He was really showing promise of becoming a masterful swordsman. D.M. noticed her expression, "What?" he smiled, seeing that he had surprised her.

"That was pure genius!" Her eyes lit up, "I've never seen anything like it. I didn't think anyone your size could be so agile."

D.M. laughed heartily, "I'm full of surprises!"

"Yes, and they will keep you alive too!" She lunged at him again.

Dusk reached the base. The snow had stopped, leaving everything blanketed in another foot of fluffy white powder. The team waited inside the roof hanger of the building. A sleek, black transport helicopter hovered into view about fifty yards from the building and moved slowly toward it. Landing lights blinked on the hanger deck and the helicopter edged forward and touched down. Snow blew into the air making it almost impossible to see. "All right, let's go!" D.M. hollered and started out the door. The others were right on his heels, ducking low to avoid the spinning rotors. He slid open the side door and helped the rest of the team in. Once everyone was in, he closed the door and crawled forward into the co pilot seat. Strapping in, he grabbed the headphones and put them on. "Okay, we're set." He gave the thumbs up sign. Eagle nodded and brought the helicopter up and banked away from the building. D.M. sat looking at the controls, "So what do you call this thing?"

"This is the Warhawk, our transport helicopter. It's built on a Sikorsky 76 airframe with heavier engines and armor plating. It can carry some weapons like a twenty millimeter gun in the nose and a fifty on the door. Stub wings can be affixed to carry more ordinance."

They flew for nearly two hours before reaching their prearranged refueling location. As they were fueling up, everyone made a restroom stop and stretch break. A full moon tried to poke through the clouds, but it was repressed by the sheer mass of cloud cover. Tige stood next to the helicopter looking at his watch. It was 2100. Another forty minutes and they should be at the insertion point. The plan was to be dropped about half a mile up the beach and approach on foot. He sighed, all this waiting, what could be worse? The smell of rain reached his nose. This was not good. The mission was going to be difficult enough, but Mother Nature could certainly make things worse. It was hard enough to concentrate, and being cold and wet just added to the troubles. Perhaps the coastal weather would be better.

The helicopter skimmed along the coastline. Rain came down in torrents. Their luck had changed for the worse. Eagle had to find another location to drop them off because the waves were crashing too close to the cliffs. She settled on another spot further up the beach and sat the chopper down. They performed a quick weapons and radio check. Max opened the door and stepped out into the rain, "Damn, this rain's cold!" The others climbed out and they hurried away into the darkness.

They reached the base of the stairs and stopped to catch their breaths. The rain had slowed somewhat. Waves crashed onto the sand a few feet from where they rested. Jake stood behind D.M., letting him act as a shield from the wind and rain, "You know, I could think of a hundred things I'd rather be doing right now."

Frank wiped the rain off his face, "Hell, I could think of a million!"

D.M. interrupted the conversation, "Okay, I need someone to go up and act as a scout. Let us know when all's quiet."

"I'll go," Tige stepped forward and started up the steps. He knew that if he kept moving the cold would not be so bad. The stairs were steep, and Tige took his time getting to the top. When he reached the last flight of stairs, he got down on his belly and inched up until he could just peer above the last step. Lights were on in the house, and he could see a few guards standing post. It didn't look very promising. The guards were carrying sub machine guns and it looked like there might be a position on the roof as well.

He rose up slightly to see past a bush that grew near the top landing. A team of Dobermans with their handler rounded the corner about thirty yards away. Tige knew he had to get out of there before the dogs got his scent. He scurried down three flights of stairs and hid behind an outcropping of rock. The dogs passed by the stairs, one barked a couple times before its handler stopped to look down the stairs and then continued on. There had been no mention of dogs on the intel report. Tige keyed the radio, "Lone Wolf, this is Wombat, do you copy?"

"Roger Wombat, I read you Lima-Charlie. What's your status?" D.M. answered.

"I had a bit of a look around. There are more guards than the report said, and they also got dog teams. What do you want me to do?"

"Hang around up there until everything goes dark, then let us know."

"I hope this isn't some kind of all night party, it's pretty lively up here, Wombat out."

D.M. found a small alcove underneath one of the lower flights of stairs and ushered the rest of the group under to get them as much out of the weather as possible. The rain was coming down hard again and he knew that the more miserable they were, the more chances of mistakes. He keyed the mike and reported in to Eagle, "White Feather, this is Lone Wolf."

"Go ahead Lone Wolf."

"We got a problem. Tige says there's a lot more guards up there than reported, and there's dogs too."

"What is your location?"

"We're underneath some stairs at the bottom. I have Tige up at the top scouting for us. I told him to hold his position until the place went dark, and then to contact me."

Eagle checked her watch; they were over an hour into the mission. She had hoped that by the time they reached the stairs everything would be quiet. It was after midnight, and Tige said there was still movement. "Roger Lone Wolf, continue with your plan. We only get one shot at this, so we better wait this out."

Jake sat shivering next to D.M. He tried to control the shaking but couldn't. Sam reached forward and put his hand on Jake's cheek, "Hey D.M., I think he's starting to get a bit hypothermic. We gotta get moving soon." The major peered out into the night. The rain had slowed but the wind seemed to blow with more force. The radio crackled in his ear.

"Lone Wolf, this is Wombat. All quiet. Repeat, all quiet."

"Roger that, we're coming up," D.M. checked his watch, 0115. They had waited almost three hours for the lights to go out. "Jake? You okay?"

Jake's teeth were chattering hard enough that everyone heard him, "Yyyyeeeeehhhhh," he stuttered, clenching his rifle.

"All right, let's move out," D.M. called as he slid down the embankment to the sand and went around to the bottom of the stairs. The others followed, glad to finally be moving. D.M. radioed Eagle, "White Feather, Lone Wolf, we are moving. Repeat we are moving."

"Good luck gentlemen," she said softly over the radio.

They reached the top of the stairs and met up with Tige. He had found a nook under the stairs and had managed to stay out of most of the weather. The rain had diminished to a light sprinkle and the wind was bringing the mist from the ocean ashore giving everything a salty smell.

Tige issued his report, "The last dog team went through here about twenty mike. I timed them and they were passing here about every ten. All the lights are out and I see no movement in the house. I used the night vision and infrared scope and didn't see any hidden company. It looks clear."

D.M. gave him a light pat on the back, "Good work. Can I count on you to take point?"

"Sure, no problem." He grabbed his night vision goggles and flipped them down over his eyes. The rest of the team donned their goggles and prepared to move out. Tige crawled up to the top step and crouched behind a bush. He scanned the area for a suitable route that would provide plenty of cover for them. To the right was a large grass area flanked by tall palm trees. The left held more promise. A low wall fronted a row of juniper bushes and led up to a sliding glass door, their point of entry. He looked over his shoulder at the others, "Ready mates?" Five thumbs poked up in the air, they were ready.

Tige moved low and swift to get behind the bushes. The rest of the team was right behind him. He stopped half way down the wall and waited until everyone was under cover. Jake made his way over to Tige; he knew the next part was up to him.

"You got the gizmo?" Tige asked.

"Yep...I've done this a thousand times, don't worry," Jake whispered as he retrieved a slender pry bar from his leg pouch.

"I worry. What if they have it wired?" Tige replied.

"I guess we'll find out real quick," he said as he slipped past Tige and crawled over to where the wall met with the side of the house. He parted the bushes and stepped onto the walkway. The door opened right to left, so he needed to be on the other side. Risky move, someone could be watching. Jake flattened to the ground and edged along slowly so he would not make noise or attract attention by a quick movement. The rest of the team peered through the bushes and watched his progress.

Jake reached the other side of the door. It seemed to have taken hours rather than the three minutes that had actually elapsed. He got to one knee and reached for the door. He carefully pushed at it and found that it was unlocked. "Hey, it's not locked," he whispered over the radio.

Tige turned to D.M. "This seems fishy. You don't have a dozen guards protecting your house and forget to lock the door at night."

D.M. shrugged his shoulders, "Maybe that's why he has the guards, he hates to lock up at night."

"Fat chance," Tige replied.

Jake keyed the mike, "All right guys, I'm here, what do you want me to do?"

"Should we have him open the door slowly? If it's wired, we might be able to find out soon enough and make a getaway," D.M. pondered. Tige peered above the bushes and scanned the area. They were in a good position to make a run for the stairs if the alarm did go off.

"Kingpin, open the door very slowly. If you see or hear anything, get back here quickly," Tige said softly over the radio.

"Roger that," he gently pushed at the door until there was enough room to slip inside. The curtain was drawn across the door, giving some cover, but also possibly concealing someone waiting for them. "Okay, it's open, no bells or whistles. Now what?"

"Can you give us a visual inside?"

"Oh great, how did I end up on point?" Jake hissed as he readied his rifle. He reached inside and carefully drew back the curtain. All that reached his eyes was blackness. He brought down his night vision goggles and took another look.

Tige raised the infrared scope to his eye. He could see no heat or movement inside. "I see nothing on infrared."

"I'm clear on night vision too," Jake replied.

"Okay, let's move out. Stay low and behind the bushes for as long as possible. We'll regroup once inside," D.M. whispered to the group over the radio.

"I'm going in," Jake announced and quickly slipped inside the door. He stayed low and swept right to left making sure there was no one about. "Clear, come on in."

One at a time, the men made their way inside. They regrouped and waited for further direction. D.M. was the last in the door. He pulled out a small map and laid it on the floor. The others gathered around. "We need to break up and search the place. It's a big house, the disks could be anywhere...We are here. Tige, Sam, you two take the south wing; Max, Frank, you have the east wing; Jake and I will take the north...Keep in contact, if you find them, alert the rest of us and rendezvous here."

Tige added his input, "Be very careful of eye beams and other security measures. I can't see this guy only protecting his house with guards and not have any other type of security."

"Any questions?" D.M. paused, no one had anything to say, "Okay, move out."

The teams moved silently down a short hallway and headed to their assigned locations. Max and Frank walked slowly making sure they did not set off any alarms. They had a long hall to negotiate before they reached their rooms. Every step they took was checked before taking it. The first room was only a few feet away. Creeping ever so slowly, they reached it. Frank reached out and grasped the door handle. He turned it carefully. Locked. He looked at Max and shook his head.

Max gently pulled open the Velcro closure of one of his pouches. The Velcro separated with a raspy hiss. The noise seemed loud enough to wake the whole house, but it was scarcely louder than scratching an itch through a uniform. He removed a lock pick and set to opening the lock. Frank stood guard keeping a keen eye out for any movement. After a few minutes of work, Max had the lock open. They stayed low as he turned the handle of the door. It creaked slightly as it swung open. Max crawled inside and checked the area, then waved Frank in.

They were in a trophy room filled with gruesome animal heads hanging from the walls. Once confirming the room was clear, they began their search. Frank checked the vases and decorative urns that sat on a table in front of a couch. A tiger skin rug lay on the floor underneath the table. He moved around, not seeing the head of the tiger and tripped over it. He fell to the floor with a loud thud. Max spun around and looked at him, "Hey, watch where you're going!" He whispered loudly.

"Sorry," Frank replied and got up. He went to the door and listened for signs of movement. Nothing. All was quiet.

***

Tige pulled out a small penlight and shined it down the mouth of a large vase that sat on the floor. Sam quietly shuffled through drawers on a sideboard. They were in the dining room, the second of their four rooms. The first one was the kitchen. Tige had little suspicion that Kemal would hide important military plans in the kitchen, so they had searched it quickly. The dining room was not proving to be very informative either. There was a lot of china and silver candlestick holders, but not much else. The next room would deserve more attention, it was a small den. "Sam, you find anything?"

Sam shook his head, "Do you wanna move on?"

"Yeah, I think that would be a good idea," he crept through the doorway that led to the den. Sam followed covering their backs from any accidental intrusion.

D.M. stood guard as Jake quickly picked the lock on what appeared to be an office door. The major had his misgivings in the beginning about being paired with Jake. He now realized that the man could break into anything in less than thirty seconds. Perhaps it wasn't a bad idea that Eagle stuck them together. "All right sir, the door is open," Jake whispered and waved his arm in a flourish. D.M. crept past and scanned the room with his night vision goggles. There was no one about. He stood up and took a look around. This had to be Kemal's main office. In front of him was a large desk with a computer monitor sitting on it. Shelves lined the walls filled with books and small statues. A large window faced the ocean. The clouds had parted temporarily and the moon was shining. D.M. removed his goggles and allowed his eyes to adjust to the natural light.

Jake moved quietly over to the desk. He took out his penlight and began to search around the drawers and under the desk. "Just what I thought, wired," he began to search through his pockets.

"What are you looking for?" D.M. whispered.

"I can get past the alarm, but I need something thin, flexible, and metal...A gum wrapper would do the trick."

"Sorry, left my last pack in my other super hero suit," he joked lightly and started looking for something that would work. An intricately carved wooden box sat on top of the desk. D.M. opened it carefully, discovering it was a humidor. "Mmmm, nice." Reaching inside he removed a Cuban cigar. He held it to his nose and sniffed, "Oh, I love a good Cuban," he sighed. Checking further, he found a foil packet containing pipe tobacco. "Will this work?" He said as he dumped it out.

"Perfect, hey, get one of those stogies for me too," Jake replied as he folded the foil into a strip. D.M. tucked the cigars in his pocket.

"For the celebration later eh?" The lieutenant grinned.

"Yes, now get to work, we don't have much time."

"All right, all right." Jake folded the foil into a long strip and took out a pair of wire cutters. "I need something sticky- to hold the foil down."

D.M. searched around but was unable to find anything that would work. Jake studied the situation for a few moments, "I guess I can hold it in place, but you'll have to do all the searching."

"That's fine, if you think you can do it."

"Hey man, you forget who you're dealing with. *I* am a pro," Jake quickly worked his magic and bypassed the alarm. "Okay, we should be safe. Open it slowly."

D.M. carefully slid open the middle drawer. He held the pen light between his teeth and shuffled through the papers. There! In the back of the drawer, was a small clear plastic case with two mini compact disks. "Bingo," he said, still clenching the light in his teeth.

"You found them?"

"Uh huh," D.M. replied as he keyed the radio, "All teams, this is Lone Wolf. We have the merchandise. Prepare for extraction."

Eagle keyed the radio, "All teams, this is White Feather; I will be airborne in one minute." She quickly punched buttons and brought the helicopter back to life. The planned extraction point was on the beach where they had been waiting. The tide had gone out and there was now beach to land on. She would hover just off the water not far away until they were all down. Then the plan was to land or hover so everyone could get on. They should be able to clear the area within thirty seconds.

D.M. reached to take the box containing the disks. As he picked it up, a small red light on the wall flashed and there was a beeping sound. "Shit!" D.M. hissed.

"What's going on?" Jake poked his head up from under the desk.

D.M. tipped the box over to reveal wires leading from the box, "He wired this too."

"Oh fuck!"

D.M. keyed the radio, "All teams, we have alarm activation, proceed to primary LZ," he yanked the box free and quickly put it in his pocket. Outside, they could hear the sound of guards coming down the hall. The rattle of gunfire dispelled any chance of a quiet get away. The guards must have found some of the team.

Tige hid behind a door post and fired down the hall. Several guards fell from his barrage of bullets. "Lone Wolf, this is Wombat, we're catching some serious hell over here. I don't think the primary LZ is going to be good, they'll get us before we make it down the stairs."

"Roger that Wombat...White Feather, do you copy?"

"I heard. I'm coming up. We'll try for an extraction on that grass area next to the house."

"Copy that. All teams, new LZ will be on the grass outside." D.M. went to the door and peered around the door post. Guards were converging on their position and things were about to get difficult. "Jake, we got company coming."

"We're trapped!"

"No, the window...Go out the window, I'll cover for you."

Jake picked up the armchair from the desk and threw it through the window. D.M. poked the rifle around the door post and fired blindly hoping to pin the guards down until Jake got out.

***

Eagle hovered near the edge of the cliff. The clouds had covered again and rain was starting to come down heavily. Guards were coming out from various doors and some were on the roof manning machine guns. They splattered the helicopter with bullets. Eagle said a quick prayer that the armor plating on the bird was as good as the manufacture said it was. She swung around so the helicopter pointed at the house and opened fire with the machine gun that was housed in the nose. Guards dove for cover.

"White Feather, there's four ready to extract," Tige radioed. They were pinned down behind the low wall by the door.

"Roger, I'll get in as close as I can. Get ready to run." She maneuvered the helicopter as near to them as possible. The palm trees growing next to the house prevented her from getting as close as she wanted. There was a going to be a forty foot or more run through open ground. That was the best she could do for them. Bullets continued to ricochet off the protective armor. Suddenly an explosion shook the chopper. Eagle fought to keep control. She checked the status of the armor, the display on the control panel indicated it was still intact. They must have switched to 20mm explosive munitions.

"Eagle, we're ready to extract," Tige said over the radio.

"Okay, come on. I'll open the door when I see you coming." She rested her finger on the door button. The chopper continued to be rattled by the explosions.

"Are we ready?" Tige shouted over the gunfire. The other three held up their thumbs. "Okay, we're moving!" He hopped the wall, rifle blazing, bullets impacting on walls, trees, and guards. The others were right behind him, firing at anything that moved. They ran the distance. Tige took a round in the leg and fell heavily to the ground. Max grabbed him by the elbow and helped drag him the last few feet to the chopper. Eagle had the door open waiting for them. Frank dove in and quickly took up position on the machine gun. Sam helped get Tige on board; Max held his position and returned fire before leaping inside. The rain came down harder.

Jake worked his way around the house. The dense vegetation was good cover, but very difficult to climb through. D.M. was somewhere behind him. The lieutenant dropped down behind the wall. Several guards saw him and unleashed their magazines of ammunition at him. Bullets chipped away the wall sending pieces showering over him. Jake returned fire, holding his rifle above the wall and spraying the area with bullets. "I could use some help over here," he hollered over the radio.

Frank swung the machine gun around and laid down a field of cover fire for Jake. "Come on!" He shouted into the microphone.

Jake cleared the wall and bolted for the chopper. The rain had begun to puddle on the grass and he slipped. He landed hard on his right knee, his left hand going into the air for balance. Something stung him in the hand. He ignored it and kept on running.

A glimmer from the roof top caught Frank's attention, "Eagle, we got an RPG pointed at us!"

Eagle looked out the side window and spotted the man on the roof. He held a long tube with the rocket grenade mounted on the front. Jake was over half way to the chopper. This was going to be close. Eagle knew the helicopter could not withstand the blast of a grenade. She needed to act quickly. Jake was only a few feet from the chopper when the grenade was fired. He saw it coming and made a wild leap into the air. Frank reached out and caught Jake by the wrist just as Eagle yanked up on the stick to get the chopper out of the way. Jake was lifted high off the ground dangling from the side of the helicopter. The RPG screamed under them and detonated on a tree. Frank and Max managed to finish pulling Jake inside. He scrambled over and sat against the back of Eagle's seat, "Thanks for the lift!" He shouted.

"Sorry. Where's D.M.?"

"Still down there."

The major flattened behind the wall. The shower of bullets had stopped momentarily while the guards reloaded. He took a moment to reload his rifle. "White Feather, Lone Wolf...I'm behind the wall. How about some cover?"

Frank resumed his position on the machine gun, "Roger that Lone Wolf, I'll have the red carpet out in just a second." Explosive rounds continued to pelt the chopper. Frank charged the gun and squeezed the trigger. Eagle brought the helicopter back to hovering just above the ground. She had to keep it moving somewhat or the guards would be able to get a round inside the cabin.

"I'm moving!" D.M. yelled as he jumped over the wall. The rain was still coming down hard. He ran as hard as he could, legs pumping with all their might. It felt as if he was in slow motion. Every step seemed to take forever. Half way there. He could see Eagle watching him from the cockpit. Just a little further. A moment later a great force hit him in the left shoulder, sending him to the ground. Everything went dark.

Frank watched as the round impacted on his brother's body in a flash of flame and spray of blood. "NO!" Frank screamed as he saw D.M. hit the ground in a lifeless mass, his body twisted in an unnatural position.

"D.M.! NO!" Eagle jumped up from the pilot seat, "Take it Jake!" She was out her seat and heading for the door. Jake jumped around the seat and took control of the chopper. Frank bailed out the door and ran after Eagle. Max took his place and fired cover for them. They reached D.M. and Frank grabbed his brother by the back of his web harness and dragged him back to the helicopter. Eagle supported what remained of his shoulder and arm. They hefted him into the doorway where hands were waiting to pull him in. Frank helped Eagle in. He shrieked as a bullet pierced his right biceps. Max pulled him inside. "Jake get us out of here!" Eagle hollered.

Jake tipped the nose of the chopper down and quickly disappeared below the top of the cliff. He turned right and hugged the cliffs to prevent from being easily targeted by another RPG. Eagle and Sam were busily trying to stop D.M.'s bleeding. "Sam, I need some artery forceps, quick!"

Sam dug through the medical bag and found some. He opened the package and handed them to her. Eagle grabbed them, her hands and uniform soaked in blood. She located the artery and applied the clamp. "Jake, I need you to find us a hospital. D.M.'s in bad shape."

"Okay!" He called.

Tige limped forward and sat in the co pilot seat. He accessed the computer and typed in a query for hospitals. "You want a level one trauma hospital?"

"Yes. Get on the radio and tell them we have wounded; one very serious."

"Roger."

CHAPTER THIRTEEN

Eagle stood with her hands pressed against the operating room viewing window. She watched as a team of surgeons worked furiously on D.M. She wanted to be in there with him, but the hospital would not allow it. Sam and Max stood with her. They were at a loss for what to do. The rest of the team had been taken to other operating rooms and treatment areas to handle their wounds. They stood together, but prayed silently alone that D.M. would make it.

Something was wrong. Eagle could see the heart monitor going erratic. Oh God, she thought, he's going into A-fib. The room became a blur of frantic movement. The surgeons, nurses, and technicians worked frantically to revive him. Eagle tried to get past Max to go help, but he held her firmly, "Eagle, you can't go in there. They know what they're doing, just let them work."

She struggled for a few moments before giving up. Her knees buckled and she sagged into Max's arms. He gently sat her down in a chair. She looked up at him, tears pooling at the corners of her eyes. He'd never seen her show any kind of weak emotion, let alone cry. Max knew Eagle was tough, but this had really upset her.

Sam stood at the window and watched. To him it seemed like he was watching a movie or something. For some reason it didn't seem real. He'd spent enough time training in the OR and had done many cases; this just did not feel like it was really happening. The surgeons battled harder, injecting him with countless drugs and using the defibrillator. Finally a spark of life returned to the major. His heart beat regained rhythm. Sam turned to Eagle, "Hey, they got him going."

Eagle stood up and went to the window. The OR was still a bustle of activity, but the surgeons had resumed their work on his shoulder. She watched as they removed shrapnel and pieces of shattered bone. From what she saw, the bullet had impacted on his scapula and completely destroyed it. The top part of his humerus was gone, as was most of his clavicle and upper ribs. The chances of him keeping his arm, let alone using it again, were slim to none. She had told the surgeons as they were taking him into the OR, if there was any way to save his arm, to do it. If they could at least restore circulation and get him stable enough to travel, she knew the doctors at the base had far better technology to help him.

Hours passed. Eagle had fallen asleep from exhaustion. She rested her head against Max's shoulder, who was also asleep. Sam had found a corner and dozed off. One of the surgeons came into the viewing area. He noticed everyone sleeping and reached out and touched Eagle on the shoulder. She stirred and opened her eyes. Max woke up when he felt her moving.

"He's alive," the surgeon began, "I did manage to get an arterial graft for him and got circulation restored. He's in intensive care, but his condition is not very good. After he coded, he went into a coma." He paused for a moment, allowing her to absorb all the information. "If he makes it through the day, I give him a sixty percent chance of living."

Eagle stood up and offered her hand to him. Her uniform was stained with dried blood and she had washed her hands several times trying to get all the blood off them. The surgeon took her hand. "Thank you...I really appreciate all your efforts," she said softly.

"That's what we're here for...Your group, are they some kind of Special Forces team?"

"Yes. We got into something over our heads."

"It appears that way... Should I have all the treatment records made out for John Doe? I know, according to the government, you guys don't exist."

"Exactly...And thank you again."

The surgeon turned to leave, "You can go see your men. I'd like to keep the big guy here a couple days to make sure he's stable enough to move."

"Agreed," she replied.

Over the next two days, D.M.'s condition stabilized. He still had not regained consciousness. He lay in intensive care with the left side of his face, neck, chest and shoulder heavily bandaged. What the bullet had not destroyed or riddled with shrapnel, the explosion burned. Eagle knew she needed to get him home, but she respected the surgeon's wishes. Finally on the morning of the third day, the surgeon pronounced him stable enough to travel. She had taken the rest of the team home as soon as Tige was discharged. They would be more comfortable there. Eagle returned to the hospital with Sam, two nurses and one of the surgeons. Their goal was to get D.M. home without any problems.

She watched as he was carefully loaded into the helicopter. Tubes and wires poked out of his body from all directions. Once he was secured, she climbed in and closed the door. The rotors whined to life. Eagle looked out the window as she readied for takeoff. The surgeon who had fought so hard to save D.M.'s life stood watching. She nodded slowly in appreciation. He smiled and waved good bye. The helicopter lifted off into the bright sun and headed north.

Tige balanced himself with crutches as he stood looking out the window. With exception of D.M., the team's casualties were not bad. Jake had been hit in the hand, Frank, the arm, and Tige, the thigh. They would be out of commission for a couple of weeks. Eagle was going to have the agonizing task of drawing up D.M.'s discharge orders. She could not believe that on their very first mission her trusted second in command, not to mention love of her life was lying in a hospital bed mutilated and in a coma. It was not a happy New Year.

The surgeons were going to have to operate numerous times on D.M. They would perform delicate cosmetic surgery and skin grafts on his face and neck. His shoulder would be slowly rebuilt using stainless steel, titanium and Teflon instead of bone. New muscle would have to be grown and grafted onto his frame. The medical technology at the base was far more advanced than what civilian medicine could offer. They were years ahead in cloning, growing grafts and prosthetics. What they learned from their research, the civilian world would find out about in five or so years.

D.M. was sitting up in the hospital bed. His left side bandaged from his forehead down to his elbow. He had come out of the coma four days after arriving home. Eagle sat with him. She held his hand. He drifted in and out of sleep. The massive amounts of pain medication kept him constantly drowsy.

"Eagle?"

"Yes D.M.?" She was happy to hear his voice.

"Why can't I feel my arm?" His voice was raspy and dry sounding. Evidently he had not been coherent enough for anyone to tell him.

"Do you remember the night of the mission?"

"Kind of."

"You were running to the chopper. You got hit with an incendiary round. We got you to a hospital. The surgeons managed to save your arm, but the nerves have been badly severed."

D.M. struggled and pulled the covers off his arm. It was there, just no feeling. "I can't use my arm?"

"No. I had them save it just on the chance that the technology comes available to repair the nerve damage."

"So I have an arm that's no good?" He was beginning to get angry. Eagle knew that he could cause himself more harm if he went crazy.

"D.M., please don't get upset."

"Don't get upset?! Don't get upset?! Jesus, Eagle you don't understand how I feel." His temper was starting to boil. He growled as the pain coursed through his body. The pain medication had begun to wear off. Eagle quickly retrieved his next dose. She injected it through his IV. It didn't take long before he was fast asleep.

Eagle left him to sleep; her heart ached from seeing him like that. Her emotions were mixed. Did she still love him? Could she still love him? He was a mess of scars and sutures. The cosmetic surgeon had done a wonderful job on his face; he would have just a few small scars. His neck and shoulder would bear the scars of multiple skin grafts. He might never have the use of his arm. Did she make things worse by having them save it? Would he have felt different if it had been amputated? Why did this have to happen?! It seemed like every time something good happened in her life, some force of man or nature came along and destroyed it. Just once, she wished, something would have a good outcome.

Two weeks passed by, D.M. saw the removal of more and more bandages. His face was his own again and the cosmetic surgeon had done more work on his neck. It was still scarred, but not as bad. A psychiatrist had come every day that D.M. was awake and had talked to him. The major reluctantly began to cope with his disability. He knew his days in the military were numbered. Eagle could not afford to keep him on the roster now that he was permanently out of commission. Tige would serve as second in command until another suitable replacement could be found. His days were now filled with boredom and the slow process of healing enough that he could be discharged or medically retired.

Eagle knocked lightly on the door. "Come in," D.M. called.

She quietly opened the door and peered in. This was the first time she had seen him with the bandages off his face. He smiled slightly. Her heart warmed. Yes, she still had feelings for him. And by his expression, he was happy to see her. His bitterness toward her had faded and he was just happy she still came to see him.

"Hi," he said with feeling.

"How are you doing?"

"Bored. I'm glad you came to see me. I was beginning to wonder if this was the end of things between us. It isn't is it?" His deep brown eyes searched for some sort of expression on her face.

Eagle was torn. She still loved him, but how would their relationship continue? As much as it hurt her, she was going to have to discharge him from the military. He could not stay here, civilians were not allowed; and she was not ready to give up her career.

"Eagle?" He noticed that she was deep in thought, "Is it over?"

She looked down at the floor, "I don't know."

"Talk to me, please."

Eagle sat down on the edge of his bed. What was she going to say? Yes, she still loved him, but she was going to have to put him out in the cold. There was no conceivable way to keep him here. Every option she thought of and researched just ended up in a dead end. "You have to understand my position...I'm in charge of this unit and I must uphold the rules of the base," she paused for a long moment, "Yes, I still love you, but I can think of no way to let you stay."

"How much longer do I have here?"

"The doctors estimate another three weeks."

"Do you remember the lab that was vacant?" He changed the subject. Something was working inside his head, a possibility.

"Yes, but what does that have to do with..."

"Shhh, hear me out," he held his finger up, "If you can give me that lab for a while and get my equipment up here, I might be able to work this out."

"Don't be silly. What do you plan to do?"

"I'm not completely sure yet...Please, just indulge me for a little while. If it doesn't work out, I'll go."

"And how much time do you want? I can't stall the discharge forever."

"Give me the three weeks plus one month."

"No way. I'll have Washington breathing down my neck for keeping you on the active roster and not finding a replacement."

"Place me on inactive. Shit, suspend my pay if you want. Just give me the time." His eyes narrowed with intensity.

Eagle saw the determined look on his face. He wanted to stay. She knew he could be stubborn when he wanted something. With all her options exhausted, what could it hurt? She could easily place him on inactive and still keep him on the base. But the brass would eventually ask questions. So what! She could always make something up. Creativity was one of her strong points. "All right, you got the time. Get me the information so I can have your equipment sent up from storage. There's one lab left."

"Yes!" D.M. grabbed her, kissing her hard. He could feel energy returning to his body. He wanted out of the bed and to get back to work- any kind of work.

The next day, Eagle pushed open the door to the laboratory. The others were in use by scientists funded by the government. D.M. walked in to the large room, his arm held in a sling. He wandered around looking at the facility. The walls, floor and trim were sterile white. There was a small bathroom and a couple of built in cabinets. Against the back wall was a large chamber. The only different color in the whole room was the black granite top on the nearly twelve foot long lab work bench.

"Will this work?" Eagle said, her voice echoing.

"Yeah, looks like there will be enough room for all of my equipment," he said as he walked over and looked at the chamber. Studying the small control panel he realized it was a hyperbaric chamber, "Humm, don't think I'll have much use for this. Guess it can be for storage," he turned to her, "Thank you. I appreciate you having faith in me. I'm going to do my best not to let you or the team down. I wanna stay and be part of this... And be part of your life."

"Well then major, you'd better get busy. The clock is ticking."

D.M. stood at Jake's door. He had thought long and hard about this decision. With the use of only one arm, he would need help in the lab. He had considered asking Frank, but decided that since they were brothers, there would most likely be problems. Frank was also not a quick learner; he tended to keep to simple things he knew. D.M. dreaded the thought of working with someone in the lab. He had always prided himself on being able to do his research alone. Now he had his back against the wall. If he wanted to stay, he would need help. Despite the fact he still didn't get along terribly well with Jake, he had noticed the lieutenant picked up skills quickly. During flight training, he had mastered jets faster than the others, and his abilities in a helicopter were unmatched.

The major sighed deeply and knocked on the door. Jake opened it. He held a wireless video game controller in one hand, "Well, I see they kicked you out of the hospital huh?"

"Yeah," D.M. said softly.

"What's up?" He stepped aside to let the major in.

D.M. wandered in and stood in the middle of the living room, "Eagle told me that I have roughly seven weeks to find a way to stay on the team."

"How are you gonna do that? You aren't duty fit anymore."

"All that time I was in the hospital, I was thinking... Jake, I really wanna stay on the team, this is my life now. I'm happy here."

"So what do you want from me?"

The major swallowed hard, "I need your help."

"Can't you ask Frank? I mean you guys are bothers and all, it would make sense."

"No, Frank just doesn't think fast enough to help me with my work. I've watched you for quite a while; you pick up tasks very quickly, and that's the sort of help I need right now."

Jake stood with his arms folded, "What if I say no?"

"I'd hope that you wouldn't. I know we haven't gotten along real well so far, but I'd like to think you'd put those differences aside so you could help out your teammate."

The lieutenant studied him for a few moments. He could see the dejected look on D.M.'s face and how his posture was almost sagging in appearance. He'd never seen the major so down before. "What's in it for me?"

D.M. looked up, "Maybe the satisfaction of knowing you helped someone out."

Jake walked over to the coffee table and dropped the

controller on it, "So what's your plan?"

"Well, I got one good arm, and one bad arm. I need two good arms to stay on the team…I need to make another arm."

"What the fuck are you talking about? Make another arm? Are you crazy?"

"No. Listen, I have a degree in chemical engineering…But my minor was in robotics- specifically micro robotics…I think I can do this, I just need help."

"You're talk'in way too high tech for me."

"You don't need to know anything for now. I just need you to hold things so I can work on them…Who knows, you may even learn a thing or two," his eyes pleaded with the lieutenant.

Jake turned off the TV and approached the major, "All right, I'll help you."

D.M. smiled broadly, "Thank you!"

"You're welcome…You gonna show me the lab?"

"Sure, come on," D.M. led the way down to the fifth floor. They walked down the hallway which was lined on both sides by heavy steel doors.

"Jeez, this place looks more like a prison than a laboratory area," Jake said as he ran his hand over a door in passing. D.M. finally stopped at his lab. Taking a scrap of paper out of his pocket, he held it awkwardly while he entered the code on the cipher lock. The bolts opened with the sound of a bank vault unlocking. He pushed the door open and walked inside. Jake followed, "Damn, pretty big in here huh?"

"Yeah. I have quite a bit of equipment that's coming. I hope it all fits."

"So when do you want to start this project?"

D.M. walked over to the lab counter and leaned against it, "I was hoping tomorrow. I could use some help drawing up schematics."

"Well, I may not be an industrial artist, but I'm pretty good at graffiti, gang tags, and tattoo designs."

D.M. shook his head slowly, "I can do most of the drawings. It's gonna be difficult doing it right handed, but maybe with your help I can."

Jake wandered around the lab. He stopped at the hyperbaric

chamber, "What's this thing?"

"Ever heard of a hyperbaric chamber?"

"No."

"It allows you to increase or decrease atmospheres."

Jake studied the control panel for a few moments, "Is this the thing they use for divers to fix them when they get the bends?"

"Yes, and pilots who get altitude sickness from rapid depressurization."

"Oh, okay."

"I don't think I'll have any use for the thing, but it's too damn big and heavy to take out of here. I'll probably store stuff in it."

"So when's your gear arriving?"

"I'm hoping Eagle was able to make the arrangements to get it up here. I called the storage company and told them to expect it to be picked up. I still have another storage unit there of personal stuff, no place here to put it…If it can get here in a week, I'll be happy."

The next morning D.M. was waiting in the dining room for Eagle. She strolled in, surprised to see him. Normally she was the first one in for breakfast.

"Morning," he said softly.

"Good morning major, how are you feeling?"

"All right I guess." He went to the window and stood looking out.

She joined him, "I called and got your shipment straightened out. It should be here in six or seven days."

"Thank you." He stood silently for a few moments, "Can I ask another favor of you? I know you're probably tired of me asking, but it's important."

"What?"

"Can I borrow Jake to help me? It's gonna be a lot of hours, but he said he would help me."

She looked up and caught his gaze, "Maybe if he hangs out with you enough your maturity might just rub off on him a bit."

He smiled broadly and quickly leaned down and gave her a peck on the cheek, "I'll do my best."

"I know you will."

Late one night the weather had turned and a blizzard raged outside. D.M. lay in bed trying to get comfortable. His shoulder ached. He rubbed it but nothing would take away the constant dull ache. The surgeon had said he might experience pain and discomfort with his prosthesis. His shoulder contained nearly two pounds of titanium and stainless steel. That was the best they could come up with to rebuild the lost bones. The major growled; every minute the pain seemed to get worse. He'd taken a hot shower before bed and a mouthful of pain killers. The effect had not lasted long and soon the pain was back. He was at a complete loss for something to do. All the remedies seemed to only last a few hours and then the pain was back. And what was worse, some of the nerves in his arm had grown back together and were now sending occasional intense pain signals to his brain.

Climbing out of bed, D.M. pulled on a pair of sweat pants. He trudged next door to Eagle's room and rang the door bell. He wasn't sure there was anything she could do, but it felt better if someone could share his misery. He had suffered a few minor bouts before, but tonight's episode was shaping up to be a doozie. A few moments later the door opened and Eagle stood dressed in a robe. She could see D.M.'s face twisted in pain. "Is it your shoulder again?" She stepped aside to let him in.

"Yeah, can't stop the pain," he replied with distress in his voice.

"Come on, maybe I can help," she led him into the bedroom, "Just lay down on your stomach, I'll be right back." She disappeared into the bathroom. D.M. flopped down on the bed face first. Anything she did to help him he would be grateful for. Eagle returned several minutes later with a small medical bag and a very hot towel. She quickly draped the towel over his shoulder. D.M. let out a stifled cry as the towel hit his skin. "Gotta leave it there for a few minutes while I get the poultice prepared," she said as she opened the bag and went to work mixing ingredients. A foul odor soon filled the air.

"Yuck! What is that smell?" D.M. groaned trying to cover his head with a pillow.

"It may smell bad, but it's good medicine. My people used it for all sorts of battle wounds and infections." She removed the towel and quickly spread the dark yellow substance over his shoulder. Eagle returned to the bathroom and got the towel hot again. Carefully, she placed it back on his shoulder. D.M. still writhed with pain. She sat next to him on the bed, her legs folded Indian style. The major grabbed a pillow and placed it in her lap. He then maneuvered himself so his head rested on the pillow. She gently ran her fingers over his face and through his hair. He groaned softly, not from pain, but from the comforting caress of the woman he loved. If anyone could make him feel better, it was definitely Eagle. "How's your shoulder?" She whispered.

"A bit better, thanks."

Eagle continued to run her fingers through his hair. She noticed a few gray hairs mixed in with his raven black hair. "I guess you've been under a lot of stress lately."

"I'd say so. Why?"

"You've got a few gray hairs."

"Doesn't surprise me," he replied softly and nuzzled his head deeper into the pillow. Eagle continued to caress him until she could hear him snoring softly. With the greatest of care, she slid from under the pillow and curled up next to him on the bed. Carefully she pulled a blanket over them and turned off the light.

0530 the alarm clicked on. Eagle quickly reached over and turned it off. She checked to see if D.M. was still asleep. He needed to sleep. Breakfast and morning muster weren't that important. The major had been running on fumes for so long, he needed the down time.

Quietly, Eagle slipped out of bed and went into the bathroom. She showered and dried her hair. Tiptoeing back into the bedroom, she quickly and quietly dressed. D.M. stirred a couple of times but did not wake. She pressed her fingers to her lips and gently touched his cheek before she left.

The team gathered in the dining room. All were curious where the major was. Eagle entered and Tige called the room to attention. "At ease gentlemen," she said, taking her seat. "The major had a bad night with his shoulder, so he's getting a bit of rest."

"Is he all right?" Jake inquired.

"For now, yes," she poured herself a cup of tea. She started to think there had be some way to help the poor major. Her bag of medicinal herbs would only last so long.

CHAPTER FOURTEEN

Six weeks had gone by and D.M.'s time was running out. Eagle hardly saw him. He spent every waking (and sometimes un-waking) moment in his lab. He locked the door and kept everyone but Jake out. He needed the lieutenant as another pair of hands. When asked what was going on, Jake replied that he was sworn to secrecy and D.M. would beat the crap out of him if he said anything.

The team had just settled down to lunch. Jake sat eating his food trying to hide a smile. Eagle noticed it, "All right Jake, what's going on?"

He stiffened his lips in attempt to get rid of the incriminating grin, "Nothing." He fought to keep the grin under control.

The door opened and D.M. walked in. He was dressed in his duty grays and wore his beret cocked sharply on his head. Strapped over his left arm was a futuristic looking robotic arm. He stepped up to the table, picked up a goblet made from thick glass and crushed it in his hand like potato chips. Eagle sat in shock. He'd done it! Shit, he'd really done it! The major was back in action! She rose to her feet and saluted him. A grin worked its way onto D.M.'s face as he returned the salute. The room cheered and applauded.

"I told you I wanted to stay," he said with satisfaction.

"And stay you shall!" She reached over and pulled out his chair. D.M. sat down. It was good to be back.

***

Late that night Eagle slipped out of her room. She checked the hallway and made sure no one else was about. Darting over to D.M.'s door, she knocked lightly. The major opened the door. Eagle said nothing as she stepped inside. D.M. closed the door and stepped off the landing. She caught him by the arm and turned him, catching him in an embrace. Her lips pressed against his, her tongue finding its way into his mouth. He drew back slightly, "What's gotten in to you?"

"I'm *extremely* happy you found a way to stay."

"Yeah? How happy?" He pried, wondering what she had in mind.

"I have something for you," she began to unbutton his shirt, "But I want you to take your shirt off first."

"Does this involve taking my pants off too?"

"No, you should probably leave those on," she replied.

Darn! So much for the possibility of getting her in bed, D.M. thought as he walked to the bedroom, "Actually I'm glad you came by, I was just wondering how I was going to get undressed."

"You never gave that any thought?"

He flopped backward on the bed, "Jake's been helping me for the time, but it's late and I really didn't wanna wake him up."

She slid onto the bed next to him, "So what do you want me to do?"

D.M. unbuckled the two straps across his chest, "Okay, I need you to reach behind my shoulder and unhook the cable from the box...All you do is pinch the side tabs- kind of like a telephone."

Eagle fumbled about, finally unhooking the cable from his shoulder. D.M. sat up and wriggled out of the arm. He slipped out of his blouse and T shirt and sat looking at her. "So why did you want my shirt off?"

"Mmm, just cause," she sighed, stroking his chest. Her hand passed over one of his scars and she jerked it away, "Sorry."

"No need to be, it doesn't hurt. Just looks damn ugly."

"Such a shame it had to happen to you."

"Well, we don't exactly have an office type job," he climbed back into the arm and brought the harness over his other shoulder. Eagle reached around and reconnected the cable. She took hold of the arm, examining it.

"How did you do this?"

"I love to invent stuff...While at MIT I sold a few of my ideas and got enough money to buy all the equipment, and have plenty to live comfortably on for quite a while."

"In other words, you're filthy rich."

"I'm taking the fifth on that one," D.M. pulled the chest straps tight. "All that time in the hospital I was thinking, trying to come up with something. After the docs released me from care, I got to doing a bit of research; I stumbled on a technology that is termed Brain-Machine-Interface, or BMI. I went back down to the surgeon who did his best to put me back together and we worked on a way to fuse me with a computer. After all, I am missing nearly half of my left lung, so we filled the space with it. He spliced micro fine wires into the remains of the damaged nerves further up in my neck and to the computer that drives the robotic arm. It works pretty well, but I still have some control problems. Funny to think I have a five terabyte hard drive and ten gig of ram inside me."

"And how do you power that computer?"

"Mmm, that was the tricky part. They managed to splice a wire into my spinal cord. It picks up some of the electrical impulses from the nerves, mind you, it doesn't change or block the impulses from going to their destination, it just 'borrows' some of the electricity from them. The computer is powered by that. If need be, I can also plug into the port on my back for a recharge."

Eagle stood up, "Ready?"

"Yes...Are we going somewhere?" He asked tentatively.

She walked out, opened the door, once again making certain the coast was clear and proceeded to the elevator, D.M. behind her, clueless as to what she was doing. They took the elevator down to the training floor. The doors opened to darkness. Eagle found the light switch. The lights flickered on. D.M. could see something sitting on one of the tables. Something wrapped in a white sheet. Eagle went to the table, D.M. joined her, "So is this the surprise?"

She gently picked up the object and began to unwrap its shroud. The pommel of a sword became visible, then the handle and hilt. She finished unwrapping it and presented it to him. "This sword is a warrior's sword. It bears the name Fryktløs; Norwegian for Fearless...It has been in my family for ten generations...Only the strongest of men can wield this sword...I know you're strong enough to bring honor to its name once again."

D.M. looked at the weapon. It was beautiful in a simplistic way. The pommel was typically Viking half-moon in design with three conical spikes. The handle, which was designed for two handed grip was plain leather wrapped with steel wire for grip, and the hilt's cross piece swept forward like two daggers. At the union of blade and hilt was a small enameled boss of a Viking long ship against a dark orange background. The blade was nearly three feet long, tapering to a point; and it was razor sharp.

"Eagle...This is...beautiful," he was at a loss for words. She smiled and motioned for him to assume a fighting stance. He struck a particularly bold pose and held it for her. "So is this why you wanted my shirt off? To gawk?"

Eagle smiled and leaned against the table, "No, to drool!" They laughed.

"Thank you," he stepped over and kissed her lightly, "I promise no dishonor will come to this sword."

“Fryktløs is a very special sword. You don’t find Viking swords designed for two handed grip, this is probably one of a handful ever made. Most museums would give their eye teeth for a piece in such fine shape.”

“Did your father give it to you?”

“Yes. Contrary to popular belief, my people weren’t always reindeer herders. In fact the race split, some took to the seas and became Vikings and the others continued on with the tradition of herding.”

“You certainly don’t have the reindeer herder mentality.”

“Naw, I’m fiercely proud of my Viking heritage.”

“Quite obvious in the way you fight. Most women wouldn’t take the beating you do and come back for more.”

“I may not technically be a warrior but I have the mindset for it.”

“There’s no doubt in my mind, you’re a warrior, female or not.” He swung the sword slowly trying to get the feel for it. The blade was far heavier than he had ever used.

"Thanks, I've tried all my life to live up to that," she said softly.

"And if you can make the rest of us into warriors, we'll be unbeatable."

Eagle sat in the dining room waiting for the team to come in for lunch. Tige had taken them out into the field for some training exercises. The snow had melted somewhat and the valley was starting to show some signs of spring. It had rained for nearly three days straight, everything was muddy.

The door opened and they walked in, their uniforms covered with dirt and mud. Eagle turned and looked at them, "Please don't tell me you were all out mud wrestling?"

"No, just doing field work and that's never a clean job," Tige replied as he sat down in his chair. D.M. took his place next to Eagle. She looked over and noticed what appeared to be blood on his blouse.

"Major?"

"Humm?"

"Is that blood on your blouse?"

"Yes. One of the downfalls of being tall. We were making a hasty retreat on an exercise and I was bringing up the rear. They're all shorter, so they didn't duck under the tree branch. I, however, missed seeing it and it caught me right on the top of the head."

"Are you all right?"

"Yeah, fine. Sam cleaned me up and said no stitches required."

"I guess you should watch where you're going a bit more carefully."

Frank reached out to take a drink of water, crumbs of dirt fell off his blouse onto the table, "You know, we should rename these things. They aren't 'Duty Grays' more like 'Dirty Grays' is appropriate."

Several of the team laughed and agreed with Frank. They ate lunch and discussed the afternoon's training. It was back out into the forest for more field training. Tige was making sure they could move comfortably through rough terrain quickly and quietly. He had set up firing points along the way where they would engage targets and then continue on either advancing or retreating. Despite his somewhat rough start with the team, the captain proved to be a valuable teacher in field craft. His skills in tracking, concealment, sniping, counter sniping, and land navigation were well exploited in order to make the team as effective as possible.

It was a particularly mild mid March afternoon and the men decided to play a game of football. The weather had warmed up and there were only a few patches of snow left around the building. They talked D.M. into playing, even though he resisted at first stating he was a scientist, not a jock. He ended up on the team with Jake and Frank. Jake wanted to be the quarterback. D.M. agreed, not quite ready to trust the power of his robotic arm. He'd been experiencing difficulty with control, usually in the case of grabbing things too hard and squashing them.

Sam threw a long pass to Max. D.M. was right there to tackle him. Max caught the ball, his foot slipping into a rabbit hole. D.M. hit him and drove him to the ground. The sickening sound of breaking bone filled the air; Max screamed in pain. The major quickly got up to see what happened. He saw Max's leg in the hole and immediately started to dig him out. Max continued to scream in pain. The others hurried over and helped dig, Jake ran for help. "Max, I'm so sorry, I didn't see you fall in the hole," D.M. apologized.

"It's okay, it all happened so quick," he said between clenched teeth.

They dug frantically, finally freeing him. A stretcher was brought and Max was loaded on to it. D.M. went upstairs to notify Eagle.

Eagle sat in her office on the phone to Ft. Bragg. She was conversing with the commander of the Joint Special Operations Command. "Sir, I don't see why you're tasking us with this mission. Wouldn't SEAL team six be a better option?"

"Colonel, I do not have time to paint a pretty picture for you. I got two Airborne teams in Croatia; all of the SEALs are tied up with other situations. I got no one left but you," the reply came from the other end of the line.

D.M. knocked on the door and opened it. He crept inside and stood in front of her desk. Eagle looked up and saw the worried expression on his face, "Sir, can you hold for just a second?" She punched the hold button and gave him her attention, "Okay, talk quick, what is it?"

"We were playing football... and Max stepped in a rabbit hole... I didn't see it and tackled him. His leg's broke pretty bad."

"Oh, just great," she took the general off hold, "Yes sir," she replied curtly, "Sir, the mission parameters require a full team, I am now currently short one person."

"I will talk to Westland and see if he can send a suitable replacement," the general answered.

"Thank you sir...We will be at the target in three days," she hung up the phone, "Looks like we got another job."

"Oh? What now? We're just getting healed up from the last one."

"Hostage situation in Columbia," she replied, putting some papers in the drawer, "We need to get everyone ready to go."

"Right, I'll see to it...So we're gonna get a temporary replacement for Max?"

"Supposedly."

An Army Black Hawk helicopter touched down on the hanger deck late that next afternoon. The door opened and large man dressed in Army ACUs got out. He carried an olive green duffel bag over his shoulder. D.M. stood waiting to greet him. The man stopped in front of the major, dropped his bag and saluted, "Sergeant First Class Bruce von Teufel," he stated gruffly. D.M. returned the salute. He quickly looked the man over. The sergeant stood nearly a head taller than the major, so D.M. was forced to look up to address the new troop. Muscle appeared to bulge from every part of his uniform, stretching the fabric taut, giving the impression that he might just explode at any minute. His short blond hair and cold blue eyes completed the picture of a man who could kill without remorse.

"Please, follow me," the major motioned as he headed for the hanger.

Eagle and the rest of the team were in the briefing room. She had received the information about the mission and was preparing to brief them when D.M. came in with Bruce. Everything came to a halt as they sat staring at the new arrival. How could there be anyone bigger than D.M.? Jake thought as he sized up the two.

"Everyone, this is Sergeant Bruce von Teufel, he's Max's temporary replacement," the major stated as he found his seat.

"Welcome sergeant, hopefully we will only need your services on this one outing, then you can be returned to your unit," Eagle said, collecting her papers.

"Hey sergeant, what's your call sign?" Frank asked.

"Razor," Bruce replied with little emotion as he sat down.

Eagle put a map up on the board for them to study, "All right, we have a situation in Columbia with ten American hostages. They are being held in a fortified casa not far from the coast. Miguel de Santis, a known drug lord is holding them. He wants a ransom of twenty billion dollars..."

"Uncle Sam's not gonna pay that, why don't they just forget the hostages?" Jake asked.

"Because one of the hostages is the U.S. Ambassador."

Sam spoke up, "Why was he there if it's a known drug house?"

"He was grabbed in an ambush outside Bogota. They took him and several other influential Americans back to his casa and now have them for ransom."

"Oh, duh, guess I'm not thinking this through," Sam replied, smacking his forehead.

Eagle put a map up on the computer screen, "I was looking at the lay of the land, and I think it would be prudent if we have some air support...Jake, I want you and D.M. to bring a Badger down."

"Ah, cool, real combat!" Jake exclaimed.

D.M. studied the map, "And are you going to be Jake's

gunner?"

"You're far better at it than me. I'll be on the ground."

The major stood, "No, no way, no way in hell! You're not supposed to be in direct combat and you know that."

"Yeah, well, I'm in charge of the team, and we need the most qualified people to do the jobs they're best at. You and Jake are the best in the Badger. I think I can handle one mission on the ground."

"I strongly object," he said, pacing around the room.

"Object all you want," she snapped.

"What happens if you get wounded or worse-killed?"

"Then you get a promotion I guess."

D.M. stopped his pacing and faced her, "I don't give a damn about any promotion. You're going against the regulations."

Eagle knew she had to put an end to the discussion. It was obvious D.M. was upset by her decision, but she was ultimately in charge, and her word was the final say. Yes, she was going against the regulations, but her main objective was to complete the mission. And if it meant that she had to put herself in danger to make sure the job was done, than it was her choice. "Major, I understand your concern but I can't stay hiding in the wings all the time. This mission is going to take all of us to complete."

D.M. growled and took a swing at the air. He was furious that she wasn't listening to him. How could he get it through her head that this wasn't just a training exercise? He continued to pace the room, "I guess I've been overruled on this...Can you do me one favor at least?"

"What?"

"Stick with Tige. I think he's the best person to try and keep you safe."

Eagle looked over at Tige, he looked up at D.M., "Yeah, that would be the best bet...I tend to stay back and engage from a distance. Not too far back, but far enough back to be in the shadows."

"Is that agreeable with you?" D.M. said, resting his hands on the back of her chair. He was still angry with her, but he clearly was not going to win the argument.

"Yes," she replied, knowing he was right, but also knowing

other lives were at stake.

They continued with their planning until late at night. As the team filed out of the briefing room, D.M. stayed behind to talk to Eagle. "You know, I'm still pretty upset with you," he said, resuming his pacing.

"So get over it. We have a job to do, and I'm doing my best to make sure the right people perform their parts."

He stopped in front of her, putting his hands on her arms, "I just don't want you to get hurt," he replied softly.

Eagle managed a weak smile, "I'm a big girl, I can take care of myself. I did a lot of training with the SEALs, they were very tough on me; especially because I was an officer, not to mention a woman...No, I would have never survived their whole school, but what I did go through taught me to be tough and not to be afraid."

"Are you sure that's not the Viking warrior coming out in you? I mean you've never tasted battle for real, is this your way of getting it?"

"I'm not particularly excited about the idea. Just understand that we need all the guns out there we can. You're the best at engaging targets from the air, that's why I need you up there with Jake...I promise I'll stay close to Tige and I won't do anything stupid. I want all of us to come back from this mission with as few injuries as possible." They left the briefing room and walked down the hall toward their rooms. Tige stood near Eagle's door. She approached him, "Yes captain?"

Tige leaned over and whispered, "We need to talk."

D.M. watched as they disappeared into her room. He wondered what was going on. He wasn't normally the jealous type, but something just didn't seem right with the situation. It wasn't like Tige to be very secretive when it had to do with a mission. Finally he decided they weren't coming back out so he went in his room.

"All right captain, what did you need to talk to me about?" Eagle said, sitting down on her sofa.

"How long do we have before we go out on this mission?"

"Not quite two days."

He sat down in a chair adjacent to her, "I know you have experience in simulated battles, but have you ever killed anyone?"

"No."

"Do you think you could kill if you had to?" His line of questioning was becoming more direct.

"I would hope the training I've had would kick in and I'd be able to do it."

"Wrong answer!" He barked.

"So just what do you think I can do about it? I've never had an opportunity to be in real battle. And you never know if you can do it until you're thrust into that situation."

"Not completely true…I credit some of my abilities to all the time my grandfather and I went hunting. If you can learn to take the life of an animal, then you are one step closer to being able to kill a human. Sometimes it can make it a bit easier."

"Easier? How so?"

"Because we tend to view animals as helpless creatures. When confronted by another human with the same ability to kill or maim, the decision is easier. It's either you or him. You have to decide who gets the privilege of walking away from the fight."

"And just where are you going with this whole dissertation?"

Tige stood and walked around the room, "I need to teach you to kill."

"But I all ready know how to kill."

"Yes, but have you ever killed anything?"

"Besides spiders that were crawling in my bath tub? No."

"All right, that settles it then. Meet me tomorrow morning at 0530. Be dressed in some sort of woodland camouflage." He went to the door and opened it, "If you're gonna survive on this mission, you have to be ready."

At precisely 0530 the next morning, Eagle knocked on Tige's door. He opened it, dressed in a variation of woodland camouflage and holding his sniper rifle, "Ah, good, you're ready. Let's go down to the range and get you a weapon.

"You're serious about this aren't you?"

"Dead serious." He closed the door and led the way to the

elevator. They went down to the seventh floor and Tige found a suitable rifle for Eagle to use. "Okay, that's a two-seventy Winchester magnum. It will easily drop a deer."

"Is that where you're taking me? To hunt a deer?"

"Yes. If you can kill a deer and get past the effects of killing, I can only hope that will help you on the mission."

"And what happens if I don't come home with a deer?"

"We'll stay out there until you do. There's no getting out of this. I'm doing it for your own good and safety."

D.M. stood at the window. The previous night a small snow storm had blown through leaving the valley coated in a couple of inches of new snow. It was 0610 and Eagle had not arrived for breakfast. It wasn't like her to be late. More often than not, she was early so she could have her first cup of tea and watch the news in peace and quiet. The sun was just coming up and he spotted movement in the valley below. "What the hell?" He said, leaning closer to the glass.

"What's up maj?" Jake asked.

"That's Tige and Eagle. They're heading out into the forest. It looks like they have rifles."

Bruce stood and went to the window, "I bet I know what he's doing."

D.M. turned and looked at him, "What?"

"He's doing what our fathers and grandfathers should have done with us; he's taking her out and teaching her to kill."

"You think so?"

"I'd bet you fifty bucks on it. Eagle has never killed before, so Tige is trying to initiate her into the brotherhood."

"That seems a bit on the morbid side," Sam said as he stirred some cream into his coffee.

"Morbid or not, she has to face death by her own hands."

Tige crept up to the edge of a small meadow. He knew from previous outings in the forest exactly where the deer would be. It was the survival hunter part of him that always kept an eye on the local wildlife, just in case some day he needed to hunt for food, he would know where to find it. Several deer were grazing. He motioned to Eagle to come up next to him. She carefully made her way to his side and crouched down. "This is a nice herd of young ones; mostly bucks. I want you to pick out one."

She scanned the group of nine young deer and pointed, "How about that one on the edge of the herd?" She whispered. It was a larger buck with two points on his antlers.

Tige nodded, "Good choice. That's about a three year old. Now you have to do the deed."

Eagle flipped up the covers on the scope. Nervously she shouldered the rifle. Her hands were shaking and her stomach churned. She was glad she hadn't eaten breakfast. Settling down, she held the rifle up, the scope to her eye. Tige wasn't going to let her go home until she shot a deer. Even with all her training, she was finding it very difficult.

"Come on, you'd better take the shot before they head off and bed down for the day."

"I'm trying," she whispered.

Tige flipped the covers up on his scope and shouldered his rifle, "Don't try, do!"

Eagle took several breaths. It was hard to take in a breath; it felt like her throat was being choked off. Wrapping her finger around the trigger, she prepared to take the shot.

"Either aim for the head, or just behind the elbow. You wanna make as quick of a kill as possible."

"Right," her voice trembled. Getting the buck in her sights, she fought to take one slow breath. Her hands were shaking worse and the image in her scope was now jiggling around.

"Take the shot," Tige urged.

Eagle let out a low growl. She had to take the shot. All of her Viking heritage and the training she'd received from the military just seemed to go out the window. Tige was right; it wasn't as easy as it looked.

"Eagle, take the shot," he said more firmly. He knew he was going to have to push her harder.

"Okay, okay."

"Do it."

As quick as she could, Eagle took a breath and fought to hold still. The buck filled her scope. She closed her eyes for an instant and pulled the trigger. A loud report rang through the valley as the round went down range. It struck the deer just behind the shoulder and dropped it. The rest of the herd darted off into the safety of the trees.

"Good! You did it!"

"Oh God, I did," she said, feeling her stomach churn harder. Tige flipped his scope covers down and quickly headed out to the meadow. The deer lay in the ankle high grass. Eagle joined him a few moments later.

"How do you feel?" He said, grabbing the front legs of the deer and dragging it toward a large tree.

"Quite ill right now."

"That's to be expected." He dropped his backpack on the ground and dug around in it until he produced a coil of thick cord. Letting out a length of cord, he tossed the rest over a stout tree limb and pulled it down. Grabbing the rear legs of the deer, he tied the legs together. "Here, give me some help." He handed Eagle the loose end of the rope, "Pull please while I get this thing up…Need to get the neck opened and bled out."

"Oh, uh, okay," she pulled on the rope while Tige lifted the deer.

"Now, take one wrap around the tree. Once the tension is off, I'll get the rope from you and tie it off." She did as she was told and soon the deer was hanging upside down from the tree. Tige pulled out a knife and quickly slit the animal's throat. Blood drained to the ground leaving a large red stain in the fresh snow. He then took the knife and carefully made a cut the whole length of the abdomen. Steam curled out of the animal's still warm body. Eagle watched, partly fascinated, and partly revolted for what she'd done. Tige looked over at her, "All right?"

"No, not really." She went behind a large tree. Tige could hear her retching. It was obvious that killing the deer had hit a soft spot in her. All part of the job, Tige thought as he went back to work on the deer. A few minutes later Eagle appeared.

"All right now?"

"Better I guess." She rubbed her face, "Why does killing do

that to you?"

"What? Make you have a liquid laugh?"

"Yeah, but there is nothing funny about it."

He gently worked on the abdominal cavity of the deer, taking great care not to nick any of the organs or intestines, "Your mind is not programmed to kill. Everything we are taught from the beginning is 'thou shalt not kill.' Society's been brainwashed to see death as taboo. In truth, it's not. It's just part of the circle of life. And, well, sometimes you gotta kill. If you were lost in the forest and needed food, you would kill to survive. If you lived back in the 1800's; you'd be a farm wife expected to go out and dispatch a chicken and prepare it for supper. But since you are a commander of a Special Forces team, you may be called upon to take the life of another human in order to protect yourself or your team."

"I never imagined it would be so hard. Spiders in the bathtub are nothing compared to this."

The captain laughed, "I never said it was easy…In truth, killing a human is much harder than what you just did. But this was the only way I could vaguely prepare you for what you're going to experience." He finished dressing out the deer, "Hey, can you look around and see if you can find a stout tree branch big enough we can sling this thing on?"

"Yeah, sure."

"Good, thanks. We'll take this back, give it to the chef and we'll all dine on venison tonight."

It was lunchtime when Eagle and Tige returned to the building. They carried the deer slung on a tree branch into the dining room. The rest of the team stood and cheered as they entered. Eagle wondered how they'd figured out what she'd done. She felt a stronger connection with them now. No, she wasn't proven in battle, but she had taken an important first step.

"I see you brought dinner for us," D.M. said as he patted her on the shoulder.

"Umm, yeah," she said softly.

"Hey major, I guess that means you owe me fifty bucks," Bruce teased.

D.M. smiled, "I guess not, I never took the bet."

"Slam!" Jake exclaimed. The others laughed.

CHAPTER FIFTEEN

A C-130 cargo plane arrived at the base to pick up the team. Eagle had Jake and D.M. get the Badger loaded in the back. They made the journey to Panama and unloaded. An Army Chinook helicopter waited to fly the rest of the team down to Columbia and deposit them on the beach. D.M. and Jake would wait on the beach until the team had reached the target. Despite being small in comparison to other attack helicopters; the Badger had a range of over four hundred miles when contoured external fuel tanks were added. Jake knew it was going to be a stretch. He'd removed any unnecessary equipment from the storage compartments and made sure they had enough ammunition for the mission. It was going to be a true test of the helicopter's abilities.

Jake lay on the beach stretched out enjoying the sun. D.M. sat next to him checking over the plan of attack. They had flown down earlier to secure the LZ for the rest of the team. "So, you think we can pull this off?" Jake said as he adjusted his hat further down over his eyes to keep the sun out.

"Well, we did it last time; I can't see any reason why we can't this time."

"At least we won't be in the heat of things like before...I gotta admit I was scared when all that went down."

"Me too," D.M. replied as he plotted out distances and charted their course for the assault.

"And you got the worst of it."

The radio in the helicopter crackled. The major got up and reached inside the cockpit, retrieving a set of headphones. "This is

Lone Wolf, go ahead."

"Lone Wolf, White Feather. We have a job for you two."

"Roger, and what might that be?"

"I have an intel report that says there are is a rebel faction in the area that poses a threat to our mission. They are moving in the direction of our target. There is a bridge about a mile and a half away, it crosses the river, if you can get to the bridge before them and destroy it, you might be able to buy us some time."

"You want us two to do it?" D.M. replied, turning toward Jake, "Hey, did you put the charges and caps in the storage compartment?"

"Eagle said to never leave home without them," he smiled and snuggled deeper into the warm sand.

"When are you gonna arrive with the rest of the team?" D.M. asked.

"We will be along just about dusk. White Feather out."

The major returned the headset to the seat and sat back down. He traced the location to the target and their present location. A road twisted along the route, one area definitely cutting across a river. "Hey Jake? Can I possibly tear you away from sun bathing to help me get the gear together and set a perimeter around the chopper?"

"Mmm, uh huh," he moaned lazily and got up.

After setting a perimeter around the helicopter, so any unwanted visitors would have a surprise, D.M. and Jake collected their equipment and headed into the forest. They made their way through the thick brush, all the while keeping a close watch for rebels. When the bridge was in sight, they found a good place to hide up river and observe for a little while.

"Where do we wanna put the charges?" Jake asked as he unloaded his pack.

"Definitely the two concrete pillars in the middle, they look pretty sturdy," the major replied as he looked through binoculars.

"Mmm, great, gotta get wet."

"Sorry my friend. At least the river is pretty slow moving; we shouldn't have too much trouble getting out there. If we do it right, we can just float down river with the current when we're done."

They waited until dusk and made their move. D.M. crept to the water's edge. Quietly, he waded out until he was almost chest deep. Jake stepped out of the brush and put one foot in the water. He was not a lover of water, especially any that was cold. Luck was on his side as he felt the water seep into his boot, not so cold after all. He waded out and joined D.M. They drifted down and stopped under the bridge. Just as they had started to set the charges, the sound of several vehicles reached their ears.

"Shit, we can't let them get across the bridge!" Jake hissed as he squashed a ball of plastic explosive against the concrete pillar.

One truck came out onto the bridge. Just as it appeared that they would not be able to destroy the bridge in time, a loud bang was heard and the truck stopped. Other vehicles came onto the bridge and stopped.

"Lead vehicle must have blown a tire," D.M. whispered as he wired a ball of explosive. They finished with the first pillar and quietly swam to the next one. As fast as they could, they wired the second one and allowed the current to take them down stream under the cover of darkness. The men above had taken a long time to change the tire, evidently they had run into trouble with the jack and their loud cursing echoed through the forest.

D.M. swam to the shore, but did not stand up. He allowed the water to act as his cover. Reaching in his pocket he removed the radio detonator. Jake slid up next to him. "Here, you can't say that I don't let you have any fun," the major whispered as he offered the detonator to Jake.

"Cool, thanks," he pulled the antenna up and turned it on, "One, two, three!" He pushed the button and the bridge pillars became a ball of flame. They watched as the bridge crashed into the water, men screaming and vehicles twisting and smashing into the water. The rest of the convoy, who still remained on land, opened fire in every direction. D.M. and Jake watched as the men shot at everything, knowing that they were too far down stream to be noticed, and well hidden.

Within a few minutes the shooting stopped and the rebels

became occupied with trying to figure out how to cross the river. D.M. tapped Jake and motioned him to head back to the beach. They crawled from the water and quickly disappeared into the trees. Returning to the beach, they found the rest of the team had arrived. D.M. reported in to Eagle, "Bridge is down. We caught the convoy just as they were beginning to cross."

"Good work major, I knew you guys could do it."

Jake came up to D.M. and poked him, "Uh D.M., got a little problem," he whispered.

"Nice job lieutenant," Eagle praised, knowing that Jake seemed to work better if he received due credit.

"Yeah, thanks," Jake replied hastily as he tried to tug on the major.

"What?" D.M. growled.

"Come with me."

D.M. followed Jake to an area of trees just off the beach, "Now what was so important?"

Jake pulled up his shirt sleeve, a black leech clung to his forearm, "We better check each other over."

"Oh man, this sucks," he groaned as he began to unbutton his cuff.

"No, *they* suck!" The lieutenant said as he yanked the leech off his arm, dropped it to the ground and stepped on it.

Eagle checked her watch, 1900. The casa was nearly four miles away through a thick tangle of jungle. She wanted to get the team there so they would have time to rest for a little while. "All right everyone, equipment check in five mike."

D.M. climbed into the front cockpit and started his preflight routine. Jake appeared out of nowhere, scrambled into the back seat and began his preflight as well, "So you think we're gonna run into heavy resistance?"

"Don't know, but we're not gonna have much time to assess the situation when we get there," D.M. replied in a distracted tone. He was having trouble getting the weapons system to come on line, "Hey, Jake, you know why this thing won't let the weapons panel come up?"

"Try a partial reboot of the computer. I think it's a software glitch, I'll have a look at it when we get back."

D.M. was busy rebooting the computer when Eagle's face appeared in the canopy door, "Major, we're moving out, we'll make contact again when we're about half a mile from target."

"Okay, sounds good to me, holler if you need us early," he replied poking at the keyboard, not paying much attention to her.

"Roger that, good hunting," she climbed down, disappearing into darkness.

"You too," he called softly. D.M. had serious reservations about letting her be on the ground for the attack. In a way, Eagle was right when she said that Special Forces wasn't considered woman's work. This was a man's job to go out and kill or be killed. He had argued with her about going with Jake and being his gunner, but she refused, saying that he needed to work with his teammate. The major pulled Tige aside and pleaded for him to make sure she stayed as safe as possible. The captain agreed, saying that he would do his best to protect her.

D.M. checked his watch. It was nearly 2200. They should have been there by now, he thought as he reached back and thumped the heads up display to wake the lieutenant. Jake groaned, "Is it time to go?"

"I think we should get things started up, perhaps we can get over there and take a little peek."

"You forget this is a helicopter, it makes noise, even in stealth mode."

D.M. tossed the map back to Jake, "Have a look to the east, see those mountains? They're about three clicks off. If we hide behind one of them, we can pop up and survey the place from a safe, quiet distance. When Eagle calls for us, we will be right there."

"Sounds good to me, you know I hate to wait," Jake said as he put on his helmet and closed his canopy, "Let's rock and roll."

Eagle crouched low behind a tree. The rest of the group had spread out to a distance just far enough to maintain visual contact with one another. A full moon in a cloudless sky made the use of night vision goggles unnecessary. The area around the casa was lit fairly well, something she wished were dark and quiet. Guards moved about carrying sub machine guns slung over their shoulders. This was definitely not a soft target. Things were going to get bloody and noisy. Tige inched over to her. "Psssssssst," he hissed softly. Eagle turned to see him about three feet away, he had not made a sound in his approach, his stalking skill as a sniper was unquestionable.

"What?" She whispered.

"I don't think we can follow our original plan of attack. Intel and the satellite photos didn't include all these guys."

"No, what do you think?"

Tige uncapped his rifle scope and held it to his eye. He surveyed the area for a better place to enter. "It looks pretty dark to the east side; I don't see any movement or lights."

"What about the west? Can we take it from two sides?"

"I wouldn't recommend it; they got a lot of fire power over there. If the Badger can draw their fire and keep them distracted, we might be able to use the east as an exit route." He offered the scope to Eagle who checked out the area.

"I think you're right, we'll go with that." She keyed her microphone and passed the plan along to the others. Frank and Bruce moved out to the east. Sam would make his way to the north and provide cover fire for the hostages when they came out, and also help get them to safety. Eagle and Tige would hold their position and draw as much of the fire as possible with D.M. and Jake.

Frank crept up to a door. All was dark and quiet around them; the guards were on the other side of the house. Why they chose to guard only one side of the casa was questionable, Frank was not in the mood to question. He removed a small penlight from his vest pocket and turned it on. Only a very small circle of dim light shone from it. He carefully traced it around the door checking for alarm wires. There was no way to tell if there were wires hidden behind the door frame, but at least on first inspection there was nothing. Bruce removed his lock pick and carefully worked on the door. Within a few seconds the door popped open. Frank kept a careful watch behind for any threats. He looked over his shoulder for Bruce, but found he had disappeared into the darkness.

"Are you coming?" The sergeant's voice called out in a hoarse whisper. Frank quickly slipped inside.

Westland sat in the car watching a satellite image of the drug lord's house on his laptop. The images appeared in bright colors from the thermal scanning of the satellite. Small, bright figures could be seen moving around the perimeter of the house as well as inside. "Did you brief Sergeant von Teufel of his mission?"

"Yes sir, I only had the opportunity to speak with him for a few minutes, but I made it very clear what we wanted," Lieutenant Farlow replied, taking a sip of coffee, "You know sir, we could have ended the whole thing by alerting de Santis of their attack."

Westland yawned, "Yes, I'm well aware of that, I don't exactly have any love for de Santis, he screwed me on an arms deal about two years ago, I think this qualifies as payback."

"Have you given any thought to closing the deal with Kemal?"

"I still have a couple of component plans to get hold of, perhaps in the next few months. Good technology takes time to acquire."

"Well, if there is anything I can do sir…"

"You can shut up and watch this."

Farlow slumped into his seat, "Yes sir."

The figures on the screen were moving quicker now, the barrels of their rifles glowing with heat. A helicopter hovered over firing at the men in front of the house its exhaust sending red blurs of vapor across the screen. It was obvious the team had been discovered and were trying to fight their way out of the situation. Westland chuckled as he watched them.

Tige lined up targets in his scope as quickly as he could. One by one he dropped them. He glanced over at Eagle. She was in the right position, but no bullets were coming from her rifle. "Come on, fight you bloody Viking!"

Eagle put her eye down to her sights. She was feeling again

like she did when she killed the deer. Her hands were shaking and it was hard to breathe. Deep inside she was trying to convince herself that she could so this. She had killed the deer; now she had to kill a human. Tige was right, it wasn't easy. Bullets ricocheted off the tree next to her, splattering her with bark and splinters. It was up to her to now decide who was going to walk away from the battle, and it needed to be her.

Taking aim, she found a target. More bullets impacted around her. Taking in a breath, she slowly let it out. Her finger wrapped around the trigger and she fought to concentrate. Her eyes focused and she let out a primal growl. Squeezing the trigger, the round went off. Her target lurched wildly to one side and fell. She was cherry no more.

"Good job!" Tige hollered, "Keep going!"

Eagle felt the sickness in her stomach. She didn't have time to acknowledge the horrible feeling; more rounds were impacting around her. Collecting her wits, she commenced firing, dropping several more targets. Tige occasionally glanced over to make sure she was okay. He was proud of her; she'd faced the elephant and had won. Taking a human life was never easy, but she'd proven she could do it. Eagle was now a sister in a brotherhood of warriors. She was among the men who could pull the trigger and send another human to their death.

"Hey, how about some support over here?" Sam hollered into the headset as he tried frantically to clear a jam in his rifle.

"We're on it," Jake replied, "I'm gonna swing us over to the left, Sam could use a little help."

Jake maneuvered over toward Sam's position. Bullets ricocheted off the helicopter making it hard to see. Frank's voice came over the radio, "White Feather, this is Tater; we have the hostages and are moving out."

"Roger Tater, Lone Wolf and Kingpin are in the area to provide cover fire."

Frank stood at the door and peered out. He could see the

flash from Sam's rifle in the bush about thirty yards away. The ground in between them was gradually sloping downhill and wide open. Not the perfect place to try and get ten hostages to safety from. Simply put, it was a kill zone. He turned and craned his neck above the hostages to look at Bruce, "Hey, how are we gonna do this?"

"Someone needs to go out first and lay down fire, try to get as many of them as possible, and cover the hostages," Bruce replied.

Frank checked his magazine on his rifle, making sure it was a fresh one. He closed his eyes for a brief moment, said a quick prayer, and opened the door. "White Feather, Tater, we are moving, repeat, we are moving," he darted out the door, crouching lowly. The darkness nearly concealed his presence; no bullets came his way, "Razor, move 'em out, quick!"

"Roger, we are moving," Bruce shoved at one of the hostages, "Move out now!" The hostages scurried out the door like scared rabbits. They stumbled and pushed one another in the frantic attempt to get to safety. As the last hostage cleared the door, several of the guards noticed them. They turned to open fire. Frank dropped one immediately. The others opened fire, taking cover behind a brick wall.

"Lone Wolf, Tater, I need help, I'm getting a lot of heat over here."

"I see them, will send a grenade their way," D.M. replied as he took aim, "Say bye, bye!" He pushed the trigger and sent a grenade just over the top of the wall.

Frank turned part way to see if Bruce had followed the hostages out. Out of the darkness a muzzle flash blinked and Frank felt a crushing pain rip through his body. He fell heavily to the ground and everything went black.

"NOOOOOO!!!" D.M. cried as he smashed his fist into the canopy. He had seen the spray of blood come from his brother's body and watched him fall. The major was helpless; he could do nothing but watch. His anger boiled and he stopped firing.

"D.M.! Chill out man, there's nothing you can do. You need to concentrate on helping them out down there," Jake spoke firmly, trying to get D.M. to come to his senses, "Ground Zero, Tater is down, repeat, Tater is down. Can you get to him?"

"Huh? What?" Sam had been too busy in his own firefight to notice Frank was down. "Oh God! Give me some cover, I'll get him." He broke from the brush and ran to Frank. He dropped to the ground next to him. In the dim light he could see blood on the back of his uniform. Sam grabbed Frank's shoulder and rolled him over. Blood covered the front of his uniform, a chest wound, something not simple to take care of. He reached out and put his fingers on the side of Frank's neck, he still had a pulse.

Quickly, Sam hefted Frank over his shoulder. It was not going to be easy, Frank weighed nearly two-forty, and Sam barely tipped the scales at one-eighty, plus he had all his ammunition and medical supplies, "Lone Wolf, I'm moving," Sam said as he clenched his teeth under Frank's great weight. He moved as quickly as he could. Just as he was reaching the cover of the brush, a bullet found its way into his thigh and he collapsed to the ground, Frank falling heavily on top of him. "Ahhhh, help!" He cried, trying to get Frank off him. His leg pounded and he fought to get a bandage on it.

"Ground Zero, what happened?" Jake called.

"I'm hit, I'm hit."

"Do you need assistance?"

"Affirmative. I don't think I can manage Frank by myself."

Tige quickly picked his way through the brush and found them. He grabbed Frank and shifted him into a Fireman's carry. Sam tied off the bandage and struggled to his feet. "Hold onto me if you need to," Tige said as he moved off in the direction of the pickup area. They fought their way through the thick brush, Tige using only his instinct to get them to safety. The rest of the team had taken various other routes and converged on the open meadow Eagle had designated the LZ. They waited eagerly for Tige and Sam to arrive. D.M. climbed out of the helicopter and stood scanning the blackness. "Jake, I want you to fly Frank out, you know that chopper, you can get him there safe and quick," The major's voice trembled slightly.

"Right, I won't let you down," he replied as he climbed back into the rear cockpit. Strapping himself in, he readied the chopper for takeoff.

Several hundred yards off in the brush they could hear

something moving. "Wombat, this is White Feather, is that you making all that noise?"

Tige's voice came ragged and stressed, "Yeah it's us."

Eagle motioned to D.M. and Bruce, "Go help them." The men darted off towards the noise. A few minutes later, D.M. appeared carrying Frank. He was jogging as quickly as he could. He stopped in front of Eagle, who was waiting with a medical bag. She added more dressings to the ones Sam had applied somewhere during their journey. Blood oozed from Frank's lifeless body. His breathing was shallow and his face pale.

Bruce returned with Tige and Sam. D.M. climbed up to the front cockpit and teetered on the canopy rail. "Bruce, you're gonna have to get Frank up to me, you're the only one strong enough," The major waved his arm at him to hurry. Bruce picked Frank up and lifted him. D.M. took hold and guided Frank's legs inside, nearly losing his balance in the process. He wrestled, trying to get Frank in the seat. Once he was finally situated, he hopped down and shut the canopy. He banged on Jake's canopy, giving him the thumbs up. Jake returned the sign and started the rotors. The rest of the team retreated to safety as he lifted off. They would take the hostages to a secondary LZ to meet an awaiting Chinook helicopter.

CHAPTER SIXTEEN

This was becoming a ritual that Eagle would have been happy to do away with. She sat in the waiting room of the hospital, impatient for news about Frank and Sam. D.M. sat next to her, his head bowed in quiet contemplation. The rest of the team had taken over the remainder of the waiting room and were sprawled out on the couches. Jake lay on his back, his head propped up on his gear bag. His fingers were laced, resting on his chest. He stared at the ceiling in thought, "You know, this really stinks... We shouldn't be getting shot up like this...We need to get some body armor or something."

Tige lifted his head and looked toward Jake, "If we wore enough Kevlar to keep us from getting really shot up, we would add about ninety to a hundred pounds on top of the stuff we all ready have. We would be so slow and awkward; they would pick us off like sitting ducks. Speed and maneuverability is the key to survival. We don't wear any armor for just that fact."

"There's got to be something we can do," Jake pondered. D.M. looked up at Jake for a moment, yes, there had to be a way, and the answer rested at his fingertips. Now it was time to dust off the books and recipes and see if he could finally do it.

Hours passed and finally one of the surgeons emerged from the OR. The team perked up at his arrival. Eagle stood and greeted him, "How are they?"

"The one with the gunshot to the thigh will be just fine, he did sustain a lot of damage to the muscles, and we had to do a fair amount of debridement to the wound. I suspect he will be back on his feet in a few weeks... As for the other fellow... I wish I could give you better news other than the fact that he's alive- barely. The bullet entered at the level of the tenth thoracic vertebrae, severing his spinal column and fragmenting the vertebral body. Had it continued on its original path, he would have been dead instantly. Instead, the bullet changed course and went through the outer portion of the mediastinum, and out through his diaphragm. He is very lucky to be alive."

"He's going to be paralyzed," Eagle added in a solemn tone.

The surgeon nodded slowly, "Yes."

D.M. got up and walked away, it was too hard for him to hear. It seemed like bad luck ran in the family. First it had been himself, now Frank. His whole life was clouded with misfortune. Anger filled his soul; he fought to keep it under control. It would accomplish nothing by being angry; the situation would only get worse. No, he had to be strong.

It was nearly two weeks before Frank's comatose body was

brought to the base. His condition fluctuated enough that the surgeon did not want to chance transferring him until he became more stable. The team had returned a few days after the mission, exhausted, hoping they would not be called upon anytime soon.

Eagle placed a call to Westland requesting the team be placed in stand-down status for six weeks, allowing them time to recuperate. He balked at the idea, but finally gave in to Eagle's badgering. She met the team at lunch and passed on the news, "Well, I have good news; we've been put into stand-down status for the next six weeks." Several cheers came from around the table, some sighs of relief. "This doesn't mean a six week vacation; you'll still carry out routine training and work your respective shifts in the security section." The cheers soon turned into groans. "We still have a job to do after these six weeks, and we need to be ready for it when the time comes."

After lunch Eagle sat in her office working on the computer. She contemplated the duty roster and training schedule. It appeared that Bruce would be staying on after all since Frank was out of commission. Westland made it quite clear that she would receive no one else until Frank had been properly discharged from the team.

The rest of the team tolerated Bruce, but no one was ever too friendly to him. His attitude was one of superiority; he did not belong with this batch of so-called Special Forces officers. His team was waiting back home, a group of seasoned men that had tasted the true heat of battle. And he was certainly not helping the morale of the team.

Later that evening most of the men were in the rec room watching TV. D.M. was downstairs on the medical floor spending time with Frank. Tige flipped through channels trying to find something good to watch. Jake sat in a recliner nursing a beer. Sam, Max and Bruce sat quietly waiting for Tige to decide on what to watch. He put on the Military Channel and watched for a few moments. He was just getting ready to change the channel when

Bruce spoke up, "Hey, can you leave it? That's my unit on there."

"Oh?" Tige replied, he was not particularly interested in hearing another story of how glorious Bruce's unit was.

"Yeah, the seventy fifth Ranger Regiment, third Battalion, that's my group."

"Oh yeah," Tige said with disdain, "Please no more stories of the glory of your unit. You're here with us and we don't really appreciate you rubbing our faces in it. Yes, we're a new team, but that doesn't mean you have to put us down."

"Sorry, I wasn't aware that you guys were so sensitive about it."

Jake stood up and tossed his bottle into the recycle bin, "Yes, we are. We've worked our asses off to get where we are. I mean we were a bunch of outcast jail bait that Eagle took and turned into a Special Forces team, and she did it with the deck stacked against her. We owe our lives to her, and we're fiercely loyal."

Max got up and went to the door, "We haven't had many missions, but we have the skills and the heart to make this work. So just give us a break okay?"

Eagle sat in her office and rubbed her eyes, realizing that she was getting nowhere with the job she'd been working on. A knock at the door startled her. It was a solid knock on a very solid door, which could only be one person. "Come in major," she called loudly. The door opened and D.M. stuck his head in.

"Hey, how'd you know it was me?"

"Because you're the only one who can knock that hard on the door without breaking your knuckles."

He laughed lightly, stepped in and shut the door, "Can I ask a favor of you?"

"Depends..." she replied, choosing to study the computer screen rather than look up at him. D.M. walked over to the window and stood looking out.

"Jake said something back at the hospital in Panama that got me thinking...I have a project that I've been working on for quite some time and still have not come up with a solution. Would it be possible to fore go some training so I can work on it?"

"Is it mission essential?"

"I feel my research into the matter could possibly benefit the team greatly."

"And what is this project?"

"I'd rather not say."

Eagle stood and walked over next to him, she looked out the window, not wanting to catch his gaze. She knew he was up to something, he somehow enjoyed being rather secretive. Whatever the case, D.M. was a brilliant man, who when he got an idea in his head, it was best to leave him to his own devices. Any interference and he immediately went on the defensive, making life hell for everyone else.

"All right major. I'll post the duty schedule in the dining room. Required training will be highlighted. You'll still pull your regular duty at the security section. Am I clear on this matter?"

D.M. turned to her and smiled, "Yes ma'am, thank you."

"Hey man, are you gonna eat something?" Jake asked as he watched D.M. work in his lab. It had been three weeks and D.M. had spent every moment possible in it.

"I can't figure it…I can't get the molecular composition to change…I've tried heat, cold, different chemicals… But still nothing." The major sat back in his chair, crossing his arms in frustration. The answer was there somewhere, but finding it was going to be a challenge. Jake peered into the crucible that sat over a Bunsen burner. A dark gray sticky looking substance bubbled slowly under the heat.

"What is that stuff? A new kind of dessert topping?"

D.M. sneered at Jake. He was getting more and more annoyed. "I'll be up for lunch in a little bit, why don't you go on without me," his voice was stern and insistent.

"Okay, see you in a bit," Jake replied, sensing that D.M. wanted to be left alone. He closed the door quietly as he left.

The major sat looking at his notes. Everything had been done correctly, but what was the missing link? Why wouldn't this "dessert topping" as Jake called it change structure? His eyes focused on the crucible as if looking for an answer. He had exhausted his list of options. Was this going to be another failed attempt? His gaze drifted past the crucible stopping at the hyperbaric chamber. The major had never thought he would need it, so there were boxes piled inside. "Humm..." he pondered. Grabbing one of his weighty science books, he flipped madly through the pages until stopping on an experiment done by some obscure Polish scientist. His eyes scanned the pages until he found it. "By using extreme amounts of external pressure, the atomic structure was shifted and became a different compound..." D.M. stared at the chamber, "Well I'll be damned..."

Jake joined the rest of the team in the dining room. Eagle looked at her watch, "Is he going to come to lunch today?"

"He said he'd be up in a few minutes, but you know how he is."

"I'll tell the cook to make up a plate for him; you can take it down later."

Jake nodded appreciatively. He was the only one allowed in the lab when D.M. was working, for some reason the major wanted no one to know what he was doing. Jake had proven his reliability when D.M. was working on his robotic arm, so he was the only one trusted in the inner sanctum.

The group had just finished lunch when a large explosion rocked the building. Eagle stood up and went to the window. A black cloud of smoke curled past the window. "What the hell was that?" Tige gasped.

"Oh shit! D.M.!" Jake blurted and took off out the door. The rest of the team was hot on his heels.

Surprisingly they were the first ones to D.M.'s lab; the rest of the science section had gone to lunch. Jake hurriedly tried to enter the combination to unlock the door. He kept hitting the wrong numbers and cussed loudly in frustration. "Jake, this is no time to forget the combination," Tige snapped.

"Oh, blow me, I'm working on it!" Jake took in a deep breath and set to carefully entering the combination. The door locks unbolted and he hit the door with all his force. It opened a few inches then stopped, something was blocking it. Tige and Eagle put their shoulders to the door and managed to get it open far enough for Jake to slip inside.

Dust and smoke clouded the room; he could see debris all over the place. "D.M.?!" He hollered. No response. Jake quickly cleared the debris from the door and let the others in. The whole room appeared as if a bomb had gone off in it.

"Jake, where was he when you left him for lunch?" Eagle asked.

"Over there," he pointed to a large pile of overturned cabinets and twisted ceiling beams. They concentrated on the area Jake had last seen him, quickly clearing rubble, calling his name repeatedly.

"I got him!" Sam shouted triumphantly. The rest of the team hurried over and started digging him out. The major was buried under a portion of his laboratory workbench and a large equipment cabinet that had toppled over. He was unconscious and had a large gash on the right side of his head just about the hairline. Jake retrieved the first aid kit from the back wall and brought it to Eagle. She quickly put a dressing on the wound while the rest of the men worked on freeing his legs. Once freed, he was taken down to the medical floor.

Jake stood looking at what was left of the lab. The disaster crews had strung plastic over the huge hole in the outer wall. D.M. was lucky to have escaped with only minor injuries. The biggest injury was going to be to his heart when he saw the lab. All the time, money, and creative effort he'd put in was destroyed in just a second. Jake knew he would be crushed. D.M. was the kind of person who balanced on the thin line between eccentricity and insanity. The loss of his lab would certainly take him over the edge.

The lieutenant studied the situation. What exactly had happened? The blast had no doubt originated from the hyperbaric chamber. What had the major been doing? Jake picked his way through until he stood in the middle of what was once the chamber. His eyes scanned the area looking for some sort of clue. Amongst the wreckage lay the crucible D.M. had used to melt his experiment. Jake picked it up and examined the inside. Instead of the dark, gooey substance he had started with, the crucible was coated with a shiny, dark silver, plastic-like substance. He pulled at the edge of it to try and peel it out, but the substance remained firm. Turning, Jake found a cooled puddle on the floor of the same substance. He kicked at it with his boot and managed to pop it loose.

"What is this shit?" He said softly as he turned the piece over a few times in his hands, studying it. The weight of the material was far lighter than the size of the piece would suggest. The substance resembled plastic in every way; it even maintained a small amount of flexibility found in some of the ABS plastics. Was this freak accident just the thing D.M. needed to achieve the desired result on his work? Jake thought as he brushed his hand over the piece. There was only one way to find out.

"I want you to keep him just sedated enough that he remains fairly drowsy," Eagle said to the nurse.

"But why? He seems to be recovering fine," the nurse asked as he made an annotation in D.M.'s chart.

"The major's been burning the candle at too many ends lately. His mind and body could use with some down time. I want him relaxed for at least the next seventy two hours. No human being can work the kind of schedule he does and not border on insanity."

"Yes ma'am, I'll make sure he stays just drowsy enough to get rest."

Jake made the final preparations on the sample of plastic. He had mounted it on a small clamp easel and placed it at the end of the firing range. Tige stood behind the firing line preparing a .22 caliber pistol. They had agreed to start small and work their way up through the calibers until the plastic gave in.

"Come on, it doesn't take all day," Tige shouted down the line.

"I'm just tightening the clamps one last time; I'll be up there in a minute."

Tige placed the pistol on the shooting bench and sat down in the spotter's chair. He peered through the spotting scope and made a few adjustments. Jake appeared next to him a few moments later, he picked up a pencil and paper and jotted down the beginning test information.

"I see D.M. has taught you something scientific after all," Tige jested as he took his place at the bench, "Okay, here we go, .22 cal short, distance is sixty feet."

Tige took aim and squeezed off a round. Jake kept his eye on the scope. "Target moved a bit, but no hole," he said as he adjusted the focus slightly.

"Shall we try it one more time, just in case I hit the frame? You know I'm not so great with pistols."

"Yeah, do it again," Jake put his eye back to the scope. Tige took aim and fired again, "No, you definitely hit the middle, but it didn't penetrate," he looked at Tige, a big smile curled to his lips.

Over the next two days, Jake and Tige tested heavier and heavier caliber ammunition on the plastic. The lieutenant kept careful records of their tests; he would have something good to show the major. D.M. might just be proud of him for once.

"Jake, we only got .338, .375 and .50 cal left, and we'll have to go to the basement range for that," Tige said as he hefted a large bolt action Barrett rifle onto the bench, resting it on the sturdy bipod legs. They trudged down to the basement range which was outfitted to handle the large caliber munitions.

"All right mate, we're up to the .50 cal."

"I would hope no one would shoot at us with anything bigger than that," he mentioned as he made annotations on the log sheet. The other two rifle calibers had failed to penetrate the plastic, "Are you ready yet?"

"Not quite," Tige retrieved a clip of ammunition from a drawer, stripped a round off and shoved it in the chamber. He locked the bolt, "Okay, now I'm ready, .50 cal regular."

Jake took his position behind Tige on the spotting scope. He had only heard a .50 fired on the range once before, it nearly made him have to find a clean pair of underwear. He took a deep breath and braced for the noise. Tige took aim and carefully pressed the trigger. A shock wave rocked the room as the round was loosed from the chamber. Jake jumped anyway despite his careful psyching up. As the echo died away, he resumed his position on the scope.

"Well, it put a fairly good dent in it, but it didn't go through."

"No shit? Okay, now for armor piercing," Tige dropped a round in and readied the rifle. Jake didn't bother looking through the scope, he would jump anyway. The captain took aim and fired. The rifle recoiled viciously against his shoulder. That was gonna leave a bruise, he thought. As the noise settled, Jake peered through the scope.

"That's all she wrote," he said as he annotated the result. Tige looked through the rifle scope. A large, neat hole was drilled through the top right hand corner of the plastic.

"Got to admit, it's pretty amazing stuff," he commented as he got up and searched through some of the cabinets. Tige returned a couple minutes later with a large block of ordinance gelatin, "Hey, let's see how much force transfers through the plastic."

"Umm, good idea. Even if you wear Kevlar, you still get a good kick out of a round," Jake took the gelatin, walked down to the end of the range and placed it behind the plastic. Tige stood ready to load another .50 cal round. The lieutenant returned a few minutes later and took his place. The captain aimed and fired. The block of gelatin exploded in an amber-yellow splatter. The men walked down to the target to survey the damage. "Sweet Jesus!" Jake exclaimed as he peered into the backstop. Gelatin was splattered everywhere, only a small portion of the bottom of the block remained.

"Guess that answers that," Tige replied and went to put away the equipment.

Later that afternoon, Jake went to see D.M. The major was awake, the last of the drugs wearing off. The lieutenant peered through the observation window. A nurse was attending to him.

Jake opened the door and stuck his head in, "Excuse me," he said softly, "Can I see him?"

The nurse turned part way, "Yes, I was just preparing to remove his IV." Jake stood next to D.M.; he had a handful of papers and a piece of something shiny with a large hole in it. He was sitting up in bed; his eyes still held the glassy gaze from the sedatives. Jake offered the plastic to him. The major took it and examined it. His brow furrowed in concentration, his mind still not working up to speed. He looked at Jake curiously.

"You know what that is?" The lieutenant announced proudly. D.M. looked at the plastic and then back at Jake again. "*That* is bullet proof plastic... You did it!"

The major's eyes widened, his senses coming back in full force. "But how? What happened?" He spoke slowly.

"Well, unfortunately this great little discovery cost you your lab, but here it is, the product of all those years of work."

"How do you know it's bullet proof?"

"See that hole? That's .50 cal armor piercing... Nothing else was able to get through it," he offered the sheets of paper to D.M., who took them, setting them on his lap. "Are you surprised? That's all the test data we recorded from our little experiment."

The major's lips drew tight, "Who is the 'we' part of the experiment?"

"Well, me and Tige...He's a much better shot than me."

"How dare you!" D.M. snarled as he took an awkward swing at Jake. The lieutenant easily stepped out of the way. "That was my experiment; you had no right to interfere with it."

"Fine, be that way. I just wanted to surprise you and show you that your experiment worked, there's your results!" he barked and stormed out of the room.

D.M. once again found himself on the doorstep of Eagle's office needing a favor. This time it was for permission to fly down to Los Angeles to purchase new lab equipment. The major had said his apologies to Jake and they were again on speaking terms. The lieutenant had even helped D.M. clean up the lab and sort through all the wreckage. The repair crew had fixed the hole in the wall and had ordered a new hyperbaric chamber.

The major stood for a moment before knocking, this was a lot to ask, but perhaps because he had something tangible to work with, she might give in. He was just about to knock when the door opened. Eagle stood staring at him. "Yes major? May I help you?"

D.M. thought for a moment on how to ask her, but decided the blunt truth was the best choice; Eagle did not like to be buttered up. "I need another favor...Can I have some time to go to L.A. and purchase new equipment?"

Eagle stared blankly at him for a moment, her face showing no expression. "Take Jake along. You two are really getting on my nerves," she slid past him and walked down the hallway toward her room.

"Thank you!" He called after her.

Jake wandered down the jet way, he was dressed in jeans, a white t-shirt and wore his leather motorcycle jacket. D.M. followed along behind him, dressed in dark gray trousers, an Oxford shirt, tie and matching jacket. He was not looking forward to this. Having to replace nearly all the equipment in his lab was going to be a chore.

"So you know the place to go?" Jake said over his shoulder.

"Yeah, same place I got the last batch."

"How old was the other stuff?"

"Mmm, it was probably five years old. I bought it and put it in storage since I was going in the Air Force. The equipment was brand new."

"Well, maybe there are new and improved versions."

They found baggage claim and retrieved their bags. D.M. walked over to the rental car counter and got them a car. Loading their bags in the trunk, D.M. climbed behind the driver's seat and started the car up.

"You sure you don't want me to drive? Rank has its privileges once in a while," Jake said as he put on his seatbelt.

"Easier for me, I know where I'm going."

"All right, don't say I didn't offer."

D.M. pulled out of the parking lot and got on the freeway. He drove for nearly an hour before getting off. A few minutes later he stopped at the security gate of a storage facility.

"What are we doing here?"

"Checking on my car." He punched in the code and the gate opened. He drove around back until he reached a large storage unit. Climbing out, he dug through his pockets until he found the key. Unlocking a stout padlock, he pulled open the door. Jake got out of the car. A white cover lay over something that looked old. D.M. pulled the cover off to reveal a classic car.

"Thirty eight Jag SS one hundred roadster." He said balling up the cover and tossing it on top of a box.

"Sweet!"

"Yes, I thought so." He carefully unbuckled the leather straps on the hood and connected the battery terminals. Next he grabbed a rag and checked the oil.

"Need any help? I'm a grease monkey," Jake asked.

"Nope, I'm fine. Just going through my list of things to do.

"When was the last time you drove it?"

D.M. sat contemplating for a few moments, "Shit, close to a year. Hope it still starts." He checked the tire pressures.

"Can we take it for a drive?"

"That was my idea. Need to drive it once in a while to make sure it still runs." He finished off his checks, closed the hood and climbed in. The car almost seemed too small for his large frame. Jake noticed it was a right hand drive. It was in immaculate condition; even the leather straps that held the hood closed were intact. The chrome shined and the dark green paint was perfect.

The major put the key in the ignition and turned it. The car rumbled to life. "Park the rental over there," he pointed to a parking spot. Jake quickly moved the rental while D.M. gently edged the Jag out of the storage unit. He climbed out and closed the large door and locked it. Jake grabbed their bags, put them in the small trunk and hopped into the passenger's seat. D.M. returned and got back in. He looked over at the lieutenant, "Feel a bit weird to be sitting on the left with no steering wheel?"

"Yeah freaky, never been in a British car before."

He laughed, dropped the car into gear and sped down the parking lot.

"Woooohooooo!" Jake hollered in delight as the warm breeze hit his face. They headed out on the surface streets. "How fast does this thing go?"

"In its time, it was the fastest car out there. Top speed's just a hundred miles an hour."

"Where'd you get it?"

"Bought it at auction my senior year at MIT."

Jake ran his hands over the gauges on the dashboard, "How much did this baby set you back?"

"Quarter of a million," he replied nonchalantly.

"Fuck!" Jake coughed in disbelief. "Where the hell did you get that kind of money?"

"Sold a few inventions while I was still in school…I had a full scholarship to MIT, so education money wasn't a problem. I wanted to set myself up for later."

"How much do you have?"

"I don't discuss that with anyone. Let's just say if the government found out exactly how much I had, they'd boot me out. I'd be considered detrimental to morale."

"Millions?"

"I'm not saying." He drove another fifteen minutes before turning into a parking lot in front of a large white warehouse. Turning off the car D.M. attempted to fix his windblown hair, "Ready to go shopping?" The major climbed out and headed inside the front door, Jake followed along behind. A long white counter stood in front of them with a large man behind it. He wore a red polo shirt and tan trousers. His hair was salt and pepper.

"Ah, as I live and breathe the mad scientist returns!" The man exclaimed.

D.M. offered his hand, "Good to see you again Neil," he said warmly.

Neil shook his hand with vigor, "So what do you need now?"

The major rubbed his forehead where the scar was, "I need a whole new set up."

"What happened to all the other equipment?"

"Kablooie!" Jake said waving his hands in the air.

"You blew up your lab?"

"Well, it was an accident. But it did have a positive side effect."

"Yeah, you're back here spending money with me!"

"Ha, ha, smart ass," D.M. said as he flipped through a large catalog that sat on the counter. Grabbing a pad of paper and a pen he began to write down what he wanted.

"And is this your partner?" Neil said motioning to Jake.

"Yeah. Neil Samburg, meet Jake Collins. He's been helping me out in the lab for a while."

Jake offered his hand, "Nice to meet you."

"So where'd you go to school?"

"Atlantic City High."

"No, I mean what college?"

"Mmm, working on a degree in military tactics I guess. Haven't finished it yet."

Neil looked over at the major, "And where did you fish him from?"

D.M. flipped through a few more pages, wrote down another piece of equipment and then finally regarded Neil, "I'm not exactly in the scientific community right now."

"I heard you were joining the Air Force to be a pilot. Ah, such a waste of talent!"

"I'm still in the military, just have gone down a different path. We're on a Special Ops team. Jake is my teammate. I have a lab where we're stationed with free run to do research on what I want. The other day I was working on something and it went wrong and the lab blew up." He tore the piece of paper off the pad and handed it to Neil, "How long will it take to get all of this for me?"

Neil looked over the list, "Where do you need it delivered to?"

"Just get it to Reno airport; I'll take care of the rest of the journey."

"Humm, a week okay? One item I have to go chase down but the others are all in stock."

D.M. reached in his pocket and pulled out his wallet. Taking out a credit card he tossed it on the counter, "You know what to do with that."

"Gimme a few minutes to tally this all up."

"Take your time, we're staying the night over and then heading back tomorrow sometime." The major wandered around the makeshift showroom looking at brochures and miniature models of equipment. Jake looked at some of the brochures, clueless as to what most of the equipment did.

Neil stood up and placed a bill of sale on the counter, "Okay, here's the damage."

D.M. walked over and picked up the bill. Jake appeared at his side and looked at it, "Holy shit!" He gasped.

"Just part of being in business for yourself," he replied checking the bill over, "Hey Neil, what's this?" He pointed to an item on the list.

"A new little toy that just came out. Makes mold cutting twice as fast. I figured you'd probably want it."

"The consummate sales man eh?" D.M. said with hint of coldness in his voice.

"I was gonna go over everything with you first."

"Right, let's do that." He rested his elbows on the counter while Neil ran down the list of equipment. Jake stood watching. Most of what was being said was over his head. He was just impressed at the major's business savvy. Once D.M. was satisfied he signed the bill.

"I can't believe you just spent nearly a million bucks in less than an hour," Jake said as they walked out.

"Technology isn't cheap." He climbed back into the car.

"You seem to have a lot of power in the scientific community." Jake opened the door and carefully sat down.

"Quite a few of my formulas and inventions are widely used. Once you get known in industry for providing the solutions, they look at you much differently. Yeah, if I was to go back into it, I would be highly respected and could pick up where I left off. Hell, MIT would probably make a sweet deal for me to come back, teach and continue my research." He started the car and turned out onto the road.

"And make tons more money right?"

"Yeah. But right now I have the motivation in hand to work on the bulletproof plastic for us. I'm not gonna go out and sell it, this is something that will give us an advantage. Money is nothing right now. If I had to use every penny to make the armor a reality, I would in a heartbeat."

"You care that much about the team?"

"Yes, I do. There's always more money, but human life is worth more than that to me. You're my family now, and my home is the Knight's Keep."

Jake scratched his head, "Promise me you won't take this wrong?"

"What?"

"Well, when we first met, I thought you were an arrogant prick who was just going to throw your rank around to get what you wanted. I really hated your guts. But after we had that plane crash, I realized you were actually a caring person. You did everything you could to make sure I survived, even if you didn't really like me that much. I'm sorry for ever thinking that about you. You saved my life that night. I don't know how I'll ever repay you."

D.M. laughed lightly, "Well, I pretty much thought the same about you in the beginning. Your attitude was certainly not helping. Lord knows I wanted to punch your lights out on more than one occasion. And when Eagle put us together as a team, I was even madder. But when I needed help, you were there for me. You spent all those hours in the lab helping me build my arm and you never complained. I owe my career to you." He changed lanes and made a left turn.

"Guess that kind of makes us even huh?"

"I guess so," he pulled into the parking lot of the Casa Del Mar hotel.

"We staying here for the night?"

"Why not? Gotta have someplace to lay our heads."

"Shit, this nice. Do I wanna know how much this cost?"

"It's just money Jake. I've learned that you only get one shot to enjoy life, so I'm making sure I do it." He stopped the car at the valet parking, got out and opened the trunk. Taking out the bags he set them on the curb. With quick precision he put the top up on the roadster, not wanting to risk having the upholstery wet should it rain.

"Hmm, true. Never know when we'll get whacked in a mission." Jake grabbed their bags and carried them into the lobby. The major checked in and then headed up to their rooms.

"Hey, hope you don't mind I booked rooms right next door to each other, I'm gonna need help with my arm." He opened the door and walked in to his room.

"Sure, not a problem. Come on, we lived in a World War II Quonset hut in the middle of hell with four other guys for six months, this is a far cry from that." He set the major's bag on the bed.

"Yeah true," D.M. replied, taking off his coat and draping it over a chair. He looked at his watch, "Hey, you wanna go get something to eat?"

"Sounds good to me. Lemme guess, you like champagne, caviar, and enjoy classical music?"

"No, can't drink, caviar tastes like stale fish, and I prefer hard rock to classical."

Jake laughed lightly, "So the good things in life don't always agree with you?"

"Gimme a medium rare Porterhouse steak and a big baked potato any day."

D.M. went into the bathroom, washed his hands and returned. Putting his coat back on, he grabbed his room card. "Shall we?"

"Sure. Do I need to get dressed up?"

"Do you have anything besides jeans and t-shirts?"

"Nope. I'm not that sophisticated."

"Then wear what you got."

They ate dinner at the Catch restaurant, D.M. found a large rib eye steak to his liking and Jake opted for the filet mignon.

"Hey, can we go cruising?" Jake said as he finished the last bite of his steak.

"You wanna go cruising in a quarter million dollar car?" D.M. replied.

"Yeah, maybe the chicks will dig it."

D.M. smiled, it had been a while since he had done something juvenile, "All right. I guess the car could use some good run time."

"Cool!"

The major finished his meal and paid the check. They headed out to the parking lot and climbed in. "I need to get some gas before we go too far," he said as they pulled out onto the street. He drove a few blocks and found a gas station. Digging through the trunk he found a bottle of lead replacement and dumped it in the gas tank. Swiping his credit card, he grabbed the pump nozzle and filled it up with super. "Where do you wanna go?" He said as he replaced the nozzle and climbed back in.

"How about just going up the Pacific Coast Highway? I hear that's a hot place for cruising."

"We can do that. Not sure how many hours of light we'll have left."

"Oh, I just wanna go for a bit. Not that often I get to go out in such a classy ride."

D.M. pulled out into traffic and navigated his way to the highway. They headed north toward Malibu. It wasn't long before women were calling and waving to them. Jake waved back and whistled. "Hey, D.M., can you pull over there? My, my, the girls in California are far better looking than Jersey girls!" D.M. turned into a parking lot right on the edge of the beach. Even though it wasn't exactly beach season, there were quite a few women clad only in swimsuits. He stopped the car and turned it off. It wasn't more than of a couple minutes before several women were gathered around the car.

"Evening ladies," Jake said with a smile. D.M. sat watching him, his sunglasses pulled down just enough he could see over the top of them. The women laughed and swarmed around the car. Jake climbed out and leaned against the fender.

"Nice car," one tall blond commented as she ran her finger down the hood.

"You know how much this car cost?" Jake asked.

"How much?" She played her finger over the Jaguar hood ornament.

"A quarter million," the lieutenant boasted.

"And did you guys steal it?"

"No way, the owner is sitting right there," Jake pointed to D.M. Two women had immediately gravitated to his side.

The blonde walked back, letting her finger run back up the hood, "So this is your car? You filthy rich or something?"

D.M. smiled, "I guess you could say that."

She put her hand on his shoulder, feeling the solid muscle under his coat. Leaning down, she looked into the car, her breasts not very far from the major's face. "Is it fast?" She asked in a deep voice, tracing her finger over the top of the steering wheel.

"In thirty eight it was. Now, it's considered slow at a hundred," he answered, somewhat enjoying the company. He would have preferred to be back home with Eagle, but he was having fun watching Jake enjoy himself. The woman opened the door and sat down on the running board next to him. She reached up and played with the lapel on his coat.

"My, you're such a big guy, how do you get in this little car?" She let her fingers run down until they were resting on his leg.

"A shoe horn."

She laughed lightly, rubbing her hand on his leg. D.M. was fighting the feeling that was trying to run loose though his body. Yeah, she was a good looking blond, but he had his own at home. The woman leaned forward and made a move to kiss him, her hand sliding down between his legs. He put his hand on her shoulder and guided her head past his so he could whisper in her ear, "I appreciate the attention, but I've got someone in my life that I'm very much in love with."

The woman looked at him with a hint of disgust, "Not him?" Her eyes looked toward Jake.

D.M. laughed lightly, "No, she's a beautiful blond too," he whispered.

As the sun set, D.M. reached over and tugged on Jake's coat tail, "Hey, have you had enough cruising for the night?" The women were starting to head for their cars.

"Oh, I suppose." He climbed back into his seat, "Thanks maj, that was fun."

"You're welcome. I rather enjoyed the tall blond," he said with a smile.

"Yeah, she had her boobs just about in your face!"

"And her hand making a play for something else. Mmm, I figure there was probably twenty grand in plastic swinging back and forth in front of me," he laughed.

"Gee, are you a tit or ass man?"

"I like a bit of both, preferably on the same person. And I like it all natural.

Eagle sat bolt upright in bed. Oh God, it's happening! She turned on the light and looked around. Blinking several times, she slowly got her head to clear. Yes, she'd had her first flashback. It was terrible. She could see the man's face all over again in her sights, clearly like she was still there. She could feel her finger pull the trigger and watch as the man fell. It was something she was going to carry in her mind the rest of her life. This was the part of being a member of the warrior class she wished she could do without. Nightmares, flashbacks, anger, fear, hatred and violence; they were all part of what it meant to be a warrior. She wished D.M. was there to hold her. He would understand; he would know how to make her feel better. But he would not be home until tomorrow night, and she needed him now. She debated calling him. Maybe hearing his voice would make her feel better. Looking at the clock, she decided it was too late. Turning off the light, she settled back into bed and did her best to try and sleep.

The next morning, Eagle sat at the breakfast table stirring a cup of tea. Tige wandered in and sat down.

"Morning," he said, grabbing the newspaper and flipping through it.

"I know about the demons you fight every night."

He looked up at her, noticing she looked tired. "Have your first flashback?"

"Yeah," she said softly.

"Welcome to the brotherhood." He poured a cup of coffee.

"It was positively awful…I didn't think they would be like that, so realistic."

"Oh yes, they are. And you never know when you're going to have one."

"I figured I'd have had one not long after we got back from the mission," she said, taking a sip of tea.

"No, you never know when you'll have one. I find that if I'm under a lot of stress, I tend to get them. But that's not always true...You're gonna live with them the rest of your life."

She sighed, "I now question my desires to be part of that brotherhood."

"Too late for that now. You did well on the mission, I was very proud of you. Your innocence is lost, and you managed to keep it together. Not everyone can do that, you did and you completed your mission."

"Does it ever get any better?"

"Nope." He took a long drink of coffee, "You may get more comfortable with killing, but every time you do, you're just gonna add to your growing collection of nightmares."

CHAPTER SEVENTEEN

"I think it looks better than before," Jake commented as he wiped the last few crumbs of dust off D.M.'s laboratory counter. The major sat on his favorite overstuffed couch that had somehow survived the blast with only a few injuries. He surveyed the expanse of the lab, now crowded with more equipment than ever. This was a good as it was gonna get, he mused, laughing lightly.

"Well lieutenant, I think we got our work cut out for us. What da ya say?"

"What do you mean 'we' Scar Face?" Jake teased. He had jokingly started calling the major that because the wound from the explosion had not completely healed. D.M. didn't seem to pay much heed to the teasing; he was too focused on the work at hand. They had only a short time to perfect the production process for the bulletproof plastic and to create working suits of "armor" for the team. He knew Westland wouldn't give them much more time than necessary; they would be back in the throw of things very soon.

D.M. stood up and joined Jake at the counter. He leaned over, resting his forearms on the counter top, "Well my friend, would you please do me the honor of turning on the equipment?" He paused for a moment, "Or should I say 'partner'?" He offered his hand to Jake. They shook and nodded in agreement.

"I'd be delighted!" Jake smiled as he set to turning on the equipment with a flourish.

They worked until the early hours of the morning. D.M. carefully analyzing the data he had collected from a chemical analysis of the plastic. Jake mixed chemicals and prepared batches of plastic resin to be cast.

"Hah!" D.M. exclaimed, "I got it!"

Jake put down his work and stood next to him, "What? You figured out what happened in the blast?"

"Yes. See these chemical components? They can only occur when there is a high concentration of carbon dioxide in the air."

"Pardon me for being ignorant, but you've totally lost me," Jake replied.

"Okay, here's the scenario…I put the crucible in the chamber, I also put the Bunsen burner in there too. I then proceeded to pressurize the chamber. What was I using for pressure? Carbon dioxide. Now in theory, the Bunsen burner should have been extinguished by the CO2, but what I think happened was that the pressure drove the flame back into the gas main where it exploded."

"So you're saying the explosion was just an accidental by-product of the pressurization process? And that we won't have to go on another nine hundred and fifty thousand dollar shopping spree?" Jake scratched his head.

"Yes, and I don't need to have the plastic constantly heated in order to force the molecular change, I can just put a hot mold in and it will change as it cools."

"Man, you're using more brain cells that I got in my whole head. I think I'll just remain your humble lab rat."

"Jake, I'm offering you the chance to learn by working along with me. I don't regard you as a lab rat. Granted I might have you doing some of the more menial tasks while I work on other things; but I do intend on showing you what I'm doing and helping you learn to do it as well."

The lieutenant shook his head, "But you don't understand. I don't get all of that fancy scientific formula stuff. You could be writing in another language for all I care. I just don't get it."

"Oh and what? Do you think I was born with a silver slide rule in my pocket? I didn't understand any of this when I first started. It took time. You're just as smart as me; you just have to wanna unlock the potential of your mind."

"Why do you wanna help me?" Jake asked as he sat down across from D.M.

"Because you can't live the rest of your life by the gun. Someday you'll get too old for this business, and then what will you have to fall back on?"

Jake sat for a moment in thought. He looked D.M. in the eye and smiled, "My ass I guess."

They laughed. "Okay, back to work, we're running out of time," D.M. chided as he rolled over to the computer and began to input data.

Six weeks had passed and the team was back on active alert. D.M. and Jake worked furiously on a prototype suit of armor. Once they had the "bugs" worked out, it would be full speed into production for the rest of the team. They needed only a few more days and then they would be ready to demonstrate the capabilities of the armor.

The team enjoyed a hearty lunch together, their conversation charged with excitement of things to come. The down time had done them good. They were ready to fight again. With the promise of D.M.'s new technology there was talk of being invincible, how could they be stopped? Mere bullets were not a threat anymore. It was going to take a whole lot more to bring them down.

After lunch, D.M. made his daily journey to visit Frank. He was still in a coma and was not showing any sign of coming out of it. The major sat next to the bed and talked to him, telling him of all the great things that were going on with the team. How he and Jake had managed to create the bulletproof plastic that he had been working on for so long. And that they were in the final stages of testing and it would be demonstrated to the team in a of couple days.

D.M. took solace in talking to Frank. It provided him with a quiet window in which he could examine the happenings of the day. He could relate things out loud that troubled him, or tell him of something wonderful that had happened. Not getting any response didn't disturb him; he knew Frank would talk when the time was right. But until then, D.M. felt compelled to keep his brother abreast on all the news. If Frank were awake somewhere inside, he would take great joy in knowing what was going on with everyone. Occasionally he would stop by at night, sometimes he would see Eagle or one of the others sitting there talking to Frank. He knew that his brother was well looked after, there were plenty of people here who cared for him and made sure he knew he was loved.

Jake sat at the lab counter mixing chemicals. He measured each one carefully and poured them in a large beaker. D.M. watched him out of the corner of his eye, pleased that Jake was taking such pride and care in his work. The lieutenant was far from incorrigible; he needed something to focus his attention and energy on rather than getting into trouble with it. He had great potential; it was just a matter of gaining his cooperation.

The major looked at his watch. It was 1945, he had fifteen minutes to get to the practice hall and start warming up. The question was if Eagle would take him up on his offer for a sparring round. He had left a sticky note on her door with a stick-figure sword and the time 2000 below it. D.M. knew she would know what it meant, but would she come?

He stood and stretched, his back hurt from being hunched over the counter working on blueprints of the molds. In truth, he didn't really feel like sparring, but it was one way to get Eagle alone to talk. She had been giving him the cold shoulder ever since they had left Panama. He wondered if she felt responsible in some way for Frank, or that she had had a change of heart about their relationship. At any rate, he wanted to find out.

Pulling off his lab coat, D.M. hung it on the hook by the door.

He opened a cabinet and retrieved his practice sword. He slid it from the sheath part way as if to make sure it was still in one piece. Jake looked up, he still had four more batches to mix and was growing tired. "Hey, where are you going?"

"Um, I just need to get out for a while. Thought I'd go practice a bit."

"I've never known a man to take a sword on a date."

D.M. turned around, regarding Jake with a stern face, "Did I say anything about a date?"

"I've known you and Eagle were together for quite some time... It's not like you guys are discrete to the hilt," he chuckled slightly at his pun.

The major leaned over the counter, "Do you think the others know?"

Jake shrugged his shoulders, "I don't know."

"You'd better not say anything."

"What goes on between you and Eagle is your business, we're all adults and I think we know how to handle the situation."

D.M. slid off the counter and headed for the door.

"For what it's worth major, I think you two are made for each other," Jake called out as D.M. left.

Eagle took the note from her door and checked her watch. It was five till. Did she want to practice? It had been a while, perhaps just for a little bit. She quickly retrieved her sword from the room and went to meet him.

As the elevator doors opened, she could see D.M. in the dim light. His back was turned and he was kneeling on one knee, his hands resting on the hilt of his sword, his head bowed. She thought he looked peaceful, either he was praying or in quiet meditation. The closing of the elevator doors brought D.M. from his thoughts. He looked over his shoulder, noticing Eagle. Rising up, he took the sword by the handle and turned to face her.

Eagle slid her sword from the sheath. Carefully, she placed the sheath on the floor and stepped forward to meet him. They stood silently for a few moments studying each other. D.M. tipped his sword forward, assuming the en garde position, his eyes fixed on

Eagle's. She held his gaze, bringing her sword forward to touch his. Their blades clinked together gently. This gentle meeting was by no means a sign of things to come. They always fought with great zeal, their swords crashing loudly through the hall, heavy footsteps of attacks and parries.

Tonight, however, they simply stood looking at each other. Neither felt much of an urge to fight, their hearts were not in it.

"Well major, it appears we have come to an impasse without even having come to pass," Eagle said softly.

D.M. stepped forward and swung his sword at her. Eagle blocked it, a loud crash echoing through the hall. Within a few moments they were in the heat of battle. The major used his size and strength to his advantage. Usually he held back somewhat because Eagle would grow tired quickly from having to block his blows. But tonight he felt the urge to end the battle sooner than normal. His prime objective was to talk.

He lunged at her, forcing her back against a pillar. Eagle could do nothing but try to block him. D.M. stepped in and pinned her against it. She was defenseless. Their eyes met.

"I wanna know why have you been giving me the cold shoulder lately?" He said sternly.

"Things between us were getting a bit too serious," she replied, trying to force him away. D.M. kept himself firmly pressed against her.

"What's wrong with that?"

"I'm not sure if I'm ready for a serious relationship."

D.M. pushed away from her, his sword dropping to a defensive position, "If I recall correctly, it was you who came to me last time."

Eagle stepped away from the pillar. She stood looking at the ground trying to collect her thoughts, "You might not think this, but I'm having a hard time with this situation."

"Oh, so you're finally willing to admit that your feelings have grown too strong as well?" He said as he paced in a small circle.

"Yes," she replied meekly, afraid that the announcement might be heard by the whole world, "D.M., I want you so bad I'm afraid I won't be able to keep my vow. I want to so much, but I must remain chaste until my wedding day."

The major stopped his pacing and faced her, a smile edged to his lips, "You know, there are plenty of ways to enjoy each other without actually making love."

Eagle frowned, "I know, but I don't think I could resist."

D.M. turned his sword over and let the point rest on the floor, "All right, I'll give you some help…" he knelt down on one knee and placed his right fist over his heart. "I swear that I too will help you uphold your vow of chastity until the day comes when we can consecrate our union," he rose slowly and stood regarding her with soft eyes.

The colonel smiled. She knew D.M. was a man of his word; he would keep her safe, even if her mind and flesh cried out for him. D.M. turned and collected the sword's sheath. Carefully sliding the weapon back in, he headed toward the elevator, "Meet me in my room in ten minutes if you'd like a bit of company," he called as the elevator doors closed behind him.

D.M. sat in bed reading a magazine. He had hurried home, undressed and freshened up with a bit of deodorant and some light cologne. There wasn't much time to take a shower, and if things went the way he hoped, he would end up sweaty anyway. He looked at the clock, it had been fifteen minutes. Was she going to come? He thought as he flipped mindlessly through the pages. A familiar sound reached his ears; it was the closing of his front door. He knew Eagle would use the override code, so he didn't bother leaving it unlocked.

A few moments later she peered around the corner. Her hair was down and it looked like she had taken a shower because some of it was wet.

"Hi," she said softly.

D.M. closed the magazine and set it on the nightstand, "I was beginning to wonder."

"I felt icky, so I took a quick shower."

The major laughed lightly, "Shouldn't have bothered." Eagle wandered over and sat on the edge of the bed. She still had her misgivings about the situation, but her heart really ached to hold him. He reached over and pulled the covers back partway.

"Clothing is highly undesirable in a situation like this," he reached over and adjusted the dimmer switch on the lamp down low.

Eagle sat looking at the drawn bed covers. She had never been in this kind of situation before; it was almost frightening. D.M. studied her, sensing her apprehension, "I have a feeling you've never been this far before...How far have you gone?"

She was quiet for several moments, "I guess you could say... second base."

D.M. shook his head in disbelief, "Boy, you really don't have any idea what you've been missing," he patted the bed, "Come on... You know, with all that time you teased me at China Lake, I would have sworn you were quite the randy little minx. Guess I called your bluff huh?"

Eagle undressed. She felt just uncomfortable enough that she kept her back to him until she slid quickly into bed. D.M. pulled the covers over and rolled partway onto his side so he could face her. He reached over and cupped his left hand to her cheek. Eagle flinched slightly as the cold feeling of his robotic hand touched her skin. She had felt his hand many times, but it always seemed to make her somewhat uncomfortable, she didn't know why, but it just did.

D.M. leaned over and let the tip of his nose touch hers briefly before seeking out her lips. He kissed her, feeling the passion growing in his body. Eagle resisted, her body becoming tense. "Relax, don't fight it," he said between kisses. His hand wandered down her neck to the top of her chest. Gently, he turned his hand in order to cup her breast, his kisses becoming more serious. Eagle became tenser. The major stopped and looked at her, "What's wrong?"

Eagle swallowed hard, "I guess I'm kind of scared."

D.M. raised an eyebrow, "Scared of what? That something might happen that you don't want?"

Eagle nodded.

The major propped himself up on one elbow, "I made a promise to you. I won't break it no matter what. I'll close my ears to you if you beg. And I promise again that you will be chaste until the time comes," he rubbed his forehead in concentration. "I know this is new for you, and that you're a bit worried. But consider the fact that God gave us bodies like this so we could enjoy the pleasures of each other."

Eagle closed her eyes and took several slow deep breaths. The tension in her body slowly ceased. D.M. lay back on the bed, "Okay, how about we try this…You do what you want to me, I'll just lay here for a bit and enjoy your attention," he tucked his arms behind his head and closed his eyes. Eagle lay there for a few moments. She'd never been thrust into this kind of situation. To her, it was strangely nerve wracking. All the men she had gone out with had always taken the lead. This was new and curious. Here was the man she loved lying there waiting for her to make the first move. Oh, what to do?! She thought as she rolled over and snuggled against his chest. D.M. put his arm around her. They lay together for quite some time before he spoke up, "I don't quite understand this…Here I am, the love of your life, lying completely naked next to you and this is all you wanna do?" He paused, "I thought I recall you saying that Norwegians were very erotic people."

"Well, uh, we are," she said as she inched her way up until her lips found his. She kissed him hard, feeling her body becoming comfortable with the situation. Perhaps he knew what she needed to overcome her fear. It was funny the way he could be so gentle and understanding, yet when it came down to the serious business the major was a brutal force to be reckoned with. Eagle let her hand drift down his chest to his abdomen. Her fingers passed over his navel, and she was amazed at how soft his skin was. Her hand drifted further until it reached the border of stiff curly hair. She stopped. D.M. drew back; his lips parted from one of her kisses, "Go ahead," he said softly, "It's all right."

Her hand searched further, finally stopping at the base of his fully aroused manhood. She could feel the heat from it on her fingers.

"I take it this is a new one too?" The major whispered, reaching down, cupping her hand around it.

"Medical school only had the dead ones, they weren't very interesting," she smiled and moved her hand up the length of it. D.M. laughed lightly, finding a hint of humor in the situation. Eagle was amazed at how something that was just tissue and blood could be so hard. It truly did feel as if there was a bone inside, now she definitely understood the connotation. Her fingers passed over the end and she stopped. Something was just a bit different. D.M. watched with amusement as her brow furrowed in concentration. "You're..." She began.

"Whole...Yes... Somewhere in the mix, they forgot me," He paused, "Buy the time anyone gave much notice, it was a bit late... It's okay, I'm used to it."

Eagle continued to explore his manhood. D.M. hadn't been joking when he said he was well endowed. She guessed that everything must be proportionate on him; there definitely wasn't anything small about him. Her fingers played over the tip, trying to take in the details without seeing it. She touched one particular area and D.M. jumped, "Hey, don't do that," he warned.

"Did I hurt you?" She asked.

"No, no...It's just there's a lot of nerves there, and by doing that it sends like a shock wave through my body."

She passed her fingers over the area again and he jumped.

"Come on, stop it...Or else..." he teased.

"Or else what?"

"I'll do it to you...See how you like it," he leaned forward and sought out her lips. He kissed her hard for a few moments, his tongue searching the contours of her mouth. When he finally drew away, Eagle snuggled her head against his chest and lay there quietly. D.M. wrapped his arms around her, "May I have my turn?" He asked softly.

She looked up. Their eyes met and D.M. could see just the faintest inkling of tension on her lips. He would not push the issue; Eagle would let him know when she was ready. They studied one another for a few moments. D.M. knew she was thinking the situation through, deciding if she was ready.

Closing her eyes, Eagle took in a deep breath and slowly nodded. The major smiled to himself, she was going to enjoy this. With one smooth move, D.M. rolled her over until he was lying nearly on top of her. He used his left arm to support his weight, leaving his right free to caress and explore, "Now, all I want you to do is lie there and enjoy," he said as his lips started in the center of her chest, finding their way to her right breast. His mouth closed upon her nipple and he played his tongue over it several times.

Eagle groaned and shifted slightly under him. He looked up to see her lying with her eyes closed, she had an almost sultry appearing pout on her lips. He smiled and continued on, caressing and kissing each breast.

When he was satisfied that she was enjoying herself, he sought out her lips once again. He kissed her, letting his hand drift down until it reached the soft mound of hair. The tension returned to her body. He rested it there for a few moments, choosing to distract her with more kissing. As her body relaxed, he let his fingers curl over until they found the warm folds of skin. Her legs were closed firmly together. He pushed his hand down a bit further and nudged her inner thigh, "Open your legs," he said softly between kisses. Eagle did not budge. He pushed a bit harder, "Come on, it's okay."

Eagle moved her left leg a few inches. D.M. again rested his hand on her curly mound of hair; his fingers working carefully to part the folds of skin. As he found her clitoris, he drew his lips away. His finger stroked it once and Eagle jumped. Her eyes were wide with surprise as the seemingly electrical shock went through her body. He did it again.

"Hey!" She gasped, not completely sure if this new sensation could be considered enjoyable or not.

D.M. laughed lightly; "I told you if you didn't stop, I'd do it to you." he smiled and again sought out her lips. After all, what was the old saying: "All's fair in love and war?" He thought as he kissed her in a playful manner. Eagle wrapped her arms around him, holding him. D.M. let his fingers inch down until he was able to carefully part the warm, moist folds to her vagina. He paused for a moment, waiting to see if she offered resistance. To his surprise, Eagle moved her leg further away. With the greatest care, he gently worked his index finger until it sat at the outer margin of the cavity. Eagle felt it and quickly pulled away from his kissing, her eyes conveyed her fear.

"What's wrong?" He asked.

"Should we be doing this?"

"If you're worried about your virginity, no, this won't affect it," he paused, "I made you a promise. And I would never do anything to break that."

Eagle studied him. In her mind she was trying to convince herself that what D.M. said was true. How could she know? This was further than she had ever gone with a man before. He had at least experience with women; he seemed to know what to do. Closing her eyes, she let her head rest on the pillow.

D.M. waited a few moments for her to relax. He knew she was sacred, but if she allowed him to continue, he was confident that it would all change. He edged his finger further. It felt tight, the walls of muscle resisting his intentions. He pushed a little further, Eagle let out a stifled cry.

"Did I hurt you?" He asked quickly, drawing his finger back slightly.

"Yes, a little."

"Do you want me to continue?"

She nodded slowly. D.M. leaned forward and kissed her. His finger again carefully searching for the secret spot that would fill any woman with passion. He let his finger move over her cervix and followed it down. It was there somewhere, he thought with increasing frustration. Moving his finger slightly to one side, he felt Eagle's body writhe under him. Humm, he thought, could this be the spot? Passing his finger over the area again Eagle moaned and shifted her pelvis. Bingo! He smiled and kissed her. Moving his finger quicker, he could feel her body trying to keep the contact. He stopped and drew his head back, "So how does that feel?"

She opened her eyes and D.M. could see they were soft and almost glassy, "Incredible," she gasped, wrapping her arms around his back. He let his lips return to hers, his finger continuing its motions. As he worked harder, he could feel all the muscles in her body becoming tense. He knew this wasn't the kind of nervous tension from before, this was the kind of tension a woman experienced when she was nearing climax. D.M. moved faster and even a little harder. Eagle's breathing was now short gasps followed by long periods of her holding her breath. The major wondered how Mother Nature worked. Here was a woman who had probably never experienced and orgasm, yet her body knew exactly what to do. Perhaps it was just primal instinct.

D.M. felt a sharp pain on his back. Eagle had her fingernails set against his flesh, her hands and arms rigid. It hurt, but he was more concerned with letting her get the most enjoyment. As his finger continued to move, he could hear her exhales coming as little grunts. Her cheeks had flushed red, and sweat dribbled between her breasts. He knew she was close, her lips parted and her teeth showed, bared and clinched, her breathing had almost stopped. An instant later she opened her mouth, crying out with sheer pleasure. D.M. felt her muscles contract. He cried out too, not from pleasure, but from pain as she raked her nails down the sides of his back.

Eagle lay there in a limp, sweating mass. Her breathing was fast and ragged. D.M. felt a rush of hot liquid against his finger. She had orgasmed. His back seared with pain and he felt the need to get up. Carefully slipping his finger out, he rolled off her and went to the bathroom. He also knew it was too soon to ask her to help relieve him of his own tension; that he would sort out later.

Turning on the tap, D.M. washed his hands and face. His body was covered with sweat. He could feel it trickling down his back. He turned partway to survey the damage done by Eagle. Sweet Jesus! What felt like sweat running was really blood! She had gashed him terribly. He sighed as he ran a washcloth under the water and began to dab off the blood; she certainly had enjoyed herself.

It was shortly before midnight when Eagle slipped out of D.M.'s room. She had taken one step away from the door when Jake came from his room. He was on his way to the security floor to start his shift. Eagle stopped dead; mortified that she had been caught. How was she going to explain this? Jake saw the expression on her face. He knew what she had been up to. Quickly, he averted his glance and continued down the hall away from her. Eagle darted back inside. She found D.M. sitting on the bed doctoring his wounds.

"We got a problem," she said, her voice trembled slightly.

"What?"

"I was coming out the door and Jake saw me."

"Oh, don't worry about him," D.M. replied complacently, "He's known about us for quite some time."

"If he knows, what about the others? What if he says something?"

"He won't, he already said he wouldn't," he said as he finished and went into the bathroom.

"D.M. this is serious. If this gets out, we're done for."

He stood in the doorway, toothbrush in hand, "I know that... Perhaps honesty is the best policy with the guys."

"You mean *tell* them?!"

"Sure. If they know and understand the consequences to us, they might just be willing to cover for us."

"Are you out of your mind?!" She shrieked.

The major shrugged his shoulders, "Yeah, probably...But honesty amongst us is the best policy. The ones we worry about are the brass."

"I don't know about you, but I'm not ready to end my military career just yet. I love you D.M., but please understand if we have to put this on the back burner until one of us gets out."

"It won't be easy, but I understand."

CHAPTER EIGHTEEN

The team mustered for breakfast. Everyone was seated and waiting for their food. Jake came in carrying a piece of paper. He stopped next to Eagle and leaned over, cupping his hand to her ear and whispered something. She turned to look at him and saw the serious expression on his face. Nodding, she got up and followed him out the door. They went to her office.

"Okay, what's this all about?" She asked.

"Have you had this place debugged lately?"

"It was checked a few days ago, why? What's wrong?" Her patience was wearing thin, her stomach nagged. Jake handed her the paper. Eagle examined it. He found a pen and paper, scribbling a note on it.

"I don't trust the security around here," he said, handing her the note he had written. Eagle read it silently: Unauthorized transmission last night. Message heavily encrypted. She took a pen and wrote back: Security breach?

Jake nodded, taking the paper he wrote: Let's talk somewhere secure.

"Okay, come on," Eagle led him out of the office and up to the flight deck.

She breathed in the cold air. Despite being the end of May, the weather was still chilly in the mornings. They stood by the wall. Jake had the sudden urge to smoke a cigarette, but knew better-Eagle had encouraged those who smoked to quit, saying that the only smoking area was on the hanger deck.

"Okay, I'm sure there's no prying ears up here. What's going on?" She said, trying to turn her back to the cold breeze.

"I think we got a security problem. Somebody might be spying on us."

"And your evidence is an encrypted message we can't read?"

Jake turned to face the wind. There was just something about the whole situation that didn't sit right with him. "There should be no encrypted traffic coming from anywhere else in the building. Security floor is the only place for encryption for the entire base," he paused, "I got a couple of guys that I made friends with working on breaking the code, they said it wasn't gonna be easy, but they'd try."

"For now, I think we should just keep it between those of us who need to know. If someone is sending transmissions, we want to catch them, not scare them quiet."

"Right," he replied.

Jake sat putting the final touches on his crowning achievement. He had been playing guinea pig for D.M. during the construction of the armor and discovered that being covered from head to toe in plastic was extremely hot. So he had done some research and devised an under suit that would keep the wearer at a comfortable temperature. It worked off the principal of a small circulating unit that kept a gel polymer moving through tubes that ran all over the cotton Lycra suit. The gel was special in that when it was exposed to heat above a certain temperature, it released ions, producing a cooling effect. When a low electrical charge was applied, the gel warmed up and provided warmth to the wearer.

The major had to admit Jake had really surprised him. He really hadn't gotten the whole grasp of how the suit worked, but it did. The lieutenant was growing in leaps and bounds in his education. He seemed to enjoy a good challenge, whether it was designing the under suit for the armor, or wrestling with the problems of a term paper that was due for English in two weeks.

Jake stood and held the suit up. The white material seemed too stark for what their mission requirements would be. He knew that it would be hidden by the armor, so it wasn't a bother. Disappearing into the bathroom, he appeared a few minutes later wearing it. The suit was skintight. The material he had used had just enough Lycra to give it some stretch. "Well, how's it look?"

"It's not the question of how it looks, but how does it *feel*?" The major replied glancing up from his work.

Jake opened the little "control panel" that was attached to the left forearm and poked a few buttons, "Dunno, we'll see in a couple of minutes." He walked over to his pile of armor and started picking up pieces and putting them on. This was to be the true test.

Once dressed, he retrieved D.M.'s sword from the cabinet and handed it to him, "How about making me sweat a bit?"

D.M. bit his lip. He was far too busy working on other things to help Jake. There was a pang of guilt that nagged him because it was the lieutenant who had given so much of his time to help him, he should just suck it up and help him.

"All right, but just for a little while, I really must get my work done," the major said as he waved his arm over the workbench littered with pieces of armor.

"Give me half an hour, tops. I'll even come back and help you get them together, Okay?"

"You have to stop them," Westland growled over the phone. His patience was wearing thin with person on the other end of the line. "I don't care, the troops cannot move into Lebanon. There will be a time and place for that. Until then, just stay put, keep out of sight, and I will let you know when the time has come," he slammed the phone down and turned to Lt. Farlow, "All right, back to the office," he barked.

"Yes sir," Farlow replied as he took his seat behind the wheel and started the car up. They cruised down the surface streets until they reached the Beltway. "Sir, is Sergeant Von Teufel having some problems?" Farlow finally broke the uneasy silence.

"He thinks they may be on to him."

"You can't afford to pull him can you?"

"He has to finish what he was sent there for," Westland said with a hint of finality. There had to be another mission he could send Eagle's team on, one that most of them might not come home from. He smacked his hand against the car seat; all the other missions he had sent them on they had returned- not always in one piece, but they returned. They had to suffer enough mortal casualties that the team would not be able to come back from it. He would not provide her any more replacements and then the team would have to be dissolved. Game over, he won. He may not have the eighty billion back that her team used, but he would have his base back. Westland was confident that Eagle and her merry band of pirates would not spend another winter in *his* building. It was all ready late May and he needed to put an end to them soon.

Eagle sat in her office looking at the piece of paper Jake had given her a few days earlier. The encryption was indeed very heavy and not something normally used at the base. Who was sending these messages? Whomever it was wanted to make sure that no one intercepted it. The transmission was made late at night to a direct satellite uplink. It would be nearly impossible to trace since the signal was sent via a wireless network. Or would it? She left her office and went down to the security floor. She poked her head into the office of the senior security officer, "Hey Mitch, long time no see," she chided.

"Come in colonel, what brings you down to my dungeon?" The captain joked.

“Did you see this transmission?” Eagle asked as she handed him the paper.

“Yeah, Lieutenant Collins showed it to me. Very interesting. We're working on breaking the code.”

“I have a better idea. Can you trace the wireless modem this was made from?” Eagle said as she sat down on the edge of his desk.

"It might be a needle in a haystack, but we can sure give it a try."

"Thanks, Mitch. Any idea of how long that will take?"

"Maybe a few days. But with this code, I'm guessing that it was made off a rotating number that is changed every time to prevent detection."

“So this is pretty heavy high tech stuff huh?" She looked at the paper sitting on the desk. Mitch took a long drink of coffee and sat his mug back on the desk.

"Yeah, very high tech. Not stuff you go out and buy at the local Radio Shack."

Eagle got up to leave, "Thanks again Mitch."

"No problem ma’am, we're here to help."

D.M. strapped the last piece of armor onto Jake's shoulder. It had taken them nearly an hour to get him fully dressed. The major knew that the process would have to go faster, a lot faster to make it mission effective. Jake stood looking at D.M. He felt like the Tin Man in the Wizard of Oz, his whole body covered with semi-rigid plastic panels. He took a few steps and realized just how unwieldy the armor was.

"D.M., I don’t think we could fight very well in this stuff. It's stiff, noisy and really hard to move in."

The major sat back in his lab chair and mulled the thought over. How to make the armor less cumbersome and easier to move around in? His original patterns had been based off medieval knight's armor, but back in those days there was very little need for stealth. Jake leaned over the lab counter and grabbed the laptop computer. He carefully poked the keys with a pencil; his hands were too large with the gauntlets on to type on the keyboard. After several minutes of typing he stopped and turned the computer around for D.M. to see.

"What do you think about this idea?" He said, pointing to a picture he had found on the Internet. D.M. leaned forward and studied it closely. He rubbed his chin and realized he had forgotten to shave that morning.

"Humm, intriguing," he pondered as he tapped on the keyboard to try and find a better view, "You might be on to something Jake, good work."

Yeah, I'm good for something once in a while. Now can you get me out of this stuff? I feel like I got time warped out of the middle ages."

D.M. helped Jake out of his armor and tossed it into a pile. Maybe some of the pieces might be used again, but for the most part it was back to the drawing board. He had a feeling this was going to be a sleepless night while he worked the problem out in his head. He looked again at the image on the computer screen. It showed several pictures of armor that appeared composite. There were larger plates that covered the less bendable parts of the body and smaller overlapping plates almost like scales that covered the parts that needed to bend. How could he get the scales to articulate correctly? Scale mail was made from small metal plates held together by rings of chain mail. That arrangement certainly would not work.

"Hey, are you going to come up for dinner or should I bring something down for you?" Jake called as he left the bathroom and headed for the door. He had changed out of his cooling suit and back into uniform. "D.M.? Did you hear me?"

D.M. sat staring at the computer screen. His mind was working overtime on how to fix the problem.

"Okay, I guess that lack of an answer means I'll bring you something down later," Jake said loudly as he left the lab.

Eagle looked at her watch. Where was he? It was Wednesday evening and D.M. hadn't shown up to spar with her. She knew he loved this time of the week and rarely missed it. Sheathing her sword she went to the lab floor. Jake was just coming out of the lab. "Hey, hold the door!" She said loudly.

"Aw now, come on Eagle, you know how D.M. is about having anyone but me in the lab."

"Tough shit, let me in," she barked as she barged past him. Jake shut the door quickly and disappeared. "Hey, you forget about tonight?" She said as she made her way to the lab counter. He said nothing to her; he just kept staring at the computer screen. Eagle peered over his shoulder, "Got a problem?"

"Yes," he said flatly, still fixated on the computer.

"What's the problem?" she rubbed his back gently.

"I need to figure out how to make modern day scale mail."

"And what is your boggle?" She quipped as she leaned over and kissed him on the cheek.

"Old scale mail was held together with rings. That technology is entirely unacceptable for modern day application."

Eagle playfully tickled his ear until D.M. swatted at her. She laughed and tried to tickle him in the ribs. D.M. was not in a playful mood and he couldn't figure out why Eagle had to pick this time to bother him.

"You're not thinking of all the different kinds of scale mail," she paused as she turned for the door, "Come with me."

D.M. looked up at her, his brow furrowed with concentration. What possibly could she have that would help him in this situation?

"Are you coming major? I promise it will be an eye-opener."

D.M. followed Eagle to the training floor. He hoped she wasn't taking him there to practice; he'd left his sword in the lab. Besides, he had a big problem to work out and seemingly very little time to do it in. Eagle led him to an area they had never been in before. There were workbenches with drawers under them. Eagle opened several of the drawers until she found what she was looking for. She removed a piece of scale mail and handed it to D.M. who inspected it closely. It wasn't bound together with rings, rather it was attached to a leather backing by small holes drilled through the plates at the top and sewn on.

"No rings," he smiled and gave Eagle a gentle squeeze on the shoulder.

"Does this help solve your problem?"

D.M. smiled larger. He kissed her with great zeal and in an instant, was gone, scale mail in hand.

The phone rang waking Jake from a sound sleep. He struggled against the covers and fought his way to answer the phone. "Yeah, what?" He growled.

"Jake, get down here, I need your help."

The lieutenant looked at the clock, "D.M. it's three in the morning. Unless this is a life or death matter, I'm going to roll over and go back to sleep."

There was a long pause on the other end of the phone. "Well, technically, it is a matter of life and death. Eagle gave me a great idea and I almost have a working prototype."

"Major, *sir*, I really think you need to get some sleep. You're beginning to get way too obsessive about this project."

Again there was a long pause on the other end. "You're right Jake. Sorry. I'll see you at breakfast," with that, the phone went dead.

Sam peered through the spotting scope and then scribbled down a course correction, "Okay, two clicks left, you have a crosswind of five knots." The late spring sun was warm on his back. Tige made the adjustment and settled down behind the rifle. He took aim and gently squeezed a round off. The rifle jumped to life and sent a loud report echoing through the valley. Several birds took flight out of the trees around the valley.

Sam squinted to see where the round landed, "A bit high and to the right."

Tige looked through the scope, "Sam, your calculation was wrong. It should have been four clicks."

"Sorry. I guess I'm not a very good spotter."

"You're not that bad. It takes time to get the hang of it," Tige replied as he chambered another round and made the necessary corrections. He let fly with another round and Sam checked the position.

"Dead on."

"Yup, that's why they pay me the big bucks mate," Tige said as he stood and collected his rifle. He began the long walk to retrieve the target. Sam kept pace with him.

"Why do you do it?" Sam asked as he slung the spotting scope case over his shoulder.

"What? Kill people? Well, it's a lot easier for me to do it than someone else. I look at it this way: I have perfected the skills over the years and to me it's just another target. I don't feel anything for them; I don't really have any guilt about killing them. I figure I'm all ready going to hell, and if I can spare a few souls from that torture, then maybe they will make it to heaven," he continued to trudge down the path toward the target, "The first time is always the hardest. You know that now from the last mission. Don't worry; it'll get easier every time after that."

Eagle sat in a chair next to Frank's bed. She held his hand, gently caressing it. Frank had remained in a coma since being shot. The surgeons had done everything they could to stabilize him, yet he would not awaken. Considering the nature of his injuries, it didn't make sense why he was still comatose. I guess he'll wake up when it's time, Eagle thought as she got up to leave. D.M stood watching her from the window at the nurse's station. He watched her lean over and gently kiss Frank on the forehead. She turned and saw D.M. peering through the window and smiled at him. He managed a smile in return and opened the door. "Hello major, I haven't seen you in a while," she said softly.

"Sorry, I've been in my lab too much. I feel bad that I haven't seen Frank in a few days," D.M. replied.

"Yes, you have been burning the midnight oil rather excessively lately. When was the last time you got some sleep?" She rubbed her hand across his chin, "Or had a shave for that matter?"

"Been having some trouble sleeping lately. Lots of nightmares and flashbacks. I can't get them out of my head. I keep seeing the same things over and over again. I don't feel secure for some reason," he rubbed his eyes and ran his hand through his hair in frustration. Eagle looked at her watch, it was nearly 2200.

"Spend a little time with Frank and then come see me," she

whispered as she passed by him out the door.

D.M. spent half an hour with Frank. He then went up to his room and took a quick shower and shaved. He slipped over to Eagle's room; she had left the door unlocked for him. He found her sitting on the couch reading a book. Quietly he shut the door and took a seat on the couch with her. She glanced over at him and continued to read. Once she had finished the page, she closed the book and turned to him, "Have you been down to see the psychiatrist?"

"No, not lately. I'm not sure what he can do for me. I know what's wrong, I just don't know how to fix it," D.M. said softly.

"All of us are suffering from post traumatic stress. We've seen too many awful things, and it's taking its toll. Unfortunately they can't give us drugs, we need to stay sharp and mission ready. Counseling only goes so far to help, but it will never make the problem go away. This is something we will live with the rest of our lives. The best we can do is learn to cope with the nightmares and flashbacks and try to live as normal a life as possible."

"I don't think that will happen any time soon," D.M. replied as he stood and began to pace a small circle, "I can't sleep. If I can't sleep, I can't get enough rest to recharge my brain. I'm useless in the lab, and I'll be useless during a mission."

Eagle stood and stopped him from pacing, "All right. I have an idea. You must promise me that you'll behave."

"Eagle, I'm too damn tired to be doing any misbehaving."

"Very well, come with me," she led him to the bedroom and climbed into bed.

"You can bunk with me tonight and hopefully you'll feel secure enough to sleep. If you have a nightmare or flashback, I'll be here to talk to you."

D.M. climbed into bed next to her and turned off the light. He rolled onto his side and snuggled up next to her the best he could. Soon he was fast asleep.

CHAPTER NINETEEN

D.M. sat on the hangar bay wall. A warm spring breeze hit his face. Jake stood next to him dressed in the final prototype of armor. The suit fit like a glove. The major had skillfully engineered the armor so that it matched the contours of the human body and covered nearly every square inch. It was light weight, quiet and comfortable. With the cooling suit under, it meant the armor could be worn in just about any climate. "Well major, I really think you've outdone yourself this time," Jake broke the silence.

"It appears so," D.M. said softly as he enjoyed the breeze.

"I think this calls for a celebration. Promise you won't get mad at me?"

"For what?"

Jake reached down inside the armor and produced the two cigars that D.M. had stolen the fateful night of their first mission. They were a bit tattered, but still able to be smoked. "I managed to save them from your gear." He offered one to the major. D.M. pulled out his knife and gently cut one end off. He tossed the knife to Jake who did the same. Jake produced a lighter and held it for D.M. The major took a few puffs and coughed. This was a far stronger cigar than he was used to, but it was damn good. Jake lit up and together they smoked.

D.M. carefully ground out the cigar. He'd only smoked half of it. Jake did the same. "Shall we save the rest for later?" The major said as he rolled it between his fingers.

"Yeah, after the test we can hopefully finish the celebration."

"I hope it goes well and you're still around to celebrate with."

"I'll be fine, don't worry," Jake replied as he tucked the cigar back under his armor in a nice safe place.

The major's head buzzed with a nicotine high, "Aw, shit, I don't know about you, but I got one hell of a buzz. Haven't smoked something this heavy in a long time."

"I'm there with ya!" Jake exclaimed, "Hey, let's go down and test this bitch," he pounded his fist on the breast plate of his armor.

"Are you really sure you wanna do that? I mean we *can* rig up the computer to give us an impact reading."

"A computer can't tell you how much it hurt, or maybe suggest a way to make it better," Jake said as he headed back inside, "We need to get the rest of the gang, especially Tige, I want him to test fire at me. Do you wanna get them? I'll meet you down at the range."

"Sure, I'll get 'em," D.M. replied.

Eagle sat down behind the shooting bench and pulled on a pair of hearing protectors. The rest of the team joined her. Tige stood at the bench with a variety of hand guns and a couple of small caliber rifles. Jake stood about twenty yards away. He had put on the helmet that he designed. Secretly he hoped that the clear visor would at least deflect a bullet. He had tested it to stop a .38 caliber round. D.M. was pleasantly surprised by the lieutenant's creativity.

"Ready Mate?" Tige hollered down range.

"Bring it on baby!"

Tige took aim with a .22 caliber hand gun. He gently squeezed the trigger. The round went down range and struck Jake on the breast plate. The rest of the team was on the edge of their seats. The lieutenant looked down and then back at the group, "Not a scratch!" He yelled. The team cheered. Tige loaded a .25 ACP and took aim. Jake waved his arms that he was ready. Again the round struck him on the breast plate. He jumped up and down and let out a warrior's cry, "Hoooooaaahhhhh!!! Can't dent this!" He pounded his fist against his chest, "More, more, bring it on!"

Tige continued to work his way up in hand gun calibers until he reached .45 ACP. Jake signaled he was ready and Tige fired. The round hit him squarely on the breast plate, "Aaaagh! Fucking hell!

That stung!" He grabbed at his chest and made several gyrations in pain.

"Are you okay Jake?" D.M. called as he ran down to check on him.

"Yeah, yeah, I'm fine. That got my attention," he said as he paced around in a few circles trying to gather his composure.

"That was only a .45. We haven't even moved on to the rifles yet."

"I don't think I can handle any more than that. Anything bigger and I think you'll be looking at some tissue damage as well."

D.M. checked the armor over. He could find no damage to it, just a few rubs where the bullets had glanced off. He stood thinking for a few moments. Eagle came down and joined them. She offered her hand to Jake, "Lieutenant, you certainly stand behind the major's work with confidence."

"I stand behind *our* work with confidence," he said proudly taking her hand in a gentle grasp.

"What seems to be the problem? I thought this was rated to . 50 caliber."

Tige wandered down and joined their conversation, "Aye, the armor may be rated to .50 cal, but the human behind it isn't," he playfully punched at Jake, "We did a test of ordinance gelatin behind the plastic and it blew it to hell just with the impact."

"Ah, I see. Yes, that is a definite problem. Maybe you need a jerkin," Eagle commented as she lifted up the shoulder plate and looked underneath.

"A jerk? I'm not a jerk," Jake teased.

"No, a jerkin. A padded vest that was commonly worn under armor in the medieval era," she said as she poked around at the armor. Jake looked at D.M. who stood rubbing his chin. Too much padding and it would be bulky and difficult to move in, but perhaps a combination of padding and a more impact-forgiving variation of the plastic would work he thought. He reached over, grabbed Jake by the shoulder plate and pulled him along, "Okay, come on, back to the drawing board."

***

It was 2000 and Jake needed to get to his security detail. It was only a four hour shift, but it allowed the officer in charge to have some free time once in a while. He left D.M. in the lab and made his way to the security floor. After exchanging greetings and checking the most recent duty log, Jake settled in at his monitoring station. It was basically a boring detail. Sitting in front of a computer monitor flipping through all the security data that was being gathered from around the base. Most of it was useless: a large flock of birds showing up on radar, deer breaking electric eye beams in the forest, and the occasional bear lumbering around the flight line looking for a snack. The base was so remote that it was extremely rare to find anything even vaguely human within five miles of it.

There was only an hour left to the shift when the computer beeped. Jake poked at the mouse and saw a stream of encrypted code scroll across the screen, "Damn, there it is again!" He frantically worked to save the data to the computer. The whole data stream lasted just a few seconds and Jake hoped he had captured it. After, he opened the file and looked at the data. Yes, it was like the other one he had intercepted earlier and showed to Eagle. He looked at his watch, yup, about the same time too. Whoever was sending the data was trying to make sure as few people were awake as possible. The cyber sleuths in the security department still had not broken the code. They said it appeared to be a very complex revolving code that would require the sender and the receiver to have special software on their computers in order to decipher the messages. The problem was how to find that computer? The building was a technological nightmare, nearly every office and personal room had a computer. Finding the one that had different software would be like finding a needle in a haystack.

Jake found his way to the system administrator on duty. "Hey, I got a question," he said as he leaned in the door, "Can you find a computer in the network that's had unauthorized software loaded on it?"

"Sure, what are you looking for sir?" The sergeant on duty

asked.

"Any kind of program that would provide a high level of encryption, something not used here," Jake replied.

The sergeant tapped at the keyboard. A few moments later he motioned Jake to come behind his desk so he could view the monitor, "I see a few shareware programs that aren't authorized, which I will remove, but no sort of high tech encryption program."

Jake sighed deeply and rubbed his forehead. Where else could the transmissions be coming from? Cell phone? Some kind of stand-alone device?

"Sir?"

"Yeah?"

"The only thing I can think of is a laptop that is privately owned and has a cell phone modem attached to it. If you can find that, then you will probably find what you are looking for. It's definitely not a network computer."

"Okay, thanks for checking," he left the office and resumed his post for the last half hour of his shift. He sat thinking of who on the team had a private laptop, it certainly wasn't Eagle, she was on the straight and level.

Jake sat in the dining room waiting for Eagle. He knew she usually showed up a few minutes before the rest of the team. That morning was no exception. She strolled through the door early as usual. Jake stood and greeted her, "Morning ma'am."

"Lieutenant, you're here very early. You must be starved," she smiled and sat down in her chair.

"Another transmission last night," he said quickly, unsure of when the next team member would walk in.

"Okay we'll talk after breakfast. Same location."

"Right," Jake nodded as he took his place at the table and picked up the newspaper. He rifled through it until he found the sports section and then handed the rest to Eagle. A few moments later Tige and Sam strolled through the door. They said their good-mornings to Eagle and sat down. Soon D.M. wandered in followed not long after by Max. Bruce was the only one absent. The team ordered their beverages and the cook was just preparing to take breakfast orders when Bruce walked in. He said nothing and sat down. The rest of the team talked quietly amongst themselves leaving Bruce pretty much out of the conversation. Eagle could tell that the sergeant was not even attempting to make friends. Max had pleaded with her to find someone else. He hated working with Bruce. Team morale was suffering. She would have to do something.

Eagle met Jake up on the hanger deck after breakfast. He looked around to make sure they were alone. “I need a favor,” he said softly.

“What is it with you and the major? Always needing favors.”

“Can you get the team away from the building for a few hours? Maybe a flying training mission or something?” He said as he rested his arms on the wall.

“Why? You think it might be one of them?”

“Not certain, but I need you to trust me with the override keys to all the rooms.”

Eagle stood with her arms crossed, “And just what are you looking for?”

“Possibly a laptop computer with some rather special software loaded on it.”

“And what do we do if you find it? The code has still not been broken.”

“No, but we'll know who's doing this and can keep a close eye on them,” Jake replied as he turned to leave.

“Give me a day or so to come up with something. I'll let you know what, when and how.”

Eagle sat at her desk thumbing through the mail. A formal looking envelope caught her attention. She looked at the return address and wondered who it had come from. There was a knock on the door. “Come in major,” she called loudly. D.M. strolled through the door and sat down in front of her, “What can I do for you?” She asked.

“Nothing, absolutely nothing,” he smiled, “For once I am here not to ask any favors of you, or anything like that."

Eagle eyed him suspiciously. Most of the time D.M. was straightforward, but this time she was beginning to wonder, "Are you sure you don't want anything?"

"Well, I thought that since today is a real nice day, and there isn't much on the training schedule, that maybe you'd like to take a walk in the forest?"

"Maybe," she replied as she opened the envelope and pulled out a formal invitation. She read it and chuckled.

"What's so amusing?" D.M. inquired.

"Oh, I've been invited to a promotion ceremony. General Spears is pinning on his second star next week. He's a real good guy, kind of my adopted dad," she continued reading the invitation, "Well, it looks like I get to ask a favor of you."

"Oh?" D.M. raised an eyebrow.

"Major, will you accompany me to the ceremony and the ball following?"

"A date? A real bona fide date?" D.M. smiled broadly.

"Call it that if you want, but it's really just a social engagement."

"And we have to get all dressed up right?" He said as he rested his elbows on her desk. Eagle leaned back in her chair and thought for a few moments.

"Uh oh. Yes we do. And it's a seriously formal occasion, which means our dress uniforms aren't formal enough. We'll have to go see the tailor and have him make some up. I guess I'll have to wear some sort of long skirt and jacket."

"And is there going to be dancing?"

"Yes, I suppose so," she said with a sigh. Eagle wasn't fond of dancing.

"Oh, okay." D.M. replied as he tried to hide a smile, "Hey, can we go for that walk now?"

"After we stop by clothing issue," she said as she got up and went to the door. D.M. followed her down the hall to the elevator. They went down to the third floor and met with the tailor. He showed them designs of a simple yet elegant mess dress uniform. Both agreed that it would be appropriate for the event. The tailor made a few more measurements assuring them that the uniforms would be ready for fitting a few days before the ceremony. They left and headed outside for their walk. D.M. pointed them across the open field and toward the trees. He walked quickly and Eagle was struggling to keep up, "I thought this was a nice walk- why the hurry?" She grumbled.

"We need to be somewhere soon," he said as he slowed enough to let her catch up.

"I don't get it."

"You'll see. It's pretty important," D.M. said as he traversed the narrow gap between the line of trees and the steep rock face to the east. He walked for several minutes before slowing down. Eagle noticed he seemed to be looking for something. He stopped at the base of the cliff and looked up. He then walked a little further until he found what he was looking for, a few rocks stacked on top of each other, "Okay, this is where the fun begins," he said as he began to climb the rock face.

"You're not seriously going to climb all the way up there are you? And what is the purpose of this whole exercise anyways?" Eagle called. D.M. continued to climb. The rock face had plenty of hand and foot holds so the climbing was fairly easy. He stopped for a moment and looked up. He licked his lips and whistled the first few bars of the French national anthem; a moment later Jake's head popped up from behind a boulder.

"What took you guys so long? We've been here over an hour," he called to D.M.

"We had to make a slight detour," the major replied and continued climbing. He stopped after a few feet and called over his shoulder, "Come on, we need you up here too."

Eagle groaned and started to climb. D.M. made it to the top and waited for her. He reached down and offered his hand as she reached the top. "Well, that was certainly not what I was expecting to do today," she huffed as she followed D.M. and Jake down a narrow path. It led to a cave situated high on the rock face. It was hidden by a boulder from plain sight, only someone who had climbed the cliff would have been able to see it.

As she stepped inside she saw Sam, Max, and Tige sitting on various rocks and tree branches. They all stood as she entered. "Please gentlemen, at ease," she said as she peered into the cave,

"All right, what's this all about?"

Jake walked to the center of group, "I called the meeting to discuss those mysterious transmissions that have been sent from this base." The rest of the team regarded each other with confused looks. "I think I might have figured out who it is, but I can't be completely certain," he walked in a small circle, "No one has been able to break the code, so it's obviously being used by someone communicating with someone far higher up the food chain."

"And why do you say this?" Eagle asked.

"Because it just makes sense," Jake replied.

Max sat on a rock drawing in the sand with a stick, "He's right. I know it sounds stupid to go with that logic, but he's right. And didn't you say that Admiral Westland said Bruce had to stay? That he refused to get us someone different? I bet he's feeding information to Westland about us."

"I wouldn't doubt it. I'm fairly confident Westland has it in for us. So what do you wanna do Jake?" Eagle said as she sat down next to D.M.

"The team needs to disappear."

"Excuse me?" She replied.

"If the team was to suddenly disappear, then perhaps Bruce would make contact and then we could nail him. I'll stay behind and keep an eye on him."

"And what will we do about him if you find out it's him?" Eagle asked.

"Well, I don't think we can really bust him on anything because we can't break the code that's being used. We can, however, keep a close eye on him."

"When do you want us to disappear?" D.M. said as he stood and stretched.

Jake walked to the mouth of the cave and turned toward the group, "As soon as practical I guess."

Eagle thought for a moment, "How about next week? I got an invitation to attend a promotion ceremony for a friend of mine. It's in Washington D.C. We'll need to leave on Thursday morning; which is perfect because the resupply plane comes early that morning."

The team continued to formulate their plan and worked on

details. They agreed that if the need arose, they would meet in the cave. All plans would be kept secret from Bruce and they would leave Jake behind to monitor the sergeant's actions. He would remain hidden so Bruce would think he went with the rest of the team.

CHAPTER TWENTY

Eagle stood looking in the mirror. The mess dress uniform the tailor had designed was beautifully simplistic. It was a very dark gray, nearly black in color with a short jacket that came barely to her waist. It had six small gold buttons, three on either side of the front opening, but the jacket was held closed with an invisible metal hook and eye. The collar was upright and sported her rank and service pins, a fine gold chain connecting them. She wore a white long sleeve shirt under it with tiny pearl buttons. A gold cummerbund fitted snugly around her waist had matching sash tails that hung about a foot down from the left side. Her skirt was long, nearly touching the ground with a slit that was, by her standards, a bit on the high side. The only benefit it served was she was able to move comfortably. She wore black pumps with two inch heels. The uniform was distinctive in that it did not have any ribbons or medals on it. Not even a name tag. Since it was mess dress, no head gear was required. Eagle was happy for that, it meant her hair would not get so messed up by having to don and doff her beret.

D.M. stepped from the dressing room. Eagle turned to look at him. She felt goose bumps rise all over her body. He looked magnificent. His coat was tailored similar to hers with a white shirt under. He wore a red cummerbund with sash tails. His trousers were expertly fitted and he wore simple black patent military style low quarter shoes. On his left hand he wore a black glove to help disguise his robotic arm. The tailor had certainly out done himself with this uniform.

"Wow," Eagle smiled. She was at a loss for words.

D.M. returned the smile, "Not so bad look'in yourself there boss."

The tailor came from the back, "Well, well, don't we look like we're all ready for the ball?"

D.M. stepped over until he stood next to Eagle. He tugged at the bottom of his jacket and smoothed it out, "I think I'm ready to go to a party." There was something about getting dressed up that made the major feel good. He liked to put on a business suit and be a professional. Jeans and T-shirts were something he rarely wore. He guessed perhaps it was from his childhood. His mother would dress him up smartly and send him off to school. In the beginning the other school kids laughed and teased him. As he grew older, he found it to be quite an advantage in attracting girls however.

Thursday morning arrived and the team was waiting on the cargo elevator below the flight line. They could hear the C-130 approaching. "All right, everyone ready to go?" Eagle announced. Four thumbs-up were her reply. The plane landed and taxied back to the cargo elevator. A few moments later, the doors above them opened and they were lifted into the early morning darkness. Eagle quickly met with the load master and explained that they were heading out on an unscheduled mission and needed a ride. The team climbed on board, stowed their gear and the cargo was unloaded. The plane took off and headed north to the Reno airport. The colonel had issued orders that all personnel would be dressed in smart casual attire. They needed to make a good impression for D.M.'s part of the plan to work.

Eagle approached Sam, "Did you get the 'tool box' stocked?"

"Yes, ma'am. I got five different kinds of bugs, several transmitters, the biggest frigg'in relay I could find and a few other neat goodies."

"Good. And you three have been working on a plan to gather intel on Westland?"

"Still working out some of the details, but we got a rough plan," he replied, wiggling in the web jump seats trying to get comfortable, "How come we had to get dressed up?"

"Oh, you'll see. The major is working on something rather special, and it requires us to look and act professional. We're not some rowdy group of fighter jocks heading out for a weekend on the coast."

"Probably best that Jake stayed behind then."

The C-130 landed at the Reno airport and the team unloaded. D.M. stood looking for a way to get them to the other side of the airport where they needed to be. The team had just too much gear to carry and make a long walk. Max found an Army Sergeant who was just getting ready to climb into a deuce and a half truck. It wasn't beautiful, but more than ample to take the team where they needed to go.

"Excuse me," Max called to the sergeant.

"Yes?"

"We just came in on that flight and need to get to the other side of the airport. Could you possibly give us a lift?"

"What's in it for me?"

"Fifty bucks."

"Deal."

The sergeant brought the truck around and the team loaded up. He drove them the nearly half mile to the other side and dropped them off at the executive jet area. Max thanked him and slipped him a crispy fifty dollar bill. D.M. and Eagle went inside the building while the rest of the team stayed with the gear. The sun was just coming up and the office usually didn't open until eight, but D.M. had called ahead to make sure someone was there to rent them a plane.

"Good morning," D.M. said as he approached the counter.

"Ah, you must be the guy who called about the jet, and needing it early in the morning," the attendant replied.

"Yes, that's me."

"Well, sir, normally we don't rent executive jets out to people without the pilot. Our insurance company would freak."

D.M. reached inside his jacket and pulled out a packet of papers. He thumbed through it until he found his military aircraft rating card and pilot's license. He put them on the counter and slid them over to the attendant. "As you can see, I'm qualified for single and multi engine jet aircraft. I have over three thousand flight hours and only one serious mishap, courtesy of a bird."

The attendant looked the papers over, "You're a fighter pilot. These are all military fighter jets. How do I know that you won't pull some crazy maneuvers in one of my jets and crash it?"

"Because all of us need to be safely in Washington D.C. by this evening; and back home to this area by Sunday night. If it makes you feel any better, we're all pilots."

"Not really, but you're the one with the credit card with no limit, so if you crash the thing, I'll at least get it replaced," the attendant pulled out a stack of papers and showed D.M. where to sign. Once the paperwork was done, he showed them to a small Lear jet that was parked close to the building. Eagle instructed the team to sit tight while they preflighted the plane. They walked the outside of the plane and then went inside to the cockpit. D.M. led the way, pulling the drape out of the way. Eagle was right behind him, and knowing the others were still outside, playfully smacked the major on the behind as he got ready to sit down.

"What was that all about?" He said as he looked over his shoulder at her.

Eagle smiled devilishly, "I love covert operations."

"Right," he replied gruffly and sat down. He studied the instrument panel and made mental notes of where important buttons and gauges were at.

"Think you can fly this thing?" Eagle teased.

"Well, it's no Wolverine or Stealth Fighter, but I think I can get it in the air."

"Shall I tell the rest of the gang to get loaded?"

D.M. nodded. Eagle turned and went to the door, "All right, load up. Let's get going."

Tige, Sam and Max quickly sprang into action and within a few minutes, the plane was loaded and they were finding their seats. "D.M., this is sweet!" Sam called as he buckled his seat belt and looked out the window, "How much did this cost?"

D.M. groaned, "You don't wanna know. Just enjoy the ride."

Eagle closed the door and settled into the co pilot seat. She had flown many executive jets while on duty as an attaché for a general back in her earlier years in the Air Force, so this was nothing new for her. The major made contact with the tower and taxied out to the runway.

"Do you wanna get us in the air? I'm not quite sure of the feel of the plane just yet," he asked, wanting to be more safety conscious than bravado at that point.

"Sure, I can do that." Eagle took the controls and quickly got them airborne. Once at five thousand feet, she turned control back over to D.M. "Okay major, all yours now."

"Thanks. I got it. If you wanna take a nap, I'll let you know when we have to put down for fuel."

"Yes, actually I think I will," she adjusted herself into a comfortable position and closed her eyes. D.M. made a few minor course corrections and headed them east on the flight plan he had filed. The jet was small, only a six passenger airframe, so D.M. had planned a fuel stop in Denver and another one in Lexington, Kentucky. The noisy chatter from the back soon died out and D.M. looked back to see the rest of the team asleep. He sighed and looked over at Eagle. She was peacefully asleep.

The team landed in Washington D.C. just as the sun was going down. Eagle had arranged a stretch limousine to meet them at the airport and take them to the hotel. She had booked them into the Park Hyatt and the ceremony was to be held at The Westin Grand on the next block. It also afforded easy access to the Metro and the local busses. She had instructed the team to keep a low profile and not to attract any attention.

D.M. opened the door to his room and trudged in. The porter quickly placed his bag on the luggage rack and hung his garment bag in the closet. The major pulled out a ten dollar bill and handed to him. "Thank you sir, enjoy your stay at the Park Hyatt," he quickly left. The room was nice, furnished with modern décor that employed warm woods, smooth linen and soft, neutral fabrics. He was tired and really wanted to go to bed, but his stomach nagged and he knew he needed to get something to eat.

Knocking on the adjoining room door, he leaned against the

door post waiting for Eagle to answer. A few moments later the door opened. She looked up at him, "Hi," she said softly.

"I'm pretty tired. I don't feel like going out tonight." He rubbed his face.

"Do you want me to order something from room service or do you wanna eat in the Blue Duck restaurant?"

"Oh, I guess we can go eat there."

"Tige said that they were going out to find something. I guess they're happy to get out and see something besides forest."

They went down to the restaurant and got a table. The décor matched the rest of the hotel; trimmed in smooth wood, natural elements and hints of marble. It was certainly an upscale property; no expense had been spared for the comfort of the guests. The waiter took their order. He brought out an appetizer and their drinks. D.M. helped himself, "Nice hotel Eagle. I hope the bed is as good as the food. I need some serious sleep." They chatted until dinner arrived. Both were hungry and ate dinner with enthusiasm.

"You didn't have to fly the whole way; I would have given you a break."

"Naw, that's okay. I'll be fine. The ceremony isn't until tomorrow afternoon right?"

"Yes, that's right," she replied, taking a sip of wine.

"Good, I can sleep in," he finished his steak and drank the last of his glass of water and stood, "If you don't mind, I'm gonna turn in."

Eagle glanced up at him. He looked very tired indeed. It must have been quite a long time since the major had flown that many hours in one stretch. Most of the sorties they flew were only a few hours, but this one was nearly the entire day.

"Good night then, I'll see you tomorrow sometime."

D.M. nodded and left. Eagle finished her dinner and had the bill charged to the room.

She returned to her room and started to get ready for bed. There was a knock on the adjoining door. Opening the door, she found D.M. standing in front of her, "Need me to disconnect you?"

"Yes please," he turned around and patiently waited while she worked to unhook the cable from his robotic arm.

"Okay, all done," she said, patting him on the back.

He turned around, "Thanks," leaning down; he gave her a quick kiss on the cheek, "Good night."

"Good night major."

The next morning, Eagle met with the three who were going off to gather intelligence on Westland. They ate breakfast in their room and discussed plans with her. She filled them in on what information she was able to provide and gave them hints on where and how to track him down. They headed out and Eagle returned to her room. It was nearly noon when there was a knock on the adjoining door, "Yeah, come in, it's open," she called from the table. The door opened and D.M. staggered in. He was dressed only in a pair of boxer shorts. He leaned against the door post and rubbed his eyes.

"Afternoon major," Eagle said as she looked up from her laptop.

D.M. squinted in the bright light, "What the hell time is it anyways?"

"Just past twelve. You want me to order you some breakfast or lunch?"

"I'll start with breakfast, thanks," he turned to go back in his room, "I'm gonna get a shower and wake up."

The major returned half an hour later and joined Eagle at the table. She helped get his arm connected so he could finish getting dressed. Their meals arrived and they ate. "What time did the others leave?" D.M. asked as he speared a sausage link.

"They headed out about six thirty this morning."

"Sorry I wasn't up to see them off. I guess I really needed some crew rest. I have to admit, the bed was very comfy," he took a long drink of milk and sat his glass down, "What time do we need to be there tonight?"

"Seventeen thirty. The ceremony starts at eighteen hundred."

"Right. Was there anything you wanted to do today? Shopping? Sightseeing?" The major asked.

"Not really. I think I have everything I need. I have an appointment scheduled down in the salon to get my hair done at fourteen hundred. Not often I get to be pampered," she smiled, her eyes twinkling in the sun.

D.M. rubbed his chin. He'd showered, but hadn't shaved, "They got a place down there I can get a shave and a hair cut?"

"I think its right next door to where I'm going. Do you want me to call down and book you something?"

"Yes, thank you."

Tige sat in a hedge row with his back to Arlington Cemetery. His vantage point gave him a view of two of the Pentagon's largest parking lots. His job was to observe when Westland came out and to get the license plate number of the car they were driving. Since it was a Government vehicle, it looked like the thousand or so others that dotted the parking lot. He peered through his spotting scope and adjusted the focus. Tige watched as employees arrived for work and went through security and inside the building.

Sam had gained access through one of the rush hour Metro trains. Although there was security posted at the station under the Pentagon, during rush hour they would occasionally overlook a "forgotten" security badge and allow an active duty military member inside without it. He found a nice coffee shop and was waiting for Westland to show up. Eagle had given him the ring, corridor, and room number necessary to find the admiral. Sam located the office and now had to wait for his target. His job was to alert the other team members when the admiral was on the move. He was to loosely follow him through the building and report where he was going. Eagle had also mentioned that every Friday the admiral would eat out for lunch. This would hopefully provide an opportunity for him to get inside the office and plant a few bugs.

Max sat dozing in a rental car parked in the largest parking lot. He was to tail the admiral when he went out for lunch. When they returned to the Pentagon after lunch, his job was to carefully break into the car and plant tracking devices and bugs in it as well. He wished Jake had been along on this mission, he was an expert at breaking into cars and buildings. A crackle of static came over his headset. The team had managed to disguise two way radios into cell phone bodies and used the wireless Blue Tooth headsets to communicate. The technology was so popular that no one would think anything out of the ordinary.

"Ground Zero. I have eyes on target," Sam said quietly.

"Roger that. What entrance did he come in?" Tige replied.

"Main entrance from the big lot."

"Copy. I'll keep eyes on."

Sam watched as Westland went down the hall. He finished his coffee and slowly began to follow him. The admiral stopped at his office and unlocked the door. Sam had checked the lock earlier and formulated his plan to get in. He continued past the admiral and went down the hall to the next corridor. Doubling back, he returned to the coffee shop to wait.

About lunch time, Sam looped back around until he was about fifty feet from the admiral's office. There was a bench against the wall and he waited, reading a paper. It gave him a perfect vantage spot to see the admiral leave and then be able to follow him to the door and report when he was leaving the building. At ten minutes to twelve, the door opened, Westland and Farlow walked out.

"Ground Zero. We have movement."

Tige sat up and peered through the spotting scope, "Roger. Eyes on."

Max jolted awake and started the car, "Bull Dog is hot."

Sam trailed behind and watched as the admiral left the building, "Okay, target is heading out entrance one. Repeat, entrance one."

Tige swung his scope around to the entrance, "Roger, eyes on. Target ID'd. Coming down the walkway. Two subjects in khakis."

"One carrying a black attaché?" Max said as he scanned the area.

"Affirmative," Sam replied.

"Got 'em. Bull Dog is on the hunt."

Tige watched them as they headed for the staff car, "Target is in row seven about half way down. Now getting into blue staff car," he watched as the car backed up and adjusted his scope to try and read the license plate, "Target plate number, Golf one, one, two, zero, seven, five, Fox Trot."

"Golf one, one, two, zero, seven, five, Fox Trot. Confirm?" Max said as he hurriedly wrote the number down.

"Confirm," Tige replied, "Target heading north on North Rotary road and now turning onto Columbia Pike heading north... He's now taking the clover leaf around to get on Washington Boulevard heading south...Shit, he just went right by my position!"

"I got him. On his six now," Max said as he carefully tailed the car. The two way radios the team had boasted a ten mile radius, but Max found himself headed toward the Dulles Airport area and lost contact with Tige and Sam. "Shit, where the hell is this guy going for lunch? Morocco?!"

The staff car finally stopped at a deli not far from the airport. Max watched as the admiral got out and went inside. Lieutenant Farlow sat in the car eating a sandwich. Within five minutes the admiral emerged and got back into the car. He wasn't carrying anything, which seemed curious to Max, and he couldn't have eaten lunch that fast. So what did he do in there? The car pulled off and Max continued to follow them. He finally got back in radio range, "Bull Dog. Target returning to base. ETA is ten minutes."

"Damn!" Sam cursed. He needed a few more minutes to get the last bug planted. It was in a tricky place and he was having troubles with it. In all, he had planted seven bugs in the office. That should provide enough coverage to listen in on what Westland was doing.

"I have eyes on target. Turning onto South Rotary road. Ground Zero, you have five to seven mike," Tige said as he followed the car with the scope.

"Roger. I'll be clear in two," Sam replied as he carefully slipped out the door and made his way to the Metro station. His part of the mission was completed. Now it was up to Max. Tige stuck around to provide visual surveillance for Max, hoping he would be able to alert him should anyone get curious about his actions. The team would go their separate ways and eventually meet up at the hotel.

CHAPTER TWENTY ONE

D.M. sat on the bed rubbing his face. The barber had given him a straight razor shave and it was the closest shave he'd ever had. His face was smooth as a baby's bottom and felt wonderful. Eagle was right, he thought, it pays to get pampered once in a while, and he wasn't going to have any five o'clock shadow issues tonight. He got up and began to get dressed. Getting his shirt on was always a problem when his robotic arm was not on and functioning. He had managed to get his trousers on and zipped up, but he was going to need help getting the shirt arranged correctly and the straps for his arm through the small slits and everything buckled up and connected. He was happy Eagle had booked adjoining rooms, it meant less time back and forth down the hall. Pulling his arm on the best he could, he knocked on the door.

"Yeah, come in," Eagle called.

D.M. pushed the door open and wandered inside. Eagle came from the bathroom, "You need some help?" She was dressed in her skirt and white blouse.

The major nodded. Eagle reached around and connected the wire for his arm and then helped tuck the straps through the side slits and buckled them. This allowed the straps to lay under the shirt in case the major needed to unbutton his jacket for some reason. He thanked her and headed back to his room to finish dressing.

Eagle finished dressing and sat down on the couch. Music reached her ears. She stopped and listened. It was coming from the major's room. She listened closer and realized it was Spanish music. Carefully she crept over to the adjoining door and peered through the crack. D.M. hadn't closed the door the whole way and she could see him dancing elegantly around his room. She stood transfixed watching him as he moved effortlessly. No wonder he was so light on his feet when he was sword fighting, she thought, he had picked up the foot work very easily and was smooth and controlled.

D.M. heard the door creak. Out of the corner of his eye he could see Eagle peering in at him. He smiled to himself; it was time to have a little fun. He danced out of her sight. As he passed the door, he grabbed the handle and yanked it open. "Hah! Caught ya! Come here!" He laughed as he grabbed Eagle by the hand and pulled her into the room. She squealed at first, and then joined in his laughter. He took her hands and placed her in a dancing position. He stepped in, took her right hand had began to dance. Eagle struggled and looked down to see where his feet were going. "Ah,ah, don't look down, look up at me," D.M. said softly. Eagle continued to struggle. D.M. stopped, "Let me guess, you don't dance very well?"

"No, not one of my strong points," she shook her head.

D.M. looked at his watch, "Damn, only got twenty minutes to teach you to dance. Humm, this is going to be a challenge," he took her hands and placed them on his waist, "You dance by feel. You have to feel what your partner is doing and mirror their movements." He took a step forward, "Now, did you feel my hip come forward?" Eagle nodded. "Okay, you match that by stepping back." Eagle took a step back. "Now, look up at me and go with the feeling," D.M. slowly began to move, giving Eagle the chance to keep up. "Good, good, now a little faster." He moved at a tempo matching the music, calling out the steps. Eagle kept up, becoming more comfortable with the movements.

"I didn't know you could dance so well," she said.

"My mother thought it would be good for me to experience Spanish culture. She sent me to dance school, and I really liked it. Even after she died and father refused to pay for lessons, I got a job working in the studio, polishing mirrors, scrubbing floors and playing dance partner for women who were taking lessons." He slipped her hands off his waist and placed them back in the Waltz position with his left hand holding her right hand and his right hand around her back. Eagle began to struggle again. "Just feel the movement, let me help you, you're doing fine. Keep looking up at me and hold yourself straight." He let his hand slide down to the small of her back and with gentle pressure, guided her into a circle. "Even when I was in college, I worked part time at a dance studio." He stepped in a little closer to her.

"And what are your favorite dances?" She asked.

"Humm, let's see... I love the Salsa, my all time favorite. Then there's the Tango, Merenge, Waltz, and I know many of the Flamenco dances as well."

"Well, major, we might have to work a trade. I teach you swordsmanship, and you teach me to dance."

D.M. smiled, "Yes, I think we can call that a deal," he looked at his watch, "Come on, we'd better get going."

Jake lay belly down in the ventilation shaft peering out a vent grill. He watched as Bruce pulled out a laptop computer from a drawer and sat down on the couch. Turning it on, he connected a cell phone modem and began to type. Jake hoped his bug would work. He had taken the last two days to bug Bruce's room and computer. And he was on his way to finish the job when the sergeant unexpectedly returned. Now Jake was stuck in the shaft, unable to move until Bruce left again. With any luck, the bug would pick up the transmission and he could compare it to the ones he'd seen while working security. He knew the transmission would be short, only sent after Bruce had finished typing. With the short time he had the laptop; Jake had not been able to find the encryption software. He figured that it was a buried file that he would not have enough time to find. Whomever the sergeant was communicating with was high up. And hopefully this message would find its way to Westland, who was supposed to be at the promotion ceremony as well. He hoped that the other three had completed their mission and they would have a perfect spy network set up.

Bruce clicked the SEND button and turned off the laptop. Jake watched as he returned it to the drawer and left the room. Checking his watch, he figured that Bruce was heading to the gym. Carefully inching his way forward, Jake reached the end of the vent shaft and carefully planted his last bug inside the bedroom vent grill. Since there was no way to turn around, he now had to slowly inch backward until he reached the junction segment that led to Sam's room.

Eagle and D.M. strolled through the door of the banquet hall. It was large with numerous rows of chairs laid out facing a raised stage. A dance floor was hidden underneath. Behind the rows of chairs were banquet tables decked out for the occasion. Each round dining table had a floral centerpiece with an American flag. Little silver placard holders noted the table numbers. The tan linen table cloths matched the tan silk of the wall paper. Dainty golden chandeliers hung in recessed parts of the ceiling. Everything was bright and cheery.

"Eagle! You made it! How fantastic!" General Spears exclaimed as he grabbed her hand. He was brimming with energy.

"Wouldn't miss it for the world. Congrats," she replied, turning slightly towards D.M. "Let me introduce you to Major D.M. Elliott, my second in command."

The major offered his hand and the general shook it vigorously, "Good to meet you sir. Congratulations," D.M. said in the most formal voice he could manage.

"Are you two staying for the ball?" the general pressed.

"Yes we are," Eagle answered.

"Good, I'll catch up with you later," he scurried off to attend to his other guests.

"Is he always like that?" The major asked.

"Yup, he is. His nickname at the Pentagon is 'Speedy Spears'. He's been a mentor of mine most of my career."

D.M. smiled, "I can see why. Good to have a general looking out for you." He spied an admiral coming toward them, "Isn't that Westland heading this way?" He said softly. Eagle turned and nodded.

"Well, colonel, major. Surprised to see you here. Where is the rest of your team?"

Eagle shot a quick glance at D.M. "They're off in Reno, sir. Those that wanted got a weekend pass. I left Captain St. Ivor in charge of them. I can only hope Reno is still standing when the weekend is over," she smiled as she lied through her teeth. D.M. nodded in agreement, knowing that she was setting up Westland. The other three team members had assured her that the admiral had not seen them. They carried out their mission in secrecy and returned to the hotel by completely different modes of transit and at different times.

"Yes, well, hopefully they will behave themselves and not cost the tax payers too much money," he started to leave, "Good evening colonel."

D.M. and Eagle stiffened roughly to attention as he passed by, "Sir," they said in unison as polite acknowledgment. Once the admiral was out of hearing range, D.M. turned to Eagle. He stepped close to her and leaned over, "You think he took the bait?"

"We can only hope," Eagle whispered back.

After dinner, the band began to play. The chairs from the ceremony had been cleared and the dance floor was made available. D.M. egged Eagle on. He wanted to dance. She refused him the first few songs and then finally gave in. They stepped out onto the dance floor. "Remember, just feel my movement and follow me," the major said as he took his position with her. Soon they were keeping time to the music and moving effortlessly around the dance floor. Occasionally Eagle would falter and D.M. would have to rescue the movement. Even though she made mistakes, Eagle enjoyed dancing with the major. He was such a strong partner; it was easy to forget that she felt like she had two left feet. She decided she was certainly going to take him up on dancing lessons when they got home.

The music changed to a slow dance. D.M. pulled Eagle a bit closer and gently swayed with the music. He had to remind himself that this was a professional occasion and he couldn't dance as close as he really wanted to. Still he was enjoying himself. It wasn't often that he got to have such close contact with the woman he loved. He glanced down at Eagle. Her head was level, but he could see her eyes were partly closed. She was obviously enjoying herself as well. She looked up and saw him watching her. His eyes were soft and there was the barest hint of a smile on his face.

General Spears approached the table where Eagle was sitting. D.M. had excused himself for a few minutes. He sat down next to her, "Well, are you having a nice time?"

"Yes, I am."

"How are things going with the team?

"Mmm, we have a few issues going on, but we're working them out."

"Like what?"

"I can't exactly say right now."

"Are you keeping this from me for a reason?" He pried.

"Unfortunately, yes. I'd love to tell you, but I can't just now until we take care of our problems."

"You'll tell me later then?"

"Definitely."

The general stood up, "Would you care to dance with your old dad?"

"I'd love to." She stood and he took her hand, leading her to the dance floor. They danced to a couple of songs and then he returned her to the table where the major was waiting. She sat down and took a long drink of water.

"Have fun dancing with the general?" D.M. asked, he was hoping she would want to go back out and dance some more.

"Yeah. He's quite a good dancer too."

"Wanna go back out and dance some more?"

"In a few. I'd like to catch my breath and rest my feet a bit."

"All right. Sorry." He took a drink of his iced tea.

"No need to be. I understand your enthusiasm and love for dancing." She rested for a while, watching other people. Finally she felt rested enough and stood. D.M. escorted her to the dance floor and they continued to dance.

They danced until late into the night. After saying their goodbyes to the general, they walked back to their hotel. Eagle was happy it was only a short walk as her feet were complaining about being stuffed into high heels the whole night. The cool night air felt good after being in a crowded ball room for the last several hours. She walked with her arm resting on his. "Well major, thank you for such a wonderful evening."

"You're most welcome. I had a nice time too. And with a little work, you'll be a pretty good dancer."

A noise behind them made D.M. look over his shoulder. About five yards back were two men.

"Are we being followed?" Eagle whispered.

"Yup."

One of the men hollered for them to stop in Spanish. D.M. continued to walk. The man hollered again. "D.M., that sounds like Spanish," Eagle said, worry in her voice.

"Yes. He wants us to stop, which is exactly why I'm not."

The man shouted something else in Spanish and took several quick steps toward them. D.M. continued to walk, picking up the pace a little. The other man called out something.

"What are they saying? You speak Spanish."

"I speak Catalonian Spanish, these guys are speaking Mexican. There's a bit of a difference there."

Again one of the men spoke up, "Oye agujero de asno, parar."

D.M. slowed up. The man called out, "¿Oye puto, no me oyó usted?"

The major stopped dead in his tracks raising his finger in the air, "Now that one I know." He carefully unhooked the clasp on his jacket and moved Eagle around behind him.

"What did he say?"

"Uh, never mind, it wasn't polite."

One of the men brandished a knife. "Yo no haría esto si yo fuera usted," D.M. warned. "Don't do it," he said in English, punctuating his intentions.

"Déme su cartera," the man said as he stepped forward.

"¿Mi cartera?" The major carefully took his left hand and reached inside his jacket. A moment later, he held his cocked Sig . 45 level with the man's face, ¡"No pienso tan, ahora vaya!" He said between clinched teeth, "Leave!" His finger was on the trigger waiting for the men to make up their minds. The two muggers decided it was not a good idea and ran. D.M. quickly holstered his side arm and turned to Eagle.

"Trying to rob us eh?" She said softly.

"Yeah, wanted my wallet, but I think they changed their minds for some reason," he smiled and took her arm and continued on to the hotel. He walked Eagle to her room and made sure she got inside safely. He then continued on to his room. Taking off his coat, he draped it over the back of a chair. He removed his pistol and tucked it under his pillow. There was a knock on the adjoining door. He opened it to see Eagle. She had removed her jacket, but still had her shoes on for some reason. He figured that would have been the first thing she took off.

"Yes, can I help you?" He said in a matter-of-fact tone.

"I wanted to let you know I had a wonderful time tonight," she announced. D.M. knew that she had something else on her mind.

"You told me that all ready. And I'm glad you had a nice time," he replied with a yawn.

Eagle stepped into the room and put her hand on his arm, "I thought maybe we could have one last slow dance?"

The major studied her for a moment. He was tired, but there was a part of him too that wanted to hold her closer than they had been allowed at the ball. And dance was one way of showing feeling for the other person without climbing into bed. "Okay, one last dance, and then I'm going to bed," he walked over and poked at the CD player until he found a suitable song. As the music started, D.M. slid his arms around Eagle and pulled her tight against him. She wrapped her arms around him and snuggled her head against his shoulder. As the song played, he gently caressed her back. Eagle moaned softly, it felt good, her back hurt from wearing high heels all night. When the music faded, D.M. touched her chin. She brought her head up to look at him and he leaned down and tenderly kissed her.

"Good night," he whispered, slipping from her grasp. He unbuttoned his shirt. Eagle stepped forward and caressed his chest. The major closed his eyes for a moment, enjoying the attention. As much as he wanted to spend time with her, he was tired and wanted to get some sleep, "All right, come on, you need to get some sleep. You got breakfast with the general tomorrow morning."

"You mean *we* have breakfast with the general tomorrow," she corrected.

D.M. groaned, "Good night."

Eagle stepped away from him, "Are you throwing me out?"

"Yes, now go to bed!" He spun her around and smacked her on the behind as he sent her through the doorway. He closed the door and stood there for a few moments. Reaching up, he unbuckled the straps that held his robotic arm on. He knocked on the door and was surprised that Eagle opened it immediately.

"Yes major?" She said as she stepped through the door. D.M. turned his back to her and leaned down.

"Can you unhook me?" He asked.

"Is that all you wanted?" She replied as she disconnected the cable to his robotic arm.

"Yes, thank you. Good night."

Eagle growled lowly as she stomped back through the door and closed it loudly. D.M. collapsed on the bed chuckling. It had been such a long time since he'd enjoyed himself like that. Granted it was a formal social engagement, but he could at least spend time with the woman he loved.

Tige sat in the restaurant reading the morning paper. He took a sip of coffee and surveyed the area. He made sure the table he was sitting at was tucked in a corner against the wall where he could see nearly the entire dining area. Sam soon joined him. "They not here yet?" He asked as he sat down and poured a cup of coffee.

"Nope," the captain replied as he finished his cup and poured another. Sam picked through the remains of the paper and found something worth reading.

"Did you test your little insects?" Tige said from behind the paper.

"Checked the relay and it appears that all are working fine."

"What did you tie that into?"

Sam stirred some cream and sugar into his coffee, "I found a line up in the drop ceiling and spliced into it. Rather shocking experience if I do say."

Tige smiled and continued reading the paper. A few minutes later, Eagle and D.M. came in and were seated a few tables away. They were dressed in civilian attire and didn't even look their direction or acknowledge them, they knew they were there. Max straggled in and joined Tige and Sam. The waitress came by and brought them more coffee and took their breakfast orders. They talked quietly amongst themselves.

Eagle and D.M. sat talking. They were waiting for the general to show up. He had asked them to breakfast because he wanted to visit with Eagle and protocol dictated that he not overly socialize with junior officers on a personal level, especially at an official function. Dancing with Eagle was quite close to a protocol faux pas. The major saw the general come in. He nudged Eagle on the arm. They both stood as he approached. "Good morning sir," Eagle said as she held her hand out. The general took it and turned it into an embrace.

"So good to see you my dear."

"Good to see you too sir. So how does it feel to have a second star?" She teased as she took her seat.

"Ah, a little more pay and a lot more headaches!" He said as he poured a cup of coffee, "So when are you going to pin on your Bird?"

"Whenever Westland decides to give it to me I suppose. I don't know if our manning and rank structure will permit though."

"That's a shame. I hear your team has done some pretty tough missions and came back from it."

D.M. finally joined the conversation, "Not all in one piece."

The general studied the major for a few moments. He could tell the major had been wounded in battle, it was difficult to tell how badly he'd been injured, and D.M. hid his disability well. "What happened to your hand major?"

D.M. rubbed his glove with his other hand. "It wasn't my hand, it's my whole arm. I took an incendiary round in the shoulder and lost the use of it. With some help, I built a robotic arm so I could remain on the team."

"That's amazing. How do you have the technology to do that?"

"I have a degree from MIT in chemical engineering and a minor in robotics."

The general took another sip of coffee, "Eagle, are all your team members this educated? This is fascinating."

"They're a pretty bright bunch, but none quite as bright as the major," she replied as she emptied a packet of sugar into her tea. The waiter arrived and took their orders. They continued to chat until breakfast arrived. Eagle told the general about the team and what information she could that wasn't classified.

"It sounds like you have a good team put together. Too bad they aren't here; I would have liked to have seen more of them, and my time at your commissioning was so brief I never got to meet them up close."

Eagle leaned forward until she was only a few inches from the general, "Can you keep a secret?"

"Yes, of course. You can trust me," he replied.

"Over your left shoulder, the table in the corner there are three of them. They aren't here if you get my drift."

The general casually looked around and noticed them at the table, "Yes, they look quite capable."

"On the left is Captain Tige St. Ivor, middle is Lieutenant Sam Waters, and right is Lieutenant Max Hauer," she whispered. They ate breakfast and chatted for a while longer. The general finally said his farewell and rushed off to another engagement.

D.M. sat sipping on a cup of coffee. He gazed out the window and watched the world go by, "Well, since today is our last day in civilization, what do you wanna do?"

"It's funny; I was stationed here for nearly three years and never made it to the Smithsonian."

"Do you wanna do that? I'd love to see the Air and Space Museum," he tipped the last of the coffee down, "And would you have a problem with me making dinner plans for us?"

"Not at all."

The major smiled broadly, "I just need to borrow your computer when we get back to the room."

Jake sat in his room watching the computer monitor. It was still quite early in the morning, just past 0700. He'd had the guys down in security set his computer up for monitoring. He could now keep tabs on Bruce without being seen. The code still remained unbroken, but Jake was confident that he knew it was Bruce. The lieutenant was quite bored. He looked forward to the rest of the team coming back. He missed working with D.M. and knew when he got back they would be busy in the lab. They only had one working prototype of armor and they had yet to come up with a better, more resilient version of the plastic and some form of padding to protect the wearer from heavier munitions. Since he was basically relegated to hiding in his room, Jake had done quite a bit of research on various materials that could be used as padding. Bookmarking page after page, he would show his research to the major when he returned.

Going to the refrigerator, Jake retrieved a beer and popped the cap off. He didn't care that it was early; he was so bored that he wanted something to amuse himself. The computer beeped twice and he hurried to see what it was. One of the bugs in Bruce's room had activated. Jake pulled on headphones and clicked the record button on the computer. He listened as Bruce got his laptop and turned it on. Now it was time to see if the spyware software he managed to load on the computer worked or not. It would read the keystrokes made instead of intercepting transmissions made. Perhaps this would solve the problem of the unbreakable code. Words slowly appeared on the lieutenant's computer screen. Some words appeared to be code for people and places, but the majority of them were perfectly understandable. This was unreal Jake thought as he checked to make sure the data was saved. Eagle was going to have a field day with this. He wanted so badly to contact her and tell her what he'd found, but the team had agreed on total communications black out while they were away. There had to be no possible way to let on that Jake had stayed behind. He would have to wait another day to brief her on his findings. The typing ended and he watched as the transmission was sent. He checked his watch and made a notation on a piece of paper. He continued listening until Bruce left the room. Jake finished his beer and went into the bedroom. He flopped on the bed and turned on the TV, setting the volume low.

***

D.M. picked up the phone and dialed. The line on the other end rang several times before someone picked up, "¿Hola, este es el Flamenco Restaurante?"

"Si."

"¿Puedo yo por favor haga una reservación hacia las 19h00 esta noche?" The major asked. He figured making reservations at 1900 would give them enough time to see the sights, get back and get ready for dinner.

"¿Cuántos en su partido?"

"Dos por favor," D.M. replied. He hoped they had a cozy table just for two.

"Sí, ningún problema. ¿El señor, de dónde están usted?" The man on the other end inquired where D.M. was from.

"Zaragoza," D.M. replied. Eagle sat down next to him and listened. The major chatted for a few minutes before hanging up. "Okay, dinner is set."

"Let me guess, Spanish food?"

D.M. smiled, "Now what gave you that idea?" He sat thinking for a moment. "You didn't bring any other 'going out' clothes did you?"

Eagle looked through the closet. "No, just comfortable clothes and my mess dress. And is there going to be dancing involved?"

"Only if you want. I guess we'll have to do some shopping before tonight then."

Sam sat reading the newspaper at the table in their suite, "So what do you guys wanna do today?"

"How about we go see some of the monuments?" Tige replied, "I'd like to visit the war memorials especially."

"Why do you want to go see a bunch of stones dedicated to dead people?"

"Because if it wasn't for those 'dead people' our countries would be very different. It was because of their sacrifice we have the things we do today," he pulled his shirt on and tucked it in, "I was raised to respect those who have fallen for us. There have been many lost in my family tree because of wars and conflicts, I may be no exception. But all of us are part of the warrior culture, and it never hurts to remember where you came from."

Sam and Max sat silently for a moment. They both nodded slowly. Tige was right. From the very moment they all raised their hands and were sworn to defend the Constitution, they became part of the warrior class. Even though most of their jobs had little to do with actual conflict, they were part of the century's old tradition of warfare.

"Okay, so which ones do you wanna go see?" Max finally broke the silence.

Tige grabbed a brochure he had picked up in the hotel lobby and laid it out on the table, "Well, if we catch the H1 bus down to this stop, we should be able to walk and see most of them. Plus, if we have time, there are all those Smithsonian Museums as well." He rummaged through his suitcase and retrieved a small hip flask. Opening the refrigerator, he pulled out several small bottles of whiskey from the mini bar. He filled the flask and tucked it in his back pocket.

"You're not going to get us busted for drinking in public are you?" Max asked.

"I'll try not to. It's a tradition though; you drink with your fallen brethren."

Sam studied the brochure, "Come to think of it, my dad mentioned that I had an uncle that was killed in Vietnam. I wonder if I could find his name on the wall."

"We can most certainly look. Do you remember his name?" Tige said.

"Leon Waters."

"Okay, we'll find him and drink to him."

The bus stopped and the doors opened. "Are you sure this is the right stop Tige?" Sam said as he hurriedly stepped from the bus. Tige and Max were right on his heels.

"What the information board said," the captain replied as he pulled out his map of the Mall, "We should have a little bit of a walk to get to the Vietnam Memorial."

They made their way to the memorial and Sam referenced the computer to find his uncle. The morning air was still and somewhat cool. The grass held dew from the previous night and the sun shone brightly. Noise of the morning hustle and bustle could be heard on Constitution Avenue despite the heavy stand of trees that shrouded the memorial from plain sight.

"All right, he's on panel forty one echo, line fourteen," Sam said as he wrote the information down on the palm of his hand.

"Let's start looking," Tige said as he wandered down to the correct panel. It took the threesome only a few moments to find the name once they were at the correct panel. Sam reached up and let his fingers move across the deeply etched granite letters. Tige knelt down on one knee and pulled the flask from his pocket. Max joined him. It was early enough in the day there were not many visitors and the security guards were at the other end of the monument. Sam took his place next to Tige. The captain unscrewed the top and held it up as a salute, "To Army Specialist Leon Waters. Your sacrifice has brought you peace. You are not forgotten this day, or will you ever be. Your blood mingles with the fallen warriors of past and present. You have given your life so that others may be free. We salute your sacrifice and pray for your spirit. Sleep well fallen brother," he took a sip of the whiskey and passed it to Sam. The lieutenant took a sip and then stood. He poured a few drops on his fingers and pressed it into the letters of his uncle's name. He then handed the flask to Max. Sam knelt down and bowed his head. He'd never known his uncle, yet he felt strangely connected to him now. Tige's words had struck a chord in his heart. It no longer mattered what uniform you put on, or which war or conflict you fought in; you were part of a society where death was looked upon as the greatest sacrifice one could make for their country. The threesome sat silently for a few minutes.

Sam looked over at Tige, "You have a soul after all," he said softly, "That was beautiful. Thank you."

"I may be damned to Hell for the things I've done, but it doesn't mean I have a cold heart," The captain replied as he stood, "You, me, Max, we know all the names on this wall, and all of the other monuments across the world. We are brothers in arms. We know what our actions lead to. Sometimes we live, and other times we experience the beautiful death, the warrior's death. We're all the same no matter who we are or where we come from."

Max stood up, "Shall we go pay our respects to the rest of them?" He motioned with his arm to the rest of the war memorials. The threesome visited the Lincoln monument, Korean War Memorial and then made the long walk to the World War II Memorial. Finally, they walked a bit further and stopped at the Washington monument. It had been a long walk, but each man felt a deeper connection to those who had come before them. As they walked back to the bus stop, they saw a man in a wheelchair. He was dirty, haggard and unkempt. They noticed he was wearing a dirty old style BDU field jacket that was tattered at the elbows. He wore a dirty black baseball cap with "Vietnam Veteran" written across the front. A small yellow shield with a black horse's head was embroidered below, indicating he had been with the 10th Calvary.

"Excuse me fellas, can you spare some change?" He said his voice raspy and dry. The men stopped and regarded him. They looked at one another.

"You were with the Tenth mate?" Tige asked.

"Yep. First Squadron. We got tangled up at LZ Oasis in '69."

"I've read about that," Max replied.

"Reading about it is one thing. Being there is another." The man noticed the threesome sported military haircuts, "What? Are you guys a bunch of straight-legs here on a nice little vacation?"

"No, we're part of an SF unit here to do a little intelligence gathering," Sam answered.

"Sec Ops doing recon in our own country? What has this world come to?"

"Nothing that concerns the general public. We have our own problems." Tige pulled out his wallet and gave the man a ten dollar bill, "Get yourself a good meal mate."

He nodded his appreciation, "You're an Aussie? What are you doing here?"

Tige chuckled, "Got disowned by my own country. Oh well, their loss is the USA's gain."

"And what do you do?"

"Sniper."

"Ah, I see."

Max handed the man five dollars, it was the last of what he had in his wallet as he'd forgotten to go to the ATM and get more, "Sorry it's not much, but it's all I got right now."

"I appreciate it fellow brother in arms."

Sam took out ten dollars and gave it to him as well, "And hopefully this will get you another meal."

"Thank you. I wish you all safe and long military careers."

"Thanks mate, we need it," Tige said as they headed off toward the bus stop. They walked nearly a block in silence before Max let out a low growl.

"I can't believe this government! We're country of wealth and prosperity and they can't take the time to give our veterans proper care…There should be no veterans living homeless on the streets. They should have the best of medical care. After all, they put their lives on the line for this country. And what do they get? Kicked to the curb when they're no longer needed."

"Sad and unfortunate situation," Sam said as he looked at his watch.

"Most governments feel they can just use us and discard us after we're done doing their dirty work. Back home it wasn't much different; in fact it was probably worse. No one really saw it or paid attention to them, but they were there. I saw them," Tige replied.

They stopped at the bus stop. Tige pulled out the bus schedule and checked it, "Should be one here in a few minutes."

Max chuckled, "And when have you ever seen a bus run on time in DC?"

"Dunno mate, this is my first time here."

"Well, they are notorious for running late."

"Are we in a hurry to go somewhere? I thought we were out to enjoy the day."

Sam looked at his watch, "Yeah, we are. So what if it's a bit late."

"Anywhere else we want to go?" Tige said, pulling out his map.

"How about we go find some place to eat and get a nice tall

beer?" Max replied.

"Sounds good to me mate."

It was late in the afternoon when Eagle and D.M. returned to the hotel. Both carried garment bags from their shopping excursion. Eagle hoped that her selection of dress and shoes would be appropriate for the evening. The ladies at the dress shop had been very helpful in pointing her in the right direction. Eagle wasn't one to get dressed up and go out, she preferred quiet evenings at home usually dressed in sweats and a t-shirt.

She hung the dress in the closet and then took a shower. The weather was unseasonably warm for the time and they had not packed for it. A shower to freshen up before dinner would wash away the grime from the city. Although Washington D.C. was a beautiful city in the early summer, it was none the less a city and was dirty. After her shower, Eagle dried her hair and started to get dressed. A faint knock on the adjoining door caught her attention. She walked over and opened the door.

"Oh my," the major said in a low voice, a smile curled to his lips. Eagle was dressed only in a strapless bra and panties.

"What? You've seen me in less," she replied nonchalantly, "Need help getting dressed?"

D.M. stood staring at her for a moment. He could feel his face beginning to flush, "Uuuuuhhhhhh, yes please." Eagle connected his arm and pulled the chest straps through the shirt and buckled them.

"There, all done. Now let me finish getting dressed."

The major stepped forward and caught her around the waist, "Ah, do you have to?" He grinned.

"Yes, I do," she replied and slipped from his grasp.

Ten minutes later it was Eagle's turn to knock on the door. She was dressed, but was unable to get the very top of the zipper up on her dress. It was a shiny gold dress that was fitted all the way down. The shoulder straps were extremely thin and Eagle wondered if they would even hold the dress up. She wore gold tone high heels with straps that wrapped around her ankles. D.M. opened the door and smiled, "Let me guess, *you* need some help getting dressed?"

This time it was Eagle's turn to stare. The major was dressed in a simple black tuxedo. His hair was slicked back and shined in the dim light of his room. He had carefully shaved and the tiniest hint of aftershave reached her nose. D.M. always looked good when he dressed up, but this evening he looked especially handsome. "Yes, can you get the last bit of zipper?" She turned around with her back to him. He quickly pulled the zipper up.

"Okay, you're zipped."

"Thanks," she replied and turned around, "Let me get my little purse and we can be on our way," she reached up and straightened his bow tie, "What's with the hair?"

"This is my Salsa look!" He chuckled.

Jake sat in his room bored out of his mind. He had another whole day until the team arrived home. He wanted to go work in the lab, but just couldn't risk being seen by Bruce. Oh why did he agree to stay behind and play spy? The others must be having a wonderful time; eating, drinking, seeing the sights. No, he was stuck in his room eating TV dinners and drinking the same brand of beer every night. Hopefully when the team got back Eagle would let him go to Reno to blow off some steam. He longed for the perfect margarita, a big, fat, juicy steak dinner and most of all, some entertainment.

He sat watching TV. Nothing was on and he considered sneaking over to Sam's room to borrow some movies. No, better not risk it. Just another day and they would be home. He was tired of browsing the Internet. There was only so much research he could do on armor and weapons technology. Occasionally he would stumble across an adult website and have to quickly exit out of it. He knew security was monitoring the computers, so he had to behave himself when he looked for information.

The computer beeped and Jake opened up his spyware program. He watched as the words appeared across the screen: "Dragonslayers still gone. Request further instructions." There was a long pause before more: "Affirmative. Continue current mission parameters." The transmission ended shortly after.

"Okay Bruce, what are you up to?" Jake pondered. Mission? What mission? The team did not have any current mission planned, so it had to be orders that he was following from Westland.

D.M. held the chair for Eagle as she sat down. The restaurant he had chosen had only been open six months but had received rave reviews from the food critics. The atmosphere was uniquely Spanish with walls resembling aged stucco painted in a warm yellowish tan. Large pots holding sizable trees dotted the restaurant and each table was situated to provide as much privacy as possible. Ornate black wrought iron banisters wove between the tables, giving a sense of privacy. A large dance floor sat in the center with a stage for a band behind it. The staff wore traditional Spanish clothing and most spoke with a heavy accent.

The waiter arrived and introduced himself. He presented Eagle with a menu and D.M. with a menu and wine list. "Do you want a glass of wine?" The major asked.

"Yes, that would be lovely. I'm sure you can find me a nice red to have with dinner."

"Ah, yes, let's see," he said as he perused the list, "More fruity or dry?"

"Fairly dry," she replied.

The waiter returned and D.M. ordered a glass of wine for Eagle and a non alcoholic fruit drink for himself. Eagle enjoyed hearing him speak Spanish.

"You're not even gonna have a glass of wine?" Eagle said as she looked over the menu.

"Can't drink. Makes me sick."

"How so? Does your heart beat faster? Get flushed in the face? Stomach hurt? Vomiting? Serious hangover?"

"Yes to all," he groaned, "Remember, it was two glasses of beer that got me in trouble last time. And I even blacked out with that."

"Has anyone ever tested you for alcohol intolerance? It's an imbalance of liver enzymes that prevent you from properly metabolizing alcohol."

D.M. shook his head, "Would it show up in normal labs?"

"Not necessarily. If you want, when we get home I can run the labs on you and see if that's your problem."

"Yes, please. Is there any cure for it?" He asked.

"Sure. Don't drink!"

The waiter returned with their drinks and prepared to take their dinner orders. "¿La señora qué quisiera usted para la comida?" He looked down at Eagle wanting to know what she wanted for dinner.

Eagle gave the waiter a blank look.

D.M. chuckled, "Lamentable, ella no dice el español." He explained politely that she did not speak Spanish.

"Ah, siento. Señora, what would you like for dinner?"

"D.M., what do you suggest? I'll eat just about anything and I love seafood."

The major scanned the menu and ordered for them. The waiter repeated the order and then hurried off to the kitchen. D.M. reached over and took Eagle's glass of wine and had a small sip. He held it in his mouth for a few moments savoring the flavor.

"I thought you weren't drinking."

"Mmmmmmmm, just wanted a little taste. Good wine. I used to enjoy a good glass of wine or beer; unfortunately now it turns me into a train wreck. It's not like I'm a big drinker- more of a social drinker having one or two drinks and that's all."

Eagle sat thinking for a few moments. "Well, if you wanna play guinea pig, we can see if we can come up with something that will at least let you enjoy a drink or two without all the agony. Maybe with some tinkering I can synthesize the enzymes that are malfunctioning and make a pill or shot that you can take prior to drinking."

"I'd be game," he sat looking at her, "You look absolutely beautiful tonight."

"Thank you major. Du er veldig kjekk deg i kveld," she rattled in Norwegian.

"And I assume that's a compliment?"

"Ja, kjekk nok til å spise!" She giggled.

"Okay, okay, translate please."

"I said you look very handsome tonight- handsome enough to eat!"

D.M. chuckled and picked up his glass, "May I propose a toast?"

"You may," she smiled.

"A toast to you, me and the rest of the team. May we overcome our hardships and become something truly great." They clinked glasses and drank.

"Good toast," she took another sip of wine, "Now if we can figure out what Westland is up to."

The waiter returned with a plate of mixed tapas. D.M. selected a piece of bread and a slice of cheese. He sniffed the cheese and smiled, "Mmmmm, Manchego, my favorite." He placed a slice of ham on top and offered it to Eagle, "Have a taste of my country."

Eagle daintily sampled the hors d'oeuvre, "Nice, good flavor. You are truly a man of culture."

"I'd like to think so. Although I'll never turn down a bottle of Alhambra and a bowl of olives. You know, the Spanish version of beer and peanuts."

After dinner they sat watching couples dancing to Flamenco music. D.M. was itching to dance, but he would let Eagle decide if she wanted to or not. He also had something else on his mind.

"Eagle?"

She turned away from watching the dancers, "Yes?"

"I'm just wondering. Are you happy with the way our relationship is?"

"Do you mean personal or professional?"

"I guess mostly personal... I mean we have cooled things off quite a bit. Is that okay for you?"

"Why do you ask?" She replied drinking the last of her wine.

"Because I care greatly about you and I don't want you to feel like you're being pressured into something. I'll go along with what you want to do when you want to do it. And I can't say that having a really hot and heavy relationship was going to be very easy for me either."

Eagle collected her thoughts for a few moments, "Yes, I'm happy with the way things are now. I think we have a reasonable balance in our relationship, more so friends than lovers, but just enough intimacy to be happy. I think if we have too much it will certainly affect our professional relationship. It would be too obvious to the others that we're together."

"I agree completely," he watched the dancers gracefully moving about the dance floor, "Would you like to dance?"

"I don't know D.M., they look awfully good. I'm afraid I'd embarrass you."

"Nonsense!" He stood and took her hand, "This is supposed to be fun remember? Just enjoy it." Carefully, Eagle got up and he led her to the dance floor. They danced for a few songs before returning to the table to have dessert. The waiter brought out the dessert tray and Eagle looked it over.

"Mmmmm that looks good," she pointed to a chocolate dessert, "I don't think I can eat the whole thing myself, wanna split it?"

"Sure," he ordered the dessert and told the waiter to bring two spoons. "Have you had a good time tonight?"

"Yes, of course."

"You deserve to have some fun once in a while. All that you do for us must really be hard on you sometimes."

"It can be. But I knew from the beginning this wasn't going to be a walk in the park. I knew the hours were gonna be long and there would be heartbreak and triumph, pain, and little did I know, pleasure out of this job."

"I honestly wasn't really sure what I was getting myself into when I took the orders to join the team. They didn't really tell me much besides it was orders or Leavenworth." He reached across and took her hand, "But I'm glad I did. And along with the bad is the best thing that's ever happened to me," he smiled and gently squeezed her hand.

"Well, I never thought I'd find the man of my dreams standing in front of me in the middle of nowhere dressed only in a towel." They both laughed.

"Fate does some strange things."

"Yes major, it does," she paused for a long moment, "Would you tell me something?"

"What?"

"Why'd you decide to join the Air Force when you got out of

college? I mean, you said you'd made a lot of money while you were there; why didn't you just follow your course and continue on with your work?"

"I wanted to fly."

Eagle scratched her head, "If that was the case, why didn't you just invest in flying lessons on your own?"

"I dunno. And it may sound strange now that you know more about my past, but as much as I hated my father, I felt compelled to join the military."

"You could have joined the Navy and been a pilot."

"No. Not what I wanted," he laughed lightly, "I guess I can say I fell in love with another kind of Eagle. That too was love at first sight. And with exception of the Wolverine, I've never flown anything better." He studied her for a moment, "It seems that I like to fall in love with birds. When we met that first night and you said your name was Eagle, I couldn't believe it."

"It's that fate thing again huh?"

"Must be."

The waiter brought their dessert. Eagle grabbed a spoon and quickly dug in. She took a mouthful and sighed, "Mmmmm!"

CHAPTER TWENTY TWO

The team returned home to find Jake anxiously awaiting them in the cargo bay. He followed Eagle's directions and had a bag with him. He was supposed to look like he came back with the rest of the team, "You guys have no idea how happy I am to see you."

"I'm sure you are lieutenant," Eagle replied. The rest of the team picked up their bags and prepared to board the cargo tram that would take them to the elevators. They could hear the C-130 roar off down the runway overhead.

"I got lots of intel for you. It took some creativity, but I think you'll be quite happy with what I have," Jake rattled away excitedly.

"We'll plan a good time for a debrief. Until then, just keep it under your hat. We're all tired and want to get home," she replied.

He looked at Sam, "How did your part of the mission go? Were you guys able to get Westland bugged?"

"Hopefully," Sam replied, "We'll see tomorrow."

The next morning the team gathered for breakfast. They had rehearsed their stories and made sure they were not going to give Bruce any reason to believe they had done something different. Jake even borrowed five hundred dollars from D.M. to make it appear he had won at the casino. He sat at the table playing with the money. The rest of the team chatted and drank their morning cups of motivation. Bruce came in and sat down, "Hey, where were you guys?" He asked.

"You didn't get the memo sergeant?" Eagle replied.

"No, what memo?"

She stood and walked over to the bulletin board and removed a piece of paper, "This memo. The one that stated that D.M. and I were going to Washington D.C. for a promotion ceremony, and the rest of the team was authorized a three day pass to Reno," she handed it to him.

"No, I guess I didn't get that one."

Jake tapped his wad of money on the table, "Hey, check it out, I won five hundred big ones playing Blackjack." He fanned the bills out and waved them in the air.

"Yeah, Jake, just be a gloating winner," Sam jeered.

"Well, you guys didn't win anything."

"Did too," Tige interjected, "I won fifty bucks in the slots."

The team spent several minutes bickering amongst themselves about who won what in Reno. Breakfast arrived and they finally quieted down. Eagle gave D.M. a quick glance. He winked to show his approval. It appeared that Bruce was buying the story. She was waiting for Jake to finish his part of the rouse. He'd finished breakfast and was still playing with the stack of money, "So Eagle, how did the promotion ceremony go?" He finally said, not even looking at her.

"Oh, it was very nice. Good to see 'Speedy Spears' again," she took a long drink of tea, "I think he'll do a wonderful job with his second star. Too bad it took 'em this long to give it to him."

"Yeah, and the ball afterward was pretty fun too," D.M. piped in.

"Oh, and what did you two do?" Jake teased.

"You guys have no idea of how wonderful a dancer the major is," she smiled.

"D.M. dance?" Jake started to laugh.

"No, seriously, he can really dance!"

The rest of the team laughed. Even D.M. was chuckling, "Yes, guys, I can dance. But do you want to know something funnier?" He pointed to Eagle, "She can't!" The team burst out in hysterical laughter. Eagle reached over and playfully punched him in the arm.

"Thanks a lot major," she growled playfully.

After breakfast, Jake met with Eagle on the hanger deck. He filled her in on what he'd accomplished while they were gone and gave her the messages he'd managed to intercept. She sent Tige and Sam out into the forest on a sniper training mission. They were heavily laden with surveillance equipment and were really heading to the cave. They were going to set up the listening equipment and monitor the location and transmissions of Westland. All the equipment would have to be run on battery, so various team members would have to take large batteries out to keep the equipment running. Eagle was hoping they might only have to monitor Westland for a week or so to get some useful information. Otherwise, it was going to be very difficult to keep the secret from Bruce.

Sam worked on putting together the small satellite dish. It was barely eighteen inches across and made out of camouflage mesh. He had tucked it behind an out cropping of rocks that could not be seen from the ground. Tige sat behind him plotting the azimuth, "Come on, don't you have that bloody thing up yet?"

"Almost. Why? You got the azimuth all ready worked out?"

"Yes, it's not that bloody difficult," Tige replied as he lay back against the rock face. The warm late May sun felt good on his face.

"Oh, so nice to see you have such a mastery of these skills."

"Sorry mate, just part of being an SASR Bush Bunny all these years."

They finished setting up the dish and returned to the cave. Tige carefully disguised the wire from the dish in cracks and around stones so it was well hidden. They wanted to make sure that the equipment would hopefully not be seen from the air. Sam connected wires and plugged the small laptop into the battery bank. He turned it on and waited for it to boot up. Accessing the program, he gained a connection to the satellite. "All right, we're in. I just gotta get the connection to the transmitter above Westland's office and hopefully we'll get the GPS bugs in his car too."

"Do you think the surveillance bugs Max planted will have enough range that we can hear anything?" Tige asked as he watched over Sam's shoulder.

"Not sure. They weren't really designed with a very long range. I'm sure we'll intercept anything said while they're in the parking lot, but after that, we may be out of luck." Sam continued to work on the computer. He opened several programs and started applications running, "Right, that should do it." Placing the laptop in sleep mode he closed the top and covered it up with a piece of cloth. They left the cave and continued on their way. Tige still needed to fire off a few shots to make it look like they had been practicing.

D.M. sat in his lab working on one of the armor suits. Eagle watched as he assembled the components of one of the arms. He usually didn't want any company while he was working, but on this occasion he wanted to discuss an idea he'd been formulating. Feeling that his lab was quite secure, he had invited her down.

"All right major, what's on your mind?" She asked.

"I got an idea...You wanna get a reaction out of Westland right?"

"Right."

"So how about we feed him some false information and see if we can make him jump?"

"How so?"

"Well, what if we plan a fake mission to kick the shit out of Kemal again?" He stopped what he was doing and looked at her, "You know, tell Bruce that we're going back out to the beach house in L.A. and reduce it to ashes... Tell him that we want revenge and that Westland didn't give us clearance for this mission."

"And see if he jumps, tells Westland and we get called off the mission. Then we will know that they're all in it together."

"Bingo," he replied and picked up on his work again.

"We need to do it soon; those bugs will only live for two weeks tops."

"I can feed the story to the others, that's easy enough. We can start the planning tomorrow after breakfast," the major replied as he connected a plate of plastic to the upper portion of the arm.

"This is going to have to be played carefully; we need to find a connection between Bruce, Westland and Kemal. If we can do that, and have hard evidence to prove it, we might just be witness to a treason trial," She stood to leave, "You want me to send Jake down to help you?"

"Yes please, I could use his help, and also fill him in on the plan."

"And you can get the others briefed before tomorrow?"

"Yup, not a problem."

The next morning at breakfast, Tige sat reading a copy of the *Army Times*. Eagle had ensured that along with some of the national newspapers that were brought to the base on a weekly basis, the services newspapers were also included. She felt it was important to keep up with what the other branches of the military were doing. As Tige flipped through the pages, he stopped and began intently reading an article. Slamming his fist on the table he growled, "Shit!"

"Is there a problem captain?" Eagle said sharply. She did not normally tolerate profanity at the table.

Tige shook his head, "Sorry ma'am. Just reading some bad

news."

"Oh? Would you care to share?"

"I'd always hoped that I would someday get the opportunity to train with Captain Westmoreland, the number one sniper in the world," he studied the article for a moment, "The captain and his spotter were being air dropped for a mission. As they neared their landing zone, they got caught in a down draft and were slammed into a mountain... Sergeant William Jenkins was killed on impact. Captain Cabbott Westmoreland was severely injured. He lay in the field for nearly two days with multiple fractures to his legs, pelvis and back. He's now at Walter Reed where they are trying to put him back together...If he's lucky, he might walk again."

"That pretty much ends his military career," D.M. added.

"Yes, it does," Tige replied, his voice tinted with sorrow.

"That's odd. You don't find many officers who are snipers. Usually that's a job pretty much dominated by enlisted," Eagle chided in.

"True, he's a bit of an anomaly. He's well educated, a Harvard Law man. But for some reason he was blessed with the gift of accuracy and didn't seem to have a problem with killing people. So the Army let him go to sniper school and he graduated with honors. He then begged them to go to the Marine Corp sniper school. And he graduated that with honors too."

"You seem to know a lot about him," Jake said.

"In my line of work you get to know the others who do the same job. I've been following his career for probably five years. He's renowned for his very clean shots and incredible accuracy in less than perfect conditions. I guess you can say I'm a fan of his work," Tige took a long drink of coffee, "Sad that something like that had to happen to him, he was very valuable to the Army and several other services and agencies."

The major stood and went to the window, "Well, I don't know about you guys but I want another crack at Kemal. I think I'm about ready to have a healthy serving of revenge for what he did to us."

Jake stood and joined D.M. at the window, "Yeah, that sounds really good. We haven't had a good mission in a while. Lord knows I'd like to take a shot at him."

Soon the others were joining the conversation. Bruce sat quietly listening. D.M. and Jake had concocted a reasonable sounding plan and had filled the others in. They all sat down and began working on their plan of attack. D.M. made sure that Bruce was involved in the planning of the mission. He wanted to guarantee that there was no question about what was going to happen. The major hoped that the sergeant would feed the information to Westland and then they could confirm their suspicions.

Eagle leaned against the door frame of the chief surgeon's office, "Are you up for a little adventure Jim?"

"Oh, come on Eagle, I gave up field work years ago."

"No, no field work, just a field trip. And you even get to ride in one of the Wolverines."

Lieutenant Colonel Miles stood and approached her, "Well that sounds like a tantalizing offer. Where are we headed? And why do you need me?" He was of average height and build with short cropped brown hair and deep green eyes.

"I'd like you to consult on a case."

"Does this case have a name?"

"Oh, you'll see when we get there," she replied, "I'll meet you at your room tomorrow morning at 0300."

"Why so early?"

"I'm not telling the rest of the guys what I'm up to. If this works out, I want it to be a surprise. If it doesn't, then I want them to know nothing of it."

"Right. I understand, I think."

D.M. wandered out of his bedroom and stopped at the front door of his room. Stuck to the inside of his door was a note from Eagle. He sat down on the steps and read it. "All right my dear, what are you up to?" He stood and went to the dining room. The rest of the team was waiting for breakfast. The major sat down and placed the paper on the table, "Well, it seems that our boss has flown the coop for some reason. She says she'll be back in a couple of days. She also left the duty and training schedule for the next two days. Jake, you and I are to work on the armor. Tige and Sam, you two are supposed to keep working on your scouting and sniping skills. Max and Bruce, Eagle wants you guys to do a complete equipment inventory. She wants everything stocked and ready to go for the mission."

Max groaned, "Oh that sucks."

"Well, we all gotta do things we don't like. I'll need each one of you to come down and get fitted for armor. Jake and I have most of the components done so we'll let you know when we want you down in the lab."

"Has all this new 'armor' been field tested yet?" Bruce asked.

"Not exactly. I plan on taking the prototype down to the basement range today and taking a few shots at it," the major replied as he poured a cup of coffee.

"So you don't know if this stuff will really work?"

Jake interrupted, "Of course it'll work. We've proven that all ready. It'll stop up to a .50 cal bullet. We just need to work out the impact protection of the wearer."

Sam joined the conversation, "I'd just be glad if it stopped most of the small arms fire we seem to get hit with."

"The major has redesigned the plastic into a honeycomb laminate. It's very light but extremely strong and has pretty good deflection capabilities. And with the addition of some padding under certain parts, it should give decent impact protection. I mean getting hit is still gonna hurt like a son of a bitch, but you should survive and be able to fight on."

"Sounds good to me!" Sam said with a smile.

"You're really going to challenge me with this one aren't you Eagle?" Lieutenant Colonel Miles said as he flipped though x-rays on a computer monitor. They were in the Chief Orthopedic surgeon's office at Walter Reed Army Hospital, Washington D.C. Eagle was hoping maybe her gut instinct would pay off and she would be able to surprise Tige with the most valuable asset in the special ops community.

"I didn't say this was going to be an easy job. That's why I wanted you along to consult. I don't know if we have the technology to fix everything."

"We have the technology all right, but does he have the will?"

"I don't know Jim. That's my next stop," Eagle replied as she looked at the images in dismay, "How many more surgeries do you think it would take?"

Picking up a piece of scratch paper, the colonel began to make notations. He scribbled numbers and pictures of various bones. Indexing back and forth through the images he finally put his pen down, "Fourteen is my current estimate."

Eagle lowered her head, "Oh God... Is that in addition to the ones they have planned for him here?"

"No, I'd let them do just one more they have planned and then the rest would be done by us. I'd need your help on a couple of them, they'll be big jobs."

"Of course I'll help out any way I can. I'll just have to be a bit stealthy about it."

"Understood. We can work around that."

Eagle stood up, "Shall we go see him?"

They made their way through the maze of hallways. Eagle stopped and checked the room number. "Here it is. Let me go in and talk with him first."

"As you wish."

Eagle knocked lightly on the door and slowly opened it. "Captain Cabbott Westmoreland?" She stepped inside the room. In the bed before her lay the captain. He was looking away from her out the window. She could see the outlines of all the external fixation hardware that was holding his legs in position. "Captain?" She said tentatively. He groaned and slowly turned his head toward her. Eagle could see a glassy look in his eyes; evidently he was being kept sedated for the pain. The captain looked at her and blinked several times. "Captain, I'm Lieutenant Colonel Eagle Tryggvesson."

A slight smile curled to the captain's lips, "Ah, we meet again," he said softly.

"Excuse me? Have we met before?"

"I never forget a pretty face. We ran into each other at the Pentagon over a year or so ago- literally," he said slowly.

Eagle stepped forward to get a better look at the captain, "Oh my God, that was you?"

"Yes ma'am, it was... How'd your meeting go?"

"Very well. After a few rounds of warfare with the admirals and generals. I stand before you the commanding officer of the Dragonslayers."

"I've heard of your team. Do you still have a crazy Australian SASR sniper by the name of St. Ivor?" The captain said, his voice becoming stronger as the sedatives started to wear off.

"Yes we do. Although I wouldn't call him crazy particularly. He's good at what he does and he's helped a lot in training the team."

"I was expecting him at Ft. Benning, but he never showed. I found out later he got diverted to you."

"Well, it's because of Captain St. Ivor that I'm here... He thinks rather highly of you. I've been talking to your surgeon and he says that they aren't sure they can even get you walking again... I come to offer you the possibility of walking and saving your career, if you like."

Cabbott struggled to sit up somewhat. His lower body was kept nearly paralyzed by a spinal block, "I'm game."

"I have with me the chief surgeon for the Knight's Keep. Lieutenant Colonel James Miles is one of the premier trauma and orthopedic surgeons the military has to offer. He's reviewed your case and thinks he can get you back in form again. It's not going to be easy; he said you may face fourteen or more surgeries. But if you're willing, he'll endeavor to get you in duty shape again. Our facility researches new treatments in battlefield medicine and trauma. We have at our disposal a lot of technology that's not found in conventional medicine, much of it experimental." Eagle pulled up a chair and sat next to him, "But do understand if you accept, you'll need to leave the Army behind and join us."

The captain rubbed his face and pulled his fingers through his hair. The decision should be easy, but he was finding the idea of giving up the Army strangely difficult. Granted this was a chance to get healthy and get back to the work that he understood, but he now struggled with his loyalty to the Army. He studied Eagle for a few moments, "Strange... I should think it would be easy to say 'yes', but it doesn't seem that way."

"Would you like some time to think about it?"

"No," Cabbott said, pausing for a few moments, "I'll do it." He sighed deeply, "Being able to walk again and do my job is more important than my loyalty to the Army. If I don't do it now, I'll live to regret it." He reached out and offered his hand to her. Eagle smiled and gently shook it.

"I think you made a wise choice captain. It's going to be a tough road ahead if we can get you fixed up. I think you'll really like being part of the team. I am, however, going to keep you tucked away as a secret. I'm hoping that Dr. Miles will have you up and about by Christmas. Yes, I know it's about seven months away, but with the technology we have, it's quite possible."

"Walking in seven months? Hell, I've been trying to come to terms with never walking again."

Eagle stood, "Dr. Miles has been talking to Dr. Evans. He wants to leave you here for your next surgery, which is in three days right? After, we'll arrange transport to our base where you'll continue with treatments, surgery and physical therapy," she turned to leave, "Tell me captain, how'd you manage to survive all that time after the accident? I figured with the extent of your injuries you would have died of shock or internal bleeding."

Cabbott shrugged his shoulders, "I dunno ma'am. I guess God decided that it wasn't my time to die... He decided to take Jenkins instead. I lost a good spotter that day; we'd been together four years. I couldn't even go to his funeral."

"I'm sorry for your loss. We both know what can happen in this line of work. I haven't lost anyone yet, but have one that may never wake up again."

"How do I know this will work?" Kemal said as he stood looking out over the Pacific Ocean. He was on the phone with Westland discussing the plans the admiral had stolen of the Hermes missile. It was new technology, still highly classified, that would revolutionize medium range missile attacks. The Hermes missile used technology that allowed for a smaller rocket motor that would still provide nearly a nine hundred mile range. It was cheaper to produce and could carry a small nuclear payload or a larger payload of chemical or biological weapons.

"They have all ready tested this weapon and it proved to be far better than they had anticipated."

"Good then this will be very helpful when we go to war with Iraq again. We want to put an end to them for good this time."

"I think you better find a different target. My government has put too much time and money into rebuilding and protecting Iraq. Attacking it will be like declaring war on the US."

"I can't control what my government wants to do. I can make recommendations, but they will do as they please." Kemal sipped on a drink.

"In that case, you'd better prepare for your country to be reduced to ashes."

"That may be true. In which case I'll need to get my wife out of there. My children are in England at boarding schools, they are safe."

"When can I expect payment for this information?" Westland asked. He was more businessman than military now in the latter years of his career. He was interested in building a large bank account so he could retire in style. Becoming an informant was quite profitable. He felt very little patriotism to his country. Money was what he was loyal to.

"You will have the last payment wired into your account by tomorrow afternoon."

"Good. I'm flying down to Boca Raton to look at a nice house there. I think just a few more years in this business and I'll be ready to retire."

"I hope I can say the same. I'd like to take my wife and travel the world. She has been very patient with me all these years and I should reward her for that."

"Yeah, well, I have a damn bitch I'm paying nearly two grand a month to in alimony. The only reward I get out of that is I'm finally rid of her."

CHAPTER TWENTY THREE

Eagle sat at the table reading the paper. D.M. wandered in and sat down.

"Morning," he said gruffly, rubbing his eyes.

"Good morning."

The major reached over and grabbed the coffee pot. He poured a cup and stirred in two spoonfuls of sugar. The last two days had been a marathon in the lab trying to get all the suits of armor completed and fitted to the rest of the team. He was exhausted and needed to get caught up on his sleep, "So where did you disappear to?"

"Oh, I had some business to attend to. Nothing of your concern," she replied still reading the paper.

"You know I hate it when you keep things from me, especially if it pertains to the team."

"Well major, currently it does not pertain to the team so you don't have anything to worry about," she took a long drink of her tea, "I need you and Max to meet me on the hanger deck after breakfast. I have a mission for you two."

"Don't you mean me and Jake?"

"No, you and Max."

"All right. We'll be there."

Jake sat up and looked at the clock. It was nine o'clock in the morning and he had missed breakfast. "Shit! Eagle's gonna kill me!" He jumped up, got dressed and ran down the hallway to her office. Knocking on the door, he heard her answer. Opening the door, he entered and stood at her desk, "I'm so sorry I missed breakfast. I know you expect us to be there. I don't even remember turning off the alarm."

"It's all right lieutenant, D.M. told me that you guys have been working overtime getting the armor completed. He said you really needed some rest," she finished making some notes in a file and tossed it in the drawer, "I'm sending D.M. and Max on a mission, they'll be heading out tonight."

"Why those two? Shouldn't I be going with D.M.?"

"Because they each have special skills that I need for the mission."

"I understand. I'll keep working on the armor... Which by the way I'll need you to come down so I can fit you for it," he said as he turned for the door.

"Just let me know when."

Sam sat on a rock in the cave. He held one side of the headphones to his ear. Tige stood behind him watching the laptop screen, his rifle cradled across his chest.

"Did we get anything yet?" Tige asked as he turned toward the cave entrance. Sam carefully sifted through the myriad of information that the computer had collected over the last few days. Most of it was useless and he deleted it so the hard drive would not fill up. He scrolled through the various transmissions before stopping.

"Whoa! I think I got something," he called excitedly. Tige put his rifle down and knelt down next to him. "Here, have a listen," Sam handed him the headphones.

Tige put on the headphones and motioned to start the transmission. The captain listened and then had him replay the area several times. The recording had come from one of the car bugs. Faintly, Tige could hear the admiral over the sound of the engine and the radio. Much of the recording was unintelligible, but one word managed to stick out. "Son of a bitch, I think we got him!" Tige tossed the headphones back to Sam and clapped his hands together in celebration. Sam put the headphones on and listened again. He replayed the area several times before taking the headphones off. The two men looked at each other and in unison said: "Kemal!"

"Copy that section to a thumb drive and let's get it back to Eagle. I'm sure she's gonna love hearing this," Tige said as he picked up his rifle and paced around the cave until Sam was ready to go. The men hurried back to the building and found Eagle in her office. They presented her with the drive and she loaded it into her computer. Plugging in a set of headphones, she listened to it several times. A broad smile curled to her lips as she pulled off the headphones.

"Excellent work gentlemen. Excellent work," she leaned back in her chair and stretched, "Continue to monitor and we'll see if anything else comes up. The more we have, the harder he's going to fall."

"Yes, ma'am!" Both men replied and quickly left the office.

D.M. and Max sat in the cockpit finishing their preflight. It was just nearing dusk as they prepared to head out on their mission. Eagle stood on the ladder watching them, "Are you sure you got enough sleep?"

"Yeah. Managed to get a good nap this afternoon. I should be fine," D.M. replied.

"Remember your call sign is Delta Sierra one, one, five, eight. I had the crew chief add the largest external fuel tanks we had. After you leave here, head west and buzz past Kemal's beach house and take some images for our cover. Then head east. Your first refuel will be just off the coast of New Jersey where you'll hook up with a KC-10 out of McGuire. After you cross the pond, you'll refuel again between the Azores and the Portuguese coast from a KC-135 out of Lajes. From there, get to Cairo West where I have a secure hanger waiting for you. Get some rest and head out just before dawn. Stay low and fast over the Gulf. Iranian Air Defense will most likely know you're there. Even with all countermeasures on, they can still get a visual on you. There won't be much time before they'll scramble interceptors. Make two passes and then head right back over to Cairo West. Refuel and come home. Your tankers will only loiter for an hour, so you have to stay on schedule. D.M., you are the eyes to get the target. Max, you make sure we get the footage we need and keep your ears open. I want you to listen for any possible information that we can use."

"Right, got it ma'am," Max replied as he pulled on his gloves. D.M. began the engine start up sequence. Eagle climbed down and walked to the hanger door. D.M. closed the canopies and watched as she walked away. Eagle stopped and turned back to them. Snapping to attention, she saluted the men. The major returned the salute. The plane was lifted up into the darkening sky. D.M. taxied to the end of the runway. Pushing his feet firmly on the brakes, he brought the throttle up to sixty percent and listened as the engines roared. The major contacted flight control, "Delta Sierra one, one, five, eight requesting clearance for takeoff." There was a long pause.

"Roger Delta Sierra one, one, five, eight, you are clear for takeoff. The pattern is clear."

D.M. let off the brakes and shoved the throttle forward. The plane rocketed down the runway and was soon airborne. Max let out a whoop as they cleared the mountain face. Once they were at altitude, D.M. throttled back and turned west. They flew south down the coast until they were within ten miles of Kemal's beach house.

"All right Max, you remember what Eagle showed you about the camera?"

"Yup, I got it. You just keep the belly of this thing pointed at his house and I'll do the rest."

"Roger that. Reducing speed to five hundred knots. I'll slow us down a bit more when we are right on the place. What'd you calculate our loiter time at?"

"We got three mike on target."

"Well shit, that might as well be all day! I'll make two passes and then get some altitude and make one circle above and then we can head east," he watched the radar,

"Okay, reducing speed to four hundred knots. Ten seconds to target."

"Roger. Camera ready to go."

D.M. dipped the right wing turning the plane's belly to face the beach house. Max turned the camera on. After the first pass, D.M. brought them back for another pass. He then gained altitude so he could make one complete circle above the house. "I can't figure why Eagle has us making photo reconnaissance missions over the houses. Can't she just move a keyhole satellite over and get the data that way?" Max said as he watched the video that was being captured.

"She likes fresh data. And we can give her angles that the satellite can't."

"True, got a point there," he turned the camera off, "Okay, I think we got enough of this place, let's head east."

"Roger, heading east. Ascending to angel's sixty and lighting the fires," the major pointed the plane skyward and hit the afterburners. The plane lurched forward and shook at it broke the sound barrier. "Kicking us up to Mach three. Should rendezvous with the tanker in about an hour. Take a snooze if you want. You can take us across the pond."

"Right. I think I'll take you up on the offer," Max replied as he wiggled in his seat until he got comfortable. Soon the major could hear snoring coming from behind.

"Oh, I'm not going to listen to that for the next hour," he growled as he plugged his MP3 player into his helmet jack and turned it on. Soon he was listening to his motivational flying music, a compilation of hard rock songs that were especially good for keeping him awake. He flew along in the darkness, his mind wandering with thoughts of the coming mission. How would they pull it off? Would the armor give them enough protection? Would someone not make it home alive? There were just too many questions to be answered.

Glancing down at his watch, D.M. realized they should be meeting up with the tanker in a few minutes. He looked out the cockpit and searched the sky below for the blinking lights of the plane. Nothing in sight. Reducing speed, he dropped the plane down to forty thousand feet. They were still higher than commercial aircraft so he didn't have to worry about maneuvering around them. He could see a blip on the radar. Flipping on a small penlight, he checked his knee board for the tanker call sign information, "Alpha one, three, niner, two this is Delta Sierra one, one, five, eight, do you copy?"

Static crackled in his headphones as the tanker pilot replied, "Roger Delta Sierra one, one, five, eight, we copy. What's your position? We don't have you on radar."

"We're about five miles off your six. Coming in at seven hundred knots, angel's forty," D.M. could hear the flight crew talking back and forth as they tried to find them on radar, "Alpha one, three, niner, two, don't bother with the radar. I'll come to you. Maintain your heading and we'll meet up." He was rather pleased that the electronic countermeasures worked so well. They were essentially invisible on radar.

"Roger Delta Sierra one, one, five, eight, we will hold position and wait for you to show yourself."

D.M. spotted the tanker's blinking lights and rolled the plane over to drop in altitude. Max woke up with the movement, "What the hell are you doing?"

"Meeting up with the tanker."

"Shit, that time all ready? Feels like I just closed my eyes."

"You've been snoring back there for an hour."

"I don't snore," Max proclaimed.

"Bullshit you don't!" The major brought the plane down until it was right behind the tanker, "Alpha one, three, niner, two, Delta Sierra one, one, five, eight, we are right on your tail."

The boom operator looked out the back window, "Delta Sierra one, one, five, eight, if you are here, you must be invisible."

"Oh, sorry," D.M. flipped on the running lights. The small lights on the plane lit up and the operator was shocked that they were so close.

"Holy shit! You guys are close. What the hell kind of plane is that?"

"One that doesn't exist," D.M. replied as he backed the plane off and opened the fuel door, "Okay, how about seven thousand pounds of your best vintage?"

"Roger that sir," the operator maneuvered the boom until the planes made connection. D.M. carefully held the plane in position until the boom was retracted. He let the plane slide back.

"Thanks fellas, have a good evening." Performing a smooth barrel roll, he then yanked up on the stick and hit the afterburners. The plane shot past the tanker and disappeared into the night.

The tanker pilot radioed back to the boom operator, "Did you get a good look at the plane? What the hell was it?"

"I dunno sir, it was just a black shape with a few blinking lights. All I know is its fast and highly maneuverable."

"All I saw is a streak of blue flame and it's gone."

D.M. and Max landed at Cairo West shortly before dawn. The nearly seven thousand six hundred mile journey had taken them a little over four hours. Spending most of the time flying at Mach three at sixty thousand feet made quick work out of the miles. They taxied off the runway and met up with the marshaling truck who led them to a hanger. Once the large doors were closed, D.M. shut down the plane and opened the canopies. Reaching his arms above his head, he stretched, exhaling loudly, "Oh, that feels good!"

"No, what will feel good is a hot shower and a nice cold beer," Max said from the back seat as he turned off the computers. D.M. pressed the button that let down the small ladder. He unbuckled his harness and crawled out. His legs were stiff and he struggled to get out of the cockpit, "What's the matter major? Stiff?"

D.M. turned to look at Max, "Yeah, don't seem to log the miles like I used to."

"Well, come on; let's see what facilities we have available to us in the hanger. We can't quite leave the plane unattended for very long. Although I do think we should find the Club so we can relax a bit."

"Maybe for a little while. We need crew rest. Tomorrow will come awfully early," he swung his leg out of the cockpit and planted his foot on the ladder. Slowly the major climbed down and took several steps. Max climbed down and joined him. He walked to the front of the hanger and started looking in various doors. He opened one door and went inside. D.M. walked slowly toward the front of the hanger. Moments later, Max appeared.

"Hey, I found the latrine, and it's got showers."

"Ah, good. Did you see anyone else in the hanger?"

"No, no one," Max replied.

"Good," D.M. said as he pulled the zipper down on his flight suit and pushed the door to the latrine open, "I'm gonna get a shower and then find a place to get a nap."

***

Eagle came out of the bathroom in D.M.'s lab. She was dressed in the cooling suit that Jake had designed. "My, my, this is a slinky little number," she teased as she stepped up on a small pedestal so Jake could fit her for armor.

"That's why I call it the Slinky Suit," Jake picked up the breastplate and stood looking at Eagle, "Uh, um, I ah, I'm gonna have to..."

"Jake, just fit the armor. Never mind that I am of the female gender just do your job."

"Right, sorry. Here, hold this up against your chest," he handed the breastplate to her and then retrieved the back portion. Quickly he connected the parts of the armor and soon Eagle was covered from the neck down. She stepped off the pedestal and walked around. She moved her arms and legs and found the armor quite comfortable.

"I must say, you two have done a bang-up job. It's comfortable, light, and seems quite well put together."

"Well, one thing the major's taught me is to do the job and do it right. Don't do it half-assed. Do it correctly and it could mean the difference between life and death."

Eagle sat down on the pedestal, "You know, I have to admit, when I teamed you two up, I thought D.M. would probably kill you. I know you guys didn't like each other, but strangely enough it seemed logical to stick you together."

"And why is that? You honestly thought he'd do me in? That's not very nice."

"I guess because you two were so completely different. I was hoping that the major would impart some of his discipline to you. And it seems to have worked."

Jake sat down next to her, "I didn't really wanna be in the Army. My father bailed me out of jail one too many times and thought that the Army would straighten me out. Well, that just opened up new business opportunities for me...I kept getting in trouble because I was doing something I didn't like. Then I got assigned to the Dragonslayers and I was really pissed off because I was under complete control by someone. Now I look back and realize that this was probably the best for me. I needed to find who I was and what direction in life I needed to go...I know you were very hard on me, and I didn't appreciate it then, but I do now. You and D.M. have given me knowledge and skills that I can use to better myself."

Eagle put her arm around him, "I think you've certainly shown that you can put your mind to something and get the job done. You've matured a lot in the last year."

"I know that I can do better. I just wish I'd done it sooner."

"Oh Jake, you're still young. You can still apply yourself and make a good living," she leaned over and gently kissed him on the cheek.

"What was that for?" Jake gasped.

"Because I also appreciate you not saying anything about me and D.M."

"What goes on between you two is your business. It's not my place to say anything. I just hope that someday I'll find someone that makes me happy."

Eagle hugged him tighter, "I'm sure you will lieutenant," she stood up, "Now can you get me out of this armor, I have to pee!"

D.M. and Max wandered into the base club. Both were dressed in their black flight suits. Early June in Cairo was hot and unbearable, they could feel the heat searing through their clothes. The club was small and not furnished particularly well. Several pilots sat at the bar drinking and socializing. Max bellied up to the bar and ordered a beer, "What do you want maj?"

"I'll just have an iced tea please," he found a table and sat down. Max brought the drinks over and joined him. They sat quietly drinking. D.M. noticed some of the other pilots looking at them, "Oh, I hope they don't come over and start trouble. Last thing I need is another bar fight."

"In coming," Max said as he watched two pilots approach. D.M. groaned and set his glass down.

"So, who are you guys? Oh, wait, let me guess, black jammies. You guys don't exist," one of the pilots teased.

"That's right, we don't. So you can just ignore the fact we're here," D.M. replied.

"You nobodys are sitting at our table," the other pilot joined in.

"Hey man, we just wanna finish our drinks and we'll be on our way. We're not looking for any trouble," Max said as he took a few swallows of beer.

"Maybe we should step outside and settle this," the first pilot said as he stepped closer to the table.

D.M. stood up and faced the man. The major stood nearly a foot taller than the pilot, "Look, we said we don't want any trouble. So can you please let us finish our drinks in peace? The last bar fight I got in I sent quite a few people to the hospital and I spent three months confined to base."

Max stood up, "I'd think you guys know better than to pick on guys in black jammies. Besides, how are you going to explain to your commander that you got beat up by guys that don't exist?"

One pilot elbowed the other and they retreated back to the bar. D.M. and Max sat back down and finished their drinks. "Hey, I like that, nice touch: 'explaining to your commander that you got beat up by guys that don't exist' good one," D.M. said with a chuckle. They got up to leave, "I'm glad they thought the better of it. I really didn't feel like having to finish a fight," D.M. said as he stopped at the door to put on his beret. Max pulled his beret on and they headed back to the hanger. The sun was setting and the sky was painted with streaks of salmon pink. They stopped by the small Base Exchange and picked up a few items.

Returning to the hanger, both men stripped out of their flight suits down to t-shirts and boxer shorts and lay on the cots that were brought in for them. D.M. tucked his pistol under his pillow. Retrieving his cell phone he dialed Eagle's private number, "Hey, it's me. We're in the safe house. Just waiting for O-dark hundred to roll around... Ah, you did? Good... What did you think?...Yeah?" D.M. chuckled, "Well, it's not exactly designed for that... Yeah, okay, goodnight." He hung up and lay back on the cot.

Max unpacked his laptop and turned it on. He opened up the program with the mission parameters, "Hey, you wanna go over this one more time?"

D.M. groaned, "Oh, do we have to?"

"I think we should. It'll help me make sure I get the right area."

"Don't worry, you'll get the right area. I programmed it into the nav computer. Eagle found all the coordinates and even gave me a description of the house."

"Is it just me, or does this Kemal character have a thing for beach houses?"

"It does seem that way... Damn, if Eagle would just let me arm up all the Wolverines, we could go in, blow the houses up and be done with this mess... Of course that's the fighter jock side of me talking. What I really wanna do is meet him face to face and give him a taste of vintage steel."

Max held his index finger up in the air, "Remember, if you do face him, don't cut his head off as you kill him."

"Why not?"

"I'm sure he's Muslim. For them, the only way to die in battle and get to heaven is to be beheaded."

"Okay then. Can I kill him another way then cut his head off? He'd be dead before I did it," D.M. replied as he set the alarm on his phone.

"I reckon that would keep him from getting to his forty virgins... And why do you wanna kill him like that? I'd think you'd be happy to settle for a nicely placed round in the head... Geez D.M., why so brutal?"

"I've been training with Eagle almost from the beginning. She's taught me the ways of the ancient warriors. I look at combat differently now. This is something I need to do."

"Far be it from me to get in your way. You can have him," Max said as he turned off the laptop and slid it under the cot, "Are we ready to sack out?" He said as he got up and found the lights to the hanger.

"Yeah, morning comes real early."

It seemed that D.M. had no sooner fallen asleep when his cell phone alarm went off. He struggled, dropped it on the floor, and fumbled around until he finally found it and turned it off. Max groaned and rolled over on his cot. D.M. grabbed his penlight and found his way to the light switches, “Come on, let's get this show on the road.” He flipped on the lights, “I wanna get home before the sun gets too high.” He went into the latrine to relieve himself. Max sat up and yawned. He stood and followed D.M.'s lead into the latrine. They dressed, ate part of an MRE- short for Meal Ready to Eat- for breakfast and preflighted the plane. Max found a tug and pulled the plane out of the hanger. D.M. began the start up sequence for the engines. Max climbed up and settled into the back cockpit. The major contacted the tower and got clearance for takeoff.

Once airborne, they flew out over the Persian Gulf and reduced altitude and speed. D.M. checked the nav computer, “All right, you got five mike before we’re on target.”

“Roger. Getting the camera ready.”

“I'm going to pass from north to south and then make a quick loop and come back up the coast. Eagle said we may only get two passes, so we need to make these count,” D.M. looked toward the horizon. The sky was just becoming light. Dropping lower to the water, he maneuvered the plane toward the Iranian coast, “All right, I think I'm below their radar; that should give us a little extra time. I'm going to make the passes at four hundred knots so we can get as much imaged as possible.”

“I'm ready when you are,” Max called from behind. His finger was on the button waiting. D.M. banked slowly and dipped the right wing.

“In three, two, one, fire!” D.M. said as he held the plane's belly pointed at the coast. Max pushed the button on the camera. The images were stored on a massive removable hard drive just behind the camera. He watched as the camera filmed the passing beach.

“Nice pass major. Let's get the other one and get the hell out of here.”

D.M. looped the plane around. His radar picked up two incoming aircraft, “Damn, they're quick! They must have had a patrol up all ready.”

“How close are they?”

“About two hundred clicks and closing fairly fast. This pass is going be faster. I need to get us back across the Gulf ASAP,” he tipped the left wing and pushed the throttle forward. Max held his finger on the button. "Last shot. In three, two, one, fire!"

"Got it, now get us out of here!" Max hollered. D.M. pushed the throttle forward and soon the plane was skimming above the water at Mach one. D.M. watched the radar as the Iranian planes turned back as they reached International waters. "You think they got a look at us?" Max asked.

"Naw, they were never in visual range," the major replied as he headed for Cairo West, "Cairo West, this is Delta Sierra one, one, five, eight requesting permission for a gas and go."

"Delta Sierra one, one, five, eight, are you hot?"

"Negative Cairo West. We have no ordinance. We need to gas up and get right back in the air. We have tankers loitering at two locations and need to rendezvous with them."

"Roger Delta Sierra one, one, five, eight, we will see about getting a truck to meet you on the taxiway. What is your ETA?"

"About three mike," D.M. replied as he throttled back to just below Mach. They were flying over land and he wanted to reduce the amount of noise the plane made. The sky was getting brighter and the major wanted to beat the rising sun to the west. They touched down and turned onto the taxiway, "All right, where's the fuel truck?" D.M. said as he scanned the area, "Cairo West, where's that fuel truck?"

"We're still working on it. The truck had a flat as it was leaving the fuel dump."

Ten minutes passed before the fuel truck made it out to the waiting plane. D.M. had opened the cockpit and was tapping his finger nervously on the canopy rail. The fuel technicians topped off the plane. D.M. checked his watch. They were nearly twenty minutes behind schedule. He was going to have to make up the time somehow or risk missing the tankers. As the truck pulled away, D.M. closed the canopies and radioed the tower, "Cairo West, Delta Sierra one, one, five, eight requesting immediate clearance for takeoff."

"Roger Delta Sierra one, one, five, eight, pattern is open. Take off when ready."

D.M. taxied a bit further and then turned onto the runway, "Hold on to your hat, this is gonna be a fast one." The plane barely finished the turn onto the runway and the major shoved the throttle forward. The afterburners fired and sent the plane hurtling down the concrete. Within moments, they were airborne and headed back out over the Mediterranean Sea. They quickly gained altitude and D.M. pushed the plane to Mach three, "Max, can you check climatic conditions for our first refuel? I thought I heard there was a tropical storm forming out there."

Max accessed the computer and checked the weather, "Looks like you were right, seems to be a hurricane forming over the Azores."

"Can we shift north or south and still make it to the tanker?"

"North would be better."

D.M. checked his knee board for the tanker's call sign, "Whiskey X-ray, eight, three, niner, this is Delta Sierra one, one, five, eight. Do you copy?"

"Roger Delta Sierra one, one, five, eight, we copy. You guys on your way back home? You're running late, you almost missed us."

"Affirmative...Sorry, got held up at Cairo West... I see we have some bad weather in your area. Can we rendezvous to the north of the storm?"

"Uh, Roger. We're looking for a good spot." There was a long pause, "Okay Delta Sierra one, one, five, eight, how about latitude thirty eight thirty north by zero two eight west?"

Max entered the coordinates into the computer, "That's taking us right over the island."

"Whiskey X-ray, eight, three, niner, you want us to meet up over the island?"

"Roger, the storm is going to the south. We can meet up over the island and pass fuel when we are a few miles off shore."

"Copy that. We'll be there in eight mike."

"We'll set the table for you."

"Good, 'cause this is one thirsty bird. We will need at least nine thousand pounds."

"You guys running on fumes?"

"Damn near," D.M. replied as he reduced altitude and made the course correction. Even though the engines were fuel efficient, the major had to run with the afterburners on nearly the entire way to make up time. He had pushed the plane to Mach three point five, faster than Eagle had ever flown. And despite being very aerodynamic, the plane still produced friction as it traveled through the air and soon the cockpit was starting to get warm.

"Shit major, I think you need to slow down and cool this thing off. My ass is getting mighty hot back here," Max said as he wiggled uncomfortably in his seat.

"Yeah, yeah, I'm hot too. Suck it up. I still have another minute of burn before we can slow down to meet the tanker."

"I hope we can make it and not turn into one big fire ball."

The major looked down at the temperature gauge. It was just starting to read in the red zone. Should the skin temperature get too hot, the remaining fuel on board could explode. He checked his watch, thirty seconds to go. This was going to be close. The gauge inched up a little higher. Five seconds to go. Just as the gauge was reading critical, the major pulled back the throttle and let the plane coast. He looked over his right shoulder to see a huge trail of water vapor coming off the wing. The plane began to slow and D.M. checked the temperature gauge. It quickly cooled down to the normal level. "Whiskey X-ray, eight, three, niner we are three miles off your six."

"Of course we can't see you on radar Delta Sierra," The tanker pilot said as he checked the radar.

"I'll let you know when we're ready to hook up."

"Copy that. You guys sure you won't let us have a look at what you're flying?"

D.M. moved the plane into position, "All right, we are ready to take on fuel." The sun was just beginning to creep over the Atlantic Ocean and the plane was beginning to take on shape. He knew he needed to fuel up fast and get across to the next refueling before it got much lighter. Holding position, he waited until the boom operator extended the refueling probe to them. Carefully, he made connection with the boom. It seemed like it took an hour for the plane to take on fuel. D.M. kept checking his watch. Max monitored the amount of fuel in each of the tanks.

"Right major, we're just about topped off."

"Good. We did manage to make up nearly ten mike."

"So I'm to assume that this next leg of our journey will be a hot one too?"

"Whiskey X-ray, eight, three, niner we are topped off and are breaking contact," D.M. said as he gently pulled the plane back from the refueling boom.

"Roger Delta Sierra, have a good flight home," the tanker pilot said as he watched them streak by overhead.

It was just after 0600 and breakfast time for the team. Most sat at the table reading the recent papers and drinking coffee. Eagle sat with a note pad scribbling mission notes on it. She sipped on a cup of tea. Jake sat looking out the window. The sun was just starting to come up. The valley floor below was still clothed in darkness.

"Max, what time is it? Local," D.M. said as he slowed the plane for final approach to the base.

"Uh, zero six fifteen."

"Oh, good, just in time for breakfast," he said with a hint of mischief as he maneuvered the plane toward the building.

"She's gonna be pissed if you do it."

"I gotta have some fun once in a while."

Eagle was just tipping the cup to her mouth when the thunderous roar of the plane shook the building. She spilled some of the tea down her uniform as she turned to see the plane rocket by at very close range. "Bastard!" She hollered.

"Whoa! The major's home!" Jake cheered. The rest of the team broke out into laughter over the major buzzing the dining room.

"Oh, he is in so much trouble!" She growled as she tried to dab the spilled tea off her uniform.

After breakfast Eagle went back to her room to change shirts.

She came back down the hallway and was met by Jake who had just come from the dining room.

"You see the major go by here yet?"

"No ma'am."

The elevator doors opened and D.M. and Max walked out. Eagle turned and regarded D.M. with a stern look. Max ducked behind D.M., "Oh, you are *SO* busted!"

"All right major, what the hell kind of stunt was that?" She barked.

"Oh come on, I was just having a little fun. That was a really boring mission. I didn't even get to shoot down the Iranian interceptors that were coming after us," he said, changing the subject.

"Were you seen?"

"No. Stayed about two hundred clicks from them," he started down the hall.

"I don't wanna see you pulling any more stupid stunts like that. Do you understand? I thought you were more mature than that."

"Yeah, I am, but once in a while I like to have a bit of fun too...Now if you'll excuse me, I'm tired, hungry, need a shower, shave and a nice long nap," he reached back and grabbed the hard drive from Max and handed it to Eagle, "Here's your data."

"Thank you. We'll debrief later."

CHAPTER TWENTY FOUR

Jake sat watching TV. He flipped through the channels and couldn't find much worth watching. He felt somewhat lost now that all the armor was completed and everyone had been fitted. Soon however, they would be testing it for real. It was just a matter of time before Eagle pulled together all the intel that had been collected and drew up mission parameters. Secretly he hoped it would be soon. The team had not seen much action for a while and everyone was getting itchy for a fight.

The computer on his desk beeped. Jake hurried over and turned on the monitor. "Okay Bruce, what do you have to say tonight?" He watched as words came across the screen, "Yes, yes, perfect, just what we need." Jake saved the data and waited until the transmission had ended, "Oh yeah, Eagle's gonna love this!" Printing it out, he checked his watch, it was 1930. He stopped to think for a moment. What day was it? Wednesday; which meant that Eagle and D.M. were most likely down on the training floor practicing.

Eagle and D.M. stood facing each other. "Well, what do you wanna do first, dance or fight?" She said in a matter-of-fact tone. Both wore their grey duty trousers and combat boots. They'd removed their blouses and Eagle and wore a black t-shirt. D.M. had long ago figured out that it was far easier to wear a black tank top under his blouse. With his robotic arm, t-shirts tended to bunch up and become uncomfortable.

The major crossed his arms and leaned against a counter. He thought for a moment and then chuckled, "I never thought I'd hear those two words in a sentence together."

"We are here to do both, are we not?"

"Yes, we are. Let's start with the dancing. It'll help warm us up," he reached back and poked the button on the CD player. Stepping forward, he took Eagle in his arms and they began to dance, "Remember, you need to feel my movements."

"I'm trying. This isn't quite like footwork in sword fighting," she said as she struggled to keep time.

"Sure it is. You just need to think out of the box," he replied as he guided her along. They danced for probably half an hour before taking a short break. Eagle rummaged around in a locker and returned with two sleeveless leather jerkins. They were heavy leather backed with several layers of quilted cotton padding. She handed one to the major who studied it with curiosity, "What do we need these for?"

"Tonight, you learn something new," she pulled the jerkin on and turned around so D.M. could buckle the straps behind her back, "Hopefully that one will fit you. I had the tailor make it up special so you could pull it over your arm."

D.M. pulled his left arm through and wiggled the jerkin up and then put his right arm in. It felt a bit tight, but wasn't uncomfortable. Eagle stepped behind and buckled the straps. She walked over to a counter and pulled open a drawer under it. She returned with two long daggers, "You know what these are?"

"Dirks right?"

"Yes. And what is the first rule of a knife fight?"

"Someone's gonna get cut," The major replied as he took one from her.

"Hence the jerkins," she unsheathed her sword and took the dirk in her left hand. D.M. retrieved his sword and met her in the center of the floor. "Now this gets challenging. You not only have to worry about the sword blade, you need to worry about the dagger too. Let's just see how good you can multi-task," she lunged forward and thrust her sword at his. D.M. blocked the thrust but stopped when he realized there was the point of a dagger pressed against his chest.

"Damn!" He said as he backed away and stood facing her, "You're right, not very easy. How do all those guys in the movies do it?"

"Practice," she stepped forward again and attacked. D.M. did his best to repel the attack, but soon found the dagger point at his chest again. He growled in frustration.

Eagle stood en garde, "All right, let's try this slowly." She held her sword up so he could block it. She then made a slow thrust with the dagger, giving him plenty of time to parry, "Better." She continued the movements until he was blocking her attacks regularly. Shifting tactics, she advanced on the major. He retreated, still managing to block her attacks, "Good major. Now try and defend this move," she lunged forward and quickly slid her foot behind his. D.M. tried to retreat but was tripped up. He fell backwards onto the floor with Eagle on top of him. Their weapons still locked in combat.

"Nice move," he said as he looked up at her. He could see her eyes were soft; a thin smile worked its way across her lips.

"I thought so," she leaned down and kissed him hard. He

kissed her back with equal zeal. After a few moments, their lips parted

"Am I to assume this means you forgive me for the other day?" He whispered.

"Yes, but you better not do it again," she kissed him once more. She let her weapons slide from her hands as she reached to embrace him. D.M. let go as well and the clanking sound of metal hitting the floor echoed through the training area. He wrapped his arms tightly around her.

The elevator doors opened and Jake stepped out. He walked a few paces and stopped. In front of him lay Eagle and D.M. on the floor. "Well, I guess this is kiss and make up," he said loudly. Eagle looked up; she was shocked to see the lieutenant standing there. He smiled and waved his hand in the air, "Oh come guys, you know I don't care about what you do."

D.M. strained to look behind, "What do you want Jake?"

"Oh, I think you guys will be very interested to see what I just got off my computer," He leaned down and offered Eagle the paper. She rolled off D.M. and sat up, taking the page. D.M. sat up and she held it over so he could read it as well.

"My, my. Nice catch. Anyone wanna make a bet that within 48 hours I have Westland calling me about what we're up to?" She handed the paper back to Jake. The men looked at each other and shook their heads.

"Nope, not gonna take that bet," Jake said as he walked back to the elevator, "Carry on you two." The doors opened and he disappeared.

D.M. stood and helped Eagle up. They retrieved their weapons. "You wanna practice some more?" Eagle asked as she shifted her dagger to a comfortable hold.

"Yes, I wanna learn this," he stood ready. Eagle lunged again and soon they were in the heat of battle. The major was doing his best to block her attacks. He lunged at her and tried to put her on the retreat. Eagle parried and fought him back. D.M. blocked her thrust with the sword, but missed the one with the dagger. Her blade slipped by his and neatly sliced him on the right bicep. "Ah, shit!" He hissed and stepped back.

"D.M. I'm sorry."

The major shook his head, “Not your fault. I got distracted and missed my block.” He sat his weapons down on the counter and looked at his arm, “It’s just a scratch. Bandage me up and let's get back to it.”

Eagle retrieved the first aid kit and quickly bandaged him. “You know, I do have leather sleeves made up for the jerkins, if you want.”

“No. I'll be fine. Besides, pain is a wonderful teacher.”

They continued their training for another half hour. After a few more near misses, the major was becoming accustomed to fighting with two weapons. Eagle was pleased at how quickly he learned the art of swordsmanship, “Gee major, if only I could learn to dance as quickly as you learn the sword.”

“Maybe you're missing the right motivation.”

She smiled, “Maybe I have two left feet!”

“Nonsense! You're quite skilled in your fighting foot work, now you just need to transition it to your dancing foot work.”

It was late the next morning. Eagle had sent the team out with Tige so he could demonstrate some field craft. She watched from her office window as they practiced moving about the grass. The phone rang and she picked it up, “Hello? Yes...Oh, you have?...Good...How did he do?...Right...When can he travel?...All right...There's weekly C-130 transport that brings supplies to the base. It comes every Thursday morning, quite early. Can we get him on that?...You'll need to get him to Reno-Tahoe airport to the Air Guard unit. They can then bring him the rest of the way and I'll have personnel standing by to take him...Okay, good, thanks,” she hung up and hurried out of her office. Taking the elevator down to the fourth floor, she found Dr. Miles checking in on Frank. “Hey, I got some news on our secret project. He just had his last surgery there and will be coming to us next Thursday on the morning supply plane.”

“Excellent. I have everything ready on the secure side. No one but a few of us will know he’s here.”

“I hope this gamble is worth it.”

“Worst case scenario, we can't return him to duty, but we can help him walk again. At least he'll have some functionality in the civilian world."

Eagle sat down next to Frank. All the months in the coma had made his muscles start to waste away. Even with physical therapy being done twice a day, he was a shadow of his former self. She looked at him and shook her head, "Why won't he just wake up? There's no need to be in a coma."

"I don't know. I've wondered the same thing every day I see him... Perhaps he's just waiting for the right day to wake up."

"I'm certainly not going to transfer him to some nursing home, he needs to stay here," she gently took hold of Frank's hand.

"No, you're right; he needs to be here with his family."

Eagle stood to leave, "We may be heading out on a mission next Thursday, if we do, can you make sure the captain is settled in and comfortable?"

"Sure, not a problem."

D.M. sat at Eagle's desk with her. It was nearly 2200. They had spent the last several hours reviewing the camera images from the reconnaissance flight. Eagle made notes and drawings on a pad of paper, "The only plus we have going for us is the house is right on the Persian Gulf. We can come in under radar and hopefully get out without drawing attention to ourselves."

"I wouldn't say that's going to be easy. They have patrol flights in that area. I checked on one of the satellite maps and it looks like there's a military base not far away. I'm not sure how they found us, I thought I was below their radar, and I had all countermeasures on."

"Then air is not the best choice for insertion."

"No. But water would probably work," D.M. said as he accessed an Internet map of the Persian Gulf, "Are there any amphibious assault ships out there? Or a ship that can take a helicopter? If we can find one, we can go in by Zodiac and you can wait on the ship until we're ready for extraction. That way you'll minimize your time to their radar... I know you're not trying to make an International incident out of the whole thing."

"Certainly not," she elbowed the major away from the

keyboard and opened up a program. Searching through what appeared to be a jumble of data she stopped and pointed her finger to the screen, "The USS Iwo Jima is headed up the Persian Gulf right now, how perfect is that?"

"Sounds good to me, but how are you going to get boarding permission without Westland knowing?"

Eagle sat tapping her fingernails on the keyboard. After a few moments of thought she accessed another program, "They are supposed to be docking in Kuwait. I wonder if I can contact them when we get to Cairo West? It would still be an eight hundred plus mile flight across, so we'd need aerial refueling as well. Oh, this is looking like it's going to be a tough mission to plan out."

"And having to do it entirely on the QT is not gonna make it any easier," the major replied as he stood and looked out the window. The moon was full and he could see deer grazing on the grass below.

"Well it looks like I got my work cut out for me over the next few days. Let's try and plan a meeting at the cave in a day or so. Once we get the plans for Iran hashed out, we can then include Bruce on the faux plans for the L.A. raid," She said making more notes on her pad of paper. Never before had Eagle needed to plan two missions at once; and trying to keep them straight was going to be tough.

Sam scrambled up the cliff face and hefted himself onto the narrow trail that led to the cave. His back pack contained two batteries for the surveillance program. Tige followed along carrying his rifle and a back pack with two more batteries. "You think Eagle and the others can get out without Bruce seeing them?" Sam said as he helped Tige up onto the trail.

"Dunno mate. This is getting a little hairy if I do say so." Stepping inside the cave, he dropped his pack and took the batteries out and handed them to Sam.

"Yeah, I agree. Getting harder and harder to meet without drawing suspicion. We gotta get this mission going soon," Sam set about swapping out batteries and then opened the laptop and brought it out of sleep mode. As he accessed the surveillance program he put on his headphones and began listening to the recorded transmissions. Tige stood at the mouth of the cave and watched for the others to arrive. It would take several hours of waiting before the rest of the team showed up. Max was the last one to arrive.

"What took you so long?" Tige said as he leaned his rifle against the cave wall and found a place to sit down.

"Sorry all. It really sucks being partnered up with Bruce. The guy spends most of the day in the gym. I just finished the most brutal upper body workout I've ever done. I'm surprised I could even climb up here!"

Jake stood and leaned against the wall, "How'd you give him the slip?"

"He finally finished and went to take a shower. That was the only way I could make a break for it. So excuse me if I smell a bit."

Eagle pulled out a stack of papers from her back pack, "All right gentlemen, since our time is limited, let's get down to business," she handed everyone a packet of information and then returned to her seat on a rock. "This mission is going to require a bit more planning than thought. From the intel that D.M. provided, we won't just be able to waltz in and out like the wind. We are gonna have to rely on some of the other services for some help."

"Like who?" Sam asked as he took off his headphones and thumbed through the stack of papers.

"We're going to need mid air refueling from either the Navy or Air Force, and we will most likely need the help of the Navy and Marines to provide us a platform in the Gulf to stage from. I'm currently working on getting contact information for that part of the mission. The rest, however, you gentlemen will have to work on. I'll provide as much input as I can, but you'll be the boots on the ground, so you will all need to work together to plan this out."

Tige flipped through the packet. He stopped at the first set of printed pictures, "Not much in the way of high ground is there?"

"Nope, pretty flat. Sorry," D.M. answered.

"I was hoping to have somewhere high enough that I could provide cover fire for you."

Jake thumbed through the pictures and stopped. "Hey, would this place work? It's about the only high building I can see," he pointed to it.

Tige studied it, "Yes, that might work. As long as you guys stay to the beach side."

"That's the general plan so far," D.M. said as he studied the photos, "Make our assault from the beach, go in, kill the bastard and get out before it gets too hot."

"Easier said than done, mate."

The team continued to work out the details of the mission. Eagle checked her watch. "Hey, we should be getting back, almost time for dinner," she turned to Sam, "Was there anything interesting on the surveillance recordings this time?"

"No. In fact most of our bugs have died."

"How about the GPS tracker in the car?"

"Still functioning, but it doesn't really give us anything concrete," Sam replied, closing up the laptop. The team dispersed and returned to the building by several different routes. They met up shortly before dinner in the dining room. Bruce was nowhere to be seen. Tige paced around the room nervously, "Eagle, we may have to get this going soon. I bet Bruce is getting suspicious of us."

"He is, we all ready know that," she tipped her head at Jake to go watch the door for Bruce; "He sent Westland an email last night...Jake picked it up. I fully expect a call from the admiral here in the next few days."

"What are you going to tell him?"

"That we aren't up to anything."

Jake saw Bruce coming down the hall, "Psssssst," he hissed and carefully shut the door and hurried to his seat.

"D.M., Tige, in my office after dinner," she said quickly. Both men nodded. The door opened and Bruce walked in. "Well sergeant, where were you today? We missed you out in the forest for land nav exercises."

Bruce took his seat, "Max didn't say anything about that when we were working out this morning."

"Kind of hard to get a word in edgewise with all your grunting and straining," Max replied as he poured a glass of water. The others chuckled. Bruce gave them a dirty look.

"All right gentlemen. After going through the data that D.M. and Max brought back, I think we can commence planning the mission to Kemal's L.A. beach house. So tomorrow morning after breakfast we will meet in the briefing room and start working on our assault plan."

"Ma'am, I think it would be a good idea if everyone had some time to get used to their armor. You know, wear it around, do some combat training and in general get comfortable wearing it," Tige added.

"Good idea captain. You can get everyone down on the training floor after we get done with the planning," she replied.

"Right, thanks."

Eagle sat in her office waiting for D.M. and Tige. She reviewed the plans they had worked on in the cave. Besides the logistical nightmare of getting half way around the world reasonably unnoticed, there were the necessary contacts that needed to be made to ensure they had fuel and a secure platform on which to launch the operation in the Gulf. Flying that distance in a C-130 would take forever, so Eagle called in a favor with a friend at McGuire AFB where the team would land and change to a C-17 Globemaster for the flight across the pond to Cairo West. From there they would take off and refuel somewhere over Saudi Arabia and land on the Iwo Jima docked in Kuwait. The ship would then take them back down the Gulf until they were as close as possible to Kemal's beach house. There they would insert by zodiac and get to work. Eagle would wait on the ship for their signal to extract.

There was a fairly loud knock on the door. "Come in major." The door opened, D.M. and Tige strolled in. They sat down in front of her desk.

"You wanted to see us?" Tige asked.

"Yes, I wanna do a little more planning with you two."

"Are we secure?" D.M. said as he got up and wandered around the room.

"We are," she opened the mission folder and pulled out a couple of photographs, "Well, I can see why you were so quickly intercepted. The Sixth Tactical Air Base is housed just outside Bushehr. There is also a naval base and a nuclear reactor there as well...If I was Kemal, I wouldn't wanna live there, but I guess if you're buying and selling secrets, it's probably prime property."

"That explains why we had company so fast. Although they weren't very fast in pursuit, they were fast to find us," D.M. said as he leaned over the back of her chair to view the photos.

"Yeah, that kind of worries me, since I'll be flying the Warhawk; it's not exactly a high speed aircraft."

"Stay low, really low and hopefully you won't show up on radar," D.M. said as he settled back down in his chair.

"I hope the naval base won't have any patrols out in the Gulf, they may see us going in," Tige said as he reached over and took one of the photographs. He studied the areas that Eagle had circled, "I think the Second Fleet of the Persian Gulf is based out of there. Not good. I remember when the SASR was doing some work in the Gulf, we were constantly being watched by them."

"You two are just not making me feel very good about this mission. But I can't think of any other way to get this bastard," she said, typing on the computer, accessing information.

"No, not really. Maybe by dropping the intel that we're going to strike L.A., he'll get tipped off and run home hopefully. In fact I doubt he was even there the last time we hit the place," D.M. commented as he took out his knife and picked at his fingernails.

Tige looked at the pictures again, "Yeah, bet you're right, he wasn't even there. Why should he be? We could have leveled the place."

"I wish we would have," D.M. added.

"Well, we won't have the firepower this time either. The Warhawk will only be carrying enough ordinance to get you out of trouble if necessary and hopefully back out to sea without company," Eagle said as she pulled the supply list out and checked it over. They continued their planning for another hour and then broke up.

The team met for breakfast the next morning and then went to the briefing room to plan the L.A. mission. Since Bruce had not been on that mission, it made it quite easy. The team agreed to simply reused the previous mission plan. They added a few extra touches that they wished they would have done the first time. After, all returned to their rooms and put on their armor. Eagle decided to get more work done in her office. She needed to make contact with all the other services that they would be needing assistance from for the mission. The rest of the team went down to the sixth floor to practice some hand to hand combat.

"All right everyone. Since we're only really just trying to get used to wearing this stuff, let's not try to turn this into a blood bath," Tige said as he looked the team over, "Let's divide up into roughly equal heights: D.M., you and Bruce. Sam, you and Max. And me and Jake"

Jake groaned, "You're gonna go easy on me right?"

"Of course mate," Tige smiled.

"Oh, why am I getting the idea I'm going to get my ass kicked?"

"Naw mate, just fool'in ya," the captain teased, "Right, D.M. and Bruce, you two wanna square off?"

The major stepped into the center of the mat. The two men sized each other up. D.M. made the first move by lunging at the sergeant. He drove him backward a few paces before Bruce slammed his fists into D.M.'s back. They grappled and exchanged blows. Things got more serious when D.M. took a swing at Bruce's face. The sergeant ducked out of the way and fired back with a quick upper cut that caught the major right in the mouth. He staggered back a few steps and wiped his hand over his mouth. Seeing blood on his hand just made him madder. He stepped forward and with all his might, landed a forceful left handed blow that sent the sergeant to the floor. D.M. stood over him and looked down. Bruce was gasping for air and there was a large dent in his breastplate. He turned and walked back to Jake, "Oh, that felt good," he whispered. Jake smiled and handed him a cloth to wipe his mouth. "What sucks is now I have to fix the damn armor."

The rest of the team stood silent. Deep down inside they were cheering wildly for the major. There wasn't a single one of them that liked Bruce, and seeing him get the crap knocked out of him was probably the best morale boost they'd had in a while. D.M.

walked toward the elevator, "Well, since I made the stuff, I'm quite comfortable in it. I got things to do," he said as he punched the button. The elevator opened and he disappeared.

Sam and Max stepped into the center. Bruce had finally gotten up and moved to the side. The two men circled for quite some time; neither wanted to engage. Tige stepped forward, "All right you two, this isn't a dancing lesson, get at it!" Max lunged at Sam who blocked his attack and gave him a shove. Max tumbled to the floor and quickly got to his feet. Spinning around, he lunged again and locked his arms around Sam's waist and drove him to the ground. Soon they were locked in combat with more pushing and shoving going on rather than blows being landed. Tige stepped in and grabbed Max by the back of his armor and pulled him to his knees, "Are you guys gonna fight or just wrestle on the floor? Up!" He hauled Max up to his feet and grabbed Sam and stood him up as well, "Move around, test the limits of the armor," he said as he turned Sam to face Max. He let them battle for a few more minutes before calling the fight. Both men were relieved to be done and quickly stepped out of the center. "All right Jake, come on," he waved to the lieutenant who was doing his best to hide behind Max.

"Oh, do we have to? I've been wearing this longer than anybody, remember, I was the guinea pig for the project."

"Well, then you can indulge me, because I haven't," Tige said as he lunged forward and threw a few punches. Jake quickly blocked them. "Good Jake, keep your hands up," Tige landed the occasional punch. He stepped back, spun around and let fly with a back kick. Jake closed his eyes in preparation for the blow. After a moment he opened his eyes to see a foot just a few inches from his face. "You really think I was going to kick you? Not hardly, this is just practice."

D.M. walked down the hallway toward his room. He still held the cloth to his lip. Bruce had inflicted a nastier wound than he'd expected. Eagle came out of her office and saw him, "What the hell happened to you?"

"Bruce got in a lucky shot."

She got closer and tried to look at the wound, "Lemme take a look." D.M. pulled the cloth away. Eagle reached up and carefully inspected the wound, "He cut you pretty good. Come with me and I'll get you fixed up," she led him down the hall to her room, "Have a seat on the sofa, I'll be right back." Retrieving several items from her bathroom, she returned and sat down next to him, "All right, let me at it," she said as she pulled down on his lip.

"Ow! That hurts!"

"Come on major, don't be a baby."

"I'm not, it really hurts."

Eagle inspected the wound further. She reached for a small bottle and took the top off it. "This might sting a little," she dabbed the small applicator brush on the wound.

D.M. hissed, "Shit!"

"Well, it's this or about five stitches, you pick. The sting will go away in a few moments," she screwed the top back on and reached for a small pouch. Opening it, she pulled out a small clump of dark greenish powder.

"What's that stuff?" D.M. asked.

"A bit of ancient medicine. It's a kind of moss that grows on the fjords. It's long been used for cuts and bruises. And by the looks of it, you're going to have a nice bruise with it as well." She carefully mixed the moss with a small amount of water and gently rubbed it on the wound. "There, that should do it."

"Thanks... I must admit, I did get my licks in. I hit that asshole so hard I blew him clean off his feet, knocked the wind out of him and put a huge dent in his breastplate... I think the rest of the guys secretly enjoyed it. I know I did," he said with a half smile.

"I'd prefer that you gentlemen not get any more hurt before the mission. We need all the healthy bodies we can get."

"I understand, it was just one of those things that needed to be done. A morale booster if you will," he stood to leave, "I'll be glad when we blow the whole thing open and can finally operate without worry."

"You and me both. Just the satisfaction of seeing Westland taken down will be worth the trouble. I only hope they don't give us the ax simply because we did our job *too* good," she replied.

"I doubt that. There are so many other missions we can do."

***

It was late in the afternoon and Eagle was back in her office waiting for phone calls from her contacts. The phone rang and she picked it up, "Colonel Tryggvesson... Yes... Yes sir... No, we're not. Where'd you get that information? You can't say huh? Well, I think I have an idea, and your information is incorrect... Maybe you should hire a more reliable snitch next time."

D.M. carefully opened the door to her office and slipped in. He watched as she stood facing the window talking on the phone. Quickly he realized who was on the other end of the line and listened with interest.

"Admiral, I can assure you that we're not planning any unauthorized missions...Some training missions maybe...We're planning on taking the Wolverines down to China Lake and practicing air to ground attacks...Yes, probably next week. The weather there is supposed to be good and there's no place close we can practice," she turned and saw D.M. standing near the door. She pointed to the phone and he nodded, smiling broadly. "Yes admiral, we will...Good bye." Hanging up, Eagle let out a loud primal growl, "Arrrrruuuugggghhh!!!" D.M. backed up against the door. He was just considering making a hasty escape when Eagle started to laugh, "Oh fuck it felt good lying to that traitor!" She laughed harder. The major figured she must have enjoyed the rouse, Eagle wasn't much for the use of profanity, but on this occasion she seemed to appreciate the added punctuation.

"My, my, you're such a *naughty* little colonel," he teased as he caught her by the arm and gave her a hug.

"Oh, sometimes it's just *so* good to be *so* bad!" She laughed, "Let's get ready. We go in five days."

"Roger that! They'll be happy to hear that news."

CHAPTER TWENTY FIVE

Jake grunted as he fought to lift the barbell off his chest. D.M. stood with his hands ready to help him. “Come on Jake, just one more, you can do it,” he said, cheering him on. Jake let out a low growl and put all his effort into raising the bar. Slowly his arms straightened as he pushed it up. D.M. helped him put the barbell back into the rack. Stepping around to the front, the major offered him a hand up, “Good job.” Both were enjoying their gym time.

“Wasn't sure I was gonna get it,” the lieutenant stood and wiped his face with a towel. He walked over to the large wall of mirrors and stood looking at himself. “Just think, we get it on in two days... I've been waiting for this for a while... Sweet revenge.”

“You're not the only one. This certainly means a lot for me...Look what I lost the last time we tangled with him,” he said as he raised his robotic arm.

“If you ask me, he made an improvement. That's one serious piece of hardware you got there. Not many are willing to take you on now.”

“There weren't many before,” he walked over to where Jake was standing. The lieutenant straightened up, brought his arms up and flexed his muscles. D.M. playfully stepped behind him and did the same.

“Oh, that's so not fair!” Jake elbowed D.M. in the stomach. The major gasped, doubled over and grabbed Jake, dropping him to the floor. The men playfully wrestled. Eagle walked in and saw them.

“All right boys,” she said loudly. They stopped wrestling and looked up at her.

“We're just doing some male bonding,” D.M. said as he got up and helped Jake to his feet.

“Remember I told you I didn't want anyone else hurt, not this close to the mission.”

"Oh, we weren't, we were just playing," Jake replied as he tried to fix his hair.

"You men have a funny way of showing expression."

Jake grabbed his towel and wiped his neck and shoulders, "It's a guy thing."

"Yes, it's a guy thing," D.M. added, "We fight hard, we play hard and we love hard." He picked up his towel and snapped it at Jake. The lieutenant retaliated and snapped him back. Soon they were engaged in a vicious towel fight. Eagle just stood watching, there wasn't much point in breaking it up. The whole team was on pins and needles because of the impending mission. This seemed to be their way to blow off steam and stay focused. Containing their energy was useless.

D.M. left his lab. It was late in the evening and he'd just finished repairs to Bruce's armor. Even as much as he disliked the sergeant, he would repair the large dent he had made in the breastplate. The thought had crossed his mind, and even Jake had mentioned that they should have made a set of inert armor for the sergeant. It would look and feel like the real stuff, but certainly wouldn't stop a bullet. The major, however, had a conscious and decided that wasn't the right thing to do. And maybe Bruce would help them out, just because his life depended on the success of their mission. D.M. was just nearing the elevator when he was approached by one of the other scientists that worked on the floor. "Excuse me, major?"

"Yes?"

"My name is Captain Lance Goldsmith, US Army Department of Research and Development," he offered his hand, D.M. shook it. "Sir, I hear you've had great success with your work in plastics and polymers." D.M. nodded. "I also know you're a fellow MIT alumni. I was a late starter, so I was a few years behind you, but I read some of the papers that you published. Excellent work sir." The captain was a small man in his early forties. He had short light brown hair that was receding, pale hazel eyes and a light body frame that D.M. thought almost looked sickly. His uniform hung off him as if it were two sizes too big.

"And what is it that you want?" D.M. said with suspicion. He'd learned to keep his research to himself until it came time to sell it. There were many out there who would happily steal ideas and sell them off as their own. He'd warned Jake of the same thing just a few weeks earlier. The technology market was a dangerous place to play.

"Well sir, I was wondering if I could pick your brains. I'm working on a new type of plastic resin that's to be used in rebuilding of bones in the human body."

"And what other applications?" D.M. eyed him.

"That's all they funded me for," the captain replied.

"And just how long have you been working with the government?"

"About two years now."

D.M. leaned against the wall, "I can guarantee that whatever you come up with will be exploited by the military in any way they can... It's just the way they operate... If you want, I'll take a look and see what you got," he folded his arms across his chest, "Once you start working for Uncle Sam, you sell your soul to him."

"I kind of figured that...Yes, if you would, I'd appreciate your feedback on my project." The captain led the way to his lab. D.M. looked around as Lance brought up the data on his computer, "If you don't mind me asking sir, who do you work for?"

"Myself," D.M. replied flatly.

"How do you manage that? I thought all the research projects here were government funded."

"Oh, I work for the government, but they don't fund my research. I do," the major picked up a sample of plastic and turned it over in his hands, "I refuse to sell out to them."

"How can you afford to fund yourself? All this equipment isn't cheap."

"I sold a few benign polymer recipes to the plastics industry. Made things easier for them, and padded my pockets well enough to fund my own research."

"You're so lucky...Here, have a look at this," Lance said as he put a slide under the microscope. D.M. looked at the substance. There wasn't anything that piqued his interest.

"So you're trying to do what again?"

"Make a plastic that the human body can use as a building block to rebuild bone...Instead of using titanium, ceramic or stainless steel prosthetics; plastic is lighter and porous so the body can attach and build on it."

"Sounds simple enough," he said as he walked over to a large dry erase board with a formula scribbled on it. Studying the symbols and numbers he took the eraser and went to erase part of the formula.

"Uhhhhhhhhh," Lance gasped.

"You wrote this down elsewhere didn't you?"

"Yes."

D.M. carefully erased several lines. He stood thinking for a few moments, picked up the pen and commenced writing out a new section of formula. After, he passed his finger down the lines and reviewed the whole formula. "There, give that a try."

"Just like that, you think you fixed it?" Lance said as he looked at the new formula.

"Maybe, maybe not. But this should give you a good start," he went to the door, "I covered a similar polymer in a paper during my sophomore year. Not rocket science, just a matter of playing with the ratios and getting the proper synthesis of the copolymer chains," D.M. stood in the doorway, "Good luck, I'm sure you'll have what you want in a couple of weeks."

Thursday morning. The team was up early making final inventories on equipment and supplies. The C-130 sat on the runway waiting for them. It had arrived several hours earlier and Captain Westmoreland was secretly unloaded and taken to the medical floor. After breakfast, they collected on the hanger deck and loaded their gear into the Warhawk. They piled in and Jake flew them down to the transport. Once loaded, they took off and headed east. Eagle had given strict orders to the others to keep an eye on Bruce. Under no circumstance was he to be allowed any outside communication during the mission. They could not risk him contacting Westland and jeopardizing the entire operation.

Eagle did her best to get comfortable in the cargo net seats. D.M. sat next to her trying to get some sleep. The others sat around discussing fake mission plans. After nearly an hour of flying, Bruce spoke up, "Shouldn't we be heading west?" All eyes fell on Eagle.

"Well, we've had a change of plans. So sit back and enjoy the ride," she said as she attempted to mash her gear bag into a pillow. The rest of the team grew quiet.

"You're not going to tell me where we're going?"

D.M. looked over at Bruce, "No need. Your function in the mission is still the same."

The team landed at McGuire, changed planes and was back in the air two hours later. They settled in for the long flight to Cairo West. Eagle managed to finally find a comfortable position; her head leaned against D.M.'s right shoulder. The rest of the team spread out over the cargo jump seats and fell asleep. It would be morning before they reached their destination. D.M. occasionally woke up and looked around. He was checking to see what Bruce was up to. As far as he could tell, the sergeant had not packed a cell phone, so his possible lines of communication were nearly eliminated. Of course Eagle didn't even tell him who they were going after or where. Any intelligence that got back to Westland would be sketchy at best.

The C-17 landed at Cairo West and the team unloaded. They were given the same hanger that D.M. and Max had used on their reconnaissance mission. Max was even able to find the tug so the team didn't have to push the helicopter inside. Once in and the doors were closed, they began unloading.

"Hey, major, just like home eh?" Max called as he unloaded a munitions crate and placed it with the rest of them on the hanger floor.

"Yeah, just like old times," the major joked.

Eagle wandered over to D.M., "So this is where you stayed before?"

"Uh huh. Rather 'homey' in an austere kind of way," he smiled, "And the club here is nothing to write home about."

"We're not here to party and socialize- or start any bar fights."

"Hey, I'm the one that avoided the bar fight!" D.M. retorted.

"Yes, I know, and thank you for not causing an incident." She stopped and wiped the sweat from her face. The rest of the team had stripped out of their grey duty blouses and were wearing their black under shirts. The temperature in the hanger was stifling despite the air conditioner running overhead. The late June desert heat made them all long for the cooler valley back home. Eagle conceded that she might just have to let them go to the club to cool off. The hanger was anything but comfortable, and it could end up being home for the next couple of days. She would have to do her best to keep the men focused and sharp. There were still parts of the mission that needed planning. Eagle had not been able to contact the captain of the Iwo Jima to make arrangements for landing. She hoped that she could get to the base command post and make a secure telephone call.

Jake sat in a small conference room at the front of the hanger. Several drawings were laid out on the table in front of him. He had sketched various pictures of a futuristic set of armor. D.M. came in and sat down next to him, "What 'cha work'in on?"

"Probably nothing...When you guys were all back in D.C., I was stuck in my room the whole time. I watched a lot of TV and surfed the Internet. There was this really neat program about nanotechnology, and I got to thinking..."

"Nanotechnology? Damn Jake, I think that's the biggest word I've ever heard you say," The major replied as he playfully slapped him on the back, "All right, go on."

"Well, I don't understand how they work, but some of the stuff they showed was pretty cool. I thought if we could figure out how to make them work, we could make armor that would camouflage itself."

D.M. picked up some of the drawings and studied them. A smile slowly curled to his lips. He reached over and took the rest of the drawings and scrutinized them. Jake could tell the major was getting excited as his page flipping was becoming faster and more frantic by the moment. Grabbing a pencil, D.M. was just about to write some notes on the pages when he stopped. Recognizing that Jake was the true author of the work, D.M. didn't want to step on the lieutenant's toes by making notes and changes. He'd learned long ago that it wasn't very polite to barge in on someone else's work without asking, "Do you mind?"

"Naw, go ahead. Just a bunch of dumb sketches anyways."

"Oh, I wouldn't say that," D.M. replied as he made notations and more drawings on the pages. After several minutes, he turned to the lieutenant, "Jake, this is fucking brilliant!"

"I don't see how. I was just messing around."

"You were using that wonderful gelatinous mass between your ears that God gave you for something productive. There's absolutely nothing wrong with that," D.M. smiled, put his arm around the lieutenant and gave him a hug.

"Okay, but here is where I ran into problems. One, where do we get those little nano-thingys? Two, how do we get them on or in the armor? Three, how do we control them? That show didn't really elaborate on that aspect."

D.M. started to laugh. Soon he was laughing hard enough that his sides were hurting. Jake was not sharing in his amusement and was quite frankly disappointed with the major. Finally after a couple minutes of laughing, D.M. regained his composure. Seeing the sour expression on the lieutenant's face he pointed at him, "Oh Jake, I wasn't laughing at you or your ideas. I was laughing because I'm so happy that you've let your creativity out of the bag. I think it's absolutely wonderful that you've come up with these ideas. And I promise I'll help you work on 'em, and hopefully make 'em a reality."

Jake studied the major for a few moments. He wasn't sure that D.M. was being honest with him, although to the best of his knowledge, he'd never lied to him.

"That'd be very cool. But I'm not sure how we'd make it work. I mean, we haven't found any kind of paint that would stick to the plastic, and if we mixed the nanos with the plastic, would it alter its chemical properties and make it not work?"

"Questions, questions, questions. I love questions!" D.M. bellowed.

"D.M., you're beginning to freak me out."

"Jake, you don't understand. Questions are what make science possible. If you don't ask questions, you don't have any incentive to find the answers," he got up and paced around the room.

"Well, I guess that makes sense. Never thought of myself as a man of science; unless it was the science of cutting a kilo of coke."

"I've told you all along, you're smart, you just have to apply yourself."

"Yeah, yeah, I know. Use my brain for something useful...Do you think my slinky suit could make me some money? You know, like you did with your inventions?"

"Sure. What other applications can you think of that would benefit from the technology?" D.M. replied. He was surprised, but pleased that Jake wanted to follow in his footsteps.

"Ummm... I was thinking of maybe firefighters."

"That's a good possibility, but I'm sure with a little more thought, you can come up with many more." The major had all ready come up with nearly a dozen uses, but he was waiting for Jake to stretch his imagination and figure them out for himself.

The lieutenant sat thinking for a few moments, "What about keeping divers warm when they have to do cold water rescue?"

D.M. smiled to himself, "Another good idea. But may I ask you one question? How much do you plan to sell each suit for?"

"I'm not sure; I was hoping you'd help me out with that."

"The simplest way to do it is not to sell the suits, but to sell the technology." He walked over to the lieutenant, "Most important, you need to get a patent on it first. Once you do that, you're free to advertise on the open market."

"Oh, what about soldiers having to wear chemical warfare suits?" Jake announced and quickly wrote down all his ideas. "And people who do winter sports... And tank drivers... And police officers... And other military." He stood and began wandering around the room. He stopped and looked at D.M. "I could make a fortune couldn't I?" He walked up to D.M. and clapped his hands on the major's shoulders, "With your guidance, I know I'll be a success."

D.M. nodded slowly, "But why all the sudden interest in money?"

Jake sat back down, "I got a letter from my Mom a few weeks

ago... Seems that my old neighborhood has taken a turn for the worse... D.M., I wanna make enough money so I can move my parents out of there."

The major dropped his gaze to the floor, "It's not a quick process Jake, it could take a couple of years to get all the legalities worked out."

"I need to do something soon... I feel I'm partly responsible for how things have gotten there," he rested his elbows on the table and held his forehead in his hands.

"Some more of your unsavory past rearing its ugly head?"

"Yeah," Jake replied softly.

The major carefully stacked together all the papers and handed them to Jake, "So what do you call your creation?"

"I call it 'Chameleon Skin.' Just like the little lizard that can change colors."

"That's good; I like it...Keep all of this to yourself. When we get back, I'll see if Eagle will let us take a field trip. I'll also make a few phone calls to some of my contacts in the industry and see if I can get you some front money. We'll also have to get the paperwork sent to the Patent Office."

"Thanks. I really appreciate that... Oh, and where we go'in?"

"To get your little nano-thingys."

Eagle returned from the base command post. She had managed to borrow a Humvee from the motor pool. It was late in the afternoon and the sun beat down on the concrete tarmac. The temperature was easily in the triple digits and for some reason, it felt humid. Opening the man-door to the hanger, she walked in to see the entire team flaked out on cots taking naps. D.M. opened his eyes and looked at her, "Siesta time," he said lazily.

"Don't know how you guys could sleep in this heat, but how about going to the club and cooling off?"

The major stuck two fingers in his mouth and let out with a loud whistle. The rest of the team sprang up, "Hey, club time!"

Eagle was amazed at how fast six men in various stages of undress could get dressed. She laughed at their frantic attempts to get back in uniform, "Well, well. I guess next time we have a shakedown recall that's the motivation I should use to get you all moving quicker."

"Hell, if there's beer involved, I'm right motivated!" Tige said as he pulled on his boots and yanked the laces up.

"Yeah, me too!" Max yelled as he made an attempt to jump over Sam's cot. The tip of his boot caught the edge and he fell flat on his face in to a pile of gear. Everyone laughed as he fought to get up. Sam finally reached down and helped him.

The team piled into the Hummer and D.M. drove them to the club. They tumbled through the door and were greeted by a cool blast of air conditioning. "Ah yeah, this feels much better!" Jake sighed.

D.M. spied the two pilots that had given them trouble last time. He walked over to their table, "Well, we meet again," he said politely. The two men jumped up ready to make a hasty retreat. The major held up his hand, "Relax fellas, we're not here to start any trouble. We just want that table in the back. Is that Okay?"

"Yes sir, sure, not a problem."

"Thank you. Please, sit down and enjoy your drinks," D.M. smiled. He wandered over to the bar and found Max ordering his drink, "My, those fellas are awfully jumpy."

"You just had to go fuck with them didn't you?" Max teased.

"Now Max, I was just being polite," the major smiled with a twinkle in his eye.

"Polite my ass!"

"Yeah, you're right, I just had to go fuck with 'em," D.M. grinned.

One by one the team got their drinks and settled down at a large table in the back of the bar. Eagle joined them. "Well, I made my call to the Iwo. We got a problem... They're in dock for two more days...So, rather than flying over there and spending an extra two days stuck on a ship; I figure we can stay here. I talked to someone in Civil Engineering and they're going to check out our air conditioner issues and see if they can make it a bit more comfortable for us."

"Hey, as long as we can come cool off at the club, I don't care how long we stay," Tige joked.

"I'd like to get this show on the road. The more time we're

away from the base the more Westland will be snooping on us. Our refueling connections have been made, the Navy is going to support us," Eagle said as she took a long drink of lemonade. She scowled at the flavor. The club was so cheap they didn't even use real lemons in their lemonade. The beverage tasted like it came out of an MRE package.

"I thought you told Westland that we were going down to China Lake?" D.M. mentioned.

"And in one phone call, he'll know we aren't there."

"True."

The team had dinner at the club and returned to the hanger. Civil Engineering had been by and fixed the air conditioner. While it wasn't frosty cold, the hanger was certainly more tolerable than before. The men set about organizing themselves for the night. Cots were pulled into somewhat of a defensive perimeter and they changed for bed. Even though they were tired and most had several drinks in them, they were rowdy. Eagle carried her cot to the small meeting room. D.M. saw her.

"Hey, you want some help?"

"No thanks, I got it."

"You're not going to bunk with all of us?"

Eagle shook her head firmly, "No way! I'm not gonna be part of that male slumber party. And I know for fact that several of you guys snore."

The major laughed and helped her situate the cot in the cramped room. "Right, there you go. Uh, what time are we getting up tomorrow?"

"I can't think of anything we need to get done, so everyone can sleep in- if they can."

"Okay then," he leaned over and gave her a quick peck on the cheek, "Good night."

"Good night major."

Westland slapped his cell phone shut, "Damn that bitch!" He punched the seat back in front of him, "She lied to me!"

"They aren't at China Lake?" Lieutenant Farlow asked.

"No, they're not. And no one seems to know where they've gone either. They can't just disappear off the face of the earth...Get me to a pay phone."

"Yes sir," Farlow replied and drove until he found a pay phone. Westland got out and frantically punched numbers. Eagle had to be going after Kemal and he needed to warn him so he could get out of the country.

"Blue Mole here," Westland said quickly.

"Yes? What is it? This is not your normal day to call."

"You need to get out of the country fast, she's coming for you and I can't stop her...My informant says they're going to hit your house in L.A."

"My men took care of them last time."

"They have revenge on their minds and they won't stop until you're dead. I'm not going to repeat myself again- get out of the country now!"

"All right, I'll be on the next flight to Tehran. I can be safely home at my beach house in Bushehr in two days."

"Good, do that and I'll contact you when I have her back under control...That bitch is going to find herself in a lot of trouble."

"Good morning captain, how are you feeling?" Dr. Miles said as he poked his head in the door of the Cabbott's hospital room.

"Fine, thank you. This is a great room, I love the view...Reminds me of home back in Vermont."

"Just wait until we get a couple feet of snow, then you'll really feel like home."

"You'll have to pull the curtains then. Otherwise I'm gonna want to be out on the slopes skiing."

"I'm afraid you won't be skiing any time soon, or maybe ever...We're gonna try and get you back together the best we can, but there will be some activities you'll probably never do again."

"I guess I should be happy if I can walk," Cabbott said as he pulled a rolling tray over with a laptop on it. Dr. Miles had made sure the captain would stay suitably entertained in between surgeries and physical therapy sessions. “So where did they go?”

“Not exactly sure, Eagle didn't elaborate on their mission. She only said they should be back in a week or so.”

“I miss going to work... Hopefully I can get back to my job soon.”

Dr. Miles pulled up a chair, “Eagle told me that you’re a sniper- the best in the world. How could you enjoy a job like that?”

“I don't know. I kind of consider it my duty. The Army can't figure me out, I don't fit the psychological profile of a killer, but I do the job without a second thought.”

“You do seem like a very nice person. Did you hunt much as a kid?”

“Sure. I've bagged my share of deer, rabbit, squirrel and one very angry Bull Moose. I felt more remorse for killing them than I do for killing a man.”

“How many kills do you have?”

Cabbott looked out the window for a few moments before responding, “One hundred and fifty confirmed kills in just over five years.”

“My God!”

“I got loaned out to just about every agency in the US: FBI, CIA, ATF, Homeland Security, and a few that are happy to remain nameless,” he tugged at the covers, pulling them up higher, “The mission that got me wounded and my spotter killed was a CIA hit on a militia leader... Of course they had complete deniability on the matter and said it was a training accident.”

“Of course, they're all training accidents when they're black ops.”

“Yup. Most of my career has been spent in the dark. It was hard telling my parents what I do. Dad spent all that money on a good Harvard education and his son goes out, joins the Army and kills people. I suppose maybe someday I'll put that education to use and practice law. Just couldn't see myself doing that right out of college.”

“Was your father angry that you joined the Army?”

“Oh hell yeah, pissed as can be. Didn't talk to me for a year. He finally realized that I was gonna do it no matter what he said, so he started talking to me again.” Cabbott turned on the computer, “I emailed him yesterday to let him and mom know I wasn't at Walter Reed anymore, and to let them know that I was in good hands, but it was going to be a while before I could see them again."

"You of course didn't tell them where you are?"

"No, not a word. Besides, I have absolutely no clue where I am. I was so drugged during the flight I could be on Mars and not know it."

"Good captain, let's keep it that way for now," Dr. Miles stood to leave. "How's your mental health? I'm sure you suffer from PTSD. We have an excellent psychiatrist here who is more than willing to work with you. There's no shame in it, nothing going in your record. We understand what goes on in combat and wanna help you find some peace of mind."

"Thank you. I'll take you up on the offer. I find that when faced with stressful situations on or off the battlefield that I suffer more nightmares and flashbacks, and having so many surgeries has really set it off...I even managed to undo what the surgeons had done during a particularly bad flashback, I know I have problems."

"I'll see to it that Major Lindman comes for a visit... I have your next surgery planned for two days from now. I'm going to work on reconstructing your left tibia and fibula. I wanna hold off working on your spine until Eagle gets back. That's going to be a tough surgery and I'll need her help."

"Best to keep me pretty heavily sedated for a few days after. That will lessen the likelihood that I have a flashback and hurt myself worse."

"I understand. I was planning on that, but best to hear it from you... Also, would it be possible to ask a favor of you?"

"Sure, what? I'm sorry I don't have much to offer at this stage."

"One of Eagle's team was seriously wounded on a mission. He was shot in the back and his spinal cord was pretty much severed. I was wondering if you wouldn't mind donating some healthy spinal cord cells while we're in working on your back so we can grow them, and with luck, graft them into his spine."

Cabbott nodded, "Certainly. I only hope you find enough good ones back there to get a sample from."

"I'm sure we will. Thank you," Dr. Miles walked toward the door.

"What's his name?"

"Lieutenant Frank Elliott. He's the brother of Major D.M. Elliott, the second in command."

The captain sighed deeply, "I'll say a prayer for him."

"Pray that one day he comes out of the coma he's in."

"I will."

"All right gentlemen, this is it!" Eagle hollered as she gathered her gear bag and tossed it into the helicopter. The rest of the team was a flurry of movement: checking weapons, gear, and each other several times over. Bolts on sub machine guns and hand guns clanked loudly as they were function checked. Spare stripper clips of ammunition were loaded into pouches and everything checked again.

Tige sat quietly on his cot, rifle laid across his legs. He was ready. Too many years in the SASR had taught him to be ready all the time. He reached down and checked his gear bag. An eighteen inch silencer was nestled in a special pocket on the outside. The mission needed to be quiet, and that was certainly the piece of equipment to ensure silence. The rest of the team would be going in with HK UMP sub machine guns that were threaded for silencers. Most of the combat was expected to be close range so battle rifles were not necessary. Each man also carried his hand gun. D.M. had fashioned a sheath for his sword that allowed it to be strapped to his back. He only needed to reach back over his shoulder and grab the handle to draw it.

"Five mike, let's load up!" Eagle yelled as she opened the hanger doors. The team stood ready to go. Black flight suits covered their armor. Eagle didn't want to attract any attention when they were on the Iwo, the fewer the questions asked, the happier she was going to be. Jake attached the tug to the helicopter and carefully maneuvered it outside into the bright sun. The rest of the team climbed in. Eagle took her seat in the copilot seat, deciding to let Jake fly to the Iwo. She watched as he closed the hanger doors, hurried over and climbed into the pilot's seat. He flipped several switches and the aircraft whined to life. Slowly the rotors began to spin. He plugged his helmet into the comm jack and established contact with the tower.

"Cairo West, this is Delta Sierra three, one, one. Request permission for takeoff."

"Roger Delta Sierra, pattern is clear, take off when ready."

"Copy that Cairo, heading east to Kuwait," Jake said as he pushed the stick forward and the helicopter started to taxi. He knew that because of the load the copter was carrying he would have to perform a short rolling take off rather than just lifting off. The intense desert heat did nothing to help with lift. He taxied faster until the tail began to rise. The main rotor bit into the air and finally they were lifted into the sky. "Bad air today. Not making my job any easier," he slowly climbed until they were at five thousand feet. Making the necessary course corrections Jake kept them on the heading where they would meet up with a Navy C-130 for mid air refueling somewhere near Al Jawf, Saudi Arabia.

Eagle had stripped every ounce of unnecessary ordinance off the helicopter and had the crew chief install a close fitting external fuel tank. Even with all the trade-offs, they were only able to extend the range an extra one hundred miles. This would give them some leeway when meeting with the tankers. Once they had refueled near Al Jawf, they would need to refuel again about three hundred miles from Kuwait. The trip would take them over five hours to complete. They would land on the Iwo Jima shortly before it left port. It would then be another five hour trip before they were close to Bushehr.

CHAPTER TWENTY SIX

Amir Kemal stepped off the jet way at Imam Khomeini Airport in Tehran. He'd all ready contacted his personal pilot who would have the private jet ready to take him to the small local airport in Bushehr. In a few hours he would be home sipping some exotic fruit drink watching the waves of the Persian Gulf lap at his feet. He would have his wife prepare a delicious dinner and afterward he would make love to her. Even more special was his eldest daughter was home from college abroad. Kemal had not seen her in two years. His youngest son, now twelve, was also home from boarding school.

Perhaps this was a blessing, Kemal thought as he showed his passport to the customs officer. It was rare that the entire family was together now days. His children were growing fast and becoming independent, soon he would think of retirement. Thirty years of buying and selling secrets was getting old. He looked forward to traveling with his wife and enjoying life. He certainly didn't have to worry about money. All the years of spying had paid for first rate educations for his children, financed two beautiful beach houses in two countries, and allowed him to live a life of comfort.

Kemal had just retrieved his bags off the carousel when his phone rang. He looked down at the number before answering, "Hello? Yes. I just landed in Tehran. You still have not found her? And what of your snitch? No word from him either... I will be home in a few hours. When I land at Bushehr I will speak to the commander of the Sixth TAG and let them know to be watchful. If any aircraft stray into that area, they will be met by the new MIGs that just arrived on station... All right, good bye." Picking up his bags, Kemal headed outside where he hailed a cab to take him to the executive aircraft area of the airport.

"Okay, we're topped off again. Next stop, Kuwait," Jake said as he slowly backed the helicopter away from the boom hose. Eagle sat quietly next to him looking out the window. The rest of the team was either asleep or also looking out the windows. "You look worried," the lieutenant broke the silence.

Eagle turned to Jake, "What?"

"I said you look worried."

"I am, every mission. No matter how many times you guys go out, or how much technology you have on your side, I worry just the same," she replied softly.

"Just shows you care about us."

"I know, and believe me, it's the hardest part of the job."

The team flew along for another hour before landing on the Iwo Jima. As the rotors stopped, the team looked out the window to see nearly a dozen marines looking back at them. "Anybody here speak Jar Head?" Jake teased as he finished shutting down the controls.

"Sorry mate, I only speak Royal Marine," Tige joked as he opened the door. One by one the team hopped out and stood facing the marines.

Jake held both of his hands up, "We come in peace. Can someone take us to your leader?" He said slowly. The rest of the team tried to stifle their laughter.

A major stepped forward, "Lemme guess, you guys are the bunch of black jammies we're babysitting?"

Eagle slid out from behind D.M. and approached the major, "Yes, that's right major. I'm Lieutenant Colonel Tryggvesson." The major snapped to attention and saluted her. Eagle returned the salute, "You'll only be babysitting us for a few hours. We have a mission to launch from here and when we're done; we'll quickly refuel and head home... My men will do their best to stay out of your way."

"Yes ma'am. If you would please accompany me, I'll take you up to see the captain."

"Thank you," Eagle replied as he signaled the rest of the team to stay put. She disappeared inside the ship leaving the rest of the team face to face with the Marines.

Jake looked around, "Okay, there's twenty of them and six of us. Kind of weak odds don't you think?"

D.M. put his hand over Jake's mouth, "Now lieutenant, we're here as guests. Eagle said we need to behave. Let's not get ourselves into trouble. Remember the last time we did that, we put fifteen out of the forty in the hospital," he said lowly as he leaned over to Jake. He then straightened up and addressed the crowd, "You must excuse my associate, he grew up on the wrong side of the tracks. He's used to killing three or four men before breakfast," He smiled and winked at the group. The marines laughed.

Eagle returned several minutes later. She stopped and looked at the two groups of men, then looked down at her watch, "Well, that's impressive. I've been gone a whole ten minutes and you fellas didn't even start a fight. That must be a new record...All right, grab the gear you'll need and follow me. The captain was gracious enough to find some bunks for us...Let's get some rest. It's gonna be a long night." As they gathered their bags, they could hear the local mosque announce evening prayer. The sound echoed off the buildings and drifted through the air. Everyone on the team stopped and looked around. Max looked at his watch, "That's Isha, the call to evening prayers."

"How do you know so much about Islam?" Jake asked.

"Just part of my job. You learn the language, you learn the customs…When I was doing some diplomatic attaché jobs, I ended up being sent all over the world. I quickly learned to adopt what customs were required so I wouldn't make an ass out of myself."

Sam took a deep breath in, smelling the fragrance of the local cuisine, "I hear you sometimes gotta eat some pretty strange foods too; since you don't wanna offend your host,"

"Let's not go there. Some of that stuff I really didn't wanna know what it was. That was a case of ignorance is bliss." He took in several long breaths, "Although that smells like kharoof, one of my favorites."

"What's that?"

"Grilled young lamb usually served with rice and vegetables."

"Mmm, that sounds good."

"Yes, it is quite good; and washed down with a nice hot glass of cinnamon or mint tea."

"Stop, you're making me hungry!" Sam teased.

The team followed one of the marines below deck. Jake stayed behind and waited until the Warhawk was towed to the holding area. He secured the helicopter and then found someone to take him down to the team's quarters. The rest of the team made quick work of finding bunks and were laid out trying to nap. Jake found an empty bunk and dropped his gear bag on the floor. He looked over and saw Eagle watching him, "I heard one of the guys on the flight deck saying that we may be delayed getting underway three hours. Something about a broken part in the engine."

Eagle checked her watch, "I figured something like that would happen. I padded our schedule to allow for unforeseen circumstances. Now get some sleep."

"Yes ma'am," Jake replied as he hopped up on his bunk.

The incessant beeping of her watch roused Eagle from a sound sleep. She turned off the alarm without opening her eyes. Rolling over, she finally opened her eyes to see D.M. standing with his arms resting on her bunk. His dark eyes twinkled in the dim light, "Hi," he said softly.

"Hi," she said with a moan as she stretched her arms.

"Ready to go kill people?" He said with enthusiasm.

"You're the ones going to kill people. I'm just the taxi home."

"Well, maybe so, but you are part of the team," the major helped her out of the cramped bunk, "Come on, let's go get some chow."

The team found their way to the mess hall and filed through the chow line. Most did not take very much to eat; their stomachs were flipping with nerves. They sat down at a table out of the way. Evening mess was nearly over and only a few sailors and marines dotted tables in the hall. Most paid no attention to the team. They ate, not many words were exchanged. Each man was mustering up nerve and trying to put his game face on. Eagle sat watching them. She looked at each man's eyes noticing all held a serious expression. The captain came down and found Eagle, "We're within eighteen miles of Bushehr. I've slowed us up so your team could disembark on a zodiac. If you want, I can send a man along to bring the boat back so there's no evidence left on the beach."

"I've instructed them to scuttle it just off shore. I don't want to put any of your people in jeopardy."

"Oh, I've got just the man for the job. He's well trained in this sort of business. He can loiter just off shore to make sure your team is situated before he comes back."

"What's so special about him?" Eagle said with a yawn.

"He's former Special Warfare Combat-craft Crewman. Quite capable at insertion and extraction of Special Operators."

"All right. We wanna push off at twenty one hundred."

"I'll have him meet your team at the boat."

"Thank you sir."

The team returned to their quarters and collected their gear. They made their way up to the hanger deck and retrieved the rest of their gear from the helicopter. As they stood in the near darkness, they could see the distant skyline of downtown Kuwait. They found an area below deck and made one last equipment inventory. As zero hour approached, the team was taken down to the boat ramp. A single black Zodiac sat on the boat ramp and a sailor dressed in dark digital camouflage awaited them.

"Good evening everyone. I'm Petty Officer Mike Greer. I'll be your chauffeur for tonight's outing."

Sam stood at the back of the group. He was really not looking forward to the mission. Hearing the name of the Petty Officer, he perked up and nudged his way to the front. He stopped and eyed the man, "Mike? Mike Greer? I'll be damned, it is you!"

Mike stood silent for a moment before realizing who it was, "Sam Waters?"

"Been a long time man. I wondered what happened to you after basic," Sam replied as he reached out and offered his hand. Mike shook it vigorously.

"You two know each other?" Eagle interjected.

Sam turned to the group, "Hey everyone, this is Mike. We went to basic together... We grew up only ten miles apart and had never met until we were at Great Lakes."

The team loaded their gear into the boat and climbed in. Eagle stood watching them. As they backed away, she snapped to attention and saluted them, "Good luck gentlemen!" D.M. stood and returned the salute. He always thought it was funny that she chose to salute them, not the other way around. Her position on the team dictated that she be shown respect. D.M. figured it was her way of showing her pride and sending her warriors off to battle. The boat disappeared into the darkness. She headed back up to the hanger deck. This was going to be the longest few hours of her life. Opening the side door of the Warhawk, she sat down on the door ledge and looked out over the water. In the distance she could see the faint twinkling of lights on the Iranian coast. A warm breeze blew across the hanger deck. Somewhere out there in the darkness the team was heading to their objective.

D.M. sat with his back against the side of the boat. His stomach was all ready upset with the thought of the mission, the bouncing of the boat through the choppy waters did nothing to help. Jake sat next to him. He looked up at the major and noticed that he appeared to be concentrating on something, "What's the matter major?"

"Nothing. Just trying to clear my mind and get focused on the job."

"Oh. I'd swear that you look like you're about to puke," Jake said loudly over the engine noise.

"This boat ride is not helping," he replied. A few minutes later the engines slowed and the boat settled down on the water. Petty Officer Greer was skilled at silent insertions. He brought the boat closer to shore, slowing down even further to reduce noise and wake. The team quietly made one last check of their equipment. Within a few minutes they would be stepping ashore. D.M. checked his watch. It had taken them almost forty five minutes to reach the drop off point. From there it was nearly a half mile walk until they reached the beach house.

The boat edged into the beach. D.M. and the others quietly hopped out and grouped up on the sand. Petty Officer Greer backed the boat away. No words were said, they each knew their jobs. The team hurried away into the darkness. It didn't take long before they reached the beach house. A low sea wall about five feet high provided cover while they assessed the situation. Tige had left the group in search of his high ground. He told D.M. not to move until he was in position.

"Lone Wolf. Wombat. I am in position, repeat, I am in position."

"Roger Wombat. What do you see?"

Tige adjusted his scope and settled down, "I see two just behind the wall near your position...Uh, there's another three on the long balcony that runs across the back of the house...Switching to thermal...There's two that look like they are in bed to your left...Whoa! And I think they're shagging!"

"Wombat, just the sit-rep please, not a blow by blow of what's going on in the bedroom," D.M. said lowly. He looked over at Jake who had his hand over his mouth trying not to laugh.

"Sorry. Right... There's not much movement in the house, looks like everyone is bedded down for the night... There are two more in bedrooms to the right...I don't see any guards moving around in the house... There are some that look like guards, but they're stationary."

"Can you see anything out in front of the house?"

"Negative, don't have good angle."

"Can you tell how many are in the house?

"Looks like eight or ten. Geez, this guy must be paranoid to have that many guards in his own home country."

"All right then, who do you claim for targets?" The major reached down and made sure the silencer was firmly screwed on to his machine gun.

"Ah, decisions, decisions...Well, my angle gives me a great view of the three on the balcony. I can drop maybe two before the party starts. If you guys spread out, I'll get you in position to take the two behind the wall out... Bull Dog, go to your right about ten meters. Kingpin, go left fifteen meters. Lone Wolf, Ground Zero and Razor, stand fast and prepare to pop over the wall and take out the middle one on the balcony and maybe the one on the right if you can get the shot."

"You sure this will work?"

"No, but it's the best I can come up with," Tige said as he slid the bolt forward and chambered a round. Carefully he took aim at the guard farthest from his position, "Okay, I'm going to drop the one to the far right first. As soon as he goes, you guys make your moves on the others. Hopefully in the confusion I can drop the one closest to me." He adjusted his position slightly and took a long deep breath. He brought his eye down to the scope and let his hand slide around the grip and his finger rest on the trigger. "Okay, let the party begin," he exhaled slowly and squeezed the trigger. The round struck the guard and dropped him immediately. Quickly Tige chambered another round and took aim at the other guard. The others had come over the wall and neutralized the other guards. The last guard managed to get off a couple of rounds before Tige took him out. A few moments later, more guards came out of the house firing wildly. D.M. and the others were beginning their advance across the open area of the back garden. They dropped guards as they emerged from the house and continued their advance. One of the guards hid behind the balcony wall. He was armed with an RPG. As he stood up to fire, Tige got him in his sights. Just as he squeezed the trigger of his rifle, the guard let fly with the RPG. Jake saw the grenade heading his direction and tried to dive out of the way. It impacted on the ground just a few feet from him sending him crashing against the sea wall. He landed in a heap, not moving.

"Jake! Jake!" D.M. hollered and turned to go help.

"I got him Lone Wolf, continue on your objective," Sam called as he made his way over to Jake. A spray of bullets sent him diving for the ground next to Jake. The sting of rounds impacting the armor made him keep his back to the house while he attended to Jake. Max and Bruce fell back and fired cover so Sam could get him to safety.

D.M. ran forward to the house. Bullets ricocheted off his armor. He could feel the sting but ignored it; his mind was focused on his objective. Several guards stepped in his way; he bashed one in the face with his fist, reached back, grabbed his sword and sliced another across the abdomen. The last guard leveled his Uzi and pulled the trigger. The major took a swing and cut the guard's arm off. He then used the pommel of the sword to smash him in the face. Blood splattered all over the visor of his helmet. He pulled it off and dropped it on the floor.

Sam got Jake behind the sea wall and began checking him out.

The lieutenant was out cold. Sam could find no obvious injuries; the armor had taken the majority of the blast. He took off Jake's helmet and pulled out his penlight. Checking his pupils, Sam knew Jake would have a nasty concussion. Checking his ears, he saw a trickle of blood coming out of his left ear. Most likely he had a ruptured ear drum as well.

Tige took aim and fired as quickly as he could find targets, "Lone Wolf, have you reached objective?"

D.M. stopped at what appeared to be a bedroom. He kicked the door in and stormed inside. He found Kemal backed against the wall, his wife cowering next to him. "I have objective," the major replied coldly.

Kemal stepped forward, "I know it's me you want. Please, I beg you to leave my family out of this."

"Our fight is with you. Your family means nothing. Send your wife out."

Kemal motioned to his wife to leave. She cried out and grabbed at him. He pushed her away and yelled at her to leave. Reluctantly she left the bedroom. Kemal then walked forward to D.M., "So, how am I to die?"

D.M. held his sword with the tip pointing at Kemal, blood dripped off the blade, "I'll let you fight for your life."

Kemal nodded, "You look quite adept with that blade. May I at least have the name of the man who is going to kill me?"

"Major D.M. Elliott... And I nearly lost my life because of you."

"Revenge is a powerful motivator."

D.M. walked over to the dresser. An ornamental sword rested in a decorative display stand. He picked it up and tossed it to Kemal, "Sorry, it's not nearly as good as mine, but I will be polite and give you a chance."

"You appear to be a man of honor major."

D.M. stood en garde, "Let's do this, I have a ride to catch." He waited until Kemal made his move. D.M. knew the ornamental sword wouldn't hold up to much abuse, so he would have to toy with Kemal to make the battle fair. After a few blocks, D.M. advanced, putting Kemal on the defensive. He was pleasantly surprised to find that the Iranian had some skill with the sword.

"Yes major, I studied fencing for three years at Oxford

University. I'm not as unskilled as you might think."

"Good, I was hoping for a bit of a challenge," he parried one of Kemal's thrusts and made a thrust of his own. His blade caught Kemal on the right side of his chest, slicing him neatly, "The first point belongs to me."

Kemal staggered back and grabbed his side, "And so it does." He regained his composure and lunged forward at D.M., who easily deflected the thrust. The major stepped aside and let him crash headlong into the dresser.

"You're really not making this very sporting," the major said as he made another neat slice across Kemal's back, "Come on, have you forgotten everything Oxford has taught you? That's point number two for me."

"And how many points are we going to?"

"Three sounds good to me. Like I said, I have a ride to catch," D.M. stepped forward and taunted him to engage. He knew Kemal didn't have much fight in him and he was growing bored with how the battle was going, "If this is the best you got, I think it's time to end it."

"I appreciate you giving me a chance," Kemal said as he made one last effort. D.M. made a few blocks and then made his final move. His blade found its way straight into Kemal's heart. He looked up at the major, his eyes closed and he slumped to the floor. D.M. pulled out his sword, wiped the blood on Kemal's bedspread and sheathed it. He picked up his machine gun and walked out of the bedroom, keying his mike, "Mission accomplished, prepare for extraction." He came around the corner and stopped. In front of him was a boy. D.M. guessed him to be about eleven or twelve years old, and he held an Uzi pointed at him, "Hey kid, why don't you put that down?"

"You killed my father," The boy's English was excellent. He raised the Uzi.

"Your father was my enemy. He died in a fair fight."

"And now you die!" He squeezed the trigger. Several rounds fired from the small machine pistol.

D.M. stepped back as the bullets ricocheted off his armor. The boy raised the gun and fired again, the major tried to duck but one round caught him on the left side of the temple and sent him to the ground. He lay there for a few moments stunned. The boy stood looking at him, he lowered the gun. D.M. got up, blood streamed down the side of his face. The boy raised the gun again. Without hesitation, the major pulled his pistol and fired. The boy tumbled backward to the ground, dead. D.M. holstered the weapon. He stood over the boy, "I'm sorry kid," he said softly. Making his way down the hall, picked up his helmet and went outside. He stopped at the balcony wall and rested against it. His stomach churned and he felt sick. Killing Kemal didn't really bother him, but killing his son had hit a weak spot in his soul. He never thought he'd kill a child; it wasn't something he was mentally prepared for. As he rested against the wall, his head began to spin and his stomach threatened harder. Leaning over the wall, D.M. vomited violently. He continued to vomit until his stomach wretched dry. After, he knelt down behind the wall and leaned against it for support. Blood continued to pour down his face.

"White Feather, Ground Zero, what's your ETA?" Sam said as he attended to Jake.

"Ground Zero, ETA ten mike... What is your status?"

"I got one wounded that I know of, Kingpin took an RPG blast. He's out cold, I can't find much wrong with him besides that. Rest of the team has not come back."

Tige came down the beach and joined Sam. He saw Jake lying on his side in the sand, "He gonna be all right?"

"He was a little too close to that RPG blast. He's out cold, but I think he'll be okay."

"Any sign of D.M., Max or Bruce?"

"Not yet."

Tige keyed his mike, "Lone Wolf, Bull Dog, Razor, do you read?"

"I read you Wombat," Max replied.

"What's your position?"

"Coming out the back of the house with Razor," Max answered as he opened the door and stepped out onto the balcony, Bruce following. He walked a few steps and stopped. In the dim light he could see the major slumped against the wall, "Oh shit!" He hurried over and dropped down next to him. D.M. attempted to look up, his face nearly covered in blood. Max dug through his first aid pouch and pulled out a field dressing. He held it to the wound and did his best to bandage it up, "Ground Zero, I got one more wounded. The major's been hit."

Eagle's heart jumped in her chest as she heard the news of D.M. being wounded. She pushed the throttle forward trying to get to them as quick as possible. "Bull Dog, how bad is he?"

"All I can see so far is a nasty bullet crease to his left temple. He's got blood all over him, and he's not very responsive."

Eagle keyed her mike, "Ground Zero, can you assist Bull Dog?"

"On my way White Feather," Sam said as he grabbed his bag and scrambled over the sea wall. He ran across the open back garden and up the stairs to the balcony. As he reached the top of the stairs he could see Max kneeling down next to D.M. with his hand on the major's shoulder, "How is he Max?"

"I got him bandaged up. I think maybe he got his bell rung pretty good, he's just not acting right."

Sam pulled out his penlight and shined it into the major's eyes, "Naw, if he does, it's not very bad... Come on; let's get him down to the beach." He got one arm under D.M.'s and Max got the other. Bruce carried all their weapons and Sam's medical bag. They helped him to his feet and he staggered down the stairs toward the beach, leaning heavily on Max. Sam hopped up and straddled the wall. Tige stood ready on the beach to help. They helped D.M. over the wall. He sat down in the sand next to Jake. Sam and Max jumped down. Bruce crawled over last. In the distance they could hear Eagle coming.

Two minutes later Eagle was landing the helicopter on the beach. D.M. and Jake were loaded first and then the rest of the team climbed in. Jake had regained consciousness and was lying on his back with his eyes closed. D.M. sat on the floor next to him, his hand resting on the lieutenant's shoulder. They headed back out over the Persian Gulf to rendezvous with the Iwo.

***

"Sweet Jesus! Would you look at the gouge out of his temporal bone?!" Sam exclaimed as he helped Eagle clean and suture the major up, "Another eighth of an inch and he would have had the side of his head blown out."

"I'd say he was damn lucky," Eagle replied as she tied off a stitch. D.M. lay under the surgical drape, still in too much shock to say anything. She continued to put in stitches until the wound was closed, "All right, finish cleaning him up and get him bandaged," she pulled off her sterile gloves and went to wash her hands. She then went over to see Jake, "How are you feeling lieutenant?"

"I got one hell of a headache and my right wrist hurts."

Eagle gently took his arm and examined it. Jake winced as she palpated the back of his wrist. "I think we should get some x-rays on it."

"Yes ma'am. How's the major?"

"He's very lucky to be alive. The bullet put about a two inch long gouge in his skull."

"I always knew the major had a hard head, he's certainly proved that now," he smiled weakly.

Eagle returned the smile, "Yes, I guess he has."

"Are we going home soon?"

"If you both feel a bit better in the morning, we'll head out."

Sam pulled off his jerkin and looked down at the pattern of bruises left from the bullets that had ricocheted off the armor. He was grateful that they were only bruises; the alternative would have been death. Max stood next to him, "Shit, you got the crap pounded out of you."

"The joys of being the medic. These all came my way when I was trying to get Jake over the wall."

"At least we're all still alive. Had we not had this stuff, probably Tige and Eagle would have been the only ones to survive."

"What's that mate?" Tige said as he poked his head around

the corner.

"Oh, we were just talking about how the armor saved us. If we didn't have it, you and Eagle would have been the only ones alive."

The team finished breakfast and loaded the helicopter for the journey home. Eagle went down to the infirmary to see D.M. and Jake. "Major? How are you feeling?"

D.M. moaned softly and didn't open his eyes, "Got a wicked headache."

"Would you like something for it?"

"No."

"Are you going to be all right to travel?"

"Yes," he said flatly.

"We plan on leaving in the next hour."

"I'll be up there."

Eagle made her way over to Jake. He was sitting up in bed, not looking very happy, his casted right arm resting on a pillow. "Lieutenant? How are you this morning?"

"I got a banger of a headache, can't hear out of my left ear and my f'ing arm is killing me. I guess I shouldn't complain though, the armor saved my life because it sucked up most of the blast. I figure my injuries were a lot less than they would have been."

"Well, you can certainly say it's been battle tested now."

"Damn straight!" He managed a half smile.

"Would you like something for the pain? We plan on leaving here in the next hour. You gonna be all right to make the ride home?"

"Sure. And just make sure Sam has lots of happy pills and I'll be fine."

"I'll get the corpsman to get you something for the pain. Can you make it up to the deck?"

"Yes ma'am. And I'll drag the major along with me."

CHAPTER TWENTY SEVEN

D.M. lay curled up with Eagle. It was a Saturday morning; the sun was just coming up. The team had been home three weeks from their mission in the Gulf. The major had spent nearly every night sleeping with Eagle trying to fight off the nightmares that haunted him. She didn't mind, she had her own nightmares that haunted her as well. She gently caressed his face and ran her fingers through his hair. His nasty wound had healed; the hair had grown back white from the scar. It was a visible reminder of what had happened.

"D.M.?" She said softly.

"Mmmmmm?"

"You haven't been yourself lately. What's wrong?"

He sighed deeply, "Not sure if I'm ready to talk about it."

Eagle caressed his face, leaned down and kissed his forehead, "Sometimes talking about it will help make the demons go away."

"These demons have a good hold on me, they're not going away any time soon," he looked up and studied her. Her ice blue eyes twinkled in the early morning light. He swallowed hard, trying to muster up all the mental strength he could. Telling her what happened was not going to be easy. He slipped from her grasp and sat up. It took him several moments while he collected his thoughts. "It wasn't hard...No, killing Kemal was rather easy. I made it as fair of a fight as I could," he paused for a few moments, "He died honorably... Of course I left him his head, so he won't get his forty virgins in heaven."

"What do you mean by that?"

"Max told me that the only way a Muslim can get to heaven if he dies in battle is to have his head removed. I left him his head... I suppose that wasn't very sporting of me, but I guess it satisfied my taste for revenge."

"And you're having problems with this?"

"No, not in the slightest," he stretched and rubbed his face, "It's what happened after that I'm having trouble with." His expression changed. The major's face drew tight and he tugged restlessly at the covers, "I had finished Kemal and was leaving when his young son stopped me...The boy was maybe eleven or so...He was holding an Uzi pointed at me... I told him to put the gun down, but he pulled the trigger and unloaded half a dozen rounds on me. They all hit the armor and ricocheted off... I guess he realized that the only vulnerable part on me was my head and he aimed higher and cut loose again...I tried to duck, but one round caught me and I went down... As I got up, he took aim again," he paused again trying to put the words together. Eagle could see he was beginning to shake. She reached over and wrapped her arms around him. He lowered his head, "I...I...didn't have much choice...He was going to kill me... I drew and fired...Eagle, I killed that boy," he put his head in his hand.

Eagle held him as tightly as her arms would allow. She couldn't tell if he was crying or not, it sounded like it though. The major was usually pretty tough, but this had really upset him. Deep down inside she knew he was a man of passion, and when he let his emotions out, they were true to his feelings. She wondered if his terrible past had any influence on how he felt.

"Shhhhhhhh. I'm here for you D.M." She held him for quite a while.

D.M. finally looked at her with tear stained eyes, "I didn't wanna kill him, he was just a kid. Goddamn he was just a kid!"

"I know major. I know...You didn't have much choice in the matter. Unfortunately this is something that you'll have to come to terms with someday. You did what you had to in order to stay alive. You completed your mission."

He looked at her, "I feel awful. You can't know how I feel inside."

"No, you're right, I can't... All I can do is be here for you and offer support when you need it," she caressed his back. D.M. rubbed his face and eyes. Admittedly he felt a little better after talking to her, but he was still having issues over the whole incident. Never in his life did he ever think he would have to kill a child- especially face to face. It was a different matter when he was twenty thousand feet up dropping bombs on some village in the middle of nowhere. If a child died as a result of the bombs, there was nothing he could do about it, and most likely he would never know anyways. Eagle was right when she had told him that killing face to face was a whole different mindset. Seeing the eyes of your victim at the moment you inflict the mortal wound took a strong stomach. Even killing Kemal was harder to do than he thought, revenge driven or not. And after he killed him, did he feel any better? Not really. Revenge must be overrated, D.M. thought.

Eagle climbed out of bed, "Hey, I'm gonna get a shower. You wanna join me?"

"Mmmm, I dunno," he replied, still caught up in his thoughts.

"I'll wash your back and you can wash mine," she teased.

"Are you trying to make me feel better?"

She pulled off her top and threw it on the bed next to him, "Yes," she walked to the bathroom. Just as she got to the door, she stopped, pulled off her pajama shorts and threw them over her shoulder. D.M. watched her disappear, his heart started to pound and he was certainly aroused by her little show. He could hear the water running in the shower. After a few moments he heard the shower door close. Sliding out of bed, he wandered into the bathroom. The frosted glass of the shower walls disguised her nakedness just enough. It was a large shower, quite roomy enough for two. He averted his gaze until he had quickly relieved himself-nothing worse than trying to pee with a hard on.

Eagle turned as she heard the shower door open. D.M. stepped in and let the door close behind him. It closed quicker than he thought and the cold glass bumped him on the behind, "Whooo! That's cold!"

She laughed, "I see you decided to join me after all."

"Well, gee, let me look at my options: lay in bed and be a slug, go back to my room and get a shower by myself, or get the once in a life time chance to have a shower with the woman I love. Humm, tough choice."

"Nice to know I won out over the other two options," she splashed water at him. He stepped forward and grabbed her around the waist, kissing her hard. He backed her up until she was against the shower wall. He leaned his weight against her, his mouth searching out her lips, nibbling on them. Eagle gasped as he leaned down and kissed her breasts. He stopped for a moment and looked up.

"I take it this feels good?"

"Mmmmmm, yes... But..."

"But what?" He slid his grasp and backed up.

"Remember your promise to me."

"Yeah, what about it?"

"Just reminding you."

"Eagle... I made a promise to you and I will keep it, no matter what... But you have to understand a bit about the male species...See...we, just like you women have a balance in our lives too, although far more simpler than yours. We don't have to juggle work, family, kids and all the normal female responsibilities. Na, our lives balance quite simply, it's either death or life. We either want to kill it, or fuck it... And right now I'm a bit out of balance."

"Too much killing and not enough..."

"Exactly," he stepped close to her again.

"So, uh, what did you have in mind?"

D.M. leaned down and kissed her. He reached past her and grabbed the bar of soap, "You said you'd wash me."

She took the soap and ran it under the water and worked it in her hands to get a lather. Reaching up, she started to rub his shoulders and chest. D.M. moaned. Slowly, she worked her way down his abdomen. He leaned down and found her lips again, pushing her back against the wall. Playfully, he moved his body up and down rubbing soap on her. Eagle put her arms around his waist and pulled him closer. As D.M. pressed himself against her harder, she could feel the fullness of his manhood against her stomach. He let his lips part from hers, "You gonna finish the job?" He whispered, sliding away from her.

Eagle flipped the soap over in her hand a few times. This was one of those areas that she had no experience in. The relationships she had in the past were largely casual; there was no time for serious romance when there were things she wanted to do in her life. "I'm afraid I'm a bit out of my element here," she said sheepishly.

D.M. chuckled, "No experience required, just wash and you'll figure it out... Just like when we're dancing, my body will tell you what to do," he reached and took her hand, placing it at the base, "Just wash," he whispered, "Mind your nails please." Eagle wrapped her hand around and let it slide up and down once. D.M. gasped and moaned, "My body is yours. I surrender," he whispered. Eagle moved her hand slowly, experimenting with different positions of her fingers and varying pressure. She figured she must have found something that D.M. found pleasurable, he groaned loudly and threw his head back.

"That good?" Eagle asked.

"Oh yeah, no complaints."

Eagle continued to work her hand a little harder and faster. D.M. moaned louder, his breathing coming quicker. Eagle increased her efforts. He groaned even louder. A few moments later he let out a ragged howl as he climaxed. Eagle was surprised at how loud he was, and how it seemed an almost painful experience. His face was twisted and his mouth was open, teeth bared. He gasped for air and after a few moments he settled down. He leaned forward and gently kissed her, "Thank you, it's been a while."

"A while?"

"Few weeks...Yes, we guys have to try and keep ourselves balanced somehow...I've fantasized about this moment for a long time... Nice to say it's far more enjoyable with you."

"So are you feeling 'balanced' again?"

D.M. sighed deeply and smiled, "Yes."

Eagle lathered up the soap again, "You want me to wash your back like I said I would?"

"Sure," he turned around. Eagle lovingly lathered his back and then gently ran her fingernails up and down. D.M. moaned loudly, "Oh shit that feels good! Harder!" Eagle scratched his back harder until she got tired. D.M. leaned against the wall, he started to chuckle.

"What's so funny?"

"Oh, I was just thinking. You never asked me about my call sign."

"Lone Wolf? Humm, I just figured you got that because you were a bit of a loner."

The major chuckled a bit more, "No, that's not how I got it."

"All right, how?" She continued to rub his back.

"Well, uh, during flight school, we were all billeted in dorms. I happened to hook up with a female pilot who was going through school. She was a class ahead of me. Things got hot and heavy for a little bit...The walls weren't exactly very thick, so when I'd have a pretty good orgasm, like I kinda just did, I'd let out a bit of a howl...The guy living next to me, who was in my class, heard it, and that's how I got my call sign."

Eagle was laughing, "Oh my God that's just too funny!"

"I would however appreciate it if you keep that between us."

"Of course, that's our little secret. All right, my turn," she said as she smacked him on the behind. D.M. turned around and she handed him the soap. He flipped it over in his hand a few times to get a lather. He then handed the soap to her and began to lather each of her shoulders. As he worked his way down her abdomen, he stopped.

"Sure there isn't anything I can do for you?" He said as he let his hand slide down and drift to her inner thigh.

"Mmmm, I got a lot of pleasure just giving you pleasure."

"You sure? I don't mind."

"Right now I can say I'm happily balanced. My needs aren't nearly as demanding as you male folk."

He let his hand slide between her legs, "I beg to differ. You have needs, I know you do. You're just not wanting to explore them."

She drew away from him, "Maybe I choose not to explore them... My focus remains on the team and the mission."

"That's a bullshit answer... I remember back at China Lake, you could be quite the tease...Saying Norwegians were very erotic people...Don't be afraid to live up to that," he finished lathering up her front and motioned for her to turn around.

"I guess since you've been open and honest with me, that I should be with you," she said softly.

"I'd hope so. Relationships are built on trust and honesty."

She sighed deeply, "My mother died before I hit the formidable age of womanhood. Of course that left just my father. And what self respecting male is going to give his daughter the 'birds and the bees' talk? Certainly not him. So my sex education came by the way of books and what I could get out of romance novels. Medical school did nothing but make it look less glamorous... I guess I'm afraid because I just don't know that much and I've always put work and my career before myself."

D.M. leaned over and kissed her on the cheek, "You know you can trust me to behave myself right?"

"Yes."

"Well, then why can't we have some fun? Let you enjoy your sexuality...You already got me figured out, I'm easy. You should get pleasure out of it just as much as I do," he reached down and cupped his hand around one of her buttocks, "Damn, you got a fantastic body!"

Max sat in the dining room working on the laptop he'd taken from Kemal's office. Sam and Tige watched on. It had taken him nearly two weeks to crack some of the passwords. Now he was carefully looking through files trying to find something to link him to Westland. "Hey, wait a minute," he clicked on a folder, "Well, well, what do we have here?"

"Whoa!!!" They all hollered as Max discovered Kemal's stash of porn.

"My, my Kemal, what a naughty Muslim you've been!" Sam exclaimed.

"Hey, he had some pretty good taste. Those are some damn fine bums," Tige said as he leaned closer.

"All right, enough eye candy," Max said as he closed out the folder and clicked on another, "Let's see what this one has to offer...Humm, certainly not porn."

"Looks like plans for a medium range rocket," Sam said as he leaned over Max's shoulder.

"And quite American looking too," Tige added.

"Either of you two ever hear of this in our inventory?"

"Nope," they both replied.

"I think we should show this to Eagle," Max said as he opened another folder.

Sam sat down in his chair, "She should be here in a few

minutes."

"We probably don't want Bruce to know about this do we?"

"Best kept quiet mate."

"Roger that."

The door opened and Eagle walked in. The threesome stood. "As you were gentlemen," she took her seat. Max approached her with the computer.

"I think I have something here that might interest you," he sat the laptop down in front of her and opened the file with the rocket. Eagle studied it intently.

"These are the plans for the new Hermes missile... This thing is still under pretty tight wraps. Only someone high up on the food chain would have access to these kinds of secrets."

"Westland?"

"I'd be willing to bet on it."

The door opened and Bruce walked in. Max swiftly closed the document and got back to the desktop screen, "Sorry Eagle, I think I got his kid's computer, all I can make out is games and homework assignments."

Eagle looked up and patted him on the shoulder, "Well lieutenant, you tried." She winked at him, motioning at him to take the computer away. Max picked it up and went back to his seat. He turned it off and sat it on the floor. A few minutes later Jake wandered in and took his seat. He opened up a thick text book and sat reading intently, using his casted right arm as a book weight. Tige leaned over and tried to figure out what he was reading.

"Never thought I'd see the day that your face was buried in a school book," the captain teased.

"It's not a school book. It's a book on chemical attributes and physical properties," he replied dryly.

"Awfully heavy reading don't you think?"

"No, not for what I'm working on. And the major said I need to have a better understanding of carbon compounds."

Eagle leaned forward and rested her arms on the table, "And what are you working on lieutenant?"

"I'd rather not say."

"Mmmm. Yup, you've been hanging around D.M. too much."

"Sorry ma'am. Just not sure it will work, so I'm not getting my hopes up yet."

D.M. walked in and sat down. Jake looked over and noticed the major seemed more relaxed. The tense furrow in his brow had softened and his eyes twinkled. "You're looking a bit happier," Jake said as he closed the book, "Feel like working in your lab?"

"Yeah, maybe."

"Good, 'cause I need some help."

"You've been down there working?"

"Don't worry, I haven't blown anything up yet," he joked.

"Ha, ha, smart ass. Why didn't you tell me?"

"I did, but you probably didn't pay attention. You haven't been yourself lately."

Jake sat at the lab counter working on the computer. D.M. sat with him. They were surfing the Internet looking for information on nanotechnology. "I'da thought there'd be tons of info out there," Jake said as he poked at the keyboard, "But there just doesn't seem much that we can use."

"I wonder... Do you mind?" D.M. motioned for the laptop. Jake slid it over and the major typed in a web address.

"Gee, how could I guess, the MIT website."

"Don't knock it until you try it." He scrolled through some pages until he found what he was looking for, "There, The Institute for Soldier Nanotechnologies."

Jake leaned back and crossed his arms, "I hate you sometimes."

The major chuckled and continued to look on the site. He found the MIT World site that contained online lectures, "Humm, let's see what we got," he entered the search word "soldier" and watched as two results popped up. "Well, they're a little old, but let's watch them and see if they help."

Jake leaned forward and intently watched. He took notes to reference later. "Major, this is so cool. I can't wait to work on the Chameleon Skin."

D.M. reached over and patted him on the back, "I think Eagle's gonna drag me to Washington so we can present our evidence against Westland. When I get back, I'll see if she'll let us loose for a field trip."

It was just after breakfast on a Saturday morning. Eagle was in her office sorting through papers, storage media and photographs. She loaded Kemal's laptop into her briefcase, piled the rest of the information on top and closed it with a hint of finality. It had taken over a month to compile the evidence against Westland. Max and Sam worked tirelessly extracting data from the bugs they had planted and the laptop Max had taken from Kemal. She wondered if it would be enough to get a conviction. Westland had underestimated the team's willingness to make sure justice was served. They didn't have any trouble understanding that even the most pious appearing men kept secrets and led double lives. Washington was full of spies and thieves.

D.M. knocked on the door and opened it before she had a chance to respond. He strolled over and stood in front of her desk, "I'm packed and ready to go."

"I just have a few things to get together."

"Jake's up preflighting the Warhawk."

"How'd he manage that?"

"Got out of his cast this morning. He says he's fine to fly. In fact I think he begged the Doc to cut him out just so he could get some flight time."

"Well, his fracture wasn't that bad, so I'm sure he's healed up enough."

The Warhawk touched down next to the Guard hanger at Reno airport. Jake turned off the rotors and hopped out of the cockpit. He stepped back and opened the side door, "I sure wish I was coming with you guys," he said as he helped unload their bags.

"Sorry lieutenant, you might think it would be interesting, but usually it's about as exciting as watching paint dry," Eagle said as she put her coat on. Fall was coming early to the Sierra Nevada range and a cold wind blew across the tarmac. D.M. zipped up his jacket and turned his back to the wind. It was most likely going to be a brutal winter. Grabbing their bags, they said their goodbyes to Jake and headed through the hanger to the street were a cab was waiting. As much as the major protested, Eagle insisted they fly commercial since they didn't know how long they would be in Washington. He did at least get her to fly first class, saying that the seats in coach would require a shoe horn to get his large frame into.

"You know, sometimes you can be a real pain in the ass," Eagle growled as she settled into her seat.

"Hey, I never leave home without my trusty 'American Express.' You know that," he said, patting his right side where his holster was hidden under his jacket.

"Yes, and trying to get through security is a nightmare with you."

"I just needed to get it through their thick little skulls that I happen to be one of the good guys."

"I think your level of paranoia has reached new levels," she said as she looked out the window.

"Thank the PTSD for that... Dr. Lindman says that's one of the symptoms."

"So you've been talking to him?"

"Once in a while. Actually you're better to talk to."

"Yes, but I don't have a degree in psychiatry."

D.M. pulled one of the magazines out of the seat back and flipped through it, "You understand me and you know what we go through. You're right there with us... And we need to have good communication anyways."

"That we do."

CHAPTER TWENTY EIGHT

"Good morning captain, how are you feeling?" Dr. Miles said

as he made morning rounds.

"I could probably use with some more pain meds; my right leg is really hurting." Cabbott said as he tried to finish breakfast. He'd been in bed for more months than he cared to remember and was getting extremely restless. There was still nearly five months left until Christmas, and the biggest and most difficult surgery still remained.

"I'll go get some for you right now and you can take them with the rest of your juice."

"Thanks...Hey Doc, do you think it would be possible to just get out of this bed for a while? I mean, even to sit in a wheelchair so I can roll around here a little bit?"

"I think that could be arranged. You've been very patient these last couple of months. I was wondering how long it was going to take before you got a good case of cabin fever."

"I've been in a bed so long; I think I wanna sleep standing up the rest of my life!"

Eagle and D.M. sat at the table in the hotel room working on their case. It was late Sunday night and they would be presenting their evidence the next morning. The colonel had arranged a private meeting with General Spears to go over all the information they had gathered. It would then be up to the general to decide if they had a good enough case to bring charges against Admiral Westland. If all worked out according to Eagle's plan, Westland would be spending the rest of his life behind bars.

The major stood and stretched. He was having trouble staying awake. Admittedly the information was dry and boring. "I'll be back in a few," he said as he disappeared through the door that joined his room to hers. Since their previous trip to Washington, Eagle made sure that their rooms adjoined so she could help D.M. get in and out of his arm. It also made it easier to spend private time together without having to go back and forth down the hall where prying eyes might see them. He returned a few minutes later with his half smoked Cuban cigar clenched in his teeth.

"You're not going to smoke that are you?"

"No, I need a little something to keep me awake. Sucking on

this oughtta give me just enough of a nicotine high I'll stay awake until we're done."

Eagle stacked a pile of papers and put them together with a paper clip. She was dressed in a loose Harvard Medical t-shirt and her usual pair of pajama shorts. She playfully reached up and cupped one of her breasts, "Well, had I known that, you could have sucked on these to keep awake!"

"Oh come on, it's late. We gotta get this stuff done. Besides, I'm actually quite tired."

"Are you gonna bunk with me tonight?"

"No. Gonna to try and sleep in my bed...Hard to say if I'll have a bad night or not, the nightmares don't always happen every night."

Eagle continued reviewing the case evidence. D.M. made notes and helped her organize the information. It was nearly 0100 when they finally went to bed.

The next morning Eagle and D.M. stood in front of General Spears. They were dressed in their service dress uniforms to punctuate the formalness of the situation. He stood up and offered his hand across the desk, "Eagle, how nice to see you again."

She shook his hand, "General. Always good to see you sir."

The general looked over at D.M., "And major. Looking formidable as usual."

D.M. nodded once, "Sir."

"Please, take your seats... So, what's so important that you need to see me in person?"

Eagle opened her briefcase and produced several stacks of papers. She flipped through them until she found the one she was looking for, "General, you may have remembered that I told you my team was made up of criminals and misfits. And I believed that it was Westland who selected them..."

"Yes, go on."

"I think he had every intention of making sure the team failed... Because if we did, he wouldn't be bothered by having to run our program, and he would get the vast majority of the funds back for his use."

"And what are you getting at?" The general pressed.

"My team of screw ups..." she looked at D.M., "No offense major..."

"None taken," he replied swiftly.

"...They figured out that Westland has been selling defense secrets to the Iranians."

The general looked at D.M., "Is this correct major?"

"Yes sir, it is."

Eagle passed over one small stack of documentation. He flipped through it, "Humm, it certainly looks like you have something."

"And that's not all sir. I have a laptop computer that was taken from the residence of Amir Kemal, an Iranian intelligence dealer. It contains the plans for the Hermes rocket."

"You're sure? Those are still classified on a need to know basis... And how do you know it's Westland who stole them?"

"Because when we were here for your promotion, part of my team bugged his office and car... We have audio, although not very good, of Westland talking about Kemal to his driver Lieutenant Farlow."

"Good God! Can't say your team isn't thorough."

"You taught me well sir."

"Indeed I did colonel," he sat back in his chair, "Hold on to your evidence. Guard it with your lives. I need to speak to the chairman about this. It's not often that someone as high up as Westland is charged with a crime, so this may take some careful planning."

"Sir, I think they could get him on two crimes: One, sabotage. For trying to interfere with the selection of my team, sending me personnel that he knew would not meet mission parameters. And two, treason. Stealing classified plans and documents and selling them to a country that has U.S. sanctions against it."

"I would agree on both, but the chairman may not. Your team of misfits has proven to be a battle hardened unit. They do fit your mission parameters now do they not?"

"Yes sir. But not without a lot of effort."

"And you have worked with flag grade officers enough to know that if heat is put on them, they have the easiest out in the world- retire."

The general was right. When an officer reached that high of a status, they became part of the "Good 'ol Boys" club. It gave them nearly carte blanc to do and say what they wanted without suffering any repercussions. With minor exception, they could just elect to retire and walk away without doing so much as a day in prison.

Eagle growled, "Damn that bastard! And I bet that's exactly what he'll do." She stood up to leave, "Makes all the trouble we went through for nothing!" D.M. stood and helped her collect her things.

"He'd at least be out of your chain," the general added.

"Yes, but off scott free!" She hissed as she threw papers back in her briefcase.

The general stood, "Colonel, don't lose your temper. Now of all times you need to keep a clear head. You'll have to testify against him. He can still ruin your career if you don't play this right."

D.M. slid behind the wheel and started the rental car. Eagle sat next to him, her head straight forward and eyes locked into the distance. He could tell she was angry, her body language screamed it. The question was; how long would it take her to explode? He pulled out into traffic and headed back to the hotel. It didn't take long. She slammed her fist into the dash board and launched on a tirade of profanity that would have most sailors blushing. The major had never seen her that angry before. He found a small empty parking lot at a park and pulled over. She continued to rant.

"Eagle, settle down," he said softly. She continued. He turned off the car and got out, figuring that if he left she'd settle down. There was no sense engaging her in the matter, it would only add fuel to her all ready hot fire. He put his beret on and walked over to a sidewalk and stood looking out over the Potomac River. He figured it must have been ten minutes before Eagle appeared at his side. He looked down at her, "Do you feel any better?"

"No," she huffed. They stood in silence for a few minutes.

"I was thinking... You know, it might be best if we can get

Westland to retire." D.M. said as he held his gaze out over the river. The trees were starting to turn for fall.

"And why is that major?"

"Because if we fight him; it might jeopardize the team."

"How so?"

"Like you said a while ago, they can easily take us out of the budget and then we're without jobs," he paused, "The higher ups may get worried. We took down one crook, what's to stop us from taking down more? If we get him to retire, there won't be much made of it... And once he's out, maybe we can extract our own brand of revenge."

"And what do you have in mind?"

"Oh, maybe an accidental death or something... Can't make it obvious or they'll immediately come looking for us."

Eagle rubbed her chin, "Humm. I like the way you think. I knew I loved you for more than those big shoulders."

He reached over and put his arm around her, "Yeah, well, you can cry on them any time you want."

"Thanks."

"How's your hand? I thought you were going to stick it through the dash as mad as you were."

"Hurts, but I'll live."

He let his arm slide from her and turned toward the car, "Come on, let's get back to the hotel. Maybe we can get this whole matter settled and get home soon."

"I hope so."

Two days later Admiral Westland tenured his retirement. Eagle had prepared herself for the news and fought hard to keep her composure. They had won the battle, but the rest of the war would be fought elsewhere. As Westland filed by her he stopped. D.M. instinctively reached over and grabbed the back of her coat, preventing her from launching a physical attack against him and getting herself into trouble. He knew she hated the admiral with every inch of her being.

"Well colonel, I guess you've forced me into early retirement." Eagle said nothing, she glared at the admiral. "Pity. It would have been nice to pad my bank account a bit more, but I'll have enough to get by on." Eagle growled and bared her teeth. She leaned forward and felt the restraint of D.M. holding her. "Major, I'd make sure you keep this bitch on a tight leash." Westland joked as he walked away laughing. D.M. growled; his .45 was just a few inches away. He reached up and put his hand inside his coat but fought the urge. There would be another time and place for revenge.

The team was placed on stand down for a month. General Spears was temporarily put in charge until the decision could be made on who would replace Westland. Eagle was in her office on the phone with him, "Oh come on general, there has to be something you can do... The rest of the team can't stand Sergeant von Teufel. He's an arrogant ass!... Yes sir, I understand. Well, as soon as someone is chosen, can you please bring that matter to their attention?...Thank you sir. Goodbye." She hung up the phone and sighed deeply. There just seemed to be no way to get rid of the sergeant. He was bad for morale and bad for the team. Even now that he knew Westland was not requiring his services anymore, he continued to make everyone uncomfortable. No one talked to him unless they had to. And Max only worked with him when it was absolutely necessary.

There was a knock on the door and the major walked in. He settled down in the chair in front of her desk. "Yes major, what can I do for you?"

"Well, since we are standing down for the next month, some of us were wondering if you'd approve some leave?"

"And who is the 'us'?"

"Well, Sergeant von Teufel was wanting two weeks..."

"Granted!" She said before he could finish.

"...And I was wondering if you would cut Jake and me loose for a few weeks as well?"

"I don't have a problem with that. Are you two up to no good again?" She teased.

D.M. smiled, "Always!"

***

The rotors of the Warhawk whined to life. D.M. finished stowing his gear and climbed into the copilot seat. Jake happily continued with the last of his preflight checks. "You ready for our little adventure?" The major asked over the intercom.

"Let's go baby!" Jake smiled.

"Good. This is going to be quite interesting."

"I'm looking forward to it," the lieutenant finished the last check and radioed for clearance, "Delta Sierra one, one, niner request clearance for takeoff."

"Roger Delta Sierra, pattern in clear."

"Copy control. Thanks and have a nice day," Jake eased the helicopter into the air and headed north. The early morning sun was bright and clear. They flew along the jagged mountain peaks. Jake smoothly maneuvered them through valleys and around mountains. "I can't believe Eagle let us borrow this thing to go to Reno."

"We're gonna park it in the Air Guard hanger and then get our other ride tomorrow. Eagle said she'd come down on the weekly supply run and pick it up. Then she'll come get us later," D.M. said as he looked out the window.

"What do you mean?"

"We're not just going to Reno, I've got a surprise for you," he looked over at Jake, "Do you even own a business suit?"

"You're kidding right? I mean look who you're talk'in to: Jake Collins, former gang-banger and drug dealer. Suits were not part of my wardrobe, not even for funerals."

"We'll have to fix that. I'll find a tailor when we get to Reno."

"Am I to guess we're going somewhere fancy and important?"

"We're going to do some business... And if you wanna play with the big boys, you have to dress like one.

They flew along and finally landed at the Reno airport. Pushing the helicopter inside the hanger, they went out front and the major called a cab. D.M. had found a nice hotel and booked them a room. After dropping their bags off, they found a tailor in the phone book and headed out again.

Jake walked up and down the aisles of suits trying to find

something he liked. D.M. didn't waste time finding a couple new suits and was having them tailored to fit over his robotic arm. "And you can have them ready tomorrow?" He asked as he slid out of a coat.

"Yes sir, we can. They will be ready by noon," the tailor replied.

"Excellent. We have a charter waiting for us and are heading back east."

Jake finally came to the back of the store with a suit, "Well, gonna see how this one fits." He stepped into the dressing room and a few minutes later came out. The sleeves and trousers were a little long, but he knew they would be taken up to fit.

"Ahhh, this feels nice!" Jake said as he brushed his hand over the fabric of his new suit. He had chosen a dark gray suit with fine pin stripes, "You don't think this makes me look like a mobster now do you?"

"No, not at all... And now you must remember lesson number one of being wealthy: Dress nice and act nice. Everyone will be looking at you. Now find two others that you like. And don't forget shirts and ties... Oh, and some shoes. This is not just a day trip, we have several places to go and you need to look sharp and professional," he said as he looked through a rack of ties, "Where do you wanna eat? I'm getting hungry."

"Humm, so many buffets, so little time..." Jake teased.

"I think we can do better than that. How about that seafood place we passed on the way in?"

"That real posh one? Naw, I don't like fish *that* much," Jake wrinkled his nose.

D.M. shook his head; the guy was just not getting it. Here was a rare opportunity to enjoy the good life and all Jake could think about was the buffets. "Okay, how about that steak house?"

"Yeah, sure, I love Sizzler!"

The major reached over and popped Jake on the top of the head, "No you idiot, get a clue! You have to start thinking like a man of money- now act like it too!"

"Hey, I've seen lots of rich guys eating at the buffet- nothing wrong with it."

"If I want chow hall food, I'll go visit the Army base near here.

I want a real steak damn it!" He protested.

Jake threw his hands in the air, "All right, all right, you win. We'll eat at the steak place."

"Good. You need to learn some culture anyways," he shook his head, "Oh Jake, you're gonna take a lot of work."

Sam and Max stood next to Tige as he leaned his rifle on the hanger deck wall. The bipods of the rifle were on the wall and he stood behind balancing it, "All right Sam, what's my wind?"

The lieutenant looked at the wind meter, "Uh, ten knots... Uh, full value wind, uh, three clicks left."

"Negative, try again."

"Shit Tige, I'm never gonna get this!"

"You have to keep practicing... Rome wasn't bloody well built in a day, this takes practice and patience."

Max motioned to Sam for the wind meter. He tossed it to him, frustrated by his failures. "Well, let me give it a try," he held the meter out, "Ten knots, half value wind, two clicks left."

"Yes!" Tige hollered exuberantly.

"Hey, how did you do that?" Sam asked.

"I remember that from Infantry school. Actually they were trying to groom me for a spotter position. I didn't want it; I wanted to be a linguist."

Tige turned to Max, "Well good, can you teach him then? He does okay with most things, but he has a helluva problem with the wind and atmospheric data."

"Sure, I can help him with what I remember."

The captain made the necessary adjustments and settled down for his shot. He had placed a small metal plate nearly a thousand yards up the valley. After a few moments, the rifle reported loudly. Sam put his eye to the spotting scope and looked down range. "Hit. Dead on too," he turned to Max, "Hey, maybe Eagle ought to switch us around so you can be Tige's spotter."

"I would be thrilled if she did, but that would stick you with Bruce... And I wouldn't wish that on my own worst enemy."

Sam recorded the shot in Tige's notebook. "I'd be willing to suck it up if it helped the team out."

"She won't do that. I all ready asked her. Sam, you're my pet project. I must teach you to be a spotter," Tige said as he chambered another round.

Eagle wandered out onto the hanger deck and watched them. Tige took aim and fired again. She watched as Max explained to Sam how to read the data off the wind meter and help make corrections. Tige chambered another round. Max gave Sam the opportunity to give Tige adjustments. The wind around the top of the hanger deck swirled and changed direction regularly, so it was an optimal place to practice from. She walked up and stood next to Max, "Lieutenant, I wasn't aware that you had advanced spotting skills."

"Yes ma'am. I was just telling them that the Army was trying to make me a spotter, but I wanted to be a linguist instead... I still remember a few things they taught me."

Sam turned to Eagle, "And I'm having a really hard time with all this data. Wouldn't it make more sense to team Max and Tige together?"

"No. I have my reasons... Max will just have to work extra hard in helping you learn all this."

"Yes ma'am," Sam said in a dejected tone.

"Told ya," Tige scoffed.

"And it won't hurt you Max to get practice either. Who knows when one of you will have to fill in for the other."

Cabbott wheeled around the corner of his secured area and nearly ran into Eagle. She stopped abruptly to keep from hitting him. "Uh, hi ma'am."

"Hello captain. You seem to be feeling better."

"I was going crazy just lying around in that bed, so Dr. Miles said I could do some of my physical therapy and get exercise rolling around."

"How'd your last surgery go?"

"Not too bad. Really hurt a lot though," he rolled back and forth.

"You know the worst one is yet to come."

"I know. I'm psyching myself up for that one. Because after I should be able to walk and hold myself up like a man again."

"Is there anything I can get for you?"

Cabbott thought for a few moments, "Yes, there is...Did my shipment of personal goods arrive?"

"About two weeks ago. They're down in the cargo area."

"Would it be too much trouble for you to bring me my rifle?"

"Your rifle?"

"Yeah, I know it probably sounds strange, but I miss it."

Eagle scratched her head, "Yes, it does sound strange."

"That was Captain St. Ivor up there wasn't it?" He said pointing to the ceiling.

"You're very observant captain."

"Sorry, it's my job... And I really miss it right now."

She reached down and put her hand on his shoulder, "I'll go find it for you."

Cabbott smiled, "Thank you ma'am."

"Anything else?" She said as she turned for the door.

"Ummm, if you can find my spotting scope. It ought to be right with my rifle. I'd love to spy on the captain."

"Very well, I'll bring that up too. I won't however bring you any bullets."

"No ma'am, I don't need any of those."

D.M. walked through the door of the executive jet charter. Jake followed along a few paces behind. He stopped at the desk.

"Good afternoon Mr. Elliott," the attendant said with a smile, "I have your plane waiting."

"Thank you."

Jake leaned around the major's elbow, "Your plane?"

"Yeah, I charted a jet for us. Better than flying commercial... I did that when we went back for General Spears' promotion. Easier to take all the equipment needed and no one asks questions."

"Aw, you mean I missed a cool mission and a ride in a private jet?"

"It wasn't really glorious I can assure you."

The attendant returned with the preflight check list and log book. D.M. handed it to Jake, "Preflight please."

Jake took the books and growled, "I know, you just have me along as your bitch boy."

"No, I have some paperwork to do and then I'll be out."

The lieutenant was taken out back and directed to the plane. It was the smallest executive airframe they had. D.M. figured since it was just the two of them there was no need for anything large. He walked around the plane checking off the items on the list. As he reached the port engine he noticed a small drip of brownish amber fluid. Jake reached up and wiped his finger through the liquid and then sniffed it. Yup, hydraulic fluid like he thought. He returned to the office. "Hey, the port engine has a small hydraulic leak."

"Damn, and the service crew just went on a parts run," the attendant said as he picked up the phone to call them.

"Just find me a ladder and a tool box and I'll fix it," Jake replied.

The attendant looked at D.M. "Yeah, he used to be a helicopter mechanic in his former life. He can fix just about anything," the major said as he patted Jake on the shoulder.

"Well, I don't normally let clients fix my aircraft, but you evidently know what you're doing... You'll find everything you need in the hanger."

Jake turned, "Right, thanks. Give me fifteen mike and I'll have it fixed maj."

The crate creaked loudly as Eagle pried the lid off it. She peered inside to see Captain Westmoreland's possessions. There wasn't much in the crate that had personality to it. There was a drab green duffel bag that she could tell was filled with clothes. Some smaller boxes that she found contained reloading equipment. She located his rifle rather easily- it was contained in a heavy silver case with a stout lock on it. After pulling it out of the crate she opened a few more boxes and finally found the spotting scope. She paused as she found a picture of him and his family. It was quite obviously taken around Christmas, the whole family was dressed in festive sweaters and there was a tree decorated in the background. His mother and father were in the back and Cabbott and perhaps his sister were in the front. They were all smiling and cheerful. She tucked the photo in the case with the spotting scope. The captain spoke often of his family and Eagle thought he might like to have something to remember them by.

She carried the rifle and scope to the elevator. The three who remained behind were out in the forest so there was no chance of running into them. The doors opened and she walked down the short hallway to the secure section of the medical floor. Punching in the combination on the cyber lock, the door opened and she quickly grabbed the rifle and slid in before the door closed again. Walking into Cabbott's room she found him in his wheelchair looking out the window. “Captain?”

Cabbott turned around, “Oh! Yeah!” He rolled over and took his rifle case from her. He set it across the arms of the wheelchair and quickly worked the lock. Opening the case he pulled back the silicone cloth that covered it. Eagle watched as he ran his fingers delicately over the rifle, almost as if he were caressing a woman. With a swift motion, Cabbott lifted the all black rifle out of the case and held it up, butted against his shoulder. With one hand he closed the case and set it on the floor. Rolling over to a table by the window, he flipped down the bipods. He opened the scope covers and peered through the scope, “Ah, much better,” he turned to Eagle, “Thank you.”

“Good, that should provide you with some amusement,” she offered him the spotting scope. “What is that thing?”

“Sig Tactical Two in .338 Lapua. Nice rifle. Has served me well. There’s better out there…I suppose one day I’ll think of getting something more improved.”

“Humm, you boys and your toys,” she turned to leave, “Hope this will keep you happy.”

“Yes, wonderful. Now I can hopefully keep some of my edge while on layup.”

D.M. parked the rental car in front of the Institute for Soldier Nanotechnologies, which was part of MIT. Jake sat looking at the stark white building with dark blocky windows, “So this is the little surprise you had for me huh?"

"Yup. I did some research here my senior year, quite fascinating. Normally they only do Grad and Under Grad work, but I impressed my Chemical Engineering instructor and he took me over and convinced them to let me play in their lab. It gave me the spark I needed to continue my research," The major got out of the car and straightened his jacket. Jake retrieved his coat from the back seat and put it on. Despite being early fall, the Cambridge weather was unusually warm. They walked to the entrance. D.M. opened the door and a tall blond woman strolled out. She was dressed in an off white linen skirt and jacket. She wore high heels that just made her look even taller. "Clarice?" D.M. called. The woman stopped and turned.

"D.M.?" She said as she craned her head toward him. The major smiled. Clarice walked back and offered her hand, "My God, how long has it been?"

"A while..." D.M. paused for a moment, "How've you been?"

"Great, great...I got married," her voice was tinted with discomfort.

"Really? Anyone I know?" He pried.

"Probably not, he's only been teaching here a couple of years. He's got a PhD in Mechanical Engineering."

"Excellent."

"So what are you doing here?" She asked.

"Oh, just here a couple of days for some research... Let me introduce you to my partner, Jake Collins."

Jake stepped forward and offered his hand, "Nice to meet you."

Clarice took his hand and gently shook it, "So what's your field of study?"

Jake regarded D.M. with concern. The major quickly covered for him, "He's done some work in thermodynamics. We're here to work on another one of his projects that requires nanos."

"Fascinating. Where'd you go to school?"

D.M. answered for him again, "Jake started out as my assistant and has since moved on to doing his own research and development."

"So you have no formal education?"

“No ma’am. Just what D.M. has taught me and what I’ve learned from some of his books and surfing the Internet.”

“We've all ready field tested one of his creations and it worked beautifully. I have a meeting set up with a potential buyer,” the major said as he rested his left hand on Jake's shoulder in a display of pride for the lieutenant.

Clarice noticed the glove on D.M.'s left hand, “What happened to your hand?”

“Not my hand, my whole arm... You knew I joined the Air Force when I left MIT right?”

“Yes, I remember you were very excited that they accepted you into the pilot program.”

“Well, I'm still in the military, just not with the Air Force anymore... I've moved over to Special Operations Command,” he paused, “We were on a mission and I got hit really bad. Lost the use of my arm... There was some lab space where we're stationed and I built this,” he pulled back the left lapel of his jacket so she could see part of his arm.

“Amazing. And I suppose you haven't shared this with the scientific community?”

“No. I'm not ready to give this out just yet. There's a lot more to it than it looks. I've had to undergo some internal modifications to support the technology. It's still purely experimental.”

“Yeah, he's got a computer built into the left side of his chest,” Jake added.

“Really? And how do you interface with it? Where does your power supply come from?

“Like I said, this is experimental and I'm not quite ready to share with the rest of the world.”

Clarice looked at her watch, “I've gotta get going, I have a class to teach in twenty minutes. It was good seeing you again D.M.; I wish the best of luck to you with your research.”

“Thank you. It was good seeing you again,” he turned and opened the door again and went inside.

“Lemme guess... Old girlfriend?” Jake said as they walked up to the security desk.

“Yup,” he replied smugly.

“Not bad, not bad at all. At least I know that not all women scientists are ugly."

The major smiled, "Oh, no, there are some awfully nice look'in ones out there!"

"And you obviously have a thing for blonds."

"Naw, what gave that away?!"

After signing in and getting their visitors badges, D.M. took Jake up to the first of two floors that housed the ISN. Waiting for them was Dr. Thomas, one of D.M.'s former professors. He was a tall man with a solid build. His gray hair always seemed disheveled. He wore tan trousers with a dark gray polo shirt. There was no sense in dressing up for work in a laboratory.

"D.M.! Good to see you again. I was so surprised to get your call the other day," he reached and shook the major's hand firmly.

"Hello professor. I was surprised that you're still working here."

"Yes, well, kind of hard to make me retire from the work I love... So, you come here to see me about nanos huh?"

"Well, actually let me introduce my partner, Lieutenant Jake Collins, we're here to research nanos for his project."

Professor Thomas shook Jake's hand vigorously, "Nice to meet you lieutenant," he looked over at D.M., "So this is the prodigy you told me about?"

"Yes sir."

The professor looked back at Jake, he still held his grasp, "Well son, you couldn't have been luckier to have been partnered with one of the brightest scientists I know."

"Yes, sir, the major has pretty much turned my life around from being a street thug to being a scientist that's hopefully going to make his first technology sale here soon."

"Fantastic! I always knew that D.M. could inspire anyone to greatness," the professor turned and opened the door to the research center, "Well gentlemen, how about a quick tour and then we'll get down to business?"

"Sounds good to me," D.M. replied.

The professor took them on a tour of the facility. Along the way he introduced some of the faculty and students that were working on projects. After, he took them to his office where they sat down to talk. "All right D.M., what are you up to?"

"Oh, still doing experiments," The major replied flatly.

"I remember we all thought you were crazy about the way you were obsessed with creating bullet proof plastic."

"Yeah?" D.M. reached inside his coat pocket, "Well, I did it," he offered the original piece of plastic to the professor. He took it and examined it.

"You're joking right?"

"No... That hole is from a .50 cal armor piercing round. All the scratches and scrapes are from the smaller caliber rounds that were fired at it before."

The professor chuckled, "Well, I never thought you'd do it, but here's the proof...Have you done any further testing on it?"

Jake piped in, "Sure we have. I tested the first prototype of the armor. They shot me with everything up to .45 cal and I was just fine."

"And what happened after that?"

"We had to make some modifications to the armor and come up with a better impact absorbing combination... Anything over . 45 will knock you on your ass, but you can still get up and fight... You're not going to be very happy, but at least you're not dead."

"So you've really done it. None of us was sure it was even possible," the professor shook his head slowly in awe.

"We've all ready field tested the second generation armor and it worked great. Now we're working on the third generation which looks to be vast improvement over the others," D.M. replied as he pulled out his cell phone and found a picture he'd taken of Jake wearing the armor. He passed it over to the Professor.

"My God. Covered head to foot all the way around. Isn't that hot?"

"Nope," Jake smiled, "I designed a lightweight temperature controlled suit that's worn under it. If you're hot, you can adjust it to cool you off. If you're cold, you can adjust it to warm you up."

"And how much does the whole thing weigh?"

"Depending on your size. The bigger you are, the more plastic required. Jake's suit weighs about thirty five pounds. Mine is about forty five," D.M. replied, "And it fits very close to the body so the bulk of the weight is carried near the center of balance."

The professor sat back in his chair and fiddled with the

plastic sample, "Do you gentlemen know you're sitting on a scientific Holy Grail? The military would pay a fortune to get their hands on this technology."

"Yes, we know. But we're keeping it to ourselves for the time being. Our small team needs every advantage we can get."

"I suppose I can agree with that. Why do you need nanos?"

"Jake saw a program on them and thinks that if we integrate them into the plastic that we can camouflage ourselves."

"You watched a program?" He said in partial disbelief.

"Yes sir. I thought it would be cool if we could get the nanos to change color to match the environment we're in... I'm not exactly sure how to do that, but I'd like to explore the possibility."

"We've been experimenting with that technology for quite a few years. What makes you think you can perfect it?"

"I'm sure the maj can figure out a way. He's smart like that."

"Lieutenant, I'm well aware of D.M.'s intelligence. Even he has limits however."

D.M. stood up, "I'll disagree with that... Even after suffering a terrible wound in battle I still came up with this," he slipped out of his coat and laid it over the back of the chair. The professor sat in awe of his robotic arm. Slowly he got out of his chair and approached D.M.; taking hold of the arm he inspected it closely.

"How on earth did you come up with this?"

"I was stuck in a hospital bed for a good number of weeks. I was bored and really wanted to find a way to stay with the team. So I created this."

"And how do you interface with it?" He noticed the cable disappearing under his shirt."

"I have a five terabyte hard drive and ten gig of ram running this thing. We have a surgeon who loves to experiment with technology and he managed to get my brain to interface with the computer. I don't fully understand the finer points of the technology, but it works quite well. There are times I do have some trouble, but if I stop and just think about what I want the arm to do, I can usually get the snafu solved and I'm fine."

"Absolutely fascinating!" He took D.M.'s hand, "Forgive me for ever thinking you had limits. Son, you are Einstein reincarnate."

D.M. chuckled, "Even Einstein eventually found he had limits.

I just haven't gotten there yet." He pulled his coat on and sat back down, "Now, about those nanos... We will need enough to do some testing and then once we get that worked out, enough for seven suits of armor."

"That's a lot of surface area to cover."

"Yes it is. And we have to figure out if we can even use them. The chemical makeup of the plastic is so delicate that I'm not even sure we can add the nanos to it without ruining the ballistic properties. The plastic is also so resilient we can't even get paint to stick to it. So the nanos have to be bonded with the plastic; there's no other way of doing it."

"You know those little things aren't cheap. I suggest you get enough to do research. If you figure out how to make it all work, then buy what you need."

The major turned to Jake, "Did you figure out which ones you think would work the best?"

"Uh, what do they call those things, um, carbon fiber bucky tubes right? I think those would work the best."

"We'll take some of those," D.M. said

"You know there are many companies that make them. You can just go to them and purchase all you want."

"Yes, but you were kind enough to show us the technology that makes them work. And you know I've always been generous when it comes to this institution, so I'll include a sizable donation along with our purchase."

"Thank you, we appreciate that," the professor nodded.

Jake proudly carried out a small container filled with carbon fiber nano tubes, "Can't wait to get home and get to work on the project, this is so exciting!"

"Are you sure you won't rethink your doubts about classes here? You seemed to fit right in, even though you haven't had one tenth of the education they have."

"Dunno. But if there are more beautiful scientists like your ex girlfriend here I may have to reconsider," he smiled and climbed into the car, sitting his precious container of nanos on his lap.

The major checked his watch, it was just past noon, "Hey are you hungry? I know a great place to grab a bite before we meet up with your potential buyer."

"Sure, sounds good to me."

After lunch D.M. drove them to a small industrial park where they met with one of his contacts, "You got your prototype?"

"Yeah, right here," Jake replied as he grabbed a small gym bag, "Do you really think they'll buy this?"

"Quite sure. This company has been bucking to get a government contract for quite some time. They've been struggling to find something marketable and just haven't had a lucky break."

"And I'm going to give them that break?"

"Yes. But please do me a favor."

"What?"

"Just let me do the talking. I know how to work these meetings and I can get you the best deal. You don't just wanna take the cash and run. There are stock options and other means of income to consider."

"Yeah, right, but I need some cash in hand to get my parents moved," the lieutenant said as he opened the door.

"Don't worry, you will."

Two hours later Jake sat in the car holding a check for half a million dollars, "You were right maj, that was one sweet deal."

"I told you I'd hook you up. Shit, that's one of the best packages I've ever put together. If it all pans out, you'll live well for a long time."

"Thanks D.M., this means a lot."

"How about we go find a nice place for your parents?"

CHAPTER TWENTY NINE

Cabbott sat in his wheelchair facing the window. His rifle was resting on the table and he'd put together his spotting scope. He leaned over and looked through the scope watching Tige walk up the valley to place his targets. Cabbott studied the movements of the grass and trees, jotting down notations on a pad of paper. Making adjustments on his rifle scope, he leaned down and took aim. Gently he pressed his finger against the trigger, exhaled slowly, and the bolt clicked.

Eagle stood in the doorway to the captain's room watching him, "Taking dry fire practice on my team members?" She said loudly enough to startle him.

"I'm just trying to keep my edge. I wasn't aiming at him, I was aiming at where he was going to put his target", he replied as he made another notation on his paper. Eagle noticed he was left handed.

"Humm, another south paw eh?"

"Huh?"

"You're a lefty. Major Elliott is a lefty as well."

"Well, you know they always say that us lefties are the only ones who are in our right minds," he smiled and flipped the pen between his fingers.

Eagle sat down on the edge of his bed, "Captain, may I ask you some advice?"

Cabbott turned to her, "Sure. Not sure how much advice I can provide, but I'll try."

"Well...Say you want to assassinate someone... But you want it to look like an accidental death."

"Is this up close or at distance? Clean or messy?"

"I'm not really sure what would be the best way. All I know is it would make me very happy not to have this individual on the planet anymore."

"Is this a personal vendetta?"

"Yes."

Cabbott shrugged his shoulders, "I'm cool with that." He sighed deeply and picked up his pad of paper, "Okay. You want to eliminate someone and have it look like an accident. Humm, there are quite a few ways." He began to scribble notes down, "If you can plan it out and execute, you stand a better chance. You'll need to take time to gather intel on the target. Find out where they come and go from often and what times of day..." he continued to scribble notes, "The more you know about your intended target, the better you can find a way to eliminate them. But a good assassination takes time. And if you don't mind it being messy, then just shoot them- preferably from a distance, which is my personal favorite. But there can be accidents arranged, hits done up close and personal, hits done without ever seeing the target. You name it."

Eagle was impressed by the captain's knowledge. "Tige was right; you certainly know your job."

"That's what I've been trained for."

"Do you think Tige could make the shot? You know, if that's the way it was best done?"

"From what I've seen of his target work, he seems plenty capable. He'll just need everyone else to help get intel and make sure the target is where you want it to be. And it has to be done sterile; you don't want anyone coming back to you on this."

Eagle smiled, "You're quite the piece of work captain. I can see why Tige was looking forward to working with you. I'm impressed."

"I'm looking forward to working with him. He's a rather unconventional sniper and I hope I can learn a few things from him too."

"He's taught us a lot in stalking, field craft and marksmanship."

"I've heard that his skill in the bush is almost unmatched... Well, if there's anything more you need, feel free to ask."

"Thanks captain."

***

Jake stood on the porch of his parents' house facing the door. D.M. stood with his back to Jake keeping an eye on the street; his hand resting just inside his jacket near his sidearm. The neighborhood truly had gone to hell. Gang signs were painted everywhere and junk cars cluttered the curbs. The houses all needed repairs but the occupants were too scared to be out in the open to make them. Jake knocked on the door. It was several moments before his mother called from the other side of the door, "Who is it?"

"It's me mom, Jake," he straightened his jacket and tie.

The deadbolts unlatched and the door creaked open. His mother peered through the crack in the door.

"Oh my God, Jake it is you!" She threw open the door and quickly embraced him, "Come in, come in." She ushered them inside and closed the door. "Oh Jake, it's so good to see you. Let me take a look at you," she backed up to get a good look at him, "My you look so handsome all dressed up like that."

"Mom, let me introduce you to Major D.M. Elliott, he's my team mate. D.M., this is my mother Elfrieda."

D.M. stepped forward and took her hand gently. She was a small older woman that looked frail from years of living in a rough neighborhood, "Nice to meet you ma'am."

"Oh Jake, he's so polite. Such a strapping fellow," she reached up and squeezed his bicep, "My and ever so handsome!" D.M. chuckled at her lavish compliments.

"Mom, will you quit hitting on my partner!" Jake growled with embarrassment, "Hey, where's my old man?"

"He's in the living room."

Jake wandered through the small house and found his father sitting in his favorite recliner watching a football game, "Hi dad." His father just kept watching the television. "Dad?" Jake leaned down and looked his father in the eyes. Finally the elder man looked up and held his gaze, "Hi dad, it's Jake."

"Jake, oh, it's been so long!" He carefully got out of the chair and hugged his son.

"Good to see you dad. I have a surprise for you and mom."

"What is it son?"

Jake helped his father to sit back down and then sat his mother down on the couch, "I know I haven't been the best of sons, but I've grown up and matured a lot these last couple of years. I now have enough money to move you and mom out of this neighborhood and get you a house somewhere nice."

"Oh Jake, we can't leave here. This is our home. We raised you boys here and this is where we're happy," Elfrieda said as she stood and fussed with a lace tablecloth.

"Mom, this neighborhood is full of gangsters. It's a bad place to be now. It's just a matter of time before they break in here and hurt you and dad. Please let me take you somewhere nice."

D.M. put his hand on Jake's shoulder and leaned over so his head was near his ear, "Let them give it some thought. You're asking a lot of them right now and maybe they aren't quite ready to make a decision."

"Yeah, maybe you're right. I guess we should let them sleep on it."

"We're not seriously going to stay here tonight are we?" D.M. protested as he looked at the two beds in the front bedroom.

"Why not? I grew up in this bedroom. You can have Rob's bed, there," he pointed to the bed closest to the window.

"Jake, this whole neighborhood is just waiting to explode. It's not safe to be here. Can't we just get a hotel room on the Boardwalk?"

"It's just one night. I'm pretty sure that no one knows I'm here."

"And what happened to your brother anyway?" The major said as he carefully pulled back the drape and looked outside. The street was dimly lit and he could see movement further down on the far side.

"He got tangled up in my old gang and got killed by a rival gang."

D.M. groaned, "Jake I really don't like this."

"Oh relax, we'll be fine," he said as he pulled off his tie and sat down on the bed. D.M. pulled his sidearm from the shoulder holster, checked it and then tucked it under the pillow. He undressed and had Jake help him back into his arm, "Why you wanna sleep in this thing? I thought it was uncomfortable."

"It is, but I'm not feeling particularly safe."

"All right, suit yourself," Jake turned off the light and crawled into bed. D.M. lay awake. There was not going to be any sleep tonight. Every car driving down the street had the major worried. He would listen to make sure they passed on down the street out of hearing range. Just as he was beginning to drift off to sleep the sound of screeching tires brought him to his senses. His hand reached under the pillow and grabbed his pistol. Outside he could hear male voices yelling in what sounded like Spanish. A moment later automatic gunfire erupted from the car and splattered across the front of the house. D.M. and Jake dove out of their beds and flattened to the floor. More gunfire came from the car, this time it was handguns. The window by the bed shattered. The car squealed its tires and started down the street. D.M. crawled over to the window, stuck the barrel of his pistol out and carefully took aim. He squeezed off one round and killed the driver. The car slammed into a telephone pole and the rest of the occupants got out. The major took aim and dropped the remaining three gunmen. He held his position for a few moments to ensure that no one else got out of the car. Jake peered over the top of the bed.

"I told you I didn't feel safe," D.M. said as he got up and found his trousers.

"Shit! How the hell did they know I was here?"

"They probably had someone watching the house," the major pulled on his shoes, dropped the magazine out of his pistol and slapped another one in it. Jake quickly put on his clothes and followed D.M. to the front door. Carefully the major opened the door and peered out. The street was silent. Jake had his sidearm out and ready. His heart was pounding so hard he could feel it in his throat. D.M. scanned the area and cautiously made his way to the wrecked car. It had slammed into a telephone pole that had a street light on it. Jake was right on his heels keeping watch on their back. They stopped at one of the gunmen and D.M. kicked the body over. A young Hispanic male heavily tattooed lay motionless. Jake knelt down and inspected the tattoos, "Oh shit, this is not good."

"What?"

"See this?" Jake pointed to a tattoo on the man's forearm, "That's the symbol for MS-13. This is pretty heavy shit we broke up."

"Only a matter of time before they're missed and the whole gang comes looking for them," D.M. said as he scanned the area.

Jake inspected the other two bodies on the sidewalk, "Interesting, I see several gang tats on these guys. Looks like they were part of other gangs that got swallowed up by MS-13."

"We need to get your parents out of here now."

"Agreed. We'll get them a hotel room for the time being until I can find them some place to live. I'm pretty sure they'll go kicking and screaming, so prepare for a battle."

"I'll take your old lady, she can't put up that much of a fight, and your dad is just too spaced out to know much better."

"Let's get moving," Jake said as he hurried back to the house.

D.M. carried Elfrieda to the car and carefully placed her in the back seat. Jake guided his father in next to her. They had packed up as much clothing as they could and shoved it into the trunk of the rental car. Jake drove them to one of the casinos and got two rooms. Once his parents were settled in he returned to D.M. who was on the phone with Eagle, "Yeah, it appears they were waiting for us. Jake must have one helluva reputation around here... I iced four of them... Jake says they're MS-13, bad shit...Yeah, we got his parents out and they're at the hotel with us...Huh? Are you sure that's a good idea? I think that might be a bad idea, he's wanted by just about everyone here...No, I'm quite serious!"

"What is she suggesting?" Jake interrupted.

"That we go to the police."

Jake started laughing, "Yeah, they'll have me in hand cuffs so fast your head will spin!"

"You hear that? Yeah, even Jake says he'll be arrested on sight... Bad here, very bad. This is truly one time I can't wait to get the hell out of here and come back home... All right, good night," he hung up and turned to Jake, "She says we should go to the cops."

"Maybe you can, but they'll get me in an instant...And what's to say the cops aren't crooked? They honestly don't give a damn about their neighborhood, just one more shit hole to drive by and ignore."

Eagle looked at the calendar on her desk. D.M. and Jake had been gone almost a week. Although he called her nearly every day, she was missing him. She never realized how much of a part of her life he was until he wasn't there. If she had a nightmare there was no one to snuggle up with. It was even hard to sleep without him. He wasn't the only one suffering from PTSD. She knew he must be going through the same thing, maybe even worse since he considered her his security blanket. She would be there when he had nightmares, comforting him until he fell back asleep. And he was there for her when she needed a shoulder to cry on, or just someone to talk to.

Bored, Eagle decided to go visit Cabbott. She rummaged around her office and found a small gym bag. Opening a cabinet, she pulled out a bottle of red wine, two glasses and a cork screw. Carefully she laid them in the bag and closed it. Peering down the hallway, she could hear the men in the rec room watching a movie. It was nearly 2100. Quietly she made her way to the elevator and went down to the medical floor. Punching in the code, she let herself into the secure side. She found the captain in his wheelchair looking through his spotting scope out into the blackness.

"Anything good going on out there?" She said softly.

"Mmmm, just a few deer grazing."

"Well, how about tearing yourself away from watching Bambi and have some wine with me?" She pulled out the bottle and handed it to him.

"What's the occasion?"

"I'm bored."

"That's not much of an occasion to drink to," he looked at the bottle, "And this is a very nice red, good vintage. You sure you wanna waste it on me?"

"I got a few more."

Cabbott worked the corkscrew and carefully eased the cork out. He sniffed the cork and sighed deeply. Eagle took out the glasses and put them on his rolling table. The captain carefully poured the wine.

"Why are you bored? Stand down?" He said as he took a small sip. The wine was dry with a finish of grape peel.

"That and the major is gone for two weeks. He took Jake on some sort of information gathering vacation. I have no idea what they're up to; I just know they're back east."

"It sounds like the team has a very close relationship with one another. After a while you find you can't function without each other."

Eagle took a sip of wine, "That we do. With one exception, the whole team can come together as a mighty force."

"Who's the exception?"

"Sergeant Bruce von Teufel."

"Ew! I've heard of him. Army Ranger and all around asshole-pardon the language ma'am."

"No need to pardon, asshole is right. And as soon as you're healthy and mission ready, I plan on sending him packing. He's only been here as a replacement for Max, and then Frank. The whole team hates his guts," she took a larger swallow of wine.

"Well then, before we kill off the first glass, may I propose a toast?"

"Go on."

"To getting me back together and getting me back on the job. May that help get rid of and nasty Army SOB!" He laughed lightly and reached over to clink glasses with her.

"Very amusing captain."

"Okay, I admit, I suck at doing toasts. I had an uncle who was the silver tongued devil. He could come up with the best toasts right out of thin air," he took a long swallow and sighed, "Damn good wine."

Eagle took a few more long drinks. She could all ready feel the effects of the alcohol, "I only buy the good stuff captain." They both chuckled. Cabbott took the bottle and topped off their glasses.

"So, you come down here because you're bored and wanna get drunk?"

"Partly, yes."

"And you miss the major."

Eagle paused for a few moments before answering, "Yes."

"You two must have quite a relationship. Working together all this time has made you *very* close."

She sat her glass down and regarded him sternly, "And what makes you think that?"

Cabbott shook his head, "Sorry. I've always been able to read between the lines, even if those lines are smudged or blurred... Just one of the skills I picked up going through law school. My father is like that too."

"You're like a human lie detector... And I'm a lousy liar," she said lowly.

"No, I'm very skilled at gathering intel. Listening to you talk these last few weeks, I came to that conclusion. I just happened to be right. Although I'm glad you didn't blast me for it."

"I wouldn't do that. But please just keep it to yourself okay?"

"I promise."

She took a few big gulps of wine and motioned for him to empty the bottle. Cabbott split the wine between them. They talked and laughed, both enjoying the effects of the alcohol.

"Tell me," Cabbott began, "Have you ever taken a life?"

Eagle settled back into her chair, "Yes, actually I have. We were on a mission in Columbia and I chose to be on the ground so D.M. and Jake could be in the air providing support."

"Fascinating. I haven't met many women who have killed before."

"I'm not exactly proud of what I've done."

"No but you did your job."

"Yes, I did, and I get to experience the same horrors when I close my eyes at night as you all do."

"After a while you begin to wonder if you'll ever sleep again. I've taken so many lives that there isn't much of my life that isn't haunted by them."

"I hope I never get to that point," she replied softly.

Cabbott reached over and put his hand on her shoulder, "I hope you never get to that point either. There should be only a small few of us that have to carry the burden."

"Unfortunately I'm now one of them."

"Just part of our job. This is the life you've chosen. It was just a matter of time."

D.M. stood in front of the mirror fixing his tie. He decided that being dressed professionally might go over better with the police. Jake came out of the bathroom dressed in a towel, "Hey, wait for me."

"I thought you weren't going because they would arrest you on site."

"Yeah, well, I like a good challenge. Besides, they really don't have anything to hold me on; I served all my time before I went in the Army."

"These are cops we are talking about, and possibly crooked ones."

"I'll take my chances," he replied as he quickly dressed.

"Suit yourself," D.M. said as he tucked his pistol into the holster under his right shoulder.

"You think packing heat is a good idea?"

"I don't go anywhere unarmed, you know that. The only place I don't normally carry is back home."

"Yeah, true," the lieutenant replied as he pulled on his shoulder holster.

"You however, it might not be a good idea. If you want, just hand it off to me when we get to the station and I'll hang on to it until we're done."

"All right, I'll do that."

"I just hope I don't blow my ass off," D.M. said as he tucked Jake's .45 into the back of his waistband. He walked up the steps to the police station.

"Oh, that certainly wouldn't make Eagle very happy," Jake

teased as he buttoned his coat and followed behind. Once inside, D.M. approached the desk and asked to meet with the officer in charge. Jake stood tucked behind the major's right arm. He wasn't trying to be obvious with his presence. An officer came out and showed them to the back.

"I'm Officer Winslow, how may I help you?"

"I'm Major D.M. Elliott, Special Operations Command," he offered his hand. The officer shook it.

"What can I do for you major?"

"My teammate was home visiting his parents and the house was strafed by a drive-by shooting last night."

"Well there are a lot of bad neighborhoods here and there is quite a gang problem. We just don't have the resources to eradicate all of them."

"How bad do you want the gang problem solved?" D.M. said as he looked around the shabby office.

"Pretty bad. Some of our officers won't even patrol the really bad neighborhoods," he looked past D.M. and saw Jake standing discreetly behind him, "Hey, wait a minute, I know who you are," he motioned to an officer sitting at a desk behind Jake, "Arrest him!"

D.M. put his hand up, "Whoa! Just wait a minute. He's part of my team. Uncle Sam owns him."

The officer grabbed Jake, shoved him against the wall and quickly frisked him. He found the empty shoulder holster, "Hey, he was carrying."

Officer Winslow looked up at D.M., "Are you armed?"

"Yes, of course, it's my job. I belong to the Department of Defense. As a Special Operator I am authorized to carry anywhere. Lieutenant Collins is also authorized, but in light of his past record in this city, I've asked for his sidearm while we are in the station."

"Your 'lieutenant' has a record a mile long here. I'm surprised he was even ballsey enough to show his face in this city again."

Jake shook off the officer's grasp, "I did my time, you have nothing on me. Besides, I've turned my life around and gone straight. And after what happened last night, I'm really hating what the gangs have become."

"And I'm to believe that you've turned over a new leaf?"

"Yes. Actually the major has done a wonderful job of mentoring me and I'm even working toward a Bachelor's in Chemical Engineering."

Both officers regarded the major with suspicion. D.M. nodded, "He's grown up a lot in the last couple of years. And he is working toward a degree... Look, we're here to offer you a solution to the gang problem. It appears that MS-13 has taken quite a hold of the city. The four that hit his parent's house last night were from that gang. And yes, it was us who filled them full of lead."

"You know we can hold you for murder."

"No, we were defending ourselves. They fired first. We were well within our rights."

"So what is it that you think you can do for us?" Winslow said as he sat down at his desk.

"If you wanna get rid of the gang problem, and don't care how, our team can certainly solve your problem."

"Are you saying that your Special Forces team would come in and nuke the gangs?"

"Exactly. We do the dirty work and you just turn a blind eye. Your coroner will be quite busy however."

"I'm not sure we can do that."

Jake stepped up next to D.M.'s shoulder, "Well, you guys aren't doing a particularly good job of protecting and serving. We all could've been killed last night."

D.M. took a sticky note and wrote his cell phone number on it, "We're going to be in town for a few more days. Jake has to find a new place for his parents to live. They can't go back to that neighborhood. If you'd like our services, just give me a call. I assure you that our team is very discreet, we don't go in and shoot up a whole street just to get a couple of gangsters. We have a highly ranked sniper who can put a shot on a live target with precision...And the best part is this won't cost you a thing- save for some John Doe burials."

"And your team gets some live fire practice?"

"We won't turn it down, no," D.M. said as he turned to leave.

"And how fast can the rest of your team get here?"

"If we don't have any other missions, probably a day or two."

"I'll have to consult with the mayor on this."

***

Two days later D.M. and Jake were house hunting for his parents. His cell phone rang. "Hello? Yes. Oh, hello Officer Winslow... Uh huh...He did? All right, I'll contact my commander and see if the rest of the team can come out...Yes, I'll have an answer for you by close of business tomorrow," he hung up.

"I guess they want the gang problem solved huh?"

"Seems that way. He said the mayor has gone through all the clearances from Department of Homeland Security and the FBI, so we should be okay."

"You gonna call Eagle?"

"Tonight."

Jake drove along the streets of Ocean Grove. It was a far cry from the rundown neighborhood his parents were living in. The town was small, tidy and boasted beautiful Victorian houses. He'd seen a listing on Seaview Avenue about two blocks from the shore. They were supposed to meet the real estate agent at the property. It was a modest house, nothing too extravagant but it was far safer than where they were living. The house was a newer Victorian style that was painted a soft sage green with white trim. It was three stories and had a corner round room that went the entire height of the house culminating in a castle like conical top. Jake loved the front porches, one on the first floor and another on the second where you could see the beach.

Parking on the street, they got out. The agent wasn't there yet so they walked around the property a bit. D.M. looked at the condition of the house.

"Not in bad shape. You think you can get them to move?"

"I dunno. I feel bad that I'm mostly to blame for how terrible that neighborhood has gotten. Maybe if I would have been a better son I wouldn't have to be doing this now."

D.M. sat down on the top step, "We all do things in life that we regret later."

"And is there something in your life that you've done that you regret?" Jake said, joining him.

"What? Are you thinking I'm gonna say that I regret punching the old man?"

"Well, it did get you in a lot of trouble."

"I don't regret it."

"So is there anything you regret doing?"

The major contemplated for a few moments, "I guess I regret not being able to spend more time with my mother. She did her best to raise me and teach me my heritage. And I'm sure she did that knowing my real father was Spanish."

"She didn't do that with Frank did she?"

"No. She pretty much raised him American. Ben never knew her, so he got a bit of both."

"Where is he?"

"Who?"

"Ben." Jake stood and stretched.

"I lost track of him a few years ago. Frank told me that he's kind of a wandering soul. He never finished college and has spent his life on the road. I guess he picks up odd jobs to keep his belly full."

"I'm surprised he didn't join the military like you guys did."

"No, not his style. In fact he is rather against the establishment."

A car pulled up and the agent got out. She was dressed in a pair of light gray slacks and a white blouse. "Good afternoon gentlemen, I'm Kelly Buchman." She offered her hand to Jake.

"Hello, I'm Jake Collins. I'm the one who called you about the house…And this is my business associate Mr. Elliott."

"Nice to meet you Mr. Collins. Is this house going to be for you?"

"No ma'am, it's going to be for my parents. Currently they live down in AC, but their neighborhood has really gone downhill, so I wanted to move them away from it to some place nice."

"Very well, should we start by looking at the outside of the house?"

D.M. stood up, "We got here a little early so we've all ready looked around the outside pretty thoroughly."

"Okay then." She stepped up to the door and worked the small key lock box on the door. After several tries, the box popped open and she retrieved the key. Opening the door, she walked inside, "I do apologize for the musty smell, this house is older and has been on the market for quite sometime."

Jake wandered in. His footsteps creaked loudly on the old hard wood floors. D.M. followed behind, creaking even louder with his great weight. Both walked through the front room and back to what would be considered the living room. "So what do you think maj.?"

"Nice. Not in bad shape for an older house. What are they asking?"

"Two seventy five."

D.M. went upstairs and looked around. Jake checked out the kitchen. He found it roomy and in good condition. He met D.M. upstairs and they checked out the bedrooms. "You think they would like this?"

"Shit, I like it," D.M. grinned.

"Not gonna buy it out from under me are you?"

"No, no, it's a beautiful house, but I can't see myself living in New Jersey."

"Oh, that's right, you're a desert boy. What will you do if you marry Eagle and she wants to live in Norway?"

The major stood looking out the window, "Well, if she has a shot at the throne, I guess I'll learn to dress warm. If she doesn't, I'll be begging her to find some place warmer."

Jake laughed lightly and they continued their tour of the house. Once they had looked everything over, they returned to the front room where the agent waited.

"So, what do you gentlemen think?" She smiled, trying to make the sale.

"It's a nice house, but I need to make sure I can get my parents to move before I commit to it."

"How long do you think you'll have to decide?"

"Hopefully less than a week."

"Well, I look forward to hearing from you." She offered her hand and Jake shook it. She showed them out of the house and locked it. "Good day gentlemen."

"Good day ma'am," they both replied politely. After she left, Jake walked out to the sidewalk.

"Hey, you wanna go for a walk on the beach? I need to clear my head a bit."

"Yeah, sure." D.M. sighed. They headed down the street and out onto the sand. Jake walked down a little further to the waterline where the sand was more firm.

"Do you think we can pull this mission off?" He said, watching the waves lap against the shore.

"Sure, why not? We've survived worse. Should be an easy mission for us."

"I guess this is the only way I can right some of the wrongs I've done."

"Not necessarily. But you feel you have to take care of business, and I can respect that."

"Think Eagle will buy off on this mission?"

"Probably. Since we have the proper clearances, and there is a need, I'm sure she'll go for it. Besides, she may just enjoy a day at the beach and a walk on the boardwalk."

"You sound rather confident."

"Mmm, yeah, I just need to work my magic on her."

They walked along in silence for a while. "Hey maj?"

"Humm?"

"Are we sick and twisted because of the job we do?"

"Somewhat. As Major Lindman said in one of our group sessions that to kill requires a special mentality. But as Tige put it so long ago, we aren't psychopaths because we can tell the difference between right and wrong killing."

"I sometimes wonder. It's getting easier and easier to kill...I don't feel so bad when I do it now. Is that the way you feel?"

"Yeah. It's just that we're to the point we've detached ourselves from thinking of the enemy as humans. We've been conditioned enough to see them only as a target."

"Can we ever go back to the way we were?"

"No." He stopped and looked out over the water, "Our minds and bodies are scarred from battle. We'll never be the same again. Our innocence is lost."

CHAPTER THIRTY

Eagle and the rest of the team arrived at Atlantic City International Airport. They had flown in on the C-130, landed and taxied over to the 177th Air National Guard hanger. D.M. and Jake were waiting for them with a large van and the rental car. The team walked down the ramp heavily laden with gear. Eagle struggled with her gear; D.M. hurried over and took it from her, "Hi, glad you all could make it." He tossed her gear in the back of the van. He looked around and noticed one team member missing, "Where's Bruce?"

"Oh, he asked for another week of leave. And since Westland is out of the picture, I happily granted it. Besides, I just didn't want him along on this mission."

D.M. smiled, "Excellent... Did you bring our gear?"

"Yours and Jake's gear is still in the plane," she said as she climbed into the front passenger seat.

"Right, thanks, we'll go get it." D.M. whistled to get Jake's attention, "Our gear's still on board," he pointed to the plane and then hurried up the back ramp.

The team settled into their hotel rooms. D.M. had booked suites at Caesar's for the entire team. They met down in the steak house for dinner that night. "So we're doing a 'street sweeper' mission huh?" Tige said as he took a long drink of beer.

"A very discreet street sweeper mission," Jake replied, "We need to have minimal collateral damage on this mission."

"Well, I certainly have no issues with that. I prefer to keep it target specific."

Max finished buttering a roll and set it down, "And it's MS-13 we're tangling with?"

"They seem to have taken over nearly all the other gangs.

They're the most violent and ruthless. The cops are scared of 'em," Jake took a swallow of beer, "I think if we take them out, we'll set an example and the other gangs that are left will hopefully think twice before doing anything."

Eagle looked over at D.M. He was sitting with his chin on his hand, eyes closed, "Tired major?"

"Huh? What?"

"I asked if you were tired."

"Yeah, haven't gotten much sleep this trip. And the other night has just made it worse."

"Flash backs?"

"And nightmares."

Tige rested his elbows on the table, "Well, it seems like you need your security blanket to get some sleep at night."

"What's that supposed to mean?"

The rest of the team looked at Eagle. She could feel what little color she had drain out of her face, "Why are you all looking at me?"

"We've known for a long time that you two were together," Tige said.

"Jake!" D.M. barked.

"No sir, wasn't me. I swear I never said a thing."

Max held his finger up, "No, he never said anything. We just figured it out... I mean the way you two look at each other sometimes, the way you interact, it wasn't impossible not to notice. Ninety five percent of the time you're all business..."

"If we were that obvious, I wonder who else knows?" Eagle sighed.

"I wouldn't worry about it. None of us will ever say anything. We all swore to that," Tige affirmed.

Eagle glanced over at D.M. His face was unemotional. She wasn't sure what he was thinking. This was something she hoped she would never have to face, or at least she wasn't ready to face it now, but the cat was out of the bag and now damage control had to be done.

"You two give strength to each other and that in turn gives us strength. We need strong leadership in this organization and you both provide it. If you're apart, we'll fall apart. We don't want that to ever happen. Our loyalty is with you," Tige said with a slow nod. The others slowly nodded in agreement.

"Well gentleman... I, *we,* appreciate your discretion in this matter. The major and I had agreed that our personal relationship would never interfere with our duty to the team... In truth, our relationship is almost Platonic in nature."

Jake tried to hide a smile, "Somewhat Platonic. Of course I just won't say anything about catching you on the training floor. That was the most interesting sword fight I've ever seen."

"All right, we do have our moments, occasionally," her face flushed.

"Don't sweat it ma'am. We don't care," Sam replied.

Jake carried his bags out of the suite he was sharing with D.M. and next door to his parent's suite. Eagle and D.M. came down the hallway. "Jake? What are you doing?" D.M. asked.

"Moving next door with mom and dad. You two deserve some peace and quiet. And mom told me dad has been getting up at night and causing trouble, you know, because of his Alzheimer's, so I figure I'll sleep over there and help her out."

D.M. put his hand on the lieutenant's shoulder, "Thanks."

"That's the least I can do for my friends," he regarded them with a soft smile, "Get some good sleep, tomorrow we gotta start gathering intel."

The major awoke to find Eagle all ready up. It was the best night of sleep he'd gotten in the last week. He stretched, holding it for a long time. Perhaps it was good that everyone knew they were together. No more sneaking around, no more looking over his shoulder hoping that they wouldn't be seen. They of course would always be professional in front of the rest of the team, it was just a relief that no one would say anything about what they did during their off duty time. Their relationship was at a comfortable level and D.M. knew Eagle wasn't wanting to go any further. He respected her wishes, even though there were times she left him quite hot and bothered.

D.M. climbed out of bed and went into the bathroom. He turned on the shower, climbed out of his loose boxers and stood looking at his rather stubbly face. Jake had told him not to shave because they would be going out later to gather information. This meant finding the lieutenant's old gang; and the less they looked like any kind of law enforcement or government, the better. He rubbed his face and growled lowly, the stubble was beginning to itch. Of all things he hated the most, it was a stubbly face.

Eagle sat on the couch dressed in a pair of loose sweat pants and a t-shirt working on her laptop. She was reviewing information about MS-13 and the area the team would most likely be operating in. Jake had briefed her the best he could after their arrival. D.M. came out of the bedroom dressed only in a towel. Eagle looked over her shoulder at him and laughed lightly, "Gee, not the first time I've seen you like that."

"No, you're right. Except this time I'm not so worried about it falling off!" He leaned over the couch and kissed her on the forehead, "Good morning my love."

"You look like you got some good sleep," she could see the sparkle in his eyes again.

"Yes, I did, thank you," he sat down next to her, "Mission research and planning?"

"Of course. My job."

A knock at the door quickly got the major's attention. He went to the door and stood to one side, "Yes, who is it?"

"Your lab rat," Jake said with a chuckle. D.M. opened the door and let him in. "You're looking awfully bright eyed and bushy tailed this morning," the lieutenant teased.

"Finally got some decent sleep."

"Is that *all* you got?" Jake continued to tease.

Eagle looked up from her work, looked at D.M. and they both shouted in unison, "Yes!"

"All right, sorry. Enough teasing."

The major walked over to his suitcase, "Am I to assume our uniform of the day is ratty jeans and a t-shirt?"

"Whatever you have that's close enough to that... And we need to make a stop by my parent's house. I need to see if my bike is still in the garage. Don't think mom would have sold it. Hope no one stole it."

"Bike?" Eagle said with a raised eyebrow.

"Oh yeah. Harley Davidson Softail Rocker. Bitch'in bike...Cost me a small fortune, but of course that was all drug money, so I didn't mind," he pulled out his wallet, took out a picture and showed it to them.

"You have a picture of your bike in your wallet?" D.M. questioned.

"I don't exactly have a hot woman in my life to put in there, so the bike is there to take her place... Besides, I don't have to worry about messy breakups with it."

"Only if you wrap it around a telephone pole," D.M. teased, "Of course, I can't put a picture of Eagle in my wallet; that would pose quite a security problem."

Jake looked at his watch, "Hey, the rest of the team is meeting downstairs for breakfast in twenty mike. Are you guys gonna join us?"

"Yes, we'll be there."

Jake unlocked the door of the detached garage and pulled the door up. A sea of boxes and dusty gardening equipment cluttered the entire garage. He carefully worked his way back until he was close to the back wall. Pulling up on a dusty tarp he hollered, "Yeah baby, still here!" D.M. and Eagle helped clear a pathway through the boxes. Jake pushed the bike out onto the driveway. It was black with highly polished chrome. He trotted back inside and found several rags. Carefully he dusted off the bike and began to check the oil and other fluids. "Considering she's been sitting here a couple of years, she looks to be in great shape."

"She?" Eagle said.

"Yeah, I named her Suzie after a really hot girlfriend. She had quite the 'soft tail' as well!"

Both men laughed. Eagle playfully held her hands over her ears, "I don't think I wanna hear about this!" Jake found a gas can in the garage and filled the tank. After several tries the bike roared to life. Smoke and dust blew out of the tail pipes in a cloud. Eagle once again held her hands over her ears, "My God this thing is loud!"

Jake held his hand to his ear, "What?"

"I said this thing is loud!"

"Just like Suzie!" Jake revved the engine a few times and then turned it off. A dead quiet fell over the neighborhood, "All right. I got my wheels. Major, it's time to find you some... You ever ride a bike?"

"Sure, used to be my main mode of transport in Spain."

"Good. You guys wanna follow me to the dealer?"

D.M. wandered down the rows of motorcycles. Nothing seemed to grab his attention. He never fancied himself the 'Harley' kind of guy. He preferred the larger frame street bikes. Jake was off checking out the rest of the store. Eagle had decided to explore some of the shops just down the street. He continued to browse, still not really finding anything. The lieutenant came around the corner, "Find one?"

"No, not really. I'm more of a street bike kinda guy."

"Well, then here, check this one out. It might fit with your persona a bit better." He led the major back around the corner and over to a display. A shiny solid black motorcycle sat against the wall. "They call it the 'Night Rod'- all blacked out for our kinda work."

D.M. stood looking at the bike. Its low profile and smooth lines were more appealing. Black was always his color of choice. He wandered around it looking at all the details. After, he stopped, stepped back and looked at it from a short distance. Jake watched as D.M. contemplated. The major reached up and rubbed his chin.

"Ah, the tell-tale chin rub. The maj must be doing some serious thinking," Jake teased.

"What makes you think that? My face is itchy from not shaving."

"I know that look... I'll give you two some space...I'm going to check on my bike. They were nice enough to give me a quick service."

***

Eagle returned to find D.M. finishing the paperwork for his bike. He'd taken it out for a test ride and found it quite comfortable and maneuverable. Jake sat with him.

"So I see you found a motorcycle," Eagle said as she put down her shopping bags.

"And I see you found the mall," D.M. joked.

"Oh come on fellas, I rarely get out to do much shopping. Most of this is casual clothing."

The salesman returned to check on D.M.'s progress. He handed the paperwork over. "And how much do you wanna put on deposit?" The salesman asked. D.M. pulled out his wallet and removed a credit card.

"Just charge the whole thing on this," he handed the salesman the card.

"Are you sure?"

"Quite sure. There's plenty in my account to back the card."

The salesman took the card and hurried off. "And just how do you two plan to get these things home?" Eagle broke the silence.

"Jake's paying the freight and when we get done with the job here, we'll bring the bikes back and they'll ship them to Reno for us. We got it all worked out."

"I'll get a storage unit in Reno and then me and D.M. can have wheels when we get time in town," Jake replied as he stood and stretched, "Besides, the maj might just wanna relocate his storage closer to home. That way he can drive that awesome '38 Jag more often."

Eagle turned to D.M. "You have an old Jag? Didn't figure you the type for vintage cars... I see you more as a Ferrari or Lamborghini type."

"Bought it with my first sale while at MIT. Got it from a car auction in town. Just liked it and thought it was classy."

"Let me guess, you like quiche too," Eagle teased.

"Ick! No way! Hate the stuff. Clarice used to make it for me all the time. I just never had the heart to tell her that I didn't like it... It'll be a cold day in hell before I touch that stuff again!"

"Clarice?"

"Oh, yeah, old girlfriend. Jake and I bumped into her while we were at MIT. She married some Mechanical Engineer that teaches there... Lovely woman, very smart. Can't cook to save her life!" They all laughed.

"I'd say she's lovely... Don't see many six foot tall blonds with a body like hers." Jake grinned.

Eagle looked at D.M., he smiled sheepishly, "Okay, so I have a thing for blonds," he leaned over and kissed her, "But you're my most favorite blond of all."

"I better be!" She huffed. Jake watched them and laughed. The salesman returned with the final paperwork. D.M. signed what was required and the salesman handed him the key.

"Congratulations on the purchase of your new Harley," he offered his hand. D.M. shook it firmly.

"Hey Eagle, wanna take a ride on my new bike?" He knew she would refuse, but it was fun asking anyways.

"Not on your life. I'll see you boys back at the hotel later tonight. Be careful."

"All right maj, let's saddle up and head back to the 'hood," Jake said as he pulled on his black skull cap helmet. The major noticed his call sign was painted crudely on the side. D.M. put on a new black leather jacket and grabbed his helmet- he had opted for a full face helmet, black with a dark visor. The taste of bugs was always a turn off to riding a motorcycle. They rode back down to Jake's parent's house and checked on it. Then Jake took them to one of the local haunts where his gang used to hang out. Parking their bikes on the street they went inside the seedy bar. The lieutenant looked around and found no one familiar, "Let's go back out, better to attract attention that way."

"I just hope it's not negative attention, I only brought two extra mags."

"Naw, we should be okay. Still daylight."

"Why does that not make me feel any more comfortable with the situation?" D.M. growled.

"Oh, this isn't the really bad part of the neighborhood. There's far worse I assure you."

"Great, just great."

Jake leaned against the wall. He reached down and unbuckled

his wristwatch from his left arm. He switched it to the right. D.M. noticed a small tattoo. It was in the shape of two Roman numeral fives- VV. He never recalled seeing it there before, although it obviously had been there a long while, "What are you doing?"

"Advertising. This is the symbol of my gang the 'Ventnor Viceroys.' This is a discreet way of identifying ourselves."

"I'd say so. I never noticed it before."

"Usually always keep it hidden under my watch. Not something I wanna be proud of anymore. But it just so happens that I need it right now," he dug a pack of cigarettes out of his pocket, tapped one out and stuck it in his mouth. Fishing around in his other pockets, he found a lighter.

"Thought you finally kicked that habit," D.M. said as he watched him.

"Yeah, I did. This is purely costume. I bought the most disgusting brand I could stand," he lit up, "Tastes like shit. So I'm less likely to enjoy it so much." He watched as a motorcycle pulled up and an obvious gang member got off. D.M. watched as Jake made a small movement with his hand. The biker stopped and regarded him.

"Who are you?" He said in a gruff voice.

"Double V is the key," Jake replied.

"How do you know that?"

"Because for quite a while I was the leader," He took his right arm out of the sleeve of his jacket and raised the sleeve on his t-shirt showing his Kingpin tattoo.

The biker looked at the tattoo, "No way you could be the Kingpin, we heard he got killed a couple of years ago."

"And where'd you hear that rumor?" Jake pried as he put his jacket back on.

"Chalky told us. That's who."

"Yeah, well Chalky has too damn much coke in his head to think straight. I don't even think he'd know what day it is."

"No, he wouldn't, he's six feet under. MS-13 killed him about nine months ago."

Jake lowered his head, "Son of a bitch. Those bastards are gonna pay for that... Chalky might have been a coke-head, but he was a very good friend of mine."

"Where have you been?"

"My dad forced me to enlist in the Army. He was tired of bailing me out of jail."

The biker offered his hand, "My name's Tommy DeLuca, but everyone just calls me Two-tap."

"Jake Collins. And the big guy trying to stay hidden in the shadows is D.M. Elliott, a business associate of mine."

Tommy looked toward D.M. and nodded. The major nodded back; keeping his left hand not far from his pistol. "So what brings the great Kingpin back to AC?"

"I was home visiting my folks and MS-13 strafed their house. I need to find them some place safer to live. And my dad's health is not well... After that, I declare war on MS-13. We plan on obliterating them."

"You and what army?"

"I brought one with me. If any of you guys want in on this, you have to work with me. I need intel on where they hang out, who their leadership is and any other information you can get me."

"Come 'round to the Club House tonight and we'll give you as much info as we can. That gang has brutalized us all. We've never been that violent. They kill innocent people just for kicks. At least with the Viceroys, if we had to kill someone, they deserved it."

"About eight good?"

"Yeah. You remember where it is?"

"Unless you moved it, yes," he reached his left hand out and made a fist. Tommy did the same. They touched fists.

"Naw man, still the same place... Viceroys victorious!" Tommy disappeared into the bar. Jake climbed on his bike, "Come on, you wanna get out of this neighborhood for a while?"

"Most certainly," D.M. pulled his helmet on and started up the bike.

The major trudged down the hallway and unlocked the door. It was 2300, later than he had hoped to be back. He quietly slipped inside expecting Eagle to have gone to bed. As he crept toward the bedroom she came out. Both jumped, startling each other. "Shit! I thought you'd be in bed," he gasped.

"No, how could I sleep with you out there in gang territory?"

"Actually we hooked up with Jake's former gang and hung out with them most of the night. They gave us quite a lot of information on where to find MS-13. Even his gang is afraid of them."

"And if we're here for gang annihilation, what's going to become of Jake's former gang?"

"They're small fish. Always have been, always will be. They'll be left alone in return for all the information they've given us. And they've even offered to help us in our operation," he took off his jacket and started to undress.

"I'm not so sure we would want their help."

"Jake is handling that part of the job. They will do as he says... Tomorrow we'll need to do recon of the area. Tige especially will need to find his hide. He's going to be a vital part of the plan. I told the police that we would use discreet deadly force. No shooting up the neighborhood. The Viceroys reckon there are probably thirty to forty MS-13 gang members in the area. I'm not sure about the other gangs, they said they'll try and get us some more information."

"So we'll deal with MS-13 first?"

"That's our plan. If we go after the other gangs first, MS-13 may run and hide. They're the most brutal, so they die first."

"All right. You two will brief everyone after breakfast tomorrow. We'll then plan a recon mission down to the area and see what we're getting into."

Jake yawned widely as he sat at the breakfast table. The rest of the team was quietly discussing the day's activities. D.M. studied the lieutenant for a few moments, "So where'd you go last night?"

"I went to pay my respects," He carefully inched up his right shirt sleeve to reveal a fresh tattoo, "I went by the cemetery that Chalky's buried in and said good bye. Then I found my old tattoo parlor and had them ink me a memorial. He wasn't just a good friend, he was my best friend."

D.M. nodded slowly, "Why'd he get the name Chalky?"

"His real name was Charles Lakey, so we just shortened it to Chalky, since he was such a coke-head it always looked like he had a bag full of chalk dust. He saved my life on more than one occasion... Just sorry I wasn't there to save his."

"Or your brother's either."

"No, just there for the funeral," Jake said softly.

"What time did you finally get to bed?" Eagle asked.

Jake looked at his watch, "Oh, about three hours ago. I'll be fine." He poured a cup of coffee and added four packets of sugar to it. "We should have a few hours later to get naps... Don't wanna hit 'em until after dark when they're all in their hang out."

"What time do you think that would be?" Tige inquired.

"Probably between twenty-thirty and twenty one hundred."

"Then we'll wanna slowly get into position at least an hour before."

"I agree," Jake said as he gulped the coffee down.

D.M. rested his elbows on the table, "Anyone game for a little experiment?"

"What?" Sam spoke up.

"I told the police this would be discreet. How about we do a bullet to body count ratio? Count all our rounds before we go out. Count all the bodies and then count again when we get back... With Tige on high ground, we should be able to average less than five rounds per kill."

"That sounds reasonable. We could certainly use it as a training exercise. Fire control is quite important," Eagle added.

"Aye, I've been preaching that all along!" Tige exclaimed.

Darkness fell on the neighborhood. The team crept forward to their predetermined strike points. They had put on coveralls to disguise their armor. Jake had members of his old gang positioned about a block out just in case someone got through and ran. Tige decided to use the roof of an abandoned house for his high ground. D.M. and Jake walked quietly down the sidewalk with him. The captain looked for a way up to the roof. A porch appeared to be the lowest part of the two story building. "Hey, major, can you give me a leg up?" He sat his rifle down and stood at the edge of the overhang. D.M. handed Jake his submachine gun and got into position. He linked his fingers together and bent over. Tige took several steps back and then approached quickly. He landed his boot square in the major's hands. D.M. hefted with all his might and launched Tige into the air. He landed on the roof with a thud. There was silence for a few moments before he poked his head over the side, "Blimey! What a lift! How about passing up my rifle?" He whispered loudly. D.M. handed up the rifle. "Thanks mate. I'll be ready to go in ten mike."

"Roger that. Happy hunting," D.M. replied as he collected his gun from Jake. They quietly continued down the sidewalk, "Did you come up with a way to get 'em to come out and play?"

"Yup, right here," He patted a 40mm grenade launcher, "Yeah, it's an old Thumper, but I'm dead on with it... I plan on putting a round right through their front window."

"That should certainly get their attention," he found their hiding spot and settled into the shadows. It wasn't long before several cars and motorcycles showed up. The gang had their hang out in an old abandoned bar. Jake kept count on how many went inside. They waited for nearly an hour. D.M. keyed his mike, "All right everyone, we go in five mike. Jake will fire the opening shot."

The rest of the team confirmed.

Jake popped the breech on the grenade launcher and loaded a round. He stepped out into the street and knelt down. Carefully he took aim and fired. The round sailed down the street and broke through the window. Several seconds later there was a loud explosion. The team waited for the chaos to begin. Moments later the door flew open and gang members ran out, shooting at everything. Tige quickly dropped the first two. Jake took cover behind a car and fired over the hood. D.M. stood in a porch alcove and fired around the corner. One by one the gang members fell. Sam and Max covered the rear entrance and dispatched any that tried to escape by the back door. They placed their shots carefully and within two minutes they were no longer being fired upon. "Cease fire!" D.M. called. The street was all ready quiet, the major just wanted to make sure there would be no more shots from the team. "All right, advance," he slipped from his position and picked his way down the street. The rest of the team followed his lead.

Jake crept over to the major. They stopped a few yards from the front door. "Ground Zero, Bulldog, are you in position?" D.M. said over the radio.

"Roger."

"Wombat, do you see any movement on thermal?"

"Negative, all looks quiet."

D.M. and Jake carefully walked toward the door. Stepping over a large pile of bodies, they stopped at the door. "Cover me," the major said as he raised his machine gun, "All right, going in." He crouched down and slipped inside the door. Jake poked his gun around the door jamb, providing cover for the major. In the dim light D.M. could see several bodies; and what appeared to be several parts of other bodies strewn in the front room. "Nice job Jake, you landed your shot right into the middle of 'em," he whispered. As he advanced through the old bar he kicked at each of the bodies to make sure they were dead. There was no quarter to be given on this mission. "Bulldog, are you in?"

"We're in what was the store room. All clear... Coming out your way."

Tige carefully pivoted his rifle back and forth looking for any remaining gang members. He stopped when he came across what appeared to be a bathroom. "Lone Wolf, I think you have a live one in the bathroom."

"Roger, we'll have a look. Keep eyes on."

"Affirmative."

Max crept into D.M.'s view. The major motioned at the bathroom door. Max nodded and got ready. He fell in behind D.M., who carefully made his way to the door. He stopped and signaled that he was going to kick the door in. Max nodded and held up his gun. D.M. kicked the door in with a loud crash. They rushed into the room and stopped. They could hear no movement. One by one D.M. kicked in the stall doors until he came to the last one. With a firm kick, the door flew open. The major leveled his gun and paused. Before him was a woman curled up on the back of the toilet seat. Her clothes were torn and blood streamed from her face. She was so traumatized she didn't even move. He keyed his mike, "Lone Wolf. I think we got a hotel in here."

Static crackled in the major's ear, "A hotel?" Eagle said; she was two blocks back tucked away from any danger. A hostage was just going to complicate things.

"She looks like she's had the shit beat out of her and maybe raped." He lowered his gun and reached his hand out to her, "It's okay, we're the good guys. You're safe with us."

Slowly the woman climbed off the toilet and stood the best she could. She fell into D.M.'s arms and he picked her up. He carried her outside and took her over behind a parked car. Carefully he set her down. Jake continued to sweep the bar with Sam and Max. Finally they issued the all clear. Sam came out and found D.M. trying to comfort the woman. "I got it, I'll check her out," Sam said as he knelt down and opened his medical bag.

"Thanks. We should call an ambulance."

"I make thirty four. Tige, what's your count?" D.M. said as he stepped over a body that lay next to the front door. He reached down, grabbed the back of the shirt and dragged it to the line of other bodies. Jake and the others were busily going through pockets of the dead looking for ID.

"Yes sir, I concur. Thirty four. Although Jake did make it a bit more difficult with that spot on grenade placement."

"Hey, you wanted to get their attention..." Jake barked.

"I'm not complaining one bit. You did a damn good job. I just wonder how you got so good with that Thumper," D.M. said as he picked up an Uzi and carried it to the pile of arms that were being collected.

"I found it in one of the cabinets down on the training floor and thought it might come in handy. There were several boxes of practice rounds so between the basement range and going out in the forest and practicing, I just got the knack of it. This was the first time I got to blow something up... Way cool!"

Max came out the front door, "Major, come have a look at this." D.M. and the others followed him back inside. He took them to the store room and lifted open a large wooden chest. Inside was packed with small arms. There were hand guns, machine pistols, AK-74s, and assorted sawed off shotguns. Jake reached in and pulled a few out and set them on the floor. As he rummaged around through the collection of arms, he stopped.

"Oh, no way. It can't be!" He removed a few more rifles and carefully pulled out a Thompson machine gun. He looked the gun over and then regarded D.M., "This was Chalky's gun. I recognize the etching on the butt stock...No way the cops are going to melt this one down," he tucked it under his arm and stood up.

"I suppose the cops won't miss one. And if it was ever used in a crime, it really won't matter. It's in responsible hands now," D.M. said as he piled the firearms back into the trunk.

"Thanks maj."

"Now go make it disappear, the cops should be showing up soon... Sam called for an ambulance and told them to send the cops as well. The rest of us need to fall back and meet up with Eagle. The less of us they see the better."

Jake walked down the sidewalk and headed back up the street toward where Eagle was parked. He saw Sam carefully wiping the blood from the woman's face. Slowing up, he finally got a good look at her. Despite the blood and bruising, her face looked familiar. He stopped and leaned down, looking over Sam's shoulder. The woman just stared blankly ahead; she was too much in shock. "Suzie?" Jake said softly. The woman slowly looked up, her right eye swollen nearly shut. "Oh dear God!" He quickly knelt down and took her into his arms. "Goddamn those bastards!" Jake cried.

"Jake...Jake, the ambulance is coming. You need to go to Eagle. I'll take care of her, I promise."

The lieutenant turned and looked at Sam; his eyes were red and he had tear stains on his cheeks. His lips quivered as he tried to find the words, "Please find out where she's being taken," he let his grasp slide from her and he stood up. Sam handed him the Tommy gun. Jake took several steps back, still looking at Suzie. Slowly he turned and began walking. The ambulance and police came down the street. He ducked behind a parked car and waited until they passed. The rest of the team had quickly fallen back. Sam was the only one left on the street. He'd passed his machine gun off to Max as he retreated. He was essentially unarmed for his own safety. Jake had warned that the police would come in guns drawn looking for a fight. The cars stopped and the police got out and swarmed around Sam. He held his hands up, "I'm unarmed. This woman is hurt and needs medical attention. I was the one that called you." The paramedics quickly went to work on Suzie.

"What the hell happened here?" An officer said as he surveyed the area.

"I don't know officer. I was in my garage getting ready to work on my car and I heard a loud explosion and then lots of gunfire... I stayed there until it was over and then came out. I found her and went and got my EMT bag... She's been beat up pretty good and probably raped. I think this was a gang war. I never saw anyone leaving the scene. They must have done a hit and run."

"If it was a hit and run, why are the bodies all lined up and the weapons in a pile?"

"I dunno officer. I waited a good while before I came out. I didn't want to be a casualty."

"And why didn't the other gang take all the weapons?"

Sam stood up, "Look officer, I didn't see what happened. All I know is there was a lot of gunfire going on for a few minutes. Then it got quiet. I finally came out and saw her. I called the ambulance and then you," his voice was tinged with irritation. Sam knew that he had to get out of there soon. Had there not been a casualty, the team would have retreated to a safe distance and then called the police.

"Can I see some ID please?" The officer said as he pulled out a pen and small notebook.

"I was in my garage. I didn't expect to need it. It's at home on my dresser... Do you want me to go get it? I live just around the corner." He pointed down the street.

"Just give me your name, address and phone number in case we need to ask you any further questions."

Sam quickly rattled off a fake name, an address he had seen on the way in and a fake phone number. The officer wrote it down, "All right, you can go."

"Thank you officer," Sam turned and walked back up the street. He stopped at the ambulance where Suzie was being loaded. He asked the driver where she was being taken. He then did his best casual walk down and around the corner. When he was sure no one could see him, he took off at a full run back to the van where the rest of the team was anxiously waiting. Diving in the side door, he quickly closed it and Eagle pulled away and turned down a street away from where the police where. "Oh crap that was close! Hey, next time, just leave every one where they lay. The cops were suspicious because the bodies were moved and the guns were still there... I tried to cover saying I thought it was a hit and run, but they really weren't buying it."

"Did you find out where they were taking Suzie?" Jake asked.

"AC Medical Center."

"Oh, yeah, know that place. Been there a few times myself. Thanks Sam."

"No problem. Old girlfriend?"

Jake nodded slowly, "We were a hot item for nearly two years. Had I not gotten my ass in so much trouble, I probably would have asked her hand in marriage."

The team returned to the hotel. Jake hurriedly changed out of his armor and went back out to see Suzie. D.M. knew Jake needed to make sure she was all right, so he said nothing about the debriefing they were going to have. The team assembled in Eagle and D.M.'s suite with all their magazines of ammunition. The full ones were counted and set aside. The others were emptied and counted. Tige dropped six spent casings on the table. The major counted and then wrote down the total on a sheet of paper, "Not too bad everyone. We iced thirty four MS-13 gang members and only spent fifty two rounds. Not a bad kill ratio."

"So who's next on the list?" Tige said as he collected up his brass.

"The Bloods should be next. They're bigger than MS-13 down here, but not quite as violent," D.M. replied as he pushed all the magazines and ammo into the middle of the table so the team could begin reloading it.

"Do we have any intel on them?"

"They average about forty members and we have a possible hangout for them. We'll need to do some more research though; Jake's gang couldn't provide us much information. Evidently they haven't had many dealings with the Bloods," D.M. said as he grabbed a magazine and started to push rounds into it.

Over the course of the next week and a half, the team wiped out one gang after another. The police were stumped as to who was doing all the killings, but were secretly happy to be rid of the gangs. Their mission had been successful and it was getting time to head home. Jake decided to let his parents stay in their house, but hired a caregiver to help his mother out. The Viceroys were sworn to keep their illegal activities to a minimum and to watch over Jake's parents making sure nothing happened to them. He gave them his phone number and told them to call should a violent gang move back into the neighborhood. The lieutenant also made sure Suzie was cared for. He helped her get home to north Jersey to her parents and away from the seedy life of Atlantic City.

The team was due to fly back home the next day. D.M. decided he wanted to go down and do some gambling. He stood at the mirror fixing his tie and collar. Eagle came out of the bedroom, "What are you getting all dressed up for?"

"Going down to gamble a bit."

"Why get all dressed up?"

"Because I want to."

Eagle shook her head and headed back into the bedroom, "Don't be too late, we have to fly out early tomorrow."

"Yes ma'am, I'll be home by twenty three hundred," he replied in a mocking tone.

"Earlier would be better," she hollered.

D.M. grabbed his room card and headed out. He saw Jake coming down the hall.

"Hey maj, where ya go'in?"

"Down to the floor. Feel like a little gambling."

"Mind if I tag along? Got nothing to do since mom, dad and Suzie are home."

"Sure, come on."

They took the elevator down to the casino floor. D.M. walked slowly checking out all the table games. He then went to the credit office. Stepping up to the counter he pulled out his credit card.

The female clerk looked up at him, "May I help you sir?"

"Yes, I'd like ten thousand in chips please."

"Is this a marker?"

"No, just charge it. I want it free and clear."

Jake put his hand on D.M.'s arm, "Ten grand?!"

"Yeah, so? You wanna play too?"

"Depends on what you're playing."

"Blackjack."

"Uh, okay," Jake said with hesitation.

"Can you please make it fifteen thousand total?" He called.

The clerk was just preparing to swipe the card, "You want fifteen thousand charged on this card sir?"

"Yes, fifteen... Ten for me, five for him."

"You're awfully generous sir... I'm going to make two casino checks out for you; it's easier than trying to carry all the chips through the place... Can I please see ID from each of you so I can have your names on the checks?" They pulled out their IDs and handed them to her. D.M. pulled out a crisp fifty and dropped it on the counter. The clerk returned with their checks and ID, "Here you go gentlemen. Good luck."

"Thank you," D.M. said as he nudged the fifty her direction.

"Thank you sir," she grinned.

The major turned to Jake, "All right, let's have some fun." They walked through the casino floor. D.M. finally found what he was looking for- the High Limit Room.

"Uh, maj, that's the big money room. I think the cheapest hand of anything in there is at least a hundred bills."

"Yes, well I'd like to play Blackjack with as few decks as possible."

Jake stopped and grabbed the major's arm, "Hey wait a minute, are you telling me you count cards?" He said in a low voice.

D.M. held his hand over the lieutenant's mouth, "Shhhh. Remember, where I went to school, they perfected it there," he took his hand down, "My average is about seventy percent. Good enough to win, but not so good as to attract too much attention...Just watch and I'll help you out the best I can."

"Oh, cool!" Jake whispered loudly.

"Just keep your damn mouth shut... If I make a fist somehow, that means stand. If I scratch an itch or otherwise raise a finger, that means take a card. Got it?"

"Roger that sir."

They walked through the door and D.M. looked around. Several tables were open; others had only one or two people at it. He selected one that had two seats next to each other. He passed his check over to the dealer. He took it and showed the pit boss who verified it, "Good evening Mr. Elliott. You want ten thousand in action?" He said as he motioned to the dealer to start counting chips out.

"Yes, that's correct."

Jake passed his check over after D.M. had received his chips.

"And Mr. Collins is changing five thousand?"

"Correct," Jake replied with a hint of nervousness. D.M. had selected a one hundred dollar table. "You know, I'm glad this is your money. Too rich for my blood."

"So play table minimum for a while. See how you do... Usually what I do," D.M. said as he arranged his chips and put out his first bet. Jake collected his chips and put his bet out. The dealer passed out the cards. D.M. looked at them and motioned for another card. The dealer passed one.

"Mr. Elliott is showing sixteen."

Jake looked at his cards. He held them up long enough for D.M. to glance at. The major sat back and rubbed his nose. Jake motioned for another card.

The dealer passed Jake another card, "Mr. Collins is showing sixteen as well. Anyone care to raise?"

"No thanks," D.M. said. Jake shook his head.

"Right, let's see what you gentlemen have."

D.M. flipped his card over. He had intentionally busted.

Jake flipped his card over, "Oh yeah, Blackjack!"

The dealer flipped his card over, "Dealer has twenty. Mr. Collins wins."

D.M. looked at his watch, 2300 and he was beginning to get tired. They had been playing for nearly four hours. "Hey, what say we call it a night? We have to leave kinda early tomorrow."

Jake ran his hand down one of the large stacks of five hundred dollar chips, "Aw do we have to? I was having a good time."

"Yes, Eagle is flying out with the others. We have to take the Lear jet back. And I'd like to get some sleep before we have to tackle a ten hour flight," he pushed his chips to the center of the table, "Color out please."

Jake pushed his over as well, "Yeah, me too."

"Not a bad payday maj," Jake said as he finished filling out his winnings paperwork and shoved his thirty thousand dollars into his empty gear bag. D.M. had sent him up to retrieve it. They had done quite well and there were far too many stacks of hundred dollar bills to manage safely. D.M. handed his paperwork back and then started tossing his substantial pile of bills into the bag as well. He finished and they headed toward the elevators, "Shit, I can't believe you won that much. That was a piece of work."

"Actually, I may have won nearly a hundred grand, but I lost about fifty thousand more."

"You did that on purpose didn't you?"

"Yup," D.M. smiled.

"Well, where else can you make nearly twenty five thousand dollars an hour?"

"Science pays well, but just not that quickly."

D.M. and Jake returned to the police station. This time the major left Jake with his side arm. Officer Winslow met them and took them back into a private office.

"You fellas run one hell of an operation. The coroner was a real busy guy this last week."

"Well, you should notice a large drop in gang activities for at least a while," D.M. said as he took a paper from his coat pocket. Unfolding it, he set it on the table. "We decided to make this an exercise in fire control... Here is a listing of the gangs we wiped out, the body count and the amount of rounds expended to get the job done."

"Sweet Jesus! I didn't realize you took out that many."

Jake joined in, "You said you wanted them wiped out. The only gangs remaining are the small fish. The Viceroys were left intact. They helped us out on quite a few raids. They've promised me that they'll stay as clean as possible and make sure my parent's neighborhood isn't bothered by any other gangs... Should you have any problems, just give us a call."

"I thank you gentlemen, and the mayor thanks you too."

"You're welcome. We appreciated the live fire practice," D.M. replied.

CHAPTER THIRTY ONE

Eagle, Sam, Max and Tige landed at Reno-Tahoe Airport. D.M. had radioed that he was only an hour behind them. It was early afternoon and the men lazed around on benches outside the hanger. The sun was warm and a gentle breeze blew across the flight line. They watched planes come and go and quietly discussed the events of the past week. Eagle sat inside the hanger working on her laptop. Her cell phone rang, "Hello? Oh, hi... You just landed? Okay, we'll see if we can find a vehicle to come get you... Right, see you in a few," she hung up and went outside, "Hey, they just landed."

"We know. I think Jake mooned us from the cockpit as they went by," Max said as he stood and stretched, "I found a car I can borrow. Do you want me to go over and get them?"

"Yes, please. That would be wonderful."

Once the team was back together Eagle started to make arrangements to get them back to the base. She was tired and just wanted to get home.

Jake approached her, "Do you think you would let us all stay in Reno a couple of days?"

"And for what reason is this request?" She replied with irritation.

"The major and I have our bikes arriving late tomorrow and we need to find a storage unit."

"And why does this require the rest of the team?"

"I just thought we could have a little R and R. I promise we won't get into any trouble."

Eagle chuckled, "I find that statement rather amusing coming from you."

"Really, we won't...And who knows when we'll get to see some civilization again," he begged.

"You just had two weeks of civilization."

"Most of it was doing work."

D.M. approached, he could see the sour expression on Eagle's face, "Something the matter?"

"The lieutenant here was just trying to convince me that I should let all of you stay in Reno for a few extra days. What do you have to say about it?"

The major shrugged his shoulders, "I don't have a problem with it... Besides we need to get to the bank."

"What for?" Eagle grumbled. Jake trotted off and retrieved his gear bag. Dropping it at her feet, he unzipped the bag and pulled it open.

"For all this," he pulled out several stacks of hundreds. The others gathered around and looked at the bag full of money.

"You two rob a bank or something?" Sam joked.

Jake stood up, "Naw, D.M. and I won it last night. He's one helluva Blackjack player."

"How much did you guys win?" Max added.

"Umm, not quite a hundred and thirty."

Eagle regarded the major, "You two won all this in just four hours?"

"Yeah. I won most of it, but Jake had his share of good hands." D.M. replied with a slight smile.

Eagle sighed deeply. She was more than ready to get back to the base and relax. What harm could it do to let the men have a few days off? "If I give you the time off, how are we going to get all the gear home?"

"Easy, we pack the Warhawk with our gear. You fly that home, leave it packed. When we fly home Thursday morning, we'll unpack it and put everything away. Not like there's going to be anyone there to bother it," the major responded.

"Fine, pack it up. I leave you in charge major. Anything happens and it's your ass that's in trouble."

D.M. snapped to attention and saluted, "Yes ma'am!" Eagle slowly stiffened to attention and returned the salute. The major clapped his hands, "All right guys, get the Warhawk packed with everything we won't need. I'm going to arrange us transport and find a hotel. We get two days here in Reno."

The rest of the team cheered and quickly broke off to load the helicopter. It wasn't long before Eagle was on her way home and they were on their way to a hotel.

"You know, I'm actually getting tired of living in hotels. I miss my own bed," Jake said as he carried his suitcase to his room.

"Remember, this outing was your idea. We could have just sorted out the storage and bank issues and gone home," D.M. replied as he jiggled the key card in the door. He had decided he wanted his own room, so Jake had to bunk with Max.

"I know, I know. I just thought we could enjoy a bit of guy time away from Eagle."

D.M. opened his door, "So am I to assume that this 'guy time' will include lots of drinking and strip clubs?"

"Well, maybe..."

"Count me out; I'd rather not do either."

"Oh come on, I promise we won't get too wild. Besides, you're in charge, so you have to make sure we behave," Jake teased.

The major groaned, shoved his suitcase in the door and shut it firmly behind. He was tired, wanted to get a shower, eat something and get to bed. As he placed his suitcase on the stand, he began to realize that maybe making Jake stay with Max was a bad idea. He was still very dependent on someone to help him in and out of his robotic arm. At least in Atlantic City, Eagle had been right there to help him. It was one of the few times he didn't mind asking for help, and she was more than willing to assist him. Perhaps it was time to go back to the drawing board and try to come up with another robotic arm that would be lighter, easier to control and less of a burden on himself and the others.

Jake knocked on the major's door, "Hey, it's me."

D.M. opened the door, "Yes?"

"The rest of us are gonna hit the town and find something to eat. I know you're tired and probably just wanna get some sleep. We'll probably be back kinda late. You need any help with your arm before I go?"

"Well, as your babysitter, should I not be going along?"

Jake scratched his head, "I guess if you want to, but I just figured you'd want some sleep."

"I'm tired, yes, but I also have a duty to Eagle to make sure you all stay out of trouble," he yawned widely, "Can you guys give me ten mike to get ready?"

"Yeah, sure. That'll give us time to find a cab to get us downtown."

"I'll meet you down in the lobby."

The men selected a reasonable restaurant and dined quietly. D.M. was surprised to see they didn't drink the place dry. The next stop on the evening's junket was some strip club Jake had found in the phone book. He was confident there they would drink and get rowdy. Jake leaned over and gently elbowed the major, "Hey, I know the next stop is not your idea of fun, but for some of us, we haven't had any female company in a long time."

"Yes, I know. I highly doubt any of you will get laid unless you're willing to fork out the money."

"Getting laid would be nice. I'm not crazy enough to stick it in one of the hookers on this side of town... None of us are. We just wanna have a little fun."

"That's fine. I'm planning on being as invisible as possible," the major said as he finished the last bite of steak.

"Do you mind if I ask you a personal question?" Jake said

lowly.

"It depends on how personal it is."

"How far have you and Eagle gone in your relationship?"

D.M. leaned over until he was quite close to the lieutenant, "Well, she's still a virgin and I'm still frustrated as hell."

Jake chuckled softly, "I would have thought by now you two would have taken the final step."

"No...She happens to be from an ancient royal line... She can only marry another blue blood, and she has to remain chaste until that time."

"And you bleed red like the rest of us?"

"Through some cruel and amusing twist of fate, I bleed blue."

"Huh? No shit? Why didn't you tell me?" Jake gasped.

"Never thought there was much of a reason to tell you. Eagle did a very extensive DNA test on me to find out that my real father is the King of Spain."

"You're shitt'in me!"

"It appears that my mother had a one night stand with him, ran home to Zaragosa, met a *then* Major Elliott, quickly married him and then I popped out... In a way I'm really glad I'm not related to that bastard."

"So because of your positions in the chain of command, you can't do anything until at least one of you is out."

"Right. It sucks, but you're right."

"Can't you guys just elope and we won't say anything?"

"I'll let her decide when the time it right. Until then, our relationship is on the lighter side of romantic."

Jake nodded, "I can respect that."

"I have to respect it."

"Oh come on major, have a little fun," Tige said as he took a long draw of beer and playfully smacked the waitress on the behind as she walked by. The club was booming with loud music and packed with male patrons. Women in various stages of undress danced on the stage swinging wildly around on brass poles. Waitresses hurried from one table to another bringing drinks to the men. Other dancers were moving through the crowd selling lap dances.

"Fun is overrated. Just please behave so we don't get in trouble," D.M. growled. He sat drinking a soda, not at all happy to be part of the spectacle.

Jake looked over at Tige, "Hey, leave him be. It's not bad enough that we're surrounded by scantily clad women who are dangling their boobs in our faces, but he has to babysit us all so we return home Thursday morning... And *his* significant other is waiting at home."

Tige rummaged through his pockets and pulled out fifty dollars. He flagged down one of the dancers, a tall blond, and whispered in her ear. She nodded, took the money and made her way over to D.M.

"Hey big fella. You don't look like you're having a very good time," she stepped close to him, "How about letting me put a smile on your face?"

The major turned around, "Is this your doing Jake?"

"No sir," the lieutenant replied crisply.

Tige cackled loudly. The others laughed with less enthusiasm.

"All right captain, how would you like to be a sergeant again?" D.M. turned back to the dancer, "Look, I've got someone at home that I'm quite attached to. I'm just here to babysit this bunch of delinquents so they don't end up in jail... Can I give my dance to someone else?"

"Yes, I suppose so."

"Good," he pointed at Jake, "Give it to him," he reached in his pocket and gave her another twenty, "He's been out of circulation for a while, give him a good dance."

The men walked out of the strip club. The evening air was cool and the moon was full. Jake looked up and let out a long wolf howl.

"Hey watch it there buddy, you're treading on my call sign," D.M. said as he poked Jake in the ribs.

"Sorry maj, no insult intended... Just been a long time since I've had an enjoyable night like that," He stopped and looked across the street, "Hey, you guys know what we should do? We should all get tattoos with the unit emblem."

"No way!" D.M. barked.

"I'm game," Tige quipped. Sam and Max nodded in agreement.

"Oh come on maj. It's a symbol of our fraternity. We're together as one. We fight as one, we bleed as one. And as our leader you should be setting the example."

"Don't even play those psyche games on me lieutenant, I'm just not interested. If the rest of you wanna have a permanent memento of your service, go ahead. I however choose not to mark up my body with anything other than scars, and I have plenty of those."

"All right, all right. Fine," he looked both ways and quickly darted across the street. The others followed. D.M. brought up the rear. He stepped inside the shop to find the walls covered with tattoo art. Most of it was quite tasteless, but some of the designs that were aimed at women were quite ornate and beautiful. He had never been attracted to body art. The major watched as Jake pulled out a small piece of paper from his wallet and showed it to one of the male tattoo artists. He nodded and motioned to his assistant, a wildly tattooed and pierced woman with orange and green hair. "Hey, he says he can do it, and his partner will help out. Their work looks pretty good. Whoever wants one, it's on me," he handed the paper to the woman. Tige, Sam and Max chatted excitedly and thanked Jake. "All right, where do we want it? Left shoulder where the patch usually is?" Jake asked.

"Yeah mate, that would work. Got my SASR tat on my right arm," Tige said as he rolled up his right sleeve to show it off.

"Sam? Max"

The men looked at each other, "Left."

"OK then, left it is," he looked over at D.M., "You sure you don't want one?"

"No thank you."

"Afraid Eagle will be mad at you?"

The major growled, "Cut it out Jake."

The lieutenant pulled his shirt off and sat down in the chair. Tige quickly occupied the other. After several hours the four men stood comparing tattoos. They had opted for just black ink with some shading around where the patch border would be. The scales of the dragon's head and neck were intricately drawn. Light shading was given to the background of the patch making the dragon and sword stand out. Sam rubbed his upper arm gently, "Well, for my first ink job; that was rather painful!"

"Aw, you get used to it after a while," Jake teased.

"What makes you think I'm going to have any more?"

"Tattoos are like Pringles, you can't just have one."

"Naw, one is enough. I got good will power."

Jake looked at the tattoos that dotted his arms and chest, "Guess that means I don't!" He laughed, "You sure you don't wanna join us maj?"

D.M. stood thinking for a few moments. True, he was one of their leaders, and he of all people felt a strong bond with the team. They were in a way a fraternity and common bonds just made them stronger. He looked at the others tattoos; they were only about three inches high and maybe two inches wide. Not very big by tattoo standards. Pain was certainly not a factor, that part of his arm was neurologically dead. Yes, Eagle would probably be a bit angry, but with proper explanation, she might just forgive him. He sighed, "Okay Jake, you win." The rest of the team cheered. "But I need your help for a minute."

Jake pointed to a dressing booth, "Right, come with me." He quickly helped the major out of his robotic arm and watched as D.M. slowly sat down in the chair. He used his good arm to subtly position his arm for the tattoo. The artist quickly prepped his skin and traced out the pattern. After several minutes of work, he picked up his tattoo machine and prepared to start.

"This is going to feel like someone scratching you."

D.M. sighed deeply, "Just get on with it. I won't be bothered."

As the needle dug at his flesh, the rest of the men cheered, "Ma-jor, Ma-jor, Ma-jor!"

It was shortly past noon when Jake knocked on D.M.'s door. After a few moments of no response, he knocked again. "What?!" Came a loud growl from the other side of the door.

"Rise and shine major, the bikes have arrived."

The door opened and D.M. stood dressed in his usual pair of

loose boxer shorts. His eyes were still not fully open and he looked like he had just crawled out of bed.

"My, my, did you just wake up? So much for your party animal reputation," Jake teased and strolled inside the room, "You gonna get dressed so we can go get the bikes and storage unit?"

The major rubbed his eyes and yawned, "What time is it?"

"Quarter past noon."

"Shit. Slept a little longer than I wanted to... All right, let me get a shower, shaved and dressed and we'll head out."

"You want something to eat? I can get you room service if you want," Jake handed the menu card to D.M.

"Have them send up an omelet of some sort and a big glass of milk."

"Roger that. I'll get right on it," the lieutenant picked up the phone and dialed. After placing the order, he turned on the TV and plopped down on the couch. He was watching the news when a story about the dramatic reduction in the Atlantic City gang population came on. Turning to holler at D.M., he realized that the major was still in the shower. So he watched the story with enthusiasm. When D.M. did finally emerge, Jake immediately told him what he saw, "Hey, major, you're not going to believe it, we were on TV!"

"What do you mean *we* were on TV?"

"Well, not us exactly, but there was a story about how there was a huge reduction of the gangs in AC."

"And did they say who they thought did it?"

"Either some vigilante group, or a serious gang war," he stood and helped the major into his arm.

"Good, let it stay a mystery," he finished zipping up his pants, "Did they at least get the body count right?"

"Most definitely!"

"Humm, funny, the press usually inflates the figures."

"The mayor was on and I swear he had the list that you made up for Officer Winslow," Jake said as he plopped back down on the couch.

"Hopefully that will buy your parents some time in the neighborhood."

"I hope so."

Room service arrived and brought the major's breakfast. He ate ravenously. Finishing off the last of his milk he belched loudly, "Damn good omelet!"

"Major, my God, that was the most uncouth thing I think I've ever heard you do," Jake joked.

"Oh, sorry, pardon me."

"Come on, you're a guy. You're entitled to a good burp and fart once in a while."

"My God, that's it!" Captain Goldsmith shouted as he pulled a plastic bone prototype from a mold. Running his fingers over the surface of the part, he turned it over examining it. Now he would begin the regimen of testing for durability, heat resistance, chemical compatibility and several others. The plastic was reasonably lightweight, had a surface with small pits, grooves and ridges that were designed to encourage the body to attach tendons and ligaments to. Initially, the surgical process would involve either wiring, screwing or stapling the part to the bone; after, it would hopefully grow into the grooves and become more firmly attached.

The captain took the prototype over to a standard operating room sterilizer and dropped it into the tray. Closing the door, he set the time and temperature settings, "Might as well go with the most important one- will it sterilize?" He turned the machine on and returned to his workbench to make another mold. Carefully he heated the plastic and then poured it into the mold. As the plastic cooled, the captain made notes on his computer. He then went to a small refrigerator and sorted through plastic bags containing various size animal bones. These were to test the comparative strength of the plastic bone versus a real bone of the same size and density. Once he found a few close in size, he brought them back to the workbench and removed the plastic. The bones had been stripped clean but were still fairly fresh. He placed one in a piece of equipment he lovingly called "The Torture Chamber" and turned it on. The machine was capable of creating realistic trauma to a bone by bending, breaking, twisting, compression, and impact. It provided readings in pounds per square inch of force applied and foot pounds of torque.

Taking a pair of calipers, the captain made several measurements and recorded them in the computer. "All right, let's see how much of a breaking point you have," he said as he adjusted the equipment and then flipped the switch. The machine hummed louder and louder. Within a few moments there was a loud crack as the bone broke. Releasing the pressure, the captain took his reading and quickly typed it into the computer. He looked at his watch and decided the part in the mold should be cooled off enough to test. Prying open the mold he worked the part loose and checked it over, "Now your turn." He removed the animal bone and replaced it with the plastic bone, "OK, let's see what you got." Turning on the machine, he waited for the outcome. The equipment hummed even louder than before and finally a dull crack sounded as the plastic bone gave under the pressure. Looking at the reading the captain smiled broadly, "Shit, that's more than twice the breaking strength of regular bone!" He recorded the results and set about making more prototypes for testing.

Sir, may I have a few minutes of your time? Captain Goldsmith said as he stood in the doorway of Dr. Miles' office.

"Certainly, what can I do for you?"

"Actually, it may be the other way around. I think I've perfected my plastic bone." He walked over to the desk and offered one of the prototype pieces to the colonel.

Dr. Miles took it and studied it, "It looks like it would do the job. And how did the durability tests go?"

"It's more than twice as strong as a real bone. It survived the sterilizer in excellent form. I still need to test it against various chemicals, but so far this looks like a winner," he handed a printout of the test data to the surgeon.

"And I thought for the longest time you'd been stuck. How'd you find the answer?"

Lance smiled and leaned against the desk, "Well, I found the answer in the hallway outside the labs... We have one of the best experts on plastics and polymers working right here."

"You mean Major Elliott?"

"Yes sir. I asked him to look at my formula and he made a few changes and voila! Within the week, I had a working compound."

Dr. Miles shook his head slowly, "D.M. is man ahead of his times... He had me install a massive hard drive and processor into the empty space where part of the left upper lobe of his lung used to be. With incredibly delicate surgery, we tied fine wires into the usable nerve endings that ran from his brain and into the computer. From there, we were able to create a port on his back where the robotic arm would attach to... How he came up with all this technology just blows my mind... And I have no clue what kind of operating system he's using to interface between his brain, the computer and the arm, I seriously doubt its Windows based. I only wish I could convince him to share some of that knowledge for the good of science and medicine."

"I got the feeling from talking to him that he keeps everything to himself until he's ready to sell it on the open market... I don't know how much luck you'll have getting secrets out of him," Lance added.

"I bet I could if he knew it would help his brother."

"That may get him to open up a bit."

Dr. Miles looked over the test results, "These are very impressive. When do you think you'll be ready for a human trial?"

"I still have a few more tests to run, but then the technology is supposed to be tested in animals first... It could be a year or more before it goes into a real human... Why do you ask?"

"Because I have a human in need of some new bones. I really don't wanna put titanium and stainless in him, he's going to need four new vertebrae... And seeing how much pain the poor major is in when it gets cold, it would be brutal."

"Do you think he would consent to being a test subject?" Lance inquired.

"I can ask him." He played with the plastic bone, "Do you mind if I keep this to show him?"

"Sure, not a problem, I can make hundreds more."

The elevator doors opened and the team strolled out. They

had enjoyed their two extra days in civilization and were now ready to get back to business. Eagle came out of her office when she heard the ruckus in the hallway, "Well, well, I see you have all returned."

Jake stepped forward, "Yes ma'am. And we behaved ourselves."

Eagle regarded D.M., who nodded slowly.

"We did do one thing," he pulled his jacket off and rolled up his sleeve to reveal the tattoo. The others followed suit. D.M. stood unmoving. Eagle walked over and inspected the lieutenant's artwork. She then looked at the others.

"Humm. I'm not a fan of tattoos. I guess however if you want to mark up your bodies, then the unit insignia is a reasonable choice." She stepped over to D.M., "And did you get one too?"

He stood silent for a moment, "I am part of the team. I provide leadership to them."

Eagle cocked her head, "You did it didn't you?"

"Yes," he said lowly.

She rolled her eyes, turned and walked off, returning to her office.

Jake slammed his fist into the workbench. "Fuckin' hell, why won't this work?!" He'd been working in the lab all day and it was getting late.

The major approached, "What's wrong?"

"I can't get the nanos to change color correctly. Some do and some don't. See how blotchy it is?"

D.M. gently picked up the piece of plastic that Jake was working on and turned it over. Inspecting the fine wires closely, he took a pair of tweezers and delicately moved one, "I think you got a bad connection. Let me have the soldering iron."

Jake handed it to him. The major very carefully pressed the tip down and soldered the loose connection. He then flipped the piece back over, "All right, try that."

The lieutenant reapplied the power. "Ah! That fixed it! But how are we going to control the color change?"

"Oh, that's gonna take some work. You're treading into

unknown waters there."

"There's got to be a way. I guess its back to the Internet..."

"Do you have a small piece I could take down to the range? I wanna test it to see how the nanos have interacted with the plastic and make sure it's still bulletproof."

"Yeah, sure, take the piece over there. I messed up the wiring really bad, so it's worthless."

"Thanks."

"I'd love to go watch, but I wanna figure this problem out."

The major opened the heavy door, "Good luck." He headed upstairs and knocked on Tige's door. A few moments later the door opened and Tige stood looking at him, a rolled up magazine in his hand.

"Hey, are you doing anything? Can I borrow you to test some plastic for me?"

"Oh, I guess so," he held up the magazine, "I'll just have to continue my date with Miss September later." He tossed the magazine back in his room and followed D.M. down the hallway.

"Sorry, I hope I wasn't interrupting anything."

"Just missing female company," he poked the elevator button.

"Ah, uh, umm," D.M. stammered when he figured out what Tige meant.

"At least you're lucky mate, you have Eagle."

The elevator doors opened and they stepped in. D.M. hit the button for the seventh floor, "It may seem like we have a hot and heavy relationship, but that's not true. Yeah, we may spend a lot of nights together, but usually she's just trying to help me through all the nightmares I have," he leaned against the wall, "And there's only so far she's willing to go. I have to respect that."

The doors opened and they stepped out. "Mmmm, I wonder if that kind of relationship is more difficult than a Playboy and a box of Kleenex?" Tige said as he opened a locker and retrieved a 9 mm hand gun.

D.M. chuckled, "Yes, it is. I've spent many nights a frustrated male."

"Oh, that sucks."

"Sure does. I finally got her to realize that we men have a balance in our lives too," he started down range to post the piece of plastic on the clamps.

"Gave her the 'kill it or fuck it' speech huh?"

"Yeah. That seemed to help. Still isn't going to get me laid, but she's more sympathetic to my needs." He returned and sat down next to Tige, "The hard part is I love her so much and can't really show her how I feel," he put on his hearing protection.

Tige took aim and fired. D.M. looked though the spotting scope, "Yeah, that was a hit. I see a scrape on the plastic."

"You want me to hit it with something bigger?"

"Sure, break out the .45 and the .44; let's see if it will stop it and how much damage it will take."

"That plastic looks different- darker."

"It's got a new secret ingredient. Jake and I aren't sure if it will disturb the chemical composition of the original plastic, so we have to test it."

"Right, no problem, I don't mind."

After an hour of testing, D.M. retrieved the sample. He handed it to Tige.

"What are all these tiny wires for?" The captain said as he flipped the piece over.

"Can you keep a secret?"

"Aye."

"The reason the plastic looks different is because we have infused carbon bucky tube nanos in it."

"And what the hell is that?"

"Jake's been working on this for a while. He thinks we can use the nanos to change the color of the armor to match whatever surroundings we're in."

"Just like a bloody chameleon eh?"

"Yup. He even nicknamed it Chameleon Skin."

"So what do the wires do?" Tige said as he poked at one with his finger.

"They carry a micro current to the nanos. That tells them what to do."

"And they are all over the plastic?"

"Well, yes. We're having problems keeping the connection from the power supply to the nanos. The wires just don't seem to be doing the job."

Tige handed the plastic back and went to clean and stow the firearms, "Can you put a piece of something like thin copper or al-u-min-i-um on the back to carry the current? You'd get full coverage that way."

"Al-u-min-i-um? Don't you mean aluminum?"

"Yes, that's what I said, al-u-min-i-um."

D.M. playfully punched the captain in the shoulder, "Fucking Aussie!"

"Hey, I resemble that remark!" He turned and punched the major back.

"Let me get back to the lab and tell Jake. Maybe that'll help him out... Thanks for your assistance. I'm sure with the smell of gun powder you're more than ready for Miss September."

Tige inhaled deeply trying to take in the last bit of odor from the gun powder, "Oh yeah, I'm ready now!"

D.M. took a deep breath, "Humm. Shame on me."

"What?"

"It seems to be having the same effect on me," he smiled.

Tige chuckled, "Kill it or fuck it!"

D.M. decided he better go make a quick visit to Frank. It was getting late and Jake could try Tige's idea tomorrow. He sat down next to Frank and rested his hand on the bed railing. "Hey Frankie. Just me, your brother... Look, I'm sorry I haven't come to see you much lately, but Jake and I are working on a new kind of armor. I wish we would have had it a long time ago; it might have saved you... I wish you would wake up, there's so much that you're missing. We just recently had a mission that annihilated quite a few gangs in Atlantic City. Jake's parents live there and the gangs took over their neighborhood. So we talked to the police and they got permission from the mayor for us to wipe them out... It was interesting; I never knew exactly what goes on in gangs. Some are of course worse than others. But the end result was his parents could still live in their home and we got some life fire target practice out of it." He sat in silence for a while more.

***

Cabbott sat in bed with a chess board on his tray table. Eagle had brought it down thinking he might find it enjoyable. She quickly realized that the captain was a master at strategy. He was just about to make a move when he stopped. Taking several sniffs in the air, he looked around, "Somebody's been to the range."

"What?"

"I smell gun powder. Someone in the nearby area has been shooting."

Eagle took several long sniffs, "I can't smell it."

"Sorry. Sniper training."

"Is there any sense that isn't extra keen on you?"

"I wouldn't consider my sense of taste to be all that great. MREs don't seem half bad."

"I've always been told that if you have a great sense of smell, you have a great sense of taste as well."

"Mmm, that doesn't seem to be the case with me."

She laughed lightly and prepared to make her move. Cabbott raised his finger, "Oh, I wouldn't do that. You'll just be setting yourself up for my Knight to get you."

"And why are you telling me this?"

"Well, I figure you'd like to use this as a learning experience, so if I just win, there would be no merit. If you see your errors, you may learn from them next time."

Eagle groaned, "Now you're sounding more like D.M. - he's always making everything a learning experience."

"I like his style, can't wait to meet him."

"Soon," she yawned, "You wanna pick this up another day?"

"Sure, I'm getting tired too."

She stood to leave, "Good night captain."

"Good night ma'am."

Eagle walked out of his room and down the short hall to the door. Quietly she slipped out. Just as she was closing the door, D.M. came out of Frank's room. She turned and was startled by him. "Hey, what are you doing down here?" He said as he came closer.

"Uh, nothing really."

"Nothing? What's behind the secure door?"

"Oh, just some doctors doing research. One of them asked my opinion on a new drug he's working on," she could smell the gun powder on his uniform, "Have you been at the range?"

"Yeah, Tige helped me test a new prototype piece of armor."

"How'd it do?" She walked toward the elevator.

"Just as good as the old stuff."

"Excellent. And when do you two plan on debuting the new armor?"

"Not sure, we still have quite a few challenges ahead of us." The elevator doors opened and they walked in.

"Well, I haven't received word on any missions coming down, so you and Jake spend as much time as you need to get it working. You've certainly impressed me with the other armor. It was good to only have minor injuries this last time out."

"Yeah, well I wouldn't have been one except I got so much blood on my face shield I couldn't see, that's why I had my helmet off."

"Maybe you should think to install windshield wipers!" She teased.

"Ha, ha, very funny." The doors opened and they headed down the hallway. Saying their goodnights, they went to their respective rooms.

CHAPTER THIRTY TWO

It was late October. The trees in the valley had turned for the fall. A cold wind blew from the north west occasionally bringing a few early snow flakes. The Pentagon made their decision and named General Spears their new commander. Eagle was glad that she had someone in charge who would take them seriously. The team had not been tasked with any missions in a few months and she was beginning to wonder if they'd been forgotten. D.M. and Jake worked tirelessly on creating the new armor. Tige and Sam practiced daily on shooting and spotting skills. Max usually hung out with them since Eagle had still not been able to get a replacement for Bruce.

Dr. Miles had been pressing her about Captain Westmoreland's last surgery. She knew the easiest way was to have the team gone for a few days that way there would be no questions about her being tied up on the medical floor for hours at a time. A four day pass to Reno should solve her dilemma. She decided to give them the news at dinner that night. Since it was Tuesday, they would have time to pack before the weekly transport arrived on Thursday morning. She would fly down and pick them up Sunday afternoon.

"Do I have to go?" D.M. said softly, "I'd rather stay here."

"No, you guys need to go kick up your heels. I know everyone has been working hard. A nice break should do you good."

"And why aren't you coming?"

"I have some things I need to get done here... And besides, this will be my little vacation from the lot of you."

"So this is 'mandatory fun' huh?" He grumbled.

"Yes, go enjoy it."

Late Thursday morning Cabbott sat in his room. He was anxious, yet apprehensive about the last surgery. His back hurt him every day, and he was hoping that surgery would remedy it. He knew that the recovery period was long and difficult, but it would be the only way he could possibly walk normal again. There were four vertebrae in his spine that were so damaged he could no longer even stand up straight. The surgeons at Walter Reed had placed several rods and screws in his back, but it was doing little good. The bones were so brittle that some of the screws had come loose. He prayed that the new technology would help and he could hopefully go back to his work.

Eagle scrubbed up and prepared to assist Dr. Miles. This was going to be a difficult surgery and James was going to need all the experienced help he could get. Captain Goldsmith had cast four replica vertebrae that were to be exchanged with Cabbott's destroyed ones. James figured the surgery would take at least nine hours to complete. Each of the new vertebra had a vertebral body and a neural arch that screwed on behind. This would facilitate the delicate positioning of the spinal column inside the new bone. The old vertebrae would be painstakingly cut at the arch to remove them. One slip and the captain might never walk again. Each new vertebra also had a disk made out of a tough fibrous plastic polymer. This would allow for shock absorption and movement to the spine. All the tendons and ligaments that attached to the vertebrae would have to be carefully reattached. As far as experimental surgeries went, this was as untested as ever.

Watching through the OR door, Eagle looked on as they positioned Cabbott on the OR table. While spinal surgery was not her specialty, she was educated enough to provide another set of skilled hands. Secretly she hoped for success. In all her visits to see Cabbott, she'd found him to be interesting and engaging in conversation. She enjoyed hearing his stories of going through Marine sniper school and all the crazy things they did to him because he was Army. His first kill. The last time he was home in Vermont, went skiing and nearly kissed a tree after the binding on one ski broke. For a man with so much death in his life, he was quite lively and personable.

"Ready Eagle?" James said through his surgical mask as he bumped the door open with his behind and entered, hands held bent at the elbows and still dripping wet. One of the surgical technicians gave him a sterile towel to dry his hands with. Eagle followed behind with her mask on, hands needing to be dried as well. When both were ready, they were helped into their surgical attire.

Eagle stepped near the anesthesiologist, "He still awake?"

"Yes ma'am, I'm still awake," came the groggy voice of the captain.

"I promise we'll take good care of you."

"Thank you...I just hope this works...I'm tired of the pain."

It was late the next morning when Eagle made her rounds to

see Frank and Cabbott. She found the captain in a specially designed bed, face down, staring at the floor. "Good morning captain. How are you feeling?"

Cabbott made no move to try and look up at her, "Comfortably numb at the moment ma'am. Dr. Miles did a neuro check on me after surgery. I had good responses in both legs and could feel anywhere he poked at me. Right now though, he's got a serious spinal block going. If he didn't, I'd probably be in excruciating pain."

Eagle sat down and partly slid under the bed so he could see her, "Ah, there you are! Is there anything I can get you?"

Cabbott groaned. He was quickly becoming bored of staring at the floor, but he wasn't sure he could get his arms freed up enough so he could use his laptop. "I can't say staring at the floor is very interesting, and I'm supposed to be in this position for the next three days. Something about helping reduce the pressure and swelling in my back."

"Give me a bit and maybe I can find something to keep you entertained."

"Thank you... And thank you for all you're doing for me."

Eagle searched around and found a small flat panel TV, extension cord and a long length of coaxial cable. She returned to his room to find him asleep. Quietly, she assembled the cable, disconnecting it from the TV on the wall and then attaching it to the one she had found. Within a few minutes, she had everything connected. Cabbott groaned and moved slightly. Eagle looked under the bed to see him looking back, "Did I wake you?"

"No ma'am. I can only cat nap for maybe half an hour at a time."

She pushed the TV under the bed, "I brought you some entertainment."

"Excellent, thank you."

Eagle pulled the remote out of her pocket and placed it in his hand, "Give it a try."

Cabbott worked his fingers over the remote. Finding the ON button, he turned the TV on and then found an interesting channel.

"You're pretty good with that, considering you can't even see the buttons."

"It's the same one as the one on the wall. Besides, having a great sense of touch is a plus in my line of work."

"Do you want me to see if I can find a DVD player? That way you can watch some movies?"

"I appreciate the offer, but I tend to fall asleep in the middle of most things. I just need something to keep my mind busy while I'm awake."

"All right. I need to get back to work. If there's anything you need, just let me or the staff know. We'll do our best to keep you comfortable."

Eagle stopped by James's office, "Hi, how are the nerve tissue cells doing?"

"Not bad. Not growing as fast as I would have hoped, but they are growing."

"When do you want to try and implant them?"

"Maybe in the next few weeks. I won't need your help for that, I can do it." James took a long drink of coffee, "How's Captain Westmoreland doing?"

"As he puts it: 'comfortably numb,' and bored... I found a flat panel TV and hooked it up for him, now he has some amusement if he wants."

"You always did have great bedside manner."

She leaned against the door post, "I hope this works out for him. He's such a nice guy. Even if we can't return him to full duty and he gets sent home, I can't say I didn't enjoy his company."

James wagged his finger, "Now, now, you know you're not supposed to get involved with your patients."

"I had no intention of that. But spending time with him has been certainly educational."

"How so?"

"I've learned to never play him at chess again!"

"Beat you good eh?"

"Obliterated me!" She laughed.

James chuckled and got up, "I guess I'll take my turn and go see him. You're right, even for a cold blooded killer he's a genuinely nice guy. His parents must have raised him right."

Jake sat at the hotel bar nursing a beer and intently watching as the bartender poured a layered rainbow cordial. It involved pouring the liqueur with the heaviest weight first, then carefully pouring each liqueur with lighter weights down a glass mixing rod until the lightest liqueur was last. He found the way each liqueur separated from the other fascinating. He didn't even notice a woman had sat down next to him. "You know why they separate like that don't you?" She said.

"Each liqueur has a different specific gravity. And because they are poured carefully, they tend to wanna separate," he answered back without looking at her.

"Very right."

Jake finally turned to look at her. She was fairly attractive, probably in her early thirties, her hair was long and dark brown, she had green eyes hiding behind black rimmed glasses. She looked to be of average height and was quite slender in her light gray business suit. "Hi, my name's Monica," she offered her hand. Jake took it and shook it gently.

"Jake Collins."

"Are you here for the convention?"

"Me? No. What convention?"

"The Science and Engineering convention."

"No way!" Jake ran his fingers through his hair, "Oh, I wonder if that's where my business partner wandered off to... Or he's just playing Blackjack again."

"And what do you do?" She asked.

"Strangely enough, we work together in chemical engineering, plastics mainly."

"Where'd you go to school?"

"He went to MIT; I'm just the 'child prodigy' as he calls me. The government currently owns us."

Monica ordered a drink and then leaned against the back of her bar stool, "You work for the government?"

"No, they just own us for a while. All our research is privately funded and we keep the profits of what we sell. What about you?"

"I work for a micro engineering firm in Houston," she pulled out a business card and handed it to him.

"You guys deal in nanotechnologies at all?"

"Sure, we're one of the biggest companies out there. Why? Is that your area of expertise?"

"Not really. I'm doing some work with them and I'm not having a lot of luck getting cooperation from the little buggers."

"What kind of work?"

"Trying to teach the damn things to change different colors when I want them to," he took the last few swallows of beer and sat the bottle down heavily.

Monica laughed lightly, "It's not as difficult as it may seem."

"Oh? Is this information on the open market?"

"It is," she smiled, "But if you buy me dinner, I'll let you in on it."

Jake knew he had to be careful. D.M. had warned him of "industrial spies" that would wine and dine someone just to get technological secrets out of them. As long as he said nothing further, he figured he was safe. And the information was on the market, if he just knew where to look. Monica wasn't hard on the eyes, and he wasn't one to pass up any kind of female company. "All right, you got a deal... I was waiting for some others from my group, but I think you'd be much more interesting to dine with."

"Won't they miss you?"

"Naw."

Tige grabbed Sam by the back of his shirt, "Hey, don't!" He whispered loudly over the noise of the crowded hallway. They were just rounding the corner to the bar.

"Why, what's the matter?" Sam replied as he swatted Tige's hand off.

"Look, Jake's got a lady friend. Best to leave him be mate."

"Don't you think he might wanna have dinner with us?"

Max flicked Sam in the back of the head, "No dumb ass, leave him alone. Can't you see he's working on a possible score?"

"All right, all right. What about D.M.?"

"He's off playing Blackjack. He'll eat when he's hungry," Tige said as he ushered the two through the bar and into the restaurant. Jake saw them out of the corner of his eye. He smiled slightly knowing that they were giving him his space.

"So captain, how are you feeling today?" Eagle said as she lay on her back on the floor looking up at him. Cabbott managed a weak smile. This was nearly the end of day three in the bed and he was more than looking forward to gazing out his window again.

"When are they going to flip me over? If I was a steak, I'd be burnt on this side...I'm just about to go out of my mind, TV or not, I've had enough."

"Dr. Miles will be in shortly. He had a few things to do and then he was going to round up several people to help flip you over."

"Oh thank you God!"

"Yeah, and then the fun begins: physical therapy."

"That's okay, I'll deal with that. I'm ready to get back to work."

She started to get up, "Do me a favor huh?"

"What?"

"I know you wanna get back to work, but don't overdo your therapy and make yourself worse. Dr. Miles isn't sure how many more surgeries you could take...If you can walk a little by Christmas, that's good... Don't expect any more from yourself."

"Yes ma'am."

Jake wandered into the lab and sat down next to D.M., "What 'cha work'in on maj?" Their four days in Reno were over and now they were more than motivated to work. Jake had taken the information that Monica told him and had quickly remedied the problem he was having getting the nanos to change color faster.

"New arm. I'm tired of fighting with this one. It's heavy, not very controllable, and I can build the outer skeleton with armor instead of fitting it on top," he replied as he affixed a plate of armor to the arm and carefully connected a small wire into the main matrix. Sitting back, he stretched and sighed deeply, "If I could only find a way to avoid having a cable connection. It's damned uncomfortable, the site tends to get irritated and itches sometimes, and I can't get dressed by myself which is the most annoying of all."

The lieutenant rested his arms on the counter and contemplated for a few minutes. He then picked up the laptop and perched it up on the tips of his fingers. D.M. watched him with curiosity and also hoped that he wouldn't drop and break it. "Tell me major, how is this computer connected to the Internet?"

"A wireless router," he paused for a few moments, "Yes, a wireless router!" He grabbed a pencil and paper and began to sketch out ideas, "Since it only needs to broadcast a few inches, there isn't much need for a big router. I could feasibly make one no larger than a fat credit card, place it next to my internal hard drive and then run a flexible antenna along the inside of the arm to pick up the signal. Brilliant!" He reached over and patted Jake on the shoulder, "Thanks for the intellectual kick-start."

"No problem. Glad I could be of some help," he smiled, enjoying seeing D.M. happy.

"I hope you don't mind, but I used some of the plastic with the nanos in it. I think I can program them to sync up with the rest of the armor and I'll blend together."

"Sounds cool. Maybe with your vast hard drive you can program a huge amount of colors and patterns in and then have them at your disposal at a moment's notice."

"I might not even need the control panel in the forearm then," D.M. replied rubbing his chin in concentration, "And with the wireless connection, the signal can be sent out and picked up by the matrix wires which will transmit it to the plates and scales."

"This is sounding like a fun project."

D.M. looked at Jake and smiled, "Hard to think that a few years ago you were a rebellious street punk. And now look at you, a budding young scientist."

"Rather scary isn't it?"

"Definitely."

"In truth, I never saw myself amounting to much of anything. I figured that when I got out of the Army, I'd go back home and pick up where I left off."

"And what are you thinking your plans are now?" D.M. said as he made a few more notations on his sketch.

"Now? Humm... Well, I'm happy here, so I think I'll stick around a while. Maybe I can find some online classes to take and work toward a degree in something more than just warfare."

"Why don't you try a few distance courses from MIT?"

"Are you nuts? Look at you; you're light years ahead of me. I don't think I'm smart enough for your Alma mater."

The major smiled, "Sure you are; you're plenty smart. You just have to practice a bit on your eccentricity and geekiness."

"Aw, do I have to be a geek?"

"No, eccentric will do just fine."

Jake playfully poked D.M. in the shoulder, "Naw, I can't see you as a geek, you're way too good looking to be one of them."

The major eyed him with suspicion, "Uh, what was that?"

"I meant you don't fit the profile of the standard geek."

"That's what I thought you said," D.M. said as he carefully attached another piece of armor to his new arm. He had just two more pieces to affix and the outer skeleton of the arm would be complete. The most difficult part was going to be programming all the movements for it.

"Anything I can do to help?" Jake asked as he watched.

"I'll need my USB splitter. I think it's in the drawer over there," he pointed to a desk. Jake went over and rummaged through the drawer until he found the cable. It allowed one USB cable to come from the port on his back and attach to his arm, to the new arm, and the laptop. That way he could use both hands to type on the keyboard and get the job done faster. As D.M. finished attaching the last plate of armor, he lifted the arm onto a framework that was bolted to the bench. This would allow it to be moved freely while it was being programmed and tested.

"All right, hook me up," the major said as he brought the cable from the new arm and passed it across the counter. He sat down and rested his arm on the counter while Jake disconnected it and then plugged in the splitter. Once both were connected he sat back down next to D.M. and watched with interest. He connected the last cable to the laptop and went to work. As he typed, the new arm started to move.

"How the hell are you doing that?" Jake asked, "How come

you can type with one arm, move the other and not cause conflicting signals from just one processor?"

D.M. smiled and laughed lightly, "I'm one of the few males that can multitask."

"I'm not buying that."

"Fine. If you pay attention, I type and then the new arm moves. Not simultaneously; close, but there is a time delay. I've partitioned my hard drive and have to switch back and forth to carry out the commands."

"Smart ass," Jake teased. D.M. quickly punched a few keys on the computer and the new arm bent up at the elbow, the hand closed and the middle finger extended. Jake chuckled.

"Let's see if I can do something new." D.M. typed for a few minutes and then clicked the mouse. He sat up and watched the new arm with anticipation. Within thirty seconds the arm began to change color. It slowly transitioned from the shiny dark gray to a bright red.

"Holy shit it works!" Jake exclaimed and gave D.M. a hearty pat on the back. He accessed the Internet and found a paint company that had color swatches on their website. Copying several to his hard drive he then went to a military page and found pictures of uniforms. He copied parts of the images and saved them as well. Next he went to a page with different kinds of foliage and copied more images. After, he sat back, rested his chin on his hand and had a long moment of thought.

"Now a new problem. If I don't wanna use a key pad to change the colors, how would I do it? The computer isn't smart enough to read my mind. There has to be some sort of code or designation I would use to make it change colors."

"Can you assign each color a name or number? I mean, you have your brain wired into that computer, so when you carry out a thought process, the computer interprets the signals and performs the movement. So if you give the colors names, then you should be able to think of the name and the computer will recognize that as a designation and perform the command."

"In theory, yes. Let's test that theory," he sat forward and went back to his typing. After a few more minutes he stopped and closed out the program he was working on, "Okay, let's see if this works." He closed his eyes and thought of one of the colors he'd assigned a name to. Slowly the arm began to change color. Jake sat quietly watching. His heart was pounding with excitement. He wanted to blurt out the color the arm was changing to, but he knew he better be quiet until the major opened his eyes to see if it worked. The suspense was driving him crazy. He watched as the arm turned the color of Marine Corps digital forest camouflage. The nanos were performing flawlessly.

Finally D.M. opened his eyes and gasped in awe as he saw the arm. "Yes!" He hollered at the top of his lungs, "Yes! Yes! Yes!" He laughed deeply. He turned to Jake and held his hand up in the air. The lieutenant reached up and slapped hands in a celebratory high-five.

D.M. walked down the hallway toward his lab ready to start another day of work. Captain Goldsmith caught him just as he reached the door, "Major, I have great news. With your help, I perfected the formula and now have a working prototype." He presented D.M. with a piece of the plastic. The major inspected it.

"Congrats. I knew you could do it," D.M. offered his hand.

The captain shook his hand, "I was talking to Dr. Miles and he mentioned that you have a very large amount of hardware in your shoulder."

D.M. reached up and touched his shoulder, "Yeah, got quite a bit... Every time it gets cold or the weather changes drastically I get horrible pains... Very little makes the pain tolerable...I'm not looking forward to winter again."

"If you could get rid of all that and have something put in that's twice the strength of bone and light weight would you?"

"In a heartbeat. Anything to lighten up this side of my body. It's unbalanced and is playing havoc on my back as well," The major replied as he straightened up and tried to align his spine.

"You do understand that you'll be a test subject."

"Captain, I'm a walking test subject. Just look at me," He raised his arm.

"Very true sir."

"And thinking about it, as long as they're going in to do some work, I have a few other things that need to be done as well."

"Excellent. I hope that the technology will help you out. And it seems only fitting that you benefit from the assistance that you gave me," the captain turned to leave, "Oh, when do you wanna get with Dr. Miles and have him measure you for the prosthesis?"

"I'm going down there this afternoon to see my brother. I'll get with him then. Once you have the measurements, how long before you'll have it ready?"

"About five days. I'll need to cut the molds and then get all the parts together and readied for surgical implantation."

"Good, that's about how long I'll need to finish building my upgrades."

A week later D.M. sat in a hospital bed awaiting surgery. He'd given Dr. Miles the wireless router to install and directions for making the connection. Captain Goldsmith finished the prosthesis and handed the sterilized package off to the surgical nurse. Eagle wandered in and stood at the foot of the major's bed, "You sure you wanna go through with this? None of it is proven technology."

"It has to get proven somehow."

"Well, yes, but..."

"But nothing, I'm going through with it," he sat up slightly, "I'm tired of the pain and trouble this is all causing."

"All right," she walked over to the side of his bed, "James needs me to scrub in and help him, you're gonna be a big job."

"I'm a big guy," D.M. smiled slightly.

Eagle leaned over and kissed him gently, "We'll take good care of you."

Three weeks later D.M. sat at his lab counter putting the finishing touches on his new robotic arm. Jake had to help him since the major could not wear his old arm because the surgical site needed time to heal and the new prosthetic bones needed to fuse with the remaining bones is his shoulder. It had been a frustrating and long three weeks, but now he could try out his new arm. Jake removed the arm from the framework and helped

D.M. into it. As soon as the arm was pulled up to his shoulder it started to work. He let out a wild whoop, "Hot damn! It works!" He reached down and buckled the straps across his chest.

"Well maj, how does it feel?"

"Fabulous! Much lighter and far more responsive." He put the arm through range of motion, "This is great. I wish I had this technology the first time around." Jake sat back and watched him. He hadn't seen the major this happy in a while.

"It was out there, you just never thought to use it."

"That's why science is an evolving field of study. You have to expand your mind and look for other ways of doing things."

"Hey, how about a color change test?"

"OK, what do you want?"

"How about one of those foliage patterns?" Jake said as he poked at the laptop.

"Lemme see what I can do," The major stood motionless for a few moments. Gradually the arm began to change several different colors. Within a minute D.M. looked like he had a palm frond draped across his arm.

"Bitch'in!" Jake exclaimed as he hopped off the lab stool and walked around him, "Color's good all the way around, no missing plates or scales. You have one hundred percent color saturation."

"Excellent," he checked his watch, "It's lunch time, let's go show the rest of the gang." He reverted the arm back to the normal shiny gray color of their armor. They hurried out of the lab and upstairs. Jake opened the door to the dining room and quickly took his seat. Eagle looked at him curiously.

"Is the major going to join us today?" She asked.

"Oh, definitely," he replied with a wide grin.

The door opened and D.M. walked in. The rest of the team gasped as they saw his new arm. "D.M., that's awesome!" Sam said as he put his glass down.

Eagle stood and walked around him inspecting the arm, "So this is what you've been working so long at."

"Yup...And watch this," he pulled the buckles loose, slipped his right shoulder out of the harness and dropped the arm to the floor. Eagle stepped behind him and put her hand where the cable connection used to be.

"How'd you do that?"

"That little fat credit card Dr. Miles installed was a wireless router. I have Jake to thank for that idea...Now I don't have to rely on anyone to help me get dressed." He picked up the arm and put it back on, "Ready for the really cool part?"

"There's more?" Eagle raised an eyebrow.

"Think of a color."

"All right, red."

The major stood motionless and closed his eyes. The arm slowly changed to red. The whole team broke out into wild cheers.

"Major, that's amazing!" She took hold of his arm and inspected it closely, "And this is from the nanos?"

"Jake finally figured out how to make them interface with my hard drive so I can control the color of the arm without the use of the key pad."

Eagle turned to Jake, "Lieutenant, I'm impressed. You've really put your mind to work on this project."

"Just wait until you guys see the third generation armor. It's almost finished." Jake boasted proudly.

"And when should we expect to see a demonstration?"

"Probably next week we'll have it ready. It's much better than the other stuff."

"I was impressed with the other armor. But this looks absolutely amazing," she said as she sat back down. The major took his seat and they ate, chatting with excitement over the new technology.

D.M. strolled through the door to Eagle's lab. She was sitting at her counter working intently on the computer. A bottle of red wine was opened next to her with two glasses. One was filled and she had been taking the occasional sip out of it.

"Good evening my love," he said as he gave her a quick peck on the cheek, "What have you got for me?"

"Well, after analyzing your blood and also taking some from Frank so I'd have a familial baseline, I think I might have worked out the correct amount of enzymes that will help you metabolize alcohol."

"Bring it on," he smiled.

She handed him two rather crudely pressed tablets and gave him the empty wine glass, "Go take these with some water first and then you'll have to wait a bit before you can try the wine."

"Okay." He went to the sink and poured a small amount of water into the glass. Looking at the tablets, he popped them in his mouth and followed it with the water. "They don't taste very good."

"I never said they would," she said with a little laugh. She checked her watch, "Let's give them about half an hour and then see if you get lucky."

He sat the glass down on the counter and wrapped his arms around her waist, "Humm, pills to get me lucky," he said, nuzzling her neck and playfully fondling one of her breasts.

"That's not what I meant." She tried to wiggle out of his grasp. The major held her tight, gently kissing her neck. She sighed, "Don't you have some work in your lab you could be doing right about now?"

"Nope, Jake's got a handle on the situation. I'm free and clear for the next few hours." He sensed she was not in the mood to play around. Letting his grasp slip, he stood and leaned against the counter, "So now what are you gonna do with your time since you've finally found your Mr. Right?"

"Oh, I have stuff to work on... Remember when you got beat up by Tige at China Lake?"

"How could I forget?" He groaned, rubbing his jaw.

"Remember I gave you that drug that helped you heal faster?"

"Yeah."

"Well, it's kind of been back to the drawing board on that one... After a few more human trials they found that the reaction rate was far higher than was expected...So I'm working with a couple of the other scientists here to see if we can make a kind that has a lot less reactions."

"Humm, I was fine. Guess I was a lucky one... Nobody died did they?"

"No. One was very serious though." She went back to working on the computer. D.M. pulled up a lab stool and sat down next to her. Patiently he watched and waited for the time to go by. He studied some of the data on her computer screen. Even though he was a Chemical Engineer, some of the elements she was reviewing were familiar to him. He wondered if any of his knowledge would help her on the problem.

Eagle looked down at her watch, "Okay, time's up," she poured him a glass of wine. Taking her own glass she held it up, "Well, here's to test number one. May there only be one!"

D.M. picked up his glass and gently touched it to hers. He took a sip. The wine was good but very dry, more so than he was used to. He hoped that this would be the solution to his problem. Tipping the glass to his lips, he drank the wine down fairly quickly. Setting his glass down, he watched as Eagle grabbed the bottle and poured him another glass, all without taking her eyes off the computer screen. "Show-off," he scoffed.

"What's that supposed to mean?"

"Yeah, just show off those womanly skills of multitasking."

"Ha,ha, you're just jealous that you can't do it," she smiled devilishly.

"You're right, actually I am." He leaned over and kissed her, tasting the wine on her lips. It took him a few minutes before he emptied the second glass. He was already feeling the effects of the drink.

"How are you feeling?" Eagle said after a few minutes.

"Got a nice buzz going," he said with a grin.

"How's your stomach?"

"Nothing so far. Maybe this worked." He played his finger around the rim of the glass.

"Need to give it some more time. As Tige would say that Rome wasn't bloody well built in a day." She continued typing. A few minutes later D.M. groaned. "Something wrong major?"

"Yeah, I think this test was a failure. I'm getting sick to my stomach and pretty uncomfortable."

"Damn! So much for that."

"Where's your bathroom?" He said, his voice showing signs of distress.

"Over there," she pointed to a slender white door.

He quickly got up and went into the bathroom, closing the door behind. Eagle could hear him vomiting. She rubbed her forehead in frustration. Now she would have to work on something different for the major. Perhaps it wasn't enough enzymes in the tablets? Maybe she would have to find another way to get them into his body? Pills? Injections? Transdermal patches? What was going to be the solution?

D.M. appeared after several minutes. She noticed he looked a bit pale, "Are you all right?"

"Yeah. I guess I got my hopes up too soon."

"I'll keep working on it. There has to be something out there that'll work. I'm sorry to put you through that."

He opened the door to leave, "It's all right. I'm the one who wants to be able to enjoy a few drinks once in a while. I hope you can figure it out... Although next time I'm going to bring my own booze...Red wine is not very good tasting when it comes back up."

"Sorry, it's all I had."

Jake lay flopped out on the couch in the lab. His thumbs frantically poking buttons on his cell phone as he texted Monica. He was waiting for the major so they could put the last finishing touches on the armor and hopefully show it to the team. D.M. walked in and saw him, "What are you up to?"

"Oh, just texting Monica. She's at work right now."

"You still got a thing going with her huh?"

"Yup," he smiled.

"Well, how about getting off your ass so we can get some work done? You wanna show off the new armor today right?"

"Yeah. I was just waiting on you there partner." He poked at the buttons a bit more and then tossed his phone on the table, "I told her I'd catch up with her later." He stood up and went to the metal framed mannequin that held his armor. Grabbing his slinky suit off the hook, he disappeared into the bathroom to get changed. After a few minutes he came out and started putting on his armor. D.M. worked on his own set, trying to get the rest of the armor to interface with his robotic arm and internal computer. He was hoping he could get it fixed and they could both show off their suits of armor together.

After twenty minutes of getting dressed, Jake stood next to

D.M. fully covered from the neck down in his new armor, "Well, what da ya think?"

"Looks good, how does it feel?"

"Humm, better than the old set. With the modifications you made, it's like I got a second skin on."

"Good. How about a color change?" The major said as he worked on the laptop trying to fix his interface problem.

"Any preference?"

"Whatever turns you on."

Jake opened the small panel on the inside of his left forearm. He carefully touched the screen and initiated a color change. Within thirty seconds the armor was hot pink in color.

"Barf! You trying to make me sick?!" D.M. exclaimed as he tried not to look at Jake. The lieutenant laughed and quickly changed colors to something more subtle.

"Okay, is that better?" He said as he turned around, his armor was now a pale blue, "How about a saturation check?"

D.M. stood and looked him over from top to bottom, "So far so good, how about putting your helmet on so we can make sure that works right?"

Jake grabbed his helmet and put it on. They used the same wireless technology the major had used for his robotic arm to make the helmet change colors without having to be hard-wired to the rest of the armor. "Yeah, that looks good too. Now how about a camouflage pattern?"

Jake accessed his control panel and found a pattern he liked. The armor changed to a desert pattern, "How's this?"

"Much better... How about changing to white and standing next to the wall?" D.M. said, half teasing.

Jake changed to white and stood by the wall, "I guess with exception of the face shield, you can't see me huh?"

The major glanced over, "Unfortunately you cast shadows, so I can see you. But, if I was someone looking for a specific target, I might just overlook you if you were standing still." He went back to typing, "How many colors did you load on your control panel?"

"Uh, I think there is somewhere near two hundred."

"Isn't that a little overboard?"

Jake reverted back to the normal gray armor, "Okay, okay, I

was having too much fun." He sat down next to D.M. and watched him work. It would take the major another hour and a half of work before he fixed his problem.

"Finally!" D.M. sighed and went to get dressed in his slinky suit. Checking his watch, he had almost an hour before dinner. That should be plenty of time to get dressed and have Jake check his armor over. He came out of the bathroom and went to his suit. Disconnecting the power cable that kept the nearly thirty small, flat rechargeable batteries that were hidden all over the armor charged; he began to get dressed. Jake sat back down on the couch and resumed his texting. D.M. got dressed and approached Jake for help with the last piece- an extra plate that covered his left shoulder more completely. The lieutenant affixed the plate and stood back, "Nice, very nice!"

"You're right, it's very comfortable, even with the extra weight from the batteries, you don't really notice it." He walked around getting a feel for the armor.

"Okay, your turn for a color change."

"Humm. I think something a bit more subtle than hot pink." He closed his eyes for a couple of seconds. The armor slowly changed to light gray.

"So unoriginal!" Jake scoffed. He walked around the major checking all the plates and scales for color saturation, "Looks good to me. Don't see any that aren't working."

"Excellent," he looked at the clock, "We got ten minutes until dinner. Perfect timing."

"This is gonna be so cool!"

They went upstairs and hid out in the briefing room until they were sure everyone else was in the dining room. D.M. was becoming the master of grand entrances. "All right, what color should we go in as?" The major said as he peered out the door.

"How about that really neat woodland pattern you found?"

"Sounds like a good choice," D.M. said as he made a conscious thought for color change. Jake opened his control panel and selected the pattern. In less than a minute both men were covered with an intricate woodland camouflage pattern. They put on their helmets and waited for them to change and match the rest of the armor.

"Ready?" D.M. said as he opened the door.

"Hell yeah!"

They walked down the hall and D.M. opened the door. Stepping inside, they stood together in front of the rest of the team.

"Holy shit!" Max exclaimed as he stood up. The others quickly got to their feet and rushed over to inspect the new armor.

"D.M., this is amazing!" Eagle gasped, "And I thought what you did with your arm was impressive."

"Thank Jake, the Chameleon Skin was his idea," D.M. replied

She turned to Jake, "Lieutenant, I think you've totally outdone yourself this time. You are to be commended on your efforts."

"Thank you ma'am."

Tige came over and smacked Jake on the shoulder, "Bloody fine job!"

D.M. leaned over to the lieutenant, "Change to matte black."

"Okay." He opened the control panel and found the correct code for the color. Both of their suits began to change and soon were a dull black. The rest of the team applauded.

"How long is the battery life on these things?" Max said as he ran his fingers over one of Jake's shoulder plates.

"If you don't run it continuously, you get twelve to fourteen hours. Otherwise, running it full time gets you about eight hours."

"That's a pretty good length of time. Hopefully our missions will only be that long. The more you're exposed in a hostile environment, the more chances you have of getting hit," Tige added.

CHAPTER THIRTY THREE

It was just before Thanksgiving dinner. Eagle burst through the door, grabbed D.M. by the back strap of his robotic arm and tugged at him roughly, "D.M., come quick!" She pulled hard enough the major felt like he was being lifted out of his chair. He'd been at the range part of the day and was still wearing his .45. His head was pounding with a headache and he just wanted to eat and go to bed.

"What?!" He growled.

"Come quick!" She pulled at him again. He got up, and in a flash, Eagle was out the door. He ran down the hallway after her. Finally he caught up to her as she frantically poked at the elevator button.

"What the hell is going on?" He barked.

"It's Frank, he's awake!"

The major took over poking at the button. A few moments later the doors opened and they hurried inside. "My God, he's finally coming to after all these months?"

"Yes. And..." she stopped short.

"And what?"

"And, uh, he seems to be doing well after all this time," she tried to make something up to cover her error. She couldn't say that Frank woke up after they had implanted some of Cabbott's spinal cells into his back. None of the team was to know the captain was there.

"Why does this not sound like you're telling me the truth?"

"All right, I know, I'm a lousy liar... But know that he had the best possible care."

"I'm well aware of that. What aren't you telling me?" He pressed.

"There was the opportunity to do a little experiment on him, and it worked. We don't know why, but he's awake now."

"And what was this 'little experiment'?"

"Ehhhhh, I can't say. Not right now at least. Not until we know he's stable and going to remain out of his coma."

"Will he ever walk again?"

"I don't know. That technology is still a bit out of our reach. I know what you've done with yourself is quite extraordinary, but I don't know if it would help him or not."

"I'll certainly do everything I can to help him," D.M. said as he slipped through the elevator doors as they opened and hurried down the hall. Eagle followed close behind. He burst through the door of the nurse's monitoring room and into his brother's room.

Frank was awake and watching television.

"Hey bro, nice to see you," Frank said with a raspy voice.

The major quickly embraced his brother, "You son of a bitch, you had me so worried that you'd never wake up."

Frank shook his head, "I don't know, but something strange woke me up."

"What do you mean?"

"I can't explain it. I just can't."

"Well, in time I'm sure you will... How does it feel to be back among the living?"

"Great, I'm starved!"

D.M. laughed loudly and hugged Frank again, "Yup, that's the old Frankie, always looking forward to his next meal!" He pulled a chair up and sat down. Eagle leaned against the door post watching them interact. She was happy that the surgery they had done on his back had mysteriously brought him out of the coma. Dr. Miles was completely at a loss for the outcome. The cells were supposed to help regenerate his spinal cord; instead, they somehow triggered Frank to finally wake up. She marveled at the circle of technology that made it all possible: D.M. had helped Captain Goldsmith, who intern created the artificial bone that helped Captain Westmoreland, who agreed to give up some of his spinal cord cells to Frank, who magically woke up after the implantation. This came full circle back to D.M. who was happy to have his brother back. Even though this was a happy moment, Eagle knew that it would probably not last. If Frank was unable to walk, his time at the base was limited. She wasn't banking on D.M. to come up with some technological miracle that would make him walk. Granted the major was a genius, there was only so much he could do with the current technology. She watched them for a few more moments, and then went back up to the dining room. As she entered, the rest of the team stood.

"What the heck was that?" Jake said as he took his seat.

"Frank's awake." The room broke into celebration.

"When did this happen?" Sam asked.

"Dr. Miles did an experimental surgery on him...Wasn't supposed to bring him out of the coma, but somehow it did."

"And he's talking and all?" Bruce inquired.

"Yes, he is."

"That's bloody fantastic. I know the major's happy," Tige added.

"He's beyond happy. Unfortunately it may not last. If Frank can't get back on his feet, he'll have to leave the team and the base," she poured a glass of water and gave her order to the chef. The team settled down and ate dinner. Eagle told them not to visit Frank for a day or so, giving him time to catch up with D.M. and come to terms with things.

Just as dinner was ending, D.M. came in. Immediately the men began firing questions at him. He did his best to politely answer, but he really just wanted to eat and go back down to spend time with Frank. Jake, Sam, Tige and Max hung back after dinner and talked with him. Bruce excused himself.

D.M. hurried back down to see Frank. As he opened the door to his room, he found Bruce standing next to the bed. He had just inserted a needle into Frank's IV and was preparing to attach a small syringe filled with some sort of clear liquid. Instinctively, D.M. pulled his .45 from his shoulder holster and pointed it at Bruce's head. "Just what the hell do you think you're doing?" He growled loudly.

"I'm just following orders."

"Orders from whom?"

"Westland told me to secure my position here at any cost."

"In case you haven't noticed, Westland is out of the picture. And for what reason do you need to kill my brother?"

Frank stirred, "Because it was Bruce that shot me."

"Is this true sergeant?" D.M. cocked the .45.

"I was just following orders."

"Then I order you to stand down," the major said firmly. Bruce made a move with the syringe. D.M. stepped forward, "Sergeant, I order you to stand down!" Just as Bruce connected the syringe, D.M. squeezed the trigger and put a round right between the sergeant's eyes. Blood and brain matter splattered against the wall, his body slumped to the floor.

"Holy shit! You killed him!" Frank gasped as he struggled to sit up in bed.

The major holstered his .45, "I wasn't gonna stand here and let him kill you. He hurt you once before and I wasn't gonna let it happen again."

Frank looked over at the body on the floor, "What are you going to tell Eagle?"

"The truth," he removed the syringe, setting it on a tray by the door.

"And how is she going to explain this to command?"

"Training accident."

It wasn't long before there were several nurses and Dr. Miles in the room, "All right major, what the hell just happened in here?"

"I caught Sergeant von Teufel just about to kill my brother," he picked up the syringe and handed it to the colonel.

"And how can you be sure that this is some sort of toxic substance?"

Frank butted in, "It must be, he was the one who shot me in the first place. He was hoping that I'd never wake up, but since I did, he needed to finish me off so his secret was safe."

Eagle looked at the toxicology report from the substance in the syringe, "He must have somehow gotten into the anesthesiology cart and swiped a vial of curare."

"That's some serious stuff," Sam said as he looked over her shoulder. Everyone had gathered in the dining room for a meeting.

"All right gentlemen, take your seats. We seem to have a dilemma on our hands."

"No dilemma, just a training accident," D.M. said flatly.

"Yeah, he got killed in a live fire exercise," Jake added. The others nodded in agreement.

"If that's the story we're going to use, everyone needs to stick to it," Eagle replied as she folded the report and tucked it in her pocket. "I'll notify command and have them come pick up the body."

"Good, the sooner that asshole is out of here, the happier I am," Max hissed.

"I know we've all have had a hard time dealing with Sergeant von Teufel, now in his absence I think we can relax a bit," she said, concern still tinting her voice.

"Funny. I never made the connection...His last name, von Teufel, is German for 'The Devil', shoulda figured with a name like that he'd be trouble," Max commented.

Cabbott sat in bed anxiously awaiting Eagle's visit. He'd heard the commotion earlier and knew something had gone on. No one who came to see him would tell him anything, not even Dr. Miles. It was nearly 2100 when Eagle finally stood in the doorway.

"All right, can you please tell me what the hell happened out there?" Cabbott said with agitation in his voice.

Eagle sat down and tried to think of a reasonable explanation, "Dr. Miles took the spinal cells that you graciously provided, carefully grew them, and when he had enough, he implanted them into Frank...We don't know how or why, but Frank woke up today."

"He did? Fantastic!" He smiled, "But that doesn't explain the gun shot I heard a while ago."

"Yeah, well, uh..." she stammered trying to think of something, "We've had a problem here for quite a while. Sergeant von Teufel managed to stay on by taking Frank out of the picture. He then proceeded to gather intelligence and use it against us. For months we all had to live a double life, telling him one thing and doing another. And when Frank woke up, he had the nerve to try and finish the job. Unfortunately for him, he ended up tangling with a very angry D.M. who put a .45 slug in his head."

"Gee, and I missed all the excitement," he replied unemotionally.

"Yes, well, since I've let you in on it, he died in a live fire exercise. Right?"

"Right. I don't have any problem with that."

"Thanks. How's your back feeling?"

"Decent. Got up and took a couple of steps. Feels good to stand up all the way for once."

"Sounds like you're making good progress."

"I got just about a month right?"

"Yes, but you do what you can. Don't push it too hard. I'd

rather have you start slowly than to have you up and running with the team and suffer a setback."

"I promise."

"Aw do we have to?" Max whined as he plopped down in his chair in the dining room for breakfast. It had been three days since D.M. had killed Bruce and command was coming to pick up the body later in the day.

"Yes, we have to put on a good show, remember we don't want them to think we did this on purpose," Eagle replied.

D.M. poured a cup of coffee, "And the sick part is that traitorous asshole will get buried with full military honors."

"Yeah, he doesn't deserve it, you're right," Sam added. The others nodded in agreement.

"So what's the plan?" Tige inquired.

"I have the paperwork done and Dr. Miles signed off as the provider on duty. A Black Hawk will show up about fifteen hundred. We will be wearing service dress and form a funeral detail to escort the transfer case to the helicopter. After he is loaded we will render proper military honors- even as much as he doesn't deserve it, I agree, but we must do this to help eliminate suspicion."

"We'll do as you wish," D.M. replied, "After, however; I think this should be cause for celebration."

"Just keep it together until after, then you can do as you want."

Jake sat his fork down, "Don't worry, we'll behave."

At 1500 sharp, an Army Black Hawk helicopter hovered above the hanger deck. The team stood inside the hanger waiting for it to land. An American flag draped the transfer case that held the body of Sergeant von Teufel. It sat on a gurney to make transport easier for his nearly three hundred pounds. As the rotors whined to a halt Eagle called the team to attention. Silently, they carried the body out to the open door of the helicopter. After placing it on the Black Hawk floor, they all stepped back five paces and rendered a sharp salute. The rotors began to spin slowly. Max fell out and returned with the duffel bag that contained the sergeant's personal effects. He handed it up to one of the crew.

The team marched back into the hanger and stood in formation until the helicopter lifted off and turned north. As it disappeared from view, Jake yanked off his beret and let out a loud whoop, "Par-ty!" He hollered. The others cheered. Eagle did not share in their joy, she still worried. She left the men as they headed to the rec room to celebrate. It was one of the few common areas that alcohol was allowed. Most of the time booze was served in a controlled situation. It was well known that sufferers of PTSD commonly self medicated with alcohol, so Eagle made sure there was never enough around that they could get themselves into trouble. A few beers here and there and sometimes wine with dinner was about all they were allowed.

Poking the elevator button, she thought it was time to help Cabbott become part of the team. With less than a month until Christmas, it was time to get him a uniform. The doors opened and she stepped in, turning to make sure no one was going to join her. Reaching the medical floor, she quickly entered the code to the secure side. The door opened and she strolled in. She rounded the corner to his room. "Good afternoon Captain, you look like you're in good spirits today," Eagle said as she leaned against the door post of Cabbott's room.

"Indeed I am... I stood and took a few more steps this morning."

"Fantastic! Do you think you'll be able to manage a few more in the next month?"

"Certainly," Cabbott smiled, "Was that Black Hawk the hearse to take away Sergeant von Teufel?"

"Yes it was... Since you'll be one of us soon, we should probably work on getting you fitted for a uniform... I think right now we'll keep it simple and get you some duty grays, or as the fellas call them 'dirty grays' because they usually come back from training exercises all covered in dirt, mud and blood."

"Blood?"

"They work hard, they train hard. Occasionally there is a bit of blood spilled. Most of the time it's nothing serious though." She pulled a small notebook out of her pocket, "Do you happen to know your measurements, or should I send the tailor to see you?"

Cabbott motioned for her to give him the notebook. Taking a pen off his table, he neatly wrote down his uniform sizes and handed it back to her, "That should be pretty close to right. Although I'm not quite in the shape I was."

"Well captain, I'm sure this is a good place to start... I'll go see if we have everything and bring them back for you to try on. If everything fits, I'll have your name and rank put on and you'll be ready for Christmas."

"Thank you ma'am. I must admit, I'm looking forward to being part of the team. From everything you've told me, they sound like an outstanding group."

"That they are captain. That they are."

Eagle went by clothing issue and gathered all the necessary items for Cabbott. She returned to find him sitting on the edge of his bed, "All right captain, give these a try. They should fit almost like ACUs." She laid them on the bed next to him.

"Thank you ma'am," he took the shirt and held it up, "Looks like it should fit."

Eagle leaned in and grabbed the door and went to close it, "I'll leave you to get changed." She closed the door and went to check on Frank. He was watching TV.

"How are you feeling?"

"Better," he turned off the TV, "Hey, Jake was telling me that one of the guys in Security Control is getting ready to retire... I may not be so handy with computers, but I'm willing to learn...And it's a sit down kind of job and all..."

"You really wanna stay here huh?"

"Yes ma'am, I do. I don't have anything to go back to, the Corps was my life...And now the Dragonslayers is my life... I serve my country, that's what I do... I'm not bright enough to be a scientist like D.M.; I only know how to be a soldier."

"And that's a most noble calling. I'll see what I can do. No promises."

"Thank you," he replied softly.

She turned to leave, "Take care Frank." She walked down the

hall and back into the secure side again. Knocking lightly on Cabbott's door she heard him say to come in. Opening the door she found him standing, leaning heavily on a cane.

"I think I can consider getting dressed my physical therapy session for the day," he joked, "I'm exhausted!"

"And when was the last time you put on a uniform?"

"More than a year ago. Since then it's been hospital gowns and pajamas."

"I think that's a good fit, what do you think?" Eagle said as she walked around him.

"Yes ma'am, feels comfortable."

"Good, then I'll take them back and get them finished up…Oh, what do you want on your name tapes? I didn't realize it until I looked at your personnel record that you have a hyphenated last name."

"Oh, just put Westmoreland on them. My mom was being pushy and decided her last name, Smythe, just had to go in there as well. My father's side is well known in the legal community, I'm happier with his last name…You can leave the boots here. If you can get me some polish, I'll get them shined right up. Don't have much else to do; they'll give me something to occupy my time. There are only so many targets I can pick out in the valley."

"Certainly," she turned to leave, "I'll bring you some polish and pick up the uniform...It will be nice when you can be with the team."

"I look forward to their company- not that yours isn't pleasant, but I wanna get to know them also."

Eagle laughed lightly, "Sorry, I don't do 'guy talk' very well."

"Anybody up there play chess better than you?" He teased.

"I'm sure the major would take up the challenge, I've never played him but Tige says he's brutal."

"Good, a worthy adversary."

Eagle sat at her desk doing some paperwork. It was one of the most boring Monday mornings she had had in a while. Snow was falling hard outside. The winter seemed to drag on, starting earlier than normal. There had been no missions for the team and they were restless. All the training had just made them thirsty for some action. The phone rang and she answered it, "Colonel Tryggvesson, Yes general, good afternoon sir... Snowing like crazy right now... Oh, probably three feet on the ground from the best I can tell... A what? Working vacation? Exactly what will that entail?... Yes, I think we can...five days? I'm sure they'll appreciate the change... Yes sir, if we get a break in the weather we can probably be up and out of here in less than eight hours... Yes sir, you too... goodbye." She hung up and looked at her watch. The team was due for lunch shortly; she would break the news to them then. Eagle left her office and walked next door to the dining room. D.M. was standing, looking out the window.

"Just think of it as fluffy white sand," she said as she stood next to him.

"Sorry, not buying it," he grumbled. He was tired of being cooped up in the building.

"Well, then a change of pace should suit you."

He perked up, "Oh, we got a mission?"

"Well, sort of. You like being the bad guy?"

"I wear a black beret don't I?" He smiled.

Eagle sat down at the table, D.M. joined her. Several minutes later the rest of the team arrived. She waited until they had ordered lunch, "All right gentlemen, I got a call from the general today. He has a little job for us." There were several cheers from the group. "I can't say it's a glorious task, but at least we'll be out of the building and out of the snow for a few days."

"What's the gig?" Jake said.

"We'll load up the C-130 and take the Badgers down to Twenty Nine Palms to play aggressors for the Marine Cobra pilots."

D.M. groaned.

"Hey, it's better than a kick in the pants," Tige added.

Jake drummed his hands on the table, "Awesome, this is gonna be fun!"

"For you maybe. I'm the one who has to fly with you," the major protested.

"When do we leave?" Jake asked with anticipation.

"After lunch I'll see if the C-130 can come up here. The snow's pretty bad; they may not be able to make it. And the maintainers will have to get out and clear the runway and dig out the Badger hangers as well... If, and that's a big *if*, we can, I'd like to be out of here by twenty hundred."

"That's a tall order," Sam said.

"Yes it is. Let's hope the snow lets up so we can get out of here."

It was nearly twenty two hundred hours before the team was able to leave the base. The storm had finally subsided and they could load up their equipment and head out. Eagle made a quick stop by Cabbott's room and told him they would be gone for a few days. Jake made sure the appropriate tool boxes and parts carts were loaded. Only three maintainers were going to fly down with the team. The lieutenant happily assumed the main burden of maintenance upon himself. He loved the helicopters and working on them just made his relationship with them closer. The more he knew about each copter, the better he could fine tune the machines for maximum performance. Jake had even devised special covers for the rotor mounts and intakes to prevent sand and debris from fouling them while they were on the ground in field conditions.

The team arrived at Twenty Nine Palms several hours later. The desert was cold and dark. They found the tents that had been put up for them and quickly moved in. Jake took care of the Badgers, making sure they were all covered for the night. They turned in for a short night's sleep.

Early the next morning, Eagle met with the marine commander and discussed the rules of engagement. As aggressors their rules were simple: there weren't many. The goal was to teach the Cobra pilots to think and maneuver in a combat situation. She returned to the team, who were trying their best to eat MREs for breakfast.

"Oh God do I miss the cook!" Max whined.

"Got that right," Sam added as he choked on some "scrambled" eggs.

"Sorry gentlemen, I'll see what I can do to get better chow,"

Eagle said as she fought to open her heavy plastic package with her meal inside. D.M. whipped out his knife and offered it to her. "Thanks," she cut the top open, handed him back his knife and looked inside. The packets and little brown cardboard boxes looked very unappetizing. Dumping them out on the table she picked up one of the boxes, "Denver omelet? You've got to be kidding."

"Hey ma'am, I highly recommend dumping your Tabasco sauce on it, it'll give it some flavor," Tige said as he held up the tiny bottle of hot sauce that routinely came with the meals.

"Thank you captain, I might just have to try that."

After breakfast, the team preflighted the Badgers and Eagle went over the topographical map with them. They took to the air and flew to their assigned loiter area. Eagle and Max flew their helicopters with the front seat empty. All gun controls had been switched to the rear cockpit so they could fly and fight with the others. It wouldn't be easy for them, but they needed all available helicopters to run the scenarios. The Marines planned on sending up six Cobras at a time against the four Badgers. She knew having Jake at the controls was a force multiplier. His talent in the helicopter was to be feared.

"All right boys, split up and let's make this as difficult as possible," she banked right and disappeared over a small hill. The others found similar hiding places. Jake remained out in the open.

"We're gonna play tethered goat. I wanna see what these Jar Heads have to offer."

"Fine, do what you want," she called.

D.M. picked up the six Cobras on radar, "Here they come." He made sure the straps on his harness was tight. Flying with the lieutenant was a gut wrenching experience. "Weapons on line, just waiting for you." The Cobras came into view. "Uh, we got a lock on us."

"Yeah, yeah, I hear it," he yanked up on the stick and banked hard to the left. The Badger smoothly performed the maneuver. "Come on baby, let's give 'em the slip." Pushing the throttle forward he shot past where Tige and Sam were hiding.

"You want us to get one?" Tige said over the intercom.

"Yeah, pick the one off that's on my six. I'll be back around and take on another," Jake replied as he maneuvered between the small hills on the range. Tige managed an easy shot on the passing Cobra. They immediately broke off and returned to base to try again later. Tige popped over the hill and saw one coming right at them. "Bugger!" He hollered and rolled hard to the left. Max was tied up with his own battle and couldn't help. Eagle had engaged a target as well.

Jake spun around and quickly got radar lock, "Gimme the Mongoose on line," he called.

D.M. selected the missile, "Okay, you got it."

"Get your shot lined up maj."

"Getting tone, lock, fire!" He pushed the button.

"Another one bites the dust!" Jake hollered as he yanked up on the stick and brought the helicopter around. Eagle had managed to take out the Cobra that was stalking her. Max was having difficulty getting angle to attack. "Hey Bull Dog? You want some help?"

"Yes please!"

"On my way." He pushed the throttle forward and charged headlong toward the advancing Cobra. "Hey buddy, wanna play a little chicken?" Jake lined up on them. "Go to guns. You take them."

"Right. Targeting," D.M. fought to get a lock. Just as he was preparing to take the shot, the Cobra pulled up and tried frantically to evade. Jake yanked up on the stick and sent them into a belly-to-belly climb.

"Now hang on, this is where it gets fun," he pushed the stick over to the right and let the nose fall toward the sand. As the nose pointed down he stomped hard on the left rudder and brought the Badger around so it was right behind the retreating Cobra. D.M. got a lock and fired. They watched as it flew about half a mile away and hovered low as if to observe the rest of the battle. Jake saw Eagle was having trouble, "Hang on White Feather, the cavalry's coming!" Rolling the Badger nearly upside down he engaged the target from above and easily got another kill.

"Thanks Kingpin, good flying."

Tige and Max ganged up and shot down the last Cobra, "Right

all, that's six up and six down. Let's head for home," Tige said as he brought the Badger around and met up with the others.

"Gee, that was fun, can we do that again?" Jake teased as he banked left and right in a smooth slalom pattern.

"Knock it off Jake, I've had enough for now," D.M. said as he could feel his stomach threaten.

They landed and climbed out. D.M. dropped to the ground and took a knee; never before had he been so air sick. Flying with Jake was a real challenge. In all his years as a fighter pilot, the major never had a problem with air sickness. Every time he went up with the lieutenant his stomach flipped and protested. Jake hopped down and put his hand on the major's shoulder, "Hey, you okay?" D.M. belched, hoping that it wasn't going to be something worse. He knew he probably shouldn't have eaten so much for breakfast, and now it was haunting him. He groaned.

"That MRE turn your stomach?"

"No, you did."

Jake laughed and walked off to get his tool cabinet. Eagle came past and saw D.M. kneeling, "Major?" He looked up at her. "Oh my, I've never seen you this green at the gills before. What happened?"

"I made the mistake of eating breakfast and then flying with that maniac."

"Perhaps we should send him up as a solo and you can partner with Max."

"I'm almost tempted with the offer. We're a team though and I have to stick with him no matter what."

"The offer stands if you want."

"Thanks, I'll keep that in mind." He struggled to his feet and headed back to the tent to lie down.

Jake balanced precariously on the upper housing of the engine intake. He had pulled the panel just below the rotor mount open and was leaning inside making some adjustments. A Marine major stormed through their camp and stopped at a picnic table where the rest of the group was being debriefed by Eagle. He stopped, saluted and addressed her, "Where is the crazy bastard who shot down three of my best pilots?" All fingers pointed to Jake, who had his back turned to the group. "You're joking right? No helicopter mechanic can do that."

D.M. smiled, "He can, and he can do it all day."

The major stomped by and stopped at the helicopter Jake was working on, "You! Wrench turner, did you shoot down three of my best pilots?"

Jake turned part way. He managed a rough salute while still holding a wrench, "Yes sir, I did."

"And where did you get your training?"

Jake laughed lightly, "Army training sir!"

"I doubt that. And why are you turning a wrench? Don't you Special Forces people have crews for that?"

"Yes sir, we do," he stroked the engine housing lovingly, "But I like doing this and it makes me feel so much closer to her." He playfully leaned down and kissed the housing. The major huffed and turned to leave. "Sir? If those were three of your best, you might not wanna bother sending up any more, they'll just be easy cannon fodder for me."

The major stomped off. As he passed the rest of the group he could hear stifled chuckles coming from them. Eagle did her best to quiet them but their laughter grew louder.

The afternoon sortie's outcome was much the same as the morning. The Marines fielded several new pilots in an attempt to beat Jake. Each time he sent them packing back to base in defeat. D.M. quickly learned that if he ate a small meal and took some motion sickness pills he wouldn't feel so bad when flying with Jake. The adrenaline was more than enough to shake off the drowsy effects of the pills and he could keep his head in the game. With his skill at targeting and Jake's skill at flying they were nearly unstoppable.

It was the morning sortie on the third and final day. Jake and

D.M. found themselves up against three Cobras at once. The Marines had figured out who was the hot shot pilot and made a joint effort to take them out. Jake frantically maneuvered to get out of their radar locks. The Badger creaked with the great G load the lieutenant was putting on it. "Jake if you're not careful, you're gonna fly the rotor right off this thing!" D.M. hollered as he fought to get a lock on a Cobra.

"She's fine, just keep shooting," he called back as he dove toward the ground. Another Cobra was hot on his tail. Pulling up hard on the stick and rolling to the right he looked over his shoulder to see the Cobra still in a dive. "Pull up you stupid Jar Head, pull up!" A moment later the Cobra slammed into the desert floor and burst into a ball of fire. Jake opened up an emergency channel, "Mayday, mayday, we have a Cobra down!" He spun around and hovered a few hundred feet from the burning craft. "I didn't see anyone get out did you?"

"Negative," D.M. replied.

"Son of a bitch."

The rest of the helicopters broke off their engagements and hovered near the crash site. A few minutes later an HH-64 Jolly Green Giant helicopter flew in and landed. Jake watched as the rescue crew got out with fire extinguishers tried to put out the fire. The other helicopters returned to base. "Come on Jake, let's go back. There's gonna be a lot of questions we're gonna have to answer," D.M. said as he turned off the weapons panel. They returned to their base and landed. Jake climbed out and stood looking out into the distance. He felt a bit shaken by the crash of the Cobra and the loss of the two crewmen. D.M. climbed out and stood next to him, "Hey, you gonna be okay?"

"Yeah... I feel really bad that happened."

"I do too... At least they died doing something they loved."

"That's not much of a consolation to me." Jake said as he walked off.

"Two good Marines died out there today. What do you have to say for yourself?" The Marine major said to Jake as he stood over him. D.M. sat next to the lieutenant at the accident investigation board.

"Sir, I was just doing my job. We were brought here to be aggressors and that's what I was doing. I'm sorry those men died. I don't know why they didn't pull up. I was about five hundred feet from the deck when I pulled up."

"Major, what is your input on the situation?"

"The lieutenant is an extremely capable pilot. He knows the exact limits of the craft he's flying. My best guess is maybe the Cobra pilots didn't know they wouldn't be able to pull out of a dive that deep and that fast," he paused, "Or maybe they suffered a mechanical failure of some sort."

"All right gentlemen, that's all the questions I have. The remaining sortie has been canceled. Your team may return home. If necessary, we will contact you for further questioning."

The team loaded up and returned home late Thursday night. The maintainers had cleared the snow off the runway and the hanger doors. Another storm was forecast to hit Friday morning so they wanted to get home and all the helicopters and equipment put away before the storm enveloped the valley again. They quickly got the Badgers situated in their hangers and took their gear upstairs. Little was said, they all felt bad about what happened to the two Marines.

It was a lazy Saturday morning. Eagle had informed the team they would have the luxury of sleeping in and doing what they wanted for the day. A powerful storm raged outside dumping snow by the foot. The team wasn't going anywhere fast. D.M. had decided he wanted to spend the night with Eagle. Not because he was having his usual nightmares, but because he just wanted to have some private time with her. They lay in bed together watching the news. Eagle was curled up against him with her head resting on his right shoulder. He had his arm around her. The weather report came on and they both watched with interest.

"Good heavens, it's ten below and it's colder here and we have more snow than Alaska," she said as she rubbed his chest.

"Supposed to be the worst winter in a hundred years."

"Getting supplies in could be a problem. There are nearly three hundred mouths to feed on this base."

"I would say if needed, we could keep the hanger deck clear and the Army could send up Chinooks and drop supplies to us," he said as he played with her hair.

She wiggled herself out of his grasp and crawled up on his chest, "That might be a very real option," she leaned down and kissed him and then continued to move to the left until she was lying on the other side of him. Gently, she ran her hand over the fresh scars from his recent surgery, "How's your shoulder?"

"Much better now that there's only a little metal in it. Haven't had any pain yet. And this kind of weather really would make it hurt."

"Good. I'm happy to see that Captain Goldsmith could help you out."

"I didn't mind helping him out. I remember I was in his shoes once."

Eagle played her fingers over his tattoo. He looked down at her, "Are you still upset that I got that?"

"No, I'm not," she leaned down and kissed it. Rolling over, she got out of bed and disappeared into the bathroom. A few minutes later she returned and stood by the bed, "You wanna get a shower and then some breakfast?"

D.M. smiled, "Sure, you gonna wash me again?"

"Oh, I think I can manage that," she grinned.

After breakfast, D.M. caught up with Jake and they went down to the lab to work. Eagle figured it would be a good time to visit Cabbott. As she stepped out of the elevator, she was nearly run over by Frank in a wheelchair. "Morning!" He said as he skidded to a stop a few feet from her.

"Well, Frank, good to see you out of bed. How are you feeling?"

"Not too bad. I just finished my physical therapy session."

"Good... I inquired about the Security Control job. I'm just waiting to hear back."

"Thanks, I really appreciate it," he rolled past her and back into his room. Eagle continued down the hall and into the secure side. She found Cabbott in bed, a heating pad wrapped around his right knee and an IV running once again.

"Captain?"

He groaned, "I know how the major felt. This is horrible! Nothing makes the pain go away- not even the morphine."

She walked over to his bed and put her hand on his shoulder, "I used to have some herbs that I made into a poultice and would apply it to D.M.'s shoulder when he was really bad. Unfortunately I don't have any more. And the only way to get more is to go home to Norway and pick them myself."

"I talked to Dr. Miles this morning. None of the other hardware is bothering me, just my knee. He's thinking of doing up a plastic knee and performing another total knee replacement on me."

"That sounds a bit risky."

"I'm willing to take the risk... The last couple of weeks I've been mostly pain free. That massive storm changed that... I don't think I could go on living here and have to put up with pain like that."

"When do you plan to have it done?"

"As soon as Dr. Miles can get everything together...How'd the aggressor sorties go?"

Eagle sat down, "It was going well for us. I think the Marines are sorry they took us on. Jake shot down anything that had USMC stenciled on the side of it...There was an unfortunate accident. One of the Cobras chasing Jake and D.M. didn't pull out of a steep dive and slammed into the desert...They lost two."

"Sorry to hear that."

"They still aren't sure if it was pilot error or something mechanical."

"Accidents happen," Cabbott replied as he shifted his position in bed slightly.

CHAPTER THIRTY FOUR

It was December thirteenth, just three days before D.M.'s birthday. A powerful force nagged at him. He could not put the thought out of his mind. He needed to meet his real father. The Thursday morning transport would be landing shortly. He stood in the basement hanger waiting for it. He had dressed as warm as he could: jeans, a heavy long sleeve shirt and his leather motorcycle jacket. It was 0500; the team would not be meeting for another hour. He had filled out his leave request on the computer and left Eagle a note in her lab. D.M. took the four pages that showed his DNA lineage to the King of Spain. Perhaps this would be enough proof, but maybe not. And he risked being caught and thrown in jail, but it was a risk he was willing to take.

The doors above opened and he was lifted into the cold dark morning air. A thick blanket of snow covered the valley. Crews had been out earlier to clear the runway so the C-130 could land. He hurried up the back ramp and found a seat near the front. He shoved his suitcase under it. The plane off loaded and soon they were back in the air. The flight seemed to take forever before they touched down at Reno airport. Quickly, D.M. disembarked and called for a cab. He needed to hurry; the first flight out that would get him to Denver was due to leave in an hour. From there he would catch another flight to Newark, New Jersey where he would make his final connection to Madrid. It was going to be a long day, and he hoped the TSA guards at the Reno terminal wouldn't give him a hard time about carrying a gun on board.

Luck would have it that the security guard on duty recognized him from a previous flight and the major was able to get through security easily. He sat down in his first class seat and looked out the window. Was he out of his mind? After doing several days of research, he had a plan. But would it work? There was just no way of telling until he got there, and that was nearly a day away.

0615, Eagle and the others gathered for breakfast. She looked at the empty chair to her right, "Anyone seen the major?" They shook their heads. "Jake, do you think he's still in the lab?"

"No ma'am, he came up with me last night and said he was going to give it a rest for a couple of days...You want me to check his room?"

"Yes, would you?"

Jake got up and went out. A few minutes later he returned, "He's not in his room, and his .45 and holster are missing."

"Are you sure?"

"Yes, he always keeps it on the table next to his bed."

Eagle stood and went to the window. It was still dark, the sun just starting to make its appearance in the eastern sky, "Come on Jake, let's go check the lab." They went down to the research floor and Jake opened the door. They entered to find the lab quiet, no sign of the major.

The lieutenant pulled out his cell phone and dialed D.M.'s number, "It went straight to voice mail, he must have it turned off."

Eagle rubbed her forehead, "Oh, this is not good...He didn't say anything out of the ordinary to you last night did he?"

"Not that I can think of. He was more quiet than normal, something was on his mind. You know how he gets."

"I wonder if he said something to Frank..." she said as she opened the door and headed for the elevator. Jake followed, just as confused as Eagle. They found Frank eating breakfast. He told them D.M. had said nothing to him, but it was obvious that something was on his mind. Eagle instructed Jake to get the others and search through the building. She went to her office and called the Air Guard station in Reno. She spoke to the pilot of the morning transport who confirmed that the major had gotten on. After they landed, he had hurried off, called a cab and disappeared. Eagle hung up and sat with her head in her hands, "Oh D.M., what the hell are you up to?"

***

It was 0700 Friday morning when the Iberian Air 747 landed in Madrid. D.M. yawned and looked out the window. The pilot announced the local time and the major reset his watch. He patiently waited until the person next to him had stood and filed out. With stiff legs, D.M. stood, smacking his head on the overhead luggage compartment. He groaned and rubbed his head. Carefully, he inched his way out into the aisle and headed for the door. Once in the terminal he located baggage claim. Slowly he wandered through the airport. Though fuzzy-headed with travel, D.M. felt happy to be back in Spain. Just hearing everyone speaking made him feel at home. The sights, smells and sounds, yes, it was good to be home again.

Collecting his bag off the carousel, D.M. made his way outside and hailed a cab. He told the driver to take him to a hotel he had booked on the Internet. It was within short driving distance of the palace at El Pardo. He would check in, get a shower, order some food and then take a nice long nap. That evening he would scout out the palace, looking for a way to make a quiet entrance. Then he would try to get some sleep.

The wall didn't seem too high and there wasn't any barbed wire or other deterrents on top that he could see. D.M. pulled out a small map he had drawn of the palace complex. Intel about the daily life of the King was sparse; it seemed that no one felt it too important other than to list his main speaking engagements, or they were not saying anything due to security reasons. He made his best guesses as to where the King would be found. Leaning against the wall, he rubbed his head in frustration. There had to be a better way. It was only 2000 and a few people walked about the streets in the cool evening air. He wandered down the length of the wall until he reached one of the gates. He stopped and read the sign. Here was something promising; the palace offered daily tours of the main house and gardens. Yes! D.M. thought, the easiest and most obvious way to gain access was by a tour group. He took out a pen and jotted down the tour times. If he played his cards right, he could ask some simple questions, nothing too out of the ordinary, but useful. Then he could devise his plan.

"Still no word from him?" Eagle asked Jake.

"I got nothing. He must have his phone off."

"Yeah, I got the same response," she sat down at her desk, "I don't wanna make this phone call."

"Can't you give him a day or so?"

"I'm really not supposed to. If he's AWOL then I have to report it."

Jake shook his head, "I know him well enough that he wouldn't dream of doing something that stupid. He's a 'by the letter' kind of guy."

"I know and that's what makes it even stranger. He can be secretive but he's never done anything this crazy before," she tossed the phone back on the desk, "I'll probably get in a lot of trouble for this, but I'll give him two days."

"I'm sure he'll turn up."

D.M. sat up in bed and stretched. It was time to go to work. The tour he had taken earlier in the day had proven most helpful. He was especially lucky because the King had come out of the main house and gotten into a car and left, so the major was able to get a good look at him. He was an older man probably in his late seventies, tall and broad with gray hair and plenty of wrinkles. D.M. waited outside the palace for quite a few hours to make sure the King returned. It would have been a wasted trip had the King left on some sort of diplomatic trip or function and not returned to the palace that night.

The major showered, shaved and dressed. He wore his most comfortable black suit, a black tie and he had even found a black shirt at a local store. He smiled as he fixed his tie; this was the classiest camouflage he'd ever worn. You didn't meet royalty dressed in black jammies, especially when it was your father you were meeting for the first time. He took out the pages with the DNA results and carefully removed a tattered picture of his mother from his wallet. Running his fingers over the photo, he smiled at the beautiful woman she had been. Folding the pages, he tucked them in the inside pocket of his coat. The photo was carefully placed next to them. Checking his watch, D.M. knew he had about half an hour. His stomach fluttered with butterflies. He paced around the small room trying to get his composure. Words flew through his head. What to say? How to say it? And what happened if it all failed?

Grabbing the key to his room and his cell phone, D.M. closed the door and headed down the hall. The closest hotel he could book was about eight kilometers from the palace so he had to get a rental car and drive up to the small town where the palace was. It was an easy drive of maybe ten minutes, still not enough time for the major to get his thoughts together. He was nervous, very nervous.

Stepping out onto the street he surveyed the surroundings. A few people were walking on sidewalks, but El Pardo was a quiet town so he knew anything out of the ordinary might be noticed. Quietly he wandered down the street and turned down another that led to a back wall of the palace. The street was empty, not even a car or person was about. As he stopped near his entry point at the wall, he pulled out his phone and made sure it was turned off. The last thing he needed was to have someone call while he was trying to be stealthy. After stashing the phone back in his pocket, D.M. looked up at the wall, "You crazy bastard, this is one birthday you won't forget." He walked a few feet further and found the tree he planned to climb.

Hefting himself onto the first branch, D.M. climbed until he was level with the wall. Peering over, he saw the garden was dimly lit and there appeared to be no guards about. During his tour that morning, he had not noticed any sensors or even cameras anywhere in the palace or the grounds. The Royal family must be very trusting souls he thought as he swung over the wall and dropped to the ground. Crouching lowly, he stayed motionless for a few moments to make sure he had not been detected. Scanning the area, he saw a set of French doors open on a patio. This was just way too easy D.M. thought as he quietly made his way to them. Once inside, he waited for his eyes to adjust to the darkness. He found that he was in a large library or study. Books lined the walls and there was a massive desk at one end of the room. Two couches sat in the middle of the room facing each other.

The sound of footsteps coming down the hall sent D.M. searching for a shadow to hide in. He managed to cram his large frame in between two bookcases. The door opened and someone walked in. They turned on a small light at the end of the room. D.M. remained in the shadow. He peered out from his hiding place and could not believe his luck. The King was standing in the room! Now was his chance. His heart pounded so hard he thought the whole world could hear it. Sliding out of his hiding place he stood, still hidden in the shadows, "Good evening your Majesty," he said in a soft voice. He figured that speaking English might help his cause.

"Who are you? What are you doing here?" the King said in a nervous tone.

"I am Major D.M. Elliott of the U.S. Special Operations Command. I mean you no harm. I only wish a few minutes of your time to speak to you," D.M. continued softly.

"You are American?"

"Spanish by birth and lived here the first part of my life."

The King closed the door and sat down on one of the sofas, "And why do you want to speak to me?"

D.M. sat down across from him. He unbuttoned his coat and reached into the pocket. The King eyed the gun, "You are armed?"

"Yes, just part of the job," he patted his side, "I don't leave home without it." He took out the picture of his mother and handed it to the King, "Her name was Maria Espinoza Padilla, she was my mother," he paused, "She used to work in the palace here as a maid...I believe you knew her."

The King looked at the picture and sighed, "Your mother was the most beautiful woman I have ever laid eyes on...Had I not all ready been married, I would have taken her in a heartbeat, royalty or not," he handed the photo back to D.M., "I must admit that there was a time in my marriage that my wife and I were not very close...It's not easy being royalty, the stress can be too much sometimes...Your mother caught my eye, and in a moment of weakness, we spent a night together...Just one night."

D.M. nodded slowly and took out the papers, "That one night your Majesty was all it took."

"I knew she was pregnant and didn't know if it was from that one night. To be safe, I sent her home to Zaragoza."

The major handed the papers to the King, "My commander studies genetics. She is of royalty herself, Norwegian. And she may only marry another royal. We have a rather special relationship together. I had her test my DNA to see if I was a likely match. Those papers you hold are the result of her search. She found that your DNA was a ninety five percent match. Nothing else was even close."

"So you are saying you're the result of that one night all those years ago?"

"Yes your Majesty. I am... My mother went home and quickly wed an American that was stationed at the base there and I believe tried to pass me off as his son... This very day thirty six years ago I came into the world... I think he knew I wasn't his because he always treated me different than my other two brothers."

"And what of your mother?"

"She died giving birth to my youngest brother Benjamin."

"I'm very sorry to hear that."

D.M. smiled slightly, "She was an amazing woman. She made sure I knew my Spanish heritage. I went to bullfights, learned to dance the Flamenco, and enjoyed the flavors of the country... God I loved growing up here!"

The King sat back on the sofa and sighed, "So what is it that you want? Money? Power? A title?"

"No sir. I have a Master's in Chemical Engineering from MIT. I hold patents on several polymers and compounds that I created and sold. I have more money than I know what to do with. I'm happy with my current position in the military. And a title means nothing to me...What I want is you to acknowledge my existence... Between you and me and no one else... I know a bastard son has no claim to the throne, and I don't want it."

"And the press will not know?"

"As I have said, I have no need for fame or fortune. I have everything I want in my life."

The King rubbed his chin, "I think we can have a gentleman's agreement."

"Very well," D.M. smiled slightly.

The King stood to leave, "Well my son, you know I can't just let you walk out the front door."

D.M. quickly stood, "Yes sir, I will leave the way I came in," the major lowered his head in a respectful bow. As he raised his head his eyes met with the King's, he felt almost like he was looking at himself in a mirror with quite a few years added. Their eyes were the same and even the shape of their faces were similar. He stood nearly a head taller than the King, but their builds were very much the same.

The King looked the major up and down, "Yes, I'd say there is a strong family resemblance," he smiled and put his hands on D.M.'s shoulders, "You must go, I'm expected back for dessert." He leaned forward and kissed D.M. on each cheek.

"Thank you father," he said softly. As he turned to leave, he pulled a business card from his pocket and set it on the table, "Should you ever need me."

"Damn him!" Eagle hollered as she read the note that D.M. had left on her lab table. It was just before lunch. She noticed the papers were gone and the note simply read: "This is something I need to do," and was signed with his initials. She tore upstairs and found Jake. He was sitting in the rec room watching a movie. "I found him... I need you to fly me to Reno. I need to get a flight out... I only hope he hasn't done something really stupid."

"Okay, where is he?"

"Spain... He went to see his real father."

"Uh-oh," Jake turned off the TV and got up. He opened the door, "Go grab what you need and I'll meet you up on the hanger deck."

Ten minutes later they were airborne and headed for the airport. Jake dropped Eagle at the Air Guard hanger. She caught a cab to the main terminal and quickly went to work arranging a flight. The best she could do was to land in Madrid late morning the next day. It would have to do. She tried to call the major's cell phone and still found it off. There was going to be hell to pay for this stunt. If she was lucky she wouldn't have to bail him out of some Spanish jail.

The hours and the miles seemed to pass slowly. Finally Eagle landed in Madrid. She was walking down the concourse when she spotted D.M. standing in line to check in for his flight. "D.M.?" She walked quickly over to him, "What the hell are you doing here?" She barked.

He turned and regarded her, "I might ask the same of you."

"Do you have any idea how much trouble you're in?"

The major raised an eyebrow, "Should be none."

"Oh no. How about AWOL for starters?"

"Evidently you haven't read your email for the last few days, there was a leave request in there," he replied calmly.

Eagle folded her arms across her chest, "No, I was too worried about you."

"You shouldn't have been. I'm a big boy; I can take care of myself."

"And the note you left me. Are you crazy? I had visions of having to bail you out of some dark nasty Spanish jail."

He smiled and shrugged his shoulders, "Well, as you can see, I'm quite fine and am on my way home," he stepped up to the counter, "Should I book you a seat home with me or are you too mad to fly together?"

Eagle sighed deeply, "Yes, please, let's go home."

D.M. made the arrangements. "We don't leave for another couple of hours. Do you wanna go to the bar and get something to eat?"

"That's fine. And you can tell me about your adventure."

"Sure."

"And why was your phone off the whole time?"

"Because I'd made up my mind and I didn't want anyone talking me out of it," he headed toward the bar.

"You crazy bastard," she said lowly.

The major put his hand on her shoulder, “Yes I am.”

Eagle carried Cabbott's uniform down the hall. She unlocked the door and went to his room. His usual smiling face was nowhere to be found. Hanging the uniform on the back of the door she went out and found one of the nurses, “Where's the captain?”

“Oh, he should be out of physical therapy soon. He's probably down at the pool ma'am.”

“Isn't it a bit risky to be having him out of the secure side?”

“We ensure he has a safe corridor all the way down and back. None of your team would be caught dead at the pool this time of year.”

Eagle shook her head, “Got a point there.”

A few minutes later Cabbott returned. He wheeled himself in and carefully stood. He was dressed only in a pair of swim trunks and flip flops, a white fluffy towel draped around his neck, “Hi!” He said with enthusiasm.

“Have a nice swim?” She said looking him over. Despite being basically confined to a bed for over a year, he appeared in remarkable shape. His legs, however, bore the gruesome scars of many surgeries.

“Yes I did, thank you... Did twelve laps today- my best so far.”

“Good, good for you,” she paused, “I must admit, for someone who's been in bed for so long you look very fit.”

Cabbott laughed lightly, “God blessed me with a good metabolism. I get fit very quick. The last three weeks I've been in the pool twice a day.”

“How's the knee?”

He poked at his knee with determination, “Can't feel a damn thing. Dr. Miles did some research and found just the right spot to do a block. He says he'll have to do it every couple of days, but it should get me through until I can get it replaced.”

“And when does he think he can do it?”

“After Christmas sometime. He's taking some leave to be with his family.”

“I guess I should come watch him do the block so I can do it when he's gone.”

Cabbott tossed his towel on the bed and kicked off his flip flops, "That would save me a great deal of pain. Hurts like hell when he does it, but the relief is worth the few moments of pain... I'm due for one tomorrow. He does it just after he finishes morning rounds."

"I'll try and be down here for that," she turned to leave, sensing that he wanted to get a shower, "Your uniform is on the back of your door."

"Cool, thanks!"

"Just two days to go," she smiled and left.

Jake stood next to a large plasma TV that he had mounted on one wall of D.M.'s lab. He had a cable running to the laptop and he poked at the keys bringing blue print style images of the Badger helicopter to the screen. D.M. walked in and saw him, "What the hell are you doing? And where did you get that huge TV?"

The lieutenant turned, "Ah, yes, the joys of mail order!"

"Where did you get those schematics?"

"Eagle gave them to me. I've been thinking on how I can improve the structural integrity of the helicopter."

The major rolled his eyes, "Now you've gone aeronautical engineer on me huh?" He sat down at his work bench.

"Come on, you know I love flying these things."

"Nauseatingly so," he groaned.

"I think by making a few reinforcements at selected points, this will add two or three G's in performance."

"Oh be still my upset stomach!"

"Quit picking on me. You're just mad because you can't fly them as good as me," Jake replied as he moved the mouse to change the angle of view on the screen.

"I'm not mad about that. Your skill is unquestionable. I just hate that every time we go up; I come down about ready to puke my guts out."

"But you don't get sick when you fly the Wolverines."

"No. I think it has something to do with the fact you fly like a maniac and I'm also not used to that extra dimension of flight."

"What? Backwards?" Jake teased.

"I don't know. I can only hope I 'out grow' this and can be a good gunner for you," He took down a book from the shelf and opened it.

"Well, if it makes you feel any better major, you're a damn fine gunner."

"Thanks. There were a few times out there I was beginning to question my abilities. Multiple targets aren't such a big thing in jets, but helicopters add a whole new level of chaos."

Jake sighed, "Yeah, my kinda world: chaos and mayhem." He sat the laptop down on a small table he had borrowed, picked up a tablet and made some notations. After several minutes of writing, he sat down on the couch, "Damn, that's not gonna work."

D.M. looked at him out of the corner of his eye, "Problem?"

"Yeah. If I make all the improvements I want, I'll really screw up the lift to weight ratio."

"What kind of reinforcement material were you planning on using?" The major put his finger on the spot where he was reading and looked up.

"I was thinking of titanium. It's strong and lightweight, but even that would be too heavy."

"Carbon fiber?"

"Humm, let me keep thinking. This is my pet project, I have to work this out for myself," he stood and went back to reviewing schematics.

"All right Cabbott, you know the drill," Dr. Miles said as he drew up a 10 cc syringe.

"Yes sir," the captain replied. He was sitting in bed dressed and ready for his morning swim. Grabbing a pillow, he shoved it under his knee. Eagle stood by watching.

"So, you're gonna keep him happy while I'm gone?" Jim asked as he prepped the captain's leg.

"That was my general idea. If he's been doing well with this, I don't want him to be miserable while you're gone," she stepped in closer to see exactly what he was doing.

"You give him 10 cc's. Use a two inch needle, twenty gauge is fine," he pointed to the area, "You go in there, straight down until you almost hit the hub. Inject slowly," he lined up to make the stick, "Ready captain?"

Cabbott reached down with both hands and grabbed the bed covers, knotting his fists up in them. He swallowed hard and nodded. Dr. Miles set the needle against his leg and in one swift movement, inserted it. Cabbott didn't flinch. He drew back to make sure there was no blood return. Slowly he pushed the plunger down. The captain grunted lowly in pain. Eagle could see his fists clenching the covers harder, his face twitching with pain. To her, it seemed a rather barbaric way of dealing with pain, but it would have to suffice for the mean time.

After finishing the injection, Dr. Miles withdrew the needle and handed Cabbott a small piece of gauze to hold on the site. The captain's face still showed the pain he was experiencing. Jim disposed of the syringe and turned to Eagle, "He'll be all right in just a couple of minutes. That stuff burns like hell for a bit and then everything goes numb."

"Do me a favor? Please make sure his knee is a priority when you get back," she said, turning for the door.

"On the top of my list. Captain Goldsmith is taking leave as well. He's got the mold partially cut. He'll finish up after he gets back and then we can proceed."

"All right. Thanks Jim, have a Merry Christmas."

"You too Eagle."

She left the secure side and walked down the short hallway to the elevator. The doors opened and Frank rolled out followed by a PT tech. He had evidently been to the pool. "They have you swimming?" She said in surprise.

"Naw, more like a lot of treading water. Getting my upper body stronger."

"Are you gonna come up for Christmas breakfast?"

"Actually, I have PT pretty early. Then I get a shower, shave and then have breakfast. After all that, I'm ready for a nap... Can I come up for dinner instead?"

"Sure. You remember your elevator code?"

Frank smiled, "Actually I do."

"Good, then we'll see you about eighteen hundred tomorrow."

CHAPTER THIRTY FIVE

D.M. rolled over to find Eagle just coming out of the bathroom. She was dressed in her duty grays. "Hey, you go back to sleep mister. Ms. Clause has some work to do." She held her index finger to her lips, "Shhhh, you don't want to ruin your Christmas now do you?"

"I'm sorry, I didn't leave you any milk and cookies," he chuckled and pulled the covers over his head. She reached down and swatted him on the foot as she passed by. It was 0530 Christmas morning. She needed to get to her office and get all the presents she had bought for them.

The team gathered in the dining room for their traditional Christmas breakfast. Large and small boxes dotted the dining room table. The men filed in, excited to see what they were getting. Tige sat down and looked at a blank spot on the table where his present should be. He was wondering why he was left out of the gift giving. The rest of the men quickly opened their presents and were chattering noisily. D.M. had picked up a present for Eagle. He presented it to her. It was a small box wrapped in shiny silver paper. She carefully opened it. Inside was an ornate Viking cloak pin in gold with small emeralds set around the outside. "Oh D.M., it's beautiful!"

"I saw that on one of my outings and thought you'd like it."

"I do, very much. Thank you," she hugged him gently. Turning her attention to Tige, "Well captain, I suppose you're wondering why there was no gift waiting for you?"

"Ummm, uh," Tige stammered sheepishly, "I didn't think I was that bad of a boy this year- shit, I didn't even rate coal in my stocking."

Eagle stood and went to the door. She opened it and stuck her head out into the hallway. After a few moments, she turned around, "I think this Christmas present will certainly meet with your approval," she opened the door wide. The team was quiet. Slowly, Captain Westmoreland made his way into the dining room, leaning heavily on a cane. He stopped and stood straight. He was dressed in neatly pressed duty grays and his boots shined with hours of polishing.

"Merry Christmas Captain St. Ivor, we finally meet," Cabbott said with a smile. He turned to Eagle, "Ma'am, Captain Cabbott Xavier Smythe-Westmoreland the third reporting for duty," he quickly changed hands with his cane and saluted her. She returned the salute.

Tige slowly rose. His mouth hung open in awe. Sam playfully reached up and pushed his mouth closed.

Eagle stepped over to the table, "Captain, I present to you the Dragonslayers." She pointed at D.M., "This is Major D.M. Elliott, second in command, and then we have Lieutenant Jake Collins, his partner. Over there is Lieutenant Sam Waters, he's partnered with Captain St. Ivor," she paused for a moment, "And this is Lieutenant Max Hauer, he'll be your partner."

Max stood, walked over and offered his hand, "Nice to meet you captain. Tige has told us quite a bit about you."

"Mmm, sounds like my reputation precedes me," Cabbott smiled.

"Please captain, have a seat. Welcome to the team." Eagle said as she settled back into her chair. Cabbott made his way over to the empty seat and carefully sat down.

D.M. turned to Eagle, "So was this what you were hiding from me all these months?"

"Yes. I kept it quiet because Dr. Miles and I weren't sure if we could get him fixed up enough to return to duty. I didn't wanna get anyone's hopes up. He still has one more surgery to go, and lots of physical therapy, but we think he'll be fine after a while."

"You did a real nice thing. Tige looks like he's died and gone to heaven."

"I'm not one to pass up a real asset to the team. Besides, with all the time I've spent with the captain, he's quite a nice guy... Hard to believe he has taken over one hundred and fifty lives in his career."

"So, you've been spending time with another man?" He

teased.

"Yes, major. I was."

Tige approached Eagle, "Thanks, I think that's the best Christmas present I've ever had."

"You're welcome. But please remember he's not up to mission fitness yet."

"Yes ma'am. I'm just thrilled to have him here to mentor me. I hope I can learn a lot from him."

"I'm sure we'll all learn a lot from him."

They settled down to breakfast, chatting back and forth. Cabbott sat back with a cup of coffee just enjoying their conversations. All these months he had waited to finally meet them and they seemed like a good group to be part of.

"So, uh, Captain Westmoreland, Tige tells us you have quite the number of kills under your belt," Jake said as he finished his coffee.

"About one fifty."

"Damn! How do you keep your head straight?"

"It's not easy I'm afraid. I fight the same battles you do every night when you close your eyes. Except most of mine are seen up close and personal."

Tige nodded his head, "A sniper's life is full of one to one death. You carry their faces in your mind forever."

Jake leaned forward and rested his elbows on the table. He looked across the table at each of the snipers, "Then why do you do it?"

Cabbott sat quietly for a few moments collecting his thoughts, "I guess you can say it's a calling. You know, something like being called to be a priest, a cop or some other kind of civil servant."

Tige leaned forward and looked down the table at Cabbott, "I look at it this way: I have no problem taking a human life. I'm more than likely damned to hell for what I've done, but if I can save some other poor soul from having to go down that same path, then I feel I have done a service."

"Novel concept," Cabbott said, "I just consider it my job. That's what I go to work to do and what I get paid for."

Eagle listened to their conversation. She turned to D.M., "You know, here it is Christmas morning and what are they talking about? Death."

He shrugged his shoulders, "Well, we are in that line of work after all."

"Yes, I suppose so, but you'd think they would find a better subject to talk about!"

Jake overheard Eagle, "Oh, sorry. Yes, you're right, it's Christmas and we shouldn't be talking shop," he looked back across at Cabbott, "So where are you from?"

The captain glanced at Eagle. She'd heard his life story all ready, but he figured since he was new to the group he should share. "I grew up in Burlington Vermont, went to Harvard, have a Bachelor's degree in law. I joined the Army because I wanted to serve my country. My father was really pissed that I joined; he wanted me to take over the family law business. I wasn't ready for that... I never dreamed I'd end up a sniper. Sure, we used to go hunting when I was a kid, and I was a damn good shot... I guess the Army figured they could capitalize on my skill. They sent me to their sniper school and I graduated top of the class... By then, I had a taste for it. I begged them to send me to the Marine sniper school and I came out on top there as well. I've been in about seven years. The last year and a half was spent in a hospital bed."

"Yeah, Tige told us what happened. Damn shame," Max added.

"I racked up so many kills so fast because once word of my talent got out, I was being 'loaned' to every service out there. CIA, FBI, and a few with initials that are classified, they all wanted me. The mission that landed me in the hospital and killed my spotter was a CIA job. We were supposed to be taking out a right wing militia leader high up in the Peruvian Andes."

"Ah. So that's what happened. The *Army Times* didn't elaborate on where you were when it happened," Tige commented.

"Naw, they probably said it was a training mission, right?"

"Didn't even say that. Just said you were badly injured and your spotter was killed."

"Yeah, standard red tape political BS. My poor parents thought I was dead for about a week. The Army finally got their facts straight and I was able to make a phone call to let them know I was still alive." Cabbott poured himself another cup of coffee. He was happy to be in the company of others like him. He could now tell some of his classified stories and not have to worry about anything getting leaked out.

"So captain... Tige has told us so much about you, but he neglected one detail." Jake said as he tossed his napkin on the table.

"And what detail is that?" Tige replied in an embarrassed tone of voice.

"Every SF Operator has a call sign. What's yours?"

Cabbott took a long drink of coffee, set his cup down and smiled, "My call sign is Angel."

"Oh, that's cool. Is that short for something like the Angel of Death?" Jake quipped, taking a sip of coffee.

"No, just Angel... And how I got it was somewhat humiliating."

Jake looked at Cabbott, "Oh, do tell, we love a good story." The rest of the team joined in egging the captain on.

"All right...Well, I was stationed down at Ft. Benning. Me and a few of the guys from my team went down to a local diner one night. As we were leaving, there was this morbidly obese waitress that worked there. She was having car trouble... Being the nice guy I am, I went over to help her. It turns out her battery was dead and she needed a jump. So I pulled my car around, hooked up the cables and got her car started... She was so happy, she grabbed me, hugged the crap out of me and planted a big wet kiss on my cheek and called me her dar'lin Angel... I thought the rest of the guys were going to piss their pants because they couldn't stop laughing."

The whole team was laughing, even Eagle. That was one story he hadn't shared with her. "And it gets better," he paused, "That diner was quite close to the base and had great food, so we ate there all the time... Well, every time we were in there and she was working, she would come up, hug on me and call me her Angel... And they never let me live it down."

"Bloody hell. And you never fought to change it?" Tige gasped.

"No. It suits me just fine."

Jake propped both elbows up on the table and rested his chin in his hands, "And what was the name of the fair damsel in distress?"

Cabbott grinned widely, "Bertha."

The entire room erupted in laughter. They laughed long and hard. It was evident that they had been holding back a lot when Bruce was around. Now they could freely express themselves. Eagle thoroughly enjoyed seeing them happy. It was time to be a team again.

During the day, the men had given Cabbott a tour of the areas he hadn't been allowed to see. He marveled at the technology of the basement hangers and the aircraft he would learn to fly. They relaxed in the rec room having a few beers and watched a movie. Most of the time they spent telling stories of their missions. It was obvious that they all felt very comfortable together.

Eagle sat in her office finishing the transfer paperwork for Cabbott. The next duty day she would call General Spears and inform him of the change in manning. She figured he might be a bit angry since she didn't even tell him what she was up to. He'd get over it. They had a solid enough relationship that something like that wouldn't create too much flack.

There was a knock on the door and D.M. walked in. Eagle looked up, "Done partying with the animals?"

He laughed lightly, "Actually they're being quite well behaved... But that's not what I came to talk to you about."

"Oh, what is it?"

"What's going to happen to Frank? I have some of his things packed up in his room, and I didn't want to show it to Cabbott because of that."

"Just sit tight for now. It'll get sorted out soon enough."

Eagle hurried into the dining room. Most of the team was present. D.M. of course was nowhere to be found. She needed some help, "Captain, come with me."

Both Cabbott and Tige looked at each other and in unison replied, "Which one?"

She stopped for a moment, "Oh crap, that's right, there are two of you now. Tige, come with me," she opened the door and they quickly hurried out. They went right next door to her office where she unlocked and opened a large cabinet. It was filled with racks containing bottles of wine.

"Whoa! The boss's private stash!"

"Can't very well leave them lying around, you guys would drink me dry... And this is NOT cheap wine!" She pulled out three bottles and handed them to him. Taking another two out, she closed the cabinet. They returned to the dining room where they gave the wine to the cook to uncork and serve with dinner.

It was just after 1800 when Frank rolled down the hallway. He pushed open the door to the dining room and found the whole team seated. As he rolled in, he noticed a new face in the chair where he once sat. At the end of the table was an empty space for him.

"Hey Frankie, glad you could join us. Take the spot at the end," D.M. motioned to the end of the table. Frank rolled over and took his place. There was an envelope with his name neatly written on it. He looked down at it and then at Eagle.

"Merry Christmas Frank. Open it," she said softly. The room got quiet. Frank picked up the envelope, tore the flap open and pulled out a letter. He sat reading for a few moments before looking up.

"I got the job?"

"Yes. I had to pull a lot of stings, but it's yours."

Frank let out a loud whoop and threw his arms in the air. The rest of the team clapped, not exactly knowing what they were celebrating. Eagle got up and went to Frank. She wrapped her arms around his shoulders and hugged him.

"Thanks ma'am, this means a lot."

"You're welcome. You're also going to be sent TDY starting next week for training. You'll be gone probably six weeks."

"That's okay. It's worth it."

She returned to her chair but remained standing, "All right, now that everyone is here, I can *finally* let the cat out of the bag."

D.M. looked up at her, "Keeping secrets again?"

"Of course," she paused, "I'd like to share a sequence of events that none of you have known about, but has led up to this very moment... Tige, you started it all off. You told me about Cabbott. I took a big chance and brought him here. Dr. Miles and I worked together to get him back in shape. Then there is D.M., who helped Captain Goldsmith perfect the polymer to make plastic bones. He intern helped you out by making you a new shoulder and Cabbott by making him four new vertebrae. Cabbott here, being the nice guy he is, graciously donated some of his spinal cord cells so we could grow more and then implant them into Frank. We did that, and didn't exactly achieve the desired results, but Frank, you woke up. This of course made D.M. very happy. He no longer suffers from horrible pain in his shoulder, and he has his brother back. Jake, you happened to hear that there was going to be a job vacancy in Security Control. You told Frank, who told me. I made some phone calls, and Frank now has a new job- guarding the base," she let out a loud exhale and plopped down in her chair.

"Ho-ly shit!" Jake exclaimed, stood and started clapping. Soon, the others were on their feet clapping. Eagle and Frank remained seated smiling at each other. This was a merry Christmas indeed. They all ate, drank and socialized until late into the evening. There couldn't have been a happier family.

Eagle wandered into her office. D.M. followed. They had been down on the training floor working on fighting skills. A red light blinked on her phone. She picked up the receiver and poked the message button. The general's voice came on, "Eagle, it appears we have a situation here. I need you to come to Washington ASAP. You have unique knowledge of the task at hand. Bring your over sized bodyguard if you wish." The message ended.

She hung up the phone and turned to D.M., "It appears our presence is requested in Washington."

"Uh-oh, you didn't tell him about Cabbott did you?"

"Not yet. But whatever it is, we have 'unique knowledge' of the task. Oh, and I was told to bring my 'oversized bodyguard' if I wanted."

D.M. laughed lightly, "Well, I assume that means me. I'll go get packed."

***

Washington D.C. was cold, bleak and gray. The temperature was at least well above the minus ten that the base hovered at. D.M. was happy to be out of the snow. As they drove to the Pentagon, Eagle looked out at the landscape. She always hated the winters in Washington. The trees looked dead, the people were miserable, and whole place felt like doom and gloom. "So you have no idea what he wants huh?" D.M. said as he pulled into the largest of the Pentagon's parking lots.

"Nope, not a clue. But whatever it is, we have the skills he's needing."

"Good, I'm bored, I wanna go to work."

"I know, all of you are just itching to get some action."

He found a parking spot and pulled in, "It's what we've trained for; it's what we live for." He got out, hurried around and with a gentlemanly flourish, opened the door for her. They were dressed in a class B version of their Service Dress, nothing fancy. It was a simple uniform that with exception of the upright choker type collar on the coat resembled a dark gray business suit with rank. Eagle had it made up for occasions when there needed to be a level of discretion. This meeting with the general proved a perfect time to try it out.

They walked for quite a while before heading up the ramp into the building. Showing their IDs to the guard, they continued on until they reached the general's office. The secretary showed them inside. They stopped in front of his desk and saluted crisply. The general stood, quickly returned the salute and stepped from behind his desk, "Good timing, let's go get some lunch," he grabbed his hat and coat, "You have a car here?"

"Yes sir," D.M. replied, "I'll go get it." He left the office and started on the long walk back to the car. Eagle and the general walked slowly down the corridor.

"Sir, I need to tell you something, but promise me you won't be mad?"

"What have you gotten yourself into now?"

"Nothing bad I assure you. I just made a decision without your approval. Well, without anyone's approval really."

"And what decision was this?"

"To take on another team member to replace D.M.'s brother."

"Sergeant von Teufel was there to replace him. At least until he met with his untimely death in a training accident," he replied in a suspicious tone.

"I took a big gamble and I think it'll pay off."

"Who did you get?"

"Captain Westmoreland, the number one sniper in the world."

"Humm, he was deemed unfit to return to duty and was going to be medically retired. The doctors said he would probably never walk again. What do you think you can do with broken merchandise?"

"Medical miracles. He's up and walking," she smiled.

"And the Army handed him over to you just like that?"

"Yes sir, they were tired of caring for him. He'd been at Walter Reed for nearly a year. The poor guy has gone through so many surgeries his legs are just a mess of scars."

"And you think he can perform for your team?"

"I do." They reached the door.

"All right then. Yes, I'm a bit upset with you not getting approval. But on the same token, if he works out, you made a smart business investment."

"Yes sir. Thank you."

D.M. stopped the car and got out. He stood ready to open the door for the general. A light cold rain had begun to fall making the day even more miserable. They hurried down and got in. D.M. slid back in the driver's seat, "Sir, where would you like to go for lunch?"

"Find something that looks good major. Frankly I don't care. The real business will take place after."

"Yes sir," he put the car in drive and pulled out onto the street. It didn't take long before he found a suitable restaurant. They ate lunch, talking only about non-business related items. After, the general directed D.M. to find a location where they could talk in private. The major selected the park he'd stopped at when Eagle had her meltdown after finding out about Westland. The rain had stopped so they could get out and walk. The park was empty.

"The reason I asked you here is we seem to have a problem,"

the general started off, "And you both are very familiar with this problem."

"It got a name sir?" D.M. asked.

"Rear Admiral Richard Westland, retired... He seems to have forgotten that he's retired and is once again back in the information business."

Eagle looked at the general, "How's he managing that?"

"I don't know. And he's getting more and more heavily classified information. This has got to stop. National security is on the line here."

"What do you want us to do sir?" D.M. asked.

"From my mouth to your ears only- make him go away."

"Permanently?" Eagle said with a dark tone of voice.

"Yes. I know you hate his guts for what he did to you and your team... You must promise me this will not be traceable. Make it look like an accident if you can. We can't get dirty on this."

Eagle smiled broadly, "Don't worry sir; we can certainly devise an accident that will take the poor admiral out of the picture... I've been talking to the best."

"Captain Westmoreland?"

"Amazing what that man knows about killing people."

"Fine. I don't want to hear anymore about it," he waved his finger at her, "I just wanna read an obituary... Enjoy your revenge colonel," he walked a little further, "Major, would you excuse us for a little bit?"

"Uh, yes sir. I'll be by the car," D.M. turned and left.

General Spears continued walking. He waited until he was sure the major was out of hearing range. "Eagle, I've known you almost your entire military career."

"Yes sir."

"And you've almost been like a daughter to me...You were there to comfort Rose as she was dying, and you gave me comfort knowing she was cared for with the greatest respect... And as a father of two other daughters, I've learned the telltale signs of when one of my daughters was hiding something from me...Especially a boyfriend."

Eagle sighed, lowering her head, "Is it that obvious sir?"

"Not to the untrained eye...But as a father, I can see it," he stopped and turned to her, "Is this relationship worth the jeopardy? Is he the one?"

She looked up slightly, "Yes, he is...His father, the King of Spain had a brief affair with one of his maids, his mother... Granted, the major is illegitimate, but he's still of royal blood... And I love him with all my heart."

The general nodded, "All right. As a father I understand. I want you to be happy in your life, so as a father, I give you my blessing...As your commander, you must understand the position I'm in. I cannot in good conscious endorse the relationship from a professional aspect. You will keep this quiet. If I hear anything from anyone other than members of your team, I cannot defend you. Is that understood?"

Eagle snapped to attention, "Yes sir!"

"Good, now that we have that settled, come give your adopted dad a hug," he held out his arms and she embraced him, "I'm happy you've finally found someone to share your life with. He looks to be a very good man. Take care of him," he let his arms slip away from her. As he stepped back, he could see tears in her eyes.

"Thanks dad," she said softly.

They returned to the Pentagon and dropped the general off at the ramp. Eagle climbed into the front seat. They were just pulling out of the parking lot when she started to giggle. Soon the giggle turned into a laugh, and then to something that D.M. thought sounded rather possessed, almost demonic.

"Okay Eagle, you're really scaring me now. How about you cut that out?"

Slowly her laughter subsided. She reached over and squeezed his arm, "Finally we get to bury that bastard!"

"Hey, I'm a bastard. Don't go putting me in the same class as him- I'm offended!" He teased. Although being considered a bastard was considered quite derogatory, D.M. was actually quite proud of his *bar sinister* status. Not many could say their father was a King and really mean it.

"All right. We get to bury that asshole then. Better?"

"Yes, thank you," he stopped at a red light, "And what have you and Cabbott been discussing?"

"Oh, just ways to kill someone and make it look like an accident."

"You've been planning this all along haven't you? You just feel better now that you can do it for real."

"And didn't you feel better after killing Kemal? You planned your revenge for a long time."

"No, not really. Killing him did nothing. I still felt the hatred. There was no spontaneous gratification, just an empty feeling."

"Vikings live for revenge, it's in our blood. Westland will feel sorry that he ever tangled with this bitch. My leash is off and I'm ready to fight!"

"So am I to assume you and the good captain have a plan of some sort?"

"We've put together a few ideas. We just need to work the details out better. It will be a team effort. We all got screwed, so we can all have a part in this."

D.M. pulled into the parking garage at their hotel and found a spot. He parked the car, turned it off. He closed his eyes, sighed deeply and let out a little chuckle.

"You find something amusing major?"

"Oh, I was just thinking... If we had a full-blown relationship going what would 'revenge sex' be like?"

She punched him in the shoulder, "Hey!"

"I mean, I've heard that angry sex is good, so revenge sex must be off the charts!"

"In your dreams major!" She scoffed.

"Yes, they will be tonight," he smiled, eyes twinkling.

Eagle had just finished getting ready for bed when there was a knock on the adjoining door. Even though the major had his new arm, she still booked the rooms so they could share time together if they wanted. D.M. did his best to try and sleep in his room, but it didn't always work. He poked his head in the door.

"Yes?" She said noticing a worried look on his face, "Are you okay?"

He opened the door a bit farther, "I know I said I was gonna sleep in my room tonight, but something- I don't know what- just set me off." He pushed the door open all the way and stood with his holstered pistol cupped in his hand, "I don't know if it was a sight, smell, or sound, but all of the sudden the hair on the back of my neck stood up and I went on alert."

"All right, come on," she patted the bed next to her.

"Thanks," he closed the door, slid his .45 out of the holster and sat it on the nightstand then climbed into bed. She turned off the light and they tried to get some sleep.

Not even an hour later D.M. awoke from a nightmare. He sat bolt upright in bed covered in sweat, breathing hard. "Nightmare?" Eagle said softly.

"Flashback."

"Wanna talk about it?"

"Just the same one I keep having. The one where I blow Kemal's kid's head off. I just can't get those thoughts out of my head."

She turned on the light and reached over, gently rubbed his back, "There's not much I can say about that one. Hopefully with time it will fade somewhat."

D.M. pushed himself back until he was sitting up against the headboard, "What did General Spears wanna talk to you in private for?"

Eagle sighed, "It was a father, daughter talk."

"About what?"

"The relationship that you and I have."

He felt a sinking feeling in the pit of his stomach, "Oh shit."

"It wasn't all bad. Unfortunately his relationship with me is two sided. There is the father part, where he's very happy that I've finally found the right man. He's known all along of the promise I made to my people and just how hard that was to keep. So as the father part, he gave me his blessing. But there is the commander part, which must follow the rules of the military. He told me that if anyone other than members of the team tell him of our relationship, he cannot, and will not be there to defend it."

"I thought we've done a pretty good job of keeping our time in public strictly professional."

"Yes, we have. He's just a father of two other daughters and knows when we're up to something."

"But he gave you his blessing?"

She nodded.

"And you're okay with that?" He said slowly.

"Yes."

He smiled and climbed out of bed. Walking around to her side he stopped, "Okay then," he knelt down on one knee, taking her hand, "Eagle Tryggvesson, will you do me the honor of marrying me?"

She slid out of bed until her feet were off the side, her eyes looking straight into his, "Yes, I will."

He leaned forward and kissed her with a passion he'd never felt before.

Jake met Eagle and D.M. out in front of the Air Guard hanger. It was dusk and the sky was painted with dark blue and silver hues. He carried her bag to the awaiting Warhawk. Cabbott sat in the co-pilot seat.

"What's he doing here?" D.M. asked.

"Brought him along so he could see the sights and get to know the helicopter a bit," Jake replied, opening the side door and hefting her bag inside. He helped her up and then took the major's bag and put it in. They climbed in and shut the door. Jake took his seat at the controls, "Okay, you remember the start up sequence?"

Cabbott held up his left index finger. Reaching forward, he pushed the first button. He then held up two fingers and pushed another. He continued until all five fingers were up and five buttons were pushed.

"Good. You got that part down fast."

"I'm a quick study."

"Right, I got it from here. Just keep your hands lightly on the controls and feel what I'm doing." He contacted the tower, got clearance and took off for the base.

It was after dark when they landed on the hanger deck. The four days they had been gone brought two more feet of snow. The maintainers worked tirelessly to keep the runway and hangers cleared. Some of the team had even chipped in to help remove snow. "Jake? Do you think you could round up the rest of the team and meet us in the dining room in fifteen minutes?" Eagle called as she headed for the elevator.

"Near as I can ma'am."

More than half an hour passed before Jake had everyone assembled. The team was scattered all over the building. Tige and Sam were down in the basement range practicing and Max had been working out in the gym and was in his room taking a nice long hot shower. Once everyone was assembled, Eagle addressed them. "I know you gentlemen have been waiting anxiously for something to do. Well, we have a job. Not some training sortie, a real mission." Cheers arose from the table. "The major and I were told in strict confidence that a certain admiral has been a very naughty boy... He's up to his old tricks again. We've been given permission to handle the problem- discreetly of course."

Cabbott leaned forward, "So this is no longer hypothetical huh?"

"No captain, this is finally the real deal."

"Good, count me in," he smiled.

"Are you sure you're gonna be up to it?"

"We'll see when this all goes down."

Eagle poured a cup of tea and stirred some sugar and milk into it, "General Spears recommends this look like an accident... It just so happens that Cabbott and I have been discussing something of the sort... But to pull this job off and to do it well, we will need lots of intel. Westland's daily patterns have to be observed, his movements charted and anything out of the ordinary noted."

"How long are we looking to gather intel?" Tige spoke up.

"It could be as much as two to three weeks."

"And where's he living now?" Jake asked.

"General Spears gave me an address in Boca Raton, Florida."

"Oh glory be! A vacation from the snow!" Sam cheered. The others applauded.

Eagle took a sip of tea, she frowned as she burnt her tongue, "Not everyone will get a vacation from the snow. Just like we've done before, we're going to mix things up just a little bit... Tige, you will be in command of the recon party. Sam and Jake will go with you. Jake, I want you to find a place where you can charter a helicopter. Aerial surveillance will be very handy. Document as much as you can: routes he takes frequently, establishments he goes to, places he shops, the whole works."

"And what's the current outline for the mission?" Tige added.

Cabbott sat up, "The idea we came up with is taking Westland out in a controlled car crash. A very well placed bullet into the right front wheel at just the right time and place will hopefully lead to him kissing a tree and saying goodnight."

"Right, I think I know where you're going with this. We'll get the intel and let you sort out where the best place will be."

"Good. And if we're lucky, we might have time to do a dry run through to see if it'll really work. Then we can make necessary adjustments to the plan," Cabbott replied.

"What about the three of us who are left here?" D.M. joined in.

"Cabbott, do you need to fabricate your magic bullet?" Eagle asked.

"I'm pretty sure I don't have one. So yes, I will."

She turned to Tige, "You don't have any problem with him making the shot do you?"

"No, not at all. He's the most experienced. I'll help out in any way I can."

"D.M. and Max, you will assist Cabbott. Show him where the reloading lab is. Give him whatever help you can. Max, you will need to get up to speed spotting for him," she finished her tea, "All right gentlemen, tomorrow we start. Recon team, get packing."

CHAPTER THIRTY SIX

Jake opened the door to his motel room. It was a cheap place, nothing fancy, but it was a place to lay low and watch for Westland. Tige had cross referenced the area and found the motel was not far from the gated community where Westland lived. There was only one way in or out, and the motel was right on that road.

Dropping his bag on the bed, Jake headed next door to Tige's room. He and Sam were busy putting together the "Command Post" where they would relay information back to the base.

"Hey, is the computer up and running yet?" Jake asked.

"Yeah, sure." Sam replied.

"Good. I need to find a local airport where I can rent a chopper."

Tige checked the battery on the digital camera, "Did Eagle finally remember to give you your rating card?"

"I bugged her and she did it. So I'm legit now, I can *officially* fly helicopters." He accessed the Internet and began to search.

"Sam, did you have any luck finding information out from the DMV before we left?" Tige said as he connected a long lens to the camera.

"Negative. We'll probably have to do it the hard way- by surveillance," he paused, "But Eagle did load Westland's personnel file on the computer. We can see if that will help us out."

"Where'd she get that?" Jake said as he continued his surfing.

"General Spears gave it to her on a thumb drive. She passed it on to me to load on our laptop."

Tige finished his work on the camera, "I don't know about you mates, but it's getting close to happy hour and I'd happily like to have a drink." He grabbed the car keys, "Any requests?"

Jake pulled out a couple twenties, "Get me a case of Corona."

"Yngling, Sam Adams, or some kind of lager," Sam said as he handed Tige a twenty.

"How much you want?"

"Eh, just a couple six packs."

"Right, I'll be back in a few."

Jake and Sam decided to sit in chairs that were outside by their rooms. They could watch all the traffic going up and down the road. Even for early January the weather was warm and mild. Only a few cars went by, mostly going into the community.

"Hey Sam, you reckon those gated communities are there to keep those people in, or to keep us people out?"

"I'd bet a little of both."

A dark gray Mercedes sedan drove by. Jake perked up and took notice.

"You see something?" Sam inquired.

"Maybe. That guy driving looked an awful lot like the picture Eagle had showed me."

"Anybody with him?"

"Not that I could see." He got up and went to the room, Sam following. "Pull up Westland's file; I wanna look at a few things."

Sam quickly found the file, "Here ya go." Jake took over and scrolled through the file. He stopped when he found a recent photograph.

"Maybe, just maybe." He took a tablet and wrote down his possible lead.

Tige returned and started bringing in the beer, "A little help here would be appreciated mates."

Sam got up and helped him, "Sorry, we were sitting outside and a car went by and Jake thought he recognized Westland."

"Did you get the plate number?"

Jake looked up, "Shit Tige, I barely got a look at the guy driving, gimme a break!"

"Right, sorry. I was just hoping to make this a bit easier." He unscrewed the cap off a beer and took a long drink, "Mmmmm, happy hour."

The next morning the threesome headed to the local municipal airport. Jake had phoned a charter company and reserved a helicopter. They showed up to the hanger. "So what's our cover story?" Tige said as he grabbed the camera bag.

"Here on a photo shoot for a home and garden magazine. I told them we'd be around flying low sometimes," Jake replied.

"Fucking brilliant!"

"I have my moments." He opened the door to the office and

walked to the counter. A clerk came from the back. "Good morning, I'm Jake Collins, I spoke to someone in regards to renting a helicopter for a few days."

"Yes sir, that was me," the clerk replied, "May I have your credentials please?"

Jake pulled out his wallet and produced all the documentation required. He also handed over a credit card, "Here, just stick it on this, the company will reimburse me later for it."

"Not a problem sir." He reviewed Jake's rating card, "Well, you're qualified to fly the Apache, the Sikorsky 76 and the Bell 222. That's a nice resume."

"Yeah, was an Apache pilot for a few years, then I made a job move and went a bit fancier."

"Yes, I can see that. Will you be comfortable in a Bell 206?" He handed several papers over for Jake to sign.

"Oh, I can fly anything with rotors, just may take me a few minutes to find all my instruments and get orientated."

"Not a problem. I can have one of the mechanics go over some things if you want."

"I appreciate the offer, but shouldn't be necessary."

After all the paperwork was done, they went out to the tarmac. Sam and Tige hopped in while Jake performed the preflight. Once in the air, Tige looked over at Jake, "Well mate, Eagle certainly beefed up your rating card!"

"The Apache part was right, but she was having a hard time finding a civilian equivalent to what we really fly. So she had to be creative about it."

"Hey, it worked," Sam said from the back seat, "Are you really gonna get reimbursed for renting this thing?"

"No, but I have enough money now that it doesn't matter. Can't trace any of this back to the government." They flew over the gated community and Tige pulled out his map. He traced the streets off and triangulated until he found Westland's house.

"There, that one with the two big palm trees out front and the dark red gar-age door. Damn, no car parked outside."

"Gar-age?" Jake teased.

"Yeah, I know, fucking Aussie. D.M. gives me shit too."

Sam peered out the window, "Maybe he's not home."

"I think we'll have to do some close up surveillance. Jake, take us up higher so I can see where the wall is closest to his property."

"Roger that."

Sam sat in the back taking as many photographs as he could so they could pass the intel on that night.

"Good job gentlemen," Eagle said as she reviewed the information from the day's recon mission, "Take your time, be thorough."

"Yes ma'am," Sam said as he sent another file through, "Here, this one is of his house. We didn't get any photos of the car. Tige is on foot to stake it out and hopefully get a license plate number and description for us."

"Yeah, he had to go right by a swamp. We hope the gators didn't get him," Jake said as he took a long drink of beer. He was happy they had not managed to get the video conferencing working, so they could only communicate via audio on the laptop. Eagle would have been mad had she known how many beers they had gone through.

Tige felt something crawl across his head. It felt big whatever it was. He thought about swatting it off and then decided it might just be something poisonous that would bite or sting him. He tried to ignore it and remained motionless. From his vantage point in a neighbor's bush across the street from the house, he could see no one was home. He checked his watch; it was 2100 on a Friday night. It was going to be a long night. Keying the mike on his radio, "Kingpin, Ground Zero, this is Wombat, do you copy?" He said softly.

"Yeah this is Kingpin, I read you Wombat. So the gators didn't get you after all?" Jake teased.

"Negative. I would have made a nice meal out of one."

"Hah! Try the other way around."

"You didn't drink all my beer did you?"

"No. I only made it through half my case. I'm pissing so much I can't think straight."

Tige stifled his laughter, "I hope this bloody fucker comes home soon. There are things crawling around in this bush and I'm really hungry."

"Just be field expedient and eat what's there," Jake replied as he took a big bite of a sub sandwich.

"Fuck off! Wombat out." He tucked the radio back in his pocket. Another hour and a half would pass before the admiral came home. The car pulled into the driveway and the garage door opened. Tige grabbed his starlight scope and quickly zeroed in on the license plate. Taking a pen out, he wrote the numbers and letters down on the inside of his forearm along with the time and date. He waited until the door was closed and lights came on in the house. Carefully and quietly, he climbed out of the bush and kept to the shadows until he reached the wall. Taking out his radio he keyed the mike, "Wombat here. Got the plate number. Dark Mercedes. Good catch Kingpin."

"Roger that," Sam said as he grabbed the radio.

"And someone call for a pizza, I'm starving."

"Sure, what's your ETA?"

"I'll probably beat the pizza delivery guy."

"We'll get right on it. Ground Zero out."

"Good, and make sure it's got everything on it. I just passed a gator and it was looking mighty appetizing."

D.M. stood next to Cabbott watching him work. "So what exactly did Eagle mean by your magic bullet?"

"Oh, nothing magic about it really. I just have to pour a solid lead bullet, no jacket."

"And the reason for that?"

"It will have enough impact to blow the tire, but should it get lodged inside, it will quickly distort and look like a tire weight that fell off. If it goes through and hits the road as planned, it will nearly disintegrate and probably never be found. The best way to cover our tracks."

"She was right, you do know a lot about killing people."

"The Army trained me up to be a sniper. In truth, most of my kills are done with the rifle. But having been loaned to the CIA, they taught me a few other things."

"Oh, like what?"

"I can kill you with a handshake," Cabbott offered his hand. The major was reluctant to take it. "Oh come on, I'm not going to do it, I don't have the equipment unpacked yet."

D.M. took hold of his hand. Cabbott squeezed gently, "Didn't feel anything abnormal did you?" D.M. shook his head. "Now here's the difference," he squeezed again but this time pushed a bit harder with his fourth finger. "Feel that? I have a ring that has a few small pins on it that when dipped in some unsavory poison will usually deliver death within twenty four hours." He released the major's hand, "I'm not just a sniper, I'm a rather well trained assassin."

"Shit."

"I can kill you from afar, up close and personal, or not even have any contact with you and you'll meet with an untimely death."

"Now you're scaring me."

Cabbott chuckled, "I think my all time strangest assassination was what I called 'death by condoms'."

"Do I really wanna hear this?" D.M. said as he went to find another block of lead to melt for a projectile.

"Ah, it's a good story. I've never been able to share it before. Now that I'm in like company I can let out some of my dirty little secrets."

"You're far more sick and twisted than me... Go on."

The captain popped open the bullet mold and dumped the projectile out, "I was working for the CIA...They needed a double hit done. There was a husband and wife spy team... After lots of intel gathering in which I broke into their house several times and even went through their garbage, I realized they were quite the randy couple. I found three or four condoms in the trash each week. So I put together a nice mixture of botulism and salmonella toxins in a rather slippery medium. I loaded it up in a syringe with a 25 gauge needle and went back to their house. Carefully I slid the needle right into the package and injected five or six of them. They were dead in less than a week."

"Okay, now you've really got me worried."

Cabbott smiled broadly, "Just be happy I'm working for this side."

"Yeah, I pity our adversaries." He dropped the lead block into the smelting crucible and lit the burner below. He watched as the dull gray metal slowly melted and became shiny silver in color, "How many of these do you want?"

Cabbott screwed the mold back together. "Oh, maybe a dozen. I need a few to practice with. The ballistics are just a bit off from what I normally shoot, so I'll have to play with my figures to get the right point of aim. Really I only need one to do the job."

"And you're confident you can do it?"

"Much as I can be. There's always room for error. We only get one shot for this battle plan. If we fail, there is always plan B."

"What's that?"

"He gets done up close and personal."

D.M. nodded. He picked up the small crucible and poured the lead into the mold. Cabbott tapped the mold and motioned for D.M. to pour more.

"You really don't have any problem killing people do you?"

"No. The first couple were hard. After that, your head gets so screwed up that no matter what you do or how many you kill; you're a head case... I've just learned to deal with that. Most likely I'll never be able to function in society ever again."

"Probably none of us will. Then what becomes of us?" D.M. said softly.

"In the perfect world of the US Government, they would be happy if we were killed in action, or through other methods, were eliminated from the planet... We're the biggest threat to the people and politicians of this country, the government knows it."

"So what do you plan to do if you make it to retirement?"

"I bought a cabin high up in the mountains in Vermont. I plan to live out my life there and hopefully be left alone... What about you?"

"I wanna get married, maybe have a kid and live someplace quiet too."

"At least you have someone who understands."

D.M. eyed him suspiciously, "What's that supposed to mean?"

"Sorry. I'm quite good at reading people. Eagle was visiting me one day and just the way she said something I put it together. But mind you, the average person would not have picked it up. I've been well trained. She swore me to secrecy."

The major shook his head, "Good God."

"Your secret is safe with me sir."

D.M. sat in the dining room reading the paper. It was a bit early and he didn't expect anyone else to come in so soon. The door opened and Eagle walked in. He was just about to get up. "As you were major." She stood behind his chair. Reaching in her pocket, she produced two transdermal patches. Pulling the paper backing off one, she grabbed his collar and shoved her hand down his shirt, placing one of the patches on his chest.

"Oh! You're a bit forward this morning!" He laughed.

"Come on, I'm just trying a new kind of enzyme patch on you."

"Baby you can patch me anytime!" He said with a big grin.

Eagle pulled her hand out and peeled the backing off the other patch. Once again she put her hand down his shirt. D.M. grabbed her hand and held onto it. She laughed, trying to pull it out. He growled playfully and refused to let go.

The door opened and Cabbott walked in, "Whoa! Isn't that supposed to be the other way around?"

"This isn't what it looks like captain," Eagle said as she finally wiggled her hand loose from the major's grasp. "I'm working on a project to see if I can give the major enough enzymes in his blood to be able to metabolize alcohol."

"Huh?"

D.M. straightened his blouse, "I have a chemical imbalance. I don't make enough of the right enzymes to metabolize alcohol. I suffer from alcohol intolerance."

"So that's why I never see you drink."

"Yeah, as much as I'd like to have a beer or glass of wine once in a while, it wrecks me up pretty bad."

"Oh, that sucks," Cabbott replied as he took his seat.

Eagle sat down, "Okay, wear those all day and then tonight we'll give it a try."

"Hope this works better than the last try. And I'm bringing

my own booze this time around."

"That's fine. I know you didn't get on very well with my selection last time."

Later that morning Cabbott sat on the treatment table dressed in his swim trunks. His knee was screaming in pain. He'd tried to ride out the pain but finally decided he needed to have another injection. Eagle drew up the syringe and approached him, "I got a phone call from Dr. Miles this morning. He's going to take some more leave, his mother passed away."

"I'm sorry to hear that."

"That means you'll have to wait until after the mission to get your knee done." She prepped the area.

"If we're going to be in Florida, I should be fine. I've just been spending a lot of time in the basement range and it's pretty cold down there."

She set the needle against his skin, "Ready?"

Cabbott groaned, "No, not really." He grabbed onto the side of the table, closed his eyes and took in a deep breath. Eagle inserted the needle and slowly started to inject. The captain growled lowly trying to bear the pain. After the injection was done, Eagle handed him a piece of gauze. Cabbott held the pad down until she returned with a piece of tape. His face was twisted in pain.

"Hopefully we won't have to do this much longer," Eagle said as she put her hand on his shoulder and patted gently.

"I'm so used to living with pain, I wonder what it feels like not to hurt."

"Well, they all say that pain is God's way of telling you that you're not dead yet," she disposed of the syringe in the sharps container.

"If that's the case, then I'm more alive than I care to be," he hopped off the table and headed for the pool.

Jake maneuvered the helicopter high above the trees. The sun was just setting. Tige and Sam were following on the road below. They were keeping a tail on Westland but doing it from nearly a mile back. "Okay, he's turning right. Just wait for my mark... Uh, next intersection, make a right." He flew in a circle to stay with Westland. "He's headed west... Shit, I just lost him in the trees. Stand by." He hovered and waited, "Okay, got him. Continue west. Now the road bends and forks, take the right fork, repeat, the right fork." He hovered again, watching. "About a quarter mile up, he turned into a parking lot. Looks like some sort of bar or club, can't really tell from this distance."

"We got it." Sam replied. They drove by slowly. "Affirmative, some kind of club."

"Can you find a place to stake it out for a bit and see what the clientele is?" Jake said as he hovered a distance from the club. His view was partially obscured by all the large trees that lined the road.

"No place to park but the lot."

"Well, then park, get out and become shadows... I'm getting low on fuel, I'm heading back. I'll catch up with you back at the room." He turned and headed back to the airport.

Tige parked the car as far out of the way as he could. They got out and headed for a nearby tree line. "Let's see if we can get around back, maybe there are windows where we can get a view," Tige said as he stepped into the shadows. They watched the front door for a while. Several cars pulled up and it was quite obvious that the women who got out were working girls. "Did Westland's file say he was married?" Tige whispered.

"Divorced."

"Right."

They continued on until they were around the back. A patio deck and BBQ pit were in the back with a large sliding glass door leading out to them. Inside they could see older men and the working girls mingling. Tige was just about to settle down and watch the show when he heard a hiss behind him. He turned, and in the dim light he could see a large snake coiled on the ground. Sam stood stone still, "Uh, Tige?"

"Yeah, yeah, I'll handle this." He found a stout branch. Reaching forward, he caught the snake behind the head and pinned it to the ground. He stepped on the branch to hold it down. Whipping out his knife, he cut the head off in one swift movement.

"There, problem solved," he threw the snake further into the brush.

"Not gonna take it home and cook it?" Sam teased.

"Eat shit," he hissed as he crouched down. Sam inspected the area and then settled down next to him. They watched for several hours.

"Is it just me, or all the men in this club over fifty?" Sam observed.

"Humm, yes, appears that way."

"I'm sure Eagle's gonna want one of us in there."

"Oh, probably so. Guess we need to find a costume shop," Tige said as he slowly stood.

"You're the oldest; you stand the best chance of getting away with it."

"Age and treachery will always overcome youth and skill."

Sam stood, "No, you just look old."

"Asshole."

"Just telling it as I see it."

They hopped in the car and Sam jotted down the notes from their observation. Returning to the room, they found Jake on the computer.

"Hi guys, how'd it go?"

Tige opened the refrigerator door, grabbed a beer and twisted the cap off. He took several long drinks, "Bloody club is for old farts."

"Come again?"

"The bloody club is a gentleman's club for old men. We saw the hookers go in and everything."

"You're joking right?"

"Nope," Sam said as he grabbed a beer.

Jake typed a few more lines on the computer. He then pressed his fingers to his lips and touched it to the screen, "Goodnight my dear."

"Hey, what are you up to?" Tige said as he walked around behind Jake to see what was on the screen.

"I was just instant messaging a wonderful woman I met in

Reno."

"Oh, that bird at the bar?"

"Yeah, that 'bird' works for a micro engineering firm in Houston... And I really like her."

"Long distance relationships rarely last," Sam added.

"Maybe so, maybe not. I'm going to play this through and see."

"What's her name?"

"Monica Lowenstein. She's thirty."

Tige raised his bottle, "Oooohhh, going for the older woman eh?"

"Tige, leave him alone. At least he's got someone, even if she is half the country away," Sam said as he finished off his beer.

"High and to the right," Max called as he looked through the spotting scope. Cabbott sighed deeply, adjusted his scope, reloaded and leaned down, taking aim again. A few moments later the basement range echoed with the shot.

"Just a bit high this time, one ring off."

"Okay, it's been a while."

"Just take your time. We literally do have all day."

Cabbott made another adjustment and settled down again. Shooting from the seated position was far from his favorite, but he was just not able to comfortably lie down prone yet. Another round went down range.

"Hit! Dead on!"

"About damn time," he counted the number of empty casings next to him on the table, "Yeah, I'm sorely out of practice, never takes me more than eight rounds to sight for zero. Took me eleven this time."

"Picky, picky," Max teased.

"In this line of work, you have to be exact. It could be the difference between taking out your target, missing completely, or taking out an innocent bystander. Collateral damage is unacceptable in my books," he replied stiffly.

"Yes sir," Max said, feeling a bit like he had his toes stepped on.

Cabbott chambered another round, leaned down and took

aim. Max watched as the captain became nearly motionless, the only part of his body that moved was his finger as it slowly curled around the trigger. The range was cold and Max could see Cabbott exhale long and slow. It seemed an eternity before he let the round fly. Checking the spotting scope, Max turned to him, "Dead on again."

"Good. Now for something different," he picked up one of the solid lead bullets and dropped it into the chamber. Closing the bolt he settled down again and repeated his silent ritual. The round struck the target.

"Low and to the left."

Cabbott sat up and made a note on a pad of paper, "Mmm, I thought so." Ejecting the spent case, he loaded another and made a few adjustments to the scope. He leaned down, took aim and fired, "How's that?"

"Up two, right one. Try it," Max said as he leaned back and stretched.

The captain made the adjustments and loaded another. "All right, this one better be on. I'm getting tired." He leaned and fired again.

"That was good, right on this time."

"Excellent," he looked at his watch, "Lunch time, good I'm hungry too." He packed up his rifle and returned it to its case. He would clean it after lunch.

Max packed up the scope, "You're not much for conversation are you?"

"Not when I'm working. I must stay focused on my job."

"Oh, I understand. Sorry, I'll remember that."

"I've got plenty of stories to share, but when I'm on the range or on a job, I'm all business."

"The Old Salty Dog Club? You've got to be joking!" Eagle said with exasperation.

"No ma'am, that's the name of the place. We saw Westland in there having a wonderful time socializing with a working girl," Sam said as he snatched a piece of pizza from the box Jake was carrying by.

"And how long did he stay there?" Cabbott inquired.

"He was there probably four hours. Didn't take anyone home with him, he just was there to chat 'em up," Tige added.

"Anything else to report?" Eagle said as she took a long drink of tea.

"We did find a good road that might work for the accident. Long, straight, and has good sized trees on each side. The only problem is the speed limit is 45," Jake hollered as he plopped down on the bed.

"That should be close enough. We can force the issue if need be," Cabbott said as he made a notation, "Is there any other activities that he does at night?"

"No, not really. Most everything is during the day. He goes and plays golf, does a bit of shopping and probably meets up with his contact while he's shopping. We've tailed him pretty heavy and can't ever catch him in the act," Sam replied.

Cabbott turned to Eagle, "I think we should bring them home so we can plan this in a secure location. I think I have enough to go on."

"Tige, did you hear Cabbott? Come on home. We'll finish planning the mission from here."

"Aw, do we have to? I was working on my tan!"

D.M. wandered into Eagle's lab. He carried a six pack of Alhambra beer. Plopping it on the counter he leaned over and gave her a quick kiss on the cheek, "Hello my love."

"You seem to be in a good mood tonight."

"I'm really hoping this works."

Eagle collected her supplies for drawing blood, "I wanna take a blood sample before you do the test, that way I can measure the enzyme levels in your blood."

"So if it doesn't work you know how much to fix it by?" He unbuttoned his cuff and pulled up his sleeve.

"Hopefully." She tied the tourniquet around his arm and prepped the site, "At least you have nice easy veins to work with." Making the stick, she drew two vials of blood. Removing the needle, she pressed a gauze pad against the site. D.M. put his finger on it until she could get a piece of tape. "All right, drink up major."

He pulled a bottle out of the pack and with his hardened titanium thumbnail, popped the cap off with ease.

Eagle looked over at him and shook her head, "Yeah, cute parlor trick."

"Hey, I'd like to see you try that. Bet you wouldn't have a fingernail left."

She sat back in her chair and folded her arms, "Are you gonna sit here all night and flap your trap or are you gonna drink up?"

D.M. ginned and held the bottle up, "Cheers!" He took a long swallow of beer and then let out a sigh, "Oh that's good!"

Eagle motioned to him for the bottle. He handed it to her and she took a sip, "Not bad. I'm not much of a beer drinker though." She handed it back.

"Maybe it's not so much the taste, but the fact that it reminds me of home...Just wish I had a bowl of olives to go with it." He quickly downed the bottle and sat it on the counter. Grabbing another, he popped the top off. Just as he was getting ready to take another drink, he belched loudly, "Ooops! Pardon me." They both chuckled. Eagle took the two vials of blood and began to process them. The major sat watching her, working on his beer.

"Well, how are you feeling?" She said as she pulled a vial from the centrifuge.

"Okay so far," he looked at his watch, "And this is longer than I made it last time."

"Good, let's hope we're making some progress."

"Hey, have you had any luck working on that super healing drug?"

"H.C. 15?"

"Yeah."

"Some. We're still wrestling with a few issues. Maybe we'll get back to clinical trials sometime in the next few months."

After an hour of waiting to see if he would have any reaction, D.M. was getting tired. It was late and he knew they would have a busy day tomorrow. "Well, so far so good. I think we can call this test a success."

Eagle took two empty vials and set them on the counter, "Can

I draw some more out of you so I can get another reading?"

"Sure," he pulled up his sleeve again. Eagle found a different vein and drew the blood. "If you're done with me, I'm gonna call it a day," he yawned.

"Yes, I think that's all. Hopefully this will be the solution for you."

"I hope so. It would be nice to enjoy a few drinks once in a while without all the agony that goes with it."

The men returned home two days later. The snow had let up and they were able to land with minimal effort. The maintainers had cleared the runway and the hangers. It was just a matter of time before the next storm hit. Eagle was doubting herself that the base was the perfect place for the team. Maybe she should have opted for someplace warmer with less extreme weather. Well, they were there now and would have to deal with it.

The team spent the next several days working out the plans for their mission. All were feeling that they could pull off their respective parts. It was just a matter of fine tuning the details and ensuring that every bit of intel was gone over to ensure accuracy. Equipment was checked and rechecked; plans were committed to memory and rehearsals performed where they could be. They all wanted the mission to be a success.

D.M. rolled over and looked at Eagle. She was curled up on her side facing away from him. He inched over until he was curled up against her. With the impending mission, he'd been fighting more nightmares so he'd been sleeping with her. Sometimes she would wake up from a nightmare. D.M. realized she suffered from them too, although not as bad. She moaned and looked over her shoulder at him, "Morning."

"Morning," he replied and snuggled closer.

"You sleep okay?"

"Yeah, actually I did. Got nearly a full night," he leaned over and kissed her on the cheek.

"Good. We gotta do some more planning today."

"How much do you know about Captain Westmoreland?" He said, changing the subject.

"Why do you ask?"

"Oh, just talking with him, he's on the spooky side of things."

"What do you mean by that?"

"I mean the good captain is far more than just a sniper. He's been heavily trained by the CIA as an assassin."

"Humm, no, he didn't mention any of that. I guess he wanted to make sure he was going to be part of the team before he said anything."

"Maybe so, but that guy can kill you six ways from Sunday. He scares me!"

Eagle rolled over part way and looked at him, "I didn't think there was anyone alive that scared you."

"There's always a first."

The team sat down to breakfast. They ate quietly, knowing that after there was more mission planning. Cabbott leaned forward and looked down the table at Eagle, "Ma'am?"

"Yes?"

"The major was telling me that there are labs down stairs."

"Yes, on the fifth floor."

"Are there any vacant?"

"There might be, why?" She said as she poured another cup of tea.

"I have some things that really should be kept in a secure lab away from the general public."

"Like what?"

"Oh, just some tools of my trade."

Eagle knew now what he was talking about. The captain needed some place to store the rest of his assassination equipment. "I'll check after breakfast before we start planning. Will you need any of the equipment for this mission?"

"I have something in mind. Yes, I will."

"Absolutely not!" D.M. said loudly as he paced around the

briefing room table.

"She'll be fine," Cabbott replied, trying to smooth things over.

"I'll be fine D.M., it's my choice to do this," Eagle threw her weight into the conversation.

"And what if you get hurt?" The major retorted.

"I can take care of myself, you know that."

D.M. paced harder, "I don't like it. I just don't like it."

"Major, sir. She's the best person to start this whole operation. She can get into the club and get Westland started down his final path."

Eagle stood and approached D.M., "Just like you needed to kill Kemal, I need to do this. I'm entitled to my share of the revenge too."

"And Tige will be right outside. He can keep an eye on her," Cabbott added.

The major looked down at her. He could see the serious determination in her eyes, "All right. But the first sign of trouble you get the hell out of there. Okay?"

Eagle nodded slowly. She knew D.M. was only trying to protect her and it wasn't worth the battle to say anything more. Even though they weren't exactly husband and wife, she knew this was one time she didn't want to disobey him, military rank or not. They both returned to their chairs and listened as Cabbott continued with his briefing. Each member of the team was given a specific job. They listened and took notes on what their part of the job was going to be.

Max raised his hand, "Sir, are you sure you want me spotting for you?"

"Do you feel you can do it?" Cabbott replied.

"I'm not sure. Maybe Tige would be a better choice. I'm not sure how good I would be spotting in the dark."

Cabbott looked over at Tige, "How would you feel about that? Can you spot for me?"

"No problem mate. Just have to work with you a few times to get your rhythm down."

"All right then, change of plans. Max, you stay with Eagle and mark the admiral's car with the infrared paint. D.M., you'll be the aggressor. Sam, you will push from behind to keep him going.

Tige, you spot for me. Jake, you're air support and surveillance," he jotted down a few notes, "Right, any questions?... I think we should plan to be out there a few days before so we can have a dry run through and to get everything we need."

A large crate sat in the lab next door to Eagle's. Cabbott carefully unpacked the contents. D.M. helped, not feeling very comfortable with handling all the equipment. He leaned down and reached into the crate, retrieving a smaller crate, he lifted it up and sat it on the counter.

"Be very careful with that. It's got the lethal stuff in it," Cabbott warned.

"Good, then you can open it," he pushed the crate so it set firmly on the counter.

"Just leave it there, I'll get it."

"I'm not so sure I'm happy you have a lab right next to Eagle's. You truly are death walking."

"Nonsense. I have very tight control over what I'm doing. You don't have to worry. I only let the genie out of the bottle when I absolutely have to." He opened a box and shuffled through its contents, "Ah yes, there they are!" He pulled out a small bag containing several gold rings.

"Are those the killer rings?"

"Yes. Well, they are when the correct poison is added to them."

"How does the wearer prevent from being poisoned by their own ring?" D.M. said as he leaned against the counter.

"I have a special hand gel that's put on prior. It makes a protective barrier. I can't say it's a hundred percent safe, but it does help."

"So Eagle's gonna give him the handshake of death?"

"That was my thought. I'll have her come down and practice so she can be as safe as possible. I also want her to slip Westland an LSD mickey in his drink. Make him just a bit paranoid. That will hopefully make your part easier."

"And you're gonna make me up the special blanks for my .45?"

"That's next on my list."

"You need any more help?" D.M. said as he turned to leave.

"No sir. Thanks for your help."

The sound of an approaching helicopter got Eagle's attention. She looked out the window to see a black Bell Jet Ranger approaching. Picking up the phone, she dialed Security Control, "Hello, this is Colonel Tryggvesson. Are you picking up that incoming helicopter? Do they have clearance?... Humm, they do? Thank you, I'll go see to them." She hung up and left her office. D.M. was coming down the hallway toward the elevator. "Well, it appears we have some unannounced company coming in, will you join me in seeing what they want?"

He nodded and they went up to the hanger deck. The helicopter was just touching down as they came from the hanger bay. The side door opened and two men dressed in black suits got out. They looked completely out of place in the cold, snowy environment. Approaching Eagle and D.M., they pulled out their identification badges.

"I'm agent Fields, and this is agent Marks, CIA. We understand that Captain Westmoreland is here. We require his services. He will need to come with us," one of them men said as he flipped his ID wallet shut and shoved it back in his pocket.

Eagle looked up at D.M. and then at the agents. She was not amused. "Just who the hell do you think you are? You do not come barging into my base and take my personnel as you wish. This is a secure location. And just how did you know that the captain was here?"

"The Army informed us ma'am."

"Yes, well, he is no longer part of the Army. The contract you had with them is null and void. Captain Westmoreland is part of our team now. I suggest you go find another assassin to do your dirty work," she turned on her heel and walked back into the hanger. D.M. followed. She poked at the elevator button and watched over her shoulder as the two men got back in the helicopter and left. The elevator doors opened and they stepped in. D.M. leaned down and gave her a quick kiss on the cheek.

"What was that for?" She said, a tone of surprise in her voice.

The major laughed lightly, "I love it when you're assertive."

"Mmmm, bitchy more like. I'm not gonna roll over like the Army did and give the captain up whenever they need him. We've got too much invested in him to let him go back out and get ruined."

Cabbott groaned. Even with a fairly thick shooting mat, the concrete floor of the basement range was still cold and hard. He could feel every ounce of metal in his body. Tige had all but one small light out and they were practicing in near darkness. The target was three hundred yards down range and was painted with infrared paint. He settled down to take another shot. A few moments later a loud report sounded through the range.

"Hit. Just a tad high though," Tige said as he peered through the spotting scope. He was intrigued by all the equipment Cabbott had: infrared scopes, special paint, poisons, and a host of other goodies all used for the sole purpose of assassination. He was thoroughly enjoying all the time he was spending with the captain.

Cabbott made a minor adjustment, "Damn, this floor's cold." He lined up and took another shot.

"Dead on," Tige called.

"Good. I'm pretty frozen," Cabbott said as he struggled to get up.

"Need some help mate?"

He lay there for a few moments, frustrated, "All I can get."

Tige helped him up, "You know, I wonder if you can borrow a slinky suit..."

"What the hell is that?"

"Jake came up with it. It's a rather nifty deal. You put it on like long johns and it has controls where you can adjust the temperature to keep you either warm or cool."

"Sounds good. How do I get one?" He said as he lowered himself into a chair. He could feel every bone and joint complaining.

"I think you and Max are pretty close in size. You can borrow his; he won't be needing it any time soon. You'll get your own once they fit you for a set of armor."

"Thanks."

"I'll get it and you can try it after lunch."

CHAPTER THIRTY SEVEN

The team loaded up on the C-130. Jake carefully strapped down the Warhawk in the back. D.M. had gone to the storage unit and returned with his motorcycle. They were flown to Homestead Air Reserve base on the south east coast of Florida. From there, they took the Warhawk and landed at the local municipal airport in Boca Raton. D.M. didn't have any reservations about riding his bike the eighty plus miles up to Boca, the weather was nice and he looked forward to a road trip. He had tried to convince Eagle to go for a ride, but she of course, refused him. It was a good way for him to get his mind cleared and focused on the mission.

They rented cars to allow them freedom to move about the city. After checking into the same motel the recon team had used, they gathered for a meeting in one of the rooms. It was early evening and they had just returned from dinner. Cabbott sat at a small desk, the others arranged about him on beds or the floor, "Okay everyone. With tomorrow being Tuesday, I think we should do some more surveillance to make sure Westland's patterns haven't changed. By Thursday, I hope we can do a dry run through that night to see if our plan will work. We'll need to go out and get some disguises. Tige, you know where the store is right?"

"Yup. Right in a big shopping mall."

"Good. I think the one who needs the most elaborate disguise will be you ma'am."

Eagle laughed lightly, "Most likely. I've never had the occasion to dress as a hooker before!"

Cabbott pulled up a few pictures Sam had taken of the women they saw at the club on the laptop, "Well, at least they appear to be higher class. So it's just a matter of finding the right attire for you.

We'll go out tomorrow morning and see what we can come up with. Then we should practice a bit on your handshake."

"Sounds like a plan."

The next morning D.M. was digging though his gear bag. Jake sat up in bed and watched him, "Why'd you bring all your armor?"

"Two reasons: one, I'd rather play it safe just in case Westland happens to be armed and takes a shot back at me. Two, in case he manages to bump me or something and I wipe out. I want as much protection as I can."

"That's reasonable. What are you gonna hide the armor under?"

"Not sure. Can't fit it under my jeans- just a bit too tight."

"How about a pair of leather pants? That will give you even more protection."

"Good idea. But I don't have any," D.M. replied as he disconnected some of the parts that he didn't want to wear.

"I'm sure we can find a place to get you some. I'll go over and check after breakfast."

"Thanks."

The team returned from breakfast and broke off into groups to get supplies or to resume surveillance. Eagle, Cabbott and Max were to go and find the right disguises. Sam and Tige would go out and see what Westland was up to. D.M. and Jake had shopping of their own to do. Everyone was in the parking lot getting ready to go their separate ways. Jake came out of the room with directions in hand, "Okay, got 'em."

D.M. swung his leg over his bike, "Are you gonna take the rental car? Or do you wanna ride bitch with me?"

Jake looked around at the others. He quickly darted over to D.M., "Oh major, I'll ride bitch with you any day baby!" The rest of the team laughed hysterically. Jake hopped on and grabbed the sides of the major's jacket.

"Why do you have to keep embarrassing me like that?" D.M. said as he started up the bike.

"Because it's so much fun to see you blush!"

D.M. reached back and swatted the lieutenant. Jake laughed and hung on as they sped out of the parking lot.

Cabbott opened the door for Eagle. She slid into the passenger seat and he closed the door. Climbing into the back seat, he buckled up and motioned for Max to go. Since it had been so long since he'd driven a car, he figured it was safer to let Max take the wheel. They drove to the large shopping mall and found the costume store. Cabbott went to work selecting the proper disguise for Eagle. He wanted to make her as completely different as possible from her normal self. The less she looked like herself, the less chance that Westland would recognize her. He perused a long line of wigs, "Humm, how do you feel about being brunette?"

"I don't exactly fancy the idea, but you're the expert," she replied as she poked through some racks with various costume dresses on them. Cabbott wandered back and forth until he found a wig he thought would suit her. He bought it over for her to try. Eagle balled her hair up and the captain carefully helped her with the wig. He stood back and looked at her.

"Does make you look a whole lot different. Just need to color in your eyebrows and that should work."

Eagle looked in a mirror, "I guess it'll work." She wanted to face Westland as herself, but the danger was just too great. She would have to settle for the satisfaction that she'd be the one, who if all else failed, would give him the handshake to Hell.

Cabbott saw the look on her face, "Well, you only have to do this once and then you can be happily blond again."

She snatched the wig off her head, "All right, let's get the rest of the stuff we need."

They made their purchases and then Eagle found a dress store. Cabbott and Max sat in chairs near the dressing room and waited for her to appear. She figured it would have been more fun had D.M. been there, but they were men, and she hoped they would see something they liked that would work for the mission. Cabbott had helped her select dresses that were roughly the same style as the ones the girls at the club wore. He wanted her to blend in.

Eagle stepped out of the dressing room. She was wearing a

tight black dress with a low cut neck and spaghetti straps. The dress barely came to the top of her knees.

"Yes!" Max exclaimed. He'd never seen Eagle that dressed up before. On a normal day, she was never hard on the eyes, but in this dress she was a knock out.

"No," Cabbott said.

"What's wrong?" She said as she turned around once.

"We need to hide more of that pale Norwegian skin."

Max looked over at Cabbott, "No we don't!"

Eagle laughed as they bickered back and forth.

Cabbott finally got the upper hand, "Can you try the other black one. The one with the little jacket that goes over it?"

"Oh, all right," she went back and changed again. She came out in another black dress, this one a little longer and had a short, scalloped front jacket that went with it.

"No!" Max said.

"Yes!" Cabbott barked. And they were back bickering again.

Eagle stood waiting for them to stop. She wished D.M. was there, he would have picked the one he liked right away. She returned to the dressing room and tried on one that she had picked out. It was another tight little satin black dress that had long gloves that went nearly all the way up her arms. The neck was cut to show what cleavage she had and the shoulder straps were thicker, hiding a little more of her skin. It was a longer dress, nearly coming to her ankles and there was a long slit up the left side to the middle of her thigh. She stepped out of the dressing room. Cabbott and Max took one look at her, then looked at each other, "Perfect!" They shouted in unison.

"Good, I was thinking I liked this one the best anyways," she replied, returning to the dressing room.

D.M. stood looking in the mirror. They had found the local Harley Davidson shop and Jake managed to find a pair of leather pants that would fit him. "This feels really weird," D.M. said as he tugged at the leather trying to get comfortable.

"You got enough room for the armor?"

"Yeah, feels like it," he wiggled a bit more, "Would like a bit more room for something else though."

Jake chuckled, "Well, sorry, can't help you there. You weren't planning on wearing that part of your armor were you?"

"No, can't sit the bike comfortably if I did." He went to go take them off.

"Hey, you probably wanna wear those a bit to get them broken in and more comfortable," Jake said as he tried on a new helmet, something similar to his old one except not beat up. They paid for their purchases and headed out to the parking lot. The lieutenant walked around the major's bike, "So they beefed up the springs and shocks before they shipped it to Reno?"

"And put pegs up front and back so I could stretch out a bit. I'm getting used to it. Nice bike." He climbed on.

"I thought you'd like it," Jake said as he pulled on his helmet and swung his leg over, settling down behind the major, "I'm just jealous that you got to bring yours. This place is great for bike rides."

"Coming up the coast was nice. But hey, you got to fly the Warhawk, so that can't be all bad."

"True. I'd prefer a Badger, but to get any fly time makes me happy."

D.M. put on his helmet and looked over his shoulder, "What? No rude comments this time?"

"Naw, nobody here to embarrass you in front of."

They headed back toward the motel. Along the way, D.M. noticed a jewelry store. Making a quick lane change, he pulled into the parking lot. "Why are we stopping here?" Jake said as he hopped off.

"Oh, just looking for something," D.M. said as he pulled his helmet off and looped the chin strap over one handle bar. He strolled through the front door and stopped. A large number of jewelry cases stood in front of him, "Yikes," he said softly.

"And what are you looking for?" Jake pried. D.M. stepped over to a display case filled with rings. "You shopping for a ring?" The major did not reply. "You gonna propose to her?"

"All ready did," he replied lowly.

Jake smacked D.M. firmly on the shoulder, "You shit! And you didn't even tell me! Humph! Some partner you turned out to be."

"Wasn't much to tell. I asked her, she said 'yes' and that's that." He moved away from the ring cabinets and went to look at necklaces. Finding a selection of gold charms, he looked intently for just the right one.

"Oh yeah, that's right, you can't buy her a ring, that would be too obvious."

"Yup. And we have to keep this seriously on the quiet side. General Spears knows, and he said he won't defend us if we get caught."

"How'd he find out?"

"He's known Eagle a very long time. He kind of adopted her as a daughter. It was parental intuition that busted us... He's okay with it from that side. The command side however, he can't endorse it."

"Understandable. Maybe we should remind everyone that this needs to be kept under the radar."

D.M. found a charm that he liked. He motioned for a salesman, "Can I have a look at that one?" He said pointing to a European style golden dragon with ruby eyes. The salesman took it out and handed it to him. Jake leaned over and looked at it.

"That's beautiful D.M., I'm sure she'll love it."

"Think so?"

"Definitely!"

"All right, I'll take this. And I need a nice chain to put it on."

The salesman found a suitable chain and boxed it all up. Jake leaned against the counter, "Did you guys set a date yet?"

"No, I'm leaving that to her. She's the one with traditions to uphold, so she can decide that."

"I'm really happy for you guys."

Sam yawned and put down his note pad. They had been staking out the golf course for nearly four hours. Tige had disappeared, trying to keep an eye on Westland to see if he met up with someone. It was nearly 1600 when the captain returned to the car.

"Well, did you see anything?" Sam said as he pulled the lever on his seat bringing it back up from being reclined.

"No, not much. He's a rather bad golf player. Nearly took my head off with a bloody slice. Had to hurry and find another place to hide."

"He didn't meet with anyone?"

"Nope. He was out with the usual gaggle of blokes we saw him with last time," Tige replied as he started the car. They watched as Westland came out, put his clubs in the trunk, changed shoes, got into his car and drove off. Tige followed along at a safe distance. He was certain Westland was heading home, but wanted to make sure of it. They followed him until they reached the motel parking lot. The rest of the team was outside enjoying the late day sun and having a few drinks. Pulling into the parking space, Eagle approached them.

"Any good intel today?" She said holding a glass of wine.

"Nope. Not a bloody thing."

"So there's no change in his routine?"

Sam got out and closed the car door, "Not that we can see."

Max came from one of the rooms and brought a beer for each of them. Tige quickly twisted off the cap and took a long drink, "Ah, that's better. Makes sitting in the bushes around a hot golf course all day not so bad." He plopped down in a chair next to Cabbott, "So how was your day?" He reached up and picked a leaf out of his hair.

Cabbott took a drink of beer, "Oh, just brutal. We had to sit and watch Eagle try on tight little black dresses."

Tige shook his head, "That's just not fair mate!"

"No one said this job was easy," Cabbott grinned.

Max awoke to find Cabbott sitting in a chair near the window. It was 0200. The dim lights from the walkway outside filtered through the blinds. "Don't you sleep?" Max said as he rolled over and sat up part way.

"Sleep is overrated," he replied dryly, not moving.

"Nightmares again?"

"Nightmares always."

Max sat up and turned on the light, "You wanna talk about it?"

"I've talked until I'm blue in the face, yet they still keep coming." He got up, pulled on a pair of jeans and went to the fridge. Taking out two bottles of beer he went outside. Max knew he didn't go far, he could see his shadow as he sat down in one of the chairs. Climbing out of bed, he grabbed a pair of shorts and dressed. He wasn't sure he could help the captain, but he was going to give it a try. Stepping outside into the cool night air, he sat down next to Cabbott.

"Why don't you just go back to bed?" The captain said unemotionally.

"Because you look like you need someone to talk to."

"I all ready told you that talking does nothing for me."

Max turned to him, "Look, just hear me out okay? We've been partnered up as a team. That means we're gonna spend a lot of time together... I'm no shrink, but I think we need to be as open and honest with each other as we can. I need to understand the way you think and work, and I'm sure you'd feel the same about me... I don't like talking to Dr. Lindman, but the times I did, it seemed to help a bit... So if you want, talk to me. We all have to help each other out."

Cabbott sat for a while thinking. He took a long drink of beer and held the bottle between his laced fingers, "I just can't get the thoughts to go away..."

"What thoughts? Killing all those people?"

"Yes. But the worst is the accident..." He finished one beer and twisted the cap off the other, "I had my reservations about the mission. I didn't think the Agency had planned it out very well. There were just too many variables to go wrong... But we took the mission because we were told to... I had this feeling that something was gonna go wrong from the very start... But I was basically powerless to say or do anything." He took a drink and rubbed his face in frustration, "When zero hour arrived and we jumped, there was a storm just beginning to form. The air was terribly unstable and we hit a bad down draft... Jenkins and I got slammed into the top of a mountain..." He took a few long drinks and sat collecting his thoughts. Max could see the anguish on his face. "Most thought that Jenkins died instantly... I wish he would have. Instead, he lay there for probably four hours screaming in pain as he died... I couldn't help him. God knows I tried to get the twenty or so feet to help him, but I couldn't move. All I could do was lay there and listen to my friend die." He sniffed loudly, rubbed his eyes and pulled his fingers through his hair. "Every night I lay in bed wondering if I could have gotten to him could I have saved his life?"

"You'll never be able to answer that question," Max said softly.

"I know... And still I can't get it out of my head... Jenkins was married and just had a son born. I felt responsible that he would never see them again."

"If anyone is responsible, it should be the Agency."

"Yeah, right, never happen," Cabbott scoffed.

"You did everything you could to try and make it a safe mission. You can't control the weather or the CIA; those things were just out of your hands."

The captain rubbed his face, "I guess what really makes it hard is Jenkins and I became friends. That's a cardinal sin in our line of work. I got too close to him and when he died, it really fucked me up... So I've learned the hard way never make friends with those I work with."

"You can't really say that. Yes, our team knows that as well, but we're very close together. Hell, I think it's saved our hides on several occasions. We know each other so well that we can almost think like the other person. You fight harder when you know one of the team is out there in trouble."

"I fight hard anyways... Understand though if I don't fit right in, I've still got a lot of baggage to carry around."

"We all got baggage of some sort, so don't worry. I think you fit in okay for being here such a short time. At least you interact with us. Sergeant von Teufel managed to destroy our morale and we all wanted him dead."

Cabbott looked over and cracked a weak smile, "You did get your wish."

Max smiled back, "Yes, and I think I was celebrating the most... I mean I've worked with some assholes before, but he really took the cake."

The captain tipped down the last of his beer and stood. He was walking nearly all the time without his cane and getting stronger ever day, "I'm not the asshole type. But forgive me if I'm not always warm and fuzzy- if you know what I mean."

"Yeah, I understand. And you can talk to me anytime you want. We're all in it together," he offered his hand and Cabbott shook it.

Eagle pulled into the parking lot and turned off the car. D.M. and Jake were outside chatting. She got out and carried a white Styrofoam food container into her room. The rest of the team had decided on sandwiches for lunch, but Eagle had other ideas. A few minutes later she reappeared with her container. Sitting down in the chair in front of her room she proceeded to open it and prepare her lunch. The major wandered over, "Decided against sandwiches huh?"

"Oh, yes. I found a place that sells Norwegian food," she picked up what appeared to be a tortilla of sorts and put a piece of fish on it.

"And what's that?" D.M. said as he sniffed the air, "Doesn't smell very good."

"Lutefisk, laks, lefse and grønnerter stuing."

"Do I really wanna know what all that is?"

Eagle took a mouthful and smiled, "Mmmmmmm."

"Norwegian comfort food?"

"Ja!.. Lefse are these- potato pancakes," she held one up. "Laks is just smoked salmon... Grønnerter stuing is stewed green peas. Lutefisk is the true Viking food... It's dried cod that has been soaked in lye."

D.M. wrinkled his nose, "That sounds absolutely revolting!"

Eagle laughed. Taking a lefse and some laks she rolled it up and offered it to him, "Come on, it's just smoked salmon on a potato pancake... I'll spare you the lutefisk for now."

The major carefully took a bite, "Humm, not bad." He finished off the small pancake, "I'm just trying to figure out why you would eat fish soaked in lye."

"It's a Viking delicacy. An old folk tale says that when the Vikings invaded Ireland, the Irish put lye on the raider's dried fish thinking it would poison them. Instead, they found it to be quite tasty. I guess the old adage holds true that what doesn't kill you makes you stronger. At least I'm not Icelandic Viking, they eat hakarl."

"I'm almost afraid to ask what that is."

"Rotted shark meat."

"Gross!"

"Yeah, a bit too much for me!"

Cabbott came from his room carrying a small gray plastic case. He walked over to D.M. and handed it to him, "I think we need to make a small change of firearms."

"Why?"

"Because if you use your .45, it will eject the spent case and leave possible evidence.

D.M. opened the box, "You've got to be kidding me!"

"No, that's the perfect weapon for the job. Small, short barreled, and still quite lethal. The benefit is that because it's a revolver, you won't lose a spent case."

"Oh come on, a snub nosed .38?"

"Easier to draw and conceal." He pointed to a plastic bag with six bullets in it, "These are special rounds, they have a glass projectile instead of lead. It should be just enough to break Westland's side window and not be found... I tested some like it back home and they worked well... Come up on him from a forty five degree angle and aim toward the dash board. You don't really wanna hit him with the projectile, just splatter him with glass. That should freak him out pretty good."

The major examined the contents of the bag, "Thanks, hopefully that'll do the trick."

"I loaded them pretty loud and bright, don't look too much at him when you shoot, you'll lose your night vision," he stepped over to Eagle and offered his hand. She took it and practiced what he had taught her, "Good. And having those gloves will be a bonus. You'll have an extra layer of protection against the poison."

"You think I can pull this off?" She said.

"Sure. Just keep your wits about you and you'll do fine."

Max and Eagle sat in one car in the parking lot of the club. Sam waited down the road about two hundred yards. It was rehearsal night. Max got out, quickly painted the right front wheel of the car with infrared paint and climbed back in. "All right everyone Bull Dog here, are we ready?" He said as he started the car.

"Ground Zero here, roger, I'm set.

"Lone Wolf, I'm in position."

"Kingpin is high and mighty with eyes on target."

"Wombat and Angel are on our bellies," Tige reported.

Max backed out of the parking space, "We are rolling." They pulled out onto the road and it wasn't long before he saw Sam trailing behind. Jake flew overhead keeping an eye on progress. D.M. was waiting for Jake to cue him to start his part. The road was dark with only a few cars on it.

"Lone Wolf, Kingpin, target approaching. You have maybe fifteen seconds."

"Roger. I see them."

Sam sped up and closed the distance. The cars passed and D.M. pulled out on the road. He quickly caught up to the car and prepared to come down the side to make his simulated shot. Max had the window down. D.M. drew the pistol and aimed, "Fire! Fire! Fire!" He said and quickly reholstered the gun. Max stepped on the gas hoping that would be the response Westland would do. D.M. backed off. Sam kept right behind, preventing the car from slowing down.

"Angel, they'll be to you in twenty seconds," Jake called as he looped back to watch. He had the Warhawk in silent mode and was struggling to fly so slowly. With the rotors flared the helicopter had less lift so Jake had to do some fancy flying to keep it in the air.

"Roger Kingpin," Cabbott peered into his scope, "Wombat, you got anything yet?"

"Affirmative. Four hundred yards and closing pretty fast. Nice paint job."

"Good. Call it," he wrapped his finger around the trigger.

"Two hundred. One hundred. Mark on us," the car passed their position, "Now one hundred out, two hundred, three hundred."

"Fire!" Cabbott called.

Max immediately slowed down and pulled to the side of the road, "Yeah, that put us right into the area with the most trees."

"Excellent," Cabbott answered as he rolled over and got up, "Let's all meet back for debriefing."

Jake was the last to arrive for the debriefing. The municipal airport was nearly half an hour from the motel and he had to make sure the Warhawk was secured. He finally strolled through the door at 2200.

"Nice that you could join us lieutenant," Max teased.

"Hey, not like the airport is just down the street," he grabbed a beer out of the refrigerator.

Cabbott sat in his usual spot at the desk. He had a note pad and pen ready to take any notes, "All right, feedback everyone."

"I think it went well. Admittedly, D.M. scared the shit out of me coming down the side of the car like that," Max said.

"Good, nice to see I have the desired effect," the major smiled.

Cabbott pointed at Jake, "You didn't have any trouble keeping everything straight did you?"

"Nope, just had a little trouble in the beginning since there are a lot of trees hanging over the road in that part. Otherwise, I got it."

"Sam? You fine with being the pusher?" Cabbott said as he made a couple of notes.

"Yeah, I think so. Did it seem like I was close enough?"

"From what I could tell, yes. Just be prepared to break off when he loses control otherwise you may end up in the back seat," he looked over at Eagle, "Ma'am, how do you think it went?"

"Like clockwork. I must compliment you gentlemen, you all came together to make this work. Let's hope it goes this well in two days."

"Oh, Tige, what was the execution time on the whole operation?"

Tige pulled up his sleeve and looked at the data he had written on his forearm, "Four minutes and thirty five seconds."

Cabbott dropped his pen on the table, "Damn, I'm not used to having something go so well! And the fun part is we are doing this pretty much like an Agency hit. So if anyone does realize that it was an assassination, they'll be looking at someone else to pin the blame on."

"Are you sure? I mean you're the architect of this one. They know you belong to us now, so it might only be a matter of time," D.M. replied as he stood.

"Hmmm, true. I can assure they won't figure it out."

"How so?"

"Destroy any evidence by fire."

"Sounds gruesome, but effective," Eagle said as she got up to leave.

D.M. sat up in bed shaking, breathing hard and sweating. He'd been lucky and hadn't had any flashbacks in a few days. He always found it harder when he was away from home. Sleep was difficult enough as it was, and being somewhere unfamiliar made it worse. Jake rolled over and looked at him, "Hey, why don't you go next door to Eagle?"

"No, it's late and I don't wanna wake her. Just go back to sleep, I'll be fine." He settled back into bed and lay there staring at the ceiling. Jake closed his eyes and went back to sleep. It wasn't more than half an hour when he startled awake. D.M. looked over at him, "Your turn now huh?"

Jake rubbed his eyes, "Yeah."

"Well, since we're both awake, you wanna talk about it?" He reached over and turned on the light.

Jake rolled over onto his stomach in his bed, grabbed a pillow and shoved it under his chest, holding himself up on his elbows, "I keep getting these strange dreams. Sometimes they're bad, other times they're psychedelic... I'd almost swear I was on drugs or something."

"The human mind can really get crazy sometimes."

"I get a lot of flashbacks of getting blown up at Kemal's place."

"That's to be expected. Traumatic events like that seem to get stuck on replay in the mind. God knows I have quite a few that haunt me at night." D.M. sat up, leaning against the headboard. He rubbed his face, "So what was this one?"

"Got blown up again."

"That one is your worst right?"

"Yeah, I've been pretty fortunate so far. That was my only real big 'oh shit' moment."

"Count yourself lucky," D.M. said as he turned off the light, "As Eagle says, you can only hope that with time it fades somewhat... Of course with this job, it's just a matter of time before another one gets thrown on top of it."

"Great, can't say I'm looking forward to that."

"Can't say that I do either. Part of the job though."

Eagle pulled on black coveralls. It was Friday night and Tige was taking her to the club for some surveillance. She wanted to get as much intel on the place and the girls that worked there as she could. The recon team had found out the girls only came on the weekend. The rest of the week the club was mostly inhabited by a few old war horses that had nothing better to do with their lives than to hang out, tell war stories and get drunk.

They were just getting into the car when D.M. approached, "What time do you think you'll be back?" He said leaning down to her window.

"Why? Don't want me out past curfew?" She teased.

"Well, umm, I was just wondering."

Eagle reached out and patted him on the cheek, "Don't worry major, we'll only be a couple of hours."

Tige leaned over, "Yeah mate, and I promise I'll check for snakes." He started to back out.

"Hey, what's that supposed to mean?!" D.M. took a few steps toward them.

The captain laughed and quickly left the parking lot before the major could catch up. They drove the few miles to the club and parked in the darkest part of the lot. They sat for a while observing the front door. When all was fairly quiet, they got out and disappeared into the tree line. Tige took her around to the back where they could watch. He checked the area before motioning for her to take a seat on an old log.

"So was that what you meant by checking for snakes?"

"Yeah, met up with a rather unfriendly inhabitant last time. Best guess it was a four foot long Copperhead."

"That must have been exciting."

"Naw, not really. Pinned it down, cut its head off and chucked it back in the bush."

They sat in silence for a while. Eagle had a small pair of binoculars and was doing her best to see what the girls were doing. She spotted Westland. He was sitting at the end of the bar with his back to the patio door. A tall brunette woman came up to him. Westland pulled the bar stool out for her and signaled the bartender to get her a drink.

"Bingo!" Eagle whispered.

"Got him?"

"Uh huh. And he's with a brunette."

“Lemme have a look if you don’t mind.”

She handed him the binoculars. Tige scanned what area he could see through the door, “Humm, I see a couple of girls that were there last time, but there are some new faces too.”

“Do you think there’s a pimp that runs them?”

“I haven’t ever seen any guy in there or in the parking lot to suggest it. And the girls only show up on the weekend.” He handed the binoculars back to her.

“Humm, I wish I had some time to get dressed up and see if I can get in there.”

“The major would be pretty pissed if you did that.”

“Yeah? So? I’m a big girl and I need to make sure my part of the mission goes smoothly.”

“Maybe so, but I don’t think D.M. would approve. Besides, your part may be the kick off of the mission, but it’s not exactly the most vital part.”

“It’s important to me. This is my chance to get revenge for all the things Westland has done to me,” she paused for a few moments, “One day after the committee had finished, I was getting my things together. We were the only ones left. I had just finished packing up my bag when I felt him behind me…” she took in a long, deep breath, “He grabbed me from behind and pushed me against the table…I knew I could fight back, but I didn’t. Something in me knew he wasn’t going to rape me, but he wanted to make it very clear that he was in charge of the situation, dominating me...He's done nothing but try to intimidate me the whole time I've had dealings with him."

"Bloody bastard."

"Please, please Tige, don't tell D.M. about that."

"I won't. That's for you to tell him when you feel the time is right."

"Yeah, maybe after Westland is done for...I could see the major getting the chance and ripping him apart."

"And that wouldn't please you?"

Eagle looked through the binoculars at Westland, "I'm not sure that would really please me. It's my time for vengeance."

"I can respect that ma'am."

She continued to watch for nearly two hours. Finally it looked like Westland was getting ready to leave, "Tige, can you hurry around front and see if she gets in the car with him?"

"Yes ma'am, on my way. I'll meet you back at the car. Be careful out here." He quickly picked his way through the dark forest and appeared at the corner of the building. He watched as Westland got into his car and left. No woman with him. He waited a few more minutes to see if maybe the woman would come out and leave, but she stayed inside.

Following along the tree line, Tige stepped out onto the asphalt and stood next to their car nearly out of sight. A few minutes later he could hear Eagle coming toward him. Walking slowly, she was trying to be careful. The last thing she wanted was an encounter with the native wildlife. She stopped near the front door and observed for a few minutes. There was a formidable looking bouncer at the door. He was roughly as tall as D.M., but probably weighed nearly three hundred and twenty pounds. His head was shaved and he sported a black mustache and goatee. A car pulled into the parking lot. Two more women got out and walked up to the door. One was a tall blond dressed in a skin tight leopard print dress and stiletto heels that must have been five inches high. The other was a brunette dressed more reasonably in a less tight dark red dress with lots of jewelry. It was obvious they were working girls.

"Hi ya Bobbie, how's it going tonight?" The tall blond asked.

"Busy night tonight Gabriele, almost think we need some more girls to go around," he replied with a thick Brooklyn accent.

"Well, maybe I'll see if I can find a few more for tomorrow night, since Saturday is the best night anyways," she reached up and gave him a kiss on the cheek.

"I'm sure there will be plenty of work to go around for all the girls."

The brunette pulled out a cigarette and lit up, "Ick, Gabby, I really hate coming here. These old guys are crude, rude and have no class at all. Can't we find a better place to work?"

"Shut up Marty, I don't like this gig either, but when you get them real drunk, they pay well. And half the time they get so drunk they can't even get it up."

Eagle took in as much information as she could. Perhaps the intel she had just heard would make getting in there easier. Continuing on, she finally reached Tige. Stepping out of the trees, she made her way over to the car. The captain saw her and opened the door.

"Well?" She said.

"Went home stag. The bird stayed inside," he said starting up the car.

"Humm, that's curious. Why do you come to a club, socialize with hookers and go home alone?"

Tige turned onto the road, "Maybe he's just looking for female company on social terms... Or better yet, his Willy's wore out," he said, his accent still very strong after all his time with the team.

Eagle looked over at him with a rather confused expression.

"You know, his Willy's worn out...Uh, his pecker's pooped...Uh, his dick is done for."

They both started laughing. "You know, you're probably right," she finally said after regaining her composure. "I overheard two hookers talking about that."

"Aye, that's the saddest day of a man's life. When the Willy stops working, life might just as well be over!" They laughed even harder.

"Makes me wonder just how much he could've pressed the

point if can't even get a rise."

"Sometimes a bloke will try and cover it up. Bet he was just trying to throw his power and position around to intimidate you."

"Sorry, I would have none of it. I'm not easily intimidated."

"Ah, you're a feisty enough Viking you probably would have broken him anyways!"

As the car pulled into the parking lot, D.M. came out. Eagle got out of the car still giggling a bit.

"What's so funny?" The major said as he looked at his watch.

"Oh, the captain has been a rather entertaining tour guide tonight."

"What do you mean by that?"

"Ah, Tige, what was it you said about Westland?" She leaned back into the car.

The captain got out and locked the car, "Oh, I said that he probably goes to the club and chats up the birds but doesn't take 'em home because his Willy's wore out." They both started laughing again. D.M. wasn't very amused.

Eagle finally stopped laughing and looked up at him, "Sorry. You kinda had to be there to fully appreciate it." She yawned, "All right, let's hit the hay, we got a big day tomorrow."

CHAPTER THIRTY EIGHT

Everyone was up bright and early. They were ready to go to work. It would be nearly eighteen hours before they would complete the mission, yet they were all ready checking equipment. Jake fired up the Warhawk and flew several surveillance patterns over the area looking for anything out of the ordinary. He was also working on his timing. Cabbott and Tige found an area right next to the hotel where they could hide in the brush and target passing cars. This gave Tige extra practice with the rangefinder scope and Cabbott time to get his sight picture down. As far as both captains were concerned, there could never be enough practice. The others rehearsed their parts the best they could.

By early evening they were putting the finishing touches on the operation. As the sun went down they slowly began to leave out for their designated locations. Jake was just coming out the door of his room to leave for the airport when Eagle stuck her head out, "Jake?"

"Yes ma'am?"

"Can you send the major over? I need some help."

"Sure. I think he's just about dressed. I'll have him come right over when he's done."

"Thanks."

Jake went back in the room, "Hey, Eagle said she needs your help when you're done getting dressed."

"Okay, I'll be right there," he said as he struggled to get his leather pants over the thigh portion of his armor. It was a tight squeeze but he finally got them all the way up. He buckled his belt and then put on his jacket. Grabbing his room card, he left the room and headed next door. Jake was leaning against the car talking to Cabbott and Tige.

D.M. knocked on the door. Eagle opened it. The major thought his eyes were going to pop out. She stood dressed in the tight little black dress; her face was made up to bring out every ounce of beauty. Her hair was pulled up but a few tendrils fell on her shoulders. He stepped inside and closed the door. His mind was going crazy. Without much thought he grabbed her in his arms and kissed her passionately. Eagle didn't refuse him. He nudged her backward toward the bed. Using the same tactic Eagle had used on him during one sword practice, he tripped her up and dropped her on the bed, falling on top of her.

"Major!" She gasped. He let his weight rest against her and kissed her hard, his hands feeling the smooth satin of the dress. It didn't take long before Eagle could tell he was quite aroused by the situation. "D.M.?" She tried to dodge one of his kisses, "Major, please."

"What?" He whispered in a deep voice.

"I think we need to get to work."

He kissed her hard again, "I am working."

"That's not what I meant."

His hand found its way up the slit in her dress to the garter belt she was wearing. She had decided to complete her ensemble with fine black fishnet stockings. He wanted so much to undo everything she'd done, but she was right, they needed to get to work. Eagle groaned under his great weight. D.M. slid off her and knelt on the floor at the foot of the bed. She sat up and looked at him.

"Shit you look hot tonight," he said softly.

"So, I assume you approve of my choice in dresses?"

He smiled and tipped his head to one side, "I'd pay good money for you!"

She laughed lightly and put her hand on his cheek. He leaned up and kissed her gently. "I have something for you," he said as he reached in his jacket pocket. Taking out a long slender box he held it out, "Well, since we're engaged, and I can't really get you a ring to wear, I got you this," he opened the box to reveal the necklace and charm.

Eagle gasped, "D.M., it's beautiful!" She kissed him. "Oh, here, put it on me."

"Maybe you should wait until after this is over. Don't give Westland any reason to be suspicious."

"I suppose you're right," she stood up, "Can you zip up my dress and help get me into my wig?" She turned around so he could get at the zipper. D.M. stood and playfully unzipped the dress most of the way down. "I said up, not down!"

"Down is more fun," he let his hands wander inside the back of her dress, caressing her gently. After a few moments, he pulled the zipper up, wrapping his arms around her waist, he pulled her close, holding her, "I love you," he said softly.

"I love you too," she tipped her head back and nuzzled him. Finally he let his arms slide off and Eagle retrieved the wig. She worked at tucking in all the stray blond hairs as D.M. carefully placed it on her head.

"Ew, I don't fancy you as a brunette."

"Only temporary," she pinned it with some bobby pins, "Thanks, that was all the help I needed."

"You're welcome... Uh, maybe you can *help* me out later," he said as he tried to adjust his pants to be more comfortable, "I seem to have quite a problem right now." He was still very aroused. Eagle giggled at his obvious discomfort. Leaving her room he walked over and climbed on his bike. Jake approached him. He could see D.M. shifting uncomfortably.

"Problem?" Jake asked. He knew from the major's expression when he came from Eagle's room that he was definitely bothered.

"Yeah, big problem. That really neat Harley Davidson belt buckle you got me for Christmas is pretty damned uncomfortable right about now."

Jake chuckled, "Good hunting major," he patted him on the shoulder and walked off. D.M. put his helmet on and quickly started up the bike. He made a hasty exit from the parking lot. The major knew he had to get his mind on the mission, and hanging around waiting for Eagle to come out would have been pure torture.

Cabbott stood outside giving final instructions to everyone as they left. Jake climbed into the car and headed for the airport. Sam got his final instructions and left for his position. Max waited for Eagle to come out.

"Got the plate number?" Cabbott said as he ran down his checklist.

"Check," Max answered.

"Paint?"

"Check."

"Radio?"

"Check."

"Hooker?"

"Uh, not yet!" Max laughed. Cabbott looked over the top of his clipboard and cracked a devilish smile. A few minutes later Eagle appeared. Those that were left stopped what they were doing. There was just no way they could be inconspicuous. Each man stood with his jaw hanging open.

"Bloody hell!" Tige gasped.

Eagle giggled at their boyish expressions. Cabbott was the first to snap out of his trance, he quickly opened the car door for her, "You look lovely this evening ma'am."

"Thank you captain."

He reached in his pocket and produced a small plastic bag. Two rings and a very tiny bottle of poison were inside. "Here is what I want you to do... Put the first ring on. Do the deed and then find some way to excuse yourself to the bathroom. Take that one off carefully and dispose of it. Then take the other ring and put it on. Don't put any more poison on it; what you gave him will be sufficient. You got the LSD pill right?"

"Yes."

"And what cover name are you using?"

"Elkie Sraeps"

"Kind of funky don't you think?"

"Elkie was my nickname back home, and Sraeps is Spears spelled backwards."

"Devious, I love it... Good luck ma'am. I know you can do this."

He carefully closed the door and went around to Max. The lieutenant still stood transfixed.

Cabbott elbowed him, "Hey, time to get the show on the road."

"Uh, yes sir," Max stammered and climbed in the car. He did his best to keep his attention on his driving, but he found it hard not to occasionally glance in her direction.

"So lieutenant, how's my camouflage?" She said in a professional tone.

"Ma'am, If I didn't know who you were, I'd never recognize you."

"Good. Let's hope Westland doesn't know who I am either."

They drove along and finally pulled into the parking lot of the club. It was especially busy just like the bouncer said it was going to be. Cars were packed into the small lot. Max parked at the far end and turned off the car. They sat quietly for a few minutes. Eagle gathered up her nerve. Max scanned the parking lot to see if he could locate Westland's car.

"Do you see it?" Eagle said as she slid the ring on. She would put the poison on just after she got inside and had a look around. Jake radioed that he had followed Westland to the club.

"That may be it over there. Can you pass by it on your way in and verify?"

"Sure."

"Thanks," he looked over at her, "Are you ready?"

Eagle took in a deep breath and nodded. Max keyed his mike, "Attention all. White Feather is going in." He got out and opened the door for her. Eagle struggled a bit getting out so Max offered her a hand. She wasn't used to walking in such high heels, so the journey across the uneven parking lot was going to be difficult. "Good luck ma'am," he whispered as she started off. He sat back down in the car and watched her walk across the lot. He knew she was having trouble, but there was nothing he could do. Eagle passed by the car they thought was Westland's. She looked down at the plate, verified that it was his and then glanced back over her shoulder at Max. She nodded once and continued on. The bouncer was too busy talking to some other girls to notice what was going on around the parking lot. Trying her best not to misstep, she walked up the three steps to the small landing where the bouncer stood. The other girls had gone inside.

"Hi," she said softly.

"Hi," he replied, stepping closer, using his height to look down the front of her dress, "Haven't seen you here before."

"Oh, I'm a friend of Gabrielle. She told me that it was gonna be busy and there'd be plenty of work tonight."

"And what's your name sweet cheeks?"

"Elkie. Elkie Sraeps."

"You sound like you got a bit of an accent. Where are you from?"

"Sweden."

"Mmm, Swedish girls are always so hot."

Eagle played her finger up and down his shirt, "So, what's your name?"

"Bobby," he replied.

"And you have an accent too, where are you from?"

"Brooklyn."

She laughed lightly, almost making it sound fake, "Oh, I would have never guessed." She ran her hand down his arm, "So, you think I could go in and do a bit of fishing?"

Bobby chuckled, "Sure, there's a bunch of old Navy farts in there, I'm sure you'll catch one or two."

"Thanks." She pressed her fingers to her lips and gently touched them to his cheek. Bobby smiled and opened the door for her. Eagle strolled inside and got her first real look at the club. It was dimly lit, and with the smoke from all the cigars and pipes, there was a haze that clouded the whole place. She wrinkled her nose at the smoke. A strong whiff went up her nose and she sneezed. She held onto her wig to make sure she didn't sneeze it off. Ugh, the place was gross, she thought. The furnishings looked like they had come from some defunct seafood restaurant, very nautical in a cheap sense. There were some tables to sit at, and a fairly long bar that ran down the right side of the building. A kitchen door was next to the end of the bar. Eagle shuddered to think of what they would call food here. And it was obvious from the clientele that they were there mainly for boozing and picking up broads. The club was noisy and quite crowded considering the average age of the male clientele was over fifty. Working girls hung all over the men, trying their best to ply them with alcohol. There was a jukebox belting out moldy oldies; hardly the music one would expect to be good for picking up women. The girls didn't care, they were there to work and make money.

Through the haze she could see Westland sitting at the far end of the bar. From her observations the night before, that appeared to be his designated spot. She looked around and spotted the bathroom. That would be a good place to apply the poison to the ring. Pushing the door open, she noticed several girls at the long sink. They had small mirrors, rolled up dollar bills and were doing lines of cocaine. Eagle averted her gaze and walked toward one of the empty stalls. Closing the door, she opened her little black purse and pulled out the bag with the other ring and the bottle of poison. Carefully she unscrewed the top which had a tiny brush attached to it. With utmost care, she dabbed the tiny pins on the underside of the ring. All she had to do was touch Westland with a fairly firm hand and the deed would be done. She shuddered; the thought of touching him turned her stomach and all the stench of smoke was really not helping her out. Replacing the cap on the bottle, she put it back in the bag and into her purse. If all went according to plan, she hoped she would be out of there in a couple of hours.

***

Cabbott and Tige reached their location and settled down. They knew it was going to be a wait, but they would continue to practice in the mean time. Cabbott keyed his mike, "All units, this is Angel, report please."

"This is Kingpin. I'm airborne and hanging out."

"Ground Zero here, I'm in position two hundred yards out from the club."

"Lone Wolf, I'm at my designated location. Awaiting go."

"Bull Dog. White Feather is in the club. Going around back to observe."

"Bull Dog, watch for snakes," Tige added.

"Roger that," Max replied as he followed the tree line around to the back. It was several minutes before he reported in, "Angel, I have eyes on White Feather and eyes on target. She has not approached him yet."

"I wonder what's taking her so long," Tige said as he looked through the rangefinder scope.

"I don't know. Maybe she's not trying to be so obvious," Cabbott replied.

"Guess we have to leave her to work."

Max watched through the patio door. He had lost sight of Eagle for a while, but managed to keep Westland in view. He was just beginning to wonder what happened to her when she appeared. She approached the bar and took a seat next to Westland. From what he could see, she had not yet spoken to him. He saw Westland turn and start talking to her. She offered her hand and he shook it, then leaned down and kissed it.

"All, Bull Dog. Handshake delivered."

"Excellent!" Cabbott whispered loudly. It was just a matter of time now.

Westland let his hand slide from hers, "My, my, you're quite lovely. Richard Westland. I'm a retired Navy Admiral."

"Elkie," Eagle replied, trying to act as civil as possible and biting her tongue when needed. She hated his guts, and now she was facing the fact she was going to be spending the evening with him. But at least she had the comfort of knowing that this would be his last night. "Oh, you're an admiral eh?"

"Yes, well, retired. Humm, Elkie, that's an interesting name."

"Ja, I'm Sweeeeeedish," she drew out the words trying to disguise her natural accent.

"Oh, I don't think I've ever seen a brunette Swede."

"We're out there. Some say we're considered extra lucky in situations."

Westland put his hand on her arm, "Lucky huh?"

Eagle bit her cheek, "Yeah, lucky."

"Well, do you think you may be lucky for me tonight?"

"All in what you consider luck." She could feel her nerves starting to get at her. Waving at the bartender, she ordered a brandy. As soon as it was delivered, she took a long drink. The alcohol burned as it went down, but she didn't care. Ideally, she didn't want to get too intoxicated and make a mistake, but her nerves were really bad and she at least wanted to settle them somewhat.

"So what brings you to this country?" Westland said, moving his stool a bit closer to hers.

"School. I'm just finishing up my Master's in Fine Arts."

"Mmmm, yes, I'd say you were definitely some fine art."

Eagle looked down at her drink trying not to let her emotions get the best of her. Westland was not only an asshole, he had lousy pick up lines as well. She was beginning to see why the woman didn't leave with him the other night. And if this was the way he behaved around women, she could clearly understand why he was divorced. None of the dealings she'd ever had with him were civil. He always treated her like a second class citizen.

Westland reached up and let his fingers play with her hair, "Humm, you look a bit familiar, do I know you from somewhere?"

"No, I don't think so. This is my first time in this club."

"Oh. I'd swear I knew you from somewhere."

"Ja, you know, we Swedes all look a bit alike."

"Yes, well, maybe…I know this Norwegian, she's a real bitch."

Eagle clenched her jaw so hard she thought her teeth would break, "Ja, dem Norweeeegians, they can be a bit on the tough side." Oh, she was furious, but could not show it. She reached her left hand under the bar and clenched her fist, her fingernails biting into the thin gloves and then her flesh. She had to keep it together.

Westland tipped back his drink, "She had no business being in the military, let alone on my budget committee."

"And what's wrong with women in the military?"

"It's a man's job. They should be home having children and taking care of their husbands. And that bitch managed to ruin my career."

"And do you think that about all women?" She said stiffly.

"No. There are some women who do best to be out in the workforce providing the pleasures that you do." He put his hand on the side of her face.

Eagle tightened her jaw again; the touching of Westland coupled with the thick smoke was really turning her stomach. She needed to get away to dispose of the ring as well. Westland waved at the bartender, "Hey, more drinks here!"

She stood, pushing the barstool back, "Excuse me for a few minutes admiral, I need to use the ladies room." She made her way to the restroom. The ladies who had been doing drugs earlier were out working the floor. The place was all hers. Carefully she worked the tainted ring off her finger and wrapped it in a paper towel. Depositing it into the trash, she stepped into one of the stalls and closed the door. Her stomach threatened more. Eagle sat down and took several long, slow, deep breaths, fighting off the nausea. Although the thought still ran through her head that she had poisoned the admiral, she didn't feel particularly bad about it. She knew he would die one way or another. The ill feeling in her stomach started to subside. Gaining her composure, she returned to her place at the bar.

Max continued to watch as Westland bought another round of drinks. He'd seen Eagle take a few swallows and then excuse herself. Max knew she'd gone to the bathroom to dispose of the first ring. A several minutes later she reappeared and joined him. The lieutenant almost wished that Cabbott would have placed a wire on Eagle; he was dying to know what they were talking about. He keyed his mike, "All, Bull Dog. White Feather has swapped out her ring. Just waiting for the pill to be placed."

Eagle ran her finger along the rim of her drink. She was trying not to drink very much; she needed to keep a clear head. Westland did his best to try and impress her. He started telling old Navy stories about how he had been in command of a battleship and how it had the biggest guns in the fleet. It sounded to her like he was trying to make up for an inadequacy in another area. Oh well, she was not impressed. Try as she might to remain interested, she still ended up letting out a yawn.

After an hour or so of chatting and drinking, Westland excused himself to the bathroom. Eagle quickly took out the small LSD pill and dropped it in his drink. It dissolved almost immediately as Cabbott said it should. She was growing tired of the admiral and wanted to finish this. He returned and continued with their conversation. Half an hour had passed and she noticed Westland looking a little odd, "Are you okay admiral?"

"Humm, I don't seem to be feeling myself. I wonder if it was the clam chowder I ate."

"You do look a bit pale. Maybe you should call it a night. I'll be here tomorrow," she said, lying like she had never done before. Her heart raced and she fought to keep her composure.

"Yes, maybe I will... You've been most wonderful company this evening Elkie. I look forward to seeing you tomorrow." He reached down, took her hand and kissed it. Eagle fought back the urge to vomit. Westland was a vile man and she resented being touched by him. But it was all part of the operation and she had to deal with it. All the rude and rotten remarks he had made when she was at the Pentagon were going to be buried shortly. Vengeance was to be hers tonight.

"Good night admiral," she said in a deep voice, a smile curled to her lips. Westland walked past her and headed for the door.

"All units, Bull Dog. Target is on the move. Repeat, target is on the move." Max started to make his way toward the front of the club.

The rest of the team shifted gears, it was time. Jake turned inland from his time-killing tour of the coast. The air was stagnant over land and it made flying more difficult. He would be on target in a matter of seconds. Sam started the car. D.M. checked the little .38 and reholstered it. He buckled the bottom strap on his jacket and zipped it just far enough he could get his hand inside, he didn't want it blowing open in the wind possibly exposing the fact he was carrying a firearm. Starting up his bike he moved from the deserted parking lot to down the road to a stop sign. He would wait until Westland and Sam passed.

Max hurried through the brush to get around front of the club. He got to the corner just in time to see Westland get into his car.

"Bull Dog, target is moving."

"Roger Bull Dog, I'm waiting," Sam said as he put the car in drive and kept his foot on the brake. The adrenaline was pumping through his body and he fought to keep it under control. He had to remain calm and do as he was told.

"Kingpin, where are you?" Cabbott called.

"I'm ten seconds from target area. I got pretty bad air up here. Flying in stealth mode is a bitch."

"Just get your eyes on target," Cabbott barked.

"Yes sir," Jake replied crisply. He adjusted the throttle and changed the pitch of the rotors slightly trying to make flying a bit better. Making a big circle of the club area, he saw Westland's car pull onto the road, "Kingpin. I have eyes on target."

Sam took his foot off the brake and rolled forward, "Ground Zero, I'm moving out with caution."

"Affirmative, just keep your distance for now," Cabbott warned.

Eagle came from the club and did her best to hurry over to the car. Max had the door open waiting for her. She climbed in and grabbed his radio. He closed the door and hopped in next to her.

“You got Westland’s car tagged?”

“Yup, waited until the bouncer went in to take a leak.”

“Good job Max.”

"Looks like you did a good job in there too."

"Yuck, it wasn't easy. That man is positively vile."

"Well, at least you didn't have to go home with him and try and off him there."

"Yes, thank heavens. And that bar is disgusting. They should have the health inspectors close it down."

They sat listening to the operation as it played out. There was no need for input, their part was done. He waited a few minutes then left the parking lot. They would cruise along well behind the operation until they made a turn to head back to the hotel.

Jake banked around watching Westland's car, "Lone Wolf, you got maybe thirty seconds to pick up."

"Roger Kingpin, I'm ready."

Sam picked up his pace. He needed to close the distance to get ready for D.M. to come out. He accelerated a bit quicker until he was within one hundred feet of Westland's rear bumper.

"Good position Ground Zero. Lone Wolf, they're coming by," Jake said as he throttled back and tried to hover.

"Target acquired," D.M. said coldly, pulling out on the road. The stretch of road they had chosen was not well traveled. D.M. could see no oncoming traffic. It was the perfect place. He revved the engine and gave the bike some gas. It took just a few seconds before he was in front of Sam. He swung out into the oncoming traffic lane and sped up. Pulling alongside Westland he glanced over. The admiral had surprisingly not seen or heard him. He drew his pistol and fired. The glass shattered, startling the admiral. He swerved erratically, narrowly missing the motorcycle. D.M. took evasive measures and dropped back slightly. Westland gained control of the car and sped away. They continued to follow him, keeping him moving fast.

"Angel, Lone Wolf. Target is rattled and he's moving faster than planned. We are doing eighty, repeat, eighty."

Jake flew down the road and turned, "Angel, you got maybe fifteen seconds to target."

"Copy," Cabbott replied, "All right Wombat, get ready."

"I'm ready mate."

Cabbott settled down behind his rifle. The round was in the chamber ready to go. He peered through the scope awaiting Tige's direction.

"Wombat, have you acquired target?" Jake asked as he flew back up the road so he could tail Westland from behind.

"Negative."

"He's coming fast."

Tige watched through the scope, "I have target. Range five hundred, four hundred, three hundred, two hundred, one hundred. Mark. One hundred out, two hundred out, three hundred out."

Cabbott exhaled as he saw the tire appear in his scope, "See you in hell," he said as he gently squeezed the trigger. The round went off and struck the tire on the outer part of the wall just where he wanted it to. It blew and immediately Westland lost control. The car hurtled down the road, the tires screeching loudly. It ran off the road and impacted the stand of trees that the team had found. The loud crash of metal and glass breaking echoed through the area.

"Shit, it worked!" Cabbott said as he quickly got to his feet, grabbed his rifle and headed down to the crash site. Tige turned off the scope and followed. They hiked through the edges of the tree line along the road trying to remain hidden. Sam and D.M. passed by, not stopping. If there was any more work to be done, it was Cabbott's responsibility. A few minutes later, Eagle and Max went by. They slowed slightly but did not stop. The road was empty. Jake had seen the accident and was heading back to the airport.

Cabbott walked up to the remains of the car. It was a clean head on collision with a very large oak tree. He couldn't have planned it any better if he tried. Westland was slumped over the steering wheel. Cabbott pulled on a thin rubber glove and reached inside. He felt Westland's neck for a pulse. Tige stood back in the bushes watching. Cabbott changed his hand position a couple of times then he looked over the roof of the car and shook his head.

"Angel here, target eliminated." He walked to the rear of the car and looked underneath. The gas tank was still intact. He continued on to the passenger side and looked under the car. A fuel line close to the engine was dripping fuel. He looked up at Tige, "Hey mate, you gotta light?"

Tige smiled and tossed him a lighter, "One admiral on the barbie." He retreated further into the trees. It was all up to Cabbott. The captain found a handful of dry leaves and lit them. With one quick flick of the wrist he threw them under the car and made a hasty retreat to where Tige was standing. A few moments later they watched as the car was slowly engulfed in flames. A car passing by stopped and the passengers got out. One had a cell phone and called for the fire department. Cabbott knew the nearest fire station was more than nine minutes away. The car would be charred remains by the time they got there.

They hid in the dense trees until satisfied that the job was done. The fire crew finally showed up and put out what was left of the fire. A police car arrived and the officer got out. They could hear him talking to the passerby's about the accident. The officer took out his flashlight and walked part way up the road. He found skid marks and a few bits of broken glass. He returned to the group and informed them that it appeared to have been a drunk driving accident.

Returning to their car, Cabbott held out his hand, "Mighty fine spotting there captain."

Tige took his hand, "Mighty fine shooting there captain." They laughed, shook hands and then loaded their gear in the trunk.

“Max?” Eagle said, her stomach was not feeling well.

“Yeah?”

“Do you think we can go find something to eat? I'm afraid all the alcohol, smoke, and the stress of the mission have not made my stomach happy.”

“Sure, any preferences?”

“No, just go find something simple. Any place without smoking.” She took out her cell phone and dialed General Spears' number, “Good evening general...Yes, the job looks like it went well...Another assignment? What? Humm, I told the CIA they can't have him anymore. I guess they just can't take ‘no’ for an answer. Can you see about talking to them? I'm just afraid Captain Westmoreland will get sent out on another mission that will get him hurt, or worse, killed... Yes sir, the team is currently one hundred percent. Oh, I see. Right, I'll check the computer when we get back to the base...What's our timetable? Humm, I think we can manage that, provided we don't get snowed in...Yes sir, I will. Goodnight." She turned to Max, "The general congratulates us on a job well done."

"What was all that bit about the CIA?"

"The army used to loan Cabbott out to them for jobs. In fact they came to the base one day looking for him."

"They came all the way out there?!"

"Yes."

"And what did you do?"

"I, with the major's formidable presence, made it very apparent that we were not going to give him up to the CIA anymore."

"Bet they weren't very happy. He told me that he did quite a bit of dirty work for them."

"And I told them that the deal they had with the Army was null and void. He's part of our team now and I'm not gonna loan him out to just anyone."

Max stopped at a red light. They were just a few blocks from the motel. "Why do I have the feeling that the CIA isn't gonna take 'no' for an answer; like you said to the general? I'm sure they're trying to think of a way to get him back on their roster."

"If I have my way that'll never happen. I've gone through too much hell to get him here, fix him up and get him back on his feet so he can work for us. Granted I may sound a bit selfish, but I think since we put forth the effort, we should keep control of him."

"You're making him sound like chess piece rather than a human being."

"Sorry, I'm not meaning it like that. Cabbott's a really great guy. I spent lots of time with him when he was healing from surgeries. I got to know him quite well. But from a management stand point, I did what I thought was best to bring a very skilled asset to the team."

"He certainly does have the skills, and the ability to use them."

"And I hope for our sake and his that we can avoid battles with the other services and agencies. They can go out and find another sniper, or train one of their own."

“Gee, we got pretty lucky. We got two of the best in the world on our team.”

Eagle and Max pulled into the parking lot. The rest of the team was waiting. She had called D.M. to let him know she was getting something to eat. The events of the evening and all the alcohol had not made her feel very well. Having gotten something to eat, she was feeling better. Cabbott opened the door for her, "Mission accomplished ma’am."

She stood and the rest of the team gathered around her, "My compliments gentlemen for a fine operation. You did the general proud."

"We didn't do it for the general, we did it for you," Jake announced. She stepped away from the car and was met by the major. Reaching up, she pulled out the bobby pins that held her wig on. D.M. took it off her head.

"This gentleman prefers blonds," he said in a deep whisper, dropping the wig on the ground. He played his fingers through her hair, trying to tease it loose.

Eagle looked up and smiled at him. Pulling the last few bobby pins out of her hair, it fell back down to her shoulders. D.M. put his hand on her cheek, “That’s much better,” he said softly, his eyes shined with the fire that burned inside him.

She knew what he had in mind, "All right gentlemen, it's late. We'll discuss all this in the morning. The general also mentioned some more work for us in the coming days." She turned and headed for her room, D.M. next to her on the left side. He let his arm drift across her back and rest gently on her hip. The rest of the team watched. Eagle pulled out her key and opened the door. They disappeared inside together.

"She's not gonna debrief us?" Cabbott said in a confused tone. Although he was well aware of their relationship, he tended to prefer staying blissfully ignorant.

Jake leaned against the car, "No, but I'm fairly confident that she and the major are gonna be doing some *serious* debriefing of their own."

They all laughed.

THE END

Hand gun: Sig Sauer P220- 45 ACP Elite Dark with threaded barrel 8 or 10 rnd mag adjustable combat night sights 30.4 oz w/mag

Sub Machine gun: Heckler & Koch UMP45 in 45 ACP 600 rnds/min 25 rnd mag

Battle rifle: HK 417 in 7.62 X 51 mm (308) with AG-C/EGLM grenade launcher 500-600 rnds/min 16 in barrel

Cabbot's Sniper Rifle: Sig Tactical 2 in .338 Lapua range 1500 m+ 4 rnd mag

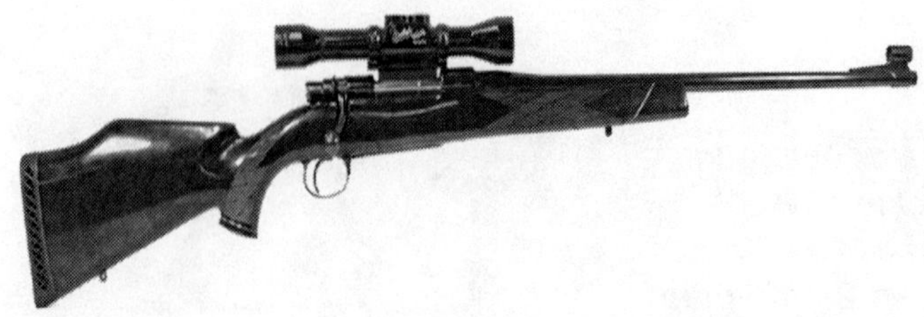

Tige's- .375 H&H magnum- belonged to his grandfather- he has changed the stock out for a camouflaged composite stock. Able to maintain impact point with wide range of bullet weights. 200-300 gr bullets.

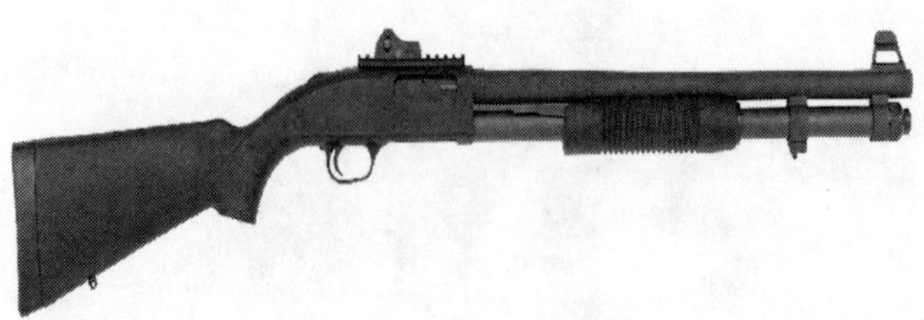

Shotgun: Mossberg 590 Special Purpose 9 shot with collapsible stock in 12ga

LaVergne, TN USA
08 February 2010

172351LV00001B/1/P

9 781935 605072